Coven C

David Clark

Table of Contents

The House of the Rising Son ... 4
1 ... 5
2 ... 9
3 ... 15
4 ... 23
5 ... 27
6 ... 35
7 ... 46
8 ... 53
9 ... 58
10 ... 67
11 ... 71
12 ... 76
13 ... 80
14 ... 84
15 ... 97
16 ... 105
17 ... 114
18 ... 122
20 ... 128
21 ... 133
22 ... 137
23 ... 139
24 ... 144
25 ... 149
26 ... 156
Blood Wars ... 161
1 ... 162
2 ... 169
3 ... 177
4 ... 188
5 ... 194
6 ... 199
7 ... 203
8 ... 207
9 ... 211
10 ... 223
11 ... 228
12 ... 233

13	238
14	244
15	253
16	258
17	267
18	274
19	279
20	285
21	291
The Revenge of the Shadow Witch	298
1	298
2	305
3	311
4	316
5	322
6	327
7	335
8	341
9	345
10	349
11	355
12	360
13	368
14	374
15	381
16	387
17	393
18	401
19	407
20	414
21	420
22	423
23	427
24	434
25	438
26	442
27	447
28	456
29	461
30	468
31	477

The House of the Rising Son

1

"Just have a seat."

Several sets of hands ushered me inside to the closest chair. I fought each of them away. Despite the room spinning, I felt I was more than capable to find my way to the chair on my own. I was wrong, and would have completely landed on the floor if Jen hadn't caught me and moved me a few feet to the right to the chair that I never sat in as a child. It was one of those things that was nice to look at, but not something you sat on. A fact that made it a constant joke between my mother and father, but now I was sitting there, and the joke was on me. "How?"

The room was full of silent stares, but I felt a few struggling to withhold their sarcasm.

"If any one of you starts with the birds and the bees, I am throwing you in to the next state, and trust me I could do it." I held up a hand, showing one of my newest tricks. There wasn't just a glow. There were lines forming patterns and runes.

"I have heard of this before, and it is not that uncommon," said Theodora. She strutted across the room and sat on the loveseat that was next to the chair I sat on. She crossed her legs elegantly and leaned as close as she could to me. "The father is human, correct?"

I gave her a 'duh' look, and then I shot a warning at the rest of the room before anyone clarified he was human at the time. Nathan was no longer a member of the human species and was well on his way to becoming a vampire.

"That's a yes," assumed Theodora.

"I've heard about it too, but I've never seen it before," Marie said curiously. "It usually reversed, though. A human female carrying the child of a male vampire."

"That's true," agreed Theodora. She leaned back away from me and then looked at Marie Norton. The glance had a shared understanding between the two women. It reminded me of the days sitting in Mrs. Saxon's residence back in the coven, watching her and Jen or Mrs. Tenderschott carry on a conversation about me, but without me. Oh, to be back there. Those were simpler times.

"Everyone out," ordered Marie. "Everyone but Theodora, Jen, and Larissa. Everyone else get out now!" I had never seen or heard her this forceful before. She walked around and ushered a few stragglers out. Apryl tried to linger just outside the door, but Marie put a stop to that, and gave her a little shove from behind to move her down the hall.

"Larissa, I want you to relax."

That wasn't going to happen. I guess Theodora didn't know that I wasn't a relaxing type. Especially not with the world exploding around me, witches and vampires assembled outside, and the love of my life upstairs becoming a monster. Yep, there were plenty of reasons to relax.

"Can you feel it?" Marie asked.

Jen Bolden stepped into the center of the room and nodded.

Theodora nodded as well.

"What?" I screamed at them all.

Marie Norton walked over and kneeled in front of me. She laid her hands on my legs and looked up into my eyes the way she had for years. The look on my mother's face, or foster mother's face, was one of concern. Seeing it just added to my own. She then moved her hands up and over my stomach. I flinched backwards when she yanked her hands away from me and gasped. "It's there. I feel it. It has a pulse, but how?"

"Dhampir pregnancies have an accelerated gestation period. Some as short as a month," said Theodora. "But this is not one of those."

"Dhamp-what?" I asked. All I knew was that the word sounded both funny and terrifying at the same time.

Theodora leaned toward me again, and reached over with her long slender hands, taking mine in hers. "Forgive us Larissa. As strange as all this is for you to hear, it is also new to us. A Dhampir is what we call a child that comes from the union of a vampire and a human. No one knows why, at least not medically, but those pregnancies have a much shorter term. I have heard of ones as short as a month, and others a few months. I have never witnessed one personally, but..."

The three women exchanged looks again. I was beyond tired of this little unspoken language they had, and I leaned forward in my chair and allowed my head to drop into my hands. "But what?" I exclaimed. "Will someone tell me what is going on?"

"Larissa honey," started Marie Norton. "The problem is this is a little different. In those, the woman is human, not the other way around. That is a crucial difference. When we become vampires, our bodies stop changing. We stop aging. We stop growing. We stop everything. And... well, our bodies can't adapt to carry a child."

Maybe it was the stress of the situation, or the bizarre situation with everything else going on around us playing in my mind, but my first thought wasn't about what she had said and what it meant about my situation. My first thought was about the conversation I had had up on the rooftop one night, and I looked right at Jennifer Bolden and said, "Well, we have our answer." The last word passed my lips at the same time as the realization of what that answer meant entered my brain. The answer converted into a question. "Wait! If my body can't change. How can I give birth?"

"Yes," started Marie. "This leads to a ton of questions, and I don't have any answers," she finished, looking around at the others.

"I could try to ask around, but I'm not even sure who to start with," remarked Theodora. "It is possible this is a miracle of sorts."

Right then another wave hit me, and I leaped out of the chair and ran across the parlor and back out to the front porch, where again I heaved nothing more than a few strings of yellow foam.

"Dry heaves are the worst," Jen commented from behind me. I turned around and gave her the look from hell. She didn't know the half of it. I remembered dry heaves from when I was sick as a child once. The feeling of the gagging, and the constant rolling and squeezing of your stomach as it tries to empty whatever contents it had left. This was worse, way worse. The squeezing was there, with an enormous cramping that followed, almost paralyzing. Then came the heaving that felt like my stomach was being ripped from my insides.

"So, if everything happens faster, how long will this morning sickness last?" I asked, hoping to hear it would only be minutes, but then I heaved again in front of the large audience still gathered in front of the house.

Marie reached down and helped me gather myself, and then walked me back into the house with a supportive arm around my shoulders. We didn't stop at the parlor, and I let her guide me down the hallway to the kitchen where most of our new house guests were. A bit of dread set in. Was she wanting to make some grand announcement to everyone? I wasn't ready for this yet, not that most hadn't already heard Theodora's announcement on the porch earlier.

Amy pounced on me and grabbed me around my waist as soon as I entered the door. "Larissa, are you okay?" She squeezed me firmly, and I stroked her hair.

"I'm fine."

"You sure?" she asked, looking at me with her big blue eyes.

I nodded while I smiled and tried to be more convincing than I felt.

"I want to do a test," Marie said as she approached me with a glass of water in her hand. Apryl and Brad stared at the glass like the Wicked Witch of the West, fearful of melting. "Take a sip."

"What?" I asked in disbelief. "I've been dry heaving, and you want me to drink this?"

"Yes, I want to see something." She handed it to me.

"No thank you." I put the glass down on the table. "Are you trying to get me to vomit even more?"

"Larissa, trust me on this." Marie reached down and picked up the glass and gave me that look that only parents seem to have mastered. The type that told you they would not take no for an answer and would stand there until the end of time until you finally did what they wanted. For most, that wouldn't last more than a few minutes or maybe an hour at the most, if the parents were persistent. We were immortal, so that timeframe would be a little different.

I had done this a few times before. Some as an experiment when I was, I guess, what you would call–younger. Another when I made the mistake of swallowing after I brushed my teeth to freshen my breath. Just a few drops of water in my stomach caused a tossing and turning unlike anything I had ever felt, and then it rolled back up faster than the speed of sound, bringing up blood and anything else that might have been in there. I braced myself and took the glass, while looking at Marie for confirmation.

"Go on," she urged.

I tipped my head back, but stopped. My stomach was already turning. Either it was another dry heave coming or the anticipation of what was about to happen. To be on the safe side, I moved close to the backdoor. Pamela moved out of my way.

"What's going on?" asked Jack from the door.

"Larissa is about to spew," announced Apryl.

I didn't even bother with a dirty look or any comment. She was right. I was about to spew, but there had to be a point to this, or Marie wouldn't make such a request. I knew she wouldn't ask me anything that would be dangerous. She basically gave her own life to protect me. It was that trust that allowed me to raise the glass to my lips. It took a little more than that to tip it far enough for a few drops to pass over them.

Maybe it was curiosity. Maybe it was a lapse in judgment, but I did it. First a drop, then a second, and then what I guess most would consider a sip passed over my lips and into my mouth.

My lips clamped shut instinctively, and Pamela moved away even further from the back door.

"She's about blow!" Apryl warned, and everyone scattered.

It was cool and moist. A feeling of comfort flowed over and around my tongue on its way through my mouth, and a quenching of a thirst, that I didn't know I had, exploded when it hit my throat. That was it. After that, the feeling disappeared, and I braced myself for the rolling. My hands grabbed at my stomach, ready to hang on, but the loud gurgling I expected wasn't there. It was silent, really silent. It hadn't been that silent in almost a day. Then, amidst a room full of gasps and horrified looks, I took another sip, and after another uneventful reaction, I drank the entire glass, and then sat it down on the table.

2

After my little make-the-water-disappear-without-it coming-back-up trick, I left everyone down in the kitchen to examine the glass and prove to themselves it was just an ordinary glass. I wish it were as simple as a trick or magic, but I actually drank that water, and it tasted good. It was as simple as that. I wish what was upstairs was that simple as well, but it wasn't. Nathan wasn't just asleep, taking a nap, or playing some cruel joke on me. He was going through hell, no matter how peaceful he looked, laying there in my bed.

I went in and sat on one side of the bed. Jennifer Bolden sat on the other side. Her look answered the question I had. There had been no change, at least not outwardly. Changes were going on inside, and I felt it when I reached down and interlaced my fingers with his. He was cold, even to me. Gone was the warmth I so enjoyed feeling. Rough, almost paper-like, tissue had replaced the soft and supple feeling of his skin. This was temporary, but disturbing all the same. The light pulsation of fluid moving through his fingers was gone as well. They were now nothing but just gray fleshy protrusions off of his hand that laid limp between mine. I prayed to feel them move. Even a little flinch, or a stroke of one of his fingers against the side of mine like he did so often. It was a comforting sensation when he did it. Now, I wanted to be the one to give him the same comfort, so even though he felt lifeless, I kept on holding his hand with one hand while the other either stroked the back of the one I held, or I stroked his hair. I wanted him to know I was there. I needed him to know I was waiting for him when he finally wakes up.

All that comforted me was knowing at this moment he wasn't aware of what was going on. He already felt the worst of it, at least until he woke up. When it happens, you feel yourself die slowly, one part at a time. The pain of each adding on to the next, flooding your consciousness with nothing but an agony that pushes out any chance of seeing your life flash before your eyes. There is no room for thoughts of loved ones that may miss you, or ones you know you will miss. There is no time for thoughts of regret. The only flash you see is when the light disappeared and the blackness takes hold, and then it's all gone.

I don't really remember anything of when I was out. If it felt like I was sleeping, I don't know. I just wasn't there, and then I woke up with no sense of how much time had passed. Had it been minutes, hours, or days? I didn't know. I didn't care. What I felt was an insatiable burning deep inside and Marie ran me out the backdoor to the woods behind our house to help me take care of it.

"You know, Gwen would just die if she knew you were pregnant with his child," remarked Jen.

I looked up in shock and quickly held a finger over my lips, urging her to keep it quiet.

She looked back at Nathan. "He can't hear us."

She was right, and I knew it, but that didn't make talking about him or things like that in front of him any less weirder. My mind told me he was still there, and I rubbed his hand as an apology for being so callous. Then I smirked.

"You know I'm right."

"Yes, you are," I admitted, not taking my eyes off of Nathan this time. "I didn't think you thought about things like that. Apryl? Yes. You? No."

"I would be lying if I didn't say that prima donna witch didn't get on my nerves more than a few times. I am sure she is sitting up in the coven enjoying the fact that everyone but the witches were exiled."

"Probably buddy-ing up to Mrs. Saxon..." then a question hit me, and I turned to look right at Jen. "Jen, she is still in charge of the coven, right? Please tell me she is."

"Yes, why do you ask?"

My shoulders slouched. "They threatened to take it from her before because of me, and now all this. It kind of proved all the points Mrs. Wintercrest tried to make back in those trials." My voice trailed off as I imagined them removing her.

"Stop!" ordered Jen. "None of this is your fault. Not a single thing... and, if you really think about it, Rebecca kicking all of us out probably helped her standing with the council. That Mrs. Wintercrest was there with a few others just before Rebecca told us to leave."

"Maybe," I said, unsure if I really believed her or not.

"Demius and Mrs. Tenderschott tried to talk her out of it, but she refused to even listen to them. The council members that were there agreed with her actions. I wouldn't be too worried."

"Okay," I said, but I still wasn't sure. I could see Mrs. Saxon being so upset over Nathan that she threw everyone out, but I could also see her being forced to by the council. Either was plausible. Which was the truth? Only Mrs. Saxon would know. I knew her well enough to know she would put up a strong showing either way. If it was all her, I couldn't blame her. A shudder went through my body when I thought of what I had cost her, and it had nothing to do about my suspicions about the coven. Nathan was her everything, thus the unwritten rules, which I had broken every single one I knew about, and probably several I hadn't heard of yet. There was something extra vile about that thought. Could it be? I had only found out I was pregnant a few hours ago. Was I already seeing things differently?

"Don't do that to yourself."

"I'm fine."

"No, you're not. I see that look on your face, and I know what's running through your head. Now stop it." She leaned across the bed and placed a hand on my shoulder. "Focus on what is in front of you right now. Don't worry about the past. Nathan will need you, and well... you need to stay calm for your little one."

My free hand reached up and instinctively rubbed my stomach. I could have sworn it felt different. A little bigger. Was it even possible? In just a few hours?

"You know, I've been giving your situation a little thought. I think it's his fault." She nodded her head in Nathan's direction.

There was no way she was that naïve. She was older than me, at least physically, and she was married. She was the one that offered to have the conversation about the birds and the bees with me. I gave her my best 'duh' look back.

"No, I mean about how it happened."

Again, I gave the same reaction. There was no other suitable response.

"Not like that," she corrected. "Everything they were talking about downstairs involved a human female, which makes sense. Her body can make the adjustments to carry a child to term, and ours can't, but we are missing one factor about you and Nathan. You're a witch and his mother is one too. Who's to say Nathan doesn't have a little in him that manifested this way? It's a big unknown in the equation we can't ignore."

"Can it do that?" I asked, and then spouted out another question. "Oh, you don't think..."

"What? I don't think maybe Rebecca lied to everyone, including Nathan, to protect him?" Jen shrugged her shoulders and scrunched her face up. "Anything's possible. She is a very private woman when it comes to her husband, and as you know better than ever, very protective of her son."

Looking back at things, she was right to be protective, and the idea Jen had just floated was possible, but not all that probable. Magic had a way of making itself known. If Nathan had anything in him, it would have, should have, come out by now, even accidentally. A random thought that triggered something to happen–like throwing an annoying classmate in the pool. An event that still brought a smirk to my face. Even something simple, like something magically materialized out of thin air. Anything at all. Maybe it had. I had only known Nathan for a relatively short time. Even by human standards, it had only been just a few months.

I looked back at his blank face, and wondered, could he be hiding something from me? The thought prompted a quick headshake. We didn't have secrets. Well, I didn't have any secrets I kept from him. That was a promise I made to him after I snuck out looking for Marie, and I kept it. Then the list of situations that I had kept from Nathan played in my mind, prompting a feeling of guilt. I didn't really like it. I had a reason for not telling him each and every time. They weren't exactly secrets. I was just delaying when I told him. That attempt at rationalization did nothing to squash my guilty feeling. The situation with Clay wasn't really something I was delaying when I told Nathan. I didn't know how to tell him, and really just hoped it went away on its own. It didn't, and then it blew up right in my face. Whether I would have ever told Nathan, I wasn't sure. It was another hit to the fabric of who I thought I was. I thought I was an honest and open person with the man I loved, but in reality, I wasn't. I was a briar patch of rationalization and selective openness. They say strong relationships are built on a foundation of truth, and I hadn't really held up my end of things. Was it possible he wasn't either?

"What secrets are you hiding?" I whispered, and then reached up with my free hand to caress his cheek.

"Don't do that to yourself, Larissa. I see those wheels turning."

"It was just a question."

"No, it wasn't," remarked Jen. "I know you. You have probably already analyzed every moment you and Nathan spent together for any signs that you might have missed and any times you think he may have tried to mislead you, and wait…" she held up a finger as soon as I opened my mouth. "You also went through every time you haven't been completely truthful with him. Just stop and wait for him to wake up. Then, when the time is right, ask him. Considering the situation," she glanced down at my lap. "I am sure he will understand and will answer honestly, if he knows."

"Too bad we don't have those stones Mrs. Tenderschott has. I could put one in his hand right now."

"You could. You could walk out to any of those witches that are camped outside and ask them if they have something like that. Your Master Thomas probably could find something like that if you asked, or you could show Nathan some trust, and just wait. Which is what I would do, if you want this old woman's opinion."

"I'm older," I snipped back

"You know what I mean."

"Yep," I agreed. She was giving me relationship advice, and she was absolutely more experienced there than I was. "Oh, guess what happened downstairs after you came up? You'll love this. Marie had me drink a glass of water, and I didn't vomit."

"A whole glass. Not just a sip?"

"A whole glass, and it tasted good."

Jen regarded me with a curious and concerned look. Without warning, she reached across the bed and yanked my hand away from Nathan's and held it in her own palm up. Her thumb pressed hard into my wrist and then she waited.

"Jen, what are you..."

"Quiet," she snapped. Her thumb searched, and then she released me. "No pulse. You're still one of us."

"I could have told you that," I said and yanked my hand back.

"Your child is all human, though. It has a strong rhythm."

"Why can't I feel that like everyone else?"

"Remember when you first arrived at the coven? You were a girl of mystery. You still are."

If there was anything within an arm's reach, I would have thrown it at her, and conjuring something took too much energy at the moment. I didn't want to be that girl anymore. All that mystery was tiring and stressful. Oh, how much I desired to just be normal.

"How is he?" asked Lisa from the doorway. She was bracing herself with one hand, the other arm wrapped around her ribs.

"Lisa, you need to go get some rest."

Lisa didn't follow my orders and stumbled into the room and over to the side of the bed, where she gingerly sat down next to Jen.

"He is fine, and you need to get back to bed and rest. Kevin believes at least one of your ribs is broken."

"I don't doubt that." She groaned as she shifted around on the bed to get comfortable.

She looked at Nathan the same way everyone did when they saw him lying there; like they were looking at a dead body. If I hated people looking at me with pity, I morally despised anyone looking at Nathan that way, and I had to remind anyone who wasn't a vampire that he wasn't dead. That didn't stop the looks. Neither did my attempt to banish everyone. Everyone continued to stop by to check on him.

"So how much longer will he be like that?"

"Hard to say. It's different for everyone," explained Jennifer. "The biggest change is done. Now his body is preparing for its new state."

"Larissa," Jack called from the door. I was about to spin around and tell him no more visitors. I wanted Nathan to be left alone. "Master Thomas needs to talk to you downstairs for a minute."

With no hesitation, I declined. "I will be down there once Nathan is awake."

Jack took a step back from the door, but then stepped back to the door and added, "He was rather insistent."

I was about to become rather insistent myself when Jen looked over and said, "Go on. Lisa and I can watch over Nathan."

"All right, but come get me if anything happens." I stood up but waited for a response before I moved.

"Absolutely."

I took one more look at Nathan before I slowly walked to the door.

"Hey Larissa, is it true?" asked Lisa. She rubbed her stomach with one hand. I nodded, and Lisa smiled. "I'm glad. Gwen would have a cow if she knew."

"Why does everyone keep saying that?" I asked rhetorically.

"She'd have a whole dairy farm," remarked Jack as I passed him going out the door and down the stairs. Now that got a smile from me.

3

"Master Thomas," I called from halfway down the stairs.

"How is young Nathan?" he asked from where he stood down in the foyer.

"No change," I said.

"How are you feeling?" he asked, brushing right past my response about Nathan as if he didn't really care and was only asking to be polite.

It irked me a little and caused my answer to be abrupt. "Fine."

"Good, I have someone you need to meet." Master Thomas turned and walked out the front door without another word. Leaving to assume I was to follow him.

We walked out the door, and off the porch across my battle scarred yard. The yellow line of runes I had put there yesterday was still present. The bright intensity of the line prompted a small smile as we crossed it.

Just beyond it were two camps. Opposing armies, it appeared. These weren't the Union and the Confederate armies camped before a great battle. Though one occurred here on this very property many years before I was born, or so my grandfather told me. On one side, there was a camp of vampires that hung back close to the trees. They lurked in the shadows, which completed the image that most of the world had of us. We weren't heading in their direction. We were going to the other side, but that didn't mean the vampires weren't taking notice of our presence.

Where we were heading resembled something of a circus or a fair. Some had put up tents, but everywhere you looked small campfires burned, with several people gathered around them for warmth. Some played instruments like guitars or flutes, while others sang and danced. They all looked in our direction as we passed. Most gave a respectful nod to Master Thomas. It was an understandable acknowledgement of respect considering who he was. I, on the other hand, received looks of indifference from those that ventured close enough to look me in the eye. Many seemed leery of me and only looked in my general direction.

Master Thomas stopped at one tent, and I stayed a few steps behind him. "Is he in?" he asked.

"Yes, but not for you," answered the man, who was slightly taller than Master Thomas, and also a lot thinner. He looked like a human skeleton with a black robe draped over it. Only his face with pronounced cheekbones and a scruffy beard were visible beneath its hood.. He stepped to the right, moving his thin frame in between Master Thomas and the tent. The two men were inches from each other, and the aggressive stranger's jaw twitched. Master Thomas was his usual statue of stoic calm.

"Let him in," called a voice from inside the tent.

"Maybe next time," grumbled the thin man, and he stepped aside, letting Master Thomas pass by. When I stepped forward, he took an aggressive step toward me. I grinned, showing the points of my fangs. Not that my black eyes weren't a dead giveaway. He returned a similar grin, and I searched his eyes for the familiar emptiness, but what I found were bright brown eyes with flecks of gold glittering in them. I had seen that only three times before. The first was when Mr. Markinson knocked me unconscious outside the coven.

"Larissa, come on," Master Thomas called, holding open the tent's cloth door. I stepped through and expected to see the inside of a small tent, but this was not like any tent I had ever seen before. It was rather spacious. I needed to learn to drop any expectations of the world and just go with the flow. Stepping in through those dilapidated doors and into the coven should have taught me that. At the other end of this room, across the white oak hardwood floors, and behind the burgundy sofa stood a rather regal looking man, or so he seemed from behind. He wore some type of black cap with locks of black curly hair protruding out from under it.

"Guard dogs?" asked Master Thomas.

"One can never be too careful, Ben." He turned around holding a coffee cup, and my mouth dropped open. The man was gorgeous. I mean Greek god gorgeous with striking facial features chiseled from stone. His striking blue eyes were an exotic contrast to his dark complexion and jet-black beard and hair.

"You," he said, regarding me. "I must commend you. You are either somebody, or just somebody with a death wish with how you went after Madame Wintercrest. I applaud your audacity, and your stupidity." He held up his coffee cup as a toast. "Would you like some coffee? I grow my own beans." He motioned to the windows behind him, where a field of coffee plants stretched as far as the eye could see up and over a distant hill.

"Oh, she's somebody," remarked Master Thomas.

Our host put his cup down on a table and walked around the red couch, and approached me, taking a better look. I felt like a bug under a microscope. "I see," he said curiously, and then pointed right at me and asked Master Thomas, "Is this her?"

"It is. Marcus Meridian meet Larissa Dubois." Master Thomas handled the introductions.

"So, you're the one that this old folk keeps babbling about. The one that can help restore the natural order of things." He reached out and offered his hand.

My hand trembled all the way to meet his. I was more than a little star struck. That name was one that any witch would, or should, recognize. I did as soon as Master Thomas said it. "You're a M-M-Meridian," I stuttered, and was too shocked to even care.

"The last time I checked my driver's license, I was." He let go of my hand, but mine hung there in the air.

"I don't understand," I said, and tried to pull myself together. The tremble was gone, but the realization I was standing here in front of a Meridian still had me out of sorts. I wasn't sure if I should bow or something.

"What's not to understand? This is my castle."

Master Thomas chuckled. "No, she means why you are here, among the rogue elements?"

Marcus smiled, and I felt the world light up around me. "That's both a funny story and one that is not that interesting." He walked back to the table he placed his coffee cup on and picked it up, taking a sip. "You aren't the only one who isn't on the best of terms with Wintercrest, or the rest of the council. Let's just say several generations back, my family had a difference of opinions with most, if not all, of the council, and we now find ourselves on different sides."

"That is putting it mildly," said Master Thomas. He moved forward and took a seat on the couch, and did so without an invitation. I found that odd considering we were guests, and who our host was. It was almost like he was comfortable. "Your great grandfather was called a heretic. Do I have the term right?"

"You do," agreed Marcus Meridian. He sat on the other end of the couch and sipped at his coffee. He crossed his legs and sat back casually.

"They even wanted to do that ceremony to strip your family of any magic. Do I have that right?"

"Yes, I guess." Marcius Meridian dismissed the question flippantly with a hand. We were talking about a stain on his family's history. An event that forced a great family, make that one of the greatest families in our world, into a disgraceful hiding. I knew the name. We all talked about it with the reverence of a royal family, and, in every sense of the word, they were royalty. There weren't any true kings or queens of the witches, but there were those dynasties that sat atop the council for generations. Those families whose names became synonymous with greatness; the target for what everyone should strive to be. This should be akin to sacrilege, like criticizing the Pope, but yet I was here watching Master Thomas do it with no hesitation. "To be true, I doubt that ceremony works, anyway. I believe it is more of a pomp and circumstance thing."

"Probably so," responded Master Thomas. "And help me remember, there was a single family that stepped up to stop it."

Marcus nodded.

"What was their name? Do you remember?" prompted Master Thomas. He was egging him on. I could tell by the way he looked at him, but I didn't understand why.

"Larissa, why don't you take a seat in that chair behind you? I have a feeling we are going to be here for a while."

I was about to point out there was no chair, but when I turned out of the way so Marcus could see, there it was, just a few feet behind me, a red velvet chair. It wasn't there when we first came in. I knew that was a fact. I would have stumbled over it if it had been. I sat down as nonchalantly as possible.

"So, Marcus, do you remember the name of the family that helped you? The family one might say you owe a little debt to."

Marcus Meridian looked away from Master Thomas and exhaled. "Are we really doing this?" His head jerked back toward Master Thomas, and he looked at him sternly, almost like a warning.

"We are."

"Fine. Fine." He resigned himself and stood up and walked around the couch back to the table he was standing at when I and Master Thomas first entered. He picked up a square bottle of brown liquid and popped off the top before pouring a liberal amount of the libation into his coffee. "If you are going to ask me to go through all the sordid details of my family, then I am going to need something stronger than this coffee." He gave his coffee a little stir with a finger and then leaned back against the table, facing us.

"Where to start? Where to start? My family disagreed with the direction the council was taking. Their purpose was changing pretty drastically. One might say it was a one-hundred-and-eighty switch. They were no longer a group focused on protecting and teaching our kind. They wanted to govern and control. Something they were never meant to do. The council's single purpose back then was helping and assisting. It was to bring our community closer together. I will tell you what I heard my grandfather say once." Marcus stopped and took another healthy swig of his drink.

"The world was expanding. The new world was growing in size every day, and life was changing in so many ways. Things such as religion and beliefs were taking a back seat to prosperity and drive. Where your life *was* focused on community and helping others, now it became all about the person. We, as a people, and I mean the larger group of humanity, were losing everything that made us great, everything that made us strong. Our community of witches wasn't immune to this, and it was more important than ever to focus on our people. To continue to help one another. To continue to teach and pass down our identity, but the modern plague took hold, and many of our people saw their position on the council not as a responsibility to help, but as an opportunity to rise up and place themselves above all others, and then just to be safe, they set rules in place to make sure they stayed there for generations. Before, they granted your seat on the council based on the works you performed, not what you could do. Then the whole thing shifted to protecting your seat, which meant corruption, and..." Marcus exploded forward, and leaned against the back of the couch. "Larissa, have you ever read Plato's Republic? It really is a wonderful book about the search for the truth. Have you read it?"

I had more than read it. My father assigned it to me one winter to read. It was more than a suggestion. Every night we talked about what I had read, and what I felt it meant, and what it meant about life. At no other time had my father ever assigned me anything like that before, or taken such an interest. That included magic. My mother did most of the drilling where that came, but to my father, this seemed important and now the pieces of the puzzle of why fell into place. "Yes, my father had me read it."

"And what did you take away from it?"

This was a simple question. There are four points I remembered more than any other my father and I discussed. We discussed these four over and over again and even continued to do so long after I finished reading the book. "The importance of being just and true."

"Yes, but what does it say about leaders? He has some very specific tenets. Do you remember them?

Did I remember them? I had them drilled into me. There was no doubt about that. "A true leader should always keep an eye on tomorrow, share it, and drive toward it. That vision should be realistic and achievable. This was what my father called avoiding setting yourself up to fail. Another point he often reminded me from the text was a leader should always think of themselves as a teacher and a learner. That a person with knowledge to pass on who does, or believes there is nothing left to learn, is a fool. And to be wary of the leader that wants to be a leader. A leader should be truly altruistic. We should question anyone who is driven to seek power."

Master Thomas gave a polite and quiet clap.

"Very good. Your father taught you well," said Marcus Meridian. He let go of the couch and walked around it, retaking his seat. "Would it surprise either of you to know the council was failing on all of those points?"

That answer for me would be an emphatic no. After my recent involvement with the council, it wouldn't surprise me in the least.

"That is what my great grandfather saw, and he pushed back harshly. He challenged them. He challenged every one of them," Marcus said forcefully. He appeared agitated and had ignored his coffee and its additive. Perhaps he needed a little shot of it to calm down. He was making me uncomfortable, but Master Thomas appeared to be as cool as a cucumber, sitting there listening. I knew him. He had an end in mind, and this was all part of the path. That was how he worked. What the end was here, I didn't know yet. "What did they do? How did they react? They accused him of creating a schism and took him into custody and threatened to strip him of all of his magic, sending shockwaves through the others that felt the same way forcing them into silence."

"Can they do that?" I blurted.

"Do what?" asked Marcus.

"Take away someone's magic."

Master Thomas leaned forward and held up a hand toward Marcus, cutting off his attempt to answer. "I'm not sure. They say there is a spell that can strip it away, but I have never seen it and it has never been used, to my knowledge. Not that the threat isn't, or its possible existence isn't, an effective deterrence to keep people in line. Luckily for Marcus's family there, someone stepped in to help. Didn't they?"

Marcus groaned and looked away.

"What was their name?" Master Thomas asked again. He leaned toward Marcus Meridian to urge his answer to emerge. I wondered what was so important about the name. There was one option, though my mind had already considered, and the more I thought about it, the more it made sense. The family name had to be Wintercrest. They spared his family in a show of mercy, and instead, just exiled him. I was sure that would earn them a substantial amount of respect, and probably helped her family rise to the position they had.

"Dubois," muttered Marcus.

I was still working over the thought that it was Wintercrest when I heard my own. My body jerked up straighter than I normally sat, and my head cocked to one side as I stared right at Marcus with my black eyes.

"Yes Larissa, it was your grandparents that saved the great and powerful Meridians. You have never heard that story, have you?"

I shook my head, still too shocked to talk. The Meridians were legends in our world. They were the Supremes of the Supremes, but never held the role by their own choice, which made them even that much more legendary. My family knew them. They not only knew them, but they also helped them.

"Well, they did, and the way I see it, he owes you a debt of gratitude."

"Next time you see your grandparents, tell them thank you." Then it was his turn to stop and look surprised. "Wait, the math doesn't work." He held out his hand and a bright light with blue sparks hit me, causing my skin to tingle. He watched intently as it moved up and down me, then he got up and walked closer, trying again. It didn't hurt. It wasn't even annoying, but I still didn't like it and was ready to get up and do something about it, Meridian or not, but he stopped before he pushed me over the edge. "This isn't a trick?" he asked, now looking at Master Thomas.

"No trick."

"The math still doesn't work," he proclaimed.

"Oh, it works. You should know your history, and should be more observant. Look closer," urged Master Thomas, and Marcus Meridian did just that. He looked closely, and again I was not a fan, and grew more uncomfortable by the second, but again he stopped just in time. This time he jumped backward, and I saw a glow start in his hands.

"Don't try it," I stood up in a blink, and warned. "I will have you against the wall before you can raise your hands."

"Knock it off, both of you," Master Thomas bellowed. "Marcus, yes, she is a vampire, but not what you are thinking. She is also a witch. And she is the answer to all of this."

"The answer?" asked Marcus Meridian. He stood poised to attack me, but hadn't. I wasn't sure if it was my warning or Master Thomas's request, but I hadn't dropped my guard yet. He would have to make the first move either way. "What the hell is the damn question?"

"Is she the same girl in that picture of your grandfather back there on the table? She is." Master Thomas sat calmly, almost smugly, while Marcus jumped over the back of his couch and retrieved a large golden picture frame. I couldn't see the picture in the frame, just the back side of it, but I had a clear view of how intensely his eyes studied the picture, and then studied me.

"This... is you?" He turned it around so I could finally see it. Even from where I sat, I could see it clearly and recognized the grainy black-and-white photo of my family and the Meridians standing outside our house. I think I was eight there. This was one moment my mother didn't hesitate to remind Mrs. Landry of often.

"It is. I was eight."

"Impossible!" Marcus took another look at the picture, and then a look at me.

"Jean and his followers turned her eight years after that picture was taken. So, she is now a vampire, who retained her abilities as a witch." Master Thomas reached over the back of the couch and took the photo from the slack jawed Marcus Meridian. He put it back in its original place. "Which means she is also the answer to the question your grandfather was trying to answer."

Marcus attempted to say something once or twice, but no sound came out. His eyes took a few side glances at me, and then down at the picture. There was comfort in seeing that. It meant I wasn't the only one confused as hell by what was going on.

"That is where your debt comes in." Master Thomas got up off the couch and walked around to the table where the coffee was. "I think I will have some. Would either of you care for some? Marcus, can I freshen your cup?" he rattled the bottle that Marcus poured into his coffee.

"My debt? I think I get it." He looked right at me as compassionately as anyone had looked at me in a long time. Maybe since Mrs. Saxon did that first night in the coven. "I heard what happened to your betrothed, and I am sorry to tell you, I can't help you. Only one substance can reverse vampire venom, and I'm afraid yours is still red." He pointed at the blood charm dangling from my neck.

"She knows that, and if there was a spell or a potion to reverse it, trust me, she would have already done just that. In many ways, she is far more powerful than you. Just a little unrefined, but we have been working on it." The spoon Master Thomas stirred his coffee with rattled against the cup as he stirred, and his last comment stirred me. I was unrefined?

"Then," Marcus threw his arms up and bobbled his head. "What is it Ben? What do you need from me?"

"I want you to help me train her. Help me refine her."

"Why?"

"Because she can fix it all."

4

Marcus Meridian and Master Thomas talked about what *ALL* meant for the rest of the morning. I just listened as neither really asked me to contribute. I was the thing in the room that they talked about and pointed to as a piece of evidence in some presentation before a court. At times it appeared the court accepted the argument and at other times there were objections. Those objections created other conversations. When logic appeared to fail to sway Marcus, Master Thomas threw on the weight of his family debt to my family, tipping the scale back in his direction.

"I thought you were my teacher," I said on the way back up to my house.

"I am, but I will need help, and his involvement will go a long way toward your acceptance," replied Master Thomas.

"My acceptance?"

"Larissa, this goes far beyond magic." The porch floorboards creaked as we both stepped up on them, and that sound brought a thundering herd through the door to meet us.

Mike and Apryl both tried to fit through the door at the same time, bumping and jostling each other. Apryl eventually won and knocked Mike out of the way and grabbed my hand.

"Come. Hurry. It's happening," Apryl blurted. She grabbed my hand and yanked me hard through the doors and up the stairs.

Rob and his brothers stood at the bottom of the stairs and appeared to be on edge. Laura held Amy. Both had a concerned look on their faces. A look that had been commonplace here for some time now. Marie Norton and Theodora stood at the top of the stairs waiting for me. When I saw the look on both of their faces, I understood what Apryl had meant. I yanked free from her grasp. Now it was my turn to knock her out of the way as I rushed up the stairs. I felt woozy when I reached the top.

Nathan wasn't awake when I arrived, but he no longer looked dead. There were changes happening. The final changes. His hair had lost its straw-like texture and was full, lush, and more colorful than before. Darker than the darkest black. Gone was the ashen look of his skin. It was still pale. The pink and peach hues of the living would never again be present in his complexion. I wanted to check one last thing, but I couldn't. I wouldn't. At least not until he woke up. Of course, once he woke up, there would be no more questions. It would be complete then, and we weren't far away from that now. I didn't know how long, but it didn't matter. Now I was going to sit here with him until that happened, and neither Master Thomas nor wild horses could drag me away from him. The queasiness that was rolling around inside me was something different, and I asked Marie to bring me a bucket or pot from the kitchen, just in case.

The sun set, and darkness flooded the room. Who was standing at the door, or just inside it, changed throughout the night. Amy came in and slept on my lap for a portion of the night, but she eventually left to go to my parents' bedroom to sleep comfortably. I never left. I didn't even stand up to stretch; that wasn't something I needed to do. What I needed to do was what I was doing. I held vigil over him, wanting to be the one there when he woke up. To be the first person he saw.

And, while I sat there, my mind rehearsed what I would say to him when he finally did. I went back and forth between throwing my arms around him, confessing my love, and crying, or apologizing and begging his forgiveness. I had to be careful. This was a moment he would remember forever. That first moment when he opens his eyes and experiences the world more vividly than he ever had before. The colors of the world are all brighter, like high definition on steroids. The sounds deeper and more complete. It's a full symphony with layer upon layer stacked up, exposing you to depths you never knew existed, where before, you were only hearing one instrument play the song of the universe, missing most of it.

For me, it was overwhelming at first. Everything flooded in on me all at once. Then the thirst, a burning down my throat, hit me like a freight train before I had a chance to absorb everything else. It was blindingly painful. Like the world's brightest spotlight shining right into my irises while the loudest concert blared into my ears. That was why the Nortons grabbed me and rushed me outside to hunt. There was no way I would have made it out there on my own. Nathan would go through the same once he woke, and he would need someone to help him, and that had to be me.

I watched over him for the rest of the next day, and the crowd at the door continued to rotate. Everyone stayed at the door, except the others like us. They all ventured in. Some checked on me, but all checked on him. I thought about this for a bit during one of the many moments of silence while I waited for him to rejoin us, and I had a theory of why this was. The others didn't understand what was happening to Nathan, and their distance was a show of either respect or possibly fear. For the rest of us, it was personal. We had all gone through it; we understood it better than anyone.

"If you want a break, I can watch him," offered Apryl. She sat on the other side of the bed from me. Nathan's body jerked. I jumped and grabbed both of his hands with mine. They were still limp.

"Sorry," Apryl apologized, and shifted again, causing Nathan to move.

"It's fine." I let go of one of Nathan's hands, but I kept a firm grip on the other, and laced my fingers with his.

"Why don't you take a little break?" Apryl offered again.

"I'm fine," I insisted.

"It could still be hours or days."

"I know."

"Can I point something out, just as a friend?" Apryl asked. There was a humorous, almost snarky tone to her voice.

"What?" I asked, curiously. I cut my eyes in her direction and saw her lean over closer to me.

"I know you want to be here when he first opens his eyes. I would too, but when was the last time you showered? Remember, senses are on edge when you wake." She smirked.

I sniffed at myself, but smelled nothing. That didn't mean I didn't stink. It had been a few days and the world around us had a way of adhering to us as we passed through it. Then I turned to check the mirror. Holy crap! I was the volcano of hot messes. Makeup streaks down my cheeks traced the path my tears had taken. Yep, all of the senses are razor sharp when a vampire first wakes. If this was the first image Nathan saw when he woke, he would run, and I wouldn't blame him.

"Go. I got him," Apryl said, and I rushed out of the room, happy no one was standing at the door to hear our conversation.

I took the quickest and hottest shower in the history of showers. I wanted the heat to melt away the grime and the pain of the last few days. It took the grime, but left the pain. All of that still existed, and it would for who knew how long. It would persist even after Nathan woke. It might even be stronger. Seeing him in his new form would be a potent reminder of what all had happened.

When I returned to my room, Amy was at the door, and Apryl was still on the bed. I asked Amy if she wanted to help me with my makeup. Magic wasn't going to work for me this time. Not that I couldn't use it easily. I could, and if I did, what Nathan would see would be better than any make-up artist could ever do, but there was something about it that felt fake, and I didn't want to be that. I wanted to be real.

After a few minutes of trying, I felt I had made a mistake. What I had applied so far made me look like a clown. Amy had managed to at least apply some blush to my cheek and blend it out correctly. She, at her young age, had more of a skill at this than I did, and that was surprising. I saw Apryl snickering behind in the mirror and shot her a harsh glance. She stood up and walked up behind me.

"Let me give you a hand."

I looked up at her and snipped back, "Since when have you become a make-up expert?" I both felt and heard the thump on the back of my head.

"We can't use this old stuff," she said, looking down at the contents of powder-based cosmetics I had Laura retrieve from my mother's dresser the night of the holiday ball. "Be right back," she disappeared in a flash, but returned just as fast, carrying her own bag. Her hands rummaged around in it, pulling out two vials of some flesh-colored liquids, a single compact of powder, and a single tube of lipstick. I knew what to do with that. It was basically all I had ever used when I was with the Nortons, and before that, my mother permitted me to use a little blush and light lipstick. That same blush was what I was trying to apply on my own, but obviously had forgotten how over the years. The lipstick, pink chiffon was the shade, was now nothing more than a solid stick of dried up color.

"Hold still." She grabbed my head and began tilting it back and forth to give her the best angles. I now knew what a mannequin felt like. I must have made a few faces or something while Apryl worked. Amy giggled a couple of times. I couldn't really see what she was doing. As soon as I could glance at the mirror, she was turning my head again.

"There," she announced as she backed away from me and admired her own work in the mirror. I looked and Amy climbed up in my lap to look at me in the mirror, too. It was going to hurt to do this, but I had to give it to Apryl. She knew what she was doing. I looked great. Actually, I looked better than great. I was radiant. If you ignored my eyes. They sat like lifeless islands in the middle of paradise.

"Wow," I said, and spun around, looking at Apryl.

She wiggled her fingers in the air. "See, you aren't the only one with magic in your fingers. It helps that I was a teen in this century before. I learned everything I needed to know from the mall make-up counters."

I reached up and ran my hands through wet and stringy hair. It was a mess and needed to be done. I grabbed a brush, and turned back to the mirror, but a movement, really the movement of a shadow behind on the wall behind Apryl grabbed my attention. One hand pushed her aside, while another did a quick brush through my hair, drying it and styling it into a wavy red frame around the work of art Apryl had just completed.

5

One would think a fanfare of trumpets would announce a person's rebirth. Maybe it should also be followed by symphonies and a choral hallelujah. Maybe that was what it was for those that were not cursed beings. For us, it's a silent awakening, with your eyes popping open first, then the flood of colors, smells, and sounds more vibrant than you ever remembered. Your senses are so sensitive to the world around you; nothing escapes your notice. If that sounds overwhelming? It is.

"Apryl, get Amy out of here!" Apryl had already thought of it and had her in her arms and out the door before I finished my command.

You hear everything. The wind, the creaking of the wood in the bed you are lying in as you first move, the movement of a creature over a mile away in the woods, and the rhythmic thumping of the heart in that same creature. What quickly becomes obvious are two realizations. That thumping is the more succulent sound you have ever heard. You want it, and you need it. You would run through a wall to get to it. The second observation is that there is one thumping missing from the world, and that is your own.

I quickly threw up a block to keep anyone from hearing or sensing the life growing inside me.

Nathan hadn't opened his eyes yet, but his hand moved, and his body jerked in the bed. I jumped from my chair to the bed, landing lightly to not jostle him. I grabbed his hand. At first, he stayed limp in my grasp, like he had the entirety of the last few days, but then his fingers curled and gripped mine, and I moved up higher on the bed, to be right next to his face. There was a twitching behind his eyelids. He was becoming aware of the world, and eventually they would spring open.

Mike, Clay, and Brad stood at the door with Jen and Kevin Bolden behind them. Kevin pushed through the crowd and walked in, but stayed a few steps from the bed.

"Larissa, we're here. Are you sure you're ready?"

"Do I have a choice?" Who knew if I was ready. It wasn't like I really had a choice in this matter. It was going to happen no matter what, and I didn't want to wait any longer for it. I wanted my Nathan back. I longed to hear his voice and to see that smile again. I did question if I would ever see it again once he found out what happened to him, and that was devastating to all of us. The world was a better place when he smiled, and god I needed to see it.

I also knew Kevin wasn't just asking if I was emotionally ready for this. He was talking more about the physical. He had more experience with newborns than anyone else I knew. He knew what we were in for and that was why he pushed past the others, and was in here with me. It was also why Clay and Brad made their first appearance up here. They were his backup.

"Martin took the others out of the house. It's just us."

Nathan's fingers gripped my hand firmer than before. There was life in them. I wrapped my other hand around our joined hands and rubbed his to tell him I was there. His fingers rubbed back. His thumb, doing the simple up and down as he often did when we held hands. I moved up closer to his head, about to leap out of my body and into his to drag him out of there when his head moved. It was just a simple roll to one side, but it was movement, and even Kevin Bolden moved closer in response.

His head rolled back, and then it happened. It wasn't slow. It was a spring-loaded surprise, exposing two black orbs that searched all around, trying to absorb as much of the world, the true world, that he could. The sight of them broke what was left of my heart. They were cold and emotionless. Not the pools of blue I often lost myself in the warmth and safety of. Those days were gone. That didn't stop the flood of other emotions to appear as tears, and my throwing myself across his chest, wrapping my arms around him.

Nathan's arms wrapped around me, reluctantly at first, and then he squeezed me closer, and his hands rubbed my back. His head bent forward, and he buried his face into the crook of my neck.

"It happened again, didn't it?" he asked, muffled.

"Umm huh," was all I could say.

"How many days this time?"

He didn't know. He absolutely didn't know. I looked up at Kevin and begged for help. How could Nathan not know what happened? He felt it all, but wait, that meant he felt it all before when we brought him back with the charm. Oh, my god. That is what he thinks happened again. That devastated me. Someone was going to have to tell him the truth, and it had to be me.

"Nathan," started Kevin, but I shook my head to wave him off. Nathan released his embrace, and I sat up a little and looked down at his tormented face. It appeared the realization of what had happened was settling in. Maybe his memories were all crashing in on him. I felt his body tense up underneath me.

"Larissa, you might want to move," warned Kevin. He inched forward defensively.

Nathan's hands gripped frantically at his throat. Kevin reached down for Nathan, but he threw his hand away. He then threw me off the bed and exploded toward the door. Clay and Mike had a grip on him, but both struggled to hang on. He was stronger than them at the moment. He was stronger than any of us at the moment. I was quickly up on my feet, ready to throw spells. Before I even realized what I was considering doing to my boyfriend. Kevin waved me off.

"Nathan, let us help you. You need to feed."

His head jerked back and looked at Kevin, and then at me. My boyfriend was gone, and there was an animal in his body. An uncaring, absent of love, harsh killing machine. Gone was the best of him, and the worst of me had replaced it.

Kevin grabbed him from behind and helped the others force Nathan out of the bedroom door. I heard several loud bangs and rushed out to the second-floor landing. At the bottom of the stairs was a pile of tangled bodies. Nathan was already up on his feet and out the front door.

"I got him," yelled Clay, and he sped off.

"I hope so," Mike moaned as he stood and followed, a little slower.

Kevin looked up at me and before he followed, he said, "We will take good care of him."

Jen came up and put her arm around me on one side. Pam on the other. "Trust Kevin, he knows what he is doing."

It wasn't that I didn't trust him. That wasn't what was gnawing at me. It was guilt. Nathan was in this state because of me. I needed to be part of this and pulled away from them. Theodora caught my hand and pulled me back before I hit the top of the stairs.

"Larissa," she started, and then stopped. Tears flowed down my cheeks when our eyes locked. Theodora lowered her eyes and released my hand. She didn't say another word.

Marie Norton stood next to her, and I expected her to stop me like the others, but when I searched her for her objection, she mouthed, "Go." That is what I did. I took off down the stairs and out through the field, staying away from the rogue witch encampment and ran toward the shadows and what remained of St. Claire's coven.

The vampires weren't visible until I reached the trees, which took me an embarrassing long time to reach. I wasn't winded; that wasn't possible. I just wasn't as fleet of foot as I remembered. I was now slow for a vampire.

In the trees, Jean's followers, make that Jean's former followers, stood on either side lining a path that I had to assume the others had traveled. There were no footprints to follow or any broken branches. We were too graceful to leave either when we were on the move. Like ghosts moving through the world. I glanced back, just to check my own, and felt relieved there were no footprints or signs I had traveled in through that way. I had to check. I didn't feel myself in so many ways.

When I ran out of vampires lining the way, I had to trust my instincts to lead the way. Nathan was out here for only one reason, and I followed its scent deeper into the dense woods and then turned south along the river. I came across Brad and Mike standing by a tree. They grabbed me as soon as I stepped past them.

"Let Mr. Bolden handle him," Mike said as he yanked me backward by the arm.

I yanked my arm free and took a few steps forward. Mike made another attempt to grab my arm, but all he got was air and a perturbed look.

"Where is he?"

Brad stepped forward and leaned over close to me. I dodged him, thinking he was going to grab me and yank me backwards. He stood back, holding both hands up in front of him until my glare relaxed. Then he pointed off in the distance, and I let my glare follow. I saw them. Mr. Bolden stood over Nathan while he sat on the ground. He braced his arms on his knees with his head drooped between them.

"What are they doing?" I whispered.

"Do you remember what happened after you fed for the first time?"

I did. The burning went away, and I felt renewed in a way I had never felt before. Then it hit me, "Oh," I muttered. The memory of that moment choked off the sound. That same feeling swept over me again and sent me trembling.

"Yep, that." Brad reached over and rubbed my shoulders, and I leaned into him. "Nathan will be okay. This is just something we all go through."

He was right, but that didn't make it any less heartbreaking, and knowing what he was feeling made me want to be there with him. I wanted to hold him, but I knew that wouldn't help him. This wasn't a time to tell someone that it would be okay and try to hug the pain away, and unfortunately, that was all I could offer at the moment. I remembered how I felt, but I couldn't remember how Marie and Thomas got me through it. I was sure it wasn't by holding me. I am sure they did at some point, but there was a speech, and a lot of talking, and that appeared to be what Mr. Bolden was doing now.

Nathan appeared to be listening, but he didn't appear to be hearing what Mr. Bolden was saying. There was an internal fight going on in his head that I was well aware of. When he sprang up to his feet, Mr. Bolden tried to calm him down, and cut off his attempts to leave, but then he missed, and Nathan stormed by. I stepped out away from Brad, right in Nathan's path. Nerves stirred inside me, and the urge to empty my stomach emerged again. I fought and pushed it back down, and steadied myself as Nathan approached. The look that greeted me was cold, and it had nothing to do with his now lifeless black eyes. There was no expression of recognition, just a stare that went through me. I took a step closer to his path, but Nathan walked right past me.

"Give him time." Mr. Bolden put his arm around me and gave me a half hug. He didn't appear concerned. "He has a lot to absorb. It will take time and soon the old Nathan will return. Everyone does."

He let go of me and followed behind Nathan. Mike fell in line behind him. Brad waited for me to join him, and we walked out of the woods together, with a stewing Nathan leading the way.

"Just give him–" started Brad.

"I know... time." I finished for him.

He shrugged. "It's hard. You remember that don't you?"

"I guess." My answer drew a question filled look from Brad. I had a feeling I was missing something, but I didn't ask. I sped up, and Brad tried to grab my hand, but caught nothing but air.

Mike made the same attempt as I passed him, and missed.

Mr. Bolden didn't grab me, but he whispered a warning, "Larissa, don't." I ignored it.

"Nathan," I called out to him and reached for his shoulder. My hand was about to touch him when he spun around. The frigid expression I had seen in the woods was gone, and I would have given anything for it to return. It would have been a thousand times better than the anger-fueled look that had replaced it.

Nathan spun around and seethed, "Don't." Then his eyes remained locked on mine. The emotion-filled windows to his soul were closed. Around them, his face steamed and stewed, fueled by rage and pain. I wanted to remove it. I wanted to pull that weight from him, but I couldn't, and with how he looked at me, he didn't even want me to try.

He left me standing there at the bottom step of the porch. I just watched as he walked in through the front door. Mr. Bolden passed with a simple pat on the shoulder. Brad passed by with nothing, but Mike muttered, "We tried to warn you." That earned him a punch to his stomach as his reward. Brad snickered.

Once inside, I looked around for Nathan, but he was no longer in the front entry. I checked the parlor, but found nothing. Theodora walked down the hall toward me and rounded around the newel post and glided up the stairs gracefully.

"He's up here, but give me a minute. Some things require a woman's touch."

I watched as she ascended and disappeared into my bedroom. That woman, so graceful, so beautiful, and so alone with my boyfriend. My foot was on the bottom stair before I knew it and I was at the top in a dash, but something stopped me at the doorway. I stood there and watched.

Theodora sat next to him on the bed. Her legs crossed, with one ankle behind the other. She leaned into Nathan as she spoke. A hand occasionally touched him on the leg. Each touch was light, and from my vantage point, slightly seductive. Light and delicate. It lingered in an area before being removed, only to return to a new location. They returned a little too often for my liking. Nathan's eyes appeared to study her. Her shape, her lips. I had to shake that thought from my head. She was not flirting with my boyfriend, and he wasn't flirting with her. I told myself that repeatedly, but I couldn't miss the fact that he was sitting there, seemingly enjoying her non-flirting a bit too much. I had to stop my mind from running off in that direction. Jealousy wasn't a feeling I was familiar with, and so far, I didn't like it.

The two of them spoke softly. Her tone was sweet and smooth. Whatever she was saying, which I couldn't hear, was being well received. Nathan's face had relaxed. The anger and ferocity that had been present had melted away moments after I arrived at the door. He looked more like himself, and he even interacted with her. Was he asking her questions? What were the questions? There I was, feeling jealous again. I wanted to be the one he went to. Who was she to take my role? I wanted to walk in there and assert myself and take my rightful place, but then another voice spoke to me. It was logic, and I rarely heard it over my emotions. This time, it was as loud and clear as a cannon shot. Theodora was hundreds of years my senior. She knew more and had experienced more than I had. She had seen this probably dozens, if not hundreds, of times. She was the oldest, and best prepared of all of us.

After a conversation that lasted long into the afternoon, Theodora gave Nathan a hug and then stood up and took her exit of the room. I couldn't help but notice how Nathan's eyes traced her body as she walked away from him. That was something I filed away for later. There were bigger concerns now. At least that was what that logical voice that still had control of my being said. She closed the door behind herself, and I held out a hand to hold the door open. I was going in now, or was, until she looked at me with her big eyes and pursed full lips and shook her head. I dropped my protest and stood there face to face with a closed wooden door.

"Give him some... time."

My mind completed the statement before Theodora had a chance.

"He is dealing with so much. Sadness. Anger. Name any negative emotion and that is what is going on inside of him at the moment. It will just take time."

"The first kill is always the hardest," I agreed.

She laughed. "Oh child, you think this is what that is all about?"

I nodded, believing that was all it could be, but she shook her head.

"He knows what he is, and as a result he realizes what had happened, and what it means for everything. To most, that is a frightening and depressing realization. The life they knew is gone in so many ways. You remember that moment, don't you?"

I didn't. I didn't at all. When I woke up, I didn't remember my life before. Being what I was at that moment was all I remembered. My life before, was a big black hole. She walked me downstairs and explained more, and I finally asked her what she told him. She said she told him about what she felt, which she still remembered as clearly as if it had happened just yesterday, and explained that everything he felt was natural. Then she told me what she always tells new vampires in this situation. It's a statement that slapped most of them right across the face. That everything they felt was wrong. Life is not over; it is just the beginning. Your life can be as much like your old life as you want it. It's completely up to you to make what you want out of it. She had one last point that I remembered hearing her tell me clearly on one of my visits. We are beautiful creatures and should live life to the fullest.

Theodora left me on the front porch. She needed to head back to her place for a bit to attend to her "human" business, but promised to come back tomorrow or tomorrow night to check in. The last thing she said to me before she hugged me and bid her farewell was an instruction that I felt would be impossible to fulfill. I wasn't to go to Nathan. He would come to me when he was ready. I wasn't sure if she truly understood what she was asking of me, but she was rather insistent and made me promise.

So, I sat out on the porch and waited. I fought every urge I had to run up the stairs to him. Twice I was weak and made it as far as the front door before I stopped and returned to my perch in the rocking chair. When darkness fell, the others returned home from their visit with the rogue witches. Amy seemed to think it was some kind of fair and talked about all the magic tricks she saw. Stan bragged about a few of her own tricks, remarking to me she was rather advanced for a shifter of that age. She sat with me until she dozed off and then Lisa grabbed her and took her in with her to get some sleep. Martin, Rob, and Dan stood out on the porch for a few minutes, just staring out at the sight before them. A large camp of witches on one side, and dozens of vampires hovering in the trees on the other.

"I don't really see a need for us to do a patrol, do you?" Martin asked. I agreed and sent the three of them inside.

Throughout the night, random vampires emerged from the house and attempted to make small talk. It didn't take any of them long before they realized I wasn't really in the mood for it, and they either sat there in silence or went back inside. I wanted and needed the solitude to ponder what Nathan was going through. The emotions, not from all he sensed in this new world, but from what he felt he had lost. I didn't have a reference point for that, at least not personally. I remembered the story Clay had told of those first few days. It sounded like he was a tormented soul until we, I mean the Boldens, found him. Was that how Nathan felt? I sure hope not, but feared he did.

Out among the woods, vampires mingled and as darkness set in and the witches' camp quieted. Groups upon groups mingled with one another. Some came as close as the line that used to be made of runes, just to look around before retreating to the shadows. The line had faded significantly, losing both its luster and strength throughout the day. I hadn't redrawn the line, so nothing stopped them from coming over, except choice. They were choosing not to, or that was what it seemed. Mostly, they appeared unable to make a choice. They have spent years, decades, or centuries doing what Jean commanded. Now they were on their own, and that seemed to be unsettling for them. I felt a brief moment of responsibility there and decided to talk to Theodora about it when she returned to see if anything could be done.

An hour after the witching hour, which really had nothing to do with witches except for the fact that they were all asleep at that moment, the door creaked behind me. Laura and Pam were on the swing, and out of the corner of my eye I saw both of their heads shoot toward the door before they stood up and walked inside.

"So, you and I have something in common," said a familiar voice behind me.

Tears came to my eyes at hearing his voice. "What's that?" I said, playing along, forcing my voice to sound stronger than it was at the moment.

"We have both turned twice."

"Sucks doesn't it?"

"Yep." Then he placed a hand on my shoulder briefly before he leaned down and hugged my neck.

6

He sat in the chair beside me for a long time. There was silence between us, but there wasn't distance. Which was something I worried would be there. It seemed, as absurd as it might sound to say, normal. None of the speeches I rehearsed in my head for the moment he woke up made it out. They didn't seem important anymore. The one where I apologized and begged his forgiveness seemed limp and worthless for what had happened, but at the same time, it didn't appear needed anymore. Nathan never regarded me with a look that had an appearance of hatred or blame. The one where I threw myself across him and confessed my love didn't seem to be needed either. We weren't sitting on top of each other, and hadn't shared a great embrace, but there didn't seem to need to be one. Him sitting here, with the little looks in my direction from time to time, told me everything I needed. That we, at least for the moment, were okay. That didn't stop my heart from breaking every time I saw those black eyes. We might be okay, but I wasn't so sure I was.

We sat and looked at the scene that used to be my front yard. There were still scars on the ground from the fight that occurred a few days ago. They were something I could easily fix, but hadn't. I really hadn't even looked at them before now. The shadows created by the moonlight made the indentation where I slammed Jean St. Claire down into the ground appear enormous, where in reality it was only a dent of a few inches in the ground. Looking at it now didn't bring any of the pride like I had felt before. All I felt was the painful reminder of what had happened, and how I didn't stop it.

"Witches, I assume?" asked Nathan, breaking the silence.

"Rogue witches."

He looked over at me and asked, "What?"

"Rogue witches. Ones that are exiled by the council, or disagree with the council," I explained, looking out at the camp. My mind wondered how many there were, and how many witches there were in the world? I didn't think there would be all that many, but this camp was huge, and those were just the rogue witches that were in the area.

"I thought they called those Larissa," sniped Nathan, completely deadpanning the shot while looking forward.

"That is a special level of hell. These witches haven't achieved that yet." I fired back. "It's between this and the prison." I nodded out to the camp of roque witches.

"Prison?" Nathan asked. He leaned forward in his chair and looked at me with a cockeyed expression. He thought I was kidding. Oh, contraire.

"Yes, there is a prison for the most dangerous witches. I just found out about it." It was true. Marcus Meridian told me about it. Which made me wonder why the council threatened his family with the removal of their magical power instead of just being put in prison where they couldn't do any harm to the council. Marcus told me it was to send a message to anyone that might support them. The fear of being stripped themselves would keep them from doing anything that the council might feel was a threat.

"It's a horrible place, underground in a deep cavern on an island that no one knows is there, in a place you can't find."

"Of course it is," he said, and winked.

"No, I'm serious. The sun never rises, and it always rains. Underground there are bottomless pits and rivers of lava. Anyone sent there is there for life. There is no parole, and the council is judge and jury." I looked at him as seriously as I could and his own expression changed as he sat back in his chair. I made note of how straight he sat. It was very un-Nathan like. "Yep, it's pretty much a bad place."

"And they call us savage," remarked Theodora from behind us. I turned around, but not as fast as Nathan did. His grin was expansive. I didn't remember her returning, but perhaps I was so stuck in my own thoughts she glided right by me. "I hope we aren't interrupting anything." She stepped out the door. Marie Norton followed.

"Oh, no. You aren't interrupting anything at all," Nathan was quick to say, and his eagerness ruffled me slightly, but I held my tongue, which was very un-Larissa like.

"We were thinking it might be time to go out and meet your cousins," Theodora said with a smile.

"Sounds good." Nathan stood up, again a little too quickly. This would be what I would call the Theodora effect, and I would pick an appropriate time to correct it with an equal and opposite reaction, but that time was not now.

She led the way off the porch, and Nathan wasn't far behind her. I watched, annoyed, and then turned to Marie. A realization of what we were doing had set in, and I didn't agree. I grabbed the woman I had regarded so long as my mother by the hand and yanked her close. "Mom," I caught myself, and there was an awkward glance between us. I knew this moment was bound to happen eventually, and again;

this would be something we would have to settle later. I had other concerns that were at the forefront of my mind that needed tending to. "Is this a good idea?"

Marie reached over and brushed a lock of hair away from my face. Her touch brought back so many memories of all the years we pretended to be mother and daughter. Wait, I take that back. No one was pretending. This was complicated, and it was complicating what I was trying to get through.

"It is," she answered calmly. "Theodora and I talked about it, and we both agree it would be good for Nathan to meet others like us. Others that from all appearances are just normal people living normal lives, even with what they are."

"But this soon?" I asked urgently. Nathan had just come back from it, and like Theodora told me earlier, he was dealing with a ton of emotions. "This isn't too soon?"

"It's exactly the right time. Now come on." She wrapped both hands around mine and led me off the porch. We had walked this way many times together in our backyard, back in Virginia. Usually headed out to the shed where Thomas was working on the furniture and cabinets he built for others. It felt natural and good, but odd, all at the same time. We were in the wrong place.

Marie giggled just before she let go of my hand. "Go reclaim your boyfriend."

She gave me a big shove forward, and I reached him in just a few steps. I grabbed his hand. Our fingers interlaced together perfect, like they had so many times. Now the warmth I always enjoyed was missing. I felt something cold come over me as several shadows emerged out of the woods as we approached the tree line.

"Marie?" cried a thick creole female voice. With it, I felt the glare of dozens of sets of eyes. My body tensed up. Mr. Helms had taught me well.

"Oh God, it is you," cried the voice again, and then out of the darkness ran a middle-aged blonde woman in a simple navy-blue dress that went to her knees, she wore brown leather boots which were caked with mud from the field. "It is you," she repeated.

When she was close enough for us to see the attractive features of her face, Marie ran to meet her with a cry of, "Frances!"

The two women hugged, slinging each other around one another as they spun and shrieked. A small group of vampires splintered off from the others beyond the tree line and joined the two women. There were hugs and warm embraces all around. A man grabbed Marie by the face, looking at her with what appeared to be tears in his eyes, and then bent down and kissed her on both cheeks.

Nathan and I watched the sight of Marie's old friends welcoming her home. We heard greeting after greeting with a few adding in, "We thought you were dead." It would appear no one in this crowd knew Jean St. Claire had her locked in that dark dungeon being tortured. With how they greeted her, I wondered if they had known, would they have stood up to him to do something about it?

The joyful reunion turned solemn when I heard someone ask about Thomas, and Marie's head bowed as she told them. She didn't hesitate to tell them what happened and who was behind it. Several of them turned and looked away from her as she identified the assailant that took his life. Others showed anger, with one pounding his fist into the palm of his hand. "You should have reached out to us," he exclaimed. Marie just ignored him, and tried to turn the conversation away from such a dark topic. Her next topic was, well, me.

Marie turned and motioned for Nathan and I to join her. "Everyone, this is Larissa Dubois, and..." there was a collective gasp following my name that drowned out Nathan's introduction. A few stepped back, while the others stepped forward with curiosity.

"So, this is her?" asked the same man that pounded his fist at hearing who was behind Thomas' death.

"Yes," responded Marie, then she turned and introduced her passionate friend. "Larissa, this is Fred Harvey. A dear old friend of mine and your father's... I mean Thomas'." Hearing the term father caused several odd looks and Marie waved an embarrassed hand in the air before delicately placing it just below her collarbone. Something I had seen her do many times in the past.

The tall, redheaded man with a long red beard that hung down over the vest of the suit he wore, which appeared to be several centuries out of date, stepped forward and looked me over. "You're still a witch?"

I figured the best way to answer that, and any other questions the others may have, was to show them instead of telling them. I pulled my hand away from Nathan's grasp and held both hands up in front of me. A glowing green orb appeared between them, then green flames shot from it, illuminating everyone. But I wasn't done yet. The flames swirled as I played with the strings of the surrounding universe. I allowed them to climb high into the sky, carrying the orb with it at breathtaking speed. Then a single bolt of lightning cracked across the clear sky. I held both hands up as if to say, "Anymore questions."

"She's her father's daughter," proclaimed Theodora. "Just as powerful, if not more so than Maxwell ever was."

"Well, that explains everything I guess," muttered Fred Harvey.

"Yes, it does," said the woman who first greeted Marie. The woman looked at me through the tears that had formed in her eyes. Her bottom lip quivered.

I knew her name was Frances from hearing her and Marie greet each other, but there was something familiar about her. I first saw it when my little light show chased the shadows away from her face. She walked forward and reached for both of my hands, and I held them out instinctively. Her face was familiar, and my mind raced to place it. It wouldn't have been odd if I have had seen many of these people around town, but this was more than just a casual acquaintance or a one time passing on the street. Then my mind moved her blond hair up into a bun on the back of her head, and her full name escaped in a single phrase, "Frances Rundle."

"You remembered," she beamed. "My, you grew up to be the spitting image of your mother."

Then my mind exploded with memories. Frances Rundle was the woman that attempted, albeit a failed attempt, to teach me to play piano for two years. It was all my mother's idea. An outlet that wasn't magic related. The problem was, I had a tin ear and wasn't particularly good. That's not exactly accurate. I was horrible, unless I used magic, which I never did when she was present. It was the strict rule in our house. No magic around visitors unless my parents told me they were witches, which they never told me if Frances Rundle was or not. They most certainly didn't tell me she was a vampire, and I had to wonder if she was at that time or not. This wasn't a question I knew how to ask.

Frances pulled me in and hugged me, and it felt like it always did before, all those years ago. "It's so great to see you," I said. She let go and backed away, beaming as she looked back at me several times.

Nathan leaned over and asked, "Who's that?"

"My piano teacher," I said.

"I didn't know you played."

"I don't. I stunk at it," I confessed to Nathan.

"You just never put in the practice time," said Frances as she settled back in with the group.

Dang, that vampire hearing.

The man who first approached Marie and kissed her on both cheeks walked forward, and I prepared for another introduction by searching his face for any familiarity. There was none. Not even the hint of anyone I used to know or may have seen once or twice, and much to my surprise, he didn't approach me. He approached Nathan with an outstretched hand. The man was tall and slender, a good two inches taller than Nathan, which meant he was a giant to me. His deep voice completed the picture.

I nudged Nathan, who seemed to be leery of the outstretched hand. He reached out slowly, eventually taking the man's hand. "You must be the young man that we saw Jean bite. I want to say seeing you rush and tackle him away from her," he glanced in my direction, "was one of the bravest acts I have ever seen."

It was one of the stupidest I had ever seen, and he had now done it twice, but I wasn't about to say that aloud and ruin Nathan's moment. I just stood there and smiled.

"Thanks," said Nathan reluctantly.

"I guess I should also welcome you. It will take a bit, but you will soon forget anything happened." The man let Nathan's hand go, but added. "We are all here to help."

"Thank you, sir," responded Nathan.

"Sylvester's the name. Sylvester Webb."

Theodora put her arm around Nathan and said, "Sylvester is a good person to know. He is over eight hundred years old. He knows more about blending in with human society than anyone I know."

"Three continents," he stated proudly. "I've even fought in every major war, including... the French Revolution." He threw the last bit out with a convincing French accent.

"I need to borrow these two for a moment. I promised to bring them back," announced Theodora. "I want them to meet *him*." She turned Nathan easily with the lightest of touches, and I grabbed his hand to remind him I was there.

"Nathan, everyone you just met lives in New Orleans and has rather normal lives. If you didn't already know they were vampires, would you have known?" she asked.

"Not really."

"That is something I want you to remember. We live how we want. The only difference is we don't have some of the same limitations humans do," she said as we walked deeper into the woods, passing small groupings of vampires as we went.

"You make it sound so simple."

"I agree," I interjected into their seemingly private conversation. It did sound simple, too simple.

"It is," she insisted. "It's our mind that complicates things. As soon as you free your mind to the possibilities that life brings, how simple it really is reveals itself." Theodora continued to prance proudly forward into the woods, not that she ever gave the impression she was anything but proud. This woman exuded confidence.

I looked back at Marie, who was a few steps behind us. She mouthed, "she's right." Huh. Leave it to my brain to not see it. Of course, that didn't really surprise me. The girl that over thinks everything. Simple doesn't have a chance in my world.

"Marteggo," called Theodora. She stopped dead in her tracks and went down to a single knee. Marie Norton stepped up next to me and did the same.

I followed suit and yanked Nathan down to give him the hint. I bowed my head, but then looked up slightly to see what all this was about. There were two males, dressed in the black suits and slicked back hair like what Reginald and the rest of Jean's most loyal followers wore, but they weren't the only people here. There was someone else, and he was different, very different. He sat on the roots of a grand mangrove tree, sprawled out as if it were his throne. His posture had a little slump to it, and long, black, curly locks hung down around his face and across his broad shoulders. He even dressed differently from the others. He wore boots, and jeans, and a white shirt that almost looked like a t-shirt.

"Theodora," his voice returned. "It's been a while."

Theodora stood up, and I waited for Marie to do the same before I joined them.

"I could say the same for you. We haven't seen you around these parts in what, two hundred years?"

"I didn't like the neighborhood," he grumbled back.

"Who is he?" I whispered to Marie.

"Better question, who are you?" he asked, pointing a gnarly finger in my direction.

"Marteggo, let me introduce you to the vampire that forced Jean to leave this area. This is Larissa Dubois." Theodora reached back and yanked my hand free from Nathan's, and pulled me forward toward the man that now looked more beast than man sitting there in shadows. "Larissa, this is Marteggo Dupoint."

She introduced him as if I should know who he was.

"I guess I should thank you for ridding us of that fungus, but he isn't gone, only displaced. So, I will hold it for now." He leaned down from the mangrove roots. "He will be back. Mark my words. He is after something, and has been for years. Something very dangerous."

"She's the witch," spouted Theodora.

Marteggo leaped down off the root and stomped toward me, emerging out of the shadows and crossing through several beams of moonlight, giving clarity to who we were speaking with. This was no beast; this was a man. A large burly man, with long curly black hair that flowed behind him in the wind as he walked. His face, like

Nathan's, had chiseled features, or at least what I could see did. A jet-black beard covered his mouth. Nothing hid his black eyes, which appeared to have a permanent scowl. "You? You're, the witch?"

From beside me, Theodora clarified. "She is the daughter of Maxwell Dubois. Didn't you recognize the name?"

He threw his head back as far as it would go and laughed a bellowing laugh that echoed through the woods. His clear charm dangled on a long gold chain and glistened in the moonlight. His two escorts didn't join in. Theodora covered her mouth, hiding what appeared to be a smirk of her own.

"I call that a huge and well-deserved dose of karma. Too bad it wasn't laced with some poison." he said. "You have brought me some great news, my sweets." He grabbed Theodora by the waist and spun her around. The rough exterior he had dropped away as she wrapped her arms around him. I looked at Nathan to be sure he was seeing this. Not that Theodora threatened me, but I couldn't ignore how beautiful she was. With how Marteggo Dupoint devoured her, he saw her that way too.

He dropped her to her feet, but still held on to her. She plastered herself to his side. "Now, Miss Dubois. Don't for a second believe this is the last you will hear from him. The man is not well, and you have now wounded him, yet again." Marteggo warned with a wag of a finger. "First you deprived him of what he wanted, then you defeated him, and probably worst of all, you took his world from him. That won't go unpunished."

I wanted to thank him for pointing out the obvious, but against my nature, I held my tongue. I still didn't know who this man was. All I knew was he appeared different from the others, and Theodora seemed to trust him. I needed more information before I did as well.

"And who is this big strapping boy?" He slapped Nathan on the arm and almost knocked him to the ground.

"This is her boyfriend, Nathan Saxon. He saved Larissa from Jean, tackling him to give her the opening she needed," introduced Theodora.

"Well, any enemy of Jean's is a friend of mine." He reached out, shook Nathan's hand. "A brave move. We need more like you that will step up–"

"He was human when he did it," interrupted Theodora, stopping Marteggo mid-statement.

He looked at Nathan, shocked, and ripped his hand back. "Son, were you stupid? Didn't you know who you were attacking and what would happen?"

Nathan appeared mortified standing there and stammered, trying to answer.

"Relax son. It's okay. I say we need a little more stupid and reckless abandon these days." Marteggo slapped him again. "It's great to meet you."

My inner voice escaped and asked, "But who are you?"

"Well," Marteggo straightened himself up, and tugged at his shirt. "Marteggo Dupoint at your service."

"I know your name, but who are you?" I asked, feeling there was more to this man, and why Theodora brought us to see him.

"Well, maybe I should take that question," interjected Theodora. "This will sound like some fantasy story, but it is all true."

I half wanted to say try me, considering the world I had seen over the last several months. There wasn't much I wouldn't believe anymore.

"Marteggo was a pirate that sailed the Gulf and Caribbean several hundred years ago. A vampire in Port-au-Prince bit him, and he became the legendary Vampire Pirate until he settled down here. Once word got out who he was, vampires flocked to him, and, well, he became the de facto leader here."

"Not something I wanted, mind you," interrupted Marteggo. "I wanted to find someone and suckle all that life had to offer. Not tell people how to live their lives."

"Which you never really did,"

Marteggo held up a finger to emphasize the point. "True. I didn't unless someone caused a problem. Then they stood before the mast."

Now I was confused. If I understood what Theodora had said, Marteggo was really the true leader of the New Orleans coven, and if that was true, what happened? Something had to have for Jean St. Claire to take control, or, and my head was swimming at this point, was there some kind of split, like in the world of witches? Why couldn't anything be simple?

"Then I have a question."

"Go ahead."

Marteggo righted himself and crossed his arms. He was an impressive image with a stature that demanded respect or created fear. I had a feeling either worked for him. The weight of his presence caused a hesitation on my part as I wondered if I should ask what I was curious about. "Then..." my voice cracked, but I cleared it quickly. "What happened? If you were the leader, how did Jean take over?"

The gregarious smile that had adorned Marteggo's face slipped away, and he backed away from Theodora. She attempted to hold on cautiously. Maybe that fleeting warning in my head was right. The giant man sank back into the darkness and sat on the edge of the mangrove roots he used as his throne when we arrived. There was a huff before he leaned forward against his tree trunk thighs.

"You already know Jean St. Claire, so you shouldn't have to ask that," he sneered, and glanced to the side before looking back with a pained expression. "But, since you asked, I will tell you. He was a sniffling whiner in our world. Always complaining, why do we need to act more human? Why do we need to hide? Why shouldn't we show how superior we are? Always this and that. Now, I will say, I never ruled. I refused to. I thought of what I did as leading by example, and yes, I hid what I was by blending into the world around me when I had to and avoided humans as often as I could. That is what we must do. Nothing would be gained by us showing the world our true colors, but fear, forcing us further into the shadows. Just like Theodora and many others have done. That shouldn't stop us from living the best life we can, and I wanted to enjoy life, not spend it trying to control and enslave."

Theodora smiled and nodded as he mentioned her.

"Jean was never satisfied with that, and did the only thing he could do. He couldn't physically challenge me." There was a deep chested chuckle.

"Few could," added Theodora.

"Thank you, my love. Jean knew it too, so he didn't. He did the only thing anyone like him could do. He fostered discontent in the masses. He found a few that felt as he had, and it grew. What is the saying? One bad apple ruins the barrel. He spread like a cancer through our community. Before I knew it, there were more of those than there were of us. There was no grand announcement. No election of sorts. Just a switch in the balance of power."

"Why didn't you fight back?" asked Nathan.

"Well now, that is an interesting question there, my boy. At first, we didn't. Remember, we just wanted a peaceful life, which is what you should strive for too." He wagged a finger toward the newest vampire of the bunch. "Heartache and pain comes with wanting more. There is nothing wrong with taking the best life this world offers. At first, we let him do as he wanted, and we watched. When he stepped too far and threatened to destroy that peace for all of us, there was no choice. We fought, we lost, and they hunted us until we gave up and left. It's why some of us are way back here, and not with the others out there. Distrust still runs deep, but hearing the news that someone forced Jean out, we had to come see for ourselves." Marteggo stood up and left his throne of roots. "Don't take my presence as a return to power. It's quite the opposite. I hope it is a return of the peace."

I hoped he was right too, but nothing at that moment felt like peace. It felt more chaotic than normal, and sitting out there threatening to pour more chaos on it was Jean. My mouth went off without a filter again to point out that fact. "Jean is still out there."

"It's Larissa, isn't it?" Marteggo asked.

I nodded.

"I know, and his absence might only be temporary, but it still gives a moment of peace and maybe enough will enjoy that. If enough do, it may dissolve any chance of him finding support when he returns."

I felt it coming, and I knew I needed to push it back down. It wasn't another bout of nausea. That would have been better. The pressure built up inside, and nothing was going to stem it. It needed to be said. Even while happiness and warmth appeared to return to our group. Marteggo embraced Theodora. Nathan put his arm around me and pulled me close. I should have just let it go, but I didn't. I shook off Nathan's arm and took a step forward, and let out the storm cloud that had bumbled up inside. They had to know.

"I think he has the support of the witches."

I looked around, expecting to find expressions of doom and gloom, but I heard laughter. First from Marteggo, and then from what I believe were his escorts that stood on either side of the mangrove.

"Good, let them deal with his ass," replied Marteggo. "If you ask me, they deserve him. They are no better than he is. Them and that council. Neither are happy with just being who they are. They all want more."

Theodora joined in with a reserved snicker. Even Marie giggled at the comment. Nathan and I were the only ones that didn't. I knew the truth. This wasn't just a relocation of the problem of Jean to someone else. This was taking two colossal problems and creating one gigantic issue, but I let it drop, at least for now. There was a part of me that believed this was more of a witch problem.

"You seem so serious. This is all good news." Marteggo let go of Theodora and came over, wrapping Nathan and I in the largest embrace I had ever felt. We were like dolls against his massive frame. "This is good news." His voice sounded muffled, with my head buried against his chest. "Come, let's drink and tell stories," he said as he released us both. Then he put a single hand on Nathan's chest. "Well, we drink, you don't. You are still much too young, but you can listen."

He walked around us, laughing as he continued out of the woods toward the other vampires. Theodora joined him and walked with him hand-in-hand. Marie fell in behind, and I found Nathan and I were the only two left, so we followed as well.

7

The first rays of morning were cutting through the openings in the canopy of branches overhead when we headed back up to the house. The night was great, and I had to swallow a little crow and admit that Theodora and Marie were right. Letting Nathan meet others like us helped. It helped him realize his life wasn't over. If anything, as many pointed out, the best parts of his life were ahead of him. I hoped I was part of that picture, not that I had a lot of reason to doubt it. Most of the night, Nathan held me in his arms as we listened to stories and gems of advice from those that had been vampires longer.

Mike, Jeremy, and Brad were out on the porch, horsing around when we arrived back at the farmhouse. I wanted to remind them there was a house full of others sleeping behind them, but every light except the parlor was off, so no one seemed to be bothered. The three of them straightened up as soon as they saw us approaching and stood at the rail grinning.

"Where have you kids been?" asked Mike. He stood right at the railing with his arms crossed, tapping his foot. Of course, being a vampire, it sounded like a woodpecker on speed.

"You could have called. We have been so worried." Brad said, struggling to keep a straight face.

"Oh, knock it off," cracked Pamela from behind them in the door. "They were the same place you guys were. Out there with the others, enjoying life."

The three of them turned and watched as we walked by. Mike grabbed Nathan by the shoulder and whispered something into his ear. I couldn't hear it, but I saw the grin grow on his face, and then felt him grip my hand and yank me through the door, almost trampling Pamela. "What the hell?" I asked, and I didn't get an answer.

We were one foot on the stairs when Nathan jerked to a stop. The grip on my hand tightened, and his head snapped. I was so used to what had his attention, I never really noticed it anymore unless I focused on it. The years of being like this had desensitized me. To a newborn, there was no ignoring it. Its presence overrode your thoughts. Your body just reacted to its presence, just like Nathan was now. I spun around on the stairs as he ran for the parlor. In there,

Laura had sprung up from the settee and rushed to meet Nathan at the door. Amy, who had been sleeping soundly in her lap, was now startled awake. The first sounds of a scream left her mouth. I watched as he shoved Laura against the wall. Mike, Brad, and Jeremy rushed through the front door, but they would never catch him. He had a head start, and being a newborn was still faster and stronger.

My hand reached to grab him, but he was too far. That was when I squeezed the vibrations of the world and shoved them forward, knocking him facedown on the floor. He didn't lay there stunned as long as I had hoped. He jumped back up to his feet in an instant. I had one trick up my sleeve and pulled it out. He stopped and stood there, confused.

Amy crawled back behind the settee and screamed. Laura pulled herself along the floor to Amy. Each movement appeared pained, but that didn't stop her from reaching Amy and pulling her close. Nathan stood there, clueless. I had cast the spell so fast; I couldn't even remember what I had projected for him to see. This wasn't the simple trick I played at Theodora's making Master Thomas appear to be a vampire. That was my first choice, and albeit easiest, but I couldn't trust that Nathan would stop, even when the feeling disappeared if he could still see her. This way, there was no doubt. She wasn't there, and neither was he.

The scream had woken the entire house, and Rob and Martin bounded down the stairs. Steve joined them. I saw the concern on his face as soon as he took in the scene.

"She's okay. I have Nathan under control," I said, standing right next to Nathan, just in case I needed to intervene again. Steve pushed down the stairs the rest of the way and pushed through Mike's shoulder to get through the door. Mike hissed with the thud of the impact, and Steve growled. Martin and Rob took another step down the stairs, but backed off when Mike didn't follow Steve into the parlor. He made a beeline for Amy, who was in Laura's arms.

"She's safer with her own kind," he said with a coldness I hadn't seen in him before, but it was common from Ms. Parrish. Steve wasn't just making a suggestion. He reached down and yanked Amy from Laura's grasp. She went willingly and stopped screaming. She sniffed as they passed us. I reached out and stroked her head while she looked leerily at Nathan standing confused in the center of the room. Laura shot me a look of disdain that I couldn't explain at the moment. It was both pointed and targeted. There was no mistaking that.

I ushered Rob and Martin back up the stairs, not waiting to take any chances at all. As I expected, both protested, stating they could handle things themselves, but I urged them as nicely as I could to go back upstairs, not wanting a fight inside. They didn't listen. At least not to me. When Pam and Apryl both made the same suggestion, they reluctantly headed upstairs. I gave it a few seconds to be sure before I let Nathan return. His head jerked around, taking in the parlor, and probably wondering where what he saw went.

"What happened?" he asked.

"You tried to eat Amy," sniped Laura.

Nathan's jaw dropped and his hands reached out into the room for an explanation. He looked around the room, which was now all vampires. "I didn't."

"Oh, you did," responded Mike.

Apryl hit Mike with a sharp elbow. "She's okay, Nathan. You couldn't control yourself. It's not your fault at all," she explained.

He looked back at me, horrified and shaken. "How could I?"

"Nathan, darling." I reached up and caressed his cheek. "You couldn't help it. Things are too raw right now for you to stop yourself, but she is okay. I did a little." I waved my hand in front of his face. "You were someplace else and didn't even know she was here."

Nathan collapsed in the chair in the corner and held his head in his hands. "How could I?" He repeated, more mournful this time.

"Nathan, you will learn to control it. Trust us," Jeremy said.

I wanted him to look up. If he had, he would have seen an entire room of smiling vampires, and boy were we a sight, fangs and all.

Apryl walked over and kneeled down next to him. She looked around at each of us cautiously, and her attempt to be the peacemaker drew some odd looks from the room. Apryl would be the last person I would pick, but she was the one that stepped forward. Compassion and her were an odd couple. "Trust us, in time, you will learn how to handle it. We all have. Remember, back in the coven, we were all in the same classes, and I never once wanted to attack anyone."

"None of us did," added Mike.

"Well, except for Gwen," concluded Apryl. There were smirks and a few admonishing looks in her direction at that comment.

I had refrained from smirking and motioned for her to get up and took her spot next to my boyfriend. I reached up and pried a hand from his head. It still shook, as his mind tried to process what had happened. I thought of what Clay had told me about his encounter with his parents in those first two days after he turned. It was the same thing, and if he were here, maybe hearing about that could help get through to Nathan, but Clay, Marie, and the Boldens were still outside with the others. It was up to me, and to be honest, I wouldn't have it any other way.

51

"Nathan, she's safe. None of us would let anything happen to her. Trust us on that. In time, what you feel now will stop feeling like an uncontrollable raging fire, and turn into nothing but an itch that you can easily ignore, but... until then. I can help you like I did tonight. I can mask Amy and the others."

"Can you?" he asked through his remaining hand. I stroked his other between my own.

"I'm a witch, remember?" I wanted him to look up at that comment and see me. I wanted him to see how serious I was and feel reassured by it, but he didn't. He kept his head buried in his hand. "I did it when Master Thomas and I met the other vampires at Theodora's that night, and it worked perfectly, and if that doesn't work, I can do what I did tonight to you, and to Clay a few weeks ago."

"And it works?"

"It did just now, didn't it?"

Nathan didn't answer verbally, but he looked up. The pain of the memory of what had happened still tore at his face. We all sat there in quiet for a while, just letting Nathan process things. Theodora said silence would be the great healer here. The more Nathan processed and adjusted to his new life, the better. He needed to get past the emotional shock of the moment, or moments as it was in this case, and really understand. When he finally leaned back in the chair, I felt he was coming around. He still didn't look like the old Nathan, or even the vampire Nathan who had just woken up yesterday. He was still heavily distressed. I could see it and feel it in how vacant his touch felt when he rubbed my hand as I held his.

"How long does it take? How long does it take to feel normal again?"

Blank stares were in abundance in the parlor. No one had an answer, least of all me. I felt anything but normal, and even then, I was so far away from normal I wasn't sure I could even use that word. It was a fact that I knew Nathan needed to hear, but I also knew I didn't have the heart to tell him. How badly he needed someone to say he would feel normal in just a few days, or weeks, was clear on his face. I felt a true terror about telling him and ruining all Theodora had done to calm him down earlier. I didn't want to be the one, but I had to be. It had to be me. He was my boyfriend, and most importantly, he was like this now because of me. I owed that to him. Even if it set him back, which I didn't doubt it would. That smile I had seen reappear a few times tonight would be gone again. I just had to swallow it deep, do it, and deal with the consequences later.

"Define normal?" asked a voice from heaven. Hearing it lifted the weight of the dread I felt. Nathan looked at Kevin Bolden standing in the door with his wife. Marie and Theodora were behind them. "Seriously Nathan, define normal. What do you believe normal feels like?"

Nathan appeared dumbfounded by Kevin's question, as did the rest of us.

"It's difficult to answer, is it?" asked Kevin. His question appeared directed at more than Nathan. We were once again the students and class was in session. "Ignore what you know about your situation. How do you feel that is different from normal? Mike, in what way do you feel any different from how you did before?"

Mike looked like someone had punched him. His mouth hung open. I hoped that was a sign he was working the problem in his head, but it was Mike. He gave no outward signs of being a deep and introspective person. "I don't know," was his answer, but coming out of his mouth, it sounded like more of a question.

"Apryl, what about you?"

Even Apryl hesitated with her answer. She looked perplexed.

"Oh, come on," urged Kevin. "Anyone? Really think about this."

"I don't feel any different now than I did before," responded Brad.

"Exactly..." Kevin Bolden started to celebrate the response, but Brad quickly interrupted with more to his answer.

"But, at first, I did. I felt like a raw nerve, irritated by the simplest of sensation, and my impulses were stronger, sending me from calm to aggressive in the blink of an eye."

"That's an excellent answer, Brad. See if each of you search your feelings. You'll have what you need to help Nathan and others through these issues. The secret is your own experiences. We are a community. We have to help each other. No one else can." Kevin looked right at Nathan and stepped into the room. "It's just going to take time, Nathan, and then you will feel what you believe is normal again. Look around you. See all the people that have gone through this. Lean on us."

Thank you, Mr. Bolden. Not only did he save me there, but he also opened a door I could walk right through.

"Nathan... lean on me. Let me help you through this." My hand caressed his, and I waited to feel that squeeze of recognition or to see him looking into my eyes, wanting to pull what strength I had to help him. I had to be strong for him. Which meant I needed to hide what a mess I was on the inside from him, and our other little secret. Even if just for a little while, or until I understood it more. Nathan was dealing with so much right now. Telling him he was going to be a father, especially when I couldn't explain how, might be a touch too much. There was still time.

Nathan's head turned toward me. Here it came. He was finally going to look at me. He was finally going to see me as his rock to help him through this. We would tackle this together, just like I wanted to take on any challenges we face for the rest of time. Come on, turn a little more and look at me. See the strength I have in my eyes? Those black, emotionless eyes that are staring up at you beseeching you to let me help you. Yes, he's almost there.

"Lean on all of us Nathan," commented Theodora from the doorway, drawing Nathan's eyes right to her.

If my looks could kill, that woman would be in a casket.

I felt the little squeeze from his hand, and then he finally looked down at me. He looked lost and confused, and why wouldn't he be? He was new in this strange new world.

"It's going to be okay," I said.

"I need to apologize to Amy."

Well, that could be a problem. I doubted Steve and Stan would allow us anywhere near her at the moment, but I couldn't tell Nathan that. He felt bad enough as it was. "Just give her some time. We can talk to her when she wakes up."

"Okay," he agreed reluctantly.

"Why don't you go take a shower? Clean your body and your head." I stood up, pulling his hand with me, and he stood up and followed as I led him out of the room.

Laura grabbed my shoulder before we reached the door.

"Just because you have yours, don't ruin things for me." There was venom in her words, and I caught her glance down at my belly, and it hit me. The realization of what it meant knocked me for a loop. She let go, and I pulled Nathan through the door.

"What was that about?" he asked.

I didn't answer, and pulled him up the stairs and to the bathroom.

Nathan stood there, silently, as I ran his water. A hot shower always helped clear my mind. Not to mention, having him do something normal might help him. It's not like he could sit down and eat a greasy hamburger and fries, or gorge on junk food while watching TV, like he used to do before. Which I never really understood, well maybe I did. There was the bacon. He needed to do as many things he used to do as possible.

Once the water was hot enough, I laid out a towel and started for the door. "Take your time. We won't run out of hot water."

He replied, "Good," and then grabbed my wrist. "I wouldn't want us to get cold." He pulled me in close and kissed me, and boom. Holy Jesus Christ, and what the Hell, all rolled into one. There were fireworks, sparks, and explosions the moment our lips touched. He let go first, and I tried to pull him back in, but not before Nathan said, "He was right."

"What? Who?" I asked weakly. My mouth searched for his. Each attempt to find his missed.

"Mike."

"Mike what?" I asked. My lips finally found his, and there it was again. The fuse was lit, and I was ready to explode, but Nathan pulled back again and held just a hair's width away. His body shuddered. "He said it was more intense," the last word barely making it out before he pulled me in closer, and then pulled me into the shower with him, clothes, and all. It wasn't long before those were nothing more than a wet pile of fabric on the floor, and he hoisted me up in his arms, feeling more alive than I had ever felt in my life.

8

That magic smile returned to Nathan's face. It was my sun, and the world felt warmer with it present. His eyes kept watching me as I dried off, but he wasn't the only one doing some watching. I was watching him. This was only the second time I had seen Nathan naked, make that the second and a half. I had walked in on him once. There was something about him now. Maybe it was the glow left over from what I could only call an electrifying experience. Even without the sun kissed tan he had; he was a feast for the eyes. Best of all, this is how Nathan would look for the rest of his life.

I found myself lost in my own bliss and hoped this would help put him over the hump. Maybe feeling us together, better than ever, would keep him from missing anything or feeling depressed about what he had lost. There was so much more that he had gained, some of which I didn't even know existed. I jumped when his arms wrapped around my waist, and then I allowed myself to sink back into him. If I could have sunk further and become one with him, I would have. There was nothing that sounded better than that union. His hands caressed my skin lightly, and I felt the desire in his fingertips as they roamed. I closed my eyes and let the feeling consume me. They didn't pause as they traced the shape of my body, teasing every inch of me, and I had a feeling he knew exactly what he was doing to me. How he returned to several spots of my body confirmed it, and no matter how much I tried to hold still, my body betrayed me and quivered. Then I froze.

His hands stopped on my stomach and stayed there. They were no longer caressing. Instead, they were just... well.. there. I let my eyes open and looked down. My stomach was no longer flat and taut, like it had been for years. There was a paunch there. If he noticed, this was going to be more than a little problem. I wasn't ready to tell him yet. He needed more time to adjust, and I needed more time to understand how this happened. My only saving grace sat with the fact that he had only seen me naked once before. Maybe, just maybe, he didn't see, or remember, what I looked like then.

Inside, I begged for his hands to move, but they didn't. They just stayed there while he stood behind me. Before he was nuzzling against my neck, but even that had stopped. My gaze drifted up and met the reflection of his in the mirror. I didn't wait long enough to read him. I didn't want to. I didn't want to know if he had noticed and had a question there. My own hands met his and pried them off just enough to allow me to spin around and meet him face to face. Again, our lips met, and that electricity was there. I pushed the kiss deeper, hoping it would chase away anything he may have noticed. I was pretty sure this would work. The heavenly bliss was already making it hard for me to remember why I was doing this. I almost didn't care why anymore as he led me back over to the bed and leaned back.

I laid there in his arms, realizing I could lie here forever and not have a care in the world, and that didn't sound all that bad. What would be wrong about a life lived in bliss? I was sure somewhere someone was living life just that way. Why shouldn't we? The complications of our lives, that's why, answered my mind, and I wanted to yell at it to hush. By now, I had learned enough to realize that if I rolled over and kissed Nathan again, I could chase all of those issues away for another brief period of time. If I kissed him well enough, that period could be extended, but that solved nothing, and I had this nagging feeling of responsibility sneaking its way back in, dragging dread with it by the hair. What I needed to fix or do was too long to list, or at least a list I didn't want to play in my head at the moment.

I rolled over and swung my legs out of the bed and looked up at the clock. A panic reminded me of one of the issues with being what we were. Time wasn't the same for us as it is for others. Not that we had more hours in the day or anything, but being immortal, the feeling of five minutes to us, was not the same as to someone that only lives 80 years or so. The last four hours felt like just minutes, heavenly minutes, but still just minutes, and I had missed an appointment, more of a promise I had made. Nathan's hand reached for my back as I stood up.

"Don't leave," he begged.

"I have to. I promised to meet with Master Thomas this morning," I said and quickly got dressed the traditional way.

"Witch stuff," scoffed Nathan, as he did the same.

"Yes, witch stuff. I am a witch, and part of the problem out there is related to witches. So, yes." I ignored his scoff and finished getting dressed. "I won't be gone long. I will ask Mike and Clay to..." I caught myself before I completed the statement. I realized how it sounded in my head, but I had already sent enough that any reasonable person in Nathan's situation could make the leap.

"In case I get out of control again?"

"Yes," I said, regretting I even brought it up. I could have just asked them to help without Nathan even knowing it. The left over buzz of our bliss dripped away from his face, and seeing it stole mine along with it.

I walked over and placed a hand on his cheek. When he tried to turn away from me, I grabbed the other side of his face to take control of the situation and help center him. "Look, it is just for a bit. I promise, it won't be long before you have control over everything."

He tried to pull away from me, but I maintained my grip, knowing now I couldn't hurt or even bruise him. It was quite the opposite. "Nathan, don't do that. Don't get frustrated, that will just lead to other emotions boiling over. The best thing for you now is to stay calm, and work past this period with the help of all of us. You heard Mr. Bolden." His body relaxed and conveyed his agreement. "I won't be long, and tonight I want to take you some place I used to love going at night around here. Just the two of us, okay?"

"All right."

I gave him a quick kiss, emphasizing on the quickness of it to avoid being pulled back in, and then departed while he pulled his shirt on over his head. I went down the stairs, looking for the first of the two stops I needed to make, on my way out to meet with Master Thomas and Mr. Meridian. I found the second of my stops first, standing out on the porch under the eaves and out of the sun.

"I got to admit Larissa. This is a real nice farm here. Peaceful and beautiful," said Mike as he looked out at the property. "That is, if you ignore the two large camps of opposing forces," he added sarcastically. Both Jeremy and Clay snickered from the rockers they sat in.

"Then let me show you something." I walked up next to Mike and slid my hand over his eyes.

"You going to push me over or something?" he asked. There was a leeriness in his voice that I found humorous. He was actually frightened of me.

"No, just watch." When I removed my hand, I heard a gasp from him. He then walked out of the shadows and out into the sun, taking the tingling sensation that came with it without even a wince. "That is what it looked like when I was a child." Okay, the picture I projected for him may have been a memory from spring and not winter, so sue me, but it looked great.

"I want to see it," demanded Clay as he pounced out of the rocker.

Jeremy followed with a "Me too."

Why not? I thought, and I grabbed Clay by the arm and put him next to Jeremy. Then, from behind, I reached around them with both hands and covered their eyes and performed the same glamor trick on them than I had on Mike. All three were now seeing the same image.

Field after field of lavender and lilac in bloom. Tractor rows clearly cut through the field, and every building on the property was newly painted and well maintained, not that I hadn't already fixed those after I arrived.

I let them spend about a minute in that memory before it disappeared, revealing the real world before them.

"Mike's right Larissa. It is a sight to behold," said Jeremy. It was heartfelt, and I slapped him on the back as his head turned in my direction when he said it.

"Thanks. I need to ask a favor of you three."

"Watch Nathan?" asked Mike.

"Yep, can you?"

"We were already planning on it. We discussed it with Mr. Bolden after you two went upstairs. We have him. You don't need to worry about anything."

"Good. Thanks." I said and started for the stairs, but then I stopped and headed back for Mike. I placed a hand on his shoulder and leaned up and whispered into his ear, "And thanks for what you told Nathan."

Mike grinned from ear to ear before he covered his mouth with his hand. I was smiling too as I left the porch, but I wasn't about to turn to let any of them see it.

Out in the old lavender fields, which didn't look anywhere near as well kept and bright as they did in what I had just shown Mike and the others, I spied my next stop.

Seeing Amy running around the fields holding the doll I gave her for Christmas, chasing a dog, make that a wolf, was an adorable and somewhat normal scene. Rob had let his wolfy side out for the moment and bounced around like a hyper puppy. If he rolled over and let her give him a belly rub, I would lose it. I did a quick check and saw both Stan and Steve not far away with Cynthia. They were keeping a watchful eye over things, but neither appeared too concerned with my presence, at least not at the moment.

When Amy saw me, she didn't run to me like she usually did, and that hurt. It told me something had changed between us. She didn't run from me either. I kneeled down and straightened up her clothes with a tug here and a tug there, while Rob stood behind her. I looked him right in the eye. I needed him to know I wasn't there to harm Amy. That it was quite the opposite. He didn't appear all that concerned.

"Is Nathan okay?" Amy asked. Her voice quivered and trailed off.

"Yes," I said, and it wasn't a lie. He was and eventually would be even better. "He is just different now," I added, thinking that explaining the birds and the bees might be easier than this.

"So, he's like you now?"

I nodded. "He is exactly like me and Mike, Clay, Apryl, Jeremy, Brad, Mr. and Mrs. Bolden, and Laura. So, there isn't anything to worry about, or to be frightened of." Well, there was, and I struggled with how to describe it without making her fearful. The truth. They say that never hurts, which they are wrong about that. I have been told the truth many times, and it skewered me. "It's just all new to him, so he needs to understand what all he is feeling and how to deal with it, but," I quickly added. "It won't be long before he is the Nathan you remember, and we can get back to sitting on the porch reading stories and all, okay?"

It was her turn to nod, but what I didn't see was that infectious little girl smile.

"Everything will be all right, honey." I reached up and stroked her hair.

"Will you still have room for me?" she asked, with the question slapping me right across the face.

"Of course. What makes you think I wouldn't?" I asked.

"The baby," she said, and I about fell backwards on my ass. Behind her, Rob phased back into his human form and stepped up close behind her.

"Yes, of course we will darling," I responded.

"Amy, just think of it like having a little brother or sister," Rob pointed out. "It's great. I can't imagine life without my brothers."

"But we aren't real brothers or sisters. I'm not really your child." Her bottom lip quivered, and my heart sank hearing those words.

I pulled her in for a hug and didn't even check to see if Steve or Stan would have a problem with it. If they were over there glaring at me like Ms. Parrish used to, I didn't care. "Amy, stop thinking like that. You are our child in every way that matters, and that is all that is important."

"And I'm your uncle," added Rob.

"Yep, and Rob is your uncle," I agreed. "Every family has one of those crazy uncles."

Amy giggled, and that was what I needed to hear. I kissed her on the forehead and stood up. "Now you play with Rob, and I will be back later. I need to go meet with some witches." She hugged my leg.

"Mike and the others will watch him today."

"Jack can't do your little trick to make him think he is somewhere else?" asked Rob.

I shook my head. "Not yet. It takes practice, which is where I am heading. More witch training."

"More school? Didn't we just leave a school?"

I just shrugged as I turned and walked away. I didn't make it more than a few steps before I heard the squeals of happiness behind me.

9

Marcus Meridian's little watch dogs out front didn't even raise an amber flecked eye when I passed them and approached the tent's opening. I paused with my hand on the canvas of the tent and looked at each of them for some kind of reaction. They sat off to the side on old wooden crates playing cards and acted like they didn't even notice me, but I saw the side glances they gave me. One finally looked up from his cards and with a deep chested chuckle said, "Go on in, you're late."

I pulled the canvas flap open and stepped into his chalet, just like before. I had to wonder if all the other tents were the same. Did they lead to some other place?

"Master Thomas, I'm sorry I'm late. Time got away from me." He sat alone on the sofa, waiting.

"It's fine Larissa," responded Marcus Meridian from the hall to my left. "Oh, and he isn't a Master anymore, and you are not a witch. At least not one the council recognizes." He waved a folded piece of paper with a wax seal out in the air in front of him. "When did this arrive?" he asked Master Thomas.

"This morning."

"Shall I?" prompted Marcus.

Master Thomas didn't respond. He just sat there, almost looking annoyed.

Marcus unfolded the paper and held it out in front of him at arm's length. He gave the paper a little pop and then cleared his throat with an over-exaggerated cough.

"It is the decision of the council that Master Benjamin Thomas be stripped of his seat on the council and all the rights and duties adorned to him. He is now exiled from our community."

The world fell in on me. This was another life that I had a hand in destroying. I turned and apologized, "I'm sorry–" but Marcus interrupted me.

"Oh, just wait."

"Larissa, I knew what I was getting involved in. I did this knowing full well what could happen, and I was prepared. This changes nothing, it's just hot air."

"Can I continue?" asked Marcus. He popped the paper with a finger.

Master Thomas and I both turned our attention back to Marcus. "It is also the council's decision that Larissa Dubois be exiled and categorized as a hostile element in the magic community. She is to be apprehended and transported to Mordin as soon as possible." He closed the paper and balled it up. "Oh, it's signed, Supreme Wintercrest." He tossed the ball of paper up into the air, and it burst into flames, burning up before it hit the ground behind him. "So, now shall we get started?"

I fell down to my knees, surprised the ground was there to catch me. The world felt like someone had yanked it out from under me.

"Oh, come now Larissa," commented Marcus. "Welcome to the club." He extended his hand and helped me back up to my feet. "Everyone here is an exile. That is why we are here, and there are many more of us out in the world. Anyone that doesn't kiss the ass of Madame Wintercrest, or the council, are considered such. This changes nothing. It actually makes things better."

"Um, how so?" I asked, more than a little curious how my being called a hostile magic entity and to be sent some place called Mordin made things better. I didn't even know what that was. "And what the hell is Mordin?"

"Oh good. Get mad," Marcus said as he sat down next to Master Thomas. "I knew I liked this one." He smiled like a proud parent.

"Mordin is the prison for witches and other magicals. Like the Coven, it exists between the real world and the magical world. Those that have committed crimes against—"

"Those that are the biggest threat," interjected Marcus.

"... crimes against the rules of our community, or against another witch are there," completed Master Thomas.

My body shook under me, and I felt I was about to hit the floor again and moved over to a chair and used the back for support as my mind kept repeating that word repeatedly. Prison! Make that a magic prison! What is that?

"It's nothing to worry about," Marcus dismissed flippantly.

"It's everything to worry about," disagreed Master Thomas.

"Nah," retorted Marcus.

"If she is there, she can't do anything she needs to do."

"True," said Marcus as he rolled up off the sofa and stormed toward the door. "Come on," he said and yanked my arm when he passed by. "You too, Ben."

We walked outside and his guard dogs immediately snapped to attention and everyone in eyesight went down on a bended knee.

Marcus let out a loud sigh at the sight. "Up! Get up!" His voice echoed across the land. Everyone stood. "Let's hear it. What do you think of Mordin?"

There was a loud grumble across the camp.

"Okay, that's unanimous. No one likes it." He turned and remarked to Master Thomas and me, "but watch this."

"Who here has been sentenced by the council to be sent to Mordin?" He raised his hand and turned his back on the crowd and faced me. Every single person in camp behind him raised one of their hands. Marcus walked back into his tent with his hand still up in the air.

I stood there and took in the scene until the crowd dispersed. There were dozens, if not hundreds, of people here. All sentenced by the council and considered criminals of some kind. I had to wonder what their crimes were, but that was probably a question I couldn't walk right up to someone and ask. That didn't stop me from wondering as I made eye contact with a few of them before I went back inside.

"Any more questions?" Marcus asked. He sat casually on the sofa waiting on our return.

I had a ton of them, but none I felt comfortable asking.

"That doesn't dismiss the threat of Mordin," stated Master Thomas. "It is a very real place, and it houses some of the worst criminals of our world." He looked at Marcus Meridian sternly. "And I'm not talking about those that have crossed the council, I am talking about those that use magic to murder and terrorize. Neither is to be tolerated in our world."

"No disagreement there, Ben. I just wanted to show that the threat of imprisonment is one of Mrs. Wintercrest's favorite tools, and she uses it against anyone that might push back or become a pebble in her shoe. I think Larissa has made it more than a little uncomfortable for her and I find that absolutely fascinating." Marcus examined me with a curious gaze. "Shall we find out what she can do?"

He again got up and walked past me and toward the door, where he waited.

"Well, that is what you are here for, isn't it?" Marcus asked.

To be honest, I wasn't sure why I was here anymore. Let me see if I can sum up my current status. I was being hunted by an old vampire, who was still alive. I came here to confront him, and did, only to be stopped from killing him by the Council of Mage's Supreme. My boyfriend was attacked and is now a vampire. I am now an exile and criminal with a prison cell waiting for me. These two, basically magic royalty and Master Thomas, want me to save the world, and I am also pregnant, which who-the-hell knows how that is even possible. That about summed it up.

Marcus walked through the camp, and everyone he passed kneeled or bowed. He asked them to stop a few times, but eventually gave up with a headshake and continued out beyond the edge of camp and into a field.

Something familiar caught my eye around a campfire off in the distance. There, with a group of six other rogue witches, laughing and smiling, were Jack and Lisa. It felt good to see them with what I guess we could call our cousins, much like how Theodora had referred to the other vampires. They needed to be around others like them, their own tribe. This would help them grow. God knows I was letting them down in that responsibility. I was too consumed in my world to help them grow as witches.

"Stand here," instructed Marcus. This reminded me of a session with Mr. Helms or Master Nevers, so I readied myself for anything.

He kept walking and Master Thomas stayed with him. They were talking between themselves. Marcus was asking how much I knew, and Master Thomas was trying to explain what he had covered so far, but then he said I was still raw, and that hit a big inflamed raw nerve within me.

"You know I can hear you."

"Yes, we do," Marcus echoed back.

The two men stopped and kept their back to me as they talked. Their discussion was now a whisper or something lower. I couldn't hear them, which at this distance I should be able to hear them clearly, but there was something else missing. I couldn't hear or feel their heartbeats. Tricky, tricky witches. I adjusted my stance.

Marcus spun around and slung a fireball in my direction, but I was ready for it, and I didn't just deflect it like any witch would. That would be too simple and elementary. I wanted to impress him. To truly show him what I could do. I felt the vibrations around me and squeezed them together, trapping the fire ball halfway between us. It hung there in the air, spinning and pulsating. I looked over it at the two men and felt pretty proud of myself. He probably expected me to just move out of the way, or deflect it with one of my own. Not pull out what I felt was some advanced stuff they don't teach anymore. I did everything but bow before Marcus flipped his wrist and I got knocked over by a flash.

"Don't assume your opponent doesn't understand the fabric of the world, too. Everything you can do, can be undone."

I picked myself up off the ground and brushed the grass off of my jeans while I listened and fully understood what I assumed was lesson number one. Out of the corner of my eye, I picked up some movement around the front of the house. It was Nathan, Mike and Clay leaving and heading out into the vampire camp. That wasn't exactly what I had in mind when I asked them to watch him, but maybe this was a good thing. Nathan's visit out there yesterday seemed to help him cope. They hit the tree line, and a few vampires came out to meet them. The greetings were friendly, but one was a little too friendly for my comfort. The hug Theodora gave Nathan appeared to last a little longer than acquaintance level. It was more in the realm of close personal friend, or more. I watched as her hand lingered on his shoulder as she introduced him around. I was so focused on them; I didn't notice the long line of others leaving the house for the woods, led by Kevin and Jen Bolden, followed by Marie Norton with Pam and Jeremy bringing up the rear. Theodora didn't greet any of them with the same warmth she had Nathan. I felt something burning inside me, and even my skin felt warm, and it was getting hotter. A fireball knocked me to the ground, and I rolled around, putting out a few flames on my clothes and in my hair.

"She's good, but raw," I heard Master Thomas remark.

"I see," chuckled Marcus. "Get up. Get up," he commanded and waited while I stood up, calculating how and when I would get him back for that.

"Now try to hurt me," commanded Marcus. He stood facing me, with his arms crossed in front of him.

"What?" I asked, not exactly understanding what he wanted me to do.

"You heard me."

"All right," I agreed, rather reluctantly. I wasn't sure he really knew what he was asking. He might not be able to defend himself because I was faster than most witches. I added a little flare and spun around, slinging my own in his direction. The man never even moved, and my attack veered off into the ground beside him.

"Not attack me. Try to hurt me. Do you understand?"

I didn't, but a feeling I hadn't felt in years soon remedied that. A paralyzing sensation sent me to the ground. My insides were being squeezed. The uncomfortable pressure graduated to full on pain, which was a sensation I hadn't missed. My hands clawed at my body to find the source, but there was nothing. Then, as quick as it came on, it all stopped.

"Do you understand now?" Marcus asked.

I pushed up on my elbows but still struggled to speak. The memory of the pain I had just felt was still fresh and caused me to groan with each movement I made to get back to my feet.

"We haven't covered that yet," Master Thomas said.

"What exactly are they teaching in covens these days?" sniped Marcus Meridian. He seemed to enjoy this. "How about some of elemental magic? Let's try this."

The ground rumbled underneath me and started to glow. A crack opened up. I jumped to avoid being swallowed, but weeds and blades of grass grew up and grabbed me, pulling me back toward the crevasse that had formed. My fingers clawed at the ground, but I slipped closer to the edge. I had had it with the games, and my mind drew a combined symbol made up for the solar cross and besom. One of the few combinations I had already figured out, thanks to my father's notes. The hole closed, and the weeds turned brown. In the distance, Marcus Meridian hit the ground, and Master Thomas laughed smugly.

"You can thank her father for that."

"Yea well. I won't let that happen again," Marcus brushed off his black slacks, and then rolled up the sleeves of his white shirt. "Not bad Larissa. Not bad at all. You can make your own magic. I'm impressed."

"Thank you," I said, then the ground rolled toward me, but stopped just short of me, and again Marcus fell to the ground.

"I should have told you; her runes are strong." Now it was Master Thomas who seemed to enjoy this more than anyone. He reached down and helped up his counterpart. "Larissa, go ahead and drop it."

I did as he requested and let the symbols leave my thought.

"Okay. That's good to know." Marcus shot a look at Master Thomas and then walked away from him, putting distance between him. "That's actually very good Larissa. It means your ability to apply curses and enchant objects is very strong. How about your potions? Have you mastered that?" He continued to walk, now circling around me, almost stalking.

"I know some basics, but I have not mastered it. That I am sure of."

"Good, knowing your limits is very important. I have people that can help you with that. What about spells?"

My mind went back to Mrs. Saxon's on Elemental Spells 1 and 2, and the ones my mother taught me. I felt I had a good handle on them, but in this company, I had to wonder. "I know a few."

"Like what? Humor me."

I was better at doing them than listing them. Kind of like a spelling test in normal school classes. I knew when a word was spelled correctly, but don't ask me to be the one to spell it. I had to think. A few came right to mind. "Teleportation. Levitation. Glamor."

"Good, those are important ones, and there are many variations of each of those. Tell me, do you still say the words that go with it?"

I shook my head.

"Thank god," he said and threw his hands up exasperated. "Too many young witches pay attention to the movies. It's a wonder they aren't all running around with sticks waving them when they cast a spell nowadays." His hand made wild circles in the air, but then stopped and pointed right at me. "But you, you aren't a young witch, and you have great promise. But what do you say? Let's stop messing around."

This was messing around? I was confused. He was acting like the test hadn't even begun. Was this just fun for him?

"Take that rock there, on the ground beside you, and throw it at me." Marcus wagged a finger and then cautioned me, "Don't use your hands."

I looked down at the rock. It was rather small, but size had nothing to do with his request. At least I didn't believe so.

"Come on. Don't look at it. Pick it up and throw it," he urged. Master Thomas watched curiously, and I looked at him for support. If I really threw it at Marcus, I wasn't sure he could get out of the way in time. "Do it!" Marcus ordered.

The rock lifted off the ground and then propelled itself toward Marcus Meridian. It never got close to him before he dismissed it with a simple wave of the hand, but that didn't mean he didn't jump out of the way.

"One," said Master Thomas. He held up a single finger on his hand.

"Yep, but that was a simple one. If she couldn't do that, she couldn't really call herself a witch, could she?"

Master Thomas smirked.

"And, actually, that is two," Marcus corrected Master Thomas. "Pyrokinesis."

"True," he agreed, and raised another finger.

"Two?" I turned to Master Thomas and asked.

He held the fingers out in my direction as if I needed to see them clearer. I knew the count was two, but two what, and why were they counting?

"Pay attention." He said and pointed toward Marcus Meridian.

If I wasn't annoyed before, I was more than a little annoyed when that rock flew back at my head. I moved and felt foolish when it stopped and fell several feet short of me. I shot two quick looks at both Marcus and Master Thomas. Each was unapologetic, and that just turned my heat up a little more.

"Turn that rock into a tree," ordered Marcus.

At that moment, I would rather melt it down and send half of it at each of them. I stood over the rock, looking down at it, and then at the two of them. Then back at the rock.

"Larissa, do you know how to change one thing to another?"

"Yes," I barked back. I did. My mother had taught me, and that was why I always had roses for my mother on Mother's Day, even though we grew nothing but lavender and lilac on the farm.

"Well, then, we are waiting."

I looked down at the ugly rock. It was gray and lifeless. Just like the stone floor in Mr. Demius' classroom. The same floor that I turned into a thick, lush carpet of green grass. I leaned down over it, and closed my eyes, and imagined the elemental symbol of fire, just like I always had before. A flash emitted from my hand toward the rock, and the ground around it changed. Roots extended out and into the ground. Then the trunk projected up, and the first branch took shape, forking off at the top. It continued to grow until it was taller than me, and the first leaves sprouted, giving it the look of a tree in early spring, not the dead of winter like the ones that surrounded my farm.

A third finger on Master Thomas' hand went up. "I think we can pass on number four. I've heard from others she has done it before."

"Nope, I need to see it."

"Oh geez," sighed Master Thomas. His shoulders slumped.

"I won't let her do too much."

Both hands extended out palm up and then dropped to his side. "Do your worst," he said, sounding resigned to his fate, but why did I feel his fate was now in my hands?

"Larissa, I want you to make Ben dance. Not by moving his arms and legs, but by controlling his mind."

"You mean consumption?"

"Now that's a term I haven't heard in years, but yep, that is what I mean. Make our pal Ben there do the Charleston or some modern dance kids do today."

I looked at Master Thomas apologetically. I didn't enjoy doing this. The only times I had done this before were for schoolwork, but technically, this was. It was a test, but that didn't mean I enjoyed the thought of doing this to someone I looked up to. It didn't take much to plant the thought in his head. No Charleston, or modern dance. Just a little soft shoe style shuffling of his feet, with a new arrangement of fingers on his hand. It no longer showed three fingers, but now a single one, the middle, was pointed up in the air. I didn't keep control of Master Thomas long, just enough to make my point.

When I released him, Marcus Meridian conceded, "that's four."

"Four what?" I asked.

"Four of the seven wonders," replied Marcus.

"What?" Wonders? What the hell was he talking about? We were witches, not God. I knew what the seven wonders were. In fact, there were two sets. The ancient and modern ones, and none of them had anything to do with what I just did. The only wonder I felt about any of this was about why I was being asked to perform them.

"The test of the Seven Wonders. Larissa, if you are going to challenge for Supreme, you better know the test of the seven wonders. You have just finished four of them: telekinesis, transmutation, pyrokinesis, and concilium, or what you called consumption. There are three left, which I don't doubt you can perform. That is with the right training. They are a little more advanced and need to be performed in more supervised settings than this."

"What are those wonders?" I asked.

"Divination, Descensum, and Vitalum Vitalis," Marcus spouted.

"Diva-whats-it, Dec-a-whose it, and... can I have that in English?"

"Divination is the ability to see or have knowledge of the future," Master Thomas stepped forward and began his explanation in an academic tone. It reminded me of the many times he and Mr. Demius conducted my secret classes. "Descensum is astral projection to send your soul to the nether plane. Lisa might be able to help you with that."

"Good, I never once cracked the stack of books Edward placed next to my bed on the topic." I neglected to bring up the warning he gave me about how dangerous it was to try.

"Now she has performed the last one. I was there."

This seemed to surprise Marcus. His stalking of me, his prey, stopped, and he turned to Master Thomas and pressed a single finger to his lips. It remained there until he spoke. "Are you serious?"

"What is the last one? The Vital Vitamins thing?" My attempt to pronounce whatever the double-V item was, appeared to humor both Marcus and Master Thomas.

"Vitalum Vitalis," repeated Marcus Meridian. "It's the hardest of all the wonders. It's the ability to create life."

"The duck," I mumbled.

"Yep, the duck," repeated Master Thomas. He then continued to explain the incident to Marcus Meridian, who seemed to be in a state of disbelief and asked Master Thomas to repeat and explain several parts. Inside, I was no longer thinking of the duck. I was considering another possibility.

10

After a few more rounds of the game Marcus-says, we returned to the camp so Marcus could, as he said, make several formal introductions. That didn't mean I wasn't also subjected to dozens of other less formal ones as we walked through the camp. Everywhere we walked, people greeted and gushed over Marcus and Master. The welcomes I received bordered on downright frigid. No where even close to the warm welcoming I saw Nathan receive out in the tree line moments earlier.

Things didn't change much once we reached the first person Marcus said I needed to meet. She was a peculiar-looking lady. Her brown hair sat atop her head in tight curls, clearing her glum face of any hair, giving me a clear view of her bright green cutting eyes and her rather small mouth. It just hung there on her face, pinched together. Her leather boots and long-sleeved reddish brown gown looked out of place in modern fashion. Like me, she appeared to be a woman time had forgotten, though her attire would have fit more in a time well before my own. She wore white gloves on her hands with the fingers removed. Her name was Mary Smith.

I reached my hand forward when Marcus made the introduction, and in return, I received a once over, and not a pleasant one at that. There was a scoff that accompanied it.

"Mary Smith will help you with astral projection." Her death-like glare appeared to disagree with Marcus's offer, though she didn't protest, and by the way she bowed at his request, which Marcus sighed at, she would run into a raging fire if he asked her to.

"James," bellowed Marcus.

A man with long dark hair three tents down stood up. He stepped out away from the group he had been sitting with and sprinted towards us with dozens of eyes following him. On closer inspection, I was a little surprised. This man wasn't much more than a boy. He couldn't be much older than I was, or was supposed to be. With a rare chance, he could be early twenties and just look young. He was slim, making his skinny jeans a tad bit baggy on him. He wore a bright red hoodie over a white tee and sneakers. There was nothing witchy looking about him.

"Still working the streets?" Marcus asked as the two men exchanged handshakes.

"Some, but I keep it fair." He flashed a killer smile at Marcus.

"Larissa, meet James O'Conner, street swindler."

"Hey now, I take offense to that word." James laughed and extended a hand to me. His welcoming was a tad warmer than old Mary back there. She was still glaring in my direction. "You can call me a hustler or vendor, but never a swindler."

"My mistake. James here will be your guide to divination."

There he was with the big words again, and I had forgotten to take notes, which explained the blank expression on my face.

"The ability to see the future," Marcus leaned forward to explain. "James here runs local shell and card games on the street."

"But," James interrupted and stepped in front of Marcus. He slapped his hands together and displayed that killer smile again. "I never, and I do mean never, use any magic during my little profession, but if you need to learn how to see things that hadn't happened yet, I'm at your service." He spread his arms out wide and curtsied, and remained bent over.

"I guess I do," I admitted, reluctantly.

"You absolutely do." Marcus grabbed me by the arm and rushed me away. I looked back behind us, and James was still bent over. "And you need to perfect your potions."

We walked deeper into the camp and up to a tattered tent. Marcus didn't stop at the door, and pulled me through the opening. Where we emerged was a room that looked oddly familiar. Shelves cluttered with containers of all varying sizes and colors lined every wall, just like Mrs. Tenderschott's classroom. Then the oddness of the moment went up another notch, when a woman that could have been her twin emerged, and I almost screamed her name.

She gasped and placed a hand over her heart. "Marcus! It's not nice to sneak up on an old woman."

"I know. I'm sorry, Gladys. I have someone I wanted you to meet."

"I see that. You must be Larissa Dubois. You're something of a celebrity around here." She didn't hesitate to walk right up to me and give me a big hug. Once the shock wore off, I did the same. "It's so nice to meet you." She pulled me in closer, not the normal reaction when someone was in the presence of a vampire. Hugs didn't happen often, and definitely not ones this close. When she let go, she kept one arm wrapped around me, and spun to my side so we were both looking at Marcus. "So, I take it this old fart is here because you need help with potions? That is usually the only time he stops by."

"Not true," protested Marcus.

The rotund woman narrowed her eyes and tilted her salt-and-pepper covered head down. It was a universal look that all parents used. I know I had felt it more than once in my life, by both sets of parents.

"Not entirely true," he conceded sheepishly. "I do promise to stop by more often."

"Nonsense, you're a busy man. I just enjoy busting your chin a bit." She leaned over and said in my ear. "Did you enjoy watching him turn red as much as I did?"

"I didn't turn red."

"You did. Didn't he, Larissa?"

"Yep," I agreed because he did, and small beads of sweat formed on his brow. His heart even skipped a few beats.

"Well, any who, I'd be more than happy to help you with potions. Have you had any training?"

"Some," I said.

"Well, some is better than none. We can cover some basics starting tomorrow and get an idea of where you are. Then we go from there. How does that sound?"

"Sounds great," I responded. What else was I going to say? Marcus Meridian, someone who was practically royalty in our world, if you ignored his family's current standing with the council, was assigning people to help tutor me. And none of them were asking why. They were just agreeing to do it, some less enthusiastic than others, but they still agreed.

We stayed and chatted with Gladys for a few minutes. Some of it was what I would call shop talk, which appeared to be an attempt to feel out where I was with potions without actually testing me. Hearing that I understood the purpose of some of the foundational elements seemed to make her happy. It probably meant I had a solid base to start with.

By the time we left her tent, night had fallen, and the moon was high above us. Most of the witches had turned in. The need for sleep did not restrict me like my fellow witches, but that didn't mean I didn't relish the break. There had been something on my mind since Marcus and Master Thomas brought up the seven wonders. In fact, it was around one particular wonder they defined that brought on a full on feeling of panic that I worked to hide from both of them.

"Do you know where Nathan and the others went?" I asked Jack and Rob, sitting in the parlor watching television.

"No, but I heard Apryl saying something about a vampire pirate," responded Lisa as she walked down the hall from the kitchen with an apple in hand. The bruises of her first encounter with Jean St. Claire were still visible. I brushed the hair out of her face to expose more of them. "I'm fine. My ribs barely hurt anymore." She twisted around and then did a quick spin, trying to hold back a wince. But I clearly saw it. "So, what was this about a vampire pirate?" She asked, and took a bite of her apple. Her question had Jack and Rob sitting on the edge of their seats, literally.

"It's a long story, but yes, there is a vampire that used to be a pirate. I'll explain more later. Did they say when they would be back?" I didn't really care when the others would be back, but I wanted to know about Nathan. I had something planned, but also had something I needed to do to clear my mind.

"Nope. They didn't even say bye."

"Hmm." My hands found my hip as I hoped Nathan hadn't forgotten, but that gave me a few moments. "Where is Amy?"

"You'll love this," Rob started as he sat back in the chair and returned his focus to whatever he and Jack were watching on television. "Steve picked up right where Ms. Parrish left off." As if I hadn't noticed. "They're out somewhere refining their skills."

"So be careful about kicking a rock down the road. It might be one of them," remarked Rob with a laugh.

I let his joke go without a comment. I was too focused on what I needed to do next. I turned to Lisa just before she took another bite of her apple. "Is there anyone in the kitchen?"

"Nope, it's all clear. You going to do your visit home thing?"

I nodded.

"One day, I want you to take me with you. I would like to meet the woman who gave birth to you. Family roots are important."

"One day. I promise."

11

"Mom."

"Well, hello there. I was wondering when you might come for a visit." My mother turned around. She was again at the sink, right where she had been every time I visited. That brought a horrifying thought regarding her eternity.

"Mom, you're always at the sink doing the dishes or something when I arrive. Is that where you spend all your time when I'm not here?"

She walked over and took her usual seat at the kitchen table. She had a humorous smirk on her face as she waited for me to do the same. When I finally sat, she gave me her answer. "I don't know. You will have to ask yourself about that. I am where you expect me to be. Is that how you remember me?"

That left me stammering. I searched my mind for any memories of my mother not at the sink. There were plenty. Even more than those when she was at the sink, but then I realized something. There was a unique characteristic about the memories that involved me sitting at the table and my mother at the sink. All were the same, and it was at that moment it all made sense, and it was my turn to have a humorous smirk on my face. "No. I have tons of memories of you doing all sorts of things, but every time I came to you for your advice on magic, life, and even boys, it was here, in this kitchen. I would sit right here, and you would stand at the sink until you would come join me at the table to talk."

She looked down at the table, and then back up at me. "Then that would be why you find me here. It's driven by the reason for your visit. This is all up to you."

"Huh," I replied as I pondered this. "So, if I came here to work in the field, I would find you out there?" I had to ask to be sure I understood how this thing worked.

"Perhaps," said my mother. She leaned across the table and whispered. "But let's not do that. Maybe something where we are sitting on the porch with a cool breeze."

"Deal."

She smiled back, "So since we are here, what are you looking for my advice on today? Is it magic, life, or... boys?"

"Kind of magic and boys," I squirmed. This was not going to be an easy conversation to have.

"Okay, I can help with those. I am kind of an expert in at least one of them. What are your questions or problems?"

"Well," I started, beating around the bush, and hemming and hawing. The question sounded simple in my mind, but every time I started to ask it, it took a detour somewhere between that easy spot and my mouth.

"Larissa, what is it? I haven't seen you this uncomfortable since you told me you broke the window in your room."

To a seven-year-old, having to tell on yourself was about as traumatic as it could get, and to be honest, it wasn't my fault. There was a bug on the outside, and I wanted it to move, so I threw my shoe at the window. The bug moved. Oh, for the simpler times.

"Mom, I'm pregnant," I spat out like ripping off a band-aid.

My mom sat straight up, while in slow motion her eyes increased in size, larger than I thought was humanly possible. Her hands went up to her mouth and tried to hide the wide grin that was forming. "My baby is having a baby!" she crowed, and then jumped out of her seat and wrapped her arms around my neck, hugging me. She was surprisingly quick. She kissed my cheek. "This is great news. Congratulations. You and Nathan must be so happy." Then she let go of my neck and backed away and asked, "It is Nathan's, right?"

"Yes, mother!" I exclaimed, shocked she would ask such a question. "What kind of girl do you think I am?"

"Not saying that, and I don't know how long it's been since you last visited. I'm so happy for both of you. I'm sure you are both over the moon about this. I remember how your father reacted when I told him about you..."

"He doesn't know," I said, interrupting her gushing.

"What?" The happiness and glow drained from her, and she sat back in her chair.

"Mom, it's a long story, and a lot has happened."

"Wait, I remember now. What ended up happening with Jean and your plan?"

"It went to hell in a handbasket." And even that was putting a positive spin on it. I sat back in the chair, and my shoulders slumped. Something that happened here without really having to think about it. "There is so much to tell you that you need to know." I let out a loud sigh and collapsed forward onto the table, letting my arms catch my head. The abridged version. "The plan worked, and we removed the curse from New Orleans. Jean walked right into our trap and gave me the conflict I wanted without breaking any witch or vampire rules." Or so I thought. Technically, I still hadn't. It was all self-defense no matter how you looked at it, but with all I know now, why would I expect Mrs. Wintercrest and the council to respect the rules? "Jean got away with the help of Mrs. Wintercrest. Let's leave it at the council and I aren't on the best of terms right now, and all of Jean's followers are camped on one side of the yard out front, and all the rogue witches are on the other." I paused and thought about it for a moment. There was a lot to cover, without going blow by blow into the details of what happened. "Yep, that covers it."

"Oh, dear!" gasped my mother before she covered her mouth with her hands.

"I wouldn't worry too much about any of that. There are some very smart witches helping me, and about as bad as that sounds, that isn't my biggest concern. The pregnancy is."

"Okay. Okay." My mother repeated it a few more times before she calmed down. "I understand. I can help you with that." She took in a deep breath, "What's a mother for?" Her voice shook.

"Mom, I'm not sure you can, but I hope I'm wrong and you can."

"Try me." She straightened herself up and sat with her hands clasped together on the table.

"How is it even possible?"

I saw the same shocked look on her face I had seen on the face of others when I asked that same question. "Larissa, we had that talk. Don't you remember?"

"No mom, it's not that." I wished it were that simple and bowed my head before I explained further. "Mom, think about what I am now. That is the problem. How could this physically happen?"

"Oh," she said, and then she stood up and exclaimed, "Oh!" Her chair skittered across the floor. "How is that possible?"

"I know, right? My body can't change any more. It won't age. It won't get sick. And it most definitely won't change to support a womb and a child."

My mother grabbed her chair and slid it back to the table before sitting back down. "I've heard of the opposite situation, where a male vampire and a human female had a child."

"Dhampir," I interjected.

"Yes, but never this way. I assume you have asked some vampires about this." Question marks dripped from her voice.

"Yep, some that are very old, and they are just as stumped as you are, which is why I came to you."

She looked at me curiously.

"I am not just any woman or vampire, I am also a witch, and do you remember the situation with the baby duck when I was nine?"

"Yes." The single syllable word took several seconds to leave her lips as she glared across the table at me. "Oh Larissa, you didn't? Did you?"

"I don't know... I might have... I don't really remember... but it's possible." I stuttered, trying to remember if I had. "We were–" My lips clamped closed as soon as I realized what I was about to say, and who I was about to say it in front of.

"You were what?"

Why did she have to ask? "We were," I tried, but I still couldn't say it, at least not by name. "We were," I squirmed, trying to complete the phrase, "doing something of a personal nature, and I might have thought about having a baby and family with him at that moment." God, I hoped she understood my cryptic explanation. It was embarrassing enough to say it one time. If I had to repeat it or provide any clarifications, I would just die, if that were possible.

"It takes more than just thinking about it, but," she held up a finger. She had a point to make, and I was all ears. I leaned forward for her expert guidance. "It is possible when you are in the correct mental or emotional state, either distress or elation, for something to slip, but you would have noticed it. Did you feel that flash of warmth as the fire of creation ignited?"

Oh, I felt a flash of warmth all right. I wasn't sure if that was it or not. "I might have." That was as much as I was going to admit to. If that was it, there was something that didn't make any sense. "When it happened before, the duck just appeared in my hands. If that was it, wouldn't a baby just appear there, like the duck?"

"Should have, or I should say, could have. It all depends on what you were thinking about. Maybe you wanted to go through the childbearing process," she suggested. "It's hard to be specific without knowing what you were thinking about at the time."

"That has to be how," I conceded. My thoughts were all over the place, like they usually were. There was no telling what I was thinking and if that idea had slipped into my mind. It was the only explanation, no matter how crazy it might have sounded. I had to accept it. What choice did I really have? I was pregnant. This was really happening, and now I had an explanation of how. The next question in my mind... what the hell was this pregnancy going to be like? Theodora and Marie had already told me vampire pregnancies were accelerated, and in just a day I was already showing. That should have taken weeks. I was probably a few days from not being able to fit through the door. Now the next part of what seemed like a dark daytime soap opera drama, I had to tell Nathan. "That is why I haven't told Nathan yet?"

"You wanted to understand how."

"Not wanted to," I corrected with a shake of my head. "I needed to. He was going to ask. What could I tell him?"

"Do you think he will believe you?" She looked at me cockeyed.

"I think so. He grew up around witches." In reality, I hoped he would. I was still having a hard time believing it myself, but I found myself in an Occam's Razor moment. This was heavily improbable, but all other possibilities had been removed.

"The only other question left is how are you going to tell him? I fixed your father a nice dinner and told him after. You could do the same. It would have a sense of symmetry from generation to generation. Almost a tradition."

Oh, yeah, that was one detail I hadn't shared with my mother yet. That would make that a terrible idea. I shook my head and braced for her reaction. She had to know, and there really wasn't any point in holding it back. "Jean bit Nathan, and Nathan is now a vampire." I paused and let that sink in for a moment, and braced for a load of questions, but the lengthy silence meant there were none. The shock of the news must have knocked them out of her. "He is fine and acclimating to things rather nicely." My mother's face was stone still. No twitching and no blinking. "And, it at least solved a problem. There won't be any awkward eighty-year-old grandfatherly looking man kissing on a teenage girl moments when he aged, and I didn't."

The stone expression on my mother's face cracked slightly, but not entirely. "Well, that's something."

"I already have an idea of how to tell him." Now I just needed Nathan to cooperate.

12

It took quite a while for my mother's shock to wear off, and our conversation return to something of a normal mother daughter chat. Well, scratch that. There was nothing normal about us or our chats, not when you compared them to those others probably had, but we weren't exactly normal. She showed a lot of concern for Nathan and how he was adjusting. I told her about the Boldens and how they were experts in this, and that Theodora had taken a lead. Both pieces of news appeared to make her feel better. Of course, I mentioned many times that he had me to help him. I had over eighty years of experience in being a vampire. This was a point she continually brushed past without so much as a smile or comment.

After I left my mother, with many promises to stop by throughout my pregnancy, I went out in search of Nathan to put my plan for telling him into action, but he was nowhere to be found. My home was quiet, with people sleeping in every room upstairs. Downstairs, the kitchen was dark, which was how I found it when I left my mother. Someone must have turned off the light while I was sitting there. I didn't know why, but Jack, Martin, or Rob seemed to be the most likely suspects to me.

The parlor was the only downstairs room not empty. It was dark, with only the flicker of the television illuminating its sole occupant. I went in and plopped down next to Laura on the sofa. She had the show down low, and the sounds of crickets and the low rumble of the river rode a cool breeze in through the windows.

"Whatcha watching?"

"No clue, whatever that was on when I turned it on. It's not half bad though," she replied without breaking her stare.

I would have never picked Laura for a fantasy romance fan. This had kings, castles, and fancy dresses, and lots of big words that no one would ever say if they weren't trying to mock Shakespeare. And even though I felt like mocking it when I first started watching it—I doth think the girl protest too much—I got lost in it after a few cheesy lines.

"Where are the others?" I asked, staring at the screen, and feeling a little lovelorn for the old days.

"Don't know. Probably out there with Theodora and Marteggo."

"So, you met him?" We were two girls gabbing while watching a sappy romance movie. The only thing missing was a big bowl of popcorn.

"Oh yeah, we all did."

"What did you think?"

I turned and looked at her to see her expression. The flicking light of the television highlighted her naturally beautiful features. She stayed focused on the screen, where the woman, Frances, or some frilly name like that, cried because of the contents of a note a royal messenger handed her. The contents of which were still a mystery to us, adding to the intrigue. "Interesting fellow. Exactly what I would imagine a pirate would be. Tons of ego. Tons of macho attitude, but just enough of a soft edge to swoon someone like Theodora."

She nailed it. That was exactly my read as well.

"He and Mike hit it off instantly and started some stupid macho feats of strength competition or some crap like that. That was when I headed in. Nathan and Clay had joined in when I left."

Somehow, none of that surprised me. Not even hearing that Nathan was involved. He was a guy, and I couldn't remember how many stories he told me of the stupid sports or challenges he, Rob, and Martin engaged in. It was just how guys were wired. They were also wired to win. Jen and I talked about it once, when I complained how stupid it was, and she told me all men, no matter the age, will always be little boys, always competing to show whose is bigger. That made me giggle at the time. Not so much now.

"So, Nathan will probably be out there for a while," I said out loud sounding disapprovingly a lot like little Frances, who was a wilting lily on the screen.

"Probably, had plans?"

"Kind of." I did, or make that, we did. We had carefully constructed plans, and he knew it. I told him I had something special I wanted to show him tonight. The fact he hadn't returned home yet burned a little. There was still time before dawn. So, I couldn't lose complete faith in him. But that faith was waning. I expected him to be waiting for me when I got back. Not out with the others. I felt an urge to slap my selfishness right out of me. Where it came from, I had to chalk it up as that more mature voice that often crept in and told me when to keep my mouth shut and when not to. Not that it spoke often, and sometimes when it did, it was nothing more than an easy to ignore whisper. It was good for Nathan to be out with the others, and I needed to trust my boyfriend. He knew we had plans and would be back. He hadn't ever let me down before. All I could do was sit and wait, and watch this show that I was starting to become rather involved in.

Would she and her beloved be allowed to be together? Forbidden love, the story as old as time, and something I knew a little bit about. I doubted Frances was the type of girl to break all the rules to be with him, like I had. I also doubted she would be the type to hop in the shower with him. What had occurred this morning was never far from my mind. How could it be? The feelings and sparks I felt were intoxicating. It made me wonder, and I just happened to be sitting next to someone that might be able to provide me a few answers.

"Laura, I have a question... and it's kind of a personal one."

"Okay, what is it?"

"Did you ever, you know, do something before you became a vampire and then found it was more intense after you became one?"

"You mean sex?" she asked directly.

"Mmm hmm." Maybe it was the time I grew up in that made me such a prude that I even had a hard time acknowledging that was what I was asking about.

"Oh yes," she replied without so much as even a glance away from the television. "Night and day. And not just any day. Christmas day. Your birthday. Halloween. Name any other special day. It is like that. And don't worry, it doesn't diminish, ever. It only gets better as you learn to let yourself go more." She leaned over next to me. "Just enjoy. It only gets better from here."

It gets better? It was going to get better? I wasn't sure I could handle that. What I had already experienced had blown my mind, and as it would seem, caused me to lose a little control.

"So, you never had it before?" asked Laura.

"No," I answered in a rush. "Remember, I was only sixteen."

"So?"

"Times were different," I said, then I pointed up at the screen. "They were more like those times."

"What times?" asked Marie. She was standing in the arched doorway with Jen and Kevin Bolden.

"What are you two talking about?"

"Oh nothing," I quickly answered, and even caught myself straightening up a little.

"Just girl talk while we watch this movie," added Laura.

Marie moved around so she could see the screen. "Oh, I love these old movies. Mind if I watch with you guys?"

"Not at all," replied Laura. "The more the merrier."

Marie took a seat on the chair to our right and settled in.

A movie night sounded good and reminded me of what we used to do up on the roof in the coven. I had other plans, and a participant in those plans was missing. "Jen, do you know when Nathan is coming back?"

She looked at Kevin awkwardly before answering. "Sorry, Larissa. I don't. He, Mike, Clay, and Marteggo went off somewhere a little while ago. I haven't seen them since."

That faith that was waning took a little more of a hit.

"Don't worry Larissa. I'm sure he is fine," Marie said in what was an obvious attempt to comfort me. "The guys and Theodora won't let anything happen to him. Remember, worry brings stress, and right now you don't need any of that." She reached over from the chair and rubbed my belly. "How are you feeling?"

Before I could answer, Laura popped off the sofa with a huff and stormed out of the room. Prompting an odd look from Jen and Kevin as she passed them and left out the front door.

13

The sun came up and Nathan still hadn't returned. I meandered downstairs to the kitchen and took the opportunity to spend some time with Amy while she ate breakfast. Steve and Stan had taken over her care in what I viewed as an understandable, albeit hostile takeover. There were benefits to the change. Amy and Cynthia seemed to have become closer. Both girls were the same age, and as they sat there at the table, one next to the other, they appeared to have their own language, made up of looks and hand motions. Which worked fine. It allowed them to communicate while Cynthia ignored my existence like she usually did.

I missed my time with Amy, and my heart melted sitting there while she ate cereal, and I munched on some dry toast. Why had I picked it up and tried it? I didn't know. After it didn't repulse me, I tried some more. A sight that caused that little girl giggle from Amy and more than a curious look from Stan, who was not hovering, but was still there with us. Cynthia, again, could have cared less. Stan was a little easier to talk to today than the last time I tried. I explained I could protect Amy, and he said he didn't disagree. He was concerned the others couldn't do the same when I wasn't around. I didn't have an answer for that, but there were two people in the house I could teach to take up some of the slack.

His friendly demeanor changed when Nathan walked down the hall past the door. Amy's did too, but she didn't go on the defensive like her older counterpart. She was still afraid, and I reached over to grab her hand to comfort her. In the corner of my eye, I saw Stan jerk in our direction, and I looked right at him.

"Sorry, my bad," he apologized.

It almost was bad. Not that I would have attacked him right there in front of Amy if he made the mistake of trying to separate me from her, but there would be a time later that I let my feelings out.

"Stay here with Stan and Cynthia," I said and kissed Amy on the forehead before I ran out the door, or tried. Her grip on my hand was as strong as mine, and it yanked me to a stop. I bent down and kissed her again. "I promise. You and I will spend some time together today, okay?" My eyes looked up over her head and directed the question to Stan, who just nodded. Amy eagerly agreed and let go of my hand.

"I have some training"—my hands made air quotes– "with the witches today. Would it be okay if she came along?" Amy spun around and looked at Stan. He was already smiling and just gave me a wave of his hand.

"I'll be back," I said, and this time I made it through the door in search of my boyfriend, who was hours late. It was easy to find him. All I had to do was follow the noise. They were back in the library talking loudly. Just in a few seconds, I heard the name Marteggo more than a few times. Seven, to be exact, but who was counting.

The secret door in the bookcase was open, and Jack was inside at the desk with a journal open. It was a common place to find him lately. Master Thomas was normally in there instructing him, but this morning he was nowhere to be found. I knew I needed to spend more time in there studying as well. It was the promise I made myself to continue my father's work, but before I could, I needed to catch up with him.

I stopped in the middle of the room, between the sofa and the coffee table, and this brought the rambunctious proceedings to a stop. You could have heard a pin drop in the library. As proof of that, I could hear Jack turning the pages of my father's journals.

"Nice of you to come back," I said, glaring right at Nathan.

I heard Mike chuckle from the chair he lounged in. Jeremy, Clay, and Brad stayed frozen where they were. Their eyes raced back and forth between each other. A brief spark from my fingers brought Mike back in line.

"We had plans," I said, and then added. "Important plans."

"I'm sorry. I guess we lost track of the time."

"Lost track of time?" I asked, my voice verged on a yell, but I held it back and under control. No matter how infuriating the stupid grin on Nathan's face made me feel. This was not that smile that melted me. Not that smile that made my brain stop working. This was one of those what-are-you-bugging-about-we-were-having-a-good-time smiles. Not one Nathan had ever shown before. It was something more common on Mike's mug. "We had plans. You were outside. Lost track of time? There is this great big ball light in the sky that comes up during the morning and goes down at night. How can you lose track of the time?"

"Relax Larissa. It's a little overcast. The sun wasn't too bad," replied Mike.

I turned and faced Mike. My control was teetering, and a small glow emanated from both of my hands. I heard the room clear behind me. Mike sat up in the chair and pushed back as far as he could get to add some distance between us. "Nathan and I had plans. Stay out of it." A tad bit of the piss and vinegar had made it into my tone, and it rubbed hard enough on Mike that he followed the rest out of the room, but circled around me as far as he could.

"We can go do whatever you wanted to do now. Like Mike said, the sun's not that bright, and he said it really isn't much more than a tickle when it hits you."

"First, for your education newbie, it is more than a tickle. Ask Marie who spent months locked in Jean's dungeon with the sunlight focused on her as torture. It's why we only went out when it was cloudy at the coven, and before you remind me of the times you and I went out to the cove or walked around in full sunlight, remember I am a witch. You shouldn't forget that, like ever." I caught myself and made myself take a moment to calm down before I sounded too much like something that rhymed with witch. "Second, we can't just go do whatever I wanted to do,"–sparks flew from my fingers as I added the air quotes–"last night right now. This was a special spot that I used to go out to at night when I was younger. I wanted to show it to you."

Nathan dropped that stupid grin from his face. "Sorry, we can go right now."

I crossed my arms, forgetting to stop the sparks in my fingers and giving myself a little jolt. I did my best to hide it and covered by thrusting them down in frustration. "No, it's not the same during the day."

He stood up and walked over to me. Ignoring the heat and energy flowing through my hands, he grabbed them, and pinned them behind my back, and looked down into my eyes. "Then tonight. I'm all yours."

Behind those big black eyes, I could see the passion that was my boyfriend. The same I saw before, and I knew he was sorry. He knew he messed up. I knew that even before he leaned down to kiss me, but if there were questions left, they were gone when our lips touched. When he released me, we were no longer alone in the room. Jack was still in my father's study. But there was another presence in the doorway. One that drew Nathan's attention a little quickly for my comfort.

"Is everything all right? I heard yelling." Theodora asked while leaning on the door frame seductively, which I didn't even know you could do. I know I couldn't. Not like her. If I tried, I would look like a drunken sloth hanging on to the doorframe for support. Not her. She was there like a movie poster. One hand extended up to the top, her long legs angled out toward the other side of the door, with the slit in her skirt riding high on her hip. Nathan's eyes took it all in.

"Everything's fine," I said as I pulled back from Nathan, but I kept a firm hold on his hand. A reminder for both Nathan and Theodora.

"No, it's not," said Nathan. I turned my head toward him in shock. Things were fine. We just made up, and I was letting him off the hook. What the hell was he talking about? "I messed up and missed plans that Larissa and I had last night."

"Well, that's okay," dismissed Theodora, which the words and her dismissive tone rubbed me the wrong way. "You guys have eternity together, Nathan. Don't sweat the small stuff. Now are you coming?"

Maybe I should be relieved that Nathan looked at me first before answering, but seeing he didn't explain or ask, I wasn't. He just turned back to her and answered, "yep," and bolted for the door.

"Wait!" I cried. "Where are you going now?"

"Marteggo invited us to come back. There is someone he wants us to meet," replied Nathan. Then it looked like a lightning bolt hit him in the head. He offered, "You should come too. It would be good for you to spend some time out there with the others."

"Yes, Larissa. Marteggo is very interested in getting to know you better."

I looked up at the clock on the wall and ducked my head. "I can't. I have training to do."

"More witch stuff?" Nathan asked.

"Yes, with Master Thomas and Marcus Meridian."

There was a gasp, and it wasn't from Nathan, or even Jack. Though if it came from the room behind me, it would have been understandable. Jack would have known the family name like I did. Everyone in our world should.

"Marcus is here?" asked Theodora.

"Yes, he is out there in the camp. Why? Do you know him?"

"We do," was all Theodora said, and she attempted to change the topic all together. "Let's not keep Marteggo waiting." She reached out and guided Nathan by the shoulder out the door with a lingering look back at me. "Larissa, don't forget you are a vampire. You should be with your own kind." Then she turned, and I watched as her hand ran down Nathan's back. If it had stayed there, she was going to meet my witch side in a way she would not forget.

"What was that about?" asked Jack.

"No clue, but I don't like it."

"She's something else."

I just rolled my eyes and stormed out, leaving Jack with a "Not you too."

14

"I promise I will watch after her."

Stan's over protectiveness around Amy grated on me. When we were at the coven, he barely acted like she even existed. She was always with me, and other than Ms. Parrish, not a soul had any concerns about it. "What's the worst that can happen? It's all witches, and she spent how long surrounded by them in the coven?"

There was no reply or objection from Stan as Amy took my hand and skipped enthusiastically down the hall behind me. It was a cool day outside. A strong breeze added to the chill. We stopped upstairs first to make sure she was properly dressed, not that she had an extensive wardrobe here. None of us did, and especially not with winter clothes. Us vampires didn't care. We were never hot or cold. An advantage. The same with Rob and Martin. Well, they were always hot, a benefit of who they were. It could be freezing outside, and they would be out in shorts. Shapeshifters and witches weren't so lucky. So, I made do. I imagined a few cute outfits and jackets and made sure they would be in the closet when we arrived upstairs. My own heart felt warm when I saw her all dressed in cute white leggings, boots, and a coat with fur around the collar. We took a moment to pose in front of the mirror, and I took a moment to suck in my gut. It didn't work.

Amy was more eager to be out around the witches than I was. She practically dragged me down the stairs. It took all I had to throw on the brakes at the door to the parlor, where I saw something unexpected. I believed all the vampires had left for more fun with Marteggo. A name that if I heard again, I might just vomit. Sitting there, like some sitcom scene, was the feminine contingent of our little group, minus Theodora, of course. She would undoubtedly be at her mate's side. "I thought you would be out with the others."

Laura was the first to break her gaze from the television. "Too much testosterone. There is only so much of Mike embarrassing himself I can take."

"Where are you two off to?" asked Jen.

"We are off to see—" I caught myself singing it as if we were about to skip down some yellow brick road. "I have more witchcraft training, and Amy wanted to come along."

"There's more to learn?" Laura asked with a tilt of her head.

"More than anyone can imagine," I replied and sighed.

She got the point and smiled. "Well, there might be more you need to learn about vampires, too."

I restrained a snarl in her direction. Yes, it was something I had always worried about, but this wasn't the right time for it to be thrown in my face. The solution to all of our problems was on the witch side. If it meant my vampire friends felt a little slighted by my showing favorites, then that was how it would have to be. In the end, they will see why.

"I'm curious," Marie said as she sprung up. "Care if I tag along?"

Well now, that was a curious proposition. I wouldn't mind showing Marie my other side. She only knew the vampire me, and never really saw the witch me. The presence of my vampire half in the witch camp already drew enough odd looks. Having her walk through it might push things a bit. Of course, there was a solution.

"Come along, but first, we need to make an adjustment." I raised my hand.

"Wait! Let me!" Lisa bounded down the stairs and went right up to Marie. Without hesitation, she raised her hand, and a golden glitter covered the woman. When it cleared, there was a pink hue to her skin, and an unfamiliar thumping in her chest.

"Nice!" I gave her a high-five.

"I'm coming too. I like it out there."

"You would," remarked Apryl.

I ignored her, chalking it up as just more sour grapes.

"The more the merrier." I reached back and ushered Lisa to join us before she responded to Apryl's comments. There was no sense in letting Lisa get pulled in and struck with any crossfire from the barbs aimed at me.

The four of us headed out. Amy held my hand the entire time. Lisa was on her other side. Out of the corner of my eye, I could see the little girl sneak a few glimpses up at Lisa. She wasn't afraid of her, and they had been around each other a lot, but I have to imagine her dark appearance might be a tad offsetting to young kids. It wasn't an accurate depiction of what she was truly like. Lisa was a sweetheart, and one of a few who I think actually understood me. It was more than just we had both ascended recently. We are both looked at oddly for who we are, or who part of us was. My being half vampire and witch, and she, a witch but, of the dark magic variety, who talks and plays with dead things variety. Slowly, Amy reached up with her other hand and grabbed hold of Lisa's hand.

Closer to the camp, I glanced out at the edge of the woods. I couldn't see anyone particular out in the open, but I knew they were there. I knew for sure there were five somewhere out among the trees.

The sight of the dozens of tents of various colors and the columns of smoke rising from campfires drew Amy's attention. She pulled hard on my arm, wanting to reach the camp faster. As we entered, I watched to see if anyone took any notice of Marie, and they didn't. They still took notice of me. There was no doubt about that.

"What's in the pots?" Marie asked.

Most of the campfires had pots suspended over them on metal frames or makeshift wooden ones. Inside, something boiled.

"Eyes of newt, and frogs' ears," answered Lisa, and she did so with a straight face and tone. A feat I would have struggled to pull off.

"Really?" Amy asked, and hearing the curiosity and wonderment in her voice, I felt guilty for not cutting Lisa's little joke off before it went too far.

"No, not really. It's just their breakfast."

I heard the sigh of disappointment come from Amy. Even though she spent a lot of time around us, I believed she still had this fantasy image of what we were.

"Plus, frogs don't have ears."

"Spoiled-sport," objected Lisa.

I didn't care. I wanted to show Amy and Marie what it was truly like, and a realistic view of witches was what they were going to get. That in itself will be magical enough.

"So, are we meeting Marcus Meridian?"

"Not sure Lisa. He might be there, but he might not. We are going up here, to the yellow tent, to see James O'Conner. He is going to teach me how to see the future."

"Divination?" asked Lisa. I wondered if I was the only witch that didn't know that word.

"Yes, that."

"Why would you..." Lisa clamped her mouth shut and let go of Amy's hand. She spun around in front of me and took a few steps backwards before stopping and forcing me to stop before I ran her over. "You aren't...," she started, stuttering her way through both words. "The seven..."

"Stop," I said, and slammed my hand over her mouth. I shook my head, but her eyes widened, and I felt a grin growing under my hand. "Just stop." I released my grip. "I'm just learning new skills. That is all. We should never stop learning. Isn't that what Mrs. Saxon said once?" I wasn't sure if she had or not, but it sure sounded like something she would have.

Lisa's grin turned into a quirky, lopsided smirk. She wasn't buying it. I knew her well enough to know that, but I also knew her well enough to know she was going to drop it. When we were alone, this would become a game of twenty, or more, questions. I grabbed her shoulders and turned her around. "You know, James is kind of cute." Then I gave her a little shove. That was all it took for Lisa to lead the way up to his tent. She didn't even pause at the opening, and marched right in.

I ducked through the opening with Amy and Marie. Our first meeting was outside, not inside in his tent. I didn't really know what to expect, but I definitely didn't expect an apartment overlooking a bar on Bourbon Street in downtown New Orleans. The combination of old southern brick walls and wide plank pine floors and industrial metal railings and accents was both stunning and beautiful. I took a few notes for my use later. It might be time to update the farmhouse, which would be as easy as a snap.

"You came, and you brought friends." James announced as he came down the stairs that I guessed led up to his bedroom. There were no obvious sleeping quarters in the open floor plan room we were in. His kitchen was tucked against the far wall, and a large spacious living area in front of the wall of windows that overlooked party central below.

"I did," I said, as he walked right past Lisa, creating a scowl. "This is Amy O'Neil, and Marie Norton."

He bent down to Amy. "It's very nice to meet you Amy. You ready to be a big sister?"

Amy giggled. Lisa gasped, and I about died. "Did Marcus tell you?"

"Nope, you will in a few days. Now you don't need to." He grinned, and held up his hands, and pushed up his sleeves, showing there were no tricks up them. "And I know all about Amy, and completely understand the situation. Something else you will explain to me when I make a similar comment. It is an easy assumption for people to make, with how you feel about her and all."

I pulled Amy close, not to protect her from James, but because he was right. I felt so deeply for that girl, like she was my own.

"It is fascinating to me. She must have learned and picked up that caring trait from you." He turned to Marie. "You did the same thing so many years ago and raised a wonderful woman. The world thanks you." He bowed and took her hand.

This could become tiring.

He then stood up and turned toward Lisa. "Hi Lisa. Don't worry. We have a pleasant conversation in two days, and I have already decided I don't mind teaching you too." Lisa looked back at him as confused as I felt, and he just cracked that wide smile again.

"So," he turned back and clasped his hands, and stretched them in front of him, cracking his knuckles. "Shall we get to it? But wait, there is something we need to take care of first." He bent back down to Amy. "It appears you have something in your ear."

I watched as his hands flashed around in front of Amy, and he palmed a quarter before he slipped his hand by her ear. His other hand pointed up at me. "Don't ruin it for her."

I stepped back.

"How are you going to hear all this Amy, with this in your ear?" He pulled out the quarter, just like birthday magicians had done for years, but that didn't matter. She still looked at his hand in awe, even after all the magic she had seen. Then the quarter fell, and another twenty followed it before disappearing onto the floor. He was showing off. I just wasn't sure for who.

"All right. Let's get to it." He hopped up. "Divination, or what others call, the art of future telling. First, you don't need a crystal ball or anything. None of those fortune tellers really can see anything. The crystal ball is just a distraction. I call them fortune guessers. Ask a few questions and watch the reaction. Then they build on it. Knowing about future events, or things that are more random, is where the trick is, and that is what I am going to show you, but I need you to put something in your mind. It won't make a lot of sense to you right now, but one day it will. Time is not a when, it's a where. No one can truly travel into the future, but some of us can see far enough down the road in front of us to see what is coming. Does that make sense?"

"Sure," I said with a head full of scrambled eggs.

"Come, let's have a seat while I explain. First, can I get you anything? Amy? Lisa? Would either of you like something to drink?" His refrigerator popped open, showing a wide assortment of sodas and juices. "Help yourselves. Larissa, I'm not sure what you and Marie may like, but feel free to conjure whatever it is that would be."

"Wait? You know what Marie is?" Lisa asked, as she examined the options for her and Amy.

"Yep, but relax, not many will be able to see through it. I can see it because I saw when you did it, and I can see when you will remove it."

"Huh," I remarked and had a seat on the black leather sofa and admired the view outside the windows. James sat on the front edge of a matching lounge chair positioned catty cornered to my right. "I'm serious. Stop thinking of time as the hands on a clock going around. It's not a when, it's a where. Think of a road. You can look back and see where you just came from. What is right behind you is easier to see, thus it is easier to remember. What is way back there, miles away, is just a spot in the haze on that hot summer day and is harder to see, and your memories are less clear. That is, unless something happened at that spot. Like you visited an amusement park or something. That spot is a little bigger, with more signs reminding you of its location, so those memories stick with you longer. It's the same with looking forward. You can see what is coming ahead of you, but the difference is, when you are looking back, you have been there. You won't actually be at that spot ahead of you until you get there, but that doesn't mean you can't see it. Does that make sense?"

That was both a big *hell no*, and a *hell yeah*, which only added to the spin in my head. It was a simple explanation for one of the most complex problems in the world. Not even Einstein could explain time, but this was magic, not science, and those laws didn't apply here. Here, there were no laws. Now the question was, how to take what he just explained and use it. "I guess. I mean, I get it, but I don't understand what to do with it. Is there a spell or something?"

"Nah, nothing that fancy." He sat back and looked to be in thought. "Have you ever had hunches about something, and then found out you were right?"

"We all do," I answered. What he just described was human nature.

He exploded forward in his seat and leaned as close to me as he could, bracing his arms on his legs. "No, we all think we do, but we don't. Yes, everyone has hunches, or gut feelings as they are called, but they are rarely right. What I am talking about is hunches that are mostly, or always right. They may even be something you dismiss. I need you to think. Have you ever noticed that? This is important."

"Maybe. I don't know."

"Think back. This part is important." Then his arm jerked up and pointed a single finger at Lisa.

"I have," spouted Lisa. "I've had visions and feelings that have come true. Not often, but I've had them."

James got up and walked over to the lounge chair Lisa sat in. "I know, and as we will talk about in a few days, your grandmother exposed you to this practice many years ago. She would use tea leaves and auto-writing to view events yet to come, but you found another way that is easier. Which it is. Using something like Celtic runes and bones, are just magnifiers. It is better if you learn how to do this without."

"James, won't all this telling me about what we will talk about in a few days, change what we talk about?" asked Lisa. It was a good question, and one I had wondered about earlier when he preempted all of my introductions.

"Not at all. I'm careful about what I expose to avoid changing the natural flow of the world. I use this gift to observe, and not to manipulate. It would be irresponsible to do anything else." From the center of the floor, he stood and looked at us both. "Here is the first instruction. I need you to clear your mind. A cluttered mind clogs up the senses. If you need to do some kind of meditation, do it. Some cultures use substances as part of a ritual just to clear one's mind, but I prefer not doing that. This needs to be something you learn how to do at a moment's notice so you can use it when needed." He took a deep breath, raised his hands up to shoulder height and then slowly pressed them down to his side as he let it out. "Clear your mind. Now try it."

"Try what?" I asked, still unclear about what he was describing. Okay, clear my mind, and then what? Clearing my mind would not be a trivial act as it was. It was going to be an impossible act if I was sitting here wondering what the next step was.

"Just close your eyes."

"All right," I said, and then watched Lisa as she sat there in what looked like complete peace. Oh, I was so jealous.

"Larissa, close your eyes." I must have been a little too slow for his taste. Imagine that. Me being too slow at anything. I closed them. "Now clear your mind. After that I will tell you what to do next. Trust me, this will work. I've already seen it."

A simple, but impossible task with my mind still focused on what was next. How to clear it was also cluttering it up. I was the true portrait of irony. It took a bit, but I fought against the thoughts of what was next, and won. With that out, I felt a little more relaxed. My mind was clearer, but not completely clear. There was too much going on in my world to actually be vacant of all thoughts.

"Okay, I'm ready," reported Lisa. My natural sarcasm called Lisa a showoff, further clouding my thoughts.

"Just a few more moments. Still giving Larissa a little more time before I give her a booster shot."

"A what?" I demanded. My eyes opened in enough time to see James's thumb hitting me on the forehead, and then everything went black and my mind was clear.

"Now, imagine you are standing on that road. Where you are standing is here in this apartment with all of us. Just behind you are the moments when you sat down, walked in through the door, and even just a little further back than that is when left your home to come here. Each of those are clear as they just happened. Things that happened last week, not so much. Do you see the road?"

"Yes," answered Lisa.

"What about you Larissa? Do you see it?"

"I guess," I answered knowing full well I didn't.

"Larissa, open your eyes and look at me."

I did what James directed and opened my eyes and looked right at him. His face was just a foot or so away from mine. His kind eyes reached out to me. "This is not some imaginary or metaphysical road. This is one of the few times us witches can be literal, like the runes. Imagine an actual road. It can be any road. Straight. Winding. What ever kind of road you want." He reached out and grabbed my head gently. "Now close your eyes again, and imagine that road."

I did, and imagined a long straight road that cut across open fields. It disappeared off into the distance ahead of me. I turned and looked back and it did the same in that direction.

"Got it?" asked James."

"Good. Now look ahead of you. Out there lies every event that hasn't happened yet. Every milestone of your life and the lives of those you know are out there. Think of one. See if it will come to you, but try to not be too eager. Pick something close. Something right there in front of you."

The clutter returned to my head, but instead of crowding out what I was trying to do, event after event bounced around, wanting attention. I just needed to pick one. Which would I choose? My baby? My future with Nathan? As I ran through them, there was one that shadowed over all other questions. Its shadow loomed over my entire future. I thought about it, and all other thoughts cleared, except that one. Excitement built inside me. The possibility of finding an answer, of clearing this cloud away from my path, was almost too much to contain. But even with all that focus, my head was full of a black nothingness, and this wasn't some magical realm or potion created space like Mrs. Tenderschott took me to. This was the emptiness of my head coming up with a big fat nothing.

"All right Lisa. Keep it to yourself. Larissa needs some more time."

"You know I can hear you," I reminded him.

"I know. I also know how much longer it is going to take for you to get it." He said, his voice was close to me. Almost right in my face. I opened my eyes. "Don't open your eyes or the world will come crashing down around you." I slammed them shut before I saw how close he was. "You hold the fabric of the world in your hand." His voice boomed all around me.

I felt my body tense up and wished he had told us this before we started. Having that kind of responsibility might have been something I would have passed on.

"Just kidding," he laughed. "But I don't want you to lose the frame of mind you are in."

My body relaxed, and I stuck my tongue out at him, keeping my frame of mind steady and clear.

"Also, maybe I should have told you to just sit and let something come to you. Or think of something really short. Like what I am holding in my arms when you finally open your eyes. Trying to focus on an event of your choosing is hard, especially one so far ahead. Remember the road analogy. From where you are right now, Larissa, you can't see the on ramp for that decision. There are hundreds of intersections to cross before you get there, all of which are also too far away to be within view."

I let my disappointment out with a huff. Yes, he should have mentioned that earlier. That would have saved me time and frustration, but I had noticed a lot of what I would call the witch-way involved frustration. Instead of telling you exactly how, it required you to struggle through a series of mistakes first, then you hit the jackpot. That feeling of accomplishment made the successes all the better and helped cement the lesson inside of you, and it worked. I could attest to that with so many examples, but that didn't mean I had to like the method.

"I am going to have you keep your eyes closed for another minute. Think about what you are going to see when you open them. A minute in the grand scheme of time is just in front of your toes on the road. Three minutes, a grain of sand further. It's not that far to look. If you focus, you can see it from here." His voice took on a melodic tone. "What did my apartment look like when you closed your eyes? What will it look like when you open them again? What will it look like in three minutes?"

I saw his apartment. The style I liked so much, and we were all there, just like we were when I closed my eyes. Was I seeing a memory or the future? It was hard to tell. Had anyone moved since I closed my eyes? If not, then this was the past, or was it? Maybe they had moved, which made what I saw the future, or maybe I saw them where they were earlier before the moment I closed my eyes, which would be the past. It required a lot of that term I couldn't stand, focus. You had to remember all the details and then compare. It reminded me of an activity book Edward once pointed out that Amy would like. It was full of pictures. After looking at one picture, you flipped the page and tried to identify all the differences in this version of the picture. I scanned around the image in my head. Nothing seemed to be different. I looked back to the side. Coming in and out of focus. There was something on the couch next to me that wasn't there before. I opened my eyes and looked right at the spot between me and Amy. It was empty.

Confused, I looked up at James. "Just wait, and that confused feeling will eventually go away." He pointed back at the spot on the sofa. I watched, as did everyone else in the room.

"Give it another half a minute," said Lisa. "I saw the clock."

"What clock?" I asked.

Lisa pointed up to the digital clock on the table behind the sofa. Its big blue neon numbers said it was 11:07 AM. I hadn't looked up that far in my vision, but I was now. I watched as the ':' flashed on and off, denoting the ticking seconds. To my left, Lisa was whispering a countdown.

"Three. Two. One."

Right on cue, a black cat hopped up on the table and then down on to the sofa, and curled up next to me.

"Oh, a cat," cooed Amy. She reached over tentatively.

"Don't worry. Archimedes doesn't bite. He likes to be scratched between the ears."

I leaned back and pointed, while Amy gave him a good scratching. The cat leaned into her hand, wanting more. "You conjured that there, didn't you?"

"Nope. Archimedes is a real honest to God cat, and before you suggest the next question, I know you are going to ask, did I cause him to hop up there through some training? Try training a cat and tell me how that goes. What you saw was just a few moments into the future. By the time we are done, you will be able to see quite a ways into the future, and it won't be a struggle. It will take work, I already know that, but you will get it. Just trust and do what I am saying. Can you do that?"

I reached over and gave Archimedes a scratch. At first, he acted leery of my touch. It was probably the coolness in my fingers, but after he felt the scratching, he acted like he didn't care anymore.

"Remember, you have nothing to lose. I have already seen the outcome." He raised his eyebrows up and gave me a goofy grin.

"All right, you're on." I agreed.

"That's great. Now you two have the gift, but you will never be as cool as me. I see everything a few seconds, minutes, or even days before it happens."

"That sounds like a headache," commented Lisa.

"It is until you learn how to filter things. Then it's an advantage. No matter what it is, you see it coming."

"Did you see Larissa coming?" Lisa asked.

"Or me?" piped in Amy.

"Oh, absolutely little girl. I knew an adorable little girl was coming. Cuteness glows red in my visions." He winked in my direction. "I knew something was coming. I didn't know what it was, but I had visions of Jean retreating in fear, and others coming out of the shadows. Not all my visions are crystal clear. Some are just flashes. Some are full conversations. You have to learn how to save them and pull all the details you can from them. Let's try again."

"Okay," I agreed.

James looked at Lisa for an agreement, and I had to wonder why he did. If what he just said was true, he already knew what her answer would be. Then, remembering back to the crazy introduction session we had when we arrived, I understood. As unnerving and messy as it might be for him to see the world that way, it would be even worse for those around him. Imagine interacting with someone who was always several steps ahead of you. I imagine trust wouldn't be that high. So, he must be going through the motions for everyone else's comfort.

"I'm game," added Lisa.

"Now this time, Larissa, don't think of a question like you did before. Just let it flow and tell me what you see. I will help you to interpret those visions. Lisa, just do what you did last time."

Over the next several hours, Marie and Amy kept Archimedes busy, or vice versa. There was a lot of giggling in the background. Marie made Amy some lunch, with James's help. All of this happened while Lisa and I played a magical game of red car, blue car. We sat at the window trying to predict what cars would drive down the road at various points in the future. We started with shorter time intervals, and then progressed to ten minutes, twenty minutes, and then multiple cars over thirty-minute intervals. James said this was a game he played with himself to refine his skill. Then he started working on predicting every person who would walk into the bar across the street and when, hours before they even arrived.

His routine for training started every day at noon. He would sit at the window and focus on that night writing down the description of everyone he saw and logging when they would arrive using the time shown on the same clock Lisa had used to tag when Archimedes would appear. He explained that the list, at times, would be as long as several hundred people, with full descriptions of what they were wearing, if they arrived alone or with someone, and if they left alone or with someone. Even how two strangers would have paired up before they left. If some of his visions were longer about a particular person, he would actually go down and sit at the bar to watch and see how much of what he saw was correct.

To me this sounded like perfecting an ability, but then James put the cherry on top, and explained he had stretched it to something that happened several months into the future, eight months being the furthest. Of course, referring back to his road example, what he could see wasn't all that clear and precise. More of a feeling and some fleeting details that he could put together over the next several months.

"Now just pick your method for testing yourself daily. It's like a muscle. You have to use it to strengthen it."

"We could pick who is going to drool on the floor first, Rob or Martin?"

Amy laughed at Lisa's proposal, and James appeared to be confused. It was nice to see the shoe on the other foot, but I let him off and explained, "Werewolves."

"Ah. Stop by in two days and we will work on it again together."

"Will do," responded Lisa and she helped gather up Amy so we could leave. Amy had chased the cat upstairs a little while ago.

"Now, Larissa, you have a question you are going to ask me."

"I do?" I asked, unsure of what he was referring to.

"See, you did." He chuckled, humored at himself. Being the butt of what I felt was an ill delivered joke didn't amuse me. "But that wasn't it. Earlier you were trying to see how all this ends up for you. Don't try. You can't see your own future like that. You can see those that are around you and might infer what happens to you from them, but you can't see your own future. You are just observing that point. Remember, you haven't really been there, but you can see what is out there."

"Wait." That didn't make any sense to me. "If I am there observing, then I am there."

"No," he shook his head. "You aren't there. You are here, looking at that spot through a huge telescope. Don't force it to make sense right now. The more you do it, the more sense it makes. Especially once you start to see what I call the conversations."

"Okay, I'll have to trust you on that," I conceded, reluctantly. "I have one last question." I was very hesitant to ask. Hearing that I couldn't see my own future was a hard buzz kill to the question that drove me earlier. It explained the big empty nothingness I found when I searched for that moment in time. It was also possible I just wasn't skilled enough, or unable, to see that far yet. Either was possible, but James gave me another avenue, or angle to explore. Lisa probably wasn't there yet. She was learning this skill with me, but James was an expert.

"Go on."

"Shouldn't you already know?" I sniped back, trying to cover the nerves around what I was about to ask.

"Well, we could play it two ways. I could tell you I do and give you the response without you ever asking, or you could ask, and I tell you the same thing. Which would make you feel better?" I expected to see his signature Cheshire cat type grin that carried an annoying level of arrogance, but I didn't. This was serious James, and it was the first time I had seen this side of him. I didn't much like it.

"I'm okay with either," I said, trying to pull his jovial nature back to the surface.

"Marie, can you take Amy out into the hall for just a moment? I need to talk to Larissa and Lisa privately."

I failed. I completely failed. The room felt like it grew colder, though it probably hadn't. I wouldn't know if it really had. It had definitely become darker, and that had nothing to do with the sun going down outside. Lisa even looked like she felt it. She sat back down slowly, with her hands tightly clasped on her lap.

"Most cannot do this. Lisa, it is part of the dark arts, so it makes more sense for you to have this ability. Larissa, it's probably a family trait. You both need to realize this is a gift, and it shouldn't be abused. Don't use it to manipulate anyone, human or witch. That should go without saying, and that is not the most important warning. You need to be careful what you try to look at with your gift. You might not like the answer you find. Which is why you should never attempt to find out about your own future, or ask anyone else to tell you. Imagine if you found out the worst news you could think of, but there was nothing you could do about it from that day until the day it happens. That is a true hell that has caused many a witch to live a tortured life. Divination should never be used selfishly. During the test of the seven wonders, the why you use it is as important as the ability."

He stepped forward and offered me his hand. I took it and he pulled me out of that hole the weight of his words plunged me into. I swear I felt a shake in my knees as I stood there.

"Do I know your future?" he asked out loud. "I know bits and pieces of both of your futures, but that is my gift, and scar to bear, and I will not tell you or anyone anything about it. Your destiny is not as important as the journey you will travel to get there."

15

"Oh, my word! You guys should have seen Larissa today," Marie gushed with all the pride of a proud parent. I wasn't really sure why though, and why she cheered every time either Lisa or I made a correct read. Yes, those reads were impressive to us because we knew what it meant, but I had to imagine from the outside it was a rather boring show. Two girls sitting there with their eyes closed, calling out various claims waiting to find out if we were correct or not. I imagined she would be more awestruck by balls of fire flying across the land at one another, or something appearing from nothing. I made a note to show her some of that one day. That would give her something to truly gush over.

"Did she set a dresser on fire?" mocked Apryl. "You know she did that once. Remember that Larissa?"

"Oh, I remember. I remember, but at least I didn't set you on fire."

Apryl responded with a single and loud, "Ha!"

The rest of the room basically ignored me, and at the moment, I was okay with that. I didn't need or want, to be the center of attention. That occurred far too often for my liking already, no fault of my own. And, if Marie planned to continue to retell our adventures of the day, she would have to do it without me. I had important and already once delayed plans, but first I had to kill two birds with one stone.

I walked over to Laura, who did her best to look around me until I blocked her view of the television. Behind me, I was sure there was some old movie playing. These seemed to be a source of fascination and bonding for Jen and Laura.

"Can you watch Amy for a bit? At least until Stan or Steve come to get her." I could have asked Lisa, Jack, or one of the werewolves to do this, but I remembered how the episode the other night with Nathan stung her.

"That won't mess up your perfect little family?" she asked. The question about knocked me over. I was trying to be nice.

"Laura, what's wrong?" I asked. Not really wanting to get into it in the middle of everyone, but she opened that door. I wasn't about to just shut it and lock away whatever issue she had behind it. It needed to come out.

"Nothing," she spat, and then held out her arms. "Amy, come sit with us. You'll like these flying monkeys."

Amy hesitated for a moment and held her place next to Lisa. Laura took notice, frowned, and then looked straight up at me with a lot of venom. I ignored her. We needed to hash out whatever this was, but I didn't have time now. This had to wait. "Amy, why don't you sit with Laura and watch this movie before dinner is ready?"

Lisa urged her forward. "Go on. I'm going to go help Jack cook. Hopefully it will be edible tonight."

Amy shuffled her feet slowly and when Laura reached out for her again, Amy appeared to relax and walked into her waiting arms, only pausing slightly to look up at me when she passed.

"I have something to do with Nathan tonight," I explained.

She looked back again, just before Laura picked her up and sat her between her and Jen Bolden. "What about story time?"

"Tomorrow, I promise. Plus, you don't want to miss this movie." I didn't know what the movie was, but it was old, and I was sure Amy had never seen it before.

"This is a classic," added Jen. "You'll love it. I first saw it when I was your age."

Marie walked into the room and looked at the screen. "Oh, I love this movie. Can I watch with you guys?" It was a rhetorical question she had directed at Amy, who nodded wildly and moved over to make room for Marie.

"Go," Jennifer Bolden mouthed in my direction, and I took the moment of distraction to leave before Amy noticed, but I wasn't fast enough.

Laura reached up and touched my belly, which now both looked and felt larger than I remembered from this morning. "Showing there a bit, aren't you?"

The entire room shifted its focus to me, including Amy. I backed away and left, longing for the protection of the hallway from the collective gaze that followed me and made me feel like a freak.

Lisa had already departed for the kitchen, and I could hear the sounds of something happening in there. There were a few smells wafting down the hall. I was thankful I didn't need to eat.

Waiting at the top of the stairs was who I was looking for, and I quickly crossed my arms across my stomach to hide our new growing addition.

"I'm present and accounted for. Ready?"

"Give me a minute. I want to change. Wait for me out on the porch, okay?"

Nathan reluctantly agreed and tried to embrace me once I reached the top of the stairs, but I spun around to avoid it.

"I will be ready in just a minute." I couldn't risk him seeing it, not yet. I was already using magic to keep him and the others from feeling its heartbeat. I wasn't sure if I did anything to hide my bump if I would harm the life within. If I was right, magic created this. How would it react to more? I didn't know.

My self-created wardrobe wasn't exactly what I needed for the occasion. Form fitting clothes meant to get and hold his attention were not what I needed at the moment. I needed to hide something, something that was bigger than this morning, and now strained against the waistband of my pants. Looser jeans were in order and soon appeared. Of course, they fit perfectly. How long they would continue to fit? Who knew? Theodora said vampire pregnancies were accelerated. Compared to other pregnant women I had seen, I believed I was now about two or three months along, even though it had only been three days. The last thing I threw on was something I had never worn before in my life. Hell, by morning I could be another month along. For some room to grow into, I pulled on a hoodie for the first time in my life. Hoodies weren't a thing when I was growing up, and since then, I didn't really wear anything baggy. I walked down the stairs looking more like Apryl than myself and hoped to slip past the door with no remarks.

If there were any comments, I didn't hear them. I was down the stairs and out the door in a flash. I grabbed Nathan's hand in full stride and yanked the poor boy off the porch. It took him a few steps before he caught his footing, but he soon joined me stride for stride as we headed around the house and passed the barn. We didn't stop there. We kept going across the field. My father would have freaked if he were alive and had seen us. We cut right through the old planting areas and didn't keep to the walkways he created. I felt Nathan slow down after we hit the trees. Probably a habit from all the trips he had made with the others recently. "Come on," I called, and gave him a good yank.

We kept going from what I knew was about half a mile. The destination was a place I knew well. Or I did a long time ago. I hadn't considered if it was still there after all these years, or if I could even find it. My directions were, head to this tree, and then to that tree. I was sure those trees had grown through the years, or may have even been knocked down by a storm. Could I even still find them? That was a big question.

To my surprise, I found the first tree with no issue. Then the second. The third was bigger, and leaned more than I remembered, but it was absolutely it, and I knew my destination was just a few feet away. Well, should have been just a few feet away. Now it was a few feet away, and a few feet up. A wide crook in an old Live Oak tree that made the perfect seat to just sit and listen to the river under the concert of crickets and frogs. To me, this was the most peaceful place in the world when I was a child. My father and I found it while out on our many walks, and he lifted me up and placed me where the trunk split into two, creating the perfect seat. I remember sitting there, with one leg draped down, leaning back against one large, towering branch. He would climb up and join me. Looking up at the spot now, I doubted he could climb up there now. Hell, I would have been a challenge for him to lift me up that high.

I pointed up and started my ascent. Which wasn't much more than a jump and a grab. Nathan stood there at the bottom of the tree and looked up. I motioned for him to follow and watched as he studied the tree. I guess he hadn't completely tested his limits yet. He was going for the more traditional attempt at climbing up. His shoes slipped on the bark each time he tried. I couldn't help laughing at his attempts, and that seemed to frustrate him. I thought he would have seen how I got up here, but he went back and again tried to climb the trunk, this time, trying to reach as far around the trunk as he could, which wasn't far. This tree was probably twelve to fifteen feet around.

"Don't be silly. Just jump up here," I suggested from high upon my perch.

"Jump?"

"Yes, jump. Like I did." I backed up to give him room to land.

It was now more than obvious he hadn't tried to jump as a vampire. He backed up and got a running start. Which was good for jumping a long way, but not for height. He found that out the hard way, smacking the trunk of the tree, sending a shudder up and through its limbs, before falling flat on the wet ground. Now I had to sit down. I was laughing so hard; I would have fallen over if I hadn't. Nathan slammed the ground with his fist before standing back up.

"Just stand there," I tried to suggest, but I was laughing too hard. I waved my hands around hysterically in front of myself, as if that would help me regain my composure. It didn't. At least not at first, but eventually I pulled myself together enough to lean down, offering a hand and suggested, "Just stand right there, and jump straight up. Trust me."

Nathan stood up and brushed off the leaves and dirt he gathered when he fell to the ground. He looked up reluctantly and then looked back at the tree.

"Come on," I encouraged.

He finally jumped, and didn't put his all into it either, coming up a few feet shorter than I expected. Luckily, I had my hand held out, and I caught him. I yanked him up the rest of the way and sat him against the large branch. I sat down next to him, and let my leg dangle off like I used to.

"So, this is your special place?" Nathan asked.

"Wait!" I held up a finger. "Just wait and listen."

I nuzzled next to him, and we just sat and listened. In the silence, there it was. An old familiar tune. The Mississippi River rolling down the river with a low roar. The crickets welcoming the coming night. It was more fantastic than I remembered. My new vampire hearing, that tool nature, or whatever created us, gave us to hunt, had opened the door, allowing new and subtle sounds to fill out the chorus. The rustling of leaves in the breeze, the clicking of barren branches.

"This is it," I whispered.

It didn't take long before Nathan got it. His eyes and ears chased every sound, and took it all in.

"My father and I found this spot when I was seven. We came out here often to just sit and listen. When I got older, I would come out here myself. I even snuck out of my room a few times late at night to come out here and look up at a full moon." I looked up through the branches, just hoping to find a sight of it, but a layer of clouds obscured my view. Only the glow of the celestial orb was visible. It was still magical without it, but I wanted, needed, this night to be perfect. I waved my hand across the sky and uttered two simple words from one of my father's journals, "Etre visible." It was French, which many of the spells in my father's journals were. The clouds parted and revealed the glorious moon behind it casting long shadows along the ground. Now it was all perfect.

"Nathan, I have something to tell you." My insides flopped around uncontrollably. I wrapped my arms around my stomach, hoping to hold things together long enough to tell him. My god, was I bigger?

"What is it?" he asked.

I caught a whiff of something on his breath. Like many a woman throughout the history of the humanity, I smelled a telltale smell that interrupted my train of thought and stopped our conversation right there. No, it wasn't the fragrance of another woman on his clothes. No, it wasn't the acidic or sweet smell of alcohol. If it were, I might have made a comment and let it go in the end. It wasn't all that important, and I didn't believe we could get drunk. One of our benefits. At least we couldn't get drunk off of alcohol. There was something we could become inebriated from and develop a strong and devastating addiction.

"Did you feed again today?" I sat up and peeled myself from Nathan's side.

"Yeah, why?"

"I can smell it on you. That's what, twice in three days?" This wasn't good. He was giving in to his urges. Kevin should have covered this.

Nathan held up three fingers.

"Three times?"

"Yep." He announced it proudly.

"You can't do it that often, Nathan. You need to develop control. If you don't, it will control you." Oh my god, I sank inside when I realized how much I sounded like Marie when she lectured me on the same topic. The difference, I hadn't fed three times in three days. I hadn't even fed twice in three days. It was just once a week at the most. At that point I had only fed once, ever, but her point was clear.

"Nah, it's fine. Marteggo said it is. He said it's how we gain our strength."

"Nathan." I turned toward him and held his face in my hands. "It is what gives us our strength, but if you feed too much, you are feeding the urges instead of learning how to control them. That will make it difficult or impossible to be around humans."

"So, what's the problem with that?"

"Plenty," I said, letting go of his face and backing up, doing everything but placing my hands on my hips. Not only couldn't I believe what he said, I couldn't believe how he said it. He was obstinate.

"Hello," I screamed leaning over him. "Wake up and smell the world. It's full of humans. People with a pulse. How are you going to learn to live with them if you are constantly wanting to feed off them?"

"Who says we have to?"

Well now, that was the five-year-old logic I expected from my boyfriend, not. I couldn't decide rather to scream the obvious at him, or slap him across the face until he realized how stupid that question was. My slaps might not feel like much to someone so well fed, and newly born, so I opted for another path. "Are you stupid or something? Are you feeding on slugs and snails or has your brain slowed down like that all on its own? The world is full of them. We can't really avoid them."

"But Marteggo says the best life is one with a little house out away from everyone. A place all our own, where we can be what we are and around others that are like us. He has lived that way for years now and loved it."

"A life of exile. That is what he has lived. Remember, they forced him out. Before that, he lived in New Orleans with everyone else." A part of the story that Nathan was conveniently forgetting at the moment.

"That's not how Marteggo described it."

Hearing that name made my skin crawl. I saw where this was going. A charismatic figure that everyone looked up to in the past, and some still did, described this beautiful freeing life to someone who had been a vampire all of three days. Just three days. What wasn't to like about the description of heaven? Even I had to admit there was an aspect to it I found wonderful. Thinking back to my life with the Nortons, that was basically how we lived. We were off, away from anyone, doing our own thing. About as far on the outskirts of town that one person could get before being in the next town, but even then, our paths crossed with others. We weren't completely isolated. Nathan had to realize that, or was Marteggo's glow blinding him?

"I don't care what Marteggo says. We...," I pointed back and forth between the two of us. "We need to learn to live in the world around us. Not isolated to just vampires. Remember, we have friends who are not vampires."

"Maybe we shouldn't," he said, and grinned sheepishly.

"What did you just say?" I asked, shocked that something so preposterous came out of my boyfriend's mouth.

"Maybe we should only be with other vampires."

"Might I remind you that you have several friends that are not. Rob. Martin. Remember them? Oh, and what about your mother, who I believe one day will be part of your life again?" Then I exploded on him, "What about Amy?" In reality I wasn't thinking about her. Well, I was, but I wasn't. I was thinking of the other child in our life. The newest child. The one I wasn't sure if they would be human, or vampire.

"I don't know," he confessed. I felt relieved. We were finally getting somewhere.

"See..." I started, hoping to bring him back around, but then he opened his mouth and blasted me right in the gut.

"Amy should be with Steve, Stan, and Cynthia. They are shifters like her."

That was it. I hopped down out of the tree and marched away from it. I just couldn't take anymore. My boyfriend. The man I thought I knew better than anyone. Someone I thought I knew well enough to know what he was going to say before he ever opened his mouth was different now. Yes, he had been turned into a vampire, which was my fault. That was the physical change, and that was heartbreaking enough. But I thought that was where it stopped, and had even looked at this change as a positive. Well, not entirely, but it had its good parts. He would never age. He would never get sick. He would never die. When, and I hoped, there was a point we would, we finally said 'til death do us part, it truly meant we would be together forever. I never expected to lose the best of him. The strong and compassionate person he was.

I looked back in the tree's direction as the first tear rolled down my cheek. I was too devastated to laugh at the sight of him trying to shimmy down the trunk, clinging to the bark like a damn squirrel. He could have easily jumped down in one move, like I had. He saw me do it too. I kept on marching. Even when I heard him approaching through the leaves behind me. Stealthy he was not. My body flinched when he touched my shoulder from behind. Not that normal melting his touch brought.

"Wait," he requested, almost remorseful.

I didn't turn as his touch commanded. I stayed facing away, but I stopped.

"Maybe that's a little extreme. "

I crossed my arms and kept my back to him. He had a lot more to say to repair the damage he had already caused. I needed to hear him. I needed to hear my old Nathan.

"But it's necessary."

"What the hell did you just say?" I whipped around to him, and he backed up several feet once he saw my expression. "Seriously. What the hell did you just say? And please," my arms flung out and waved a fist at him. "Don't you dare say it is because Marteggo said it should."

I could tell he was trying to answer, and from the shape his lips made, I knew what the answer was.

"Let me stop you there. If Marteggo was such an outstanding role model, such a great leader, then why did he just run off when Jean challenged him? Why, over the course of several hundred years, did he never once come out of hiding? Not until I cleared the way for him. Huh? Tell me that. Tell me why you should take his rules of how to live as gospel?" I didn't wait more than half a second before I charged again. "Tell me!"

Nathan stood there with a dumbfounded expression on his face. There was no logic that supported those ridiculous and infuriating statements, at least not any I would buy.

"Let me tell you something else. I am sick and tired of hearing that name. I don't care if he is Jesus Christ of the vampires. What he told you makes no sense. We have to learn to live with others, Nathan. We have to. There is no way to truly isolate yourself and never encounter others. It's just not possible, and for those situations, you must have control. Feeding whenever you want is not that way to build up that control. You have to work at it. You... have to work at it."

Nathan looked away from me and appeared to be thinking something over. Maybe I hit a few points that made more sense than the great Marteggo. In my mind, that wasn't a hard task, but I was battling a naïve vampire that was looking up at someone with the charisma of any great cult leader.

"But..." Nathan started, still looking away from me at something off in the woods. I knew what word was going to follow that word, and I cut him off before it made it out into the open.

"What does his philosophy of life say about this?" It was a knee jerk frustration motivated reaction, and in no way in any universe, this one or any parallel one, how I planned to spring this on him, but it happened. I pulled up the sweatshirt and exposed our growing bump.

16

That wasn't even close to how I had planned to tell Nathan we were having a baby. I wanted to whisper it in his ear as we sat in my special tree, listening to the sounds of night. Then I was going to drop my little magic shield and place his hand on my stomach so he could feel and hear it. When I played that scenario out in my head, which I had countless times, I expected his reaction to be one of surprise and then joy. Of course, tons of questions would follow. I tried, an exercise in futility, to use what I had learned earlier from James to see how this would play out, but nothing came to me. I wasn't sure if it was my inability or if it was because I was trying to see my future. Of course, if I had seen how it would actually turn out, I might have changed my approach. But, like James said, that is why we can't see our own. It didn't mean I would try to cheat and see if I could.

When it finally hit Nathan what I was telling him, and it took a while, I think the shock won out over joy. He almost fell back on his ass. And probably would have if I hadn't grabbed him first. His blackened eyes stared a hole right through my belly.

"My eyes are up here," I reminded him. "Look up here." I used my hand to guide him up to my eyes. Once they were locked on to mine, I reassured him, or tried to.

"Nathan, relax, please. We are going to be fine. We are going to get through this together."

It took me a second to realize I just made this sound like some tragic disaster that we just needed to 'get' through until it was just a distant memory. I sounded frantic as I tried to correct my statements.

"It's a beautiful thing. A beautiful thing."

Jesus, if I couldn't get my thoughts and emotions together, I would never calm Nathan down any. I did what Jen taught me once and faked a deep breath. That gave me the pause my brain needed to calm down.

"What I mean is... this is wonderful and beautiful. It's nothing to be worried or afraid of. It's the start of our family."

To me, it still didn't sound any better, but it was the best I could do under the circumstances. Nathan still looked like a deer caught on a freeway full of headlights. I went with the last move I had left and dropped the little block I had up to keep Nathan from sensing its presence in me. When I did, his entire head jerked down in a split second, and his hands reached out, but stopped before they touched me.

"Go ahead." I would be lying if I said I didn't feel some apprehension about this moment, but I avoided taking any sort of defensive stance until I had a reason, and I felt I could have defended myself if he had lost control and tried to eat me. I just stood there, sweatshirt pulled up, out in the chilly night air, which surprisingly, I felt a little of against my skin. I also felt the touch of his icy fingers as they brushed across our bump before they retracted.

"It's human. I can feel the heartbeat, but how?"

Oh, lord. I knew he was going to ask that. I just hoped it wouldn't be so soon. I let my shirt down and crossed my arms over the bump. Something I had found I was doing more and more of recently. "It's kind of hard to explain, but it involves what you were before.. human.. and the other part of me... a witch."

"So, it's a witch?" He asked with a touch of vinegar.

"Slow down there. I don't know yet. Even if neither of us were vampires and were just like any human and witch having a child, there is a chance the child is born with limited or no magical abilities, like you were." I paused and let that sink in for a second, and also to see if he took that as a slight against him. It wasn't meant to be one, but even I realized it sounded that way when I said it. He didn't, or didn't show it. I think the shock of my other news had numbed him for the time being. I continued, "If they are, it takes a few years before we really know. All I know for sure is I am carrying your child, and I couldn't be happier. We are going to be a family." I realized I was now smiling from ear to ear, and not doing my normal half smile to cover my fangs, but I didn't care. He had them too. This is who we are. "Don't you want that? We talked about it once."

My boyfriend backed up, and his hand reached up and rubbed the back of his neck while he studied the situation. "Uh yeah, I just didn't expect so soon... we only.. you know... one time." And there he was. I saw it in his expression. My Nathan was back.

"Well," I said as I walked over and took his hand. "It only takes once. Didn't your mother have that talk?" I asked, in an attempt to add some levity to the situation.

"Yep, it must just be me. I'm awesome that way."

I fought the urge to push him off that pedestal of sarcasm he just stepped up on, and just appreciated the fact that was the most Nathan like thing he had said in a few days. Plus, once I tell him how this all really happened, I could remind him I am awesome in that way. That line was going into my memory tagged for use later.

"This is why you have to learn how to control things," I reminded him, bringing this all back to where we started.

"I absolutely get it now," he said without hesitation.

I wondered if he was just agreeing with me or really meant it. I hoped he did. There wasn't a clearer way to explain it to him. If he still had another opinion on the matter, it just would not work. I guess, yes, I could spend years using magic to make him see our child as a vampire, but that won't help the first time there was a paper cut or skinned knee. That I couldn't control, and what if I wasn't there? A thought that sent a shiver through me.

"You okay?" He asked, and then in a reflex of who he used to be, he put an arm around me and pulled me close.

"I'm fine." The temperature wasn't the source of my chill. Neither was the strong breeze that just blew through. It was the thought of raising our child alone if Nathan made the wrong choice. That was not a prospect I wanted to consider, but the choice really wasn't mine.

"Us, parents," he wondered aloud.

"Crazy, isn't it?" I asked, and tensed up, not knowing what his answer would be.

"Not really. I don't know about you, but I thought about it some. Just wasn't sure how it could happen. Then Amy came into our lives, and I thought maybe she was that answer. I never knew this would happen."

It was an excellent answer, and I all but exhaled. We were on the same page. Then it was his turn to tense up. He froze, and his arm fell from my shoulders.

"Crap. Amy," he whispered. "I need to get a handle on this." He looked up at me longingly. "I need to be more like you."

I turned and wrapped my arms around him. He did the same across my lower back. They were looser, not the tight embrace I am used to.

"You will," I whispered back into his ear. "I can help you. We all can. Kevin and Jen are experts at this, and Marie is the one who taught me. It just takes time." His arms tightened and his head collapsed against my shoulder.

"Thank you. I guess this life isn't as easy as others were making it sound," he bemoaned, muffled against my shoulder.

"Life is hard for everyone. Ours is just difficult in different ways than others." I cringed at how similar that sounded to something my mother said to me when I was younger.

"I guess."

"It's not a guess. It's a fact," I reassured him, and released my hold of him, backed away, and looked at his face. He was unsure about everything. This was what I expected to find once he finally woke up. I guess, just like anything else, it just took time. Having a large rowdy crowd showing him the best parts of this life and filling his head full of blissful images of what life should be like didn't really help him develop a base in reality. That would now be my job, and I had some help. But right now, I didn't want him to wallow in this. I grabbed the sides of his face and leaned in and kissed him. He kissed me back, and I felt the sparks between us, but his expression remained glum. So, I took a different path to break him out of it. I kissed him again, but before I pulled back, I said, "We're having a baby. You're going to be a daddy."

There was a spark in his eyes, and the beginning of a smile on his face. "I'm going to be a daddy. Oh god!" he gasped.

"Yes, you are. We need to celebrate this." I winked, hoping he would get my hint.

"You're right. We need to tell the others. We need to tell everyone." His face lit up, and he grabbed my hand. "Come on!" He took off running, dragging me behind him. This was not what I had in mind, but I sprinted alongside him and went along with it. Putting on a little spell while on the move to protect our bundle of joy. I wasn't ready to fight off a horde of vampires away from its beating heart.

We made our way through the shadow filled forest and continued our sprint across the fields and raced toward the house. Much to my surprise, we didn't stop there. We didn't really need to. They all knew our news, but Nathan didn't know that yet. It seemed those were the friends he intended to tell our news to. We continued straight across the field and out toward the trees where the vampires hung out. It was night, but they still sat back in the shadows and watched as we approached. Which meant they weren't staring at the witches' camp.

Nathan led us back into a clearing where the light of the full moon created a single spot surrounded by darkness. I forgot I had cleared the clouds for my little moment with Nathan. There was no point in letting the clouds return now. Nathan wanted to make an announcement, and this was the stage he chose. By all means, let's give him the spotlight.

"Marteggo! Marteggo!" he yelled. I thought he wanted to tell everyone, but it seemed he only wanted to tell one person. His summonsing attracted many others in the woods to come forth and step to the edge of the light. Among them I spied Mike and Clay. It wasn't long before Marteggo emerged from behind them with Theodora wrapped around his arm. The crowd parted as he stepped through and into the center.

"Master Saxon, good evening."

"We have great news," started Nathan. He looked down at me, bursting at the seams. I looked at Theodora, who looked like the cat who ate the canary. "We are going to have a baby. Larissa is pregnant."

Marteggo looked at him curiously, then bellowed a hearty laugh. "Me thinks young Nathan here drank blood from a local drunk." The assembled mass of vampires laughed. That was all except three. Theodora, Mike, and Clay knew the truth.

"It's true, I tell you," insisted Nathan. "She let me feel its pulse. It's there." He hastily reached for my shirt, and I slapped his hand away. I wasn't ready for him to yank my shirt up in front of this large of a crowd.

Marteggo laughed again and released Theodora before circling around the spot of moonlight, taking center stage. "It's all right Nathan. We've all had it happen before. Those that walk Bourbon Street are easy marks, and depending on what they drank, they can be really sweet." He walked up and threw an arm around Nathan. "Now come. Let's go tell more stories and find a feast."

Nathan shook the man's arm off, and there was a collective murmur among the gathering. Everyone stepped back, and Marteggo turned and regarded Nathan sternly. This was bad. Nathan had disrespected Marteggo. He didn't mean to, and I knew that, but that was how it looked to everyone else. I tried to take a step in between the two men, but Nathan forced me back behind him.

Clay and Mike had left the group and moved forward. I had seen that look in Mike's eyes before. Things were escalating, and you could feel the egos of each man approaching their boiling points.

"It is true," said Theodora. Dozens of heads spun around and looked at her. Marteggo was the last. She stood there in the moonlight, almost leery of the collective gazes. "It is true. How we don't know, but Larissa is carrying Nathan's child. I was there when she found out. I felt the child's presence myself."

"You're sure?" Marteggo asked her gruffly.

She nodded and shrank as he walked toward her.

"So, it's true?" he asked, towering over her.

"Yes," she replied as his large hand reached under her chin and tilted her head up forcing her to look into his eyes. She shied away from his gaze when she answered. He held her there for a few moments, waiting for their eyes to lock, but they never did. The love I saw between them before was all but gone. Her head shook in his grasp, and I realized there was a different dynamic between them. It was the first time I had seen it. Then I realized it wasn't just between them, it was with everyone. There was an electric tension in the air, so thick you could cut it with a blunt knife. When Marteggo finally let go of his beloved's chin, it ratcheted down, but just slightly to an uneasiness. Everyone waited for his reaction as he backed away from Theodora slowly. There was a low growl that evolved into a quiet but deep chuckle. It increased in volume and intensity as he turned around with a wide grin.

"Then we must celebrate," he announced and threw his arms out. The gathered masses cheered and rushed in to offer their congratulations.

Mike made his way through the crowd and hugged me like so many others had. He held on longer than the others. He pulled me closer and whispered, "What the hell was that?"

"No clue," I replied. I didn't really have one, but I was just as curious as Mike was, if not more so.

When he backed away, he looked at me and at Marteggo. I had seen that face before. It was the same look Mike had regarded Clay with the night we first met him up on the roof. Marteggo had lost Mike's trust.

I kept a close watch on Marteggo as I endured the parade of hugs. He kept one eye on me the whole time and kept his distance.

I spent hours hearing prospective baby names from all the women. Some had had children before they became vampires. Others were extremely jealous, never having the chance themselves. A few were uncomfortably jealous. Not really making eye contact when they talked. Just kind of looking to my side and being polite as their friends gushed. I had a feeling they came along to avoid being the one or two that hung in the darkness during what appeared to be such a joyous occasion. I understood. The jealousy, not the coming along with their friends. Well, maybe I understood both. I wasn't exactly that excited to be here. Being mobbed was not exactly my cup of tea, but I was here because of Nathan.

Once the mob cleared, the night turned into rounds of singing and dancing. I conveniently used my condition as an excuse to avoid both. Everyone bought it, but it also backfired. Throughout the night I was once again mobbed, well not really mobbed more like had my peace interrupted by the rather frequent visit of someone asking if I felt okay and comfortable. Each time, I said I was, which I was, except I was being bothered. I just wanted to sit there and watch.

I could see why Kevin had said Nathan was coming along well. He was in the middle of it all, with no hesitation. The social butterfly, as it were, with his girlfriend, the wallflower sitting over here on a stump. It was good to see, mostly. Seeing how he followed Marteggo around like a lost puppy made my skin crawl. He wasn't the only one.

Men and women alike hung on every word of his stories, and boy did he have stories. I never once saw that man not in the center of a large group with his mouth flapping.

"Doing all right?"

I looked up at Clay. "If another damn person asks me that, they might get punched."

"Yep, you're fine," he remarked and sat down next to me.

"What? Are you tired of the Marteggo show?"

"I'm not much for large groups of people, plus..." Clay stopped.

"Plus, what?"

"I don't know. Maybe it's just me, but there is something about him I don't like. Something about all his stories. They are just too over the top."

"Doth he exaggerate?" I asked, going a little over the top with my old English myself.

"1000%. If he is what he says he is, how did Jean ever push him out?"

"Exactly!" I exclaimed, causing a few to look in our direction. I just waved in return and turned my head toward Clay. "Sorry, but that is exactly the same question I have."

"I know he said it was something about Jean getting the masses behind him, but I bet Marteggo could have yanked that string bean of a man's head off before he even knew he was there. All you have to do is look through history and you know the masses follow whoever holds the power. The masses would have followed him, again."

"Why Clayton Lindsey, what an astute observation." I all but fanned myself. I had to admit my southern drawl was getting better.

"Hey, world history was my favorite class back in school," he smiled back, but that smile was short-lived. He slumped next to me. "Man, that was just a few months ago, but it feels like a lifetime away."

"I know Clay." I draped my arm around him and gave him a comforting squeeze. "I know. Just being here brings back so many memories, but they don't feel like mine anymore. It's like I am looking..."

"At someone else's life?" he asked.

"Exactly."

"It's strange," remarked Clay. "Speaking of strange." His head jerked to the right and mine followed. He was right, here comes strange. Marteggo was coming in our direction.

"I should give you guys some privacy," suggested Clay. He stood up.

I grabbed onto his hand and yanked him hard back down toward the stump. "Don't you dare."

"You'll be fine, and I won't be far." He yanked free and meandered away, and he was right. He wasn't far away. He found a comfortable tree just a few yards away, but far enough to not look like he was lingering or hovering. His eyes watched Marteggo with a suspicious gaze. Marteggo didn't appear to notice that Clay, or that anyone else was even there. It was just me and him.

Marteggo stopped right in front of me and waited. Was I to stand, or stay seated in his presence? I didn't know. So, I stayed seated, and watched his reaction. There was no mistaking it. He was studying me, and I didn't like it. His magical charisma may have wooed Nathan. It had no effect on me. I saw a man who was a walking irony.

"I want to give you my congratulations," he said and clicked on the charm.

"You already did. Don't you remember? Right after Nathan told everyone, you came up and gave me a hug," I replied flatly. I wanted to see how he would respond to someone correcting him, and it appeared I was the only one that had the guts to try. Everyone else hung onto every word that parted his lips, like it was the gospel.

He didn't seem to like it at first, and hesitated before he responded. Was he trying to remember back to see if he had or was there another thought going through his head? Maybe trying to think of a response. Maybe thinking of how to dispose of me quickly. "I did, didn't I," he said, and again attempted to turn on the charm, and then sat next to me on my stump. He didn't even ask.

"I must say, I am still confused how it happened. I have met several humans carrying the child of a vampire, but never two vampires. Perhaps it has something to do with you being a witch."

I had to give it to him. He was smarter and sharper than I expected. He made that leap faster than anyone else.

"It's a possibility we have to consider. My being a witch brings many things into play." To give him a little of a reminder, I held open a hand in front of him and let a small flame dance across the surface. The sight mesmerized him. Like so many, he fell victim to the shiny object phenomenon. Show them something they haven't seen, or don't see often, and you will have them eating out of the palm of your hand, at least until the next shiny object appeared.

"Speaking of. I hear you are still undergoing training with the outcasts." He pointed out of the trees and in the direction of the orange flickering glow of the witches' camp.

"I am. Several of the rogue witches," the second time I corrected him in a very short time, and I still had my head, "are helping to

117

provide me with refreshers. I spent so long away from the world of magic after Jean's followers turned me. I have forgotten a few things."

"That's good," he started, and then shifted and turned toward me. "But don't forget, you are a vampire. You really should spend time out here with Nathan and the rest of us learning about us. If I remember correctly, you were raised in isolation by the Nortons. I'm sure they did the best they could, but that is no way to raise a vampire."

Did he really just insult the Nortons and me? Could he really be that full of himself? It was time to knock him down a rung or two, respectfully, or as respectfully as I could. "If you are talking about knowing what we are, knowing how to hunt, and knowing how to control things so we can be part of the world, we did just fine. I have been around others for a while now with no issue and can go weeks in between feedings without losing control." I tamped down how offended I felt by his assertion, and tried to the best of my ability to not sound overly proud or boasting, but I was afraid that slipped out at the end.

"Several weeks?" He asked, almost scoffing. "Impressive. But what I speak of is not about knowing how to control yourself. It's about knowing who and what you are, and suckling up to the world to repay you for this curse it gave you."

"I'll pass. I like the way I'm living my life."

"As a witch," he added to my statement.

"As both a witch and a vampire," I corrected.

Marteggo groaned and placed both of his huge hands on his knees and pushed up off of my stump and stood up and stretched. "That was what I meant."

I was sure it wasn't, and he was trying to save face. I wasn't keeping score, but this was the third time I had corrected him in the last several minutes.

"Tell me? Is Marcus Meridian one of the witches instructing you in that camp?" he asked, without turning to face me.

"He is one of many," I replied shortly.

"Huh," he grunted, and then walked back to the crowd in the middle of the clearing

17

I wasn't sure how long the impromptu party went on, but I left well before dawn. I pleaded for Nathan to come back with me, but he resisted, wanting to stay for a while longer. I tried to explain that I couldn't. Before I went out for my daily training, I wanted to take a shower and spend some time with Amy. That brought on another round of his tantrum about how much time I spent with the witches and ignoring my other side. My little sarcastic wave of my hand around at all the vampires I had spent all night with didn't seem to make the point I wanted. Nathan used to understand how important all this was, but the great and wonderful Marteggo had clouded his vision. Mike and Clay promised me they would look after him, but I got a feeling they were going to watch more than that.

By the time I had showered and changed, the more traditional way because it just felt more normal, the rest of the house buzzed with activity. There was the normal jockeying for the one and only bathroom. A detail I hadn't considered as much of a problem before. At least not until Mrs. Saxon sent the others here. Now it was a problem. But it was a problem that could be easily fixed from the comfort of my room with a little magical renovation. I hadn't learned how to make my own magical space like the coven or my father's office yet, so I stole the coat closet in the hall and made it into a small bathroom with a standup shower in it. It was cramped, but effective. Steve was the first to discover the renovation, and yelled down the stairs, "Hey guys, did you know we have two bathrooms?"

Once the stampede up the stairs finished, I left my bedroom, silently. I think Martin and Cynthia noticed me as I walked by. It was the first time, other than when she was around Amy, that I had seen that girl do so much as crack a smile. I went downstairs and started fixing breakfast. Now that was a first, or make that a first in the last eighty years. The smell didn't bother me as much as it had before, and I even snuck a strip of bacon. To say that everyone was surprised when they entered the kitchen and saw me standing over a table with all the fixings.. well, they were. But I didn't care about everyone. I cared about that smile Amy had on her face. She was 'the *why*' to why I did all this. It had nothing to do with that nagging voice in my head that complained over and over about my neglecting her. Okay, maybe it did.

I sat across the table from her and drew a smiley face with butter in her grits. Then I used a piece of bacon to make a smile on another plate with two eggs as the eyes. That produced the third smile, the one I wanted to see most of all. The one on that girl's face.

When I stole the strip of bacon off her plate, she attempted to snatch it back from me, but she was a little too slow for me. I wasn't really trying. Maybe I should have been, though. Amy fell back laughing in her chair when the bacon left my hand and floated back onto her plate. I looked down at the end of the table at both Jack and Lisa. Neither was owning up to being the one that robbed me of one more taste of that salty paradise.

Luckily for them, I forgave both of them quickly. Lisa had told Jack of our little adventure the day before, and now he wanted to come along. Which wasn't really a problem. Jack had been out to the witches' camp several times, but hey if he wanted to come along today for our new version of witch's school, then class was in session.

Amy came along as well. I tried to tell her no. Today wasn't going to be as much fun, even though only portions of it were fun yesterday. It was mostly frustrating. James appeared to be the only one enjoying our little session, while Lisa and I struggled to master the skill. I can't even consider it that. We were so far from any form of mastery of this skill, it wasn't even funny. We were barely beginners, and I had already failed to follow through with my promise to practice on my own last night. I doubt James would accept my excuse of being a little busy. Of course, if he was the master he appeared to be, he would already know it was coming.

Lisa spent the entire walk into camp bragging about all the homework she had done last night. She even had Jack wondering if he could perform the same feat. Lisa didn't hesitate to throw a wet blanket over his hopes, reminding him how rare of a skill it was.

Where we were going today was a far rarer skill, and I would be lying if I said I didn't feel a few butterflies about it. It wasn't the morning sickness, or whatever it was called either. I hadn't gotten sick in about a day in a half, which on this accelerated schedule, I guess, was more like a few weeks. Maybe it was the bacon I had consumed. That was a possibility, but the most likely source was all the warnings Edward had given me about this very topic. The stack of books he produced on the same topic still sat next to the bed in my room in the coven.

As we entered the witches' camp, I noticed something odd off in the distance. There were always vampires lingering just inside the shadows of the tree line. Some watched the witches, and others didn't. They were just there. Today was a little different, though. The crowd was larger, and there was no denying it. They were all watching the witches' camp. Especially one particular vampire. Marteggo was at the front of the line. He appeared interested, watching us as we walked from the house to the camp.

"So, we aren't seeing James today?" Lisa asked, annoyed. Her head twisted around and looked at his tent as we passed by.

"Nope, but if you had been practicing, you would have already known that."

She ignored my little jab. I believe there was something more personal that had her distracted. The deep sigh behind me confirmed that. Now I was the one that should have seen that coming. He was rather easy on the eyes, and rather, well, electric to be around. I'd be lying if I didn't feel the charge.

"Today, we are going to see Mary Smith. She's a rather pleasant person." I said with a straight face. The one and only time I ever met Mary, she didn't appear to be a fan of mine. It wouldn't be farfetched to say she would rather burn me at the stake than hug me. "Her specialty is descensum."

The rhythmic footsteps that had followed me all the way from the house vanished. I only heard Amy's and mine. There were also two rather panicked thumpings behind me. I turned and saw two very slack jaw witches staring back at me. "You guys coming?"

"Larissa, you do know what that is?" whispered Lisa.

I nodded. "Yep. Astral project, and trust me, I know how dangerous this is. Edward told me all about it once."

"Nooooo." Lisa shook her head back and forth violently, and she wasn't whispering now. She reached over and grabbed my arm and pulled me toward her. "Think about the word. Descensum."

Lisa stared deeply into my eyes. Searching for understanding, which I had to admit, I didn't have a bloody clue what she was getting at.

"Descend?" she asked, with a hand pointing down.

I stared back, "And?"

"Larissa, she means down under," interjected Jack nervously. "The afterlife. The underworld. The nether. The place where souls go when you die."

"Oh. OH!" The term finally hit me. I was to descend to the world of the afterlife and come back. That was a detail Marcus Meridian and Master Thomas had left out, and probably for good reason. That sounded all sorts of Halloween ghost story and horror film creepy. The more I thought about it, the more the second thoughts grew about taking any visits to the world of the dead. Even if it was just a short one. Then a thought occurred to me and all but swept those away. "I've already done it," I whispered to myself. "I've already done it," I said louder and looked at Lisa. Then I said it again while looking at Jack. "My visits to my mother. Don't you see? I've already done it. I've done it dozens of times."

"No. No, you haven't. Not this," Lisa explained. Panic dripped from her voice. "That is a family connection. It's different. I had an aunt that did this to connect people with lost loved ones. Larissa," she grabbed both of my hands, and lowered her head. "After she did it, she wasn't right for several days, and even then, she was different. It took something out of her, and she refused to talk about what it was like. She only told the family what their relative said, nothing more."

Well, if the prospect didn't sound exciting before, it definitely didn't now. I only had to do it once for the test. Well, maybe twice. Once in practice to know I could do it, and then once in the test of the seven wonders, or whatever that thing was called. Too bad it wasn't multiple choice, and I couldn't just identify what the wonders were. This was a damn essay test from hell, with one paragraph dedicated to a visit to either heaven or hell. Then that had me wondering. Which would I visit? Which brought another question. Were there really two different places? Holy spinning confusion, Batman. I was now pondering the existence of life after death. A topic discussed and argued in so many forums, from art to religion. If I did this right, I might have some answers. I wasn't sure I really wanted those answers.

"Maybe someone should take Amy back to the house," I strongly suggested.

Amy rejected the notion just as strongly by wrapping herself around my leg with a death grip. I felt each of her fingers pressing through my jeans. Luckily, I didn't bruise. Neither Jack nor Lisa volunteered to help there.

"Well..." I stuttered as I tried to think of an excuse not to continue forward. There were a few. Maybe more than a few, but they were all selfish and temporary. I had to remember that this was just a step on the only path that will solve the problems that stood between me and any chance of a peaceful life. I had given up on the notion of a normal life. This step was just a very unpleasant sounding one, but there was no avoiding it. As I saw it, it was a trade-off. A little temporary terror now to avoid long-term hell in the future. Not that looking at it that way made it any less frightening of a proposition. I just had to do it. "Let's go."

We walked right up to Mary Smith's tent. There was no one outside waiting for us. There wasn't really anything outside except a string of what appeared to be a wash. I wasn't sure if we should walk right in or not. Our last encounter wasn't exactly welcoming. The problem with tents? There are no doors to knock on. I guess I could knock on the flap that blocked the opening, but I doubt that would make any noise at all. Lisa gave me a slight poke from behind as I stood there, trying to decide how to proceed. I hate to tell her. If she pokes me again, I was going to throw her through the flap, solving our problem.

I settled on what I thought was the only acceptable option. "Mary Smith, are you home?"

"Yes. Yes," her scratchy voice responded from behind the flap. "Come on in, I guess."

So far, the same warmth as before. I tried to imagine what I might find beyond the flap. A large estate like Marcus's tent? Perhaps an apartment like what I saw when we visited James. Both appeared to be too stylish for this woman, but one never knows. Appearances can deceive, though I had my doubts. I stepped in wondering about a third option, but arrived in one that never crossed my mind, and it probably wouldn't have. I moved in further and let the others join me in the small tent. It was just that, a tent. The same patchwork tent we saw from the outside. Candles and lanterns were everywhere, casting a host of flickering shadows of the tent posts and furniture against the fabric walls.

"You brought others," she said with a hint of disdain. Mary walked in, wearing a black dress and a shawl over her shoulders. A large green pendant hung from her neck, and small glasses struggled to hang on to the end of her nose as she studied the others.

"No vampires. These two are witches, and this one," I placed my hand on top of Amy's hand, "she is a shapeshifter."

"I know that. I'm not stupid, you know. Do they know what you are here for?" she asked suspiciously.

"Yes."

"And they know what this really is?" she asked, and then pointed a gnarled finger at Lisa and said, "I imagine you do. The darkness is within you, but you have firm control of it. Good. Good." She almost sounded pleased when she turned her attention to Jack. "You, on the other hand, are just a witch." Mary turned her back and walked around the center post in the tent.

I looked back at Lisa who struggled to hold in the grin at that little slap. I put that one away to use later and hid any joy I felt about the grimace on Jack's face.

"Well, come on. If we're going to do this, we need to do this right." Mary motioned for us to follow her. Where were we going? I wasn't sure. There wasn't much room in the tent, but then I realized. She wasn't here when we first walked in. She came from somewhere. So, we followed her around the center post, and toward a dark void that appeared in the side wall of the tent.

If we were some place different, I wasn't sure. It was possible we were still in the tent, just another part of it that was on the back of it. This wasn't a large space, and there were no windows or anything to give a sense of where we might be. It was dark, except for a single candle in the middle of a symbol I recognized quite well. We all did, but for different reasons. It was a pentagram.

"Each of you sit at one of the points. I will sit here," she said, her voice gravelly and wandering. "Sit quickly."

Lisa and Jack both picked a point. I maneuvered Amy to the two open ones, making sure she sat between me and either Lisa or Jack. Since we entered, or make that since Mary entered, Amy had clung to my side. Something about her presence, and maybe her appearance, made Amy leery. I completely understood. This whole thing made me leery.

"You probably all know what this is, and I am sure you think you understand its significance, but you are probably wrong, so I will tell you to make sure you don't do anything stupid. This is a pentagram. The perfect shape. It is made up of ten interlocking triangles. Each triangle is the perfect ratio. That perfection solidifies the strength and the protection the symbol provides us." Her hand traced over the shape drawn in white. Each line shimmered as her hand passed over it. "This symbol is not the source of any darkness. It is protection against the darkness, and it will protect those of us that travel to the other side and help guide us back." She leaned forward and leered at the three of us. "Now leave any stupid misconceptions you have about this symbol, and accept what I have told you. You have to do that or leave."

She paused as if she were waiting for someone to walk out. None of us moved other than to look at one another.

"Okay, then. Let's begin. First, you need one of these." Mary waved her hand over the candle in the center. A haze surrounded it, and when it disappeared, a wide black candle appeared. The flame that was there before lost its yellow hue. It itself was black and danced around. A fine line of black smoke rose from it and circled around the room overhead. It was strange looking. Unbroken, like a string, or a thin thread.

"This is a reunion candle. Its smoke is the guide for your astral self. It rises and weaves like a single unbroken string. Focus on it. Follow it. There is nothing in this world but it. It will lead you to the afterlife and back. It's up to you to follow it. To become one with it, but, and you must not forget this, don't let go of it. If you do, you will be lost and will never return."

Mary paused after the warning, and I watched the smoke rise and circle around the room. It was beautiful and creepy all at once. It danced like one of those cobras in a basket. Its movements were slow and fluid, almost poetic.

"Watch the smoke. Grab hold of the smoke. When you feel it pulling you, don't resist. Go with it. Just don't let go."

It happened almost instantly as the smoke circled around me. I was moving, but my body wasn't. It was a weird sensation, to say the least. I was floating, but I still felt like I was sitting firmly on the floor. When the smoke passed by, I reached out and grabbed it. My physical hand never moved, but I had a firm hold on the smoke and as it continued by, I followed it.

"You feel it, Larissa? Don't you?" Mary asked. Her voice had lost the disdain and scratchiness it had when we first arrived. Now it was clear and smooth. Almost rhythmic.

"I do," I replied, but my voice said nothing. It was just a thought.

"Good," Mary said, or thought. She was there with me, wherever I was, just like Mrs. Tenderschott was when I used those potions. "Now yank the string. Yank it hard."

I looked down at the string. I had a firm hold of it, but didn't feel it. Even though it had wrapped itself around my hand and up my arm.

"Larissa! Yank it! Now!"

I gave it a firm yank, and I found myself again sitting on the floor at the point of the pentagram. Behind me, Amy lay asleep with her head in Jack's lap. He was almost asleep, too. Mary was not on her point. She was sitting right next to me, looking at me. Her expression and body language were not one I had seen from her before.

"Congratulations Larissa. You just did your first free float." Her hand reached out and touched my shoulder. "How do you feel?"

"Okay?" I said, but it was really more of a question. I didn't have a clue what she was talking about, or how I was supposed to feel after I did whatever it was she said I did. "Was that it?"

"No," she said. Then Mary looked at Lisa. "Welcome back Lisa." Mary blew out the black candle, and it changed back to the tall white one. She removed it from the center of the pentagram and then took its place, sitting in front of me and Lisa. "That was not it. That was just the first step. Unfortunately, Jack doesn't have the gift." She looked through the gap between the two of us and back at Jack to address him. "Don't take it hard. All witches are different. They all have different talents. Some are better at some types of magic than others." She pointed at Lisa, but smiled when she did. "Lisa comes from the dark side of magic. This is more natural to her." Then she turned to me. "You don't, but you have the talent. This was just your first step out of your body. Simple astral projection. You didn't go far. That was because I wouldn't let you. At least not yet. I had control of the smoke. I needed to see who could, and how easily they could. Now that I know, we can take a few further treks, and then make the one you seek. If that is what you want."

She stood up out of the center and extended her hands to both of us, helping us up to our feet. "You need your rest now before we make any further attempts." She looked directly at me with a smirk. "She needs her rest. You don't, but you should wait a little longer before trying again."

"Thank you, I said, trying to forget the woman I first met, and take in the one that was here now. I liked this one better. I gathered Amy off of Jack's lap. She was still sleepy, so I picked her up and carried her. It was no problem. Jack yawned when he stood up. We followed Mary back into her main tent and to the door. When we stepped out, night had fallen, the moon was high in the sky, and campfires illuminated the camp. I turned around, surprised.

"How long were we here?"

"Too long," Jack said between yawns.

"About ten hours," replied Mary Smith. "It didn't seem like more than a few minutes, did it?"

I shook my head. It didn't. It didn't feel like more than a minute or two.

"That's the danger of projection. You can lose track of time, place, and your own existence if you go too deep. While you were under and taking the first steps to separate your consciousness from your body, Amy and Jack and I had several nice conversations and we even had lunch."

There was that feeling that I had a little too much over the last several months. The spinning head of confusion. Ten hours in just a few moments? Wow! Losing track of time was right. I felt completely lost as it was. One of Edward's warnings played in my head. It was about getting lost, and not doing it for more than an hour. What was it I read about that? Oh yea, the fact that the world would have moved too far for you to find your way back to your physical vessel. But wait! I had been out for ten hours and still managed.

"Larissa, are you all right? You look pale, even for a vampire."

I looked right at Mary and asked, "How was that possible? Ten hours. I have heard... I mean, read that if we are away from ourselves for anything around an hour or longer, we can't find our way back."

Mary lit up. "You have studied this before. That's great."

"Just some reading. I don't understand how..."

"The smoke," interrupted Mary. "The smoke created a construct you could hang on to find your way back. When I told you to yank it, that pulled you back. Remember, I told you to never let go of it. If you had, you could have been lost."

18

Amy slept in my arms all the way back up to the house. I wanted to wake her when we got there to make sure she ate, but she was so soundly asleep, I hated to wake her. I took her up to her own room and laid her down. I'd make sure she ate when she woke up. There were no set meal times in this house. Except for Rob and Martin. They explained they had to eat every four hours to keep up their awesomeness, and man did they eat. They mowed down a table full of food quickly, but yet there wasn't a pound of fat on their frames. Now that we weren't at the coven, they ran around in not much more than a pair of shorts and shoes. Being what they were, I wondered why they even bothered with the shoes.

I closed the door carefully after taking one last peek at Amy. She looked so peaceful, and I had to admit, I was a bit envious. To have just one moment like that would be wonderful. I made my way to the stairs and found someone waiting for me at the bottom. And knew this would not be one of those moments.

"You didn't have to leave," said Nathan.

He didn't look pleased. Talk about holding something in. It had been well over twelve hours since I left that little party. I held a finger up to my lips, but he missed the message.

"Why? What was so important?" he demanded.

I grabbed his arm when I was on the bottom step and yanked him into the parlor. "Amy's asleep," I said and closed the double glass doors behind us. "Keep it down, please."

At that, Nathan looked a little sheepish, but that didn't deter his inquisition. "You left our party. Everyone was celebrating something that never happens, and you just disappeared." He marched toward me, and I was having nothing of his little display, and met him halfway with a hand on his chest.

"First!," I emphasized to make the first of many points I had. "I never asked for that party. I just wanted to tell you. Most everyone that mattered already knew. *THEY* were awake when I was sick and had the first signs." I should have thought about that point a little more before I made it. I only meant to say I didn't ask for a party. The rest of it just kind of came out, but it took some of the air out of his sails. "Second," I said, this time with a little less punch, "I told you I was leaving. I had an appointment."

"I know. More witch shit," he snapped.

"Yes, more witch stuff," I corrected him, and then turned to put some space between us in the hopes it might lower the tension in the room. "Remember, I am part witch, and I also shouldn't have to remind you about everything that is going on. Remember Jean St. Claire? The one who turned you into this? Mrs. Wintercrest, who isn't really my biggest fan, and now an ally of Jean St. Claire? Then there is the problem Master Thomas and Mr. Demius have asked for my help with? All of these... every one of them, is something standing in the way of our long and happy life and requires me to learn and master more magic. So, yes, more witch stuff. It is a mandatory part of life."

He paced back and forth, stewing. I wondered if I had gone too far with my first point, but it was how things happened, and eventually someone was bound to slip up and say something. It was better he heard it from me.

"Do I need to remind you? You are a vampire, too?"

"You don't, and if you think you need to, then you are stupid." There was no regret in using that word. Everything reminded me I was a vampire. Everything. "There isn't a moment that goes by that doesn't remind me. I have been one for eighty years, you have been one for a couple of days. Don't you dare lecture me." My finger wagged at him, and I had to resist the urge to let something else enter this discussion. Sending him against the wall wouldn't accomplish anything.

"Then why not focus on that for a bit? Spend more time with me out there with them. Help me get to know them, and myself."

Nathan's eyes begged, and I felt a little of my frustration melt. There was an olive branch I could offer that I hoped would end this. "If I promise to spend more time out there with you, will you understand why I need to spend the time I do with the witches? This is bigger than you and I, but it directly impacts what kind of life *we* will have." I did something I had only seen in movies and rubbed that bump of a belly I had to remind him that the *we* I referred to was more than just he and I.

"I think I can accept that," he agreed reluctantly.

I dropped my guard and walked over to him with every intention of making up the best way I could. Only to be stopped by the utter stupidity of his next comment.

"If you would consider a future without magic. We could live away from everyone and not have to worry about anything."

"Wait right there!" I stepped back for his own benefit. "We already discussed this."

"No!" he interrupted. "We didn't. We talked about my need to learn control because of our child, and I agreed. We never discussed not living secluded from others, for our safety and theirs. Marteggo's lifestyle has some benefits."

"I never want to hear that name again!" I turned away and squeezed my hands at the end of my very straight arms.

"Why? He has valid points."

"Seriously?" I asked with my back still to him. Points were running through my head, and some were rather childish and hurtful. Not really beneath me at the moment, but again, it wouldn't accomplish anything, and I needed to end this discussion with Nathan agreeing with me. That was the only acceptable outcome. But what if he didn't? What if he never bent on that? What then? That was a question that had only one answer, and it was one I didn't want to face at the moment.

I turned around, doing my best to appear loving and understanding, but God help Nathan if he mentioned that man's name one more time. Actually, I was going to commit that sin, but only once, and I hoped that would be the end of it. Hopes rarely reflect reality and his proximity out there, and the constant visits the others made told me that the name was going to be a fixture for the time being. Maybe I could diminish how it was used.

"Nathan, Marteggo didn't live that lifestyle until Jean forced him to leave! Before, he lived in the city and enjoyed everything that early New Orleans offered. So don't fall for what he is selling. He settled. But let me remind you of something I shouldn't have to. The Nortons tried that, and they still found us. It doesn't work. If it did, I would have never come to the coven. We would have never met, and this moment would never happen." Now, let's see Mr. Dreamboat comeback at that with any pearls of wisdom from the great and powerful Marteggo.

He pondered that for a few seconds. I saw the wheels churning in his head. Which caused mine to turn and anticipate whatever counter argument he was evaluating before he said it aloud. I hoped he was carefully considering everything. If he was, then he would realize there was nothing he could say. I was the living example of that theoretical life. An experiment gone very wrong, with the same variables at play. Someone was trying to find us while we were hiding. Mr. Markinson would be so proud that I remembered the scientific method, though I doubt he would have ever thought this would be how I applied it.

"True," he reluctantly conceded, and I felt the weight of the world leave. That left the other half-a-dozen worlds I was still involved with pressing on me, but at least one was gone. I inched forward, feeling victorious. "But can't you leave magic behind and just be one of us?"

And to think I was about to reward him with a kiss. "Why? Please, oh please tell me why? What and whose great wisdom has led to request that?" If I heard that name, forget restraint. Nathan was going into the wall behind him. Maybe it would knock some sense into him. I was ready for it, and I practically dared him to say it.

"Questions are the search for reason. It was just a request. A lot of our problems come from you being a witch." He paused, and then I watched his lips form that name, but he stopped before he said it. "I believe life would be easier if you just picked one."

"If only it were that easy." I saw the look on his face and knew I had just walked into something. Something I should have seen it coming from a mile away before I threw that softball at him. I had to stop it before he took the opening. "Uh. Uh. Uh. Before you say it is. Think about it like this. Biologically, I am a vampire. I can't do anything about that, no matter how much I wanted to choose otherwise. Magic flows around and through me. It's like breathing to a human. I can't ignore it. It's in everything we do. You should understand that. Your mother is a witch."

"But you could just ignore it. It can still flow," he flailed his arms in the air, "around you, but you just ignore it. Isn't that what you do when you blend in?" Nathan put air quotes around the words blend-in, and I knew what he was trying to say, but I was about to drop a bomb-shell on him that might think otherwise and remove any of that brainwashing hogwash the last few nights surrounded by vampires might have infused into him.

"Remember, vampires stop acting like vampires to blend in, too. Jen and Kevin teach an entire class about that. It goes both ways, with one exception. Magic is wonderful. Why would I want to ignore that?" I shouldn't, and nothing he or anyone could say would convince me otherwise. It felt it was the side that gave me life, and I couldn't even believe he was trying to talk me into leaving it behind. Why? To become something that lives in the darkness? One of the world's despised and feared creatures? But I had one more card to play, and it was, I hoped, a mic drop moment. "Plus, magic is why we have this." My hand patted my stomach.

Stunned wasn't the right word for his appearance. Shocked? Knocked for a loop? About to pass out? Those might be better, but still seemed to fall short. He stood there, visibly shaken, looking right at what I had directed his attention to.

"Why would I want to ignore magic?"

"You..." he started and then looked up at me. Words escaped him as he attempted to construct a sentence that anyone who spoke English would understand. "... created that?"

I guess I needed to explain and wondered if I needed to go into the biologics involved with being a vampire, but I didn't want it to sound like a science class. "Kind of," I started while I searched for how. Whatever he had that robbed him of the English language seemed to be contagious. The basics. Just the basics. I reminded myself. "When you become a vampire, your body stops changing. So, a female vampire's body can't change to carry a child."

"So, you created one!" he exclaimed, pointing violently at our child.

"No," I urged him to slow down and let me finish. "I didn't. Not in the way you mean. It is ours. When we were having sex, I let a thought slip through, and the magic took over."

I felt that should have explained it well enough for him to understand that it was ours, but it only existed because of magic. Hopefully, he wouldn't look at magic as something we could just ignore or want to live without, no matter who was filling his skull of mush with anything different. Hopefully, he would look at something other than my stomach. I was about to remind him where my eyes were when I saw his face turn grim.

"That's an aberration," he screamed. Then Nathan's body crashed into the far wall, pulverizing the plaster behind him. I let both of my hands hang out away from my body, glowing, to remind him to choose his next words carefully.

Rob and Jack rushed in through the double doors. "What the hell?"

They stopped and looked at Nathan, who was nothing but a groaning pile of humanity under a plaster dust cloud.

"Ask him." I pointed right at Nathan to make sure they knew the *him* I was referring to. "He seems to think our baby is an aberration. That's the word you used, right?"

"Larissa, put it away." Jack held up a hand defensively in my direction and I dropped my hands, and with them, the bright glowing orbs they held.

Now others had joined the crowd at the door. Mike, Laura, and Apryl were the first to come. Brad and Clay were next.

"Sure everyone, come on in. It's just a private conversation. That is why the doors were closed." I motioned toward the doors that Rob and Jack had opened.

"Well, you're the one who about brought the house down," remarked Apryl. Mike and Brad helped Nathan up to his feet. He kept his distance, and he was smart to do so. I loved him, but he had a lot of thinking to do and needed to start saying the right things.

"That child she is carrying. It's magic. It's not real."

Every head in the room swung around first in my direction, but when I held up two empty hands, they turned back to Nathan with shocked expressions.

"Nathan, it's a real child. Flesh and blood. We have all felt it." Apryl turned to me. "Did you let him feel it?"

I nodded.

Apryl turned back to him. "Then you felt it too. What the hell are you talking about? Yes, maybe magic that let her conceive and carry the child, but that doesn't mean it isn't real, and it is yours. You two made that baby. Just like anyone else." She lectured him harshly, and he didn't seem to appreciate it. He looked at her at first, but then avoided eye contact and squirmed where he stood.

By now others had joined the party, and Jennifer Bolden had taken up position behind Apryl. She had obviously heard what our little disagreement was about and appeared none too happy. When Apryl gave her an open, she pounced like a protective mother would.

"Look Nathan. No matter how that child came to be. You and Larissa are having a miracle. You should both be happy. Now get whatever stupid thoughts you have out of your head, and man up. Your mother would have expected better from you. You and I both know that."

Jen meant well and had a room full of nodding heads. But one head didn't follow suit. She lit a fuse inside that one that went off violently. "My mother would have sided with the witches because she was one. There is a better life out there without magic. You all are just too blinded by the lies of the witches to see it." He pushed free of Mike and Clay and knocked Apryl and Jen down on their way. Mike took offense to that and went to grab Nathan. Nathan tossed him aside with little effort. Clay thought he had him, but Nathan swung around and grabbed him by the throat. His throat strained under Nathan's grip. There was nothing stopping him from popping Clay's head off just by squeezing, like the top off a tube of toothpaste.

A chorus of voices called for him to stop, and I screamed at him to let Clay go. I was ready to strike when Rob hit Nathan with a tackle in the ribs that loosened both his grip and more plaster from the wall. Clay slipped to the floor and retreated. His hands explored his neck for proof that his head was still attached. Apryl ran to him. It was a good thing too. She restrained Clay and kept him from following Nathan as he fled out the door and out of the house. We all knew where he was heading, and to me that felt more devastating than what had just happened, and that had me collapsing down on the settee with my head in my hands. Jen was quick to my side with a comforting arm around my shoulders.

I felt someone kneel in front of me. "Don't worry. I'll talk to him. I've dealt with this before and can bring him around."

When I looked up, I felt tears rolling down my cheeks. The onslaught of tears blurred Kevin Bolden from my view, but I knew he was there. I recognized his calm and confident voice. Which was much stronger than my own when I choked out, "Thank you." I bent my head back down after I watched his blurred shape disappear out of the room.

20

Throughout the rest of the night, I debated going after Nathan myself. Well, let's correct that. It wasn't that much of a debate, and each time I tried, Jen or Marie either blocked me at the door, or distracted me in some way. Which wasn't really that hard in my current state. My mind was going in a hundred different directions all at once.

Speaking of my current state. There were two consensus in the house of where I was in that current state. Those that wanted to be sarcastic and take little shots at me, like Mike and Rob, who both agreed I was officially fat. Stan even got one in, and I had to remark that I didn't know shifters had a sense of humor. He promptly turned himself into a clown, and not a funny looking goofy clown. A horrifying fat clown with messed up teeth. He turned back when I told him I could freeze him like that. I wasn't sure if I could or not, but it was a nice threat, and he got the point.

Everyone else agreed I was between three and five months. It appeared I had progressed two months or more in just a few hours. There were no experts on this around. The only one that was familiar with the situation, albeit in reverse, was Theodora, and she hadn't been up to the house in more than a day. I had to assume she was out there with her beloved Marteggo.

I thought about sending one of the others for her, but I doubted she would actually return with them. I knew these thoughts Nathan was having weren't ones he came up with on his own. There was someone behind them, and his constant reference to the vampire pirate told me exactly who. That made me wonder. Did Theodora feel that way too? I wasn't sure. I remembered when we all sat outside at her place, while the elders discussed my problem. She said we are beautiful creatures that live a long life, and we should embrace all that life offered, or something to that effect. Could it be Theodora doesn't blend in as well as I assumed she did? Perhaps she lived more like a vampire than as a normal human. She had her own stock of blood, which I never asked how or from where.

I even visited my mother in the early morning hours, just to get her opinion. She guessed the same, but then asked me how many days it had been, stating the same the others said about how accelerated vampire pregnancies were. Of course, she couldn't tell me how sped up they were. How could she, or anyone, know that? It appeared I was the first, and I was getting really tired being the first or unique. I wanted to be like everyone else. My mother reminded me I was always different growing up and had that motherly smirk when she said it. I guess all parents see their children as different, or more special, than others. I just don't think she understands how bad it really was to be this different.

When the sun came up, I found myself on the porch, watching the edge of the woods for any sign of either Nathan or Kevin. There were vampires out there. Lots of them, and Marteggo was right there with them, watching the witches' camp again. It even appeared there were more vampires today than I had seen before, but that didn't matter. The two particular vampires I was interested in weren't among them. That didn't stop me from leaning against the banister for hours, looking until Lisa came out and asked if I was ready to go. At first, I didn't know what she was talking about, but then I remembered. Our next session with Mary Smith. If I could have skipped it, I would have. My mind was absolutely not into any training today, and especially not this. We almost made it off the porch before Amy caught us. I tried and tried to get her to stay behind, but even reminding her that yesterday was so boring that she fell asleep didn't deter her. She was insistent about coming and latched hold of my hand. In the end, I didn't mind. Feeling her there with me was the reminder I needed to take that walk and try to put everything else behind me. Jack made it rather clear last night he wouldn't be joining us. He seemed to lose interest after being told he didn't have the gift.

Mary was more welcoming today than I remembered her ever being in the past. She even greeted Amy with a hug when we arrived. She quickly ushered us back to the same room, repeating over and over, "we have a lot to do today." Now the biggest question was, could I focus on all we needed to today? Without being prompted, Lisa and I took our spots at two of the points on the pentagram. Mary didn't waste any time and produced the black candle. The smoke wrapped itself around the room in a single, continuous, string-like column.

"Today we are going to drift a couple of times. Each time will be further away from this place, pushing your limits with each trip. What I want you to develop is that feeling where you know where you are and how long you have been there. Then you can pick a place and time and drift to it, and you can find your way back. Now, close your eyes, and grab hold of the smoke. Do not let go of it for any reason."

I didn't know if it took me all that long or not before I felt it. I probably wouldn't know for sure until Mary told me. It was the same with how far I had drifted. I knew I wasn't within myself. I just didn't know really where I was. What was certain was the floating string of smoke was firmly in my grasp. I had even had it wrapped around my hand to make sure I didn't let go. Without Mary asking, I gave it a yank and returned to the room.

I opened my eyes, and I looked right at her. "So, how long, and how far?"

"You tell me."

I knew exactly what she was doing. She wouldn't tell us. She needed us to tell her. That was the whole point of this. I thought about it and realized I didn't have a damn clue. I looked over at Lisa, and she was still there with her eyes closed. Amy was looking through a book Mary Smith had obviously given her, but she wasn't asleep and didn't seem bored. That gave me something to work with. Not that it really helped me to narrow it down too precisely, and it wasn't exactly how Mary expected me to figure out how long I was gone. I knew we were within the range somewhere between an hour to minutes. So, I did all I could, and took a guess that lacked a lot of commitment behind it. "Twenty minutes."

She shook her head. "Try three hours, and you just barely made it out of the tent. Lisa, there has been out and back about nine times so far. You have this within you, but you need to do two things."

"All right. I can do that," I eagerly agreed, but maybe too soon. "What are they?"

"First, loosen up on the death grip you have on the smoke. Don't let go of it, but use it to move around. Pull yourself back and forth on it and treat every inch as a step. Judge your distance that way. Second, you need to focus more. Feel what is around you."

There was that word again. I hated that word. Each time someone said it, they were lecturing me about something I was doing wrong, and worse yet, they were right. I set myself to my task. Not really struggling to slip off. It seemed to happen pretty fast. Just as fast as last time, which I just heard took me hours. This time, I didn't wrap the smoke around my hand. Instead, I maintained a steady grip on it, and once I felt I had pulled free from myself, I reached up the smoke with my other hand, grabbed it, and pulled myself forward and released my other hand. It wasn't a big step, but it was still a step, and what a step.

I looked around through a translucent fog and realized the step I took was bigger than I thought. I was now looking down at the tent from fifty feet or more above it. Strangest yet, I could almost see through it. I could almost see through everything. Shadows and shapes hinted at what was inside each tent in the camp. I reached up the smoke again, and pulled myself up another length of my arm, and discovered I had a fear of heights. I was still above the tent, but now hundreds of feet above it. There was nothing below me except the little specks that were the tents, and the roofs of my farmhouse and barn. My feet kicked for the ground, but they just swung in the nothingness that was there. I had never been this high before, and I didn't really like it. I stayed there until I relaxed some. Once I had the nerve up, I wanted to explore further, but I didn't really want to go higher. I reached up and grabbed the smoke and pulled while hanging on with my other hand. I wanted to see if I could bend it, and wham, it bent at a spot just below my hand. I then messed with it some more. I could turn it in any direction I wanted. So, this is how I could move around. Fascinating. I made a quick pull down it and I was now miles away, and a light bulb went off in my head.

Pride welled up inside of me, and I needed to tell someone. I gave the smoke a yank and zipped right back to my body. It happened too quickly for me to notice each of the previous times, but now that I was further away, I was aware of what happened, and I saw what was beneath me on my trek back. Below me, witches moved and ran through the camp. Strange, I didn't remember there being that many. I sank down into my body and emerged with my mouth opened to tell Mary Smith what I had experienced. The woman was nowhere to be found. I looked around and saw Lisa standing with Amy huddled behind her. Lisa had a defensive stance, and I heard explosions outside the tent.

"Thank god you're back!" screamed Lisa. "Get up! Get up!. The vampires are attacking us."

"What?" I screamed back. What she said didn't make any sense to me, but neither did the sounds of the war zone outside. I jumped up and ran out of the tent's opening. Several bodies laid on the ground just outside the tent. I had to assume they were witches. Screams and yells were all around, along with the sounds of explosions and impacts. I knew those were witches taking shots at the vampires. I didn't know why this was happening, but I didn't care.

Before I charged into the fray, I went back to Lisa and Amy in the back of Mary Smith's tent. Lisa started to ask, "What did you see– "

"You can't be here," I said, interrupting her question. Then spun up a portal and pushed her and Amy through before closing it. They were now back in the house.

I made my way back out of the tent and looked around. Another body now laid motionless on the ground with the others. He was a witch. There was no doubt of that. I loaded both hands with fireballs, blue ones, and went on the hunt. If I found a vampire attacking a witch, they were going to pay a price. Understanding why this happened would be a matter for another time.

It didn't take long to find the fighting. I recognized both the witch and the vampire, but didn't know their names. I didn't care, and I didn't wait. I hit the vampire right in the back, setting him ablaze. It didn't faze him. He turned his attention to me. With one hand, I grabbed him without touching him, and threw him out of the camp into the woods. The landing wouldn't kill him, but it might sting a bit. It at least removed them from the fight for the moment. I reached down and helped the witch up off the ground. She looked at me with frightened and frazzled green eyes. Why wouldn't she be? She had just been attacked by others that looked just like me.

"You're okay. I'm a witch–"

A strangely familiar slap in the center of my back interrupted my attempt to assure her she was not in any danger from me. It sent me flying forward, over the green-eyed witch I had just saved. My landing was not a graceful one. I just flopped on the ground, hard, but instead of popping up and returning the favor at whatever misguided witch attacked me thinking I was a vampire, my hands reached down for my stomach. It felt even bigger than before, but that wasn't why I reached for it. I was worried the landing hurt my child. That concern drove an uncharacteristic move on my part. I slowly sat up, with my hands in the air, turned around, and pleaded, "Stop. I'm not one of them. I'm a witch too, and I'm pregnant." I finished that plea before the shock of who I saw standing over me set in.

"Pregnant?" asked Miss Sarah Julia Roberts. "Now that's a gas. No matter."

I was about to knock her so hard it would send her back to the 90s where her dark stringy hair, leather boots, and mono-chromatic clothing she wore would fit in, but something pressed me back flat against the ground with my hands behind my head and held me there. No matter how much I strained, I couldn't move, roll, or twitch. Even odder, I couldn't witch. I tried. I tried everything from opening the ground below me to give me some room to opening the ground below her to scare her and make her release me, to floating away. Nothing happened. Then I realized she wasn't in control after all. A tall, sulking older man leaned over me from above.

"Don't bother fighting. You can't do anything now. Now come on."

My body floated up waist high on him and followed as he walked through the witch camp. Miss Sarah Julia Roberts followed.

"Let me guess, It's the Saxon boy's?"

I wasn't going to tell her, but I couldn't even if I tried. Whatever this was, kept me from talking and saved her from the barrage of insults I had lined up.

21

He paraded me around the camp slowly like some trophy kill strapped to his hood, except there was no hood. I just floated in the air immobilized. Out of the corner of my eye, I saw the bodies of witches everywhere. They were probably caught by surprise and didn't stand a chance against the vampires. With all that had happened over the last few days, they had probably dropped their guard. I know I had. I didn't see either camp being a threat to the other, but I was also not a good judge of that. Being both, I didn't have a clue why either was a threat to the other. It made no sense, but I remember Mr. Lockridge, the history teacher here in the New Orleans coven, once saying that wars never made sense. This one didn't, but it was clear who was winning. That was a lot clearer to me than the sides. At least two witches were helping the vampires, but why? This slow walk to wherever we were going, and the inability to move or talk, gave me a lot of time to think. Unfortunately, I found no answers. Just more witches that were injured or dead on the ground.

We finally stopped, and my captor tilted me up onto my knees, which bent all on their own. I thought this might have given me an opening, but there was nothing. No matter how hard I tried. Nothing moved. I tried a few spells and tricks, and nothing worked. Not even something as simple as setting a blade of grass on fire. There wasn't even a flicker or a spark.

My captor shook off his hood, revealing a pitted face and long dark beard. His dark eyes were hollow reflections of what I had to assume was a hollow soul. Physically, he was a mountain of a man, and cast a large shadow across me. He stood there, stoic, as if waiting for something. What? I didn't know. It was just him, me, and Miss Roberts. Or that was all I could see. If anyone was behind us, I couldn't see them. All I could see were those in front of me, and a shadow approaching. When I saw the source, I wasn't all that surprised. It was Marteggo. What I saw with Marteggo shattered me. Another witch, dressed like my captor, led a floating Marcus Meridian to my side, where they placed him on his knees just like I was.

"I believe this satisfies the agreement?" Marteggo asked.

Miss Roberts stepped forward. "It does. In return for these two enemies of the council, Jean St. Claire will never be set free. You have our word."

Marteggo grinned. "Good, but just remember what you see here today. If you fail to uphold your end of this agreement, it will be you next time."

"There is no need for that threat," barked my captor. He stepped in between Miss Roberts and Marteggo. I never thought I would see anyone larger that Marteggo, but I just did. He had several inches on him in both height and width. That didn't mean Marteggo backed down. He seemed to bow up and viewed the man as a challenge. It would be a one sided challenge from all appearances though. My captor didn't pay him any attention and turned to Marcus Meridian.

"I told you one day you would be a prize in my trophy case. I just didn't know I would add a second one." His blank eyes cut in my direction.

There was so much I wanted to do to him and Marteggo at the moment, but I couldn't. All I could do was think about all I wanted to do to them, but God help them when I finally get the chance.

"Wait!" cried a voice in the distance. "Marteggo, what the hell is going on?" I knew it was Nathan before he came around my side and reached down and tried to lift me up. No matter how much he strained, he couldn't budge me. I couldn't even move my lips to mouth any words to him. All I could do was move my eyes, which I darted in Marteggo's direction several times to tell him who was behind all this.

"Boy, leave my prisoners alone," barked my captor. He reached down and pushed Nathan aside, rather easily.

Nathan rolled on the ground and scampered to his feet. Then he got right in Marteggo's face. "Marteggo, tell him to let her go."

"I can't. We've made a deal that will keep Jean locked away forever," he said proudly.

"A deal?" Nathan asked, incensed. "Tell him to let Larissa go. Now!" Nathan shoved Marteggo with enough force to knock that smug look right off his face and send him stumbling back several steps. He recoiled right back at Nathan. Kevin Bolden forced himself between the two men and walked Nathan backwards.

"Nathan, don't take my company to mean your opinion matters," Marteggo sneered. He tossed his curly locks over his shoulders and away from his face. He composed himself, but was nowhere near the congenial person he always appeared to be. "I made a trade. Two fugitives for the council's help in keeping Jean locked away forever. It's for the good of everyone."

So that was it. That stupid decree Marcus had read to me a few days ago. That was why Miss Roberts and the other witches were here. He turned us in. That rat, that... he turned us in. No, that wasn't it. I corrected how I was thinking about the situation. The council knew exactly where we were and they could have come to get us at any time, but it wouldn't have been without a fight, and they knew that. Now the vampires, on the other hand... Yes, that was it. My mind put it all together. The vampires were the muscles. They gave the witches an opportunity to storm the camp and grab us. It was a battle of sheer numbers and force.

"Let her go!" Nathan screamed. Kevin fought like mad to hold Nathan back, but it didn't take long before Nathan got free and rushed at Marteggo again. There was no demand this time. Not that Marteggo was going to hear it. As soon as Nathan was within striking range, Marteggo planted his right fist into Nathan's head with a thud, sending Nathan to the ground.

I felt it. I felt every bit of that force against my own face, but there was nothing I could do. I couldn't even scream or beg Nathan to stop. He wouldn't have listened anyway. That punch didn't deter him, it only delayed him. He was up again, and this time delivered one of his own to Marteggo, and then to the two humongous men that had taken me and Marcus into custody. The strike sent both men to the ground, but not Marteggo. He stood there firm and didn't even flinch from the impact. Nathan punched him again, with all his might, and then I realized we were surrounded by the vampires as several rushed forward to grab and restrain Nathan, pinning him against the ground.

Inside, I screamed, "Get off of him! Let him go!" Nothing came out, adding to my panic as I watched this scene unfold. I screamed and struggled to get free. There was no way I was going to just sit here and watch them attack Nathan. The tears that rolled down my face told a different story. One where I didn't have a choice. Nothing worked. I couldn't even feel the vibrations of the world around me. I knew they had to be in chaos at the moment, but even then, I could have used them to do something. If only I could feel them.

Nathan struggled against the horde that seemed content with just restraining him.

"In time, you will understand," Marteggo said flatly.

Nathan spit at him in response, which prompted a chuckle from Marteggo.

"I believe our business is done here?" Miss Roberts asked.

"It is. Take them," replied Marteggo with a flip of the hand.

Two blurs knocked the group off of Nathan. He went after my captor first, but never reached him. There was a kind of barrier up.

Not a rune for protection. Nathan would have felt that and kept going, no matter the pain. I could see that in his eyes. It was as if he hit a brick wall. Mike and Clay came out of nowhere and each made their own attempt to get to me, but they both hit the same wall. My captors didn't flinch on this side of the barrier as they watched the three make attempt after attempt.

"Go!" ordered Marteggo.

Neither of our captors appeared too motivated by that order. They lumbered back and gathered Marcus and me up off the ground. I was back to the floating slab of humanity with a full view of the war waging behind us. Kevin Bolden had entered it, and lightning bolts struck the ground, sending vampires scrambling. I couldn't see Lisa, but I knew she was out there. Marteggo stood there in the middle of Armageddon, unfazed. Even the appearance of four large wolves snarling and stalking him did nothing for his demeanor. I recognized two of them, but then I remembered Marcus' guards. Their attack was short-lived. Marteggo stood proudly, almost laughing as they laid whimpering on the ground, as a large spinning portal opened up ahead of us.

I fought with everything I had to grab for the ground. To scream out to Nathan, or anyone. Nothing. I was just an observer of the most painful event I had ever seen. Everyone I cared for was fighting to save me, and losing.

Nathan walked through the wounded but once again stalking werewolves. "Boy, don't make me beat this stubbornness out of you. This is all for the greater good. Don't you see?" There was an edge to Marteggo's voice, a frustration. He rolled up the sleeves on both arms while the werewolves growled and nipped at him. A large fireball drove Marteggo to the ground, but not for long. He got up quickly, but it was just enough.

What I watched over the next few seconds sent shivers down my spine for several reasons. My head and body screamed, but I was the only one to hear it in my trapped state. Just before we entered the portal, I watched as Nathan leaped on the distracted Marteggo and relieved him of the burden he carried atop his shoulders, his head. Just like what happened to Mr. Norton. Marteggo's body slumped to the ground and turned to ash. Bits of it floated in the wind and the portal closed behind us.

22

We floated down a narrow rocky path carved into the side of a cavern that extended up as far as I could see. Marcus was behind me. One captor led us down the path. The other followed behind us. A fiery orange light from below cast ominous shadows on the craggy surface of the wall. We traveled down so far I eventually lost sight of the place we exited the portal at. I wasn't sure if we were at the bottom when we entered a dark cave that turned into a tunnel leading to another similar scene with a path that was nothing more than a wooden footbridge across what appeared to be a river of molten lava. Another cave or tunnel awaited us on the other side of the bridge. Beyond that tunnel was a cold, damp, and dark world. Hundreds of torches hung in the space overhead. They did little to chase away the shadows, creating points of light framed by larger spots of darkness.

We finally stopped at the end of a path that extended out into the middle of the dark cavern. Neither of the captors spoke. They stood together and motioned up in the air with their hands. Two of the torches above fell toward us. I watched as the flames atop them danced in the wind created by their movement. Two, huh? There were two of them. I made a wild leap that our two captors would use these torches to light the way for the rest of our journey to wherever. The closer the torches came, the larger they appeared, and more of our surroundings came into view. Large, winged creatures flew back and forth across the space. The flickering flames from the torches reflected against their slick and scaly skin.

I didn't have long to ponder what they were before the next amazing or terrifying sight came into view. It was the torches, which weren't torches at all. They were rooms or cages, with a blazing fire atop them. They both descended to the end of the path and their doors opened. Flames dripped down each side of the structure, disappearing into the darkness below. I floated into one of them, and Marcus into the other. Once inside the door, my body collapsed to the hard, cold floor. I could move again and I pushed up off the floor.

The captor that took me stepped forward and once again pulled the hood away from his face. "Welcome to Mordin. Save yourself the trouble. There is no escape, and there is no magic. Each cell cancels whatever spell you try. If you don't believe me, try it yourself. You will have plenty of time to experiment, as you will spend the rest of your life in this cell. Don't bother trying to scream. The cells are soundproof, not that anyone could hear you, anyway. The cell will take care of your basic needs. Food three times a day, water, a bed for sleeping, a place to bathe, and clean clothes." With a flick of his wrist, the door on Marcus's cell closed and rose in the cavern toward its original spot. Our less than gracious host turned to and addressed me specifically. "Miss Dubois, we will monitor and provide assistance when it is time to give birth. We are not savages, but I am afraid your sentence also applies to your child, and they will serve that time with you in this cell for the entirety of its days."

"Wait! No!" I held both hands out to the man. "Don't do that. Let it live free."

He flicked his hand in my direction, and the cage door slammed shut, and up I went.

I collapsed to the floor of the cell and sobbed. Behind me, a simple bed with a single sheet appeared, but I settled for the floor. I needed something to pound against. Each smack of my fist against the floor produced no sound at all. The sounds of my own cries echoed back at me from the cage. I peered out, and the spot I had just left was no longer in view. There were hundreds of others of these cages dangling in the air. Some of their occupants were just going about their own business, sitting on the bed, or the floor, not reacting to anything. Others were watching me, the new arrival. I wiped the tears from my face and looked for Marcus. I couldn't see him in the sea of cages. He was out there somewhere.

One man with a mane of white hair on his head waved in my direction, and I returned a halfhearted wave. He picked up three pieces of bread and happily juggled them. I let my head collapse into my hands, and the tears rolled. This was it. This was where I was going to spend the rest of my life, except that was the problem. There was no end to my days. This was going to be forever.

23

Forever was right. The only problem was days and nights were not two definitive times. There was no sunrise or sunset to separate each. There was just darkness surrounding the light illuminated by the flame atop our cages. Some slept while others were awake. Food seemed to arrive when you needed it, and not at set times. Mine hadn't arrived yet, and I was curious what would arrive when it did. Did this thing know I was a vampire? Would it? Could it? It already produced a bed for me, and I don't sleep. Maybe it was just so I could have a place to sit. Even more concerning, what would I do if it didn't know what I was? I couldn't exactly eat a ham sandwich if that was what arrived.

A bathtub appeared later on the first day, and the water was lukewarm. For some reason I expected it to be just as cold as our surroundings. Not that the cage I was in was cold, or would get cold. I bathed while it was there and sat in the tub trying to let the warm water relax me, like it used to when I was a child. Come to think of it, I hadn't sat in a tub like this since when I was a child. The relaxation didn't come. My body didn't absorb the warmth of the water like I used to before. I didn't need it. Around me there were too many reminders for me to forget where I was, even for just the briefest of seconds, and I felt the tears flowing again, which made me mad.

"Stop it, Larissa!" I yelled at myself. I wasn't the type to sit around and cry when something bad happened. Okay, I admit, calling this bad was a bit of an understatement, but still, that wasn't me. That wasn't me by a long shot. I was always the person who struck out. Either with words or actions. Why should now be any different?

I looked at the walls of my cage. Small bars pressed closely together with just enough room to see through with little obstruction, but definitely not wide enough to slip through. If I were able to slide through, then what? I was hundreds, if not thousands, of feet in the air above that small path. They said magic wouldn't work here. Wait, no, that's not right. They said magic doesn't work in the cell. If I could get out, I could use it to float down? Something I imagine everyone in these cells had thought of, or tried at one time or the other. Why was I different? One fact pushed that self-doubt aside in my head. Because I am a vampire. If I fell, I wouldn't die. The others, if magic didn't work outside the cell either or was somehow limited, they would fall to a certain death. So, now how do I get out? I reached a hand out of the tub and grabbed on to a bar. I don't know what I was expecting, but I braced myself at first. There was nothing. It was nothing. Just a simple metal or iron bar.

"All right."

I got out of the tub, dried off, and put my clothes back on, which were remarkably clean again. I needed to test something. I walked right up to the wall of my cage and grabbed hold of two bars, one in each hand, and pulled hard. They didn't give. Not even a simple bow before snapping back into place. I tried again, and again. Then tried to push, hoping my augmented strength as a vampire would give me a slight advantage, or enough of one to spread them so I could slip through. There was nothing doing. These things were solid. So, I scratched that thought out of my head. What was next?

Ideas whirled around my head while I paced the floor. There weren't many, but there were some, and some was better than none. One particular idea kept being dismissed quickly over and over and yet kept coming back with the voice of my mother. "That's stupid," I mumbled to myself, and it was stupid, but that didn't make it a bad idea to try. There was no way to know for sure.

My mother once told me about why she exposed me to all worlds, both that of a witch and a human. In her explanation, she told me about a baby circus elephant that grew up with a single string holding its leg to a stake. As it grew up, the circus used the same small string and stake to hold it in place, even though the elephant was large enough to easily snap that string anytime it wanted to. They conditioned it with that restriction in place when it was young, and because of it, he would be forever limited by that string. She explained, only showing me one side of the world would restrict my view on the world and she didn't want that to be my string. Now that string had nothing to do with what I was thinking about, but the restriction did. What if they were bluffing about the cell canceling out magic? Like the string on the baby elephant. Establish a boundary we would never test. There was only one way to find out.

I stood in the center of the cage and tried to open a portal back to the farmhouse. I was glad no one I knew was around to see me achieve nothing but a sore shoulder, which even then I wasn't sure why it was sore. I shouldn't be feeling things like that. Perhaps this little bump I was carrying had something to do with that. Of course, using the word little wasn't that proper anymore. I was at least equivalent to someone that was six or seven months pregnant now. Its size grew exponentially every day.

Maybe something simpler, like setting the pillow I don't need on fire. That should be easy enough, or not. Nothing happened. Just like the first time I tried back at the coven, but unlike that time, nothing sparked out of my frustration either. At this point I would have accepted accidentally setting the entire bed on fire.

So, they weren't lying about that. There had to be something, some way. Something I wasn't thinking of. I went back to inspecting every inch of this cage for a weakness. Nothing was perfect. That was a statement I tried to believe while inside I begged for this to not be perfect. I climbed up on the bed to reach the top of the cage, hoping for a weakness up there, but another sensation sent me falling to the bed. There was a kick. A kick from inside. It was the weirdest sensation I had ever felt, and all I could do was sit there with my hands on my belly waiting for the next one, so I didn't miss it.

I didn't. I felt it do it again and again. It was such an amazing feeling. The feeling that there was life inside me. A life that I would do anything to protect. The bliss of the feeling gave way to a panic. I tried to fight back against it, but it finally won, sending me sprinting from the bed to the door, pulling as hard as I could. There was no way my child was going to spend their life in this cell. I couldn't doom them to that miserable existence. I had to get out. I had to. My hands banged and pulled on the bars, but they didn't budge. Even climbing up and putting my body weight into it didn't help. Maybe they needed something more forceful. I picked up the bed and tossed it at the closest wall. The bed disappeared before it hit the bars, and then reappeared right where it was normally placed. The cell was working against me. I threw both hands down to my side and screamed. All I needed was one more enemy.

Options were running short. I tried throwing the bathtub, and it returned to its normal place, full of warm water. Maybe something was perfect, and I just found it. Why couldn't my life be what was perfect? Or my relationship with Nathan? I collapsed on the bed, my once projectile, and tried to pull my knees up to my chest, but I couldn't. Something was in the way, so I just collapsed sideways and laid there, looking up at the top of my cage, watching the flames dance above it. I was sure somewhere in this place someone else was doing the same. With a turn of my head, I spied four others that were just lying in their cage doing the same thing, and those were just the ones I could see. There had to be others. There wasn't much else to do.

How much time had passed while I laid there, I wasn't sure. There were no clocks, and the passage of time never really registered with me. I couldn't tell you if I was sitting there for five minutes, ten minutes, or fifteen minutes. To me time was more of an anticipation.

That excitement, or dread, I felt while I waited for an event to happen. Maybe it was meeting Nathan, or Mr. Norton coming home. Once the event happened, then it was about waiting for the next. It was the same way before I became a vampire. Looking forward to when my father came in from the field, for dinner, for the nightly family time. Now, there was nothing to feel anticipation for. There was no next event, just this.

I wondered if I could teach myself to sleep. That would be a great way to lose myself for some time. A break. Maybe I could dream. I had slept before, and had slept since, and yes, I was a human both times, but that didn't mean it wasn't possible. I just needed to let my consciousness relax, and possibly lose myself in one of my many daydreams. Make that my reality for a bit and allow myself to enter a trancelike state where I stayed for as long as I could. Just a few moments of joy out in the fields as a small child, or an evening with Nathan. Either could mean the world to me, to my sanity, which I had already wondered if I could keep it intact for the rest of eternity. I looked around and saw others sleeping and felt jealous. They made it look so easy.

To test it, I closed my eyes and took in the darkness. I laid there and tried to immerse myself into a daydream. Just a little fantasy, and while my mind entertained the idea and took in the other reality I had created, the actual reality was still there. I couldn't block it out. It was always there, and it was more than just a nagging. It was right upfront as a reminder that the other world, my created world, wasn't real. That didn't stop me from trying. I went back to my alternate reality for a while.

I repeated my experiment many times, and each time I ran into the same issue. The real world was still there, no matter how much I tried to leave it behind. That didn't mean I didn't receive some benefit from this, though. There was some relaxation that came from it, but that was short-lived. The minute I stopped, the reality of my situation collapsed down on me, along with the realization that none of that was real and that it would never be real again. I did a lot of crying after each time, but that didn't stop me from doing it again. I needed it, and when I considered an eternity like this, I could only hope to lose my sanity one day and remain in my fantasy world.

I thought I had done just that when I felt I was moving, but when I opened my eyes, I saw I was. My cage was descending, and those winged creatures I spied earlier were following it. Their yellow eyes stared through the bars at me. I stood up off the bed and moved to the door to see who was below waiting. There was a hooded figure standing there. Of course, there would be, and I doubt they were delivering good news. There was no pardon waiting for me. The only reason for the visit I could imagine was my child. A checkup of some type. Like my captor said, they weren't savages. My cage settled on the edge of the path, and the door opened under the watchful eye of the winged creatures. They hadn't come this close on my arrival and appeared to be watching me. Perhaps these were the prison guards. That thought made a little sense to me. They flew and roamed in the air just below where the cages floated. If anyone got out, they would have to fall through their airspace to escape. The only question left was, would we be a nice and tasty morsel for them, or would they put us back in our cage once they caught us?

I waited for instructions, but none were given. Instead, the figure, much shorter than my original captor, walked forward, and then grabbed me by the shoulder, and threw me out the door. I tumbled toward the ground, but never hit it. A portal opened up in front of me, and I fell into it head over heels until I landed on a wooden floor. A quick glance up, and I wasn't so sure I hadn't lost myself in one of my imaginary worlds.

24

"Mordin is no place for my grandchild to be born in," remarked Mrs. Saxon. She pulled the dark green hood off of her head, revealing her white hair and clear blue eyes. She leaned down to where I was on the floor, and placed a finger under my chin, and tilted my head up, and looked me over. "Are you all right?"

I nodded. That was all I could muster. My voice failed me. I felt like a little girl that was in so much trouble.

She tilted my head from side to side one more time, checking me over, and then gave me a yank forward. I collapsed into her and wept, and her arms wrapped around me.

"You're safe now."

"I'm so sorry," I blubbered.

"It's all okay." Her hand patted me on the shoulder, and then she pulled me in harder.

That was not the reaction I was expecting. I was practically responsible for the death of her son. Well, not his death, but he was now a vampire. I had destroyed so much of what she had worked for with the others. I had betrayed her and left the coven against her command, and my departure was rather forceful. Why this warm welcome? It didn't make any sense and made me feel uncomfortable. I pushed her back and looked into those bright blue eyes.

"No, it's not. I'm sorry about Nathan. I am so sorry about what happened." Tears continued to fall from my eyes. She didn't change. In fact, she had a little of a smile on her face. Now I was confused as hell. Which was how I felt the first time I came here.

Mrs. Saxon stood up and dropped her green robe to the floor, and offered me her hand. I took it and she promptly pulled me up to my feet and guided me over to my bed, where we both sat down. She, like so many times, crossed her hands on her lap, and sat up straight. I wished I could do the same, but the worry about when she was going to unload on me had me struggling to hold myself together.

"Larissa, it's all right. It's all okay." She stopped and then sat back even straighter than before. "Do you remember the first night we met?"

"Yes, the train." How could I forget what, at that point, was both the worst and strangest night of my life? There were other nights in contention for both titles now.

"Do you remember asking if your mother told me you were coming, and I told you I knew you were coming as soon as she put you on the train?"

I nodded weakly, clearly remembering that night and conversation, but my confusion was growing. Why was she bringing this up now? Why was she acting like this? She should be livid and trying to tear my head off. There was only one answer. I was right earlier. I had lost it, and I was stuck in my daydream, and that might not be all that bad.

"Larissa, I knew you were coming. I knew everything. I knew what you were. I knew what you were going to do. I knew you and Nathan were going to be together. I may not have known who you were," she tilted her head to the side. "I had to discover that along with you, and when I did, more of your future opened itself to me. I'm a witch, remember?"

"Divination," I whispered.

"Yes, so you have heard of it?"

I nodded again, realizing I must look like such a little girl only nodding in response to her questions. "Someone has been showing me."

"Wonderful," she clapped both hands together.

"Oh, I'm not very good at it," I blurted.

"Of course, you're not. It takes a lot of practice to master it, but you don't need to be great at it for the seven wonders. You just need to show you can do it."

"You know about that?" I asked, both surprised and worried. My special training with Master Thomas and Mr. Demius was supposed to be a secret. They both mentioned about keeping it from her, but now I wondered if she knew. Maybe she didn't. She never attempted to put a stop to it. Unless... I stopped my thought right there. It was as if a lightbulb went off over my head. A big ass lightbulb the size of the sun. If she knew. If she really knew everything, like she seemed to now, then she knew and let it happen. She may have even encouraged it, but kept it hidden from others to avoid anyone on the council knowing. What a sneaky little witch. I felt a little proud of myself for figuring that out. Now I hoped she was right.

"Yes, I do." She leaned forward. "And I can help you with that and the others. Which ones are you still struggling with?"

"Wait. Wait." I waved my hands and stood up. The realization I made pushed away some of the worry I had, and most of the confusion. Other confusion replaced it, but this was something that could be cleared up quickly. "Let me get something right. You have known all along that I was going to challenge Mrs. Wintercrest for supreme one day?"

Now it was her turn to nod, but instead of doing it slow and unsure, like I had been. She was confident and responding eagerly.

"Did you know about the training Master Thomas and Mr. Demius were doing?"

"It was my idea," she answered and sat back proudly. "We needed to know what you remembered, and what you needed to learn."

"But they said it needed to be a secret," I pointed out, hoping she would confirm what I believed. If she did, the cloud I felt in my head may finally evaporate.

"We couldn't let anyone find out. You never know who might tell the council. Which speaking of," she stood up from the bed and walked over to where I stood in the center of my room. She placed both hands on my shoulders. Any joy that was in her face before had left. This was the serious woman I had grown to know. "You need to stay in this room for a while. This isn't like before where I told you not to leave the coven. Many things have changed since you left. Mrs. Wintercrest is here, staying in a room down on the ground floor. Jean St. Claire is here, locked away in a room under her protection."

My body jerked toward the door. Mrs. Saxon's grip on my shoulders tightened, and I felt something else holding me in place. Something more magical.

"Larissa, there will be a time to deal with him in the future. That time is not now. There are bigger tasks at hand. Now, you can't even go up to the roof. You need to stay out of sight. We cannot have Mrs. Wintercrest finding out you are here." There was a knock on my door, and she let go of my shoulders and walked over and opened the door.

Mrs. Tenderschott rushed in and mugged me with a hug that pushed me back to the bed. "Larissa, I'm so glad you're home." She held on to me tightly and swayed back and forth. God how I missed this. Behind her walked in both Master Thomas and Mr. Demius.

"Marcus is settled in. He understands everything," Master Thomas reported to Mrs. Saxon.

"Good."

"You rescued Marcus Meridian?" I asked.

"Yes," Mrs. Saxon answered, looking back over her shoulder at me. "We rescued and retrieved everyone. Apryl, Mike, Clay, Brad, and Laura are back in their rooms. Amy is sharing a room with Cynthia for now."

"They seemed to have grown comfortable with each other," added Mrs. Tenderschott. I understood. I had seen the start of that myself.

"Steve and Stan are back, as are Rob and his brothers. Jack and Lisa are on the witches' floor, but isolated from the others for now. I am more concerned about one of the witches becoming suspicious or hearing something they shouldn't and then speaking to the council or Mrs. Wintercrest about it."

"Gwen," I muttered harshly.

"Yes, Gwen, or anyone else really, but yes, primarily Gwen." Mrs. Saxon pulled the chair out from the desk that I never used. She sat down and sighed. "Gwen is a good witch, and I don't doubt she would lay everything on the line for any of us. Possibly even you, Larissa, but she also has ambitions for something greater, and that clouds what I can see of her future. Too many possibilities to play out. I honestly don't believe any of the others would, but I just don't know."

"They wouldn't," added Mrs. Tenderschott.

"I would hope that to be true," responded Mrs. Saxon. "Marcus is in a room that only I and Master Thomas have access to, and it will stay that way until all of this is settled, and he can be allowed out and possibly restored to his family's place on the council. Anyway, Marie Norton is just down the hall from you. Master Thomas, Mr. Demius, and I will continue your training."

"Stop," I demanded, rather loudly, startling everyone in the room. There was one name she hadn't mentioned. The only name I really wanted to hear right now. The only name that I thought would have mattered to her. "What about Nathan? Where is he?"

I watched as three witches immediately diverted their eyes from Mrs. Saxon and myself. This freaked me out. If there was good news, they wouldn't have reacted that way.

Mrs. Saxon sighed again and leaned back in the chair. Her shoulder slumped. "Larissa, you were in Mordin for seven days. During that time, I have tried everything I can to find Nathan. Kevin and Jennifer have too. We can't find him. After he killed Marteggo he disappeared with the other vampires."

"Tell her. She needs to know everything," insisted Master Thomas.

"Tell me what?" I asked, while I felt myself breaking inside. He was dead. I knew it. After he killed Marteggo, the others carried him off and killed him for killing their beloved leader. Oh God. My knees shook, and the room spun.

"We don't know anything for sure," she started, and I reached back for the post of my bed for support. "Jennifer and Kevin heard several rumors while they were searching."

"Oh, no," I cried.

"After he killed Marteggo, his followers began following Nathan. He seems to be the new leader down there, but those are just rumors. We don't know for sure, and we don't know where they went."

"We need to find him," I exclaimed. My hands instinctively went to my stomach, and all the eyes in the room followed. "We have to."

"I know Larissa. I want to find him too, and I will keep trying, but we also need to take care of you, and keep your training. Trust me. This all works out."

"How? How does this work out?" I asked. There were many answers to that question. It could be I give birth and raise the child myself as the new supreme. Nathan and I could end up together. Maybe we don't but he is part of our child's life. Those were only a few of the options. Hearing that it all works out, didn't tell me anything.

"Larissa, you know I can't tell you that. Just trust me."

Right then the baby kicked me from the inside, and I jumped, again startling the room. I moved my hand around to feel it do it again, and it did.

"You need to stay calm. The baby will feel the stress you feel."

I needed to calm down. No duh, really? Some things are easier to say than do, and that without a doubt was one of them. The weight of the world was on me, thanks to Mrs. Saxon and everyone else's master plan. Worry ate at me, and it wasn't taking little bites. This stuff was chomping away at me, and it continued to do so. I didn't even know I had anything left for it to chomp away on.

"Trust me." Mrs. Saxon leaned forward in the chair and reached over for me. Her hand landed on my leg. "This is all going to be okay. I can't tell you how. I can't tell you if everything is going to work out perfectly how you want it, or if there is even going to be a happy ending. What I can tell you is it all works out, and right now you need to focus on that baby."

"But I need Nathan," I whimpered.

"I know," she responded, and then her eyes left mine and arrived at my stomach. "I know you do. If I knew how to find him, I would bring him here to be here with you."

"I think I know," I said, and I did. If he was their new leader, there was a logical place to look first, and there were two people here that knew where that was, but I could only talk to one of them. "I need to talk to Marie."

25

Our welcome home party moved down the hall to Marie's room. If I was right, she was one of two people currently in the coven that might know where Nathan was. The other, I wasn't sure if I could be in the same room without trying to kill him, and there was the problem about getting past Mrs. Wintercrest to see him. Not to mention, I doubted Jean would willingly give up the information. Of course, there were a few potions that I knew of that would get him talking. I was sure Mrs. Tenderschott knew others, but she was more humane than I was and wouldn't opt for the ones that might torture him a little.

When we walked in, Marie jumped on me like so many have in the last few moments. It was a good thing I liked this sort of thing, or I might feel assaulted.

"We need your help," I said, and she stepped back away from me, but that didn't mean she released me. Her hands ran down my arms and gripped my hands. This was the Marie I have known for years. "Where did Jean keep you?"

She looked at me, confused every way the human face could. Tilting, skewed, and scrunched. "Why?" She looked around the room, searching the others for answers.

"We think Nathan got himself elected as the new leader of the New Orleans coven when he killed Marteggo. Where would they have taken him?"

"Kevin and Jennifer heard a rumor while searching for him," added Mrs. Saxon. "I think Larissa is right here."

I smiled proudly. "He must have had a house or mansion he stayed in. I saw the inside a few times when he projected into my head, but I never saw the outside, and I don't know where it was. If what they heard was true, they might have taken him there."

Marie looked back at me, not as sure about my idea as I was.

I shrugged. "It's all we have to work with." It was. I knew myself. I tried all the magic and spells I could find to locate Marie. The best I could do was find out if she was still with us or not. It wasn't until Jean slipped up and sent Clay after us that we had a window into his world, and I could see her. But even then, I didn't know how to find her. Well, there was another option, but that stack of books still sat in my room, and Mary Smith wasn't around to help me like she was before. I wasn't even sure if she survived the vampire's attack on the camp.

"He did. It's in the Fourteenth Ward, on Audubon. It's number 18 or 16. I can't remember. It has been so long since I actually looked at the number. I just knew where it was. You can't miss it. It's solid white, with large columns."

"Thank you." I spun around to Mrs. Saxon. "Just one trip. That's all I need."

Marie grabbed my shoulder and spun me back around. "You're not thinking of going there?"

I felt like a top spinning back and forth. "It's the only option."

"Larissa, you can't. You wouldn't make it ten feet in there without being killed."

Now it was my time to grab her shoulders. I looked right into her loving eyes and explained, "That was before. I have spent hours around all of them, and Jean isn't pulling their strings anymore. It's different."

That appeared to strike a chord with Marie, and many others in the room.

"He probably doesn't know I am free, or even alive," I said and turned to Mrs. Saxon. "Just seeing me will make him come back. I know it." I did. In my mind, the reunion had already occurred. He would run to me the moment he caught sight of me. Then he would take me in to his arms, and kiss me. Then all would be right with the world. Or at least that small part of it. At the moment, that was the only part I could fix. It was all that mattered.

"I don't know." Mrs. Saxon looked lost in thought. She was considering it, but something about the look on her face told me she wasn't a firm believer.

"I don't see any other way." Master Thomas both sounded and appeared indifferent about his vote, but I understood. I was believing with my heart this would work. He was thinking with his head. The only sure thing here was this was the only option we had.

"I agree," Mrs. Tenderschott stated. "I don't believe any other way. Plus, love can conquer all. No matter what has happened, once Nathan sees her, it will all change."

"Just one trip," I begged Mrs. Saxon. "I know the street. I can put myself right in front of the address and go right in. No one will see me until I am there." I looked right into those clear blue eyes, and added, "Please." Once this idea came to me, I didn't expect to have to plead so hard for her permission. This was her son we were talking about. I thought she would have jumped on any idea that could bring him home, no matter how big the risk or how miniscule the chance of success was. This plan had a high chance of working, at least in my opinion. I didn't see how it wouldn't. I saw how he reacted when he saw me being taken away.

"Okay," she agreed with her back still to us. "But you won't go alone. I want Jen to go with you, and," she stopped and thought, tapping her foot as she turned toward us. "I want another witch to go with you, too. Jack."

"Why not Lisa?" I asked. Not that I really objected to Jack. Any issues Jack and I used to have were short-lived, and we were rather friendly. He was one of a few that I think really got me, but going in where we were going, if I needed another witch, I would prefer it to be someone who had dark magic on their side.

"I'll go," volunteered Master Thomas.

Okay, I'll accept that.

"I'm on the outs with the council anyway. If anyone sees me, there is no harm."

"All right. Master Thomas it is, but remember both of you, it is straight in, and back," warned Mrs. Saxon.

I answered, "Yes ma'am." I hoped Master Thomas didn't mind me answering for both of us. "I need to change first."

Mrs. Saxon agreed, and I headed to my room, which was just two doors down. I stopped and winced at my door. A sharp pain is such a unique sensation for someone who hadn't felt pain in decades. It almost sent me to the floor, but I recovered quickly and kept going. Another one hit me just before I reached my door.

Two doors back, I heard Mrs. Tenderschott volunteer, "I'll get Jen." The familiar sound of her steps started toward the door, and then emerged in the hallway. I grabbed hold of my door handle and forced myself to stand up straight. The pain hit again, but I shoved it back as deep as I could. It would have been easier if I could have skipped into my room before she passed by, but I was afraid to let go of the door handle.

Mrs. Tenderschott looked at me curiously as she hurried by. "I'll get Jennifer. It won't take me more than a minute."

"Okay," I forced.

When she finally made it out the door to find Jen, I collapsed to the floor, and reached up and pulled down on my door handle. It opened, and I slowly slithered into my room on my back. A flick of my wrist shut the door behind me. I tried to reach my bed, but I couldn't before another bolt of pain hit me. It took all I had to stifle a scream. Again, I reached for my bed and attempted to pull myself up by the spread. The pain was excruciating. Drops of moisture developed on my brow, and I felt both a great squeezing and pushing at the same time.

"Holy crap!"

I let go of the spread on my bed. There was no way I was going to pull myself up there physically.

With a palm placed flat on the floor beside me, I said, "levioso", and floated up, but another shot of pain hit, stronger this time, and I crashed down to the floor with a thud. I was afraid to move at that point. Every attempt I had made so far had resulted in pain. I move. I hurt. That was my theory. Why I was hurting was a mystery? Then my theory failed. I was sitting still and another shot of pain, more intense than the others, hit me, and a fist pounded the floor.

"Larissa, are you okay?" Mrs. Saxon asked through the door.

"I'm fine," I called back, half writhing, and realizing I wouldn't even believe myself. There was no surprise when the door burst open, and she rushed in.

"Marie! Mrs. Tenderschott!" she yelled back at the door. Marie showed up in an instant. Mrs. Tenderschott wouldn't hear her. She was probably midway down the stairs looking for Jen.

"Let's get her up." Marie bent down and cradled me in her arms. She didn't wait for Mrs. Saxon to help. She lifted me up on the bed.

"Is it too early?" Mrs. Saxon asked Marie.

Before I ever thought about what she was asking, I asked for her to clarify, "Too early for what?" I knew. I knew the moment I said it. I knew it the moment Marie placed her hands on my belly.

"No," answered Marie. She leaned down to listen and then sat up smiling. "Its heartbeat is strong; I feel and hear it. It's ready to come out and see the world." She turned to Mrs. Saxon and repeated something I had heard way too much recently. It still lacked the specifics I was looking for, and I knew Mrs. Saxon was too. "Pregnancies by a vampire are unpredictable. Sometimes it's weeks to months, but never the full nine months. Larissa is unique," Wait! Did I just see Mrs. Saxon smirk at that. I was about to call her out on that when another pain sent me bucking back against my mattress. Both women attempted to comfort me. It didn't work. "She is the only vampire I have ever known to become pregnant. We believe..."

"Magic," Mrs. Saxon replied. She looked down into my eyes. "Mr. Demius told me about the duck. Did that happen here? Is that what this child came from?" She asked caringly, but that didn't take any of the uneasiness out of my answer. She was the mother of the boy I slept with. She was assuming this was something I created out of my own desire. Now I needed to tell her what really happened. Another sharp pain shot to me, adding to the discomfort of the moment, and I groaned and screamed. That scream saved me from further unpleasantry.

"Mrs. Saxon, we believe magic only played a part of this. They conceived the child," Marie started, and then stumbled slightly as she approached the next part. She was doing a lot better at this than I would have. I would have choked on the first word. "Traditionally. Magic just added it. A loss of concentration, if you would."

The look between the two women when Mrs. Saxon finally realized what it meant was priceless, and I realized I had seen this scene in several movies and sitcoms. The mother of a girl, informing the mother of a boy, that her son knocked up her daughter. A classic on many levels. I just didn't enjoy being the main character when Mrs. Saxon looked down at me. I braced myself for some motherly comment, but there wasn't one. Her face lit up, and she bent down and kissed me on the forehead. "So, it's really his?" she asked in my ear.

"Yes. All his," I replied, and then I screamed again. That shot was the most severe yet.

"Well then, how do we do this? I wasn't awake when I gave birth to Nathan." She looked over at Marie, who just shook her head.

"I never had the chance."

"This would be a good time for some magic," I started and then finished with a scream.

"Is there a doctor you trust?" Marie asked.

Mrs. Saxon rolled her eyes. I knew what she was thinking. How exactly would you explain all this to the doctor? Hey Doc, we need your help to deliver this child. The mother is both a witch and a vampire, and she has only been pregnant about two weeks.

"Wait," she jumped off the bed. "There isn't a doctor, but we do have a nurse." She disappeared out the door, leaving me and Marie alone.

Marie pulled me up higher on the bed and let my head lay on the pillow. It was soft and really comfortable. I had never used it before, but I think I might find a way in the future. Then she yanked off my pant and covered me with a blanket.

"Let's do this." She bent my legs, putting my feet flat on the bed. It felt a little better. Not as much pressure. Maybe she knew a thing or two, but then I realized she was doing the same thing they do in movies, but she had missed two things they always ask for. She hadn't asked for boiling water and towels.

By the time Mrs. Saxon returned, Marie had me propped up and as prepped, as if either of us really knew what we were doing. The pain was coming strong and fast, and I had given up screaming with each impulse. Now it was just a continual groan. Seeing who walked in the door added to that groan.

"Larissa. Relax. Ms. Parrish was a registered nurse before she came to our world. She still tends to the scrapes and bumps of our students."

She didn't say a word or even cast me a look. She just took position at the end of the bed. I felt her cold hands and wondered if she would have warmed them up first if she had actually liked me. "Good, we can do this naturally," she said from behind the sheet Marie had placed up and over my knees. "How far along are you?"

Before we went through that explanation again, I answered, "About two weeks."

Ms. Parrish didn't miss a beat. She kept doing what she was, and replied with, "You're lucky. Shifters carry for three years before the baby is full term."

I let out a loud groan as another wave ran through me.

"Larissa, on the next one, I want you to push," she said.

In the background, a stampede came down the hall, and Mrs. Saxon flicked the door shut. "Classes are over," she said as Marie looked toward the door. "They won't be able to hear anything with the door shut."

"That's not what she is concerned about, Rebecca. There is going to be a lot of blood."

Mrs. Saxon snapped around. From where I was, I saw her hands move, and then watched both the door to the hallway, and the one to the closet staircase to the roof glow. She had sealed them with runes. There was no chance they were getting through that.

I craned my neck to the side so I could see around the sheet. "Mom," I caught myself, but didn't correct it. "Are you going to be okay?"

My question prompted a glance from Mrs. Saxon, and I felt Ms. Parrish stop doing whatever she was down there.

She gave a terse nod of her head in my direction and then glanced at the others. Tension filled the room, and I believed we were about a second from Mrs. Saxon zapping her to the other side of the door. Inside, I debated with myself whether to stop her. I wanted her there with me, but also knew the risk. Marie saved herself by remarking, "Who do you think taught Larissa her control?"

I heard two large exhales, right before my next wave of pain.

"Push now?" I asked.

"Yes, Larissa. Push hard," commanded Ms. Parrish. Her next order was for Mrs. Saxon. "Rebecca, I need towels and hot water. You think you can whip that up?" Before she even finished the request, both were there.

"Oh my," Marie said excitedly.

"What? What's wrong?" I cried.

"Nothing," said Ms. Parrish. "When I tell you, I want you to push again, and don't stop until I tell you. Got it?"

"What's wrong?" I asked. Something was wrong. I knew it. Why else would Marie have reacted that way? I craned my neck again. "What's wrong Marie?" She never looked at me. Oh God.

"Larissa," snapped Ms. Parrish. She looked up over the top of the sheet. A light sheen of red on her hand. I didn't even flinch at its sight. "Nothing is wrong, but there is going to be a problem if you don't do what I say. Now when I say, push, and don't stop until I tell you to stop. Got it?"

I nodded back, and she ducked back down behind the sheet. "Now push. Push. Push. Push."

I pushed with everything I had for as long as she said the word. The bedframe let out a loud crack under the force, and I felt it dip to the floor, but that didn't stop the order of "Push" and I didn't stop pushing, and then she stopped, and I heard the most magical sound in the entire world. A small little cry.

26

"Are you sure you're ready for this?" Jen asked as the three of us stood in front of the white columned entrance of 18 Audubon Place.

"Larissa, you just gave birth. Maybe take a day or two to recover," suggested Master Thomas.

"I have to do it. It's more important now than it ever was." There was so much more at stake. So much had changed in just the last few hours, and I saw the world through a different light. I needed Nathan. We both did, and every moment I delayed, robbed the three of us of those moments, those opportunities to be a family. "Not to mention. I'm fine. It's been what, two or three hours? That is weeks in my time. Remember, I just gave birth to a child that I took to full term in just two weeks."

I led them up the steps and to the door. Before we arrived, I had already debated whether or not to knock. I had decided not to, and twisted the handle, prepared to force the lock open, but I didn't need to. It was unlocked. The three of us walked into the large, spacious white entry. There was a staircase and hallway ahead of us, with hallways on either side. There were no heartbeats to follow, and no smell of fresh blood. Traces of old stale blood were everywhere, and smelled putrid to my senses. Jennifer noticed it too and walked around the room, checking.

I was about to just pick a hallway to follow when we saw movement in the one to our right. Two vampires that I vaguely remembered from the nights out in the trees came around the corner and slid to a stop when they saw me. They smelled or felt Master Thomas and wanted to make a quick meal out of the intruder. My presence changed the menu, and they ran back the way they came.

"This way."

Jen and I ran after them. Master Thomas followed the best he could. A few turns through the house, and the clean white look changed to something more old world. Dark woods and such. We passed a hall of French doors. The scene I saw through their glass insets caused me to do a double take. There was the ballroom from one of Jean's visits. We kept going until we reached what appeared to be a single hallway that all the others converged into.

We stopped there and waited for Master Thomas. I didn't want him to be alone for this part. Something about it felt ominous, almost like we were walking into the mouth of the beast. I couldn't say why. It was just a feeling with a few flashes of details. All I could see in them was a room at the end of this hallway, and a hideously large wooden throne. If only I had a few more sessions with James to fine tune this new skill.

We walked, keeping Master Thomas between Jen and me the whole way. The opening to that room was just ahead, and shadows flashed back and forth across the doorway. I was the first to step through the opening, with Master Thomas right behind me, and Jen behind him. This room felt heavy and matched every detail I had seen in the flashes except the wooden throne. I couldn't see it anywhere. We were not alone either. Most of the vampires I had seen out in the woods, following Marteggo around like a lovesick puppy, stood to our sides and before us.

"Where is Nathan? Where is Nathan Saxon?" I barked, hoping Nathan would hear his own name and come forward. Who came forward wasn't Nathan, and before this pale figure in a three-piece suit and top hat stepped clear of the crowd, he spoke to another, who took off running toward the back of the room. I tried to watch where he went, but lost him several times. I last lost him when he passed a staircase made of old rocks. The shape of magic changed at that opening. It was chaotic and dark. That was when I knew. That led to the mildew covered dungeon that Jean pulled me to in one of his visions, and where he kept Marie.

"You have a lot of nerve coming here after what your kind caused." The top hat gentleman looked right over me and at Master Thomas. "You should leave," he warned, and I felt Master Thomas take a step back. I reached back and grabbed him by the hand.

"Our kind," I said, emphasizing the first word for all to hear. "Shouldn't you be saying that to yourself? You attacked the witches' camp and killed how many of our brothers and sisters? I was there, remember?"

The man didn't even look at me. He stayed locked on to the only non-vampire in the room. I felt him attempt to back away again, and again I pulled him back in line. I wasn't trying to show solidarity with the only other witch in the room. This was for his safety. If we offered them any opening, he would be a goner before he had a chance. There were too many of them for one witch to fend off. Even too many for two vampires to fend off, but these had all seen what I did to Jean before Mrs. Wintercrest interfered. They knew not to push.

The man laughed, and those behind him joined it. Before, when I considered all the probable outcomes, having to fight our way out of this was not one of them, but that didn't mean I wouldn't. My legs hunched down a bit, and I let go of Master Thomas's hand to avoid hurting him. A red glow glared from my hands, and several of the vampires backed up. But not old Mr. Top Hat. He stood his ground right until another vampire pushed him aside and grabbed me, hugging me tightly. I even felt one of his hands let go long enough to give Master Thomas a pat on the shoulder.

"You're free. How did you get free?" Nathan asked.

"Long story," I said, and squeezed him tighter. Over his shoulder, I saw our welcoming party back up and disappear into the gathered crowd. "Your mother can explain. Let's go home," I said feeling a little weepy eyed.

"What? My mother? Home?" Nathan asked, confused, and let me go, backing up a few steps.

"Yep. Your mother rescued me and allowed everyone to return. Let's go home." I reached out for his hand, and he moved it away.

"Larissa. You should stay here with us. You and Mrs. Bolden. Master Thomas, you will have to leave." He backed away a few more steps.

"Don't be silly. Now come on." I reached for him again, and this time, not only did he pull back, but he also turned away.

"Nathan?" Jennifer stepped forward. I put my hand on her and held her back. This was my fight. She was only here for the muscle.

"Nathan, what's going on?" I walked forward to him and attempted to place my hand on his shoulder, but he shrugged it off as quickly as it landed.

"You already know. We have had this conversation before." He turned around. Any happiness he had about seeing me was gone. What was left was unrecognizable. "You are a vampire. Your place is with other vampires."

"Not this again," I huffed. Marteggo was gone. The source of all the crap that was filling Nathan's head had been cutoff. I had him pulled back. What happened?

"No, it's not this again." It was his turn to huff now. "It's not the same as before at all. It's all different. It's all different because of what your kind did." He first pointed at Master Thomas, and then at me. His other hand shot up over his head and snapped. "I admit, seeing the life in the coven, things look amazing, but there is a dark side to the world of witches that makes us look civilized. Master Thomas told you about the war with the rogues, and I saw it. That was the first in a long list of examples that show the true darkness in the world of witches. If it doesn't fit, they must rub it out. You saw how many rogues showed up on your doorstep the minute they felt there might be a power shift, but you didn't fit, and your own kind made a deal with us to have you and Marcus imprisoned."

"Nathan, that is not it. Mrs. Wintercrest sees me as a threat," I tried to explain, but he walked up to me and held a finger right up in my face. His gaze cut deep.

"A threat because you are different. Just like I am different. Just like we all... are... different."

"Nathan, you have it all wrong. It's not that. I am a challenge to her seat..." he cut me off again.

"It is that. You can't see it because all the whispers of saving the world Master Thomas and others feed you have blinded you from the truth."

"Nathan! You know that's not true. What I am doing is trying to fix all that. That is all Master Thomas and the others want too. And your mother is in on it." He turned his back to me, but I ran around him to look him right in the face. "You have to believe me. You know this is true." I pleaded, and placed both hands on his shoulders. Then I threw my arms around him, and waited for him to do the same, but I never felt them. I looked up, and he wasn't even looking at me, he was looking over me. "You have to believe me." I let go and stepped back so I could look up into his eyes. I needed to ignite that connection again.

"Tell me, did my mother know about this?" He reached behind him into the crowd and pulled back a fist full of gold chains. Blood charms of various shapes and sizes dangled at the end of the chains. "After we did the dirty work, and you were taken, the witches turned on us, killing thirty-seven of us. Why? Because we didn't fit in, even though we made an agreement with them. So, tell me, does my mother know about this? Let me guess, that bitch Mrs. Wintercrest is there in the coven with her."

I didn't answer. I didn't have to. My lack of a denial appeared to have told him all he needed to hear, and he exploded, thrusting the fist of chains toward me, stopping just inches from my face. "Take a good look! This is what the witches did to your brothers and sisters. They betrayed us. You have a choice to make. You can be with us, where you belong, or you need to go and never come back."

I had already made the choice, but felt too broken to make it known. There really wasn't a decision at all. There were larger things at stake, more lives, than just the two of us that needed to be considered, but that didn't make it any easier to say. The eyes of everyone in the room wore away at me, and the first tear fell, again. I had been crying a lot lately, for various reasons, but all of them paled in comparison to this. I had one more card to play. It had worked before, and I needed to play it again. I needed to get him away from here. Somewhere we could talk, and I could help him understand, away from all these influences that I knew were pulling his strings. They had to be.

"Nathan, come back with me? Come back and talk to your mother? See what she has to say and if you decided to come back..." I almost couldn't get this out, "I will send you back."

"Sure, you will," he marched away from me, and the crowd parted like the Red Sea. Back against the far wall, I finally saw it. The wooden throne, with lion's heads carved into each armrest. Nathan walked right up to it and sat with one leg slung over the armrest. The blood charms still dangled from his fist. "I go back, and you or her throw some runes up and I can never leave. I see how it all works. Sorry, we trusted you once, and this happened." He shook the charms. "Larissa, your place is here with me. We have a connection unlike anything, but I can't go back to that world, and you shouldn't either." He almost sounded tender and caring. Not the hostile person who had stormed around making claims for the last five minutes, but that was short-lived. "Now you have to decide. Stay here and live the life you are meant to have, or leave and be one of those backstabbing witches. What's it going to be?"

I threw my shoulders back and braced myself for what I was about to say. More for my benefit than for anyone else's. I didn't expect to be able to say it without breaking down in a heap on the floor, but it was the only choice.

"Well, what's your choice?" he leaned forward.

"I am both a witch and a vampire. I can't turn my back on either part of who I am," I said as calmly as I could. Inside, I was about dead.

"Then be gone," and with that, the crowd closed in around us. "Witches aren't to be trusted. You should know that better than anyone else. Remember how the council has treated you."

"I can say the same for vampires. Jean spent decades hunting me," I spat back, which was probably not the best of ideas in the mixed company.

"Go, you have made your choice."

My arm spun around weakly, and a portal opened to the coven. Master Thomas practically jumped through it. Jen went through but stood there on the other side, waiting for me. I stepped in with one foot, but stopped before I stepped in with the other. "Yes, I made my choice, but it is not because of you or them, Nathan. It's because of Samantha, our daughter, and she is a witch too."

I stepped through and closed the portal.

Blood Wars

1

"I don't understand how any of this will help."

I thew my arms up, making my aggravation clear. They fell back down and slapped the top of the table. The impact echoed throughout the library. Of all the places she could have picked, Mrs. Saxon chose this one to add to my house arrest. Not the pool. Not the woods. Not the cove. The library. All because no one ever visited here. If they needed something, they summoned Edward to their room, or wherever they were. It wasn't like anyone would question a locked library door. Not that anyone would try to open it.

"You have been through a lot, and Mrs. Saxon believes that talking to someone about it might help," replied Edward from the spot his head hovered over.

"I don't need therapy!" I pounded the table with each word.

"Of course not, and I'm not a therapist. Do you see a couch anywhere? Am I sitting on a leather chair with my legs crossed and a pad of paper sitting on my lap ready to take notes with?"

"No. I don't see a couch, and I don't," I paused and looked away from Edward before I pointed out the obvious. My hand motioned to the space under him, "and I don't see any legs."

"Touché Miss Dubois. Touché." He circled around in front of me and looked me in the eye.

I felt embarrassed at my comment; It was a childish joke born out of the frustration of this, our third pointless session. "I'm sorry." I looked up at him sheepishly.

"It's no worry, Miss Dubois. Emotional stress often causes people to lash out. Now, shall we continue?"

"Sure," I agreed. Not that I had a choice. "Where were we?"

"The same place we started two days ago, Nathan, and how his turning into a vampire made you feel. Let's start there, please."

He was right. That was the first question he asked me during our first session, and the same question he had asked me several dozen times since. All I did each time was deflect. I believed that was a term a therapist would use, though Edward never did. Why there? Despite asking multiple times across multiple visits, including now, I still didn't understand. It was time to ask again. "Why do we need to start there?"

"Do we have to go through this again, Miss Dubois?"

If he was going to ask that question again, then yes, we would have to go through this again. This time I held my tongue, and propped my head on my arms, and prepared myself for Edward's answer. It had been the same answer for the last two sessions. I was sure it would be the same this time, too. Edward didn't disappoint.

"Miss Dubois, you have been through a traumatic event. Talking to someone could be beneficial, and as Mrs. Saxon and most of the others here in the coven are emotionally invested, I'm the best option. Not to mention I am a good listener. I am mostly ears." His head twisted back and forth, displaying the ears on either side of his floating head. "Beyond that, you need to bring your emotions in check if you are to continue with your training. Might I ask how that is going?"

My arms collapsed on the tabletop, along with my head. "Miserable," I said. The table muffled my voice.

Nothing was working. Not even a flash or flicker. Several of my old standbys, the things I could do as a young girl, were no shows. Telekinesis was one of my earliest discoveries, and now poof, it had vanished.

I didn't doubt Edward on his theory about the connection between my emotional state and my magic. I had even tried to address it on my own last night by attempting some meditation. That was something James had mentioned as a method of clearing my mind during my divination training in the witch's camp. It cleared my mind. That was for sure. It created a lot of room for thoughts of Nathan to come crashing in. All that did was send me into an emotional tailspin. The more I thought of him, the emptier I felt. A true and tragic irony. My head would be full of thoughts of him, but that empty feeling hole his absence created grew larger.

"Let's identify what it takes to put you back on track. Shall we?"

My head nodded against my arms, and then I sat up. "I don't disagree, but maybe we are focusing on the wrong starting place."

"Why do you think that?" he asked presumptuously.

Oh, how very therapist-like of him.

I needed to prepare myself. Once we got into this, there would be a bunch of and-why-do-you-feel-that-way questions, and I would have to tell him. If I'm being forced to endure this, then I need to get something constructive out of it. Didn't I? Mrs. Saxon gave no indications she would drop this idea soon, and my magic was a mess.

There was no way to avoid it. "I was fine when Nathan changed. I mean... Was I upset when it happened? Yes. I was devastated. Why wouldn't I be? The man I loved died trying to save me."

I held up a finger to stop Edward from stating the obvious.

"I know. I know. He didn't die, but you know what I mean. But I could still function. My magic was on point. Even stronger than before. Wouldn't the troubles have started then if that was the reason?"

Edward looked away and then floated around the room and back. Then he did it again. It was almost as if I could see a body underneath his head pacing while his arms and hands rubbed his chin in thought. "It's possible. Though your emotions could have driven your magic to continue, like a shot of adrenaline that kept you going following a traumatic event."

"Is that even possible?" I wondered out loud. "I mean, I know what you are talking about. Or let me correct that. I remember what you are talking about. That burst of energy that keeps you going even when you are exhausted." I remembered it clearly from my youth. We woke up one night to a fire in our fields. We never figured out how it started. All I remember was hearing my father screaming to wake up his farm hands at a little after three in the morning. The exhaustion I felt when I went to bed just hours before was gone. I was up, alert, and running to the field to help shovel dirt on top of the approaching flames. We worked well into the next day without stopping. I felt my exhaustion set in once the flames were out, but not before. I was driven and energized the whole time.

"But does that exist for magic? And" I stood up from the table. "Would that last for several days? I was doing quite well during my training down there. There wasn't even a hint of a problem. Not until... I returned after..." That was it. It hit me like a bolt of lightning. I didn't even know why this was a mystery. That moment was so painfully etched into my memory, I couldn't even speak of it. I couldn't say it out loud. That was the moment everything went on the fritz. It wasn't immediate, but the first small failings started then.

"The moment he refused to come back with you. Yes, I am well aware of the proximity of that event to the start of your problems, but in my experience," Edward rotated around to face me. "Which is considerable when you consider how many years I have been around, and all the generations of witches that have come through my doors. It is never that simple. Therefore, I think we need to go back. So, humor me." Edward rose a few feet and looked down his nose at me. "How did you feel when Nathan turned?"

And here we were again. We were stuck in this vicious cycle. I actually thought we were on to something this time. Yes, Edward had a point. I was falling into the trap of a simple causality. Because one thing happened after another, then it must have caused it, but in this case I felt it really did cause it.

"I just told you," I said with a shake of my head. I wasn't sure why we were going back through this, considering I just bared my soul to him about that moment.

"What a little bitch," exploded Mrs. Saxon as she entered through the formerly locked library doors.

Hearing that tone, and that term, from her put me on the defense and I backed up into a table, pushing it and its chairs back a few noisy feet. "I'm sorry," I said, and readied myself to fall to the floor and beg for her forgiveness. She must have been watching us all this time. I knew that the warm welcome I received when I returned wouldn't last forever. How long it had lasted already had me amazed.

"Oh no. Not you, Larissa," apologized Mrs. Saxon. Visibly frustrated and flustered. "That little..."

"Witch?" I interjected, to save her from the other word I felt was on her lips.

"Yes, witch. Thank you, Larissa. That little witch Miss Sarah Roberts."

I second guessed my choice of correction. I should have let Mrs. Saxon stay with her original term.

"Every time I try to ask Mrs. Wintercrest about what happened in New Orleans, and the rumored attack on the vampires, Miss Roberts steps in between us and turns it around. Then she questions my motives now that my son is a vampire. What gives her the right?"

"She is a council member."

"Thanks for pointing that out, Edward. It's not like I didn't already know that," sniped back Mrs. Saxon. She walked up to the closest table and pulled out a chair and collapsed into it. "I'm sorry Edward."

"No apology needed, ma'am."

"No, I am sorry. It's not you, it's them," she huffed. "They aren't even trying to lie or deny things. Every time I direct the question at our supreme, she just stands there and smiles while someone else steps in and deflects it. Never answering the question at all. Not even with a lie, which any attempt to deny it is happening would be at this point."

"Is happening?" I asked for a clarification that I hoped was just a poor choice of words by Mrs. Saxon. Not that she made that kind of mistake often. She was a proper person when she spoke.

"Yes, Larissa. Is happening. What happened wasn't isolated to New Orleans, and it is continuing. Jen and Kevin are hearing from others about isolated attacks on some of the smaller vampire covens. Most are those that are just a single-family unit or a few families together, but that doesn't matter. It is happening, and it shouldn't be."

"What about New Orleans?" I asked as I rushed over and took the chair next to her.

"I don't believe there has been another attack since the last one, but I don't know for sure."

"There has to be someone we can talk to. Someone that can stand up to the council and put a stop to this." I pounded the table to add an exclamation point. It echoed through the cavernous library. I couldn't believe this was happening. Witches. The council at that. They were openly attacking vampires, but why? That was a stupid question. I knew why. Nathan had already told me, and he was right. They were different, and a potential threat to the witches, like how they viewed me, and now that Jean was gone, sort of, and Marteggo was definitely gone, there was an opening, and no one to stand in their way, but that is too simple. It explained what happened in New Orleans. Jean and his coven were a problem, and so were the rogue witches. An opportune time to solve two problems. That didn't explain what they were doing now.

"There used to be. That was Master Thomas," responded Mrs. Saxon. "But not now, and I'm afraid it is too risky to approach anyone else."

"What about Mr. Nevers?" I spouted, remembering his constant presence during my training here and again in New Orleans.

"Not even him, I'm afraid." She walked over to the table that I pounded in protest. "I don't doubt he would listen to us, but what could he really do?"

Nothing. That was what he could do. I knew it, and approaching him would be a onetime thing. The moment he spoke out against anything that was going on in the council, they would likely kick him out. Just like they had with Master Thomas. This was hopeless, and I felt it as I collapsed down on the table.

"Larissa." I heard the legs of the chair beside me squeak on the floor as Mrs. Saxon slid it out and sat. "I don't want this to sound like I am putting more pressure on you, but really, our only way out of all this is to complete your training, and then challenge for supreme." Her hand reached over and stroked the top of my head.

Nope, she wasn't adding any pressure on top of me. Nope, not at all. She was only laying all the pressure in the world on me. It sounded so simple when she said it. It was way too simple, and yet, she was right. It would solve everything. I looked up. "How exactly can I do that? Challenge for supreme? I am a fugitive that escaped from a prison they sent me to for crimes against all witches... oh wait, they labeled me a hostile entity. I seriously doubt I can walk right up and make the request."

"Well," started Mrs. Saxon, and then I saw something I had never seen from her the whole time I had known her. Her eyes darted around the room and avoided mine. Even her body language changed. There was a slight slump in her shoulders, and a small slow exhale before she finished her answer. "I'm still working on that." Then there was a lengthy pause. I looked up at Edward, who hovered above the center of the table. He was also waiting for a further reply from Mrs. Saxon. This was a pretty significant step in the plan. Hearing she was still working on it was disheartening.

"Under normal circumstances, any witch can approach the council and request permission to take the test of the seven wonders," she continued.

"Well, these are most certainly not normal circumstances." That was the understatement of eternity. "But say, these were, and I wasn't me. Then what? How does it normally work? Just because I can perform them, I replace the supreme?"

That had been a question in my head for a few days now. Lisa could do some, if not all, of the wonders. I was sure there were other witches out there that could. The fact that I can, and Mrs. Wintercrest can, means at least two witches can perform all seven. Who decides who is supreme then?

"It's not that straightforward."

"It never is." Edward's remark earned him an admonishing look from Mrs. Saxon.

She straightened up and turned toward me. "There are two paths. One, if you show greater ability than the current supreme, then the appointment as supreme is automatic and unchallenged. I believe that is your path to becoming the supreme. Mrs. Wintercrest is aging, and as a witch ages, some abilities become diminished. Now if there is no discernible difference between the two witches. It becomes the choice of the council where they are to take other factors into consideration. They would consider the person, their deeds, and how they would benefit our community."

I looked right up at Edward. "So, a popularity contest."

He nodded.

"Well, I ain't winning one of those with that group anytime soon."

"I don't disagree, which is why your training is so important."

"Yep," I conceded. What else could I do?

"On that topic, any major breakthroughs?"

"Well, ma'am, today I believe Larissa fully embraced our sessions, and I believe we will..."

Mrs. Saxon raised a hand, cutting off Edward. "That is fine, and an important part of her journey, but I am more curious about her magic. Larissa, how is that going? Any improvement since yesterday?"

"Not really. It's still inconsistent."

"How inconsistent?"

I had hoped she hadn't picked up on my choice of words there. Inconsistent was really stretching it. "Basically, not there at all. What does come is a surprise."

"Not good. Not good at all," Mrs. Saxon said as she stood up from the table. "It's all the turmoil in your world. You need to put all that back into order for everything else to fall in line."

"I know." I honestly did. It made complete sense to me. That word I hated so much, focus, described exactly what was absent from my life.

"I hate to do this, but we need to double your sessions. You will meet with Edward twice a day. Once down here, and again in your room. We can't risk anyone walking in after classes and seeing you in here."

I held my scoff inside. No one would ever come in here.

"We will also double your sessions with Master Thomas and myself. Mornings before my first classes, and then evenings. In the meantime, I will talk to Mrs. Tenderschott about a potion to help you. It won't be a cure. Just a temporary solution so you can train. You won't be able to use a potion or anything during the seven wonders. They'll know."

"Okay." What else could I do other than agree, no matter how much I didn't want to do the double sessions? I didn't mind the training, but this therapy session was out-and-out torture, and one big reminder of everything that was going wrong. I didn't need any reminders of that.

"Head on up. I will be up shortly." Mrs. Saxon turned and spun her hand, opening a portal up to my room. It had barely materialized before Samantha ran through the portal and wrapped her arms around my legs. Then the one-month-old who was going on five years old hopped up on her grandmother's lap while giving Edward a rather cautious wave.

"You need to remember who you are fighting for. It's not you, me, Master Thomas, or anyone like that." Mrs. Saxon stroked Samantha's auburn hair as she said it.

2

"Please!" I begged, not being shy about how desperate I sounded. Not that I liked how it sounded, but I needed Master Thomas, Marie, or anyone else sitting around me to hear the anguish I felt.

Master Thomas threw his arms out and twirled around. A cold winter gust swept through the open space, sending the hem of his overcoat floating up around him. I didn't share the same enthusiasm, and ran my hand across my face.

"I got you out. See? Convincing Rebecca to allow this took a while." He gestured towards the barren trees around the clearing. Winter had long ago stolen their foliage. He was right. It took a week of him talking to Mrs. Saxon for her to grant what Master Thomas called small, supervised-field-trips to the woods. He suggested that Samantha should experience more of the world. It seems, while Mrs. Saxon found it easy to deny me, she found it harder to deny her granddaughter. He also gained permission to include Marie Norton and Jen Bolden. He sold them as chaperones who weren't witches and wouldn't be able to whisk me away someplace.

He was rather proud of his accomplishment and didn't quite understand the disappointment that sent me running to my bed when he first told me. This wasn't what I had in mind when I said I wanted to leave. I wanted his help to go find Nathan. A feat that if I could, I would have already done it for myself, but I couldn't, so I hadn't. He ignored the dozens of plans I told him about how I would convince Nathan to return with us.

"You know what I meant," I complained.

"Of course I do, and you know as well as I do, that is completely out of the question. That is also why there are no other witches as part of your little escapades. Just me. And I'm not about to open any portals to any place but back to your room."

"Sam is a witch," I remarked, just to remind him.

"Yes, she is, but she is… too young to open a portal."

"You tried to pick an age, didn't you?" I teased after hearing him stumble in the middle of his statement. I looked back at my beautiful daughter as she ran back and forth between Marie and Jen, giggling the whole time.

"I tried, but I am not sure. That is something beyond my comprehension."

"Something you don't understand?" I quipped, enjoying the chance to needle him a little.

"This is one of the many things in the world that I don't understand. She looks between four or five, but I know she's not."

"That's my guess too. Just going based on how she looks and acts." I looked at him eagerly and asked, "So, when do we start her training?" I wasn't sure who that question caught more off guard. Me or Master Thomas. I felt his heart skip while I wondered to myself why I had even asked that question. The more I considered it, the more it became a valid question. A very valid question.

"Let's focus on getting you back to training first," he replied.

"I wasn't much older than Sam when I started. I think I was six."

Master Thomas's tone turned stern, and he turned to look right at me. "As much as you ask me to help you find Nathan, or to help stop what is going you, recovering your own abilities and your own training should be your focus. That is the only path to what you seek."

"I know. That's what Mrs. Saxon said too."

"You need to remember that and stay focused." He paused and looked at Samantha. "But yes," his tone softer and friendlier. He sounded like the Master Thomas I remembered, with a touch of curiosity. "She looks and acts like a six-year-old. That is usually the age when formal training starts. We don't know what her true age is. She may really only be a one-month-old. It is one of many things we don't know." Master Thomas hesitated and extended a hand toward Samantha. "I mean, we don't even know what she is."

"What the hell?" I huffed. "She's a child. My child. What do you mean we don't know what she is?"

"Exactly." Master Thomas glanced in my direction.

I wasn't sure if he was being funny or serious. Either way, it burned.

"We know she is at least part witch. That much is sure, and like her mother, she is primarily a telekinetic."

Just two weeks ago we gave her the test all young witches go through. I stood there a nervous and anxious mother, watching my daughter grab hold of that crystal. When I saw the same brilliant blue light that I had seen just several months ago, I fought the urge to cheer. I don't remember going through a similar test when I was younger, but perhaps I did when I was her age and was just too young to remember.

"So, what else is there to know?" I asked, not knowing where he was headed with this. The question was always would she be a witch or not? Now we had our answer.

"Whether she has any vampire in her?" Master Thomas stated flatly, standing facing me with his hands clasped in front of him.

Wow. I could honestly say I wasn't prepared to hear that. That thought had never occurred to me. Why would it? She breathes. I feel the warmth of her breath against my cheek when I snuggle with her at night as she sleeps. Which is another thing. She sleeps. Let's not forget about how she shivers when she feels my icy touch. Something I had learned to mask with lots of blankets. Her heart beats. Something we had all felt. Mrs. Saxon even had to put up a block around my room to keep the other vampires from sensing her as they passed up and down the hallway. Blood flowed through her body, giving her cheeks that wonderful rosy complexion. Something her mother no longer had naturally. "She's human. That's plain to see."

"Is it?" Master Thomas asked while again giving me a side glance.

"Absolutely," I responded, almost a little defensive.

"Yes, she has a heartbeat, and appears human, but take her growth rate. That is more than a little accelerated, and I don't believe we can chalk it up to any of the magic that may have contributed to her being here."

"Why not?"

"It's quite simple." Master Thomas turned and addressed me directly. "The same reason the baby duck appeared when you thought about it. If you had thought about a child at a certain age, they would have appeared at that age. If magic were at play in Samantha's conception, then you imagined having a baby with Nathan. It's a logical understanding and progression of facts. Her progressive aging is something else."

"You're right," spouted Marie, as Samantha collapsed into her arms. She wiggled as Marie attempted to hold on to her before finally letting her go race toward Jen.

"Well, don't keep us in suspense."

"Yes, Marie, do tell," I prompted curiously. I wasn't even aware she was listening to us. Our conversation wasn't exactly private, but she appeared occupied with Samantha.

"You're right. It is something else." She stood up as Samantha returned to crash into her. This time she crashed into her legs, laughing. Marie reached down and rubbed her head before she sent her off toward Jen, who full on tackled her and started tickling her, causing an eruption of laughter. "I'm, I mean we—Jen and I–, aren't saying she is a vampire, but Larissa, do you remember Theodora saying vampire pregnancies were faster than those of humans?"

I rolled my eyes. How could I forget that? She said it all the time, and I lived it. Man, did I live it.

"While you and Sam are completely unique, births to a vampire male and human woman are rare, but they happen."

"The Dhampirs that Theodora mentioned?" I interjected.

"Yes, Dhampirs. Those pregnancies usually last for only a few months. Much shorter than a normal human pregnancy, but it doesn't stop there. Once born, the child ages faster than a normal human child would. How fast is different for everyone. Some I have heard of age quickly through the first few months. Then they reach an age when everything returns to normal. It's usually at a really young age. Maybe five or six. Those children are pure human. There are those who reach an age and stop aging completely. They inherit some of the vampire traits from their father. Immortality. Their speed and strength. Their enhanced senses. Even their ability to consume blood. Who's to say that…"

Three sets of eyes looked in Samantha's direction, finishing the question Marie had started. Was it possible? The roles were reversed here. Did she inherit more from me than just being a witch? How the hell could we find out? "I am guessing there isn't a crystal we can have her hold?"

"No," laughed Marie.

"We just have to watch her," said Jen. "See if she shows anything on her own."

"Wow," I said, and walked over to a stump to have a seat. "I never considered the possibility she could be both."

"You may not be the only one anymore," remarked Master Thomas.

I was unsure how to feel about that. It had nothing to do with losing that unique distinction of being the only one. That was something I couldn't have cared less about. I just didn't want her to have to go through what I was going through.

Dang it! Another life screwed up by me, and another life that hung in the balance of everything I had to take care of. Not that Samantha's didn't already rely on me completing this greater task that Master Thomas, and I guess Mrs. Saxon, had assigned me. Everyone was relying on me. But if Samantha were both, now she was part of the Jean problem. If Jean ever found out there was another one like me, I already knew what he would do.

"I cursed her." I thought I had whispered it, but I obviously hadn't. Everyone, including Samantha, looked over at me.

"What is it mommy?" Samantha cried as she ran in to my direction.

"Oh, nothing," I said, brushing the hair back out of my eyes before she arrived. Then I reached down and picked her up onto my lap. "Nothing. Mommy is just being silly. She does that from time to time."

"It's about time she realized it too," remarked Jen.

I stuck my tongue out in her direction. Samantha did the same, but she was more enthusiastic about it than I was.

Master Thomas motioned for me to make space for him on the dead tree trunk I sat on. I did, and he sat down. Until he sat next to me, rigid back, and all, I hadn't realized I was slouching. Since when had I started doing that without having to force it? Maybe that was a good thing.

"Now, she is what she is. We'll have to wait to find out what she really is. I will start her training as a witch. You, on the other hand, know what you are, and we must return you to that. This is your afternoon training session. Let's get started."

"Do we pick up where we left off this morning?" I asked, knowing that it didn't really matter. This morning's session was just Master Thomas working through a litany of various spells and hand magic. As we went spell by spell, he provided an example, and then asked me to perform them. These sessions irked me more than a little. I knew each of these spells, and had performed most of them a couple of hundred times in my life. I knew how. That wasn't the problem. It was my performance that was lacking.

"No, let's start back at the beginning, with what comes naturally to you. Once you can control that, we will build upon that foundation."

With a little pat on the bottom, Samantha went back to Jen and Marie to have fun. I needed to return to my misery.

We had already tried this several times this morning. Each time, Master Thomas floated something in front of me and asked me to push it away. Each time I couldn't. This afternoon was no different. This time it was a dead branch with three lonely dead leaves clinging to it, not that there were many other options out there in the woods on a winter day. The cold winter winds had blown away most of the leaves and left the ground barren

I went back to basics, or what Master Thomas called basics, and closed my eyes. In my head, I imagined the object he held in front of me, the branch. I could see it clearly. That was never the problem. I even felt it. That wasn't the problem either. I could even feel the surrounding universe. That wasn't a problem anymore. It was at first, but not now. The problem was that the universe was a huge, knotted ball of string. The harder I tried to make sense of it, the worse it got. Like a demonic Rubik's cube that reshuffled itself when you were close to solving it, not that I was close to solving anything.

For this test, I didn't need to make complete sense of it. I just needed to imagine a wind projecting out away from me and pushing the branch. I focused, a term and state I had loathed, but now I knew was necessary.

"See the branch, Larissa," prompted Master Thomas.

"I do."

"Now, project out."

I squeezed my eyes harder, as if that would help, and I even felt my hand give a little shove forward, but I sensed nothing coming out. When I opened my eyes, I wasn't surprised to find nothing had moved. The dead leaves still dangled on the branch. They were taunting me. Maybe I should imagine the leaves are Jack, or better yet, Gwen.

"I need a booster shot," I mumbled at the sight.

"You need a what?"

I shook my head, disheartened by another failure, and explained weakly. "James, in the witches' camp, pushed me hard on the forehead when I had a problem focusing during his lesson on divination. It worked and brought everything into focus."

"Huh?" Master Thomas wondered aloud.

"I can see it, but... I don't know. The world around seems to be in so much chaos I can't even do the simple things that don't require me to pull on any of the strings. I can understand why the hard things being a problem, but the simple ones?" An involuntary huff escaped out from my mouth.

"Huh?" Master Thomas repeated.

"I mean, this is stuff I was doing long before you explained how to reshape the fabric of the universe to create new magic."

"Huh?" He repeated it for a third time, and this time I jerked around and looked right at the side of his face with an intensity that could have cut a diamond.

"Will you stop saying that?" I barked. "What is it?"

"Your booster shot idea," he said, as if he was questioning himself. "That might be a possibility here." Then he finally turned and regarded me, adding me to the conversation. "It is possible. Think of it as a more forceful form of consumption. We might be able to clear some of the clutter away, and you could..."

I reached over and grabbed him by the shoulders and screamed. "Do it now!" Then I closed my eyes and leaned my head toward him to give him a clear shot at my forehead. I wanted to feel his thumb's thump, like I had with James. All I felt was Master Thomas removing my hands off of his shoulders and placing them back down on my lap.

"Larissa, I am afraid that's not the solution to our problems. That will only clear the confusion in your head temporarily. It won't unravel that chaos that surrounds you. You may be able to do simple hand magic and some spells, but nothing complex and you absolutely won't be able to train for the test of the seven wonders. Not until we unravel things."

I felt what little hope I had inside shrink. I should have known it wasn't that easy. Nothing in the world of witches was. Make that nothing in my world was, but my mind hung on to a small piece of what Master Thomas had explained. "How long would it last? If you were to do it?"

"A moment. Maybe a few minutes to an hour," he shrugged. "It's hard to know. It depends on you and what is on your mind. Which it would help to know–"

"Don't start analyzing me," I interrupted. "Edward does enough of that as it is." I glanced over at Samantha playing with Marie and Jen. "It's not like it is any big mystery," I muttered.

"No, it's not. At least not to me. But we have to find a way to clear it, or you won't be able to address it."

"Thank you, captain obvious for pointing out the universe's catch-22." Realizing I snapped at my mentor, I jerked up straight and turned to him. "I'm sorry."

Master Thomas brushed it off with a smile. "It's all right. I've been waiting to hear a little of the old Larissa slip out. Maybe that would help, but," and he held up a hand to block any attempt I made to interrupt him, "if you want to talk about it, you can talk to me. I am a good listener, and I was there with you, so I would understand more than Edward or Mrs. Saxon may. It's just an offer, not a command."

I accepted it with a sheepish nod. I knew he meant well, and he was right. They all were. I was tired of being surrounded by so many people who seemed to know how to run my life better than I did. What made it even worse is they were right. But, it wasn't as simple as "do step a," and then "do step b", followed by "step c". I knew what my problem was. It was Nathan, and that ache I felt inside every time I looked at Samantha. His absence had created a hole that grew with every thought, and knowing about the war just multiplied the sense of dread I felt.

I used to feel guilty for hoping the vampires got a few shots in at the witches, but no longer. Well, that wasn't exactly true. I still felt guilty, and I hoped there weren't witches blindly following the orders of their council. Those were the ones I felt for. The ones that knew full well what they were doing were the ones that I hoped got what they deserved.

"Can we try?" I asked politely. "Even if it is just for a few minutes." I watched Master Thomas' face contort and twist as he considered my request. I needed to give my case a little booster to push him further to my side. "Perhaps feeling things flowing again would lead to better clarity."

"All right," he agreed reluctantly. "There may be potions that would extend things. Mrs. Tenderschott should be our next stop, but here goes nothing." James had used his thumb against my forehead, but Master Thomas gripped my head at the temples and boom. There it was, that wonderful nothingness. The lines of the universe were still the biggest knot I had ever seen, but inside, there was a section of nothingness. A spot not occupied by my larger task, or worry about Nathan, or schemes of how to put my family together, well not exactly. If I could find a way to make this clarity last longer, this might open a few doors.

"Now. The branch."

I didn't have to close my eyes this time. I saw it, I felt it, and better yet, I felt a force projecting outward from me. It wasn't as strong as before, but it clearly moved the dead leaves that dangled from the branch he levitated in front of me.

"Come on, you can do better than that," challenged Master Thomas.

"I wasn't trying. I just wanted to see if I could move anything."

"Really focus Larissa. See the branch. Feel its presence. Feel the energy surging inside you and project out. Push with your hands if you need to."

The way he treated me as a novice witch grated on my nerves. Determined to silence his doubts, I gracefully released a single leaf, sending it soaring high into the stratosphere. In that moment, I displayed not only raw power, but also an undeniable mastery over my abilities. I was proud of myself, and I had hoped he would be too. If he was, he didn't say anything. He didn't have a chance before another force sped past both of us and knocked the branch halfway across the clearing. We looked back toward its source and saw Marie and Jen with their hands over their mouths, and Samantha with her arms outstretched.

3

"Let's go. You're mine for a bit." Mrs. Tenderschott called through the spinning portal that just appeared in my room.

"But I'm not supposed to leave my room except for my sessions in the library." I pointed down at the floor to emphasize my point and left my Master Thomas chaperoned field trips out of it. I wasn't sure if they were public knowledge yet.

"Since when did you follow rules?" Lisa asked, poking her head through the open portal. Then she looked beside me and stumbled through the portal. "That can't be."

Samantha shuffled behind me to hide. She is not a shy child, though she hasn't really been around many people before, and definitely not someone that looked like Lisa.

"Jack," she called, and another familiar head poked through. He looked more stunned than Lisa as he stepped through.

Lisa stumbled a few more steps before she kneeled in front of me and peered around my legs to meet Samantha eye to eye. "She's precious."

"She's so b-b-big."

Lisa and I both gave Jack an annoyed look. Lisa turned her attention back to Samantha, holding out her hand. "I'm Lisa, a friend of your mom's."

"Sam," I said, looking down at the cowering girl. Her eyes were about to burst. I reached my hand down and rubbed the top of her head, and encouraged her to move away from her make-shift shield. "This is Lisa and Jack. They are both witches. They are both very nice." I winked at Jack.

"They are like us?" she asked timidly.

"Yep, just like us," I said, looking her right into her saucer sized eyes.

I looked at Lisa and added, "Mostly."

"Oh my god, she talks," exclaimed Jack. He quickly covered his mouth. He almost repeated the pool incident. This time he would have flown through the portal back into Mrs. Tenderschott's classroom instead of across the pool. Though I wasn't sure if Master Thomas' little booster he gave me was still working.

"Yes, she talks. Why exactly wouldn't she?" I asked. I think Jack realized how close he was to taking another flight, and held up his hands in defense.

"She's just so young," answered Lisa. She stood up, but still hadn't stopped smiling at Samantha. "I mean, she is what? A month old?"

"One month and four days."

"Accelerated," stated captain obvious.

"Yes, it would appear so," I responded to Jack. "Our best guess is she is five or six, and..." I ran across our room to my desk. The one I rarely used for homework. I threw open the same notebook that had been sitting there since I first arrived and tore out a piece of paper. I held that up away from me. "Watch this." I gestured towards Jack and Lisa, then towards Samantha. "Sam, knock this piece of paper out of mommy's hand, like you did the branch outside."

"You guys are allowed outside?" Jack asked, and I shushed him.

"Sam, go ahead. Knock this piece of paper out of my hand like you did outside with Master Thomas, Marie, and Jen."

Samantha held out both hands and at first, the paper waved back and forth. Then I felt the force push hard against it and it slipped out of my fingers.

"Holy crap!" exclaimed Jack.

"Hey, now. Language in front of my daughter, please." I scolded him.

"Sorry."

"Seriously Larissa. What Jack said. She can already do magic?" asked Lisa. Now it was her time to be wide eyed.

I nodded. "We," I looked at Mrs. Tenderschott because she was a part of this, "tested her two weeks ago and she is telekinetic. Just like me. That is all we know at the moment. We haven't tested anything else."

"Speaking of, grab your adorable little daughter and step on in. I have something that might help you with your magic." Mrs. Tenderschott disappeared through the portal and back into her room. Jack and Lisa followed her, keeping their eyes on us.

I grabbed Samantha by the hand and walked up to the portal. I looked at it, and the room on the other side. The next step I needed to take came with an uneasy feeling. So much so, I stopped and put my foot back down on the floor in my room. Mrs. Saxon had been clear when she restricted me to my room and the library. Any place outside of that was completely forbidden, as was talking to anyone else at the coven besides those instructors assigned to my training. Letting anyone else know I was out of Mordin, and here at the coven, was an absolute no-no. Master Thomas had my house arrest extended to a spot outside, but that was it. Going into a classroom and being around Jack and Lisa broke two rules at the same time. Breaking these rules would be Mrs. Tenderschott's fault, but even knowing that didn't silence that voice in my head, which was yelling at me to stop. Why was I having such a hard time with this, when just weeks ago, I practically dismantled Mrs. Saxon's runes to leave the coven against her will with everyone watching? Maybe that was why. Not to mention everything else that had happened.

"Come on," urged Mrs. Tenderschott.

"Does Mrs. Saxon know?" I asked, still unsure, and feeling like a prude.

"Well," thought Mrs. Tenderschott as she walked toward the spinning portal. She had a mischievous twinkle in her eye that I hadn't seen before. "She told me to fix you a potion. She didn't tell me I had to bring it up to you."

"And them?" I asked, remembering the stern warning about how dangerous it would be if something slipped and others found out I was here.

"Think about it like a jailbreak," Lisa said from behind Mrs. Tenderschott.

"Yep, that is what it is. A jailbreak. Rebecca isolated them to rooms away from the others, with access to a classroom or two for their studies. This is one of the classrooms, and I don't see any harm in letting the jail birds cross," reasoned Mrs. Tenderschott with a warm smile.

"Oh, but there is," I said, worriedly, as I stepped through the portal with Samantha. The aroma from her inventory of ingredients flooded our senses. It sent me down memory lane remembering the first time I walked in to here, but that trip was short-lived. As we walked further into the room, up to the front, another equally powerful stench overpowered them. It had to be a lesson gone bad. "The council is here... or at least Mrs. Wintercrest is here. She can't know I am here." I looked at Jack and Lisa and fretted. "You can't tell a soul you saw me or Samantha here. Promise?"

Lisa rushed over and hugged me. "We won't. Will you stop worrying? We kind of already knew." Lisa smirked at me.

"Master Thomas is conducting one of our classes in secret," added Jack.

"Well, that fink. He stressed many times how important it was to keep this all a secret."

"Larissa, relax," Mrs. Tenderschott said, as she pushed Lisa out of the way and hugged me. "No one is going to find out, and no one is going to see you here. The doors... are well... locked." She spun me around to face the back wall of her classroom where the doors should be, but there were no doors. As soon as I saw them, I giggled, and she spun me back around. "Now, just stop it. Where is that brazen young woman I knew that would break any rule placed in front of her?"

"That girl is gone. The price of breaking rules has cost her too much." My eyes looked away and avoided hers.

"Nonsense." Mrs. Tenderschott bent down and hugged Samantha. "Now give your auntie a big hug." Samantha didn't hesitate. She never did around her. She took to Mrs. Tenderschott like I did when I first met her. The woman had a disarming warmth. "I have something for you, too. It's up at the table."

I looked up at the front of the classroom at the infamous table that was the source of many a torture session when we were all trying to figure out just who and what I was. There, sitting in front of two stools, were two glasses. One was taller than the other, but there were two of them.

"Wait. I'm the one that needs the potion. Sam doesn't."

"Don't be silly," Mrs. Tenderschott said as she took her place on the other side of the table.

When I finally reached the stools, I knew what she meant about being silly. Mine was a potion. A vile smelling thing that looked worse than it smelled, if that was possible. Chunky red and brown. Like the leftovers from a horror film set.

The smaller glass had a sweet brown liquid in it topped with whipped crème. I lifted Samantha up on her stool, and she wasted no time running a finger through the whipped crème. She was born with a sweet tooth for food. I was the same way when I was younger, and somehow I recently rediscovered that. From time to time, I even stole a bite or two of ice cream from her bowl. I was still shocked it stayed down every time. Something had changed about me in that regard. I still didn't need to feed the traditional away, and hadn't developed the nerve yet to attempt a full meal of regular food. I doubted I ever would. Mrs. Saxon had worked out how to handle my needs in isolation better than I believed that cage in Mordin would have. One lukewarm glass of blood every three days. It worked, but wasn't as satisfying as the hunt and the kill, but it still provided what I needed. Theodora's private stash was hot and fresh, which made me a little envious of that life. This was like expecting filet mignon and getting ground chuck. It was still blood, but it didn't taste or feel the same going down. Marie was the lucky one. Jen and Kevin took her out on hunts. She was at least able to feel normal. I looked down at Samantha and remembered an earlier conversation. I had never let her see me feed, but I wondered. Should I test her next time to see if she can stomach a little sip? I shook that thought out of my head. If I was wrong, that would be a terrible experience for her, and who knew what she would think of her mother feeding on blood? We will keep it to hamburgers, ice cream, and the required vegetables for now, until she shows other vampire traits first.

"Go ahead, drink your hot chocolate," I said, giving her the permission she sat there and patiently waited for.

"Wait, she needs this... and this." Mrs. Tenderschott plopped a huge marshmallow in the middle of the mountain of whipped crème. Then she put a straw in the glass to make consuming the sugar rush easier. I was sure I was going to pay for this later.

An uneasiness overcame me when Lisa and Jack leaned over the table toward me. Both had their own cups in front of them. They were getting to enjoy the same treat Samantha was, but yet they kept glancing down at my glass, and then back at me. "What?"

Jack pointed down at my glass and asked, "You can't smell that?"

Oh, I could. I picked up a hint of it when I entered the room, and it got stronger the closer I got to it. Now, sitting there with it practically under my nose was torturous, but I did my best to act like I smelled nothing. Just once I wished a potion for me tasted good. "Smell what?" I said as I pushed it across the table.

"Nope. You have to drink it." Mrs. Tenderschott met me halfway, pushing the glass back to my side.

I looked down at Samantha and asked, "Want to trade?"

She gave me an emphatic shake of the head and took another long sip through her straw. I looked down at my glass, resigned to my fate.

"Can't you make a potion that tastes good?" I knew it was a fruitless question. Very few of the ingredients in the room smelled or tasted good, and combining them together just made them all worse. It was probably similar to that old saying, two wrongs don't make a right. In this instance, two piles of crap combined just make a bigger smellier pile of crap.

Mrs. Tenderschott replied by leaning over and pushing it closer to me.

I picked up the glass and held it up at eye level, trying to look through it. I couldn't see through the sludge. "Do I want to know what is in it?"

"Not before you drink it. Now go ahead."

Based on experiences, and what I knew about potions, that was probably for the best. I took another tentative look at my fate and then downed it. There was no point in just taking a sip. Knowing what it tasted like wouldn't make it any easier to drink. My iron clad stomach seemed more sensitive than normal. I blamed the human food I had been eating lately. It lurched at the intrusion. I held back my stomach's repulsive response and even faked a smile toward Jack and Lisa.

"So how long will it last?" I asked. That was a question I probably should have asked first.

"Not sure. I am not really sure it will work," replied Mrs. Tenderschott with a shrug of her shoulders.

"What? You don't even know if this will work?" I felt like a lab rat.

"Well," she started, and then looked at me, unsure. "You have always been a mystery. The combination of what you are always makes potions difficult. We never know if something will work until we try it. Why don't you try something?"

I stood up from the stool and backed away from the table. How to test it? I had countless options I could go with, but I felt I needed to start simple. That didn't mean I couldn't have a little fun with it. Focusing on the glass and the sludge that clung to its sides, I levitated it above the table, but I didn't stop there. The glass rose higher and drifted across the table, hovering over Jack and Lisa. That was where I used a little jerk of my hand to tilt it. A drop of the sludge slid toward the rim of the glass. Both scattered, knocking their stools over, and I returned the glass back to the table without spilling a drop.

Well, it worked, or it kind of did. After the glass settled on the table, I did a little test and wasn't too surprised to find everything still tangled up in chaos. Master Thomas appeared to be correct about this. Being right was a bad habit of his. His booster, and this potion, opened up some of my magic, but not all of it. That made me wonder about its limits. With a quick flick of my wrist, I produced a flame. It danced on the palm of my hand for a few moments before I let it turn into a ball that changed from bright red to blue. There was one more little trick I wanted to try, but not here. There was only one question that remained. "How long will it last?"

Mrs. Tenderschott shrugged. "Again, you are a mystery to us. In most witches, this could last a couple of hours, but don't fret." She walked over to a shelf to her left and retrieved a tray of glass jars that had a depressing familiar looking sludge in them. "I made extra so you can take it with you and drink it when you feel you need it. At least until you can do all this on your own."

"Larissa, do they know what has you all clogged?" asked Lisa.

"What doesn't have me clogged up?" I put air quotes around the phrase clogged up. It was really the best term to describe what was happening, and that was the best answer. It would seem everything does.

"But I don't understand," Lisa said, clearly confused as she walked back up to the table and sat on her stool.

"I don't either," added Jack. "You had it so together magically in New Orleans."

"Was it Mordin?" Lisa whispered, seemingly afraid to even say the name.

While that place definitely impacted me, it wasn't that. I knew what it was. Edward knew what it was, but I was sure it wasn't common news Mrs. Saxon shared around with everyone. Jack and Lisa didn't know I went back to find Nathan.

"I think that was it. Probably just the lingering effect of that place."

It was a flimsy reason, and I knew it, and by the way Lisa stared at me from the other side of the table, she knew it too. I needed to come up with something else to avoid digging a hole I couldn't get out.

"Larissa, what aren't you telling us?" Lisa leaned a little further over the table, pushing her point.

"Not a thing. I think you are right. It was Mordin. It was a dreadful place." My excuse crumbled right before my eyes. That didn't stop me from trying to add more details to prop it up enough for them to buy it and move on. "Dark, isolated, cold, and they block magic..."

"You can stop right there," Lisa interrupted me, and I saw the rest of it crumble to the floor. She wasn't going to buy this, no matter how much I tried to sell it. The thought of testing this potion again and using consumption on Lisa crossed my mind, but I thought better of it. That would only be temporary, and I couldn't bring myself to do it to a friend. Oh my God. Had I developed scruples?

"Chaos and disorder surround you. It's all a big mess right around here." Lisa waved her hands all around me.

"How can you tell?" Jack asked, looking at Lisa. Questions dripped from his eyes as he looked at me again. He practically stared a hole right through me with his intensity.

"It's something you can't see yet," explained Lisa.

"Why not?"

Lisa looked at me for help, but I let my eyes politely decline. She was on her own here. She said it, knowing that was a topic we needed to tread gently around, and it took the heat off me for a minute.

"You're not old enough?" she squeaked, scrunching up her face.

"You mean until I ascend?" Jack groaned.

Lisa just nodded, and Jack sank onto his stool.

"You only have two months," Lisa reminded him, but that didn't seem to improve his mood much. When she realized she couldn't console him anymore, she turned her attention back to me, much to my disappointment. I had hoped she had forgotten all about me. "Please tell me you and Nathan aren't fighting again. Larissa, he's a guy. He is going to do stupid stuff."

Lisa continued her rant, but I didn't hear any of it. My mind had checked out, and I looked at Mrs. Tenderschott. My eyes beseeched her for help. I could only hope she wouldn't decline my appeal like I had declined Lisa's just a few moments ago. From all appearances, she hadn't. There was a quick shake of her head at the question that we were both pondering, or had to be pondering. Could we tell them? That was an absolute no. We were bending Mrs. Saxon's rules enough already. That would shatter one. No one. Absolutely no one was to know what was really going on. Not with Mrs. Wintercrest and several members of the council here. There was too much to risk. Even Lisa and Jack knowing I was here was a huge risk that still made me uneasy.

"What?" Lisa abruptly asked. I think she finally realized we weren't paying any attention to her. "What happened?" Then, just as quickly as she had asked that question, Lisa seemed to find the answer on her own. Her eyes exploded open, wider than I had ever seen. Her brown eyes were lonely islands in a sea of white.

"Oh God!" she exclaimed and pointed in my direction. Then she repeated it, "Oh God!" with a hint of a wail. Lisa sprung up off her stool and ran around the table, practically tackling me with a hug. "I don't understand, but we can fix this. We can fix all of this."

"Fix what?" Jack asked, confused.

Mrs. Tenderschott and I both struggled to pry Lisa off of me. The emotionally charged room even had Samantha leaving her half full hot chocolate behind to wrap her arms around me.

"Nathan's not here." Lisa said. Her voice muffled against my shoulder.

"What? I don't understand." Jack looked around for answers.

"You of all people should–" replied Lisa, but Jack still stood there looking as clueless as ever. I was sure he felt my anguish. An emotion he probably chalked to any of the many events he knew about that could have, and probably should have, caused it. If he had known, he probably would have asked. I wouldn't have told him the truth if he did. I was still in the mode of the least they knew the better.

I hoped Lisa didn't really understand everything either, but I had a sinking feeling that somehow she did. There was more to this than her just putting two and two together. To truly make the leap to the truth, she would have needed help. That was assuming she actually knew the truth. It was entirely possible she had assumed that something else happened to Nathan. Like he had died in the skirmish shortly after I was taken, and before Mrs. Saxon saved everyone. A logical leap, and one that even just the thought of came close to breaking me, not that I wasn't already broken. That would explain her reaction.

"Do you know where he is? We can go get him." Lisa said as she finally released me. Well, sort of. Her hands traced down my arms until they reached my hands. She gripped them and looked deep into my eyes. Hers were compassionate and caring. I knew she meant it. She truly meant she would help in any way possible. Mine, I feared, were like a deer caught in the headlights. So were Mrs. Tenderschott's. We both knew we needed to know what Lisa thought she knew.

"It's all right. He will show up soon." I looked over her shoulder again at Mrs. Tenderschott for help. The vacant stare she returned told me she was just as lost as I was.

"Larissa!" Lisa jerked my hands. "How can you say that? It's dangerous for him to be out there with all that is going on. What if the witches attack New Orleans again? The only way to protect him is to bring him here."

Mrs. Tenderschott grabbed Lisa and turned her around, gently. "Lisa, why do you think they are going to attack New Orleans again?" When she asked, she glanced at me.

"Oh... I don't know. They did before. Jack and I both saw it start just before Mrs. Saxon pulled us back here. They might again."

Mrs. Tenderschott and I let out a collective sigh of relief. I even let a little air pass my lips.

"You saw it?" I asked and pulled her away from the table at the front and to the first row of tables. I pulled out two chairs, and she sat without a suggestion.

"Yes."

"What happened?"

Lisa pulled within herself. I had seen her do this before. She was remembering back to that day by taking herself back to it. Something she could do by tapping into a little of the dark magic she possessed. Her head looked up at the ceiling, then she spoke.

"It was only a few hours, maybe two, after they took you to Mordin. Jack, Laura, Apryl, and I were helping the wounded witches. More witches showed up, and we thought they were here to help. We were stupid enough to have some false hope that the council was going to look past the fact that these were rogue witches and actually help them. They didn't help. They didn't even come to the camp. They headed off into the woods. We saw flashes of every color and heard thunderous impacts and screams. Oh God, the horrible screams. Jack and Mike ran into the woods to find Nathan, but several witches attacked Mike before they made it too far. Jack defended him, but the attack eventually forced both of them out. After the witches left, Jack and I went and searched for Nathan. We didn't find him. We didn't really find any vampires that were still alive. Beheaded bodies littered the ground. We were still searching when Mrs. Saxon arrived at the farmhouse to bring us back here." Lisa's eyes cleared as she looked back at me.

"Larissa, we really tried to find him. We did. When Mrs. Saxon arrived, we told her what had happened and about Nathan, but she wouldn't let us go search again. We begged and begged. She told us he was still alive, and she would send someone to find him."

"Divination," I said, and Lisa looked back at me curiously. "That was how she knew. It seems Mrs. Saxon is rather expert at it, and she did send someone to find him. Jen and Kevin asked around and discovered he was the new coven leader."

Lisa let out a sigh, and her body shuddered. "Good. I was afraid he was still missing, and she was just telling us that to make us come back with her." Then she smirked and leaned forward, tapping me on the knee. "I used it myself to see you weren't going to see him later tonight. That was how I knew he wasn't here."

"Dang, you're getting really good at it."

"Practice," responded Lisa, while she polished her knuckles against her black hoodie. "But seriously. Let's go get him if you know where he is.

"What are you waiting for?" asked Jack. "The Larissa I know would have already yanked his ass back here."

"Well," I paused and wondered if I was going to cause any issue with telling them what I was about to. They already knew about the attack, and that he was okay. They don't know about the ongoing war between the witches and vampires, which, from all I was hearing, was a one-sided affair. My glance wandered over to Mrs. Tenderschott for any warnings as I started just in case my judgement was flawed. "I tried, and he wouldn't come back."

"What?" Lisa screamed, startling Samantha.

I picked her up and put her on my lap. It comforted her, but it comforted me more so. Lisa reached over and gave Samantha an apologetic rub on the arm. "We tried. Right after I gave birth to Samantha, Jen, Master Thomas, and I went back to New Orleans and found him in the mansion Jean ran the coven from. I tried to convince him to come home, but the attack by the witches, the one you saw, turned him against all of us. He doesn't trust any witches, even his mother, and he flatly refused to come back with us. Then he made us leave."

"You're kidding, right?" asked Jack.

I hugged Samantha a little tighter. "Nope. I wish I was, but I'm not."

Lisa pointed at me, and then stated, "That explains the chaos that surrounds you. That has to be it."

I nodded and then ducked my head. "That's what I think too, but I don't know what to do about it."

My head was still dipped down, with my chin buried on the top of Samantha's head. I gently kissed it. When I looked up, both Jack and Lisa were looking at Mrs. Tenderschott. "I'm sorry. There may be potions for matters of the heart, but there is nothing for this. She has no choice but to handle this the hard way."

"That's me, the hard way," I remarked.

"So, what now?" asked Lisa.

"Well, we wait." I didn't expand on what we were waiting for. Nathan? My magic? Some other miracle?

"Do you think he'll come back by himself?"

"I don't know." I didn't. It was one of a million things I didn't know. "I can only hope, but I don't know." I stood up off the stool, carrying Samantha. Her hot chocolate induced sugar rush had worn off, and she had become extremely comfortable and sleepy in my lap. "What I do know is I have an exhausted little girl here who needs a nap?"

Samantha offered a mild protest, but her own yawn ended it. Lisa walked over and gave me a hug. Jack acted like he wanted to do the same, but left it with a rub on the shoulder. "I'm sure Nate will come around. He has always been stubborn, but smart."

"I hope so." Hope was something I used to rely on, but lately it seemed so far from something real, I had lost my belief in it. Things that were concrete were where I focused. "I need to get this little girl back upstairs. Mrs. Tenderschott, could you?"

"Of course." She twirled open a portal into our room, and I stepped through it without hesitation. "Don't forget your goodies." Mrs. Tenderschott stepped through and placed the tray of glass jars containing all she had made of my little focus booster on the top of my dresser. I didn't want to forget those, but almost had. They were important to something I wanted to try later.

4

Oh, how I was jealous of my sweet little angel. She slept so soundly every night. It would be heavenly to close my eyes and drift away like she did, even if only for a few moments. Nights were the worst for me. Before, I had the activities on the roof to distract me. Even in New Orleans, my mind was constantly occupied. Even if some of that was self-inflicted drama, and lord knows, I was guilty of that from time to time. Now, there was nothing. Just me, holding Samantha as close as I could while she slept, and my nightly war against the thoughts that threatened to destroy my solitude. It was a battle I lost most nights. I even tried flicking through channel after channel of television shows with the volume down to avoid waking her. Nothing really helped. The thoughts always came. The hole where Nathan should have been always opened up, pulling me closer to the edge of a bottomless pit. My soul ached.

That was the most fitting description. It ached. I used to wonder if I even had a soul, being what I was and all, but losing Nathan like this answered that question loud and clear. I had one, and it was a large part of who I was, and every ounce of it was in pain. It screamed out for Nathan, and he wasn't there to answer. One night, I wondered if it might have been easier if he was truly gone. In some ways, it might. I would still miss him badly, but it would be easier to accept. Instead, he was out there choosing not to be with me. He was choosing to not be with me for a stupid reason that he was wrong about. Making matters worse, there were others manipulating him. They wouldn't let him open his eyes enough to see past all the lies. I knew in my heart if he did, he would come home, but I also didn't see that happening. Everything that had, and was, happening out there just fueled his anger and confusion. Like gas on a campfire. He was probably now a full on forest fire raging out of control.

I no longer wept with the ache. For a while, I thought I ran out of tears, but occasionally Samantha did something that would bring a tear or two of joy surging forward. I now believed the pain I felt was too deep for tears. That it was so deep that it suppressed the activity of crying, along with everything else, including my magic. All I could do was sit there, staring off into nothingness, letting the world whirl around me. That was me, a stone in a creek with the rapids of life crashing around me, wearing down my edges. That was even me when I held Samantha all night long. While I sat there, thoughts after thoughts flooded my mind. All about Nathan. All missing him. All tearing chunks at the edges of the hole I felt in my soul, making it larger and pulling me further into it. I needed him. I needed him with every fiber of my being, and so did Samantha. That always tore at me badly, but it wasn't the worst of all. What really tore large gapping chunks from the edge of the hole was how badly Nathan needed us. He really needed us. So much of his life had changed, and he needed us to help him adjust. He needed his family to show him the way, to show him why he was important, to show him we love him. To know we weren't there for him hurt me worst of all.

That was why I was sitting here pondering something that I knew was wrong. Well, wrong was relative. What I was considering was strictly forbidden, and it may be a moot point. I wasn't even sure it was possible. That didn't stop me from trying. I stood up and walked to the center of the room, still arguing with myself about what I was about to do. The argument wasn't about whether I should do this from a perspective of right or wrong. I had already rationalized that part of it, like I always did. I had concerns about being able to pull it off. That was why I leaned back and peeked with one eye when I spun my arm around and thought of the cove. There was a little spark and the hint of an opening, but I stopped before it fully formed. That was enough to answer my question. Mrs. Tenderschott's horrible tasting potion gave me enough juice to open a portal.

I looked at Samantha and knew this was for her. That was what I told myself, even though I knew full well this was also for me. Using some of my restored ability, I witch-whispered through the wall to Marie. "Can you come over?"

She entered my door in seconds. She and Jen were the only people Mrs. Saxon had excluded from her spell that locked my door. Everyone else that knew I was here was a witch, and could just use a portal.

She hugged me instantly, and I asked, "Can you watch her for a few minutes? Just in case she wakes up."

"Yes. Yes, of course," she answered, confused. Which I knew she would be.

"And don't tell a soul what you are about to see."

Now that request received a look even more confused than the first.

I held my hand out and thought about the mansion in New Orleans on Audubon, but stopped before my arm moved. One of the many nagging questions about my current state had taken over my mind, and I was glad it did. I might have done something completely foolish. Not that it would be the first time I had. I just needed to be careful. The stakes were way too high.

To solve my nagging problem, I went over and uncapped one of the jars Mrs. Tenderschott had prepared. The smell hit the room, and my stomach lurched. Marie covered her nose. Samantha was sound asleep, but even she turned away from it. I was sure she smelled something rotten in whatever dream she was having. To save them from any more stink, I picked it up and gulped it all.

Marie gagged. "How can you drink that?"

"It's not the worst thing I have had to drink around here," I whispered back, remembering all the other portions they had subjected me to since I arrived at the coven. And what was Marie complaining about? She had me drink water when that usually would have caused severe vomiting.

Now I felt I was ready and took my spot in the room and spun my arm around. A portal opened to the room with the large wooden throne.

"Wait! What?" Marie grabbed my arm. We both looked back to make sure Samantha hadn't woken up. She was still sound asleep.

My hand met Marie's on my arm. "I need to go look. I have to, and now that I sort of have my magic back, I can." Or I hoped I could. I didn't know how long this lasted. Nor had I tested out everything. "Um... I'm going to leave this open just in case. Don't let anyone come through it."

"Who would come through it?" Marie asked as I stepped through.

"Don't know."

That same smell of old blood hit me just like it had before. This time felt different, though. Before you felt someone was there, and the place looked lived in. Now it was desolate, and whoever had been here left in a hurry. Pieces of furniture were strewn around, and the grand glass doors that lead to the ballroom were shattered. Even the doors that lead from the ballroom out to the outside courtyard were just empty wooden frames. The wind whipped in through the openings.

I continued down the hall and past the dining room. If anyone other than Jean had ever lived in this place, I was sure there were many grand family meals around the large dark wood table that sat in the middle of the room. Probably a few Thanksgiving feasts with turkey, dressing, and all the trimmings. Feast in our world was slightly different, and I saw evidence that one had taken place here. The smell was rancid and old, but I still knew what it was. When I passed two full goblets of blood sitting on the table, I knew no one else was here. I grabbed one goblet; it was cold to the touch. I tried to swirl the contents around, but it had mostly congealed into some mixture of solid and liquid. It had been here for days, and its source was probably the rancid smell that wafted in from the kitchen on the breeze.

I went in the kitchen to check it out. Why? Who knows? Maybe on the off chance that Nathan was in there feasting on whatever was rotting. Let me take that back. Whatever had already rotted. A single deer, or what remained of a deer, lay on the floor with the stains of its own blood pooled around it. Maggots feasted on what remained of its flesh. I sat there and watched them for a while. Their movements were hypnotic. Chaotic order. The mass moved around with a purpose. Maybe that was why they caught my attention. The order. The way the universe used to look to me. Now it was anything but. And there in that horrible smelling place, I found an example of what I was missing. That was probably why I didn't see him off in the corner, feasting on a rat that came for some of the deer's entrails. I didn't see him, but I heard him.

"You!" he screeched, as he stumbled out of the darkness. The rat dangled from his grasp. A finger on his other hand pointed at me as he screamed again, "You!"

When he crossed over into the moonlight and tripped over the deer carcass, I saw who it was and wanted to scream it back at him. It was him. Mr. Top Hat from my last visit. We didn't exactly leave on good terms, and we still weren't. I retreated from the kitchen to create some distance. But he kept coming, stumbling, and wobbling like a drunk, but he wasn't. He was weak and injured.

"You have the nerve to come back here?" he asked, falling from the door frame to the table. He knocked both goblets of stale blood to the floor. He paid no attention to the puddle of blood on the floor or the loud clang they made on impact.

"I'm looking for Nathan Saxon. Where is he?" I asked while I gave up more ground, backing into the hallway.

Mr. Top Hat just chuckled at my question.

"Please, tell me where he is."

Now out in the hall, he braced himself against the wall and lunged toward me. I stepped back, and he fell flat on the floor at my feet, and coughed, "No."

His bony hand reached out and tried to grab my ankle as I stepped back again. It shook and then fell to the floor, along with his head.

"Tell me where he is," I demanded again.

He pushed up off the floor and made it up to one knee. With labored movements, he lifted his head and threw it back proudly, and grinned widely at me. "Why? So, you can kill him? You made a mistake coming back here."

I was about to explain that I wasn't there to hurt or cause Nathan any harm, and I wasn't like the other witches. Not that I felt I could convince him I was the solution, but maybe I could convince him I wasn't part of the problem. He was probably there when I was taken prisoner by my own kind. I could have reminded him of that to help, but I never had the chance. Before I could even utter one word, he yelled, "Witch!"

The building came alive with movement. Vampires rushed in through the broken doors and windows. Maybe half a dozen or more. I didn't stand still long enough to count them. The time for talking had passed. I hoped they were as weakened as Mr. Top Hat, but if they were, they didn't show it. They were fast on my heels, and I was moving as fast as I could in those first five steps. A hand scratched down my back and I spun around. My instincts took over, and thank God Mrs. Tenderschott's potion didn't fail me. Two large orange balls of fire left my hands, hitting and sending their targets back against the wall.

In the impact's flash I saw five vampires, counting Mr. Top Hat, standing ready to fight. I felt a sickening wave come over me. Is this all that's left of the New Orleans coven? Please God no. I needed to know. "It doesn't have to be this way. Just tell me where Nathan Saxon is."

"It won't be that easy. Your kind has to pay." Mr. Top Hat declared with a finger pointed right at me. All five crept closer, ignoring the two balls of fire I had in my hands, ready to launch.

I stepped back each time they stepped forward. We had already passed the ballroom and were now entering the room with the wooden throne. The spinning portal I left cast everything in a golden glow. Marie watched through the opening and acted like she wanted to step through, but I shook my head.

"Look," I decided to try some diplomacy. "I know what the witches did." I needed to talk fast. We were no longer in the hall, and the angry horde had fanned out around me. "And they were so wrong. I promise you, in the end, we will hold them responsible, but–"

So much for diplomacy. Two vampires lunged at me from the left, and as I turned to fend them off, sending them flying against the wall, the two to my right took their shot. I still had the balls of fire in my hands and backhanded them in their direction. Mr. Top Hat rushed me from the front and actually got a hand on me before my telekinesis sent him flying up to the ceiling. On his way down, I gave him a more traditional punch to remind him I was also a vampire, and just as strong as he was. He landed on the floor with a thud. Another hand grabbed my shoulder, and I pushed it away just in time for two more to grab me. I looked back at the portal and Marie had stepped one foot through. She knew it at the same time I felt it. I was losing this fight. I went limp and fell to the floor, slipping through their grasp. Then I threw myself toward the portal, while sending a few fireballs in their direction. That slowed them down, but didn't stop them. Hatred, which was a powerful emotion, fueled them.

With a strong wind, I shoved Marie Norton back through the portal. I followed quickly behind her, but not before sending another fireball back toward the vampires. I didn't realize how close one of them was. He reached for me but missed. When I fell to my floor, I spun my arm to close the portal, and it snapped shut. His severed arm fell to the floor, and Marie shrieked, waking up Samantha. I used a quick sleeping spell, and whispered, "sonno." She fell back asleep, and I felt like the worst parent in the world. I just used magic on my child, but that felt like a better option than letting her see the severed limb flopping around on the floor. I opened a small portal to the middle of the Mississippi River and let it jerk and jump its way out before I closed it.

"Well, that didn't work how I expected." Well, not entirely. Something felt better, though. At least for a second during the heat of the fight, I felt in control. More than I had when I drank the potion earlier. Maybe it was just the adrenaline talking.

5

"What did you expect to find?" Marie asked, almost scolding me.

"Nathan." That was the obvious answer, which Marie had probably already guessed in her head.

"I could have told you he wasn't there," she answered, and then grabbed me by the hands and pulled me over to the chair. I sat without being told to. This felt almost natural, and why wouldn't it? She had done this many times over the last seventy years when we needed to have a serious talk about something.

"Jen and Kevin heard weeks ago that what remained of the New Orleans coven had splintered and left the area. Only a few stragglers remained. They checked around, and other than a few that showed up at other covens where they had family members or friends, they didn't know where they went."

Hopelessness dragged my head down, but ever the positive one, Marie reached under my chin and propped it back up. Her black eyes mastered what I couldn't. She could show emotions, deep, powerful emotions. I lost count of how many times I tried to replicate her looks in the mirror, but each time I saw the same expressionless eyes staring back at me. She told me once that how she did it was her little secret. Whatever the secret, it worked every time, and I felt her compassion wrap me in a warm blanket.

"Larissa, relax. Nathan is still alive. You saw him when you went back there, and since then, the Jen and Kevin have heard mention of him. They just don't know where he is. It's only a matter of time before he shows up, and you and her," she turned around to look at Samantha, "can be the family you all need to be." Her hand brushed up my cheek and then ran through my hair as she stood up in front of me. "In the meantime, take it easy and try not to mess things up here. Mrs. Saxon was awfully nice to take you back in. Don't betray her trust by breaking her rules. What you did tonight was stupid. What would happen if you got caught?"

I doubted it would surprise Mrs. Saxon at this point. There wasn't really a rule left of hers I hadn't broken, but there was something about confessing that to Marie that I just couldn't make myself do.

"I know. It was stupid," I conceded to avoid a lecture. Maybe it was, but I had to try, and if I had any new information about where to look, I would try again. Where could I find any new information? Now, that was the question.

"Good," Marie said. "Now, are you going to try anything else stupid tonight?"

I shook my head while I looked past her at the stack of books still on the floor next to my bed. The same ones Edward had sent up months ago with that huge warning. That warning still played in my head, but it was a little softer than before. Probably because I had made a few trips already, but those were just trips out of my body. Controlling where I was going was another question. I think I sort of understood how to move around, or at least I had the basics of it. But the biggest question was buried in books one and three of that stack. That was how to find someone and then how to get to them. Nothing we had discussed so far with Mary Smith came close to covering that. It would seem I have some reading ahead of me tonight.

"So, how do we get another chair?" Marie looked around. If she had understood how this place worked, she would have been more specific with her request. A single wooden chair appeared right next to her as soon as she finished the question. "Oh, wow!"

"You get used to it." I remembered my first few days here. I wasn't surprised when the chair arrived, but her request surprised me.

"It's not what I had in mind, though, but I guess it will do." Marie inspected the chair and then pulled it to the center of the room.

"Well, what did you want?"

"Something comfortable enough to sit down and have a good old-fashioned movie night on while I keep you out of trouble," Marie said with a wink. My plans for a night of reading were no longer an option, and I knew better than to protest. Her little statement—to keep you out of trouble—told me she would view any protest I made as me trying to get her out of here so I could get into more trouble.

"Okay then." I thought of a small comfortable loveseat, and the chair turned into a comfortable cushioned seat for two with pillows. If we had more room, I would have gone for a whole pullout sofa so we can get comfy, but this would work. "Is that better?"

"Yep." She plopped down on it and patted the cushion next to her. I rolled my eyes and took a seat next to her. She leaned against its arm, and I leaned against her. This was a common arrangement for us. We had settled in, and I was getting comfortable, just as Marie sat up a little and looked around the room. "Where's the remote?"

Now, for a while, that would have been a good question. I never used it, but lately I needed it, and I knew exactly where it was. It was on the nightstand next to the bed. I summoned it, but Marie snatched it in mid-air before I had a chance to catch it. Not that there was any question who was going to be in charge of picking what we watched.

Throughout the night, we watched five movies, all from the 1930s and 40s. I don't know why, but it's comforting to watch one of those movies. When Samantha woke, she was surprised and happy to see Marie there. To her, she was like a grandmother. I guess she was, kind of. She had been a mother to me. At some point, when I had better control of my magic, I needed to introduce her to my actual mother.

After a rather silly breakfast, Marie offered to entertain Samantha while I did what I told her was studying for my magic training. I told her I had a ton of reading to do for my next lessons with Master Thomas and Mrs. Saxon. It was related in a way. It just probably wasn't something we would cover for quite a while. Our focus was the basics, and this reading was anything but basic.

At my desk, with the giggle crew behind me, and some talking pig on the TV, I cracked open the first of the seven books in the stack. This was the second time I had cracked it open. The first time was just to skim through it. The content and the warning fascinated me. Then it was my path to find Marie. Now it was my path to find Nathan, and I was doing more than skimming the pages. I couldn't have done much more before. I didn't understand enough yet. Now I knew more. Did I know enough? That was the question.

My first two hours of reading told me one thing. There were dozens of ways to find someone, but each had its own challenges. It was easy to find a blood relative. There were simple spells you could use to find out if they were alive, and even where they were. That had me thinking. If you knew where they were, would you really need astral projection to go to them? Couldn't you just use a portal to go see them? Heck, just get a train ticket. That might be a simpler approach, but as with everything, there was a challenge. If you weren't familiar with the area and couldn't visualize it, you couldn't open a portal to it. My train ticket idea sounded better all the time.

For those that weren't blood relatives, which would include Nathan, it was slightly more complicated. Which is exactly what Edward told me before. You could use a memory of the person and track their aura, but that was extremely difficult, and even the book contained several paragraphs of warnings. It was everything from some have similar auras to issues with nailing down the time and place of the memory.

The method I read that held some hope was called, "Blood of my Blood". The name initially sounded more fitting for a vampire related spell, but after I read it, the name made sense. You had to combine biological material of the person you sought, or that of a direct blood relative, with a potion. The ingredient list of the potion wasn't that daunting. Even if it was, I wasn't about to let something like that stand in our way. This held too much promise for me to dismiss it. I had to imagine there was a hair or something in his room down in Mrs. Saxon's apartment. Then it hit me, and I felt stupid. I looked back at Samantha, who was coloring with Marie. We had a blood relative, and a source of his blood.

Now, if we ignored my current problems with magic and my complete lack of confidence with potions, then we had a solution. Or make that part of a solution. Getting back was a problem. It appeared you were all on your own and your astral projection skills. The last two books in the stack of seven covered that topic. I had to get through four books to reach those two. I wanted to skip ahead, but a little voice, Edward's, stopped me and brought me back to Earth. The weight of his warning pressed down on me firmly. Playing with the unknown seemed dangerous, not that I wasn't one to take risks or leap before I looked, but that was the old me. This was the new Larissa. One that was a little less impulsive than before. I had a lot more at stake now, and was going to have to do this by the book. That meant I had a lot of reading ahead of me, but that reading would have to wait until later this afternoon. I had a morning session with Master Thomas, then therapy with Edward. Oh, the joys of my daily schedule. What I wouldn't give to be back in classes again.

Resigned to have a day that felt just like the one before it and the ones before that, I walked over to the tray of jars and opened another booster to help me with the simple things. I still hadn't figured out how long the effects lasted. I drank one before my little adventure and then, for the rest of the night and morning, I didn't really have any troubles. The entire time I was reading, I never touched a page to turn it. I just did it using magic. It was my way of testing to see if I still had it. If I was going to have to rely on this, I needed to know its limits. Even after three glasses of this goop, I could honestly say the taste hadn't grown on me. If possible, it got worse the longer it sat there.

It wasn't more than a few moments before a portal opened in the room and Master Thomas walked in. He, nor Mrs. Saxon, bothered using the door, not wanting anyone to see them coming in and out. I was still the biggest secret in the coven, or make that one of the secrets. There were a few others besides me.

"It's a good thing I wasn't getting dressed," I remarked, half joking, but half not. There was a frustration building from my house arrest. It just added on to the frustration of not being able to control my magic. Both were freedoms I had taken for granted until they were taken away from me.

"I listened in and heard Samantha and Marie, so I figured it was safe." He said as his glance regarded Marie. I knew what the question was on his mind.

"I opened a portal for Marie. You can relax."

Marie said nothing. Thank God.

Master Thomas walked over to the tray and inspected the three empty jars. He was even brave enough to take a sniff from one. An act for which the putrid odor richly rewarded him. I had to give him credit; he held back the urge to vomit like a champ, holding his mouth shut through two lurches. At least he didn't have to drink it.

"So, these actually work?" He gagged his way through the question.

"Surprisingly, yes." I floated the book I had on the desk back to the stack next to my bed. Master Thomas appeared to be amazed.

"How powerful are the effects?" He put the last jar down and tightly screwed on its top.

"Well. I can do most of the basic stuff, but that is about it. The world is still chaos."

"Crap."

I heard it, but couldn't believe what I heard. Master Thomas just swore under his breath. I knew what he was hoping. It was the same thing as I was. If it cleaned up that side of the magical world for me, we could finally get into the training I really needed.

"Sorry," I said, feeling the need to apologize. It appeared I wasn't the only one growing frustrated with the current situation.

"Oh no," he quickly corrected me with a hand wave, and then pulled a handkerchief from the pocket in his red suede jacket. He dabbed along the edges of his mouth and then replaced it. "It's not your fault, and it's only temporary."

I kept expecting to hear him utter, "I hope", but he didn't. He straightened up his posture, almost like righting himself, and took a few steps from the tray of offending liquid. "We should take advantage of it, though. Magic is like a muscle. The more you use it, the stronger it is. Maybe this," he pointed with a thumb back over his shoulder at the tray, "can be a bridge to make you right as rain."

6

After a surprisingly uplifting morning session with Master Thomas, I survived another session on the couch with Dr. Edward. The magic session was uplifting in that I could actually do something. I was sure the potion of rot Mrs. Tenderschott had prepared for me was responsible. Nevertheless, it was something. I felt... normal.

My session with Edward went like the others, and big surprise, we had a breakthrough. The source of all my problems stemmed from the emotions I felt when Nathan rejected me. What an astute observation and take away from our many sessions. I had to wonder if Edward had read any Freud books since our last session. What I needed to know now was how to fix it? Other than the obvious, go find the boy, yank him back here, bring his heart back around to some sense of reality, stop the war, replace the supreme, and save the world from complete and utter chaos. That seemed simple enough.

I didn't tell him that I saw that as the only path to fixing my issues. I was still a little leery of my newfound trust with Mrs. Saxon, and yes, I absolutely believed Edward was reporting back to her. I knew he was. They discussed my issues openly in front of me. I had already suggested going to find Nathan and bringing him back more than once to Mrs. She warned sternly against that. It wasn't a–you can't leave the coven–warning. It was more of one of those very mature–patience will win the day–warnings. The problem was, I didn't have that kind of patience.

What I asked Edward for was help to compartmentalize, or better yet, isolate all this junk in my head so I could clear away some of the clutter and open things back up. I wasn't so naïve to think that I could go get Nathan in my current state. My last little side-trip reinforced that. Just like any good therapist, Edward turned around and asked me how I thought I could clear my mind. Thank God I wasn't actually paying him. At the end of our session, he gave me a few books. Spiritual text, he believed, might help center me. As soon as I saw the dust covered jackets, I kind of blocked out anything else he said about them. I already had some light reading that I felt was more important.

My afternoon session with Master Thomas was outside again. Another detail that made it up lifting. I had grown tired of my own four walls. Not that I couldn't change them or expand them anytime I wanted. It was the air inside that was becoming too familiar for my liking. Mrs. Saxon was out there too, but not to teach. She was there to spend time with Samantha while she cast disapproving looks in my direction each time I stumbled over something easy. Toward the end of this session, I found the expiration period of Mrs. Tenderschott's potion. It was about six hours. As it wore off, I kept trying little things. Some worked, and some didn't.

At the end of its effectiveness, I felt adventurous and when no one was looking; I attempted to throw a combination of symbols like I learned from my father's notes, just to see if I could with what little I had left. It had come easily for me down in New Orleans, but it wasn't like riding a bike. I needed to see the symbols and the fabric of the universe they rode on. I needed to see the shape of the lines it created as I conjured it, but now all I saw was a tangled mess. That didn't mean I didn't try. I went for the lunar spiral and the chalice. Neither of which I had tried before. Even just by themselves. I felt these were safe to try. The ones I knew well were all combat or defensive symbols. If something went wrong with one of those, who knew what would happen? These, I doubted anyone would even notice, and if they worked, maybe they would help. Both were related to different parts of a woman's connection with nature. I felt, or hoped, they would help strengthen what remained of that connection I used to have. But there was another part of it, too. Intuition was one of those natural abilities more associated with women. These were amplifiers of sort for it along with mindful subconscious connections and psychic abilities. Each seemed like it led to a clearer mind, and maybe, just maybe, those would offer me some clarity here. At least that was what I had hope. My father's journal had many entries around these and his usage of them. They were a way to clear his palette in between complex spells that had many steps. That was kind of what I needed, and I felt it was worth a chance. What did I have to lose?

My conjuring was rather embarrassing, and it proved I needed more practice at this, and possibly more of that pungent booster. The chalice is a cup. Basically, a drinking glass with a stem, and the lunar spiral looks like the side of a snail's shell. The best –dad please forgive me– I could do was replace the actual vessel on top of the stem with the spiral. Who knew if the quality of the combination impacted its effectiveness? Maybe it was like a potion. Miss the mixing instructions by just a bit, or maybe a stir too many, and poof, you have complete and utter crap. I had six more jars of crap up in my room.

I made room for the combination in my head and visualized it. I waited for it to draw itself repeatedly, faster on each pass, but all it did was hang there. I had almost given up when I remembered the advice Mrs. Saxon had given about Nathan. Patience. Why did that show up now? I didn't know. I checked over my shoulder to ensure she wasn't watching me or planting the suggestion as a caution. But she was off playing hide and seek with Samantha and Jen Bolden. When I focused back on the symbols, they hung there burning. A wave of excitement came over me, along with various questions. Was it possible that one of the symbols, or the combination, was what brought up the advice from Mrs. Saxon at just the right time? That was too corny and maybe I was reaching, but it was possible. Just like the calming effect I felt come over me. Was I relaxed because it seemed I did something, or was this the effect of what I did? Either way, I would take it. It wasn't the most powerful of spells, but it was something. I looked again at the fabric of the world, and it was still jumbled in front of me. There were a few offshoots from the rats-nest that tried to reach out and surround me in something that looked round. As it did, I thought about what it could mean. The shape was always representational of what it was. Attacks were sharp waves that radiated out. Defensive were surrounding shields. This was a cocoon of sorts, protecting me, but protecting me from what? The mess that was my life?

The thoughts and darkness that had consumed me for weeks moved aside and allowed a calming feeling to enter. I did it. That had to be it. It was small, but I still did it. The lines surrounded me tighter, but I didn't let that concern me. The calming feeling inside grew, and I even felt my body relax. A voice inside, one I didn't recognize, but one that was soothing to hear, told me the order of my life. It was Samantha, my magic, and then Nathan. Then, just as clearly as it told me the order, it told me not to worry about any of it. Nature had a way, and no matter what I did, I couldn't change it. Things will happen when they happen.

I heard it. I understood it, and even more important, I believed it. I completely believed it. Like a compass needle pointing the direction for me to follow. Even then I saw some strings of the mess in front of me untangle themselves and lay down, back where they should be. This was just a stupid random test of myself, but it had accomplished so much more than I had expected. With all the searching and asking of others, the answer was just this, but I didn't fret over not realizing it myself. I even laughed. No one else made this suggestion either. Of course, why would they? Only my father knew how to do this. That pride I felt before about all he had accomplished welled up inside. This was great, right until I heard a second voice, this one I clearly knew to be that belonging to Nathan Saxon. It was full of panic and pain, and it said two words: "Help me!"

The sound of his voice gave me life, but his tone and words took it away just as fast. It both lit an inferno inside me and froze me to my core, all at the same time. I collapsed into a dizzying spin. I don't remember hitting the ground. As far as I knew, I was still falling. In the distance, I heard Samantha cry a very weak, "Mom?" I couldn't respond from where I was. I couldn't even see her. It was all black.

7

The next sight I saw was the ceiling of my room. I was lying there on my bed. Something I never ever did. Samantha was sitting next to me, rubbing my forehead, and looking down at me. She looked concerned. Her eyes were red, and tears streamed down her face. One hung on her chin. I reached up and softly brushed it away. "Hey. I'm okay."

She fell down on the bed and hugged my neck. "You scared us."

"You scared all of us," repeated Mrs. Saxon, who watched from the corner of the room.

I sat up, still holding Samantha, who, if my imagination wasn't playing with me, had gotten taller. A lot taller. I had to swing her legs beside me as I sat up. No one else was in the room. Just Mrs. Saxon and Samantha, and that felt a little odd. I didn't know why. Who was I expecting to be there? I thought, and my mind still felt somewhat clear, but there was something there. Something I couldn't put my finger on. It wasn't a thought or a memory. Just something on my mind, as cliché as that sounded.

"Sorry, I don't know what happened."

"Not a problem," Mrs. Saxon said as she walked over to the bed. Samantha let go of the python grip she had around my neck and sat next to me. Then Mrs. Saxon sat on my other side. What a sweet family portrait this was. Three generations of Saxons. Well, maybe not. I wasn't officially one, since Nathan and I weren't married—yet. I was his baby momma. Which was a term Mrs. Saxon hated. I hadn't told Samantha who her father was yet. So, she had no clue Mrs. Saxon was her grandmother. That was something I wanted to wait to do until Nathan was here. Again my, probably stupid, desire for Samantha to learn about her father from her father. The only things ruining this perfect picture were the tears running down Samantha's cheeks and the look in Mrs. Saxon's eyes.

"What happened?" I turned and asked the only person in the room who likely knew or had a good chance of knowing.

Then I saw it. Another first. The first time Mrs. Saxon looked past me to my daughter, my much older looking daughter who looked about eight years-old now, and shared a knowing look with her. Now I knew it. Everyone knew what had happened, except me. As I looked at Samantha again, and brushed her long red hair over her ear, I wondered exactly how long I had been out.

"Well," started Mrs. Saxon, who fidgeted. "The better question is, what do you remember?"

What did I remember? Now that was a good question. Not a whole hell of a lot. Wait. That wasn't right. I remembered a few things. "We were outside doing training with Master Thomas, and you two," I pointed back and forth between Mrs. Saxon and Samantha. "You were playing hide and seek in the woods." And that was about it. Every time I tried to connect the dots between that moment and when I woke up here. It was like someone had erased a portion of my memory. "Then I woke up here."

"Nothing else?" asked Mrs. Saxon.

I shook my head while biting my lip. Why did I have a feeling that wasn't a good thing?

"What if I was to tell you, you had a magical overload and crossed into something you weren't ready for and passed out?"

"I'd say... it's not the strangest thing I've heard," I admitted reluctantly, and felt an uneasy inkling that this wasn't even the strangest part of this event. "With everything going on with my magic, I guess anything is possible." I shrugged. "A magical overload?"

"Yes, it can and does happen, but I didn't tell you the best part." Mrs. Saxon said with a smile, a proud smile at that. I felt Samantha squirm around to face me. "Samantha caught you. She saw you fall and caught you with magic and lowered you lightly down to the ground."

"You did?" I spun around. She sat there with a wide grin and then grabbed my hands.

"I did. I did it just like you and Master Thomas told me. I imagined a rope and wrapped it around you and pulled until you stopped."

"Oh my god," I hugged her. My little girl was growing up so fast, and becoming quite an accomplished little witch. Then I remembered where I last saw her standing, and let go of her. "Wait, you were off in the woods. You had to be a couple hundred feet away from where I was standing." I looked back and forth between the two of them, confused. To do something like that, that quick, over that distance was a truly remarkable feat. I wasn't even sure I could do something like that when everything was working right.

"She did, and yes, it was that far."

"Woooow," I said and turned back to Samantha. "Very nice." She was so proud; she could barely keep still. "Well, thanks for saving old

213

mom out there. I can't promise it will be the last time. I have a history of doing stupid things." That got a laugh from Samantha, and behind me, I heard a little snicker, which annoyed me and caused me to turn back to Mrs. Saxon.

"So, speaking of doing stupid things, what exactly did I do? I'm fairly sure I don't want to do it again?"

"Well, that I'm not exactly sure." Mrs. Saxon patted me on the leg. "See, after Sam caught you, I placed a block on your memories to stop any further damage."

I had to shake my head and rub my eyes at that. "You put a block to stop damage. What kind of damage?"

Mrs. Saxon got up off the bed and walked over to Samantha with a hand extended. She accepted it. Then she spun her other arm around and opened a portal. "Samantha, I need to talk to your mother for a minute. Why don't you spend some time with Mrs. Tenderschott? I think she wants to show you your first potion."

I heard Mrs. Tenderschott laugh and call Samantha in through the portal. My girl, my growing girl, practically ran through the portal, which closed as quickly as Mrs. Saxon had opened it.

"Is it me, or is she almost a foot taller than just a few days ago?" I asked, almost amazed at what I had just seen. Just last month, I held her in my arms for the first time. She took her first steps a few days after that. Her first words came later that same day.

"So, it isn't just me?" Mrs. Saxon asked, still staring at the space where the portal had been. "And her control of magic is advancing fast. She is easily where someone should be at age ten."

"She is my little girl," I remarked, trying to be cute and humorous, but it fell flat. Mrs. Saxon's face turned serious as she looked back.

"I asked her to go someplace else because the only way to find out what you did to put yourself in that state is to unblock your memories of that moment."

"Which... I'm guessing is slightly dangerous?" Trying to make the leap across the enormous cavern left in Mrs. Saxon's explanation.

"More than slightly dangerous. It puts you right back where you were just before your brain shut down," she explained.

Okay, so that sounded more than just slightly dangerous. I did something that overloaded me and put me out, and the only way to find out what I did was to return to the moment it happened. That would be a big no, or make that it should have been a big no. Except, I needed to know what it was, so I wouldn't do it again. I hopped up off the bed and started pacing while biting on my thumbnail, something I hadn't done since, well, long before I became a vampire. My mother used to jump me for the nasty habit, but it was something I did when I was nervous, and yep, I was extremely nervous at the prospects of what we were discussing.

"Larissa, you don't really have anything to worry about. I will be right there with you and will stop things before it becomes too much for you."

Well, that sounded simple enough, but it didn't keep my mind from racing through all sorts of crazy events and outcomes. "What if you can't stop it before it overloads me again?" I asked, as if I knew how this worked.

Mrs. Saxon stood there as confident as ever. Her posture was straighter than any vampire I knew. With her arms crossed and without a hesitation, she replied, "I can, and I will. Trust me."

My mouth opened, ready to mouth my agreement, but second thoughts kept speeding in. It was those that fueled what finally came out of my mouth. 'What if I get overloaded right from the beginning and it can't be stopped because it happens immediately upon starting? What about that?'

"Come now," she looked down her nose at me. "You don't think I would have put the block so close to the event, do you? I'm a smarter witch than that." She approached me, hand extended, just like she had Samantha a few moments earlier, and then led me back to the bed. I was still making a meal out of the thumbnail on my other hand when I sat.

"Try to relax," she suggested, and then smirked at herself. "I know. You are tired of hearing that. I'm going to enter your memories. You won't feel anything." She placed both of her hands against my temples. "Let's take a walk through your memories," she whispered and closed her eyes.

"Wait! This is going to work, right? I mean, you said you see events before they happen all the time, so you know this is going to work out, right?" It was a fair question. The woman had told me before she knew all the trouble I was going to cause, and she already knew how things would end.

"This isn't a big enough event on the road for me to even see, so it's nothing to worry about."

"The road analogy again? I get it."

Her eyes were still closed, but she smiled pleasantly. "I see someone taught you well. This isn't even a pebble on that road, so that should tell you something. Now let's start."

Her hands pressed lightly against my temples. "Wait. I have one more question. Why didn't you see it at least coming?"

"Not even a spec of sand on the road of your life. Now, stop delaying us. Close your eyes and follow me."

8

I'm not sure I really had a choice, and If I did, I wasn't sure she would have waited for me to make it. Before I knew it, the room disappeared, and we were back out in the clearing. I felt the sun from the unseasonably warm day baking down on me, but that was it. The rest of the world was still, or make that frozen.

"Now, I am going to release your memory a little at a time," Mrs. Saxon said from behind me, where she and Samantha were playing hide and seek. "Just let it go, but tell me what you feel." She approached me, her voice growing nearer with each word, and then she walked in front of me. "I will see what you see, but I cannot feel what you feel. I need you to tell me, so I know when to stop. Okay?"

I guess. It wasn't like I could answer her if it wasn't. She placed her hands against my temples, like she had before, and the world slowly came to life. A light breeze passed by, and then it picked up a little brisker. It carried the precious laugh of my daughter, which at first sounded like it was in slow motion, but then took on its normal cherub tone. I watched as my hands moved, and then an image appeared in my head. A symbol. Wait no, two runes combined, very poorly might I add, but what were they. Everything paused again with the image in my head.

"Now, what is that?" Mrs. Saxon wondered aloud.

Two runes combined, I thought, hoping she could hear me.

"I see."

She could. That was good to know.

"But why? Why would anyone do that, and what symbols are they?"

It was something my father did. I read about it in his journals and did a little experimenting on my own. It allows you to...

"Combine the power of two or more runes," Mrs. Saxon completed my thought, and then had one of her own. "Fascinating," she said with all the wonder of a child that just saw a bird flying for the first time.

Now I just need to figure out what the two symbols were.

"I might have an idea," replied Mrs. Saxon. In a flash, I saw the lunar spiral appear all on its own. Then it came to me, and since she was reading my thoughts, Mrs. Saxon knew what I saw as well.

"It's crude, but yes, that was it. The lunar spiral and the chalice."

A chalice appeared below her lunar spiral, but she kept them separate, with lots of space between them. Mine were together, and crudely done.

"I probably couldn't have combined them better myself, but they are interesting choices. Both sources of what makes a woman a woman, and taps into her abilities of procreation, and," then she stopped.

What?

"Intuition, and psychic abilities," finished Mrs. Saxon. "I'm sure you have heard stories about mothers that felt something bad had happened to their child. Those aren't just stories. Those are true intuition and psychic connections through the strong emotional bounds we form with those we care about. They may be far away, but we can still feel them. Those symbols tap into both abilities and enhance them."

She paused, and I was about to ask what was next when she said, "Let's take another step." We did. I wish I could repeat that step for the rest of my life. Oh my god, the peace I felt was unlike anything I had ever felt in my life. I could have lived in this moment forever. It would be ironic if this grand peace caused my overload. An overdose of peace. Just my luck. Maybe I am a child of chaos.

Mrs. Saxon found that thought rather humorous and could barely contain herself, letting a chuckle slip through. "I doubt this was it, but I can feel the influence of the runes. The clarity and focus they brought you. Let's keep going."

Do we really have to?

There was no answer, but I could tell we were moving again. Then I felt something coming. At first, it was way far away, but it was speeding toward me.

"I think this is it."

It was like being in a car crash you knew was coming. I saw it coming. I couldn't avoid it, and I damn well knew it was going to hurt. I just couldn't prepare myself for how badly it was going to hurt.

There it was. Two words. Loud and clear in Nathan's own voice. "Help me!"

Did I say car wreck? This was an airplane crashing into a passenger train that I was riding the front of. The world around me broke down slowly, bit by bit, but the calm and tranquility went away in a flash of heat that seared every nerve in my body, before leaving me in a cold frozen nothingness. Then it stopped. Everything stopped, and unlike before, Mrs. Saxon's voice wasn't there to fill the void.

Did you hear it?

There was no response.

Mrs. Saxon? Did you hear it?

"Yes," she finally said, then we were back in my room. Mrs. Saxon stood up off the bed, and walked away from me, keeping her back to me. Her head slumped.

"He's in trouble!" I fell to the floor on my knees. Now feeling all the panic and pain I must have felt earlier to cause my overload. She held up a hand behind her to stop me from continuing.

"Let's not jump to any conclusions."

It was a good thing she could no longer read my thoughts, or she would have seen where all had jumped, and it was only about conclusions. I had already jumped to several hundred conclusions. I had also jumped on her for being so dismissive about her son crying out for help.

"That could have many meanings." She finally turned around toward me. How calm her face looked surprised me. This was her son we were talking about. "And they aren't anywhere close to the ones you are thinking of. With both of your heightened emotional states and the enhancement of your psychic abilities from those two runes, that could have been as much as him joking to someone to help him climb up on something or anything else rather innocent. Your state, with those amplifiers, would have made it feel more dire."

"It didn't just feel that way! It sounded it!" I leaned hard in her direction, and almost fell on my face, catching myself at the last moment. What the hell was wrong with her? This was her own son.

She held her arms up, almost defensively, and motioned for me to calm down. "Larissa, let me explain something about psychic connections. This was your first time experiencing it and you need to understand some principles. First, in most instances, time is irrelevant to the connection. What you sense, see, or hear could have happened yesterday, a year ago, and sometimes, they may have not happened yet. It's not a direct connection to that person right at that moment. Second, the emotions you feel are your own, just transferred to what you see or hear. Third, rarely do you receive anything that is complete. A feeling, a word, or a vision is just that. Part of a whole, which you don't see. Take it as just that. Of course, you heard Nathan appear to reach out for help, but that could be from an event you already had with him, or something rather innocent, like I said. Your powerful feelings for him. That deep concern you feel for him painted that message in a certain way, and that is how you took it. We shouldn't read anything into it."

"What?" I screamed, finding myself in a rare state, speechless. I couldn't believe what I was hearing.

"Considering the two runes you combined to enhance your abilities and the quick switch from calm to hysterical, it's no wonder your system went into overload." She placed both hands on her hips and said, "Well, I'm glad we figured that out. Now, you and I need to talk more about what your father was working on and what you remember from those journals. That is absolutely fascinating."

She approached the door, but stopped short of it. I was curious if she was going to actually go through it. No one other than Marie had come in or out of that door since I returned, and when that happened, we were extremely careful to make sure the hallway was clear. Her hand reached for the door handle, increasing my curiosity and I wondered if I should say something, but she stopped and turned back to me. "But that is something for another time." Then she let go of the door handle and spun her hand around, opening one of her own, and walked toward it, almost cheery, with a bounce in her steps. That lit a short fuse on the bomb inside me. There was already a fuse burning from its other side, set by some of her earlier comments, and both just ran out. I bolted, cutting her off, just barely. My back was against the portal, and I was face to face with her, with only a few inches separating us. "What... About... Nathan?"

She didn't even flinch at the question. Her eyes kept steady contact with my own, and there wasn't even a blink. "That is something for another time." A force moved me aside, and she walked through the portal. It closed before I could follow, and I pounded my fist against the wall that was behind it.

9

I was still pounding on the door when a portal behind me opened up. I heard it and felt it, and was ready for Mrs. Saxon or someone to admonish my making so much noise.

"Mom, what's wrong?" Samantha asked from behind me, and I stopped my fists before they made their next strike.

"Nothing, I'm just a little mad." That was a lie. I was furious. I leaned forward and rested my forehead against the wall. In doing so, I caught a glimpse of myself in the mirror. A horror movie scene looked back at me. Eyes bulging and fangs out. All I needed to complete the picture was drool or foam dripping from the corners of my mouth. I didn't want her to see me that way, and I also wasn't sure if I could pull it together before I turned around, at least not naturally. A quick wave of my hand over my face fixed that. Thankfully, Mrs. Tenderschott's shake had some punch left in it. "Just a little mad. That is all." I tried to hide my inner madness and turned around.

"Mad about what?" asked Samantha.

Leave it to me to have an inquisitive child. Of course, I have heard all children are inquisitive. "It doesn't matter," I said, brushing it off in the hopes she will drop it, but doing so made me feel sick. Of course, it mattered. It was everything.

"Oh, alright."

The look on her face made me cringe. Wheels were turning inside her. She wasn't going to drop it as simple as I had hoped. Hopes were for fools. The cynic inside me knew that.

"Did you and Mrs. Saxon figure out what caused you to fall?" Samantha asked. She stood there with her hands folded in front of her, rocking back and forth on her sneakers.

"Yep." I nodded.

"What was it?"

"Let's just say magic is dangerous, and you shouldn't go playing with something you don't understand. I did, and you saw what happened to me."

Technically, I wasn't wrong. I was playing with something I didn't fully understand, but it wasn't the first time that had happened, and it probably wouldn't be the last. That seemed to be the best way to learn.

Did I know those two runes would enhance those abilities? Yep, of course I did. By that much, maybe, or maybe not. That was not the problem. It was all about what I heard, and nothing could have prepared me for that. Even if I had the perspective and experience that Mrs. Saxon described, hearing Nathan cry out like that still would have floored me. Of that I had no doubt. Something inside me didn't buy her explanation. It just didn't feel right, and it smelled worse than the jars over on the table.

"That is why it is important to practice under the supervision of a teacher, understand?"

"Yes, I do." Samantha ran over and hugged me. This hug was no longer one around my legs. Her arm wrapped tightly around my stomach and her head was buried in my chest. I supposed most children, or maybe I would be better off calling her a pre-teen now, would hear the beating of their mother's heart when being held like this. There was no such luck for my child. She won't even hear my lungs fill with air. Which at this moment was a good thing. I was still seething inside, despite my calm exterior mirage.

"Did you have a good time with Mrs. Tenderschott?"

Samantha let go of me and backed up against the bed. She was beaming. "The best. Another student came in after I arrived. Not a witch. Maybe my age or younger. Mrs. Tenderschott had baked some cookies earlier. We ate them while she showed me a few potions."

"Another student?" I asked, knowing darn well Mrs. Tenderschott knew our presence needed to be kept a secret. Why would she allow another student in when Samantha was there? Mrs. Saxon had my blood boiling. This turned it to steam.

"Yes, her name was Amy. She's a shifter."

I turned right around to the wall and spun my arm, but nothing happened. A quick glance over my shoulder considered the tray of jars. There were only three left. I had been downing them with regularity lately. Without a second thought, I stomped over to the tray.

"Mom, where were you trying to go?" Sam asked.

"Oh, your mother needs to have a chat with Mrs. Tenderschott."

My hand had just touched the jar when Samantha stood up and said, "Let me help you."

Right there in front of me, my little girl opened a portal to Mrs. Tenderschott's classroom, and I had a feeling this wasn't her first. Someone, her grandmother, I think, had been working with her.

"Thank you." I walked over and kissed her on the forehead. "Now can you do me one more favor and go through it and make sure there is no one else in there?"

Samantha walked right through her own portal and looked around. I heard Mrs. Tenderschott address her, rather surprised just before Samantha announced, "It's all clear, mom."

That was my clue to storm through. The portal closed once I exited into the classroom. I wanted Samantha to go back and wait in our room, but she didn't, and it was too late now. The eruption was starting, and nothing would hold this back.

"What are you doing allowing other students to see Samantha?" I demanded, looking right at a stunned Mrs. Tenderschott. "No one is to know we are here."

"It's fine. I was here and made sure your secret stayed safe. She only knows that Sam is a young witch visiting the coven. The daughter of one of the council members that are temporarily housed here. Which is the way it ought to be if you ask me." She gave me a little wink and a smirk to diffuse the storm she knew was brewing inside.

"Samantha, can you head back to our room, please? Me and Mrs. Tenderschott need to talk." I never looked back at my daughter, keeping my attention right at the person whose judgment I was now questioning for the first time.

"Sure," responded Samantha.

The glow of her portal reflected off the walls in front of me. When it disappeared, I let my true self out.

"What the hell were you thinking?" I blasted, hoping her better judgement would show up and apologize for what I saw as a true lapse in her thought process.

"She is truly amazing. Mastering her abilities at such a young age. Even at the age of what she looks to be."

"Thanks," the proud parent inside of me stepped up and interrupted my rant for a moment, but only a brief one. "What were you thinking?"

"I was thinking there would be no harm as long as Amy didn't know who she really was," Mrs. Tenderschott explained, sounding a lot calmer than I did asking the question.

"No harm? No one is to know we are here. It's that simple. All someone has to do is start asking questions about the new person they met, and start putting two and two together and..." And, I wasn't sure what was next. I was even thinking I might have gone a little overboard here. I wasn't so sure Mrs. Saxon would agree, though. This was her rule, and she was very explicit about it.

"You are worrying about nothing. No one, and I mean no one, is going to connect a new witch here to being your child, or anything to do with you. There are only a few people here that even knew you were pregnant, and most of them don't know you already gave birth. Let alone. All of them, except a small circle of people, believe you are on the run after your miraculous escape from Mordin... Which you should have seen Mrs. Wintercrest's face when she announced that. I had never seen someone turn so red before. Her head was about to pop open like an overripe tomato."

"It doesn't matter, and Amy of all people... wait, how mad was she?" Hearing that I might have irritated someone that I can say I truly detested had my attention. Mrs. Tenderschott may have found the way to defuse the bomb inside me.

"Oh, she was spitting mad. She called everyone in before the council and stood up from her chair. Her hands trembled as she did her best to look in control, but we could all see how upset she was. She said you broke out, then broke Marcus Meridian out, and made a point to say they didn't understand how, but were sure it had something to do with you being a vampire. She called you a menace and danger to our world, which you need to know not a single member of the faculty believes. Then she told us that if any of us hears from you, or hears any news of you, we are to inform the council immediately. Larissa, I have to tell you. I have never seen a person so angry before. A werewolf, yes, but not a person. Her voice must have cracked a dozen or more times, and during my interview, she couldn't control the trembling."

"I'm shocked the old-bitty didn't have a heart attack... Wait? What? Your interview?"

"Yes, my interview. She and Miss Roberts interviewed the entire staff about the incident and your whereabouts. Not a soul said anything, and we never would."

Interview? The inferno that roared inside me froze over and I felt a chill go down my spine. I should have suspected they would question everyone in the coven. Why wouldn't they? I escaped from the unescapable. They had to assume I had help, regardless of how she may have believed it happened.

Her explanation of how it happened made no sense at all. My powers as a vampire. Please. Vampires can't fly. If I had broken out of my cage, something that was virtually impossible to do, I was sure I could have survived the fall to the ledge below me. That part was plausible, but exactly how did I find and rescue Marcus? The only rational explanation was I had help, which I did. They had to know that. They would also assume that help came from this coven, which again, it did. About a dozen people here knew the truth. Some wouldn't be able to protect themselves from the memory intrusion of the council. The vampires. My stomach tossed as I asked, "Everyone?"

"If you're asking if they interviewed Mrs. Saxon, but of course they did." She walked toward me and placed her hand on my shoulder. I expected her to pull me in for a hug. A very Mrs. Tenderschott thing to do, but she held me there and looked right into my eyes. She was very... well... parental at that moment. "You have nothing to worry about. She has plenty of tricks up her sleeve. She even used them to help the Boldens. No one knew a thing. Your secret will remain safe. Larissa, you have nothing to worry about. You have never had anything to worry about here."

I felt a little better and added a question for Mrs. Saxon about how to block those kinds of intrusions in the future to my list of things I wanted to learn. There was still something bothering me. It was what brought me here in the first place.

"Okay, but why Amy? Why put her in that situation?"

"Oh Larissa." Now she pulled me in for that big bear hug of hers. "What happened to the crass risk taker I knew? You are worried about nothing. No one is going to interview her. There are so many new people walking around with the council here, no one knows who is here or who isn't. Like I said, I told Amy she was the daughter of one of our visitors. That is it. Not to mention it is good for Samantha to be around people her own age," Mrs. Tenderschott paused at that and finally released me. "Or close to her own age," she said with a wry smirk. "She's spending way too much time with you old people." She chuckled and released me and headed for her front table where there was a plate with a half-eaten cookie on it and several sets of glasses and beakers. "I don't count. Remember, you are older than I am. So, how old do you believe she is now?" Mrs. Tenderschott asked as she cleaned off the table.

"Yesterday, probably eight or nine. Today maybe eleven. I'm losing track." I really was. Some days it seemed she stayed the same age for a while. Others, it seemed she skipped a year or two. I wasn't sure where it would stop. I hoped it would. I didn't want to face what it meant if it didn't. I was too worried about missing moments with her while my mind was obsessed elsewhere.

"That's kind of what I think too," she agreed. "You know her magic is progressing quickly. She is easily equal to most of the students here in general understanding, and I heard Master Thomas has even taught her some combat training." She placed the last beaker on the shelf it came from. Then she disposed of the half-eaten cookie by finishing it herself before putting the plate in the sink.

I joined her up at the table. There was no danger in doing that this time, as there was no potion waiting for me. "How's Amy?"

"She is doing wonderfully. She isn't a witch, but I check in on her from time to time." Mrs. Tenderschott washed the crumbs off the plate down the drain of the sink, and with her back to me said, "You know Laura picked up reading to her every night." Mrs. Tenderschott choked on those words and looked over her shoulder to see if I was cringing. I wasn't, much. As much as I missed doing that with Amy, I was happy to hear someone had picked it up for her. "Of course, you wouldn't," she nervously corrected herself while fidgeting with her dish towel before folding it and placing it next to the sink, but keeping her hand on it. "You are isolated from the other vampires as well, aren't you?"

"Yes," I said, rather curious why she didn't know that.

"I wasn't sure considering..." Mrs. Tenderschott turned away from me. The woman was flat hiding something from me and that had me concerned. It was so unlike the woman I knew as the gossip queen around here.

"Considering what?"

Boy, I didn't really understand what that question would bring. It was as if the Hoover Dam gave way and the Colorado River stormed through. With a whirl, the dish towel went flying, as did her hands and her curly gray hair. "Oh Larissa, it's all a huge mess," she blurted. "They isolated the vampires away from the witches at the order of the council. Separate classes and everything. No one here knows about what is going on out there. At least none of the students do, but the council didn't want to take any chances, so they ordered the split, and *that* was a positive outcome." She slammed her hand down on the table in front of the room. "Originally, they wanted to exile them all. That wicked... whatever she is... wanted to kick them all out in the cold. Rebecca argued over and over how they had nothing to do with any of this and it would be cruel. None of that meant anything to that heartless wench of a supreme and her little mini-me Miss Roberts." Mrs. Tenderschott was practically spitting. Her finger wagged in the air, trying to keep up with every point. "It was only when Rebecca told them that turning them out would just turn them against all witches and aid the vampires that Mrs. Wintercrest," she said. That name appeared bitter to her tongue. "She *decided* it would be better to keep them here imprisoned until all this is settled and *then* they could be released out into the wild, as she said. Can you believe she used that description? It's like she is talking about releasing some kind of wild animal. It's a horrible bloody mess created by the council, and for what? I don't have a freckle of a clue."

"Wait! Wait! Wait! Come again?"

"They keep the vampires and witches separate from everyone. In fact, they keep everyone separate from the witches. The shifters, werewolves, and vampires are not permitted to be around the witches." She held up a finger and pursed her lips. "Wait here."

She rushed back through the door that I knew led to her apartment. I heard her go through another door inside there, and then it slammed shut. It wasn't more than a few seconds before she emerged from her apartment. Her hand held out a gold chain in front of her. Dangling from that chain was a charm, or make that a symbol, a solar cross.

"They charmed these and made all the witches wear them to protect us from the others. It causes pain to any non-witch that comes close to us."

I stepped back, not knowing what it would do to me since a part of me wasn't a witch, and Mrs. Tenderschott nodded her approval at my action. Then she tossed the chain on a table on the other side of the classroom. It slid across the surface and stopped just short of the edge.

"From what I have heard, it's quite painful. Gwen wasted no time in trying it out on Apryl. It sent the poor girl to the floor. Everyone has scattered and kept their distances since then." She looked at the shiny object on top of the black tabletop on the other side of the room with disdain. "I don't wear it unless the council is around. Demius is trying to counteract the spell on it, but so far, he hasn't been able to."

"Oh Jesus. This is bad. This is terrible." I repeated it a few more times, while the list of people's lives I had screwed up rushed through my head. That list was about to reach across oceans. I had always thought it was just a cliché in the movies when someone who was panicking said the room was spinning. Now I was either living that cliché or it was real. The room spun around me, and I felt my knees grow weak. I backed up into the table behind me, sending it screeching across the floor. My hand covered my mouth, but it was too late, and it slipped out. "It's all my fault."

"Now you stop that right now." Mrs. Tenderschott stormed toward me. "You stop that right now. This is all the council's doing."

I heard what she said, but I also didn't. This had nothing to do with the council. This was all my doing. All of it. Every single bit of it. I couldn't list anything that had happened that didn't start with me. If Mrs. Saxon was right, and she saw everything that was going to happen, why didn't she leave me on the train?

"Stop," she said as she reached under my chin and tilted my head up. "Just stop. This is all the council's doings. They have been wanting to do this for years, probably centuries. You need to stay focused, because you are the one that is going to fix all of this."

"Wait!" Hearing that come from her sent shockwaves through me. "You know?"

"Please. I've always known. I was there when Rebecca talked to Benjamin about it."

"Man, is anything a secret around here?" I scoffed.

"Well, there are a few. Your presence is one. Then there is your daughter, Marie Norton, Marcus, and Jack and Lisa." Mrs. Tenderschott counted it off on her fingers, and then held up her hand so I could see five fingers.

I knew of three of those five, but two of the names were a shock. "Jack and Lisa? What's their secret?"

"Their existence," Mrs. Tenderschott answered before walking away toward the table with her what I would call cursed charm laying on it. "The council doesn't know they are here. Which is why I felt it was okay for them to be around you the other day, and why they don't have one of those blasted things." She glanced over at the chain on the table. "Rebecca is concerned... rightly so, that someone might recognize those two from the fight down in New Orleans and would remember they weren't exactly fighting on the side of the witches. So, they are stuck off on their own."

Oh yeah. I remembered Mrs. Saxon mentioning she was keeping them separate from the other witches, but she said it was to protect my secret from getting out, not to protect them. Then I realized who she was trying to protect.

"You don't need to worry about that, though. You have enough to focus on, like your daughter–"

"And my training." I interrupted with the obvious answer.

"Yes, your training. Speaking of, how is that going?"

"A little better now, thanks to your potions. I might need some more or something stronger."

"How many do you have left?" she asked in a curious tone.

"Three." I held up three fingers.

Now it was her turn to be shocked. "Three? As in one, two, three?" She counted off on her own fingers.

"Yep, they are working great."

"Larissa, I just gave you those two days ago. It's supposed to be one a day, at the most."

Oops. All I could do was shrug. "It's not like there was a prescription label on them with instructions." I tried to remember if she said anything about how often I should take it. I couldn't remember any instructions besides using them to help me with my training sessions. Perhaps she assumed one per day would suffice. It probably would have if I hadn't taken part in some extracurricular activities.

"Trying a few things on your own?" she asked with a suspicious look in her eye.

"Just practicing." It wasn't a wrong answer. I was practicing. What I was practicing was going to stay my secret. "It has helped a lot. Thank you." I hoped my show of humbled gratitude would change that subject, but the look she gave me didn't change. "It even lets me throw some runes."

Now it changed to one of surprise. "Really? It helped you become that focused?"

"Yes." I nodded, "but it backfired. I think I tapped into something I wasn't ready for and..." As I explained what happened, a question came to me. A nagging I had felt since Mrs. Saxon explained to me what I had experienced and how easily she blew off any concerns for Nathan, fueled its origins. "Can I ask you something? It's about the runes I tried and what seemed to have backfired."

"Yes, of course." Mrs. Tenderschott settled up against the table in front of her and had a seat. She tapped her hand on the tabletop, summoning me to sit across from her. I didn't resist and took a seat. "So, what's the question?"

"The rune I chose tapped into some psychic abilities." I didn't want to get into the entire explanation with her about how my father combined symbols to create new ones and that I did the same with two that were involved with psychic connections while not even understanding what psychic connections were. That was a topic for another time, to borrow Mrs. Saxon's statement from earlier. Not to mention I wanted to avoid any type of lecture I might get about being careless with magic. "It was my first time doing that."

"Oh, then you absolutely weren't ready for it. Psychic connections and impulses are powerful. You need to develop a filter to keep it from overloading your own system."

So much for avoiding a lecture. "No kidding. That's what happened."

She reached over and took my hand. The chill of my touch never deterred her from showing me the same warm affection that she showed everyone else, and I always appreciated that. She treated me and the rest as if we were just people. "Good lord. Please tell me Rebecca was there to intervene."

"She was. She froze me and brought me back to my room until I recovered. Then we went through something that took us step by step so she could see what caused it."

"Good. She did the right thing. I have to tell you, if she wasn't there, it could have been damaging to you," warned Mrs. Tenderschott. "You need to be careful about trying new things on your own. Even someone as experienced and capable as you are can step into something you aren't ready for."

"That's what I need to ask you about. I want to make sure I understand what happened. When I was in what you and Mrs. Saxon called a psychic connection, I heard or felt something. That was the moment I became overloaded." I leaned forward. "When you are in that state, and you feel emotions in what you are... I guess... receiving is the right word, are those just your emotions reacting?"

"Well, yes, of course. Your emotions are going to react to what you see, hear–"

"Oh, good." I interrupted her, feeling relieved, but not realizing I just talked over a very important part of her answer until she finished it.

"–and feel. Emotions are particularly important in those connections. You need to understand what you feel while being able to control the flood you are receiving. The emotions that travel across the connection are raw and stronger than anything we feel ourselves."

My head did a double take, and I almost leaped across the table at the woman. What did she just say? "You mean the emotions you feel are real? They're really what the person you have the connection with is feeling?"

"Of course, silly," she said as if it were something obvious that everyone knew. "The psychic connection between two or more people is an extremely powerful connection, fueled mostly by emotions. That is why it is important to learn how to filter most of it out and let just a little through. Those emotions you receive are raw and very strong."

"That..." I muttered, catching myself before I called Mrs. Saxon something that even she didn't deserve. She lied to protect me. I let go of Mrs. Tenderschott's hand and propped my head on my left hand while my right one clawed at the table.

"Larissa, what is it?"

There was a momentary debate about whether I should tell her. When my mouth finally opened, I had either forgotten, or just ignored, all the reasons I shouldn't tell her. The first sound that made it out was a sob, then the words followed. "When I was under, I heard Nathan cry out for someone to help. It was just two words, 'help me', but they were strong, and the desperation consumed me. Mrs. Saxon told me those were my emotions, transplanted on top of what I heard." Now I knew different and that same desperation I felt while in the connection threatened to swallow me again.

"What did he say? What did you see?" Both questions fired from her lips. Now it was her turn to lean across the table, eager for my reply.

"Just 'help me'. I saw nothing. It was more about what I felt."

Mrs. Tenderschott stood up and stumbled away from the table. She had something to say, but struggled to find either the breath or words. When she did, there was an attempt to compose herself, and it only half succeeded. "He's alive. That's good."

"Well, he may be alive," I said. It was a statement that almost broke me in half, but I had to face the possibility.

"No. If you heard him, he is alive. What you hear is what is happening at that moment."

"What?" I jumped off of my stool and leaned hard over the table, supporting myself with both of my arms. "She told me that time was irrelevant!"

There was a quick and surprised shake of her head. "No, that is incorrect. What you see or hear is happening at that moment." Then she wondered aloud, "She knows that. I wonder why she...", but she never finished the thought.

I wasn't sure if I had steam coming out of my ears, but I should have. I was fuming and ready to go to war on my own. She lied to me. Yes, I wasn't too blinded by rage and concern to know she did it to protect me from, well, me. She knew what I would do if I knew the truth.

It seemed Mrs. Tenderschott knew too. She rushed toward me. "Larissa, don't do anything rash. I know what it seems like, but it could have many meanings."

"Now you sound exactly like her," I snapped and walked away. "You have already told me the truth. What I felt was what he was feeling at *that* time. I'm not sure how many other meanings that could have. He was in trouble and in severe pain. Both physically and emotionally." I turned to look at her, and half cried, and half screamed, "He was hurt and crying out for someone to help." My voice echoed around the classroom as I reached up to brush away the tears running down my cheeks. "And that," I left what I was really thinking out after a second of discretion, "she just ignored it. Her own son!" I paced around the classroom like a caged animal, which wasn't all that wrong.

"Now, now, Larissa. I know that is what it looks like, but I seriously doubt that." There was an edge to her voice that took some of the consolation out of it. She was both irritated and concerned. "You need to remember something about Rebecca. She is reserved and calculated. She has to be. It is required of her position, and it is just how her nature is. You are more emotional. I assure you. She is not turning a blind eye to her son and is working on something to help him." She stammered with her explanation.

She might be right, but how long would she wait before she took action? If it were me, I would have gone to him immediately. Well, there was the minor problem of not knowing where he was. A problem that had a solution waiting for me in the books in my room. I had to believe Mrs. Saxon probably already knew how to do those spells, and being his mother, she had more options to choose from. I only had one, and I was starting on that as soon as I got back to my room.

"I'm going to need more of that stuff you gave me to focus."

"I can't," responded Mrs. Tenderschott. She held up a hand defensively as I paced toward her, and it caught me off guard. Had I frightened her that much?

"Before you think I am saying I won't. It's not that. I can't. I'm out of a few key ingredients. They take about a week to make." When she lowered her hand, I saw a faint glow I hadn't seen before. She honestly thought I was coming at her. "I know what you are planning to do with it, and it is a bad idea. Your magic isn't stable right now. You shouldn't be going off anywhere until that problem is solved."

She appeared to have more to say, but I didn't let her. "But Nathan is the answer to that problem! Don't you see?"

"Wait," she responded, and I put the rest of my speech on hold. "I understand that. I truly do. I figured it was that as soon as you started struggling, but Larissa, you can't go out into the middle of a war like this. You can't defend yourself."

"Then fix me something to help," I roared, and felt bad about it as soon as my mouth shut. Not that it made up for it, I added, "Please."

"I can't. There is nothing I can make that will help. For your own good. You need to calm down and think things through. You are in no shape to help Nathan. I'm sure Rebecca is working on something."

10

Mrs. Tenderschott proved her point by having me try to open a portal back to my room, and there wasn't even a fizzle of anything as I spun my arm around. She opened it for me and sent me back through with a hug, a kiss on the cheek, and orders to sit tight and let Mrs. Saxon handle things. Sit tight in my room and do nothing. That was highly unlikely. I just needed to figure out what I was going to do, and, most importantly, how I was going to do it. I only had three jars left, and as much as I wanted to use one now, my better judgment spoke up through my raging emotions and convinced me to hold off until I really needed it.

Samantha was already asleep when I came through, and I stayed quiet to keep from waking her. It was early, but I had a feeling today's events with her mom causing a scene, falling and all, had tired her out. I motioned for the books to go over to my desk, but they didn't. Not even a budge or a jerk. I had to move them in a more conventional manner.

As I walked over to pick them up, I passed by the window in my room and paused for just a second to look out. I had done that often since I had returned. Until Master Thomas arranged our field trips, that was the only view Samantha, or I, had of the outside world. I rarely looked out the window at night. Mostly because it was dark, and I wouldn't be able to see as far. Being winter, there seemed to be a constant cloud cover, blocking any brilliant moonlit nights.

I don't know why I did it this time. Then again, maybe I did. Maybe it was what Mrs. Tenderschott told me. I looked down at the table Nathan and I used to sit at to read to Amy. There they were: Amy and Laura. Amy held the book and appeared to be reading to Laura. I was a little surprised not to see Mike out there. Then again, maybe I wasn't. This was more her thing. It brought a smile to my face, but also tugged at my heart. I wanted to be down there. Scratch that. I needed to be down there. I glanced back at Samantha, to remind myself that I had mine. Maybe this was Laura's chance to have hers. That was when something she said back in New Orleans made sense, and I felt bad that I didn't fully understand until now. Laura wanted a child. Something our state robbed us of, or should have. God, she probably hated me when this happened to me. Thinking back to a few of the looks she gave me; I think she did.

I still had every intention of Amy being Samantha's big sister. Make that her sister. I think Samantha had already passed Amy's age. I so wanted them to have that connection, but could I break up what she was developing with Laura? Did I even have too? We were all one big extended family, and the werewolves were the crazy uncles. As I looked down upon them, and how closely they sat to one another, with no Ms. Parrish watching from a distance, I had to wonder if Amy felt for Laura how she did me?

No, you can't do that yourself. I had to give myself that quick lecture and move away from the window. I wasn't being replaced. That wasn't what was going on. I could still be part of her life, and everything was going to be fine. No matter how many times I tried to imagine that picture of the perfect family, Nathan, me, Samantha, and Amy, the feeling that someone had replaced me crept in. Every so often, a question would follow it. Was it all for the best? I wasn't totally sure how I felt about that question yet.

Before any of that picture could come true, I needed to deal with the first member who was missing. I needed a plan. Something I didn't usually rely on, at least until our plan to lure Jean St. Claire into an altercation in New Orleans. Before that, I always just acted and dealt with what came. It wasn't exactly the best way to go about things, but it had worked so far. Things were different now, and I wasn't really in a condition to just go in some place with both barrels blasting. My barrels were now nothing more than popguns and I didn't really know where I was going. That was problem number one, and a timely reminder of what I was doing when I stopped at the window.

I grabbed all seven books, a rather large stack that I had to peer over the top of, as I carried them to the desk. I almost dropped them on the top of the desk, but I remembered I had a daughter sleeping just a few feet away. So, I opted for a less noisy move, and placed them down gently on the desk. Little puffs of dust escaped from between the pages as the weight of each book settled on the one below it. A sign that no one in this place had looked into these topics in a long while, if ever. Not a shock, but also a reminder of how on my own I was here.

Book one was where I wanted to start again, and it was easy to find the page I needed thanks to the dogear I folded into the top edge earlier. Sorry Edward. "Blood of my Blood". Out of all the methods I'd read, this was the most direct. According to the text, I needed a hair or some biological trace of the person we were trying to find, or the blood from one of their direct descendants. The stronger the relationship, the better. There were warnings about not going beyond first cousins. That far out, it would be shaky, and you might find the location of half your family tree in the process. That wasn't a problem for me. I had exactly what I needed. You couldn't get much closer.

An old question arrived just in time to shake my confidence on that matter. How much was our daughter really our daughter, and how much of her had been created by magic? It is entirely possible there was no biological part of Nathan in her. Not knowing how she really came to be was a problem. My hand squeezed the edge of the book harder. It seemed everywhere I turned there were questions, and not a single answer, but this was one I could finally answer. If this worked, assuming I perform the spell and potion correctly, then I would have my answer. One way, or the other.

I kept reading through all the variations of this spell for the main spell and potion. Why you put variations before the main content, I didn't understand. It was a bad book design, in my opinion, but then again, most of the magical teachings I had been through weren't exactly forthright. You had to try it and figure it out as you went.

Then, like a shotgun blast to my soul, "Help me. Please!"

It seared right through me and sent me tumbling out of my chair to the floor.

"Please!" his voice begged again, echoing in my head. More intense than the previous plea. I reached out for him, and he wasn't there. I spun around and searched the entire room. I knew it was hopeless. I knew he wasn't there. I felt it. His voice was as distant as it was desperate, but the feelings were right there with me. It was as if we shared our being, and were one, both feeling what the other felt. Which was a horrifying realization for both of us. If I felt his suffering this strongly, then he felt what it did to me. He felt that hole. That empty void that grew by the moment. He felt me tumbling into it each time I realized what he was going through. I tried to convince myself I needed to be strong for him. I needed to be strong for myself and use that strength to find him. It was a grand idea, and I even had a great speech that went with it, but that didn't stop me from sitting there on the floor rocking back and forth and sobbing for hours before I finally climbed back into the chair.

When my mind finally focused on the page, I realized the spell itself didn't seem too hard on the surface. I had to hold the thought and feelings I have for my lost family member in my heart while I recited, "Blood of my Blood. Bound of my bound. Heart of my heart. Reach to me." In fact, it sounded downright corny. I then turned the page to the next part, which was the potion, which again, wasn't that hard. Just a few ingredients that I was sure Mrs. Tenderschott had in her classroom. But when I read the next instruction, and what I had to do, I about knocked the book to the floor in shock. I had to find a four-foot-by-four-foot piece of parchment paper and soak it with blood and potion, and it would draw a map to the person. Soak?!? I was thinking a little drop. This thing wants me to slit Samantha's throat and bleed her out over a large poster. No way in hell.

This had to be a mistake. I kept reading through the variations of the potion for less direct relationships, like siblings and grandparents, and finally reached the part about using a strand of hair instead of blood. There! That was my solution to all this. I probably would have to burn it or something. Easy enough, and I was right. You were to burn the strand and... wait, and then allow your astral self to follow the smoke to the person you seek. Ah crap! My head collapsed down on to the book when I read, "only to be used if the person was within a few miles of you." Great, I now knew how to find Samantha if I ever lost her at the mall, but this wouldn't work for what I needed. As far as I knew, he was thousands of miles away.

There had to be another way. The book was thick enough to be loaded with hundreds of ways to do this. I pushed myself back up, but disappointment weighed on my head so much I had to prop it up with my arm. I flipped the page, and it listed ingredients for the other potions which were not for direct relationships like father and child. Then down at the bottom in small italics there was a note. It said, "Spells you may also need—Congero." That was a word I had never seen before, let alone spell. I flipped through the book for a page covering this spell. Of course, that would make things easy, and as I had already noted, nothing in the world of witches was the easy way. We made triumphs through struggle. I could almost hear Master Thomas' voice echoing with that in my ears.

I spun around in the chair, shutting the book. I almost slammed it shut, but remembered my sleeping daughter and caught it before the pages clapped together. I scanned the room for two books. I knew they were in here. Mrs. Saxon gave them to me the first day I found out, or the first day she told me, I was a witch, again. If only I could remember where I left them. I gave the desk another quick glance, just to be sure. I didn't remember ever reading them at my desk. Where was I? Then it hit me, and I sprinted to my bed, where I always sat or laid while looking through Mrs. Saxon's Elemental Spells Volumes I and II. I never made it to volume II. I really only made it halfway through volume I before I remembered who I was, and all that came rushing back to me. So, I wasn't sure if Congero, or whatever it was called, was in there or not. I hoped it was. If not, it was back to the library, or a special request to Edward. But could I risk that? I knew he was reporting back to Mrs. Saxon. Would such a simple request tip either of them off to what I was doing? I looked around on the bed for the books, checking under the covers that I never used, and the same with the blanket folded at the foot of it. Nothing. Then, on a hunch, remembering how things would become lost in my room when I was a little girl, I reached down between my bed and the wall. Bingo! Two books. I made quick work fanning through volume I at a speed that created a slight breeze in the room that even I felt. I took more time going through volume II, having never read it before. When I hit the last page, I let it just fall limp with the others. Nothing. Not even a single mention of that spell as part of something else. This wasn't just a roadblock. This was a brick wall that extended up to the moon. I needed another witch's help.

The biggest question was who? Mrs. Saxon was an absolute no. I couldn't risk it. Not that she would understand what I was really doing. At least I didn't think so. Of course, if her divination was as good as she claimed it was, she would already know I was doing this. That begs the question, why wasn't she up here trying to stop me?

Master Thomas was a curious consideration. I wasn't sure if he would object to teaching me something new. He might push back on putting something else on my plate until I was controlling the simple things first. I'm sure he would probably ask why, and I would say because it was part of a spell I was reading about, and then he would ask what spell that was, and the dance would go on. Too exhausting, but he might be the only option. Mrs. Tenderschott was a no. I was almost sure she would report back to Mrs. Saxon. She was already concerned I was going to do something foolish. That didn't leave me with many options. It really left only one, but I wasn't thrilled by that prospect.

There was another option, but to say it was the riskiest of all wasn't stretching it.

11

With a head full of doubt, which wasn't exactly the optimal state to perform magic, I stood up and spun my arm around. Nothing. I forgot. See what an unfocused mind causes. For just a second, I considered waking Samantha to ask for her help, but I quickly dismissed that, and not for the obvious reason. I was certain she would say no. My eyes landed on the tray on the nightstand. There were only three jars left, and I needed to make them last. Mrs. Tenderschott said it would be another week before she could make more. Of course, I had a habit of rationalizing everything, so just a sip should be enough to get me where I was going and back, so that was what I did.

I popped up the top of one jar and powered through the putrid aroma that filled the room, and took a sip, which wasn't more than a drop or two. Samantha rustled in her bed, probably from the smell that I thought could wake the dead. While that quick sip tortured my throat, I tightly resealed the top on the jar and sat it back on the tray. Was this enough? There was only one way to find out.

I went to the far corner of the room, not wanting to wake Samantha, and tried again. This time I saw a familiar gold glitter portal open. On the other side was another room, and not just any room. It was the room of a very sleepy witch who was shielding her eyes from the bright, spinning disk. I stepped through, letting it close immediately, returning the room to complete darkness. Which didn't last long. Lisa flicked a candle on her nightstand after just a second or two.

She rolled over and groaned. "I'm not sure if I should be happy that you seem to have a better handle on your magic, or mad at you for waking me up. Vampires may not sleep, but the rest of us do." She rolled over facing me, gripping her covers tight.

"Sorry Lisa. I need your help with something, and it couldn't wait." Now that I had her attention. She sat up in the bed and appeared more awake.

"What is it?" she asked, concerned.

"I need you to ask a question for me," I started, and then stopped. Was I now questioning if I could trust Lisa? I had to trust someone, and Lisa was my best option. "I was looking up a potion, and it involved a spell I have never heard of. I tried to look it up, but I can't find any other references to it, and I need you to ask a teacher about it for me." I flashed my ever so convincing grin. "Could you do it?"

She rubbed her eyes and then asked. "Sure, but what's the spell? Maybe I have heard of it."

"Congero."

"That would be a big nope. Can you spell it?"

"C...O...N...G...E...R...O"

"Can you use it in a sentence?" she asked with a giggle. She leaned forward toward her desk, which was right next to her bed, and pulled two books off the black wood top.

"That would be a big nope."

She let go of her copies of Elementary Spell Volumes I and II, and sat back on the bed. "Already looked?"

I nodded. "It was the second place I looked after I checked the text I saw the reference in."

"Must be pretty advanced. Why can't you ask Mrs. Saxon or Master Thomas? I am sure one of them would know what it is."

A logical question that I knew she would ask. Now, if there were questions left about trusting Lisa, I needed to get over them. To borrow an old saying that I heard Mr. Norton say a few times, I was about to open the barn door and let all the animals out. Why I even questioned it? I didn't have a clue. Lisa was as close to a sister as I had. "I'm sure they do too, but they would ask why I wanted to know, and I sort of can't tell them."

"What are you planning?" Her worry from before was gone, and a mischievous smile stretched across her face. I knew this was coming. The barn door was open, and here came the animals.

"You can't tell a soul."

Lisa motioned she was locking her lips and throwing away the key.

I went over and sat beside her on the bed. "Remember when I first got here, and I was trying to find Marie?"

Lisa nodded.

"Well, Edward gave me some books on how to locate loved ones and then use astral projection to go find them, but warned me about how dangerous it was. I only looked through them once back then and set them aside. Now I have another use for them, and I found a spell and potion combination that might help me find Nathan."

"Wait, you aren't thinking of going to him in the astral plane, are you? Not only is that extremely dangerous. We only tried it, what, once, maybe twice? Larissa, you can't seriously be considering–"

I was sure Lisa had more points to make, but I didn't need to hear all the leaps she had made and put a single finger over her lips to hush her. "I'm not. This isn't this kind of spell and potion. This will draw a map to where he is, but there is a catch. I have to use a little blood from someone who is a direct relative of the person I am searching for." I may have understated the amount of blood I needed, but that was intentional. "I am supposed to mix that with a few other ingredients and soak a large piece of parchment. Then say the spell while thinking of the person I am searching for, and it will draw a map to them on the parchment."

"Oh wow, do you think it will work?" she asked, wide-eyed.

"I guess," I responded with a shrug. "I just need to solve one problem. That large piece of parchment is really large. Like four-feet-by-four-feet, and if you think about what I told you, I need to soak it with Sam's blood." I didn't need to finish. The horrified look on Lisa's face said it all. She got my problem. "I'm hoping Congero has something to do with it."

"I'll ask during our private classes tomorrow." Lisa looked around the room for a minute and then suggested. "I can tell them it was something I read about. They won't suspect a thing."

I put my hands on my hips and cocked my head to the side.

"Right," she agreed.

"They wouldn't suspect a thing until you gave them that explanation. We all know no one goes to the library, and it's not in any of the assigned text or reading. Remember, they don't know I'm here visiting you right now, so they won't suspect anything."

But Lisa was right. If it is something special or some kind of restricted magic, they would be curious about where she heard about it. I had no clue how old those books were. Maybe it was like the runes. Something that wasn't supposed to be taught, but I had a way around that. Something that would sound both innocent and likely, considering her background. "Tell them you heard your mother speak of it before."

Lisa considered this for a second while lightly nodding. I think she realized the genius of my idea.

"So, you'll do it?" I asked eagerly.

"Of course," responded Lisa, without hesitation. "There is just one question. Once I find out what it is, how do I tell you?"

"That's easy." I raised my eyebrows a bit. "How did I come see you?"

"Oh yeah. I must be tired. My mind was thinking about our current restrictions, but that doesn't stop us," Lisa said, adding air quotes to the last two words.

"Once you have it, just come see me in my room. Deal?"

"Deal," agreed Lisa.

"Okay, I need to get back." My focus was on Lisa as I reached back and spun a portal open and stepped back through it. I should have known something was wrong. The telltale light it usually produced was rather dim, and Lisa's eyes were huge as she called my name just before I stepped through. It closed, leaving me standing in the middle of the hallway on the witch's floor. Worst of all, I heard voices coming from the commons room. One was an overly perky voice that sent chills down my spine.

Quickly, I attempted to open another portal, but nothing. Not even a fizzle. That sip hadn't lasted as long as I had hoped, and now I was in trouble and stuck on the other side of enemy lines, as some might see it. There were two choices. The door, which was a terrible idea. It lead to the stairs out in the grand entrance. Not exactly a place I wanted to walk if I intended to remain hidden. The other option was having Lisa help me, which was the obvious choice. My hand had already made that decision and was turning the handle on the door behind me.

"Dang it," I muttered. The room was dark and empty, completely empty. This wasn't Lisa's room. It wasn't anyone's room. I looked down the hall and saw Lisa's door. It was just two doors away. I thought of bolting for it, but the sound of Gwen's voice bleeding out from the commons room stopped me in my tracks. I heard other voices, but hers was the one that stuck out. Maybe it was how it grated against my nerves, but just hearing it made me feel ill, and my skin tingled, almost like it was burning. The feeling grew stronger, and her voice grew closer. She was coming out. I needed somewhere to hide, but the hallway was just that. A hallway with doors. I reopened the door I stood next to, and slipped inside, closing it as quietly as I could behind me.

I heard the sounds of footsteps as Gwen and whoever else was with her passed by, and the tingling I felt sent me to my knees on the floor. The tingling turned into a stabbing, like hundreds and hundreds of needles stabbing into my skin. Each hole burned on both entry and exit, and my body fell flat on the floor. There was no doubt I was feeling pain now. I reached up to push myself back up and saw my hand. My skin was just thin dry paper wrapped tightly around the bones of my fingers. I was afraid to move my fingers out of fear it would tear, but that didn't stop my reflexes from balling up my fingers into a fist with the next stabbing sensation. Then it was gone, along with the sound of footsteps. I laid there in the darkness and watched my hand return to normal. I could only assume the same happened to the rest of me.

What I felt had to be the stupid charms that the council gave all the witches. They were more powerful than I thought, and Mrs. Tenderschott left out one of their effects. Though she may not have known about it. There was a good chance none of the witches did either. How would they? They didn't see or hear the world as we do. They aren't able to hear the heartbeat of every living creature around them or smell that life giving fluid that coursed through their veins. I wasn't able to do either as they approached. I was sure Gwen wore hers around like a medal. Once the effects had passed, I stood up and cracked open the door. The hallway not only looked clear but also felt clear. There were no voices, and no sensations from the charms.

I made my way down the hallway, only feeling slight pinches and stabs from those who must have been close to their doors. This was the easiest part of my little journey. Just to be sure, I tried to open another portal, but nothing happened. Even an act as simple as drawing the all-seeing eye so I could see through the door was a big nothing. Something that should have frustrated me, but it instead struck me as humorous. Here I was panicking because I lost control of magic. I had forgotten all about my other side. The side that lived in the shadows. This should be easy. I would be out the door and up the stairs before anyone knew. This time of night, the lights would be down in the grand entry, anyway.

With a quick crack of the door, I checked to make sure no one else was out there on the stairs on our side or the boy's side. The coast was clear, and I made my way out to the stairs and sprinted up. The sound of an army thundered into the hall. I sped up, but then slowed down when I heard Mrs. Saxon's voice.

12

I felt them before I saw who they were, and not in the traditional way. The tingling and stabbing started before I saw them. Those damn charms. I moved up to the top landing and hid behind the thick wooden post. In hindsight, I should have made a break for the door. I could have been through it before anyone noticed. It would have saved me some torture, but it was too late now. At least where I was now had reduced the effects of the charms to nothing more than something like bug bites. Just an annoyance that caused my body to twitch. My hands rubbed up and down my legs and stomach to relieve the itching, but that didn't work. I made another glance at the door. I was curious about who was coming, but was I really that curious?

My answer really didn't matter. Time had answered that question for me. I forced my body to stay still while I watched Mrs. Wintercrest and that thorn-in-my-side, Miss Roberts, lead the council marching by the stairs in rows of two. Each wore their ceremonial red robes. It was amazing. Even in something so regal, Miss Roberts looked tacky. I wasn't sure which witch I disliked most, Gwen or her. That was unfair. It was definitely her. I hated her, and I just disliked Gwen. If I were allowed to talk to the witches, I might plant a few suggestions in Gwen's head about Miss Roberts and see what trouble I could stir up.

"Council members, please," Mrs. Saxon's voice yelled from down the hall. She sounded out of breath. In a few seconds, her first step hit the marble floor of the entry, and the click of her heel echoed in the grand space. Ms. Wintercrest appeared to huff at the commotion. I felt a little pleasure at seeing her irritation. "Supreme Wintercrest, if I may?" she requested.

Mrs. Wintercrest never looked back in her direction, but her mini-me Miss Roberts stepped right out of the line and turned, blocking Mrs. Saxon's approach.

"You have made your point quite clear, Mrs. Saxon." Miss Roberts leered with a point of her finger right at Mrs. Saxon.

Mrs. Saxon ignored both her and her attitude without so much as a look and attempted to walk right around her. Miss Roberts shuffled to her right to block her. The two almost collided, and Mrs. Saxon had to give ground to avoid hitting her. I looked up and down the line of council members for any reaction. Most appeared to be ignoring what was going on. Even Mr. Nevers, who I knew well from my time in New Orleans. He wasn't exactly a fan of Mrs. Wintercrest, and I couldn't imagine he was supportive of anything that was going on. Though I wasn't sure what type of reaction I expected from him or any of the other members. Mrs. Wintercrest had her thumb pressed tightly on each of them. That and the threat of exile I had already seen her use now twice. I believed that was why Mrs. Saxon danced carefully around her objections. "Just one more point, and that is all."

Finally, Mrs. Wintercrest turned, with her nose upturned, as if she were looking down on Mrs. Saxon. Something that was rather absurd, since Mrs. Saxon was a good foot taller than our diminutive supreme.

Miss Roberts stepped in front of Mrs. Saxon yet again and smiled smugly. But that expression didn't last long. Mrs. Wintercrest commanded her to move aside with a simple touch on her shoulder, and Miss Roberts complied immediately. She looked like someone had stolen her lollipop.

"Mrs. Saxon, we just spent an hour talking about this in council," started Mrs. Wintercrest. "Your attendance was a mere courtesy since we are here. Don't take your presence in those proceedings as meaning you have a say."

"I'm not, my supreme. I just believe there is a vantage point that wasn't considered or brought up. Just an omission, I'm sure."

"Probably, and it is probably not significant, or we would have discussed it. But since you interrupted us on the way to our quarters to retire for the night, what is it? And make it quick. It has been a long day."

"Yes, ma'am." Mrs. Saxon straightened herself up and backed up a few steps to face the entire council. Where they had ignored her before, they now all faced her since their supreme had given them permission. "My supreme, and members of the council. I believe we should not ignore our own history in the consideration of all actions we take. While it is the council's wish to continue this endeavor against the vampires, and you have your reasons. I must point out that we should not paint all vampires with the same broad brush as it appears you are. It would be important for each of us to remember why we each stay hidden from the rest of the world. At one time, they painted us with the broad brush and attempted to find and destroy anyone they could identify as a witch. Should we not be better than that and not repeat the same wrong that was inflicted on us?"

There were a few heads that nodded in the council, but not a single one spoke up in agreement. The perturbed look on the face of their supreme made sure of that. She let Mrs. Saxon stand there for a few seconds after she finished. The echo of her message, now just a distant memory in the rafters of the grand entry. Silence was its new occupant.

"Mrs. Saxon. The time and circumstances are different now, and-" Miss Roberts started, but Mrs. Wintercrest interrupted her objection with a wave of her hand. It both silenced her and annoyed her. A power I wish I had.

"Perhaps she has a point. One should never repeat their own history," suggested Mrs. Wintercrest. She turned and played to the other council members. They met her rather diplomatic statement with several smiles and nods of agreement, but still no one spoke. "We should consider our targets well. There is no need to-" What I saw next I would have never believed. Miss Roberts stepped forward and interrupted her own supreme. She reached forward, and with a hand on her shoulder, whispered something into her ear. From where I was, I could clearly see Mrs. Wintercrest's jaw twitch as Miss Roberts spoke to her, but I couldn't hear them, no matter how hard I tried.

Miss Roberts backed away, and Mrs. Wintercrest continued, "Mrs. Saxon, we thank you for your contribution, but I believe the times and circumstances are different, and frankly, it changes nothing. We are proceeding with efforts to hunt down and either eliminate or imprison all vampires for our own safety. You yourself should know how dangerous they are. You took in a young witch that was being hunted by a vampire." She then glanced back at her mini-me, in what I felt looked like a request for approval, which took me aback. What was this?

"Which you are giving refuge to, my supreme," interjected Mrs. Saxon.

Mrs. Saxon's observation caused a stir within the council, and Miss Roberts stepped forward. For what, I wasn't sure, but Mrs. Wintercrest blocked her, holding up her right hand, making sure we never found out. "Holding, until we can do a proper trial to determine his fate. We are more civilized than they are. Don't forget that. Rest assured, he will be dealt with."

"And what of the other vampires and rogue witches? Shouldn't they be afforded the opportunity of a trial?"

Mrs. Wintercrest received that suggestion like an offensive smell, distorting her appearance for a few seconds. Then I saw an expression that I had seen on her face too many times. Usually while I stood before her facing some odd accusation. That smug smile grew as she turned her head toward the council members. Miss Roberts leaned forward and whispered in her ear before she finally spoke. "Well, yes," she condescendingly agreed. "Those we capture will face a trial."

"Thank you, my supreme." Mrs. Saxon bowed slightly, and Mrs. Wintercrest turned to rejoin the rest of the council. "One last question, if it is permissible."

Mrs. Wintercrest stopped. She stood there for a few seconds before she turned around and acknowledged Mrs. Saxon. I couldn't see her face, but I knew she was stewing. I couldn't see the expression on Mrs. Saxon's face, either. Her back was to me, but I had a feeling she was standing there with her normal expression of quiet confidence, and enjoyed this little irritation. Something we both shared.

"Make it quick," Mrs. Wintercrest snapped.

"I believed this action by the council was targeted toward Jean and his followers, but in your discussion, I heard other areas mentioned. Did I hear incorrectly?"

"Mrs. Saxon. The council is taking up an effort to ensure our safety. That is all you need to know. This is a matter for the council, and none of your concern. Your presence was just a courtesy." Mrs. Wintercrest spun around on her heels and marched back to the front of the assembled council. The others turned forward as if to march out with her, but before she led them, she turned toward Mrs. Saxon once again. "I know what your concern is, and rest assured, if we run across your son, he will be granted certain considerations," she turned away.

"Assuming he doesn't take up arms against us," sniped Miss Roberts. She stood there and stared at Mrs. Saxon, almost as if she was hoping for a reaction from her.

I felt my body jerk at the statement. I wanted to jump up and do something, but I couldn't. All I could do was stay hidden and watch how Mrs. Saxon reacted. I was sure she had something more to say. I doubted she would plead or throw herself on the mercy of the council. Not that they had much mercy to give. I seriously doubted if Mrs. Wintercrest knew the meaning of the word. I was sure Miss Roberts didn't. I sat there waiting for Mrs. Saxon's response. This wasn't over. It couldn't be. I thought back to the few statements she had made. They were all carefully chosen points to make in front of the council. Each meant to plant thoughts and questions in their mind about what they were doing. She probably still had some hope that a member of the council would stand up and defy Mrs. Wintercrest. I didn't see a snowball's chance in hell of that, but Mrs. Saxon was more diplomatic than I was. Maybe that was why she said nothing. She just stood there and watched Mrs. Wintercrest lead the council down the hallway.

All the council members, aside from one, followed Mrs. Wintercrest into the hall almost in lockstep with one another. Miss Roberts stayed right where she was, in front of Mrs. Saxon. She appeared to be enjoying the moment. When the echo of the council's footsteps faded, she turned to follow them; striding with her head held high.

Mrs. Saxon waited until Miss Roberts disappeared down the hallway before she moved. I expected her to walk out the other way, but she turned and looked up right at me. I froze, not that I wasn't already frozen. How could she know I was here? It's not like she could hear me breathing.

I waited right where I was, still hidden behind the post, waiting for her to say something, but she didn't. She just kept her stare right up at me. Her expression was, well... blank. There was no frustration showing from her encounter with the council. None of the concerns I would have expected following Mrs. Wintercrest's last comment crept in. She turned and walked back down the hallway where she came from, leaving me with an icy feeling. Had she given up? She couldn't, could she? The Mrs. Saxon I knew wouldn't. I couldn't explain what I had just seen or felt.

I wasn't sure how much time had passed before I finally stood up and made my way to the door. I was still numb, and mostly moving on autopilot, thinking about what I had seen and what the expression on Mrs. Saxon's face meant. It couldn't mean what I thought it did. My legs moved me toward my room, while my brain considered other possibilities. None of them fit, which left me more dismayed than before. Maybe that was it. Maybe she had given up hope. It was a point I didn't want to accept, but it was all that remained. I paused at my door for the briefest of moments to wipe away a tear that had formed. I wasn't much of a crier, but it seemed over the last many months I had felt the sensation of the tear rolling down my cheek more than I had ever remembered before. I will say I was never in the emotional tempest I was in now, which had to be the principal contributor. I just didn't want Samantha to see me like this if she was awake. She was sleeping when I left.

"Holy Shit!" someone screamed behind me.

Crap! I've been busted!

13

My head collapsed forward, sending my forehead thudding against the door.

"Holy Shit!" she said again, this time her own hand muffled her voice. I heard another gasp from behind her. I turned my head and saw Apryl and Pamela in the hallway, shaking and bouncing.

"Where...? When did you get here?" Apryl asked. I stood up and hurried toward them, holding a finger up to my lips.

"Holy shit!" Apryl said again.

She wasn't going to be quiet, but I needed her to be. I took a more direct approach. I grabbed them both and rushed into Apryl's room, slamming the door behind us. Everyone on the floor was already used to Apryl slamming her door. This wouldn't draw any attention. Apryl bounced on the floor repeating what appeared to be her new favorite saying, and Pamela ran over to me and hugged me around the neck as I tried to explain.

"You two need to be quiet. Please!" I begged, keeping my voice in a hushed tone.

Apryl repeated her new favorite saying twice more before she stopped. Then it was her turn to hug me while I continued to beg.

"Please be quiet. No one is to know I am here."

Pamela stood back, grinning from ear to ear. Apryl let go of my neck, but as she backed up, her hands traced down my arms until she gripped my hands, pulling my arms out away from me a bit. She gave me a quick once over, and then looked at me cockeyed before she looked down again. "Seems you've lost weight."

I dropped her hands. "Look, a lot of stuff has been going on, but before I tell you anything. I need you to promise you won't tell a soul I'm here." I looked at Pamela, who agreed in an instant. Apryl was still looking for the baby bump that was no longer there. "Apryl?"

"This is different for you. Usually you are sneaking out, not in."

I let out an exacerbated sigh, a real one, and tilted my head and placed both hands on my hips. "Do you promise?"

"Yea. Yea. I promise," agreed Apryl, and it was a good thing too. I hadn't really considered what I would do if they hadn't. I guess I could have left with Samantha.

"I'm not sneaking back. I've been here for a little over a month."

"What?" This time it was Pamela who let the outburst slip, while Apryl bent over at the waist and then fell back on her bed.

"Where?" asked Apryl.

"In my room," I said, pointing across the hall to where my room was.

That sent Pamela into a stuttering fit as she backed up to the bed next to Apryl. "The whole time?" she asked once she pulled herself together.

"Yep," I nodded, and I figured I might as well tell them everything. "Mrs. Saxon rescued me and Marcus Meridian from Mordin and brought us back here. We've been in the room most of the time if you don't count a few trips out to the woods for training or Mrs. Tenderschott's classroom. Oh yeah, and the library."

Apryl's black eyes narrowed, and a sly grin crept across her face. "We?" she asked. "You and Marcus Meridian?"

I was shaking my head when Pamela asked, "What about Nathan?"

"No, it's not like that," and I sighed again. There was no way of getting around this now. "Marcus is somewhere only Mrs. Saxon knows. She won't even tell me." Come to think of it, I hadn't really asked. "I haven't seen Nathan since I went back to New Orleans to convince him to come home, and he said no."

"Wait. Wait." Apryl waved her arms in front of her. "You went back? When?"

"Right after Mrs. Saxon rescued me. I went back to bring him back, and because of..." I paused not really wanting to get into everything, but I couldn't see any way to avoid it, "... because of what the witches did, he no longer trusts us and stayed there with the other vampires."

"I can't really blame him," Apryl said. She winced as soon as the words left her mouth. "Sorry."

I let it go. I knew what she meant, and I couldn't really disagree, at least where the council was concerned.

"Wait!" Apryl pointed right at me and then hopped off the bed. "If *we've* been staying in your old room for about a month, and it's not that witch Marcus and it's not Nathan that means..." She cut off her own sentence with her hand, but the squeal that followed still made it through.

"Shush."

Apryl dropped her hand from her face and bounced on her feet, "I want to see. I want to see."

"See what?" Pamela asked, confused.

"Her baby," answered Apryl, with a slug to Pamela's arm.

"Baby?" she asked, still confused, and then I saw the light bulb click on behind her steadily growing smile. Her black eyes became as wide as the expanse of outer space.

"Wait! Wait! Wait!" I held up both hands to stop the rush toward the door. "Just wait!" I caught myself almost yelling and snapped my mouth shut. Both Apryl and Pamela froze where they stood, and all three of us listened for the sound of anyone else moving in the hallway or one of the nearby rooms. There was nothing except the sound of the wind blowing outside. I lowered my hands and let out another involuntary breath. With it, I tried to release the tension I felt, and calmly said, "Just wait. Look, our presence here is supposed to be a secret. It's bad enough you already know that I am here. I can't."

"You don't trust us?" Apryl asked, and the question stung.

"It's not that. There is just a lot at risk here. My life. Her life, and really everybody else's too."

Apryl crossed her arms and scowled at me. "I forgot. You're Larissa Dubois. The woman that will save the world, all alone. I also forgot that you haven't needed any of our help along the way or ever trusted us." If her first accusation of not trusting them didn't sting, this one cut clear to the bone.

"No. It's not that," I said to apologize, but in truth, it kind of was. Mrs. Tenderschott had already told me of the interrogations of the other witches. Those witches that knew about me could handle that on their own, but a vampire would be helpless. "It's just.." I explained, but then that rationalization engine I called a brain kicked in and presented an argument that was hard to ignore. They already knew about me, and that also meant it exposed Samantha to the same risk whether or not they had seen her. So, I changed my answer. "There is something you need to know. She's not what you would expect." Now how to explain this? Words wouldn't really do it justice. At least not the ones I could put together. "Can you check to see if there is anyone in the hallway?"

I didn't have to ask twice. In an instant, Apryl ran out to the middle of the hallway. Once she surveyed it up and down, she motioned for us to follow. Just to be safe, I let Pamela go first. When she waved me in, I followed, and walked straight across to my room and opened the door. There was a chorus of silent giggling behind me, and I heard one of the two whispers of the word baby. I knew what they were expecting to find, and they would have if they had been here a month ago, a few hours after I gave birth.

The door opened, and they rushed in, stopping right inside the door. I had to give them a quick shove to make room for myself while I closed the door. Samantha was still asleep on her bed. I pushed through Apryl and Pamela and then walked over to her bed, where I sat and stroked her head. That was something I did often while holding her when she slept. It was a lot easier when she was smaller. I couldn't dare say younger because that was really just a week ago. That didn't mean I didn't still plan to hold her while she slept, no matter how big she had gotten. "Sam, can you wake up for a minute? I want you to meet two friends of mine."

She roused awake, and rolled over in my direction, opening her eyes. When she saw the two vampires standing there on the other side of the room, she sat up. It wasn't an abrupt or startled move, as most might make upon waking up to the sight of two vampires standing in your bedroom. But why would I expect her to react that way? She has seen that all her life. The abrupt and startled movements belonged to Apryl and Pamela, who appeared to struggle to understand what they saw.

"Apryl. Pamela. This is Samantha. My daughter." I let my brief introduction sink in for a moment. "I'm sure you both have some questions. Sam, this is Apryl, and Pamela. They are two of my closest friends."

"Mom?" Samantha asked curiously. "I thought we were supposed to be hidden."

The sound of her voice invoked another reaction from our two visitors.

"We are. Let's just say I messed up. I will explain later." I looked back at Apryl and Pamela. "Not what you were expecting?"

Both shook their heads and looked dumbfounded.

"Remember what Theodora told us about vampire pregnancies? It doesn't stop once they are born." I reached over and stroked my daughter's hair. I swear she had aged a few extra years since I left, and now looked only a year or two younger than myself. "Jen thinks she will hit an age and stop if she is a vampire. We just have to wait now."

Both of their jaws dropped to the floor, and I knew what that was from.

"Yes, she could be a vampire. We haven't tried anything to be sure, and before you both ask," I said with a finger up. "She is a witch. A very capable witch." I added with a great sense of pride, and I think Samantha felt that radiating from me. She, without any prompt from me, held open her hand as a whirlwind danced around on her palm before disappearing with a bright flash.

"So, she could be both, like you?" Pamela asked eagerly.

I nodded. "Could be. We just aren't sure." I replied, feeling odd talking about her like she wasn't in the room and yet she was sitting there in the bed next to me, while I still stroked her hair. So, I added my almost teenage daughter to the conversation. "Are we?" I asked, looking at her.

"Not yet. I don't crave blood, but I haven't really been around it. I eat normal food like everyone else here. I really love cheeseburgers, but mom," she stopped and stammered while she turned in the bed a little more toward me. "There are a few things I haven't told you yet. I have been experimenting on my own."

"You have?" I asked, sounding worried, but I was more concerned than worried. I hadn't seen Samantha look grim at all in her entire life, yet at this moment that was how she looked.

"I have. I was curious. I can hold my breath for a really long time."

"How long?" Apryl asked enthusiastically as she stepped forward in anticipation of the answer.

"About ten minutes, and I didn't even feel out of breath when I did it. I only let it out because I needed to answer one of Mrs. Tenderschott's questions."

"Interesting."

"Yes, it is," I said, agreeing with Apryl.

"She breathes, but can hold it that long. Could it be magic protecting her or something?"

Now that was a possibility I hadn't considered, and one I didn't even know if it was possible, but there was still so much I didn't know I couldn't dismiss it.

"She breathes?" asked Pamela.

"Yes, and she has a heartbeat." The heads of two of the three vampires in the room shot toward Samantha. They were searching for what they couldn't feel. Since Mrs. Saxon put up her block to protect us from anyone feeling her, she was a hole. A big null. A void. It was disconcerting. I knew it. I felt it when she first did it, but I got used to it. I needed to let them off the hook before they started doubting their own abilities. "Mrs. Saxon charmed the room to keep any of you from feeling it. Just to keep us hidden. I can't even feel it now either, but I did before that. Trust me, it's there, and it's strong."

Apryl stepped forward and held out her hand toward Samantha. "May I?" I knew she wanted to double check for herself, and I nodded, giving Samantha a reassuring pat on the shoulder.

Samantha held out her hand, and Apryl grabbed hold of it. Then she ran her other hand up Samantha's arm. She searched up and down her arm for the feeling of blood flowing under her skin. I knew it wasn't there, another sensation blocked by the charms, but that didn't stop Apryl from continuing to search.

"Odd. It's not there, but something else is. She is warm to the touch, but my icy touch doesn't cause any goose pimples."

"It doesn't?" I yanked Samantha's arm from Apryl to check for myself. I might have done it a little too hard. "I'm so sorry. Are you okay?" I reached over and hugged her.

"Yes mom. I'm fine. It didn't hurt."

"It didn't?" I asked again, just to be sure, as I released her.

"No." She shook her head and twisted her arm back and forth to show me it was fine. I took her arm in my hand, gentler this time, and rubbed my hand up and down it. She shivered, but Apryl was right. Her skin never changed. Odd. I looked up at Apryl, amazed. Nathan's skin always went gooseflesh when I touched him. Maybe she had gotten used to it.

"I think we need to set up some vampire trials to find out."

"What are vampire trials? Are they like the seven wonders?"

Apryl burst out laughing at Samantha's questions, and I knew why. There was no such thing as vampire trials, at least nothing as formal as the seven wonders. I didn't have any idea what Apryl had in mind, but she was right on the thought. We needed to find out for sure.

14

During the night, I filled them in on everything I knew. There didn't seem to be any reason not to anymore. I was the big secret, and they already knew about that. Everything else they either knew part of or had heard rumors of going around the coven. They also brought me up on what was happening in the coven. I played dump as Apryl recounted how Gwen tortured her with the charm. To hear her tell it, the charm brought her close to death. I could see that if you were exposed long enough, and I had no doubt that Gwen prolonged it as much as she could. There were more stories they shared, some where my name was basically burned in effigy. Not all that shocking considering my standing with the council. Hearing Gwen's name in each story wasn't that shocking either. It seemed with the council here; Gwen had become more of a little "witch" than I remembered.

We did our best to keep things down to not wake Samantha up. She didn't share the same gift, or curse, we did. At least not to the level of not having to sleep. She still needed that every night, and the few nights she didn't sleep well, she was a bit of a grouch in the morning. A morning person my daughter was not. That gave us plenty of time to talk about what Apryl called the "vampire trials". We needed to find out if there was any part of her was vampire. I rejected Apryl's first suggestion. There was no way I was going to take my daughter out on a hunt to let her feed and see how she reacts. No way. No how. There had to be other ways.

Pamela, who also shook her head at Apryl's suggestion, came up with another plan which focused more on the physical attributes. Our speed, endurance, and strength. It seemed like a good approach that would absolutely do it. She just needed to promise not to use magic to improve her skills. When to do the test was yet to be decided, but where was clear. We would need to sneak out again, but I didn't think that was a problem any longer.

When they left to get ready for their classes, we did the same. It wouldn't be long before Master Thomas popped in for our morning session. My first therapy session of the day with Edward would follow that. Samantha would receive her private lessons with Master Thomas while I answered the same questions I did yesterday for Edward. I wasn't sure if he expected different answers every day or not. He knew the cause now, and he also knew what it took to fix it, even though he didn't want to accept it. This was our routine day after day, and it had a pleasant rhythm to it, which, believe it or not, had a calming effect on both of us. Samantha always appeared calm. She was the typical happy-go-lucky child that enjoyed learning all she could do in the magical world around her, unless her mother did something stupid and she needed to bail her out. For me, it filled the time and kept me from circling that void. That didn't mean some of my gloominess didn't rub off on her.

I often caught myself sitting and looking out the window, missing Nathan with every fiber of my being. I wasn't just hurting for me. I was hurting for Samantha too. She was missing all these moments with her father, and he was missing everything with his daughter. Her first words, her first steps, and not to mention her first spell. That broke my heart more than not feeling his arms around me. Things became gloomier after I heard his voice call out to me yesterday, and then again last night. It wasn't a longing or a missing that I felt. Those would feel like happy emotions compared to this. This was a loss and fear, and they physically drained me. It was no longer a wonder of where he was. It was an obsession. I even stared out the window, as if I could see him if I tried hard enough. When I didn't, I fell further into my personal pit of despair, and just like she had many times before, Samantha sensed it, and came over and wrapped her arms around me. Now they could wrap all the way around me, seeing that she was almost as tall as I was. She always asked me what was wrong, and I always told her the same. "Nothing. Just thinking."

We never really talked about her father. I mean, she knows she has one, and she knows he isn't here with us, and when the topic of him comes up, I say he will be with us soon and that is it. I haven't gone into the love story of Larissa and Nathan, the classic Greek tragedy. Perhaps either of us could be the tragic hero in that story. One day she will know everything, but not until he is here with us, and she can get to know him and hear it from both of us.

Right on schedule, Master Thomas appeared, and our day began. Samantha greeted Master Thomas with a hug.

"Morning Samantha, Larissa."

"Morning Master Thomas," Samantha greeted him cheerily. I said nothing, and just climbed off the windowsill I was perched on, and readied myself for our training, or what I saw was an exercise in futility. I hated to break it to Master Thomas. His theory that magic is like a muscle wasn't exactly working here. My magic was all tangled up in the world's biggest charley horse and no amount of work had even loosened it a bit. Only the rancid contents of those jars had.

"It looks like rain outside, so we are going somewhere else this morning. Shall we?" He didn't wait for an answer. He never did. With a quick spin of his arm, a portal opened, and he and Samantha hurried through. I started for the portal and then stopped, knowing I needed to drink a jar first. I walked over to them with the portal still spinning behind me, waiting for me. My hand hovered over the jars. Not because of the horrible tasting concoction they held, but because I knew I needed to preserve them for what I had planned. There were only three left, and I needed one for my training today. I saw this problem as an equation that would not work out in my favor, and it wasn't because I hated math. I knew a little sip would not cut it. That was a fact I found out the hard way last night. Maybe I could get away with half, saving some for another day. How long would that half last me? We were about to find out.

I drank that half and followed them blindly through the portal, emerging into a room that was all too familiar. One that had been used for secret classes before, and seemed fitting to be used for that again. The moment my foot hit the stone floor and I saw my first large stone archway, I knew exactly where I was. I was back at the scene of the crime. The place where Master Thomas had laid his master plan on me. Our secret plan, which, as it turns out, wasn't all that secret.

"Larissa, it's so good to see you." Mr. Demius, our master of the dark arts, approached me and warmly hugged me. Then he turned and hugged my daughter just as warmly. "So, have you been practicing?"

"Yes, I have," responded Samantha.

"You've been teaching her?" I asked curiously. It seemed someone else had been getting some secret training of her own.

"Of course," he said, with a look of shock that I didn't know. "We all have while you are going through your training and other sessions. She is a fast learner, just like her mother." He looked at her and did something I hadn't seen often. He smiled.

I stood there and waited for that little girl giggle I had heard from her for a few days when someone complimented her. Maybe it was her nervous laugh when she received attention. I used to do the same when I was younger. Usually when my parents were bragging about me. This time, it never arrived, and I looked to see a pleasant and confident look on my daughter's face. She was growing up, more than just in her height. How was it possible for someone to grow and mature years in just a month? I didn't know. Just another one of the mysteries of the universe that I didn't have answers to. Add it to the rather long list I had accumulated.

"Let's get started," Master Thomas barked.

"Training calls." I waved bye to Mr. Demius, but I watched over my shoulder as he and Samantha headed down to the front of his classroom for her own training. I had to admit, I was a little distracted as Master Thomas put me through the paces.

It was the same every day. Our routine was like morning calisthenics, if you subscribe to his theory that magic was like a muscle.. It was the same thing every day. We started with simple telekinesis, my specialty, and then moved on to creating fire and other elemental magic. We usually stopped with some fire tricks and maybe a little air movement, which, to be honest, I never really enjoyed before. It seemed boring to me compared to sending a huge fireball racing across the room, but just being able to do something like that in my current situation felt good.

My distracted state showed up when he asked me to try one more elemental trick by controlling water. This was something he and Master Demius had me perform before in this class. It was a three-part request. First, I had to create some in the basin against the wall. Then, I had to pull it from the basin toward me while in complete control of it, causing it to change shape and direction. The last step was one that took a lot of practice before, but again one that once I mastered it seemed impressive. Right there in the classroom, I needed to produce a small thunderstorm, by turning the water into a cloud and then compressing it harder and harder. I wasn't sure if Master Thomas intended for me do that last step today. It didn't matter; I didn't get that far. I lost a little control, make that a lot of control, while I was calling it to me, and the water fell to Mr. Demius's floor with a splash. In my defense, it wasn't exactly my fault. How could I focus on what I was doing when my daughter was learning her first rune from Mr. Demius on the other side of the room? I heard them talking about it, and he was giving her the same descriptions and instructions my mother gave me. It was hard enough not to stop all together and watch as she created a floor of grass under her feet. Too bad the water I dropped wasn't closer to them and I couldn't make the excuse I was trying to water it.

"You need to stay focused," cautioned Master Thomas, while Mr. Demius scowled at the puddle on his floor before he waved a hand, sending it back to the basin. "Push all those concerns and thoughts you have out of the way. They are controlling you."

He was clueless at what this distraction was until he finally caught where my eyes were looking, and then he turned and stood next to me, sharing the same view. "She is quite amazing, isn't she? Watching her learn and negotiate her way through spells and other witchcraft, you would think she has been doing this all her life." He caught himself, and we shared a look. "Okay, I walked into that one, but you know what I mean. She has only been at this a few weeks and is still more capable than most of those studying here in this coven."

Mr. Demius continued to drill her on creation by having her form everything from living plants to inanimate objects like chairs, rocks, and tables. I knew what he had her created wasn't as important as her learning exactly how she created such a variety of objects. Once she understood that, she could create anything. I couldn't be prouder. I only wished Nathan was here to see the young woman she had become.

"I think it's because of her family," he said with a wink. "Your family is a powerful family, and add in Mrs. Saxon's contribution. That combination couldn't produce anything but..."

"I thought it could skip a generation?" I interrupted his compliment. He was right, and it caused the pride to well up inside of me, but there was a fact to consider in there. It had skipped Nathan.

"Well, yes," he stammered. "It can skip a few generations," he continued, still stammering. "Take Nathan, for example. It obviously skipped him, but that doesn't take away from his family." He walked forward toward my daughter and Mr. Demius. "Demius, let me have a go," he offered, and at that moment, I knew my training was done for the day.

It was both a relief and a disappointment. I was tired of the same old frustrating attempts that resulted in nothing more than a few birthday party magician tricks. Okay, maybe I was being a little overdramatic and giving birthday part magicians too much credit, but it wasn't what I was used to, and wasn't what I needed. As I watched Mr. Demius let Master Thomas take his place in the training of my daughter, I had to wonder; maybe I wasn't the answer after all. Maybe it was Samantha. No! I shook that thought from my head. I wouldn't put that pressure on her. This was my job, and I needed to handle things myself, so I did the only thing I could do. I started practicing by myself.

"Still not focused?" asked Mr. Demius as he approached. I dropped my hands before I attempted my first spell on my own. I hadn't even decided what to try first.

"That's always my problem," I said, with a hint of venom. That word was one he had practically beaten into my head during our original refresher sessions.

"No. It's different this time."

I raised my hands and started again. Where would I start? I guess where I left off. Back to the elemental magic, skipping water for obvious reasons. Wind it would be. I picked a corner of the room and held out my hands as if to guide the air around in a swirl, but Mr. Demius grabbed them and placed them down by my side.

"Why don't you rest and relax for a minute? I know what Master Thomas is trying to do, but all it's going to do is compound your frustration as you struggle with things you know inside you should be able to do easily."

Finally, someone that spoke common sense around here.

He stood beside me, watching the lesson on the other side of the room. "Remember what I once said. Stronger focus makes stronger magic. The more frustrated you become, the less control you will have."

"Tell me something I don't know."

He laughed, which was the first time I had ever heard it. It was a jolly one at that. Our dark arts master. The king of everything that scared most people had a jolly laugh. "You would be the expert on that subject. From the day I met you, you have always had something clouding your mind."

Wait? Was that a shot at me? "I guess I'm complicated then," I sniped back rather shortly.

"Not at all. You have powerful emotions, and before you take that the wrong way," he warned, and it was a good thing he did. He was about to find out how strong my emotions were and how well they were dealing with everything at the moment. Mount Saint Helens would seem popgun compared to what was about to erupt, and this would be all me, no magic at all. "That is what makes you a powerful witch. Oh, sure, anyone born into a family of witches can perform magic. Plenty of examples of that have come through this coven. There are several of them here now, but how great you are depends on how much you care, how strongly you feel, and how well you can focus that." His eyes cut in my direction. "Tiring of that word, aren't you?"

"No, because it's true," I replied calmly, believing that the answer would earn me some points and make me seem mature.

"Oh, come on," he chided. "I saw the grimace on your face. We have basically beat it into you with a bat since you got here. It's only because we all know how great you could be if you can just harness it. Focusing and clearing your mind doesn't mean being void of emotions. It means controlling them. Removing the feeling of chaos and feeling the power of those emotions flowing through you. Look at your daughter over there. She is full of joy, and it shows in how easy she is performing. You right now, you're a mess, and it is completely understandable with everything you have gone through. Beating yourself up about your struggles with magic won't solve this. Give yourself a break."

"I've done everything but physically beat myself up, and nothing's worked," I huffed.

Then it happened again. Another uncharacteristic moment as Mr. Demius put a supportive arm around my shoulders. "The problem is you are doing all the wrong things. You and I both know what you must do, and there isn't anything else you can do that will fix this. There is no potion. There is no spell. There is no secret to force the magic out. It's bottled up in you with all your emotions and uncertainty, and there is only one way to unleash it."

I stood there in shock. Were he and I in agreement on this? Was that even possible? Or was this another ruse, like my secret training before, that wasn't all that secret? That had to be it, and I would not be the pawn in this game anymore and I called him on it. "Let me guess. This is all part of some plan concocted by Mrs. Saxon to tell me to do what I know I should, without her really being involved, like my supposedly secret training?"

He just shook his head. "No Larissa. This is just you and I talking. She knows what you need to do, and we have talked about it, but she is concerned that you entering the chaos that is going on will just unsettle things even more. Further hindering your chances of fulfilling what we all hope you can become." His head bounced back and forth as if he were considering two sides of an argument. Then, with a skewed smile, "She might be right, but I think interjecting a little instability into this chaos might just be what is needed. Not to mention, if you don't, this problem will never solve itself, now will it?"

He had a point that I agreed to with silence. "Does he know?" I nodded toward Master Thomas.

"He knows what you need, but he agrees with Mrs. Saxon. They are both of the camp that either Nathan will find his way here, or in time, your emotions will fade and settle all on your own. But we both know how strong that bond you feel is, especially now that you share a daughter. That won't happen anytime soon, if ever."

"But" I said rather loudly, causing a look from both Samantha and Master Thomas. I let the silence in the room settle back around us, and for them to resume their lesson before I asked what burned at the tip of my tongue. "Mrs. Saxon. Shouldn't she already know? She seems to know everything else that is going to happen."

"You mean her divination?"

"Yes. She said she saw me coming and knew how my path would lead."

"Which she may," Mr. Demius said, "I know her well enough to know how much she loves and cherishes her son. If she had any visions about what would happen to him, where he was, and when he would come back, she wouldn't be standing around. A mother's love is the strongest bond in the world. After she lost her husband, Nathan became her world. If I had to guess based on how she has been working the council, and all the questions I overhear her ask Jen and Kevin, she doesn't see his future all that clearly at the moment. If she sees it at all."

"So, it's up to me?"

"I'm afraid so."

Even after the conversation we just had, hearing his very frank answer was a shock. He was practically telling me to do everything that everyone else here was telling me not to. I was so stunned; and speechless, which was an odd state for me to find myself in. I just stood there and watched my daughter and Master Thomas work across the way, while I thought over what Mr. Demius had told me. It was what I already knew, but to hear someone else say it added more fuel to what was already burning inside.

"Larissa," he said, his voice steady and reassuring, "set aside your concerns for others. Trust your instincts and do what you believe is right. Mrs. Saxon's opinion, Benjamin's thoughts—let them fade away. If deep inside, you know it's the path to follow, then it is." He turned and gripped me by the shoulders and locked his eyes with mine. "And most importantly, disregard the council's judgment. Some may react with outrage, but once you fulfill your destiny, the rest will rally behind you. Trust me on that."

"Don't worry. I don't give a rat's ass what they think."

"Good," Mr. Demius commented while releasing me.

"Plus, there seems to be something going on there anyway," I remarked. It was just an off-the-cuff remark, but it got Mr. Demius's full attention.

"So, you have noticed it too?"

"Miss Roberts?" I asked.

"Mmm hmm," he responded. "It has been that way for several years now."

Master Thomas finished his lesson with Samantha before Mr. Demius could elaborate. As they walked toward us, Master Thomas gave her one final pointer. If I had to bet, it was probably something about focus. It was his favorite. I had heard it more times than I wanted to remember. That gave me another moment alone with Mr. Demius, and considering the conversation we had just had, I saw an opening.

"Mr. Demius. I was reading through an old book of spells Edward found for me," no lie there, "and I came across a related spell I didn't know. Congero. Do you know what that is?"

"I do. You really should study your Latin more. Congero. To amass or accumulate. It's a potion, not a spell. You can use it to increase the volume of a substance. The Italians mostly used it to make more wine." His right hand found his chin and stroked it. "Come to think of it, that is really the only use I have seen, but never mind," he gathered himself. "It's an old spell, but it works."

I waited for him to ask why I wanted to know, and what spell I was looking up that referenced that, but he never did. He just let the answer sit there until Samantha and Master Thomas finished the discussion they were having about his last piece of advice, which I was still assuming was about focus until I heard otherwise.

"Truly amazing Samantha. Truly amazing."

My daughter beamed from ear to ear at Mr. Demius's compliment. I had to admit I was beaming, too. He was one hundred percent correct. She was amazing in so many ways, most of which had nothing to do with what she and Master Thomas were just working on. She was a witch, and an amazing one at that, but she was so much more.

"This was a great session. Both of you," Master Thomas looked us both in the eye. "Students will be coming in soon, so you need to head back up to your room." He spun open a portal back to my room while he said, "I will be back up this afternoon for your second session. Don't forget your session with Edward around noon."

How could I forget? I thought as I put my arm around my daughter and started for the portal. I saw a figure waiting for us and gave Samantha a little shove forward. and turned to Master Thomas and Mr. Demius. "Master Thomas, what time is our afternoon session?" I asked as I walked backward toward the portal, doing my best to hold their attention. I knew good and well the session was at five this afternoon, just like it always was.

"Five," he answered curiously.

"Oh, that's right," I remarked, as my back foot stepped through. "See you then." I stepped through. The portal closed right in my face.

"That was close," Lisa said with a long exhale. Samantha ran over to Lisa and gave her a big hug. "I was just standing here, and the portal opened right in front of me."

"We're lucky they didn't see you. What are you doing here?"

"Mission accomplished," she said, pulling a piece of paper out of her pocket. "I know what Congero is and why it is important."

"Me too."

15

"We can use Congero to stretch a single drop of blood into all the blood we need," Lisa enthusiastically proclaimed.

"Absolutely. Why didn't I make the connection?" I wondered aloud.

Lisa and I were absolutely ecstatic! We were practically jumping out of our skins with excitement as we celebrated our discovery! This was the last piece of the puzzle. Now I just needed to put it all together and hope it worked.

"And there are only three ingredients. I know exactly where they are in Mrs. Tenderschott's classroom," continued Lisa.

My enthusiasm about my own discovery took a bit of a downturn. She had made it further than I had. I hadn't thought to ask Mr. Demius about the ingredients or how to do it. The thrill of knowing what the spell was had probably blinded me from all I didn't know, but needed to know about it. Thank God Lisa had thought about that and asked. If I went back to Mr. Demius now, he might ask what I was using it for. Though I don't believe he would attempt to stop me after our little discussion. He might even help. That was a thought. Having someone with his experience would be a boost, especially with me in my current state. But I dismissed that before I let the thought gain any more momentum. I couldn't put anyone else at risk. Too many have paid a price because of me.

"I can grab them tonight and bring them back up." Lisa leaned in and added, "I just learned a little invisibility spell. I have been dying to try."

"Invisibility?" I asked, thinking about all the uses I could have for something like that in my present status of confinement. "Does it make you fully invisible?"

"Yep. They can't see or hear…" Lisa stopped. Her enthusiasm drained away, and she looked past me, over my shoulder, with deep concern. I turned and saw a similar expression looking back at us.

"Samantha, what's wrong?"

"Oh nothing," she said. "Just listening in on some weird vampire plan. Lisa, I thought you were just a witch, not both, like my mother."

"I am just a witch. Why?" Then a big toothy grin appeared on Lisa's face, and it appeared she answered her own question. "I get it. The plan to create a lot of blooood." Lisa exaggerated the last word and threw in her best Count Dracula impersonation on top of it.

Oh, lord. She didn't have a clue what we were talking about. To her, it probably sounded as if we were planning a banquet for vampires. I guess we needed to explain our little plan to Samantha, especially since she is a major player, or piece of it.

"Samantha, it's not what it sounds like."

"Oh, it's exactly what it sounded like," giggled Lisa.

"Stop it." I slapped her on the shoulder. "The blood is not for what you think it is. It has nothing to do with vampires, and actually," I straightened up after thinking of this point and channeled my inner Mrs. Saxon. "It has everything to do with being a witch. Why don't you have a seat on your bed, and I will explain everything to you."

Samantha still looked concerned, but walked back and sat on the edge of her bed with only a slight hesitation.

"Where to start?"

"Why not start with your problem? It might help for her to understand the why."

"Yes," I agreed. Lisa was absolutely right. It was an obvious place. Understanding the why would help her understand the necessity for what we were going to do, and not to mention it would finally address the elephant in the room. Her father. It's not that she or I ever tap danced around the topic. We just hadn't discussed *everything*, and in this case, *everything* was really *everything*.

"Sam, you know how mom is having trouble with her magic?"

She nodded, then looked at the tray of jars. Two of which were still full, and another sat next to those, half full. "It's why you have to drink those before any training."

"That's right, but I'm not sure you understand why I am having problems."

"Mom. I might be young, but I'm not stupid. You miss my father, and that has you all confused and out of focus."

From the mouth of babes. She nailed it. She completely nailed it and said it better than anyone else had. Even me, but if only it were that simple.

"I've heard you talking to others, and it makes complete sense. So, you need to find him and bring him home."

Dang. I almost had to reach up with a hand to make sure my jaw hadn't dropped. My almost a month and a half old daughter, that now looked like she was going on fifteen, understood it all, or let's make that most of it. There were some details missing. Ones she would have had no way of knowing. I never discussed them in front of her.

"That's right." I swallowed hard to push down the nerves that were bubbling up inside. "But there is more to the story." I paused, worried what I felt welling up inside would cause me to break down. I took a few beats to gather myself. I looked down and locked my eyes with Samantha's. That was when I realized what I felt wasn't so much a worry about me breaking down while I told her. It was the concern that what I was about to tell her would destroy her. "Your father is Nathan Saxon."

Her eyes jerked, causing me to stop. "Mrs. Saxon is my grandmother?"

"Yes," I said, with a sigh, feeling even more guilty than I had ever imagined I would have about withholding that little detail. It was bad enough she was missing the opportunity to get to know her father, but I had also denied her from knowing who her grandmother was. Yes, she was still a part of her life, but who she was to Samantha was a secret that I had kept, until now. A secret that Ms. Saxon agreed with.

"She never said anything. I just thought she was just being nice."

"No Sam, she is your grandmother."

"Why didn't you tell me?" Samantha's eyes searched me for answers. Those answers led down a path that I didn't want to go down, but I had to. "I wanted you to get to know your father by actually getting to know your father, and not by what you might hear from me, Mrs. Saxon, or anyone else. Does that make sense?"

"I guess, but..." she started and then bit her lip and looked up at me.

"Go on Sam, but what?"

"Why couldn't I know who he is?"

I swallowed hard. I knew what I had to say. Just saying the words would tear me to pieces, but that was nothing compared to what I feared it would do to her. Whatever family image she had in her head was about to be shattered. "I'm afraid some of it is bad news." My warning appeared to have snuffed out that light. "Yes Nathan, her son, is your father."

Oh God, how do I do this? I tried to convince myself she had to know. She had to know everything, but it was something about looking into her deep green eyes that made me reconsider leaving out details. I could tell her without telling her all the horrifying pieces. But to what end? She would eventually find out, and the time needed to be now. "He was a mortal when we met," I choked out. "Which means he wasn't a witch or a vampire. A few weeks before you were born, a vampire named Jean St. Claire attacked us, and Nathan saved my life, but he was bit and became a vampire." A quiver developed in Samantha's bottom lip. I hadn't even made it to the worst of it yet.

"Now this might be hard to understand. I actually don't understand it all yet. The Council of Mages attacked us while we were in New Orleans, separating us. I have tried to find him, but the council has continued to attack them, turning him against anything to do with witches. He is lost and confused and needs us to help bring him home. Understand?"

"Why are they attacking?" Samantha asked. Every word shook as her voice cracked multiple times.

"I don't know, to be honest. I have a theory, but I don't know if I am right, and that isn't really that important. What is important is finding Nathan and bringing him back home, where he can be safe with us."

Samantha nodded, quivering chin and all. I walked over and sat next to her and took her hand in mine. It trembled.

"Now, there is a spell that will help us find him, but I am going to need your help with it."

"Okay, just show me what I need to do." Samantha wiped away a rogue tear and looked at me eagerly. She still looked devastated, but I knew what she was feeling. The hope of a resolution. The hope of ending the hurt. Even if that hurt may have just started.

"We need a drop of your blood."

She lurched back away from me, and I felt her hand jerk, but she didn't jerk it completely out of my hand. "My blood?"

"Yes, you are his daughter, and this spell needs the blood of a direct relative. The closer the relation, the better." I searched her face for understanding and found just a hint.

"So, you don't need me to help with performing the spell?"

"Oh, I will need someone's help with that, for sure, but first we need a drop of your blood. Then we will use a potion, Congero. The one you heard Lisa and I talking about. We need to use that to create enough blood to cover a large piece of parchment. According to what I read, if we do this right, it will draw a map to him on the parchment."

"Okay, let me get this right," Samantha asked, peering at me and then Lisa. "You need to use a potion to create enough of my blood to spread across a large piece of paper so another spell can draw a map on it that will lead to my father?"

"Pretty much," I nodded, and then to help reinforce it a little more I sprung up off the bed, almost forgetting to let go of her hand first, and then sprinted across the room to the desk, where I grabbed the book that was still open to that page. I sat back down and placed the book on her lap and turned it back one page to the start of the spell.

When I pointed at the top, Samantha started reading on her own. Her eyes grew in size the further she read. When she finally reached the end, she looked up, but said nothing.

"See, it's all there," I said, picking the book up and setting it down beside me, careful not to lose the page.

"Okay." Samantha let out a long and slow exhale, and cautiously asked, "How do we do this?"

"We need some ingredients," I said and looked right at Lisa, then I made my way to my desk. "You have the list for Congero, and here is the list for the rest of the spell." I grabbed a pencil and paper and scribbled the list quickly, before I handed the paper to Lisa.

16

Operation Blood-Map was in full go when the clock rolled over to nine that night. That was the name Apryl gave it when I told her about the plan. Right on time, a portal opened, and Lisa stepped through, wearing a plaid backpack over the top of a long black coat. When I saw Jack following her, I walked forward with my hands outstretched to block him.

"No. No. No. Not going to happen."

The portal closed before I could send him back through. I had already spent the better part of the last hour trying to tell Apryl she wasn't coming with me. This wasn't even a case where I had to convince her. The answer was a flat no. No one was. Just me. This was something I had to do, and I would not risk anyone else. Apryl kept arguing and even challenged me to stop her, which would be easier than she might believe. The others might be a problem. Once they knew where I was going, they could easily pop in there on their own.

"Jack needs to go back now!"

"I need some help to carry everything, and you are going to need some help. Those jars won't last you that long."

Based on my best guess, they were going to last maybe a day, but I didn't plan on using them unless I needed them. I was going there purely as a vampire, and I would have to rely on my speed and strength to find Nathan. In the plan I had worked out in my head, I would drink the half full one before I left so I could open a portal and have a little with me, but after that, I wouldn't touch it unless it was an emergency, or we were ready to come home. That was it.

"I can't ask you, and I won't let you. This is too dangerous on so many levels." Rogue witches were running around, attacking anything they believe was related to the council. Vampires were attacking anything they believed was a witch. The council's warriors were attacking both. I was walking into a war zone. The benefit I had over the others, I couldn't easily die. Not like Lisa or Jack could.

"You can't really stop us," Jack said forcefully as he stepped forward, as if some hero in a war movie stepping across a line drawn on the ground. The difference was, there wasn't a line, and I wasn't asking for volunteers.

"I can, and I will." I was bluffing, because I knew I couldn't, but I sure hoped he hadn't figured that out yet.

"This isn't Larissa against the world," he said firmly, staring right into my black eyes. I watched his expression and his chin never flinched. For a fleeting moment, I felt something for him I hadn't before. I actually had a brother. Wow, how far we had come.

"We can discuss that later." Lisa stepped between us. "I still need his help to gather the ingredients, and the last time we checked, your magic isn't that reliable. Seeing that he is the only other witch around here that knows you are even here, he was the only choice."

I looked at both of them. Their hands were empty, and Lisa's backpack hung limp from her shoulder. That meant they hadn't gathered them yet. "Where are they?"

"Still in Mrs. Tenderschott's classroom," Lisa said, and then held up a cautionary finger.

"And why? We kind of need them here." Her finger would not stop me from asking the obvious question.

"We do, but we need help."

She had already explained that as the reason she brought Jack. That was why my next move was to thrust my hand toward Jack and shake it to say—he's right there.

"No. He will help carry things, but even though Mrs. Tenderschott won't be able to see or hear us, she may notice things disappearing off her shelves. I've already popped down there twice, and she is still mulling around her classroom. It seems they have canceled the nightly tea they usually have with the council."

Tea? All sorts of odd images rolled in my head of that eclectic group sitting around with our instructions, pinkies extended while they drank tea and talked. They canceled it. I wondered if Mrs. Saxon's protest had something to do with that?

"We need either you or Sam to distract her while Jack and I do some shopping."

Okay, I saw where this was going, and I was all ready to volunteer, but someone beat me to it.

"I'll do it." Samantha leaped up from the bed and practically hopped across the floor at the opportunity.

"We both will. The two of us will be a better distraction than just one." I would not bow out that easily, plus as I saw it. One of us would need to keep a watch for where the activity was happening, so we could divert her away.

"Good then. When you're ready, head on down. We will pop down a few minutes after you."

Well, there was no time like the present. I looked at Samantha and motioned after her. Then I pointed right at Apryl. "You need to be gone by the time we get back."

Samantha immediately opened a portal and stepped through first. Then she motioned for me before saying, loud enough for everyone to hear. "It's all clear mom."

That was my cue, and I followed her through.

"Well, isn't this a pleasant surprise," cooed Mrs. Tenderschott from the front of the room. She was slaving over a stack of papers.

"I hope we aren't interrupting. We were bored and thought we'd come visit our favorite person."

"Not at all. I'm grading some tests," she explained while flipping through the stack. "I bet you don't miss this."

"I sure don't," I agreed as we walked to the front of the room and took our usual spots across the table from her.

"So, what's new with you two? Any break throughs?" she asked, directing the question at me.

"Not yet," I said with a reserved sigh. I didn't want to oversell our act, but as much as I tried not to, I caught myself being more deliberate with my speech and more animated with my arms and hands with every word. I told myself to relax. Mrs. Tenderschott wouldn't guess what we were doing in a thousand years. We had nothing to be worried about. I just needed to act naturally. Which was all fine to say, but doing it was something altogether different. I felt my body tense up, as a jar on the shelf behind her lifted and disappeared.

"I had hoped by now something would have worked. Are you still working with Master Thomas?"

"Yes. Twice a day, and sometimes Mrs. Saxon is there too. Sam is working with Master Thomas as well and is becoming quite good." I said to shift the attention away from myself. My nerves were getting to me. I wasn't sure if it was because I was deceiving her, or the worry I felt when it appeared someone almost dropped a jar behind her. They may be invisible, but graceful, they were not.

"Oh, I know. I have heard," she said, and turned her attention to Samantha. "They both brag about you often. Sam, I am curious. Does it come easy to you, or are you having to put a lot of concentration into it?"

Samantha didn't answer immediately. The floating objects behind Mrs. Tenderschott distracted her. Jar after jar lifted before being replaced back in their initial resting place. Lisa may have known where all the ingredients were, but I am guessing Jack didn't have a clue and was having to search jar by jar.

"Sam?" I whispered, to prompt her, but again she didn't answer, and now Mrs. Tenderschott turned around to follow her gaze. My hand slapped against my face, and I tried to hide my eyes and face. We had just been caught. But like with most things in the world, timing is everything. When Mrs. Tenderschott turned around, nothing was out of place or floating. It was as if they were not even there. I avoided letting out a stress filled exhale.

I elbowed Samantha, and she jerked out of her trance and answered Mrs. Tenderschott's question. "Yes ma'am. Most things have been pretty easy."

"That's a great sign. Your mother struggled at first," Mrs. Tenderschott said with a wink.

"That's not entirely true," I protested as two beakers of something brown were taken off the shelf to her left.

"Didn't you set your dresser on fire? And didn't you also burn down Mr. Helms' classroom?"

"Mom?" Samantha squealed. "Did you?"

"Yes, but..." I held up a hand to stop any interruptions before I corrected the facts here. "That was not my first attempts. I was like you and able to learn new abilities quickly when I was first learning. The second time around, I was a little out of practice. It had been close to eighty years. Hell, I didn't even know I was a witch."

"That didn't stop you from sending Jack across the pool." Mrs. Tenderschott grinned wildly. A jar jostled slightly. All three of us turned in the sound's direction, but none of us saw anything. "Probably just a top I didn't put on tightly settling," Mrs. Tenderschott uttered, and got up.

"Mom, you threw Jack across the pool?" asked Samantha, taking her turn to bail us all out.

"He made me mad."

"Well, I will admit, back then he had a way of doing that to everyone," agreed Mrs. Tenderschott. She settled back down on her stool. "Samantha, that was how we found out your mother was a witch. See, when she arrived, we just thought she was a vampire. We knew there was a mystery about her, but we didn't know that the mystery was both who and what she was. Then one day Jack made some comment to her out at the pool."

"He called me an orphan," I interjected.

"Ah, so that is what he said. Now that I know what it was, I can agree. He got what he deserved. Your mom used telekinesis to throw him across the pool. I'm sure others wish they could have done the same. Jack had a way of rubbing people the wrong way."

"He's grown on me." I added, and just cringed, waiting to hear the clang of another jar, but there was only silence.

For the next forty minutes, Mrs. Tenderschott dragged me down memory lane in front of my daughter. Some of them were embarrassing stories, but others were some of my finer moments. A few I didn't really remember as grandly as she did. I think she embellished a bit, but I didn't mind. Especially when they were stories about me getting the better of Gwen. I quite enjoyed them.

It had been a while since I had seen anything move or disappear in the classroom. I hoped that meant they were done and gone, but there was no way to be sure. I glanced around the room again and saw nothing moving. What they were after shouldn't have taken that long to gather up. Of course, first they had to find it, and she had hundreds upon hundreds of jars and boxes of things on those shelves. Just to be sure, I took another glance around, and again saw nothing. I also listened for the beating of their hearts and took in a sniff for that metallic richness that flowed through their veins. Either they were gone, or that invisibility spell Lisa used covered everything. We took her next pause between stories as an opportunity to return to our room, and that was what we did. Even Samantha seemed to know it was time and yawned, giving us the perfect out.

After a series of hugs, Samantha opened the portal, and we walked back into our dark room. Only when we stepped through did we see Jack, Lisa, and Apryl hiding in the corner. Samantha closed it as soon as we were through instead of letting it close on her own, as she usually did.

"What the hell took you guys so long?" asked Lisa, as she stomped out of the corner and over to my desk. There were three jars and two bowls sitting on it.

"You were invisible. How were we supposed to know when you were done?"

Lisa thought about that for a moment, and then suggested, "We probably should have come up with some kind of signal."

"You were invisible. What were you going to do? Wave an invisible hand in my direction?"

"Oh yeah," Lisa said, stumped.

"We could have dropped something," suggested Jack.

"You almost did," I pointed out. "Did you get everything?"

"Yep," Lisa pointed to the desk. "Everything's right here, including a bowl to mix it in, and..." she reached back inside the backpack and pulled out a roll of blank parchment paper. "Yep, we have everything except the last ingredient."

Everyone in the room knew what she meant and looked at Samantha.

"Are we going to do this now?" she asked.

"Yes," I said sternly, without explanation. When I saw both the concern and reluctance in her eyes, I took her hands in mine. "We need to. He needs our help and every moment we waste keeps him in danger. We can do this. Trust me on this. This will just show us where he is, and we can then develop a plan to go find him." I already had a plan. Once everyone was gone, I was going to go get him.

She agreed, reluctantly, and then held out a finger and I knew what she was offering. My first move was one of consultation, but not of the text. It was Apryl.

"You're supposed to be gone," I reminded her sternly.

"Not a chance. You may think you don't need me. You do. More than you know."

"Stop being dramatic, and just leave." I pointed to the door, but once I saw her shift her weight back on her heels and cross her arms, I knew it was settled and I had lost. She was as stubborn as they came, and I gave up, exacerbated. "You going to be okay with this?"

"Of course," she replied, dismissing the concern I had rather quickly, but that quickness bothered me. It seemed like nothing more than a reactive answer. I stared at her and searched her face and eyes for the true answer. I finally received it with a curt nod.

"Okay then." I looked at Lisa, and she glanced at the book on the table. There was nothing left to do but start. We walked together, nervously toward the book. I would be lying if I didn't say I felt some apprehension about this. This was next level magic. Even for me.

We arrived at the table, and I opened the book to the page. Lisa pulled out a piece of paper from the pocket of her long black coat. She opened it up and placed it on top of the page with the spell. "Congero," she said, and then began reading the instructions from her paper for everyone to hear as her finger traced each line.

"First, we put the drop of blood in the bowl. Then mix in two ground up sprigs of sage wood, two milligrams of silver dust, and a quarter cup of rose geranium infused vinegar. For every quarter cup of blood needed, we add a quarter cup of vinegar."

"Potion measurements need to be exact," I whispered, remembering Mrs. Tenderschott's daily warning before class began.

"Got that covered." Lisa rummaged through her backpack and pulled out a scale and measuring cup. "I came prepared." She sat both down on the desk.

"All right, Miss Girl Scout. If you are so prepared, how much do we need to make to cover that?" I pointed at the rolled-up piece of parchment. Lisa picked it up and then rolled it out onto the floor. It was a lot larger than I thought and seeing it didn't really help with the answer to the question. All I knew was we needed a lot.

"We could start with a quarter cup and then make more if we need it," suggested Lisa.

"No. We can't," I said defiantly. "That would require multiple samples from Sam. We won't prick her fingers more than once. We need to do this right the first time." I looked right at Lisa and saw her swallow hard.

"Okay, then," she studied the paper on the floor and then poured out one and a half cups of the vinegar and measured out six milligrams of the silver powder. Next, she pulled out six sprigs of sage wood and put them in a stone bowl. I knew where this was going. I had done it many times myself in Mrs. Tenderschott's class. We needed to grind the sprigs into a fine powder with a pestle. Getting it fine enough was the trick. Too coarse and it doesn't interact with the other ingredients, making the entire mixture off and the spell worthless. "While I do this," she looked right at me, "I need you to get the last ingredient."

I turned and looked at Samantha. She stood there, with a hand already held out for me. It shook. I took it and caressed it reassuringly before I selected a finger. Lisa, Miss Prepared, handed me a lancet and the bowl. I let go of Samantha's hand and held the bowl below it. Then spun the lancet in the fingers of my other hand and positioned the sharp edge just a breath's distance away from her finger. We locked eyes, and she answered the unasked question by pushing her finger slightly forward. I smelled it before I saw it. The first of several drops emerged and found their way to the bowl. It was intoxicating, but so was how brave my daughter was. I looked deep into her eyes and damned my own. She couldn't see the pride I had in her at that moment. Not that the finger prick was all that terrifying or torturous. It was how she took control of the situation. She knew what this was about and was as committed as I was to see it through. What I saw staring back at me started out as the face of my daughter, but then there were hints of another one. A look I hadn't seen on her face before, but one I knew well.

"Larissa!" cried Apryl, and I heard Jack start toward Apryl. "It's not me!"

I looked up at Samantha. Her eyes had turned black and shook as they searched for the source of the smell. I squeezed off the pinprick at the end of her finger and slammed the bowl back to Lisa. I didn't wait to feel her take it before I let it go. I hoped she was paying attention and grabbed it.

"Sam. Look at me," I said, taking her face in my hands. "You can do this. Just hold on and push it away. Fight that urge." Her head pulled back from me, but I held on. "You got to fight it."

"Samantha, listen to your mom," Apryl commanded. "I know this is hard. We both do. We have been there before. Fight it. Don't give in."

The smell diminished, and the blackness of her eyes followed suit. There was now a pungent odor in the room replacing that sweet metallic aroma. I pulled my daughter's face close to mine and caressed it. "Good girl."

"I covered it for now and poured the vinegar into the measuring cup. That should help until we produce the final quantity," Lisa said.

I turned around, still holding Samantha tightly. Her breath rushed in and out of her lungs at a sprinters pace, but it was slowing down, and I thought, *well, that answers that.*

Jack took over grinding the sage wood while Lisa spread out the parchment and readied everything else. She had it set up as an assembly line, and I could see she wanted to perform a quick mix and go right to the paper to avoid a repeat of what just happened as much as possible. She checked the contents of the stone bowl a few times, each time asking Jack to go finer. He never complained or objected. He just did as he was told until she finally said it was enough and took the bowl to its place in line.

"Ready?"

"Yep," I said, tightening my grip on Samantha, readying myself for a protest at how hard I was squeezing her.

We all watched as Lisa first combined the sage wood and silver powder. Then, as the instructions said, she added a half cup of the rose geranium infused vinegar for every half cup of blood we wanted to produce. So, a cup and a half. The odor was pungent to my nose. So much so, I barely noticed the smell of the three drops of blood in the bowl when she removed the cover. She didn't leave a big opening for that smell to escape before she poured in the mixture of the other contents over the top of the drops, and I breathed a sigh of relief.

"Are you ready for me to start the spell?" Lisa asked, holding the bowl.

"Let me do it," I volunteered. This was my mission, not hers.

Lisa held out the bowl for me to take, and the acidic vinegar odor invaded my nose before my hand grabbed it. I felt Samantha step back from my side, probably from the smell. Even Jack moved away. To save everyone from the assault, I stepped forward toward my desk where Lisa had prepared the potion, and then made an embarrassing discovery. Not only had I not asked Mr. Demius what the ingredients were earlier, I didn't even ask him what the spell was. "Um, I don't know it," I said with chagrin.

Lisa looked at me blankly.

"I never asked Mr. Demius about the ingredients or the spell. Just what it was."

I offered the bowl to Lisa, and she quickly took it. "Good thing I not only asked what it was, but I also practiced it with Ms. Tenderschott." She held the bowl in both hands, and quickly said, "Haec sume, fac plura. Haec sume, fac plura."

The contents bubbled and boiled to the top of the bowl's brim. The acidic vinegar smell dissipated, and the metallic smell of blood returned in force, turning the contents red. I turned and saw Samantha reacting again. Apryl wrapped her arms around her in a bear hug. "I got her. You finish this."

"The parchment."

Lisa was one step ahead of me and already had it spread out on the floor. She dribbled the contents of the bowl on the paper, and it soaked it up like a sponge. With no other way to spread it, we both began using our hands to spread the blood from edge to edge. It didn't take long to soak the material.

"Do the spell now."

Luckily, I knew that one, or knew where to find it. I sprang up from the floor and threw the paper containing the instructions for Congero up in the air, exposing the page I needed. It had both the Latin and English versions. I just imagined me butchering the pronunciation of the Latin words, so I opted for English.

"Blood is thicker than water, but runs like a river through our bonds, and keeps us always connected. Find Nathan Saxon and lead us to him."

The parchment shook against my floor. Then it spun around, slinging blood and sparks everywhere. I watched it and looked for any signs of a map forming in the blood., but nothing formed. Instead, the center of it disappeared before our eyes, with sparks forming around its edge, showering the room. Inside the sparks, I saw something appear. A place. Then I realized what this was. I made a quick check of the page, and realized I had read the wrong spell just as the ring of sparks engulfed the room, and all of us with it. Luckily for me, I had packed up the jars of my magic boosters in a bag and could grab it before it closed.

17

"I read the wrong spell."

"You what?" Lisa screamed, throwing her hands up in the air. Until that moment, everyone was looking around, exploring the forest that my mistake had landed them in, but once I made my admission, they were all looking at me in disbelief.

"The pages faced each other. There was one spell to produce a map, which was the one I wanted to read, but I accidentally read the other one."

"And what did that one do?" asked Apryl. "As if we don't know." She swiped at a bare branch on a nearby tree.

"Probably landed us in a random forest in the middle of nowhere," remarked Jack as he stomped through the underbrush.

"Mom?" Samantha asked, distressed. I held up a finger to put Apryl's question on pause while I rushed to my daughter.

"What is this line I see in front of me?"

"Line?" Lisa asked and joined me next to Samantha. "Did she ascend?"

I shook my head, no. I knew exactly what Samantha saw, and the others would have too if I had told them what the spell I read actually did. Now was the time to let them in on the secret that only I knew.

"That line is the path to your father. That is what the spell I read does. It takes you close to them and then leads you to them. The one I thought I was reading was supposed to draw a map to them." I ran a hand through my hair.

"Well, that's stupid. Why doesn't it take you right to them?" asked Jack. He stood next to Samantha and attempted to see the line himself. Of course he saw nothing and walked away shaking his head.

"This was not my plan. I wanted to create the map, and then come find him. On my own, and prepared. This wasn't how I wanted it to go at all," I sorrowfully apologized. "Lisa. Jack. I need you guys to take Samantha and Apryl back to the coven. Let me finish this on my own."

The two stubborn looks that responded were not surprising, but their presence was disappointing.

"Guys, this isn't the time to be obstinate."

"That's a word only an old person would use." chided Jack. "We aren't going anywhere, and, I seem to remember, you don't have the ability to send us back yourself." He twisted that last bit into my side with a smirk. He was right, but there was still someone that could, and she wouldn't tell me no.

I grabbed my daughter's hands and looked into her eyes. "Sam, this is something I need to do. Take the others back to the coven. I will return with your father once this is all done."

I felt her hands squeeze mine. This was her saying goodbye before she left with the others. I knew it and was about to thank her when she surprised me.

"No. I won't. You need us, and most of all, you need me. I can see the path to him. You can't, and don't you even think you can convince me to tell you where it goes."

Samantha let go of my hands and walked away, leaving me looking right at Apryl and Lisa. Never one to let a snide remark go unspoken, Apryl said, "Rebellious teenager." Then she and Lisa walked past me, following Samantha.

"Mom, are you coming?" Samantha called.

I was about to start one last protest to appeal to someone's, anyone's, sensibility, and logic, but I stopped. I knew good and well nothing I said was going to change things. My friends had already proven how stubborn they can be more than a few times, and Samantha, well, she was my daughter, and that told me everything I needed to know.

"I've got everyone's back," Jack said as he passed, joining the procession that now weaved through the woods behind me. He stopped just behind me and whispered, "But, just to be safe, you should load up." His hand tapped the bag of jars, causing two of them to clink together.

It was an excellent suggestion, and while he joined the rest of the group, I pulled out the half empty one and made it completely empty. After I put the empty back in with the others, I tossed the entire bag over my shoulder with its strap and rushed to the front of the line to walk next to Samantha. "Wait up."

She didn't. No one did, but I caught up to her quickly, and didn't waste the opportunity to admonish my little rebellious teen. "It's not wise to just go traipsing through the woods like this. If your father is here, it's a safe bet he isn't alone."

"Come on mom. I was raised around vampires. I think I can handle myself."

I admired her ego, but her naivety scared me. "Sam, what you were raised around were not vampires. They are friends who are vampires. Ones that have superb control. The ones you run into out here won't be like that. They will be vicious, and no matter how confident you feel as a witch, it won't matter. They will be on you before you know it."

I felt her glance in my direction as she continued to walk through the woods. I wish I could see what she did, but I didn't. All I saw ahead of us were dark woods with trees swaying in the wind above us. "So where are we—"

"What about my other side?" Samantha asked, interrupting my attempt to find out where the path took us. "Or are you going to avoid what happened back in the coven?"

"No, I don't guess we can." I threw my arm around my daughter. This was going to be our first big mother-daughter talk, and it wasn't what most mothers talk to their daughters about, boys. "I need to know what you felt when it happened?"

"A burning in my throat unlike anything I have ever felt."

"Ah yep. What about what could you hear or see?"

"Everything went out of focus except that feeling, and the smell." Samantha reached out in front of her and tensed up her fists. "Just thinking about it now. I can almost smell it. It makes me want to jump out of my skin and run."

"Yep, I know that feeling. What about now? What do you feel or hear?"

She let go of her tensed up fist and stretched her fingers out into the air in front of her. "Nothing, just the wind, the damp air of the night. A creak of a branch here and there when the trees move in the wind. That's it."

"You don't hear any thumping?" I asked.

"No, why?" she answered with a question, and turned to look at me.

"Because you have two witches walking behind you with beating hearts. You should be able to hear them."

"Oh," she said before turning to face forward, deep in thought. Or I assumed. That look could have been her trying to feel what I told her was there. After a few seconds of creaks and pops of the branches above us, Samantha asked, "Do you feel them?"

"Yep. I hear and feel every beat of their hearts." I glanced back and saw a very awkward expression on both of their faces. I imagine it was weird hearing a vampire talk about the sound of your own heartbeat.

"Jack sounds anxious," Apryl teased.

I didn't have to see Jack's eyes to know they rolled.

"I'm not sure why you can't hear them. I guess it's possible you have some abilities, but not others."

"Is that even possible?"

I didn't know how to respond to my daughter. Hell, I still didn't understand how I was possible. Could she have some vampire abilities, but not all of them? "I guess anything is possible."

There was a stifled giggle behind us. I turned to catch Lisa trying to hide it. I didn't see what was so funny, and she seemed rather embarrassed at being caught. When I turned back, she said, "It makes sense. You were always a mystery. Why shouldn't your daughter be mysterious too?"

There was another giggle and chuckle at that comment, and I had to admit, I even had to hold back my laughter. It was true. Samantha appeared to be the only one who didn't get the joke and even appeared confused by it. "I'll explain later."

That did little to remove her confused look. If anything, it added to it, but we pressed on cautiously.

We resembled a war movie Mr. Bolden would have enjoyed. A few steps, and a stop if Apryl or I thought we heard or felt something. We were the ones best equipped for a stealth approach, so we took on the responsibility of being the lookouts. After we realized it was just a rabbit or fox working their way through the low brush themselves, we moved on.

To be honest, stumbling across the living wasn't my chief concern. It was stumbling across those like us. That was what I was worried about. We could walk right up to them, or they to us, and neither Apryl nor I would know they were there. They would probably be on us so fast we wouldn't be able to react. I only hoped they would be friendly, or what would be the best outcome, just Nathan. In and out, and back home. That would be the perfect outcome, but you'd think I'd learned my lesson about hoping for the simple route.

"I see the end of the path!" Samantha pointed off in the distance, and I saw it too. Not the actual path. Only Samantha could see that, but I saw what was at the end of it. It had to be it.

"I don't like this," whispered Apryl. Without me knowing it, she had moved up next to me.

"Me either."

Ahead of us in the dark dense fog stood a church time had forgotten. It stood there, looking gothic and haunted with crumbling walls and broken stained glass windows. There was what I guessed was some kind of overgrown walkway up to the cracked stone steps. A tree stood proudly up through the center of where its roof used to be. The scene was haunting enough, but what really bothered me was the silence. There was nothing around it. No animals, or anything, and I grabbed hold of Samantha's hand to yank her to a stop.

"What is it?" asked Jack.

"Nothing," I said. "That's the problem. Wait here." I had only taken a step, maybe part of a second one, before there was a quick flash of a portal behind me, several screams, and then a large thud sending me to the cold ground. Someone fell on top of me, and by the sound of the groan, it sounded like Apryl.

A quick push forced me up off the ground and sent Apryl flying off my back. I was up on my feet, ready to fight, before she landed behind me with a groan. The problem was whoever knocked us down was nowhere to be found. That was another problem. The biggest problem, Samantha, Jack, and Lisa, were missing too.

"Samantha!"

"Lisa!"

Nothing except the crickets singing the night away. I remembered the flash. "I thought I saw a portal. Lisa must have taken them back to the coven."

"Maybe," Apryl said as she marched around searching the darkness like I was. "I'm more concerned about who hit us." She stepped forward and stood aggressively. Her hands balled into fists by her sides. "Hey assholes! Try it again!"

I took up a similar stance and readied a little surprise in each hand for any visitors. There was no doubt they were out there. They had to be, and I heard a light rustling in the surrounding underbrush, but I didn't feel an animal.

"Come on out, and I won't kill you," I announced, hoping to encourage a nice, peaceful surrender.

"Not likely, you dirty witch," a voice responded from the darkness.

I sent a fireball toward the disembodied voice as my reply. It kept flying through the trees, illuminating everything it passed in a bright red hue, including the image of three figures running off carrying three other limp and familiar figures over their shoulders. I took off without a word to Apryl, but she must have seen it too. She was close on my heels.

"Let them go!" I cried, resisting the temptation of releasing a hell storm on them as we gave chase. The risk to our friends was too much. The figures carrying them were fast, but not as fast as we were. We weren't weighted down. We were gaining, and I was considering how to handle them once we were close enough. Taking a page out of Gwen's playbook and giving them a little telekinetic pull around the ankles to send them to the ground would be safe enough. I was about to pull it off too, when who I had to assume was the source of the disembodied reply popped up and knocked us down to the ground again.

This time, he didn't disappear like he had the first time. He stood there, over us. "Vampires consorting with witches. You have a lot of nerve." I pushed up, but then I felt a foot press down on my back, planting me on the ground.

"Stay down," bellowed a second voice from behind us. This one was deep, imposing, and hostile and obviously the owner of the foot that was pressing me down. I glanced ahead of us and saw the figures we chased getting further and further away, and I couldn't let that happen. I pushed again, and the foot pressed me down. Then I let loose a little surprise in the form of a telekinetic push and a nice enormous ball of blue flames straight up. The foot moved, and I was up, staring face to face at two vampires.

Both were male, maybe mid-thirties, and dressed rather modernly in jeans, shirt, and rather expensive looking sneakers, which were caked with the mud from our current surroundings. One was stouter than the other and wore a baseball hat backwards upon his head. Not at all like the ones from Jean's coven that were stuck in time two centuries ago.

They both looked me up and down, almost studied me. The stout one with the deep voice made the obvious observation, "You're a witch."

"Yep, I am." Then I sent them both flying through the woods. His baseball cap floated harmlessly to the ground in front of us.

I searched the darkness for the other figures and caught sight of them as they ducked into the dilapidated church. Nathan was in there. Or so the spell said. Now my daughter and friends were in there too, so that was where we were going, and we would not be covert about it either.

With an impressive flash, I blew the rotten wooden door to splinters and ran in.

"Put them down!" I ordered. It was unnecessary. They had already placed Samantha, Jack, and Lisa on the ground. They were still alive, but unconscious. My attention was so focused on them, I hadn't taken the time to survey the room. I wish I had. I was someone who just made a very dramatic witch like entrance and was now standing in the middle of vampire central. There must have been four or five dozen vampires in the room, and from the sound of chatter that had started, my presence was not welcome. Which was completely understandable, given the current circumstances. If that wasn't bad enough, the deterrents I held in each hand had lost a little of their luster, and somewhere I had lost the bag carrying my boosters.

"Larissa?" Apryl asked apprehensively.

It was probably because she was seeing something I had never done before. I was backing up. My steps backward grew in size once I lost the fireball in my left hand. I could feel the one in my right hand on life support. The horde of vampires now crowded around us, and I could no longer see Samantha and the others. The red glow in my hand faded out, and darkness engulfed us. Now it was the horde who was taking bigger steps.

"Maybe we should–"

I wasn't really sure what Apryl had in mind, but I was pretty sure it wasn't what I did. Her squeal proved that when I dropped both hands, let my fangs show, and leaped forward, grabbing the closest vampire and stretching its neck to the point of its skin beginning to tear. "I'm here for Nathan Saxon! Where is he?"

The crowd gave room as I forced my unwilling partner forward. I had no intention of really removing the burden of his head. I just wanted to make a point. I was also a vampire, just like them.

"He's–" started a voice from the crowd, but the collapsing of the church under a great flash of purple and green muffled the answer.

18

Again, I found myself on the ground, and there was more than Apryl on top of me this time. Just to my side was the young man I had recruited moments before. He took one look at me, hopped up, and took off running. In fact, everyone scattered.

"Apryl!"

"Right here!" she screamed back. Then I felt a hand on my foot and spun around and up to my feet, offering her a hand to help her get up. Several of the scattering vampires smacked into us, sending both of us spinning like tops. When they cleared, Apryl grabbed my shoulders and spun me around once more, and then pointed. Lying on the ground were the others. Seems in all the commotion the vampires had forgotten all about their prisoners, and that was fine with me. I ran over, feeling great relief and ignoring the chaos that had just ensued.

I grabbed Samantha and offered to grab either Jack or Lisa. Apryl waved me off before throwing both of them over her shoulders and stepping right over the pile of rubble that was a wall a few moments ago. I followed, but then turned back to make one more check for Nathan. I didn't see him, but that didn't stop me from taking a second look. He had to be here. That spell led us right to him. There was another flash, sending a shower of crushed stone blocks over my head, and carried Samantha following Apryl into the trees.

Explosions of color from behind us illuminated the trees and the shapes of the vampires running through them. The rumbles followed us, closely. I grabbed Apryl and urged her to move faster. The splinters destroyed trees rained down on us. I made a few brave glances back to see if I could see what witch was responsible for this assault. When I saw a line of witches in dark cloaks walking toward us, I turned and pushed Apryl faster, causing a quick annoyed look and a huff from her. As soon as she spotted what I saw, she no longer had any question, and put the pedal to the metal. If we were a cartoon, there would be smoke coming off of our feet.

How long and far we ran until we couldn't hear the rumbles anymore, I didn't know. As far as I knew, we could have been miles away. We were also alone. There was no sign of any vampires, the line of witches, or the glow of the fires they started. I placed Samantha down on the ground and tried to wake her up. She had a scuff on her forehead but was still breathing. I pulled her head into my lap and caressed it, and begged for her to wake up, but she didn't. They had hit her pretty hard. I felt my body rock back and forth while I held her head. Rage was building inside, and while before I felt relief at not seeing the line of witches anymore, now I needed a target. Even some vampires would do.

Lisa was partially awake and complaining about Apryl's bony shoulder digging into her ribs. Jack moaned before rolling over and going back under. He seemed to suffer the worst with a large gash on the side of his head.

"What was that?" Apryl asked.

"Yea, what the hell was that?" Lisa groaned.

"Well, which time?" I snapped. "First it was vampires. They knocked you, Sam, and Jack out and took you to some old broken-down church. Then a group of witches arrived and blew the church to hell in a colorful attack."

"Oh crap. Sam!" Lisa crawled along the ground to Samantha's side, moaning in pain the whole way. She grabbed Samantha's hand and began rubbing it. "Come on, wake up." Then she looked up at me. "I should have taken her back when you asked me to. I'm so sorry."

"I thought you did."

"I tried, but... I don't know. I just remember opening a portal, then it all went black." Lisa rubbed across her face briefly and then reached back for Samantha's hand.

"I think she's okay. She's breathing." I had already tried a few times to pull the pain from her and help her wake up. A trick I learned from my mother after a rather clumsy period in my pre-teens that produced several skinned knees and elbows. She said it was a mother's touch. I had tried it once on my own when I was probably fifteen to pull the sting out of a bee sting, and it worked. It wasn't working now, but I was sure that was because I was out of juice.

"Lisa, can you help her? Please?" I pleaded, and then, feeling completely helpless, I said, "I can't."

"I think so." Lisa moved up next to Samantha's head and sat opposite me. She looked as if she wanted me to lay Samantha's head in her lap, but there wasn't a chance in hell I was going to let go of her. Lisa was just going to have to maneuver closer, and that was what she did until she was practically hovering over Samantha's head with a concerned look.

Lisa extended out her hand and let her fingers drape lightly across Samantha's forehead. She closed her eyes, and I watched as a white glow escaped between her fingers. It pulsated, like a heartbeat, and then stopped. Samantha groaned and turned her head.

"Ouch!" she screamed and tried to sit up.

"Don't," whispered Lisa. "Just lay there for a bit." When she removed her hand, that large scrape that had been there before was gone.

"Mom?" Samantha asked, looking up at me with glassy eyes.

"Stay still," I suggested with my voice, and then again with a light rub on her forehead. "I guess, my darling, you aren't full vampire."

There was a chuckle from the lump of flesh that resembled Jack. "I never thought there would be a time I was actually jealous of you guys." He ended it with a groan.

I looked around again, and both saw and felt no one around us, but there was still a tremor of rage inside, and I asked Apryl to see if she felt anyone. She didn't. "Let's rest here for a bit." It wasn't like we had a choice. Three of us were in no shape to go anywhere, and to be honest, I didn't know where to go. We followed the spell, and the attack interrupted us before we found Nathan. Where he was now was again a mystery. So close, but yet again, so far.

Jack and Lisa pulled themselves up against a tree. I was going to give them another few minutes to recover before I asked either of them to open a portal and take us all home. I didn't see that we had any other choice. Then it started. Probably because my mind was no longer thinking of plans to find Nathan, and there was now an empty spot it could slide into. When it slipped in, it pushed other things around to make room for a huge heap of regret for what had happened to my daughter, and even my friends, all because of some foolhardy plan I had, yet again.

I couldn't do this to them or myself anymore. I knew I should have listened to Mrs. Saxon and all the others who said things would work out if I just let them. Here I was, trying to rush it. I was trying to put things on the timetable I wanted, and as usual, it backfired. From this point forward, no more. I was going to just let things happen. Let things follow life's plan, no matter how slow it was, or how long it took. The only question I really had left was, could I do that?

"Are you the one asking about Nathan Saxon?"

I never heard the approach of the jeans and denim jacket wearing young vampire that bounded into the center of our recovery spot. Why would I? Most wouldn't hear me coming, either. He stood there, weary, ready to run, as Jack and Lisa jerked back and crawled up the tree to help them get to their feet. Apryl was already up, but she didn't seem that concerned. Just a little shocked, which was a look Samantha, and I both shared.

"Are you the ones asking about Nathan Saxon?" the young vampire asked again, this time impatiently, as he looked at each of us, ready to bolt.

I helped Samantha up to a seated position against the tree behind me and stood up. I looked down apologetically for jostling her such. My eagerness to respond caused me to move a little fast. That eagerness hadn't tempered any when I stepped toward our visitor. I was there next to him in an instant. "Yes. I was asking about Nathan Saxon. Do you know where he is?" I asked cautiously, trying to put up a dam against the wave of hope that threatened to wash over me.

"You're not here to hurt him, are you?" he asked, looking at Lisa and Jack grimly.

I grabbed him by the chin and turned his head to look right at me. "No," I said while shaking my head, slowly, with a lot of concentration going into the slow part. "We're family. We know his mother, and he is my boyfriend."

He looked around at us again before the tension in his face melted away. "Follow me."

I was about to ask him to slow up, anticipating he would sprint off, but he seemed more mindful of who was in our group and their current state. He even offered to help Jack and Lisa to their feet. Samantha could walk, but barely. I threw her arm over my shoulder and helped carry some of her burden. Her injuries were my fault. With everyone ready, he took the lead and didn't say another word. He just walked.

We silently followed our mysterious guest through the dark forest for what felt like hours, moving through the trees, and avoiding any roads or paths. With the cloudy skies above blocking the moon, it was hard to tell if we were moving north, south, east, or west. All I was certain of was we were heading in a straight line deeper into the forest, which became thicker with every step.

Behind me, I heard Jack and Lisa stumbling from time to time. Probably over a downed tree, or thick brush. In this darkness, they wouldn't see them. To me and Apryl, it was as bright as daytime. I watched Samantha and saw her step around or over obstacles on the ground and crossed that vampire ability off the list.

After what sounded like a very painful trip, Lisa asked, "Can I use light? Just a little glow…" Our escort flashed right in front of her face, and shock choked off her words.

"Do you want witches to find us?" he asked intensely, and without waiting for an answer, he continued. "You do? Don't you? Shine a little beacon so they can find us." The man was seething under his whisper.

"No–" Lisa attempted to answer, but again he cut her off with a finger right in her face.

"Maybe this was all a setup. I heard his mother is a witch. You all arrived just before the attack."

"Whoa, wait," Apryl whispered urgently, and she shoved her arm between him and Lisa, pushing him back a few steps. She took the opening to step in between them. "You can stop right there."

But he didn't. All he did was change the target of what sounded like pent up aggression. "Why are you defending them? You're a vampire god dammit. Do you know what they are?" His voice lost a little of its whisper before he caught it and backed the volume down to just above a breath.

"Yes, I do. They are my friends. So is Nathan, and that is why I am here. That is why they are here. We aren't part of this stupid war. Do you have a problem?" And very Apryl like, she didn't give him a chance to answer her question. "If you did, why did you come find us? Huh?"

"I didn't know they were with you." The words burst from his lips in a ferocious whisper. He looked right at Jack and Lisa, and I felt it was time to take some of the heat off of them.

"But you knew I was there, and I'm a witch too."

He looked at me, confused. I could almost see him replaying the image of me bursting through the door, ready to unleash hellfire.

"Me too," added Samantha.

My eyes cut in her direction, and I mouthed, "leave it." I knew what she was trying to do, but I didn't know this vampire, and I didn't know his intentions. If he attacked the witches in our group, she was in no shape to defend herself. None of them were.

"Don't you see?" I asked, hoping to find some rational thought inside his head buried in that mountain of anger and hatred. "We aren't like the witches that have attacked you. We are actually against all this, and just want to help our friend. Now, will you take us to him?"

For the briefest of moments, I saw "no" in his expression, but he turned around and kept walking in the direction we were originally heading.

19

For the next two hours, we marched forward with Apryl guiding Lisa and Jack every step of the way. I found a little humor in the bickering that ensued each time Apryl missed something they needed to be told to avoid. Each instance didn't last long. They were just momentary accusations that she was doing it on purpose. It was mostly from Jack. Lisa sounded more accepting and understanding, saying that while Apryl may have seen it, she didn't think it was large enough to be a problem. I only intervened once. I asked Apryl to put herself in their shoes. How would she like to be walking around out here with a blindfold on, and not able to see anything at all? I think she got my point as the amount and frequency of direction coming from her for them to step over something increased.

The feeling of being watched was neither a witch nor a vampire ability. It's something that was very human, and one of the creepiest sensations to experience. It's even worse when you multiply that by a hundred. That was how many sets of eyes I felt were watching us as we walked. I reached over and grabbed Samantha's hand, and pulled her closer. It was good timing too. Something to our side just moved through the low underbrush.

I heard a protest from behind, followed by Apryl shushing it. I glanced back. She had Jack and Lisa walking very close together in front of her. Her own head twisting from side to side at the sounds. Our escort had to hear the same sounds we did, but he never flinched. Instead, he just kept on walking, and I took that as a sign. He knew what was out there, and he wasn't concerned. That didn't stop me from being defensive and pulling Samantha even closer still.

He walked right up to a tall bush and paused a moment, and glanced back at us. His expression had something to it. I couldn't quite put my finger on what it was, but it set me on edge, and I pulled Samantha completely behind me and crouched. He pushed aside the tall bush and exposed a small clearing with dozens of other vampires standing or sitting. Others emerged from the woods as we stepped through. Each of them continued to eye us curiously, and I knew why.

My grip tightened on Samantha's hand, and she didn't mind. She tightened her grip even more and pulled herself closer to me. This crowd was an eclectic gathering of vampires. Every age range, gender, and race were represented, as well were the clothing styles of the last century. There was a large portion in more modern attire, and a few that appeared to be stuck in the 60's. The ones that had my attention were the ones toward the back of the group that were still dressed for a time that I remembered well. Our escort weaved us through the crowd, right to them.

The stares intensified when we approached them. I recognized some of their faces from New Orleans, but I couldn't put a name to them. It was clear they all recognized us. A few stepped in our way and wouldn't move when our escort tried to push through, and that appeared to be enough for him. He turned around, shrugged, and walked off, leaving us there, now surrounded. It was a moment of déjà vu for me. I had been in the same situation the last time I went back to bring Nathan home. Then we retreated. Now we didn't have that option. We were outnumbered, outgunned, and surrounded. Even if I had my crap together, it wouldn't have made much difference.

"We don't need to do this, do we? We are just here to find and help Nathan Saxon." I said, trying not to sound too much like I was pleading, but I was. They didn't seem to accept it, and a large section of the horde seemed to lean toward us. I whipped around. "Lisa, get them home!"

"Larissa! Larissa!" cried a voice from heaven. It froze me in my tracks and froze Lisa.

Frances Rundle pushed through the crowd and grabbed my hand. "Come with me!" She yanked me and Samantha through the crowd. I glanced back and made sure the others were following close behind.

Frances led us through a group of vampires to another clearing among the trees. There were more vampires there, but not nearly as many as where we had just left. As each of their heads spun in our direction, I watched as they parted like the Red Sea. Inside, Fred Harvey leaned over another vampire on the ground. Just by the looks on everyone's face, I didn't need anyone to tell me who that was, and I ran to him and collapsed next to him.

I felt a hand on my shoulder and looked up at its source. "He's burned on the outside, but healing," reported Fred Harvey. "Magic burns worse than fire."

I looked down at Nathan. He lay there motionless, with patches of charred skin covering him. I reached over and gently touched an unscarred area, and Nathan groaned. I wanted to throw my body over his and use my body to soak up his pain, but I knew that wouldn't work. He groaned louder as I gripped his hand. Every touch caused him pain.

"It's magic burns." Lisa kneeled down and looked him over. "It's still there too."

Now it was my turn to groan. I had hoped it was dissipating and he would be better soon, but as I looked up at his face, that chiseled thing of Greek gods, the charring continued to grow. He wasn't over the hump yet.

"Can you neutralize it?" I asked, as if some kind of chemical had caused this.

Lisa shook her head with a dark expression. "Yes, but not here. It takes a potion, spread over his skin."

I kept my focus on his eyes. Waiting for them to open, just as I had up in my bedroom when he first turned. They weren't opening, but he was busy behind the closed lids. "Let's get him home."

"Absolutely," said Lisa as she stood, and I gathered Nathan in my arms to pick him up. He screamed as I lifted his body off the ground and turned.

Samantha stood there, staring at her father for the first time. I wanted to tell her this wasn't what he normally looked like. The Nathan I knew was full of life, laughter, and love. His personality alone could chase away all the darkness in the world, and God knows, there is enough darkness out there. Without his light, the darkness felt heavier. That weight may have been what caused a quiver in Samantha's lips.

"He's going to be fine," I said to calm her, but inside I felt I needed a bit of convincing myself. Nathan felt like a dead weight in my arms and looked like a corpse burned to a crisp. The only signs of life were his moans, and the constant shifting of his eyes behind his eyelids, and his painful moans.

"Can you send back some of that potion?" asked Fred Harvey. The request caught both Lisa and me off guard, and we turned back to him. He was standing there, literally hat in hand. "There are lots just like him. Every attack is the same. Barrages of large, colorful blasts. Those caught in the flash end up like him. They suffer for days, sometimes a week or more. Some haven't recovered completely."

Lisa looked at me. I was just as surprised by the request as she was. Here, in the middle of all this, a vampire was asking a witch for help. I felt it was the least we could do, and gave her a quick and eager nod, and then gave our answer to Fred. "Of course. We will make as much as we can and send it back. Just as soon as we get back."

The ground beneath my feet thrusted up with enough force to toss me back against the closest tree. I held on to Nathan tightly and attempted to protect him when we landed. It was not a graceful one, and I fell on my back like a turtle holding him. Then it happened again. The sound of the great cataclysm caught up with the heaving of the ground and, in the bright flash, I saw the shadows of vampires flying. I didn't see them land before I did, but I had to assume most landed around the same time I did based on the collective groaning that filled the air.

Still holding on to Nathan like his life was my life, I stood up and looked around for the others, and I saw them. Not far away. Apryl was brushing herself off while Jack, Lisa, and Samantha appeared to land a little more gracefully. They probably used magic to aid their flight.

What I saw approaching behind them proved to me that magic was the reason we were all sent flying. That column of hooded witches had caught up with us. Behind them, the remnants of magic scarred lands that most mortal eyes wouldn't recognize. I saw it. There was a glow in the air, and the lines of the universe were fractured.

I ran carrying Nathan and screamed at Lisa. "Open it! Now." Then another blast hit between us, sending me tumbling backward. Nathan's body flew limp over my head. I tried to grab him, but missed before we both hit the ground, stunned. There was a loud ringing in my ears and a burning sensation on my back. With every attempt to rise, I was forcefully shoved down and disoriented by the loud ringing in my ears. I didn't know which was up or down. I knew Nathan was laying a few feet to my right, but that was all I was certain about and I was only sure of that because I could feel him with my right hand.

"Samantha? Lisa?" I cried out as loud as I could, but I couldn't even hear it myself over the ringing, yet alone their answer, if they answered.

My fingers gripped at the ground, trying to pull myself out from under the weight that had me pinned down. One hand crawling, the other hand dragging Nathan, but it didn't matter. The weight followed me and stayed seated right in the center of my back with every movement. My plan to fight as a vampire wasn't working. The witches weren't fighting fair, but why was I surprised? I fought the same way against Jean and his followers just a few months ago.

"Lisa? Jack? Can either of you do anything?" I screamed, in hopes they could fight magic with magic, but again I couldn't hear myself over the loud ringing. I clawed again at the ground. Needles burned through me, and my fingers turned to bones as they dug into the dirt. My skin was nothing but translucent paper. Then the weight lifted from my body, and I levitated a few inches off the ground. I hung there, just out of reach of the blades of grass that attempted to stand back up. My blood charm dangled from my neck and rested on the ground. My body then slowly rolled. I kicked and moved my arms, but nothing stopped me from rolling away from Nathan. I lost sight of him, and another face came into view, and my blood boiled. Seeing the charm that dangled from her neck explained everything.

"Now Larissa. What are we going to do with you?" sniped Miss Sarah Julia Roberts from beneath the hood she quickly pushed off, revealing her long blonde hair.

"Let me up, and you will find out."

"That's not going to happen," she tilted her hand, and I tilted up with it. "We don't understand how you escaped Mordin, but we will find out, and find out who helped you," she said with conceited confidence that grated on me. "We won't make that mistake again." She turned her attention to Nathan. "How painful the Fires of Ruel are. He will feel that pain for an eternity. Only a witch can counteract it. It's one of my favorite spells taught to me by my mother, but I bet you don't know that spell." She leaned in closer, and the effects of the charm dug deeper. "You don't know a lot of things, and you will never be my supreme," she sniped with a nasty sneer.

The hatred I felt for her caused my arms to jerk, and to both of our surprise, they almost broke free.

"Oh," she said, feigning surprise after she had recovered from her real startle. "We know all about your little plan to challenge. You just need to give up now. There is no way you could pass the seven wonders. You aren't a strong enough witch."

"Like I said. Let me out of here and let's find out." I shouted back, and again my arms jerked free. This time enough to reach out and grab her skinny throat. I ignored the tearing of my paper-thin skin as my fingers squeezed. The pleasurable feeling of her gasping for air made it all worth it. I felt my hatred for her flow through my arm, forcing my hand to squeeze even tighter. I hated her, not because of what she said about me never being her supreme. I didn't give a rat's ass about that at the moment. This hatred was all about what she had done to Nathan, and not to mention how she had treated me before.

In the distance, I saw the others held similarly by other witches. Samantha struggled against her magical bonds. Apryl was sprawled out on the ground and looked like a skeleton. Lisa and Jack appeared more complacent, which I found oddly curious, but that was something to ponder after I took care of Miss goody-two-shoes-witch. As much disdain as I felt for Gwen, she was still an angel compared to Miss Roberts. I squeezed a little more and felt her heart hammering all the way up the arteries in her neck. It matched the fear I saw in her eyes. I could easily finish the job right here and right now. Then, in the distance, the witch that had subdued the others raised her hand and threw me back to the ground. Miss Roberts' throat was ripped from my hand. Red scratches left by my fingernails marred her milky flesh.

She collapsed to the ground, gasping for air as the mysterious witch walked by her, leading the others away. "Stop playing with her and bring her."

20

This was an unpleasant déjà vu on so many levels. Frozen, floating, and frustrated to the point of wanting to kill the first person I got my hands on. I actually had that chance, but I didn't follow through. I could have squeezed just a little harder until her windpipe popped. That's not a sound I had heard before, but I imagined Miss Roberts' would have produced a glorious pop. The look on the face of the owner of said windpipe would probably have been even better

Lisa, Jack, and Samantha walked on their own. Well, they walked. I can't really say it was on their own. They appeared to be zombies that just followed this mysterious new witch. Neither appeared to be harmed more than they already were. That was good for our captors. If someone even made a scratch on them by having them walk too close to a tree branch, they would suffer more than a scratch. I figured I could remove the burden of a head from two, make that three witches before they stopped me. It was tempting to find out, especially since I had regained some movement in my hands , but I needed to wait for my opportunity.

We came to a small cottage nestled between the trees. It wasn't anything special, but it wasn't run down. The mysterious witch entered first, and then Nathan and I were taken inside. I could now move both hands and my lower arms, but that still left me helpless as I watched Samantha and the others disappear further into the woods. I lost sight of them when the door closed behind us. There was no surprise to find us some place other than the inside of a small cottage.

We were in a place right out of some medieval fairytale. Old wood floors and stone walls with fluted columns held up grand archways. Large, aged metal doors lead to the next room and to the outside where we came from. I heard its loud clang when it closed behind us. Dark, rich wood pieces of furniture were everywhere, with the pièce de résistance sitting on a platform right in front of us. A throne with spikes adorning the top of it worthy of having families fight over.

There was no surprise at seeing the mysterious witch walk up to it and have a seat. Her hood still obstructed the view of her face. Seeing Miss Sarah Julia Roberts step to her right side tipped me off, though. It had to be Mrs. Wintercrest, our supreme. Oddly, I never see her as one that would be out here doing her own dirty work. She seemed the type that would have others that were eager to prove their loyalty to go out and serve as cannon fodder.

"Mrs. Wintercrest. I'm the one you want. Help Nathan and send him back home." I threw myself at her mercy, or more offered myself as a sacrifice. Helping Nathan was first, the others were second, and I figured I could take care of myself if I needed to. What was she going to do? Send me back to Mordin?

"Hush, child," the mysterious woman said. Her unfamiliar voice echoed in the stone room. "You are right in that you are the one we want, but I am not Mrs. Wintercrest." She sat up straight on the edge of the throne and reached up with both of her ring adorned hands and pushed back the hood, revealing a much older version of Miss Sarah Roberts. "I can see how one might make that mistake. The throne and all. But that just shows your narrow view of the world. As you can see, I am not her, but as you can also see, I don't need to be to have more control than she ever will. She is just a puppet that serves me well."

"So, you're the real supreme?" I asked, confused, with my head spinning. "And you're her mother?" I looked at Miss Roberts, hoping the answer to that question would not be a yes. Miss Sarah Roberts stepped away from the throne and strolled around me and Nathan. My body convulsed as she passed with that charm. She even leaned down a little lower.

"Again, such a narrow view of the world. I expected more from someone from your family, Larissa. Mrs. Wintercrest is just who you see, but if you look below the surface. She is a shell of a witch. Her power has long left her. We are the ones propping her up for special benefits in return." She held out a hand toward her daughter, and Miss Robers bowed.

"So, she can be supreme," I whispered as the realization hit me. Then it all made sense. What I had observed before in the coven. Finding her leading the attack in New Orleans. Even how she responded and treated me when we first met.

"They always said you were a bright witch there, Larissa. Yes, that favor, among others," she continued. "The Council of Mages used to be a hallowed institution. It was comprised of the greatest families of our world. Each family had a seat. Each family ruled with dignity and strength. We were not ones to be defied or challenged. The vampires knew that. Everyone knew that. But, one by one, the houses have died off, allowing other, undeserving families to take their place. Each weakening the council's strength. We are going to set that right and restore the council to what it should be. An order that is not to be messed with. We just didn't know that at our weakest, fate would present us with the greatest of opportunities. A trifecta of sorts," she giggled with a nod to her daughter. Miss Roberts had her normal smug look on her face as she made another pass around me. The pain and searing I felt from her charm made me regret my show of restraint earlier.

"An opportunity to eliminate two troublesome families, the Dubois and the Meridian, much of the rogue witches, and the threat of the vampires all at once. It was too good to pass up. We just didn't plan for you and Marcus to be as slippery as you are, but fate," she paused and looked down at Nathan's limp body and smirked, "has brought you back. Marcus won't stay hidden for long. He doesn't have it in him. Then all the threats will be eliminated, and my daughter, not you, will ascend to supreme. Leaving one great family ruling over the council."

So that was it. That was why Miss Roberts was hellbent on making my life miserable from day one, focused on trying to have me exiled, and why she always seemed right at Mrs. Wintercrest's side, almost pulling her strings. I should have seen it before now. I always knew it was because they considered me a threat, and I thought I understood why. but I was wrong, so horribly wrong. None of that mattered now. Nothing mattered except the person lying beside me, groaning in pain, and my daughter wherever she was.

"Do what you want with me, but help him, and let my," I paused before I said daughter. Telling her there was an heir to the Dubois line was signing a death sentence for Samantha. "Let my friends go."

"The witches will be processed and repatriated once we know they aren't a threat. The vampires, including your beloved there, will be disposed of," she coldly announced.

"Disposed of swiftly," added her daughter with such satisfaction and glee in her voice, it made my insides boil.

"No! They are not a threat. Nathan's mother is a witch. He will not be a problem. Let him go back home!"

Miss Roberts stopped and hovered over Nathan. "The only safe vampire is a dead vampire." She held her hand over him. She had removed her charm and now held it just above Nathan. His body writhed.

"Stop!" I jerked my hands free from their current frozen state and lunged at her. She was out of reach. I lunged again, thinking I could drag my entire body closer, but I didn't move. Each attempt added to the size of the smile across Miss Roberts' face.

"Stop! Kill me!" A flood of tears joined my screams.

Her smile grew at that suggestion, but she never paused to even consider that possibility. I was ready to die. I would die a million times over to stop his suffering. The tears continued as my hands balled into fists. I pounded the air in front of me, hoping to connect with her just once. If I could get my hands on her just once, I wouldn't make the mistake I did earlier, and it would be quick. She taunted me the whole time, even taking a step closer. She was close enough that the air created by my swipes sent ripples through her robe, which she noticed and waved it at me tauntingly. All that ended when I felt a pulse of rage surge through me, and there was a flash, sending Miss Roberts across the room and into a stone archway. I felt it surging through me, with my anger and rage. It was back. Me. I was back. My magic was fully back. Mr. Demius may have been right. My emotions power me, and this was rage.

With a quick yank, I pulled the charms away from both witches, popping the chain from around their necks.. I crushed them into a powder in the middle of the room and then sent a hurricane gust to blow it and the two witches that wore them against the wall.

I threw a pentagram-based rune at Nathan for protection against what had happened, and anything that was going to happen, from this point forward. I saw the universe clearly, and the lines wrapped around him tightly and arched out a way to deflect any incoming attacks. This was working.

Next, I shot a barrage of fire at Miss Roberts' mother, aiming at her head. She attempted to move out of the way, but I yanked on the lines that surrounded her and pulled her back. She countered with a fast push that hit me before I saw it, and then she ducked before the balls of blue flame reached her. They crashed into the wall behind her.

Now it was my turn to return the favor, and I sent a push in her direction. She tumbled at first, but I watched as the lines around her straightened out and she landed gracefully on the floor. I was about to follow with another stern shove and a wide spray of fire, followed by opening up a hole under where she was going to land. I figured that would be something she couldn't counter, and probably wouldn't see coming. It would have been grand to carry it out, but her daughter countered with something of her own, sending me flailing into the wall behind me. I felt her magic burn, but with a single motion, I pushed it off of me and attempted to send it back where it came from. It hit her on the leg, and she went down to one knee.

Her mother hit me again, with something small, but it stung worse than anything I had ever felt, and it caused me to double over before I fell to the ground on my knees. I felt a strange draining sensation, but that didn't stop me from sending a shot back her way, that finally caught her off guard, and sent her flipping head over heels. Here we were, three witches giving our best to kill each other. I considered it a rather futile activity, being that I couldn't die, but that didn't mean it didn't hurt like crazy. Mrs. Roberts hit me again with her stinger which arrived with a trail of fire and sparkles, and it again sent me to the ground. That crap hurt, and if I made it out of here, I was going to need to learn how to do it myself.

It was two on one, but I was holding my own. I delivered two telekinetic pushes, one with each hand, sending both of the Roberts sliding across the floor. It bought me enough time to open a portal back to my room in the coven. With another telekinetic shove, I sent Nathan sliding across the floor towards it, but just as he reached it, a flash pushed him to its side, and closed the portal. Before I could see which of the two did it, another burning flash sent me back to the floor. So far it seemed I had spent more time on my knees than I had standing up.

Nathan groaned loudly. He was coming to and now his body could register the pain more. I threw variations of the pentagram at him as fast as I could, surrounding him in glowing symbols burned into the wood floor. That would protect him. At least for a little while. I think I stood there and admired my glowing handiwork for too long. A burning sensation in my back sent me down to my knees yet again. It almost laid me out flat, but I forced through it as hard as I could to stay upright to defend Nathan and myself. The impacts were coming fast and hard from behind. With everything I had, I turned to see Miss Roberts stalking toward me, closer and closer, with every round she leveled at me. I tried to retaliate or defend myself, but another impact interrupted each attempt.

Miss Sarah Roberts cackled when I was finally sprawled out on the floor under the weight of each of her attacks. She picked up the pace and walked closer. That was her mistake. While I wasn't able to respond as a witch, she forgot what else I was. A quick swipe of my hand knocked her to the ground. I was on her before she even breathed. A primal instinct inside me caused my body to lurch down with my fangs out, targeting her neck. I was inches away before I realized what I was doing and stopped. There was no way I was going to give her that gift, but that didn't mean I could use my fangs to rip a few vital arteries so I could watch her bleed out. I leaned in to feast, but her mother hit me with a rather powerful blast from behind. It attempted to pick me up off of her daughter, but there was no way I was letting go of her this time. I reached down and grabbed her by the throat and pulled her up with me. She dangled from my grasp as I leered at her mother. I was holding her daughter, but technically, she was the one who had her life in her hands. The longer she held me there, the longer her daughter would hang there, kicking, struggling to breathe. Each gasp I felt her throat make added to my leer. The panicked thumping of her pulse was music to my ears.

Her mother didn't release me. She held me right there, high above the floor among the arches, with her daughter kicking in my grasp below. Her mother squeezed me, just as I was squeezing her daughter. The only difference was, she kept her distance. From the safety of across the room, she mumbled something and then a blinding blue light hit me, and I felt my flesh burn.

I tried to throw rune after rune to protect myself, but the pain forced each image out of my head before I could put it to work. The same with any spells I could conjure, or even opening a portal. It was all-consuming. So much so, my grasp on Miss Sarah Roberts' slender throat slipped, but even if it was my last act in this world, I wasn't about to let her go free. With a quick squeeze and a very toothy grin through the pain, I accomplished what I wanted, and then tossed her aside like a rag doll.

Her mother shrieked and dropped me to the floor. I landed, and my body instantly recoiled into the fetal position from the burning. I shivered and shouted, waiting for her next attack. Then I felt an arm over me and looked up to see Nathan slinging his body over mine. Inside I screamed—NO! He was not doing this again. I pushed him away and I forced my body over his, while doing my best to look at Mrs. Roberts as she hovered over her daughter's limp body. How I wanted to spring to my feet and do the same to her, but my body was in no shape to cooperate. It was all I could do to throw myself across Nathan to guard him from any more suffering. A question flashed through my head about who would protect him after she killed me, but I ignored that as I did what I could to cover every inch of Nathan. It didn't help that he was a good foot taller than me.

I made another feeble attempt at opening a portal, and watched as it sparked open, but then it disappeared with another flash of blue that now engulfed both Nathan and me. The pain shot through me like a hot iron, burning both inside and outside.

"You will both die for that," she cried, and then did it again, and I knew she was right about our fate. I again tried to open a portal. Escape was our only option, and that was a fleeting one at that. Sparks flew, and it opened, just as another flash arrived, and my hand dropped and clutched at my chest. The portal didn't close. It opened wider, and then a large flash came through it, planting Mrs. Roberts into the stone wall behind her. Samantha and Apryl stepped forward. Apryl stood guard hissing, with fangs displayed. Blood dripped from her hands. Without a word, Samantha swiped her hand, throwing Nathan and me through the portal.

21

It would have been great if my daughter had put us back in our room, but it was possible something distracted her when she threw us through the portal. They say timing is everything. Well, timing wasn't on our side. We landed in the middle of the grand entry between both staircases just as the Council of Mages walked through. Our presence was just a momentary distraction. The real show was occurring through the portal. The sounds of a horrible battle with screams and wails leached through. I looked back through it, as did everyone else.

Apryl was doing her best to sink her teeth into Mrs. Roberts, but continued to come up short, while Samantha bombarded her with all Master Thomas had taught her. She was throwing everything at her. Fireballs. Spells. Lightning strikes. She even threw her through a wall. It wasn't more than a few moments before Mrs. Roberts reappeared. I wasn't sure how to pull that off. I even watched in surprise as Samantha gave up on her magic and opted for a more physical approach, and teamed up with Apryl. Samantha went low, and Apryl went high with blurring speed, taking Mrs. Roberts off her feet. Apryl grabbed her by the shoulders and yanked her down into her throne.

"Burn the witch Sam," Apryl yelled.

Next to me, I felt Nathan reach out for me, and I met his hand halfway, and pulled him close. His body was still burning, and I looked up to the council for help. None of them were paying any attention to us at the moment. They were focused on the battle on the other side of the spinning disk.

Samantha followed Apryl's lead. Instead of falling back on how I would have done it, she spoke several words we couldn't hear over Apryl's chant of "Burn the witch. Burn the witch." A column of flames erupted from the floor and consumed the throne. Apryl leaped back just in time. It burned for several seconds, then the flames bowed out and disappeared. Mrs. Roberts sat on the throne, untouched, with a glow only I could see around her.

The large metal door they brought us through sprang open and several more witches ran in.

"Apryl! Samantha!" I called and got up to my feet. They heard me and sprinted for the portal. Apryl had to leap over Miss Roberts' body on her way out. It was the first time any of the council had seen her, and it produced several gasps. The portal closed with Samantha and Apryl safely through.

Not fully understanding who we were dealing with, I threw up several runes that etched themselves into the walls and doors of the coven. There were no combinations this time. Just simple runes to lock the place down and block any attempts to follow us. Mrs. Saxon had done the same once upon a time to keep me in. I broke through. I could only hope they wouldn't be able to do the same.

"What is the meaning of this?" demanded Mrs. Wintercrest.

"Who are you to be giving orders?" Apryl asked as she stalked around the council, keeping her distance because of the charms they wore. Something that I quickly remedied, removing the charm from each member of the council, and sending them through my own portal to some place I didn't really care where. All I knew was it was far away from here.

"You," Mrs. Wintercrest pointed right at me. "You are exiled again to Mordin, and this time you won't be able to escape."

"Just hold your horses there, grandma," sniped Apryl, who stopped and glared right into Mrs. Wintercrest's eyes.

The commotion in the entry had drawn an audience up and down the stairs, and a murmur had developed. I could hear many of the questions being uttered by those surprised to see me. Others were concerned for Nathan, and I heard Mike forcing his way through the others that lined the stairs to get down to him. Kevin Bolden was on his heels. There was another presence that created quite the murmur. "Who was the new witch?"

There was banging on the door to the girls' side of the vampire floor, and Jennifer Bolden looked at it with great suspicion, but still opened the door. Jack and Lisa came running out and down the stairs. "Damn charmed doors," uttered Jack.

"Mrs. Wintercrest, I don't believe you are in any position to be giving any orders." The effects of the war I had just been through dripped away, and every ounce of my abilities returned. It was then I saw something that Mrs. Roberts had alluded to. She was absolutely right. Mrs. Wintercrest was weak. Why hadn't I seen it before? Then I knew. I hadn't been around her much since I knew how to read the magic in the universe, and when I had, Miss Roberts was right by her side.

"I'm... I'm... your supreme," Mrs. Wintercrest responded, all flustered. Her cheeks turned red, and as she huffed, ready to explode.

"Yes, that is the title you hold, but not what you are. Isn't that true?" I took a cue from Apryl and stalked around her and the council.

"Now wait a minute," said one member of the council. One of the Mr. Demius lookalikes that I was never formally introduced to. He stepped forward to intervene, but Mr. Nevers grabbed his arm.

"Do they know?" I asked, staring right at her as I circled around her. Her head attempted to follow me as far as it could before she had to turn her entire body.

"Does anyone here know?" I asked loudly. My voice echoed in the rafters. I studied the faces of the council members intently, hoping to catch a hint of familiarity or comprehension in their eyes. There it was. A glimpse at a few of them.

"What is going on here? Larissa!" exclaimed Mrs. Saxon as she entered the hall. Mike stood up from where he and Kevin Bolden tended to Nathan. "Nathan!" She ran to her son, falling to his side. "Oh, Nathan!"

Lisa joined them. "It's the Fire of Ruel."

"The potion!" Mrs. Saxon blurted. She looked around. "Mike. Kevin. Help, get him up and follow me."

She jumped up and headed for the other hallway. I had to assume it was Mrs. Tenderschott's classroom. Whatever they would need for the potion would be in there.

"Rebecca, you need to stay here and control your witch!" Mrs. Stephanie Morrison cried out, which I found odd, but maybe it wasn't. She was one of the few that I saw a glimpse of recognition in.

I knew Nathan needed help. That was something I knew better than anyone, but I also needed Mrs. Saxon to hear this. I was torn. Two needs. Which would outweigh the other? I remember an old movie, something Mr. Norton watched. Well, maybe it wasn't that old. The needs of the many outweigh the needs of the few. As much as it pained me to delay Nathan's help, that was what I had to do.

"Lisa! Go with them!" I ordered. "Tell Mrs. Tenderschott what she needs to do. Mrs. Saxon, I need you to hear something."

She stopped dead in her tracks and looked back reluctantly. There were tears running down her face. That was the first time I had ever seen that kind of emotion from her, but I understood. I would be there too if I wasn't so pissed off.

"I can help too," Gwen, the princess of pink, called from the witch's landing.

"No," ordered Mrs. Saxon as she choked back her emotions.

"Who here knows that a witch named Mrs. Robers, the mother of Miss Sarah Julia Roberts, has been propping up and pulling the strings of Mrs. Wintercrest for years?" I didn't wait for an answer. "Who here knows that her daughter was being groomed to replace Mrs. Wintercrest? That will never happen now. She is dead." There was a gasp up and down the stairs behind me. "Who here knows that Mrs. Wintercrest has lost most of her power as a witch, and has been relying on that family for support for years? And... that family is the one running this war to remove the last remaining powerful families in our world, mine and the Meridians, while also eliminating the rogue witches and vampires?"

I looked around at the stunned faces. "I'm going to guess," I stopped my circling of the council and walked right up to Mrs. Wintercrest. "I guess no one knew that last part."

"I am still your supreme," she spat back, as defiant as ever.

"No, you're not," I replied with the same level of defiance and walked away showing her my back as I did.

"Is any of this true?" Mrs. Saxon asked.

"No. Of course not," denied Mrs. Wintercrest, but just as fast as she entered her denial, another answer emerged.

"Yes."

First it was Mr. Davis who stepped forward, then Mrs. Okina, who even stepped forward out of the shadows of the other council members and pushed back the hood of her red robe. In all my previous dealings with the council, she never once spoke up, and even now, she seemed afraid to. She had a reason to be concerned or even scared. She was speaking up against the witch she believed was the most powerful witch in our world.

"I don't know about their involvement in the war, but it doesn't surprise me to hear what you said. I know about Sarah and her mother. Sarah was to be the next supreme. She spoke of it often, reminding us of how important her family was, and how we needed to be loyal to them." She looked down at the floor, and her voice shriveled. "I am only here because I pledged my allegiance to them."

"It's just a damn blood feud. That is all this is," mumbled another member of the council. This claim created quite a commotion among them.

"Council members? Council members?" Mrs. Wintercrest attempted to restore order, but the damage had been done. Even how they all looked at her had changed. Their respectful reverence was gone. In its place were scowls. No matter how many times she called them, the commotion and conversations continued. She had lost all control.

"Council members!" Master Thomas called as he descended the stairs. His voice achieved what Mrs. Wintercrest's had failed. "We can all agree these are rather shocking claims. Why don't we disburse with the speculation and do a hearing of fact?" He stepped off the bottom step and toward the council, but before he joined, he walked over and whispered into my ear. "I have this. You go to Nathan."

And that is what I did. I grabbed Samantha's hand, ran down the hallway. Mrs. Saxon and Apryl followed us. I heard the council members start up a conversation again, this time with Master Thomas leading. I could only imagine Mrs. Wintercrest standing there, wilting away. It warmed, but also chilled me at the same time.

***

Again, Nathan stayed unconscious in his bed for several days, and again I sat there as a vigil. I think this was the third time. Twice here and once in New Orleans. This was not something I wanted to make a habit of. The potion that Mrs. Tenderschott whipped up did its thing. It wasn't something he had to drink. It was a lotion we had to coat the burns with several times a day, which I handled religiously. Samantha offered to help several times, but I reminded her this was my responsibility. It was what I caused, and I needed to fix it. She told me I was being obstinate, and I asked her where she learned such a big word. Rarely did she leave my side, while I tended to Nathan. She even slept in there. Being there when he woke up was important to her, or necessary, as she reminded me more than once. It was something I couldn't disagree with, though I wasn't exactly sure how to handle that introduction, or better yet, when. Was it something I should spring on him as soon as he woke up? Probably not, but as my new attitude dictated, we would cross that bridge when we came to it.

I left his side once on the second day for just a few minutes to apologize to Mrs. Saxon for going against her wishes, and prepared myself for a large lecture about how bad things could have gone, but it never came. Even when she asked me to sit next to her on her stark white couch. Even after she sighed and looked up at me. What she said shocked me on so many levels.

"Larissa, you did what I thought you would, but not what I had hoped. I have to realize you have your own path to follow, and I shouldn't stand in your way. Without you, I wouldn't have my son back. I owe you a great gratitude for that." Then she hugged me. I returned it cautiously while I waited for the but that never arrived.

Neither of us spoke another word about it during my vigils. It was not for lack of opportunity. She spent just about as much time watching and tending to Nathan as I did. And, we weren't avoiding talking to each other either. We spoke. We actually spoke more than we ever had. I told her stories about my childhood and my parents. She was extremely interested in my father's journals. I showed her a few combined runes, just some basic safe ones. I felt there were a few entries in my father's journals she would really find interesting and had Edward retrieve them for me. The council's original rules regarding my father's journals restricted their removal from the library. Edward made an exception in my case, stating that the world was changing, and they were my family's property, so he felt those rules didn't apply to me. So, I guess I have gone from rule breaker to the person who the rules don't apply to.

By the end of the second day, the bluish scars on Nathan's skin had faded, and his periods of consciousness had increased. At first it was just periods of moaning and groaning, and then one time he asked, "how bad is it?" He didn't stay awake for the answer.

By the end of the third day, his eyes opened, and as much as I missed his old eyes, I was over the moon to see those empty black orbs staring up at me.

"So, am I dead?" he asked with a bit of a moan.

"No. Worse. You are human again."

"Seriously?" he shot up and propped himself up on his arms.

"Nah," I shook my head. "You're still a vampire."

He thought for a moment. "I'm not sure which is better. I liked being human, but I like knowing I am going to be around with you forever."

"Um, about that forever thing," I started, and he looked at me curiously, and then pushed himself up further and sat back against the headboard of his bed.

"Changing your mind?"

"No. It's not that. You need to understand the rules of this immortal thing. It just means you won't die. It doesn't mean you can't be killed. I just wanted to clarify that part of being a vampire for you. You have put yourself in some pretty precarious situations so far, and you have only been one of us for about two months. Keep it up, and your forever may only be six months."

"Worried?" he asked, almost laughing.

"This isn't a laughing matter. And no, I'm not worried because I am going to be here to keep you from doing anything stupid ever again."

"So, you are going to be my protector?" he asked, leaning toward me, grinning.

I leaned in to meet him. "Absolutely. Someone has to," I whispered, and then kissed him.

"Good. I think I can deal with that," he agreed before he grabbed my head with both hands and pulled me in for another kiss. When he released me, he looked over my shoulder into corner of the room at the occupant that had gone unnoticed by him until then.

"If you're my protector. It looks like you have one too. Who is the new witch who saved your ass?" he whispered into my ear.

"It's a long story." Samantha scooted her chair up next to me.

Nathan jerked back against his headboard with a bang. I don't believe he thought she could hear his question with how low he whispered it.

I reached over and grabbed his hand and prepared myself. "Well, here it goes."

The Revenge of the Shadow Witch

1

"Mom! This is so unfair!" Samantha screamed, storming out of my room and down the hall.

Finally, we had separate rooms to be thankful for. Not that I didn't enjoy rooming with my daughter. I loved it. It made us closer than ever. In fact, we were probably too close, in so many ways, and that might be a problem.

"What? Is she calling us ugly?" Apryl asked, poking her head through her cracked open door.

"Just ignore her. She's a teenager," I replied nonchalantly, as I passed by her door, giving it a quick shove to shut it.

Pamela stood in the hall, enjoying the show for some odd reason. As was Marie Norton, but I understood why she was. It was my stepparents' payback, and I was sure my mother was going to tell me the same thing. If only life slowed down enough for me to visit her.

"Look Sam..." Her door slammed in my face. She didn't lock it; we had already gone through that phase a few days ago. It lasted all of about five minutes. Her discovering that I knew how to open doors without a key ended it. It was just a simple spell any young witch learned so they could snoop around for Christmas and birthday gifts. After that, Mrs. Saxon taught it to Sam as a kind of revenge, or let's call it a grandmother spoiling her granddaughter. I opened the door and walked in. "I already told you there are two ways to handle it. Which way you chose is up to you, and you don't have to do anything at all."

Samantha sat at her makeup table, gazing at herself in a mirror. She tried her hair up, then her hair down. Then she pulled it back behind her head in a ponytail. That was the particular look I liked. It took a few years off of her, which I was all for. There was something about your daughter looking just as old as you were that I just couldn't get past. The good news was she had stopped aging. So, we were forever stuck together, forever, looking like sisters instead of mother and daughter. Something that more than a few made sure they pointed out, and a few of them paid for it dearly. We now know what sound Mike makes being thrown off the top of the coven. Fortunately, he landed on his feet. Unfortunately, that was probably where the good news ended, if you asked Samantha.

"It doesn't matter what I do," she cried.

"Yes, it does. You have two options." I looked into the mirror at her, smiling and hoping how uncomfortable I felt about what I was about to suggest didn't leach through. It did. "Really, you have three options."

"Mom! That isn't even funny," she protested at my suggestion, and reached down and slid her tray of makeup closer to her. She eyed the compact of powder and foundation, picking it up for a second before dropping it back to the table. "There isn't enough of this stuff in the world to cover this."

"Then you have the other option."

"Magic?" she complained, looking up at me.

"Yes. Magic."

She huffed, rolled her eyes, and got up from her chair and marched over to the closet. "No way, Jose. That is so fake. I can't believe you ever did that." Without touching the handle, she opened the doors, revealing the wide assortment of styles she had in her wardrobe. She and I were different in our sense of fashion. I was a jeans and t-shirt kind of girl, with a color palette that leaned heavily toward the blacks and grays. Samantha had skirts, dresses, tops, and pants of every color of the rainbow.

"Maybe if I wear something more in your style, I won't look that bad. Now I understand why they portray us how they do in the movies." She slid half her wardrobe from one side of the closet to the other. The screech of the metal hangers sent chills up my spine.

I heard a knock on the door frame and hoped a savior had come to rescue me. "What's wrong with her?" Amy waltzed into her room. Probably returning from an outing with Laura, which would explain how she got past the charmed doors.

"Your sister is having a bad day," I said.

Samantha turned and looked at Amy with a disgusted face, sticking her tongue and fangs out. "That's what. And mom, try life. This is for life. Remember?"

I was about to remind her that this life would never end, so she better just buckle up and get used to it, but I felt that might light another fuse.

"Why doesn't she just do magic like you did for the Christmas party?"

"Because I'm not my mom," Samantha snapped.

"Don't snap at her."

"Sorry," Samantha apologized, looking right at me. Disdain dripped from her eyes, but it disappeared when she turned to her little sister. "Sorry Amy. Want to come help me pick something out that will make me less ugly?"

"Yes, but you're not ugly," Amy responded, looking up at her sister.

Samantha just rolled her eyes and began pulling out outfits consisting of all grays and blacks, but leave it to Amy to pull out pinks and purples.

"How about these?" she asked.

"Oh sure. Those will just accentuate my ugliness," Samantha said, dismissing the suggestion.

"It will also make you look like a Gwen wannabe," Apryl added from the door.

"Stop," I warned, and she held up her hand defensively, but had an evil smile on her face.

"Sam, I don't know what you are so upset about. You have the best of both worlds." Apryl walked in and stopped to pose in the full-length mirror on the open closet door. "You have eternal youth. Your mom's good looks. That red hair is to die for..."

"And I look like a ghost," Samantha said, interrupting Apryl's compliment. "Just a week ago, I looked like I was alive. Rosy red cheeks and everything. Now look at me. Night of the living dead." She stiffened up her shoulders and rocked side to side, even playing like she was going to grab Amy, which produced a squeal.

"You didn't let me continue. You still have your eyes. Ask your mom, or any of the female vampires on this floor, what keeping our eyes would have meant to us."

Samantha looked at Apryl like she was going to respond, but then stopped and continued her search for the perfect outfit.

"Sam, she's right. I would give anything for it, and when I use magic to adjust my appearance, it is more for the eyes than anything. Our black eyes look so blank, and emotionless. You still have yours."

Samantha stopped her search for a moment to pull the closet door closed enough for her to look at herself in the mirror. "But they aren't even mine," she bemoaned, staring at her own reflection.

It happened as soon as we returned. What the trigger was, I didn't know. It had to be something that happened, or how she tapped into some of her vampire skills when fighting Mrs. Roberts or the witches that held her and the others. That was the only explanation that made sense, especially since it was later that day that life drained out of her skin, leaving her just as pale as the rest of us. Her only saving grace, that we were all jealous of, were her eyes. Fate did not curse her with the empty black orbs the rest of us were. Instead, she had human looking eyes. A colorful iris in the middle of the ocean of white, but instead of her big blue eyes, they were now a deep and brilliant gold, like the sunset. She hated it every time I compared them to that. I could only hope that in time she would grow to appreciate them.

"I love your eyes," Amy said, looking up at Samantha beaming, sporting her own pair of yellow eyes.

"Ugh!" Samantha turned around. "Knock that off, and just be yourself, please."

Amy turned and looked at me, sporting an exact copy of what Samantha's eyes look like and a huge smile.

"Knock it off," I mouthed back, and then gave the same warning to the giggling vampires behind me.

"Hurry up and pick something. We can't be late." I headed to the door, hoping if we were out of her hair, she might actually decide on something and get dressed.

"Yes, I know, mother," she practically seethed at me.

Amy handed her a shirt and a pair of jeans. "Here." It was something more like what I would pick, with maybe a touch more color. The shade of purple of the top was a little light for my taste, but acceptable, and what I felt was a fair compromise.

"Fine!" Samantha declared, almost defeated. With a quick shove from behind, she ushered Amy out of the room, along with the rest of us.

"Nice pick." I gave Amy a high five before pulling her close and jostling her hair. Something she hated and hastily put it back in to place.

"Why doesn't she just use magic like you?" Amy asked.

"She thinks it's being fake," I said with a shrug.

"That's silly."

I couldn't agree more, but that didn't move things along. "That's your older sister. She's silly."

"Yes, she is."

"Have fun with your witchy stuff today," Apryl commented as she walked away, waving over her shoulder at us. "I'm heading up to the deck for the day. It's nice and overcast." She turned around, and walked backwards toward her room and commented, "I could get used to this no class thing." Then she spun around and disappeared through her door.

"More?" Amy whined.

I nodded. "I'm afraid so. We'll drop you off on your floor on the way."

Samantha's door burst open with a whack, and she emerged in the outfit Amy had picked. She didn't wait for us, and just headed to the door, announcing, "I'm ready," when she was already halfway there. Amy and I picked up the rear and followed. It was all we could do. Samantha wasn't waiting for us.

Out the door we went, and my heart melted at the sight on the other landing. There he stood, waiting for us, like he had done every day since his return. Nathan stood there, leaning forward against the banister.

"Hey dad." Samantha waved as she headed down the stairs. The perfect image of the American brooding teenager. She didn't stop or even look in his direction.

"Morning Sam. How's my beautiful daughter today?"

"Ha!"

All I could do was shrug and smirk. He returned the same.

Amy screamed, "Hey Nathan." I saw Samantha's back crawl at the sound of the high-pitched scream.

"Hey there, cutie. Are we still on for more board games later?"

Amy nodded, and then added. "You're going to lose." I knew he was letting her win for a while, but he recently confessed she had beaten him a few times all on her own.

Nathan didn't bother greeting us at the bottom of the stairs or walking with us. They did not permit him where we were going. In fact, no one other than witches were. And even though things had changed here in this coven, it was still better if vampires weren't even close to our destination.

I dropped Amy off at her floor and then followed my sulking daughter down the stairs and down the hall toward the classrooms. It was just us now. The normally busy halls with people rushing to morning classes were a thing of the past. Mrs. Saxon had canceled all classes for the time being. We were mostly in a lockdown state. We still had access to the pool deck, which was protected. No one was allowed in or out of the coven, and that included witches. She said this was how it had to be, but it was just temporary. I couldn't see an end of this state in sight, and that had nothing to do with my divination skills. Mrs. Saxon even enlisted my help with the runes to lock down the coven, noting that mine were more powerful and lasted longer than hers. With everything I had put the woman through, I didn't hesitate. It didn't hurt that she practically guilted me into it by saying if anyone was going to break through them, it would be me, so why not just let me put my own up so it would be easier to get out? There was a smirk on her face as she said it.

We locked down the pool deck and a little area around the edge of the woods, knowing we needed to allow for some kind of outside exposure to fend off cabin fever. Of course, it wasn't like she locked us in a prison. This wasn't Mordin. I remembered that place well. This was an enchanted coven that created whatever your mind craved. If you really wanted to be outside, all you had to do was think about it and the room adjusted to make you think you were there.

To secure everything the best we could, I used the same type of runes I had used to hold Jean and his followers at bay. I just added a few modifications to them for a longer staying power, but that didn't mean I didn't go out at first light every day to check and reapply them to keep them in place. The only exception to my runes were the werewolves. They could come and go as they pleased, which had two purposes. One that they enjoyed, and one that they did out of obligation. They still ran checks night and day of the surrounding property for any intruders, just as they had before. The only difference now is they weren't just looking for the local drunk that had stumbled into a place they shouldn't have. They were looking for signs of witches or others approaching. The second reason was more of a compromise and suggested by Martin. Vampires had to feed, but we couldn't leave the coven. It wasn't safe. So, it had to be brought to us, which was one reason for securing a small area at the edge of the woods. Martin and his brothers would chase small game into that area, letting us feed. Martin's original idea was for him and his brothers to kill it and drag it to us, but that took the hunt out of it for us, making it less satisfying.

We walked to Mr. Helms' classroom and Samantha threw open the door, sending the occupants into a stunned silence.

"What? What are you looking at?" Samantha asked, standing there in the door's opening with her hands ready to go. When no one responded, she walked over and took her seat. Lisa looked back at me, concerned, and I wiped my hand down my face and pointed at my eyes, and Lisa nodded. She knew what was going on. Most everyone in the room did. They had, make that most of them had, tried to convince Samantha she was beautiful this way. One hadn't, and that pink princess eyed me the entire time I walked to my seat next to my daughter. This would not be a fun day.

2

I would have much rather be up on the roof, or in any of the common areas the vampires are now allowed to go, or even helping Nathan through what Kevin Bolden called advanced orientation than be down here for magic combat training. We had free run of the coven again. Gone were those evil charms the council gave all the witches. I rather enjoyed doing my part in their destruction. It was true, we could not leave the coven itself, but things felt a little more normal. Well, except to those of us that were witches.

The witches were on what Mr. Helms called a war-footing. As a result, we had daily combat training, which is where Samantha and I found ourselves this morning, just as we had every morning for the last few weeks following our return from the front lines. That was what Master Thomas called where we went. After our little discovery, everything changed.

The council still existed in physical form. The members of the council remained physically present within the coven, gathered in Mrs. Wintercrest's chambers, awaiting some royal command for them to follow. That command never arrived. It was almost as if they didn't know where else to go, or even what to do now. Many of them appeared aimless and still followed Mrs. Wintercrest wherever she went. Marcus Meridian, who was now free from his secret hiding location, believed they did so out of habit and what he also pointed out as an inability to think on their own. These people had spent their lives serving the wishes of the supreme. Now she was nothing. She was just a woman that seemed as aimless and purposeless as they were. She had lost that power, not to mention her current weakened state didn't really broadcast an image of supreme. Many of the council and supporters, including Gwen, begged her to show them she was still capable. She did and said nothing. It's not that she couldn't. If she did, they would all follow. It was that she just didn't.

The shattering of her hero all but destroyed Gwen, and it was clear who she blamed. Of course, it was me. It started out as a series of dirty looks every time we were within eyesight of each other. Then it progressed to rather aggressive bumps as she rushed past Samanta and me on the way out of class. I had to explain to Samantha that we had some history that made things worse. Apryl didn't hesitate to fill in all the gaps of our short but volatile past. She spent most of the time on how I stole Nathan from her. Though in that true story, there was nothing to steal. Nathan was never hers to begin with. He was very clear about that. Of course, her picture of the perfect life saw it differently.

Then, one day after class, I saw a collision coming and moved to avoid Gwen's passing. That may have saved me from the momentary torment, but that didn't stop her from mumbling something under her breath and ramming Samantha hard into a table. All I remembered of that exact moment was the blonde and pink blur that flew past me and against the wall of Mr. Helms' class. I looked back at Samantha, and she was ready to follow it up, but I put a stop to it. In hindsight, I wish I hadn't. Well, that was not completely correct. I needed to set a good example for my daughter, but I would be lying if my blood didn't boil when I heard Gwen scream back, "You two are nothing but filthy vampire liars. Sneaking back in here with lies to destroy us from the inside. They should hang you both until your heads pop off." Mr. Nevers grabbed Gwen and yanked her out of the room. She continued to scream all the way down the hall. "The Devil and her spawn are here to destroy us." Since then. Gwen has joined those aimless council members, spending most of her free time with Mrs. Wintercrest, her former and possibly still current idol. I was fine with that. It reduced the chances that we would bump into each other in the coven.

It didn't take long for word to spread outside the coven about what had happened, and about who was really pulling the strings. Mrs. Saxon had her connections and had actually received encouragement from others that she should step in. They believed the council needed direction. I even pushed her once to take over as supreme. This was no longer about the test of the seven wonders. This was about having someone at the wheel of our people. She gave me a disappointed look as I tried to push her. To me, I saw it as a win-win situation. To her, I think she saw it as a way for me to skirt stepping up to where everyone else believed I needed to be. She politely declined each attempt and instead deflected the role to either Master Thomas or Marcus Meridian. Neither accepted the role, but that didn't stop them from taking control. Their personalities commanded respect naturally, and with the current power vacuum we faced, everyone seemed to look to them. Both pointed out the same thing Mrs. Saxon did. Before any supreme could be safe or recognized, we needed to resolve the current issues, and restore the council and the title of the supreme to their former glory. That was how Master Thomas stated it. Marcus Meridian used the word purify. For many witches that harkened memories of the various witch trials that stained the pages of history books and the purification of fire those witches were put through. Samantha and I tried to purify Mrs. Roberts with fire ourselves.

Mrs. Saxon also saw another impediment that neither Master Thomas nor Marcus did. They never even spoke of it. All agreed Mrs. Roberts was out there and needed to be dealt with, but Mrs. Saxon felt she was a threat to our coven, and not in some kind of political struggle sense. She truly believed that Mrs. Roberts and all her supporters, which she heard there were still large pockets of out there, would come after us. She discussed it in a closed meeting that involved just the instructors and me. Why had she invited me and not any others? She didn't say. It felt a little odd being there. I felt like a student attending a staff meeting, but we weren't discussing course curriculum. What we were discussing was far from it. Mrs. Saxon was convinced Mrs. Roberts would come after this coven. There was only one throne, and it was no longer about the test of the seven wonders. This was all about power and control. As she talked about it, my head conjured the image of armies storming castles to claim the throne. With how she talked in that meeting, that image didn't seem that far off. Thus, we were here with Mr. Helms and several members of the council, learning how to not only defend ourselves but also how to fight as a witch.

"Gwen. Can you come down here for me?" Mr. Helms requested.

Ever the one who liked attention, she practically hopped out of her chair, which was in the front row. Making her walk to the front was nothing more than a few steps.

"Today I want to cover something that Gwen has mastered over the last year or so." As Mr. Helms started, the smile on Gwen's face grew. He was filling her ego to the brim with just those simple words. "Many of you believe offensive and defensive combat is limited to fire balls and a few spells. That view will severely limit what you can do and probably get you and others killed. We can use everything in either a defensive or offensive way. Even something as simple as compulsion can be useful. Though most witches you encounter will be relatively skilled in defending themselves against it. Gwen has been using something simple in both a defensive and offensive nature for a while. Let's show them."

Mr. Helms grabbed Gwen by the shoulders and turned her. She got one last leer up in my direction before her head turned. "Go stand over there and be ready."

He let Gwen turn before he unleashed hell in her direction. I had never seen so many fireballs and other projectiles fired by a single person before. There was a moment of panic on her face, then she spun open a portal in front of her that consumed everything Mr. Helms sent her way. He dropped his guard and looked as though he was ready to speak again, but then it was his turn to panic. I had seen the first move from Gwen before, and seeing it again was a good reminder for me. Her new trick caused Mr. Helms to panic. A second portal opened above his head and returned everything he had created right back at him. I watched and waited for him to repeat Gwen's initial trick, but he just flicked his wrist, causing each object to disappear and in a puff of smoke.

"Well done, Gwen," Mr. Helms walked back to the center of the room while Gwen returned to her seat. She did everything but bow.

"We are going to spend a lot of time working on how to use normal spells and magic in that way today, tomorrow, and for however long it takes you all to become masters of it, but first there is something else I want to show you. I have been hesitant about showing you this. I've even put it off several times. Many of you won't understand what this is, but those you will go up against will. I need you to see it." Mr. Helms headed for the side wall and pointed up in my direction, and motioned with his hand for me to come down. "Larissa, join me down here. Will you?"

He asked, but I knew it wasn't really a question. He, I, and Masters Thomas, Nevers and Meridian had discussed this very moment for the last several days. It's not that we rehearsed it. That would be disingenuous, as Master Thomas said. It was actually more of a discussion of curriculum. How do you teach someone something they haven't experienced yet? Well, you show them. The problem was, many of our audience hadn't ascended yet, and wouldn't see it. And there was that little thing about not talking about ascension with anyone who hadn't yet. Marcus pointed out that I should be the one to break that rule, since I had a habit of that. That earned him a little smack upside the head, but not from me. It was from Mrs. Okina, one of the council members who had always been quiet, but recently seemed to have become a fan of mine. She even volunteered to help finish any training I might need. Any thoughts of the test of the seven wonders were now on the back burner.

There seemed to be a budding sisterhood developing between her and Lisa. Both of them shared a strong spiritualism with the cultures. Japan didn't share the same voodoo and black magic-based spiritualism, but that didn't seem to matter. They both drew from it.

I got up and walked down the stairs to the front of the classroom. The feeling of eyes following me was one I was more than used to by now. Even the weight of the stare from Gwen didn't faze me. Why should it? What that little witch was about to see would blow her mind. With no instruction, I walked over to the side I knew I was to stand and took my position. We were going to show it first, and then tell. I waited for Mr. Helms to begin, but he didn't, and was actually focused more on the door in the back of the room than he was me. Why? I wasn't sure. This was to be an exhibit between me and him. When the door cracked open, and the entire room gasped, well Samantha didn't, Marcus Meridian, mister exile who spent weeks locked in a room here in the coven, and even after Mrs. Saxon released his house arrest, he never showed his face outside of meetings with the teachers, council, and me, strolled in. Jaws were on the floor, and I felt a bit of déjà vu. This time, we weren't out in my field in New Orleans.

Mr. Helms stepped aside and let Marcus take his place. He bowed to me and asked, "Ready?"

I nodded and readied myself for anything and everything. I had been here once before.

Marcus took off his black sports coat and handed it to Mr. Helms. Then, to continue his showmanship, he unbuttoned the cuffs on the sleeves of his dark red shirt and slowly rolled them up to his elbow. After a final tug on his shirt to straighten it and a pass through his hair to smooth it, here came hell. What Mr. Helms had thrown at Gwen was nothing like this. There were fire balls, lightning, blasts of air, and even a crack in the ground developing below my feet. I held to my promise, and responded by throwing a barrage of runes, making the air and ground between us look like some kind of rune-inspired alphabet soup. And while he continued to throw more, my runes held, and I stood there with my arms crossed. I even considered a little faux yawn while standing there calmly while everything he sent over crashed into the runes.

I knew they wouldn't last forever, and Mr. Helms had asked me not to produce any that would. That wasn't the point. Magic attacks whittled away at the runes, and even the strongest one would, or should, give out after the attack had chiseled away enough from it. I watched my runes and noticed I might have outdone myself. He was making progress at breaking through, but we would be here another day or two, and we didn't have that time. With a quick swipe of my hand, they all disappeared. To make sure nothing got through, I sent a besom with a powerful shove. The angled lines threw everything heading for me right back at Marcus, and he tumbled out of the way, letting it all crash into the hard, stacked stone walls of Mr. Helms' classroom.

All eyes were on me again, and jaws were again on the floor. I did my best not to smile and just stood there while inside I was screaming, "Take that, Gwen!"

"What you just saw Larissa use was called Runes," Mr. Helms started. "Some of you might have noticed them in the ceremonial room and, in recent weeks, you may have watched Mrs. Saxon put them up. They were a part of magic that the council forbade us to teach. Well, that ends today!" Mr. Helms pumped his fist. "Starting today, there is no such thing as forbidden magic. During the second half of our class today, our esteemed council members have volunteered to teach you the runes and help you perfect them." Mr. Helms didn't discuss my last little trick. Obviously avoiding the topic of ascension for those that hadn't ascended yet, which included my daughter. When that would happen was another mystery, and I was becoming used to mysteries.

"Miss Dubois," Mr. Demius called through the open door. "Can you come with me?"

I stepped forward and watched Samantha stand up. Then I realized the problem, and had to ask, "Which one?"

He chuckled. "You."

Samantha settled back into her chair, and as I walked up the stairs, I heard Jack suggest, "Shouldn't you be a Saxon?"

I was sure that dagger dug deep in Gwen.

"We would still have the same problem with two with the same last name," Lisa responded.

"When are you guys getting married, anyway?" Marcia asked.

I heard the groan coming from the front row. Oh, to have Jack's ability to feel what Gwen was feeling right now. I would just be happy with eyes in the back of my head so I could see her expression.

On my way out, I stopped by the last row where Samantha and I had been sitting and issued a warning. "Behave." I glanced sideways and saw Gwen glaring in our direction, and I felt the weight of worry settle on me.

"She can handle herself," remarked Mr. Demius when I joined him at the door.

"It's not her I'm worried about."

3

The question that caused a murmur in the class also sparked intense discussions most nights on the deck. Among the girls, it was what one might expect—a daily inquiry, often by either Pamela or Apryl. However, Jennifer and Laura occasionally jumped into the mix. On one occasion, Laura pulled me aside and flat out told me that if he didn't pop the question, there was nothing wrong with me taking charge and being the one to ask him. She reminded me that while I may have been born back when times were different; I was a woman of the modern age.

When the topic arose around the men, a collective groan would fill the air, and they would retreat to the far end of the deck, dragging Nathan with them. Or as Mike said once, "Come on Nathan. We'll save you." Everyone followed, except Kevin Bolden. He would linger, casting looks toward his wife, as if he were waiting for Jennifer's silent approval. Which, in her own way, she granted. And then he would sheepishly get up and stroll to the other end, while I sat and braced for the grilling to come.

A few times, Apryl and Pamela attempted to enlist my own daughter in their campaign against me. They had her drop hints for Nathan or take a more direct route and try to guilt me into giving her the family she deserved. I didn't disagree with that point or any other points anyone made. Neither did Samantha. That was why we both sat there stoically, looking at each other, guarding a secret that, if any of them knew, they would skewer me.

What no one knew was Nathan had already asked. In fact, he had asked me five times so far. Each time I said no. Well, my answers weren't exactly no. His first proposal happened moments after he woke up from the effects of the Fires of Ruel. He was still delirious, and I don't even think he knew what he was saying. I refrained from reacting or responding and urged him to rest, but that didn't stop the moment from grabbing me. We locked eyes, both ensnared in each other's gaze. It was a moment that most people only dreamed of. I caressed his head and prepared to hear something sweetly romantic. It was coming, and I waited. I waited for a declaration of his unwavering love, how I consumed his thoughts during his absence, and the otherworldly connection we shared. He was going to tell me the sun rose and set with my face. His mouth opened, and then he passed out. So much for that moment.

The next time he proposed, it was entirely ill-timed, and I had to fight the urge to explode with frustration. He, Samantha, and I were sitting in Mrs. Saxon's apartment. He had just recovered enough to get out of bed and walk around. His skin still had Mrs. Tenderschott's green antidote caked on it, including two spots on his face. He resembled a character from a monster movie, but he was coherent, and we needed to have a conversation. A very serious one. I asked Mrs. Saxon if we could talk to Nathan alone. She left without hesitation. She knew why we were there. That was the day I introduced Nathan to his daughter. I didn't make it a long and drawn-out affair. Hell, I could have drawn it out longer than my actual pregnancy, but just like with everything that involved Samantha, I accelerated it. I came right out and said, "Nathan, I would like you to meet your daughter, Samantha. She is a witch, and part vampire, kind of like me."

Samantha was more emotional than I had expected. Tears streamed down her cheeks as I told Nathan. Nathan was in shock. I half-expected that reaction and watched as the gears inside his head did the math. The light finally came on for him, and he got it. "Vampire pregnancy... the speed..."

"Yep," I responded, not wanting to go into too much detail. Not that I understood it that much, but I covered the basics. "She was born seven weeks and three days ago, but as you can see, she has aged to someone who is probably fifteen or sixteen, and that seems to be where she has stopped."

"Seventeen," Samantha chimed in with a giggle and a sniff, as she wiped away her tears.

"Oh yes, seventeen. We are having a minor disagreement about that. She wants to be older than me."

Nathan jumped up and hugged her before Samantha knew what hit her, but she quickly returned the embrace just as warmly.

"I have a daughter," Nathan mumbled over and over in a trance-like-state.

"A daughter that saved your ass," Samantha added. I gave her a look of admonishment, but I refrained from being too hard on her and ruining the moment.

"Yes, a daughter that saved us, as she has reminded me and anyone that will listen."

As soon as Nathan let go of her, he went down on one knee all starry-eyed, and popped it. "Marry me."

My heart yearned to scream yes. The desire was so overwhelming; I swore I felt my heart beat once again. However, there was something about that moment that felt wrong, and then he pushed it even further over the edge.

"We have a daughter. We need to get married and be a family." He looked back at Samantha and smiled.

While his intentions were in the right place, he used the one word a girl didn't want to hear in a proposal: "Need." I practically screeched the word as I walked away and out the door. Mrs. Saxon lingered in the hallway, likely concerned about straying too far away in case Nathan's condition took a turn for the worse. She had Mrs. Tenderschott mix up more of the antidote and stored it in her room just in case. I marched past her and down the hall. "He said we need to get married."

All I heard from her in response was, "Oh, geez." She then went inside, and I headed back up to my room.

Over the next few weeks, there were a lot of family moments. It was something I had planned on forcing, but there was no need. Nathan actively sought us out. He was eager to know his daughter, and he often lamented to me, privately, about how bad he felt about missing her younger days. I wanted to give him grief for it, and while I had a few lines about him missing the first sixteen years of her life planned, I refrained. He was hurting for all the time he missed. Anyone who saw them together could see it. I reminded him it was only a few weeks, hopefully relieving some of the guilt he felt. Whether or not it worked, I couldn't tell.

Amy joined us for many of those moments, and Samantha quickly warmed to her. It seemed rather natural, which was puzzling to me, but I couldn't deny the happiness I felt. A feeling that was disconcerting considering the surrounding turmoil. People had been hurt and killed, and I still carried the responsibility for it all. Why was I allowed to have a pure joyful moment?

Even Ms. Parrish's presence struck me as somewhat amusing. This time, it wasn't because of my actions. She was there, watching Nathan around Amy. I wasn't sure if word about the little incident in New Orleans had gotten back to her yet, or if she was just doing the same she had done with me at first. Nathan protested rather vigorously the first few times, reminding her she had known him since he was in diapers. She reminded him he wasn't the same person he used to be, and then once even turned to me to ask if I would watch after Amy when he was around. Of course, I agreed, but I smirked at Nathan as I did so. My how times had changed.

His next two proposals lacked inspiration. They were nothing more than causal suggestions. I ignored the first one and told him he would need to try harder. He didn't hesitate to remind me he was down on one knee before, and I didn't hesitate to remind him how unromantic that moment was. The word need still burning deep inside.

His last proposal was a little more thought out. Amy had just headed inside, and it was just him, me, and Samantha. I should have known something was up with how they exchanged glances all night long. Once the door closed behind Amy and Ms. Parrish, Nathan sprang up from his seat and was once again on his knee in front of me. Samantha extended her hand toward him. She held the most radiant ring I had ever seen. It glistened in the moonlight. I had to ask, "Magic?" That had to be where it came from. It was the only explanation I could think of, but I was wrong.

"My grandmother's," Nathan replied, holding up in front of me so I could see it sparkle in the moonlight. "My mother gave it to me to give to you." He gently took my hand, sliding the ring partially onto my ring finger. His eyes sought my own, and once our gazes locked, he said, "Larissa, you are it. As corny as that sounds, you are it. You're everything. From the first moment we met, I think we both knew this day was coming. You were different from the others, and..." he held a hand up, suppressing any snarky comeback I had for that remark, and trust me, there was one ready. "You were just you. You weren't a vampire. You weren't a witch. You were just you. You let me get to know the real you. Once I saw that person, I fell in love with that person and knew there wasn't anything in this world I wouldn't do for you. There is no place I won't follow you, which I think I have proven a few times. My place is by your side. Will you do me the honor of letting me be your partner in life? To face every challenge this world has to offer together. To love. To hold. To live as one. Will you allow me to be your husband?"

I was mush. He did it. He really did it. The perfect moment, the heartfelt speech, and the ring, which could have been the tiniest thing anyone had seen, and it would have still meant the same. It was his grandmother's, and that meant the world. This would be the joining of two families, and that was a symbol of that union. Samantha, the product of that joining, sat there watching her father propose to her mother with a grin the Cheshire Cat would have been jealous of. The moment was perfect, and that was why I said, "No."

All the magic of the moment disappeared, and Nathan ducked his head. I reached down and lifted his chin toward me and explained. "Not yet."

"Need a better proposal?" he asked, crushed.

325

"No. Your proposal was perfect." I admitted. It truly was. I couldn't imagine anything better, which was why I felt I needed to explain. "That isn't it. There is so much going on right now. The war. The council. It's hard for me to even see what my future is going to be, or if there even is one. I need to settle some things. Clear the problems away, and then, yes, I will marry you. You can even ask me again then, if you want, but not until then."

It was hard to tell if Nathan understood. I honestly expected him to blow up at me like he had before when I focused on my past. Ironically, now, it was my future that was problematic. Not the here and now, like he wanted. He got up and hugged me. I slid the ring back into his pocket and asked him to keep it safe until then. Things were a little weird for a few days after that. He was quiet around me. Talking only when he had to, but things eventually returned to normal.

Samantha blew up on me the minute we were back in our room. I tried to explain it to her, but she wasn't understanding. I felt she didn't understand and wouldn't, but just as I was about to give up, she surprised me and gave me something to think about.

"Mom, what if there is no future? Wouldn't you rather be with him now as his wife than never have the chance?"

It was a fair question, and one I didn't have an answer to. She hasn't brought it up more than a few times a day. Each time trying to talk me into running to him, and throwing myself into his arms while screaming, "Yes!" I actually considered it once, but the thought of him losing me somewhere in all this was too much. Though I had to wonder, did the ring make that big of a difference? Wouldn't it hurt him the same rather we were married or not? Then I realized it wasn't him. I was worried about feeling hurt. It was me.

4

We made our way to Mr. Demius' classroom for my "special" training. I didn't need to be in Mr. Helms' class anymore. According to Master Nevers and Master Thomas, I could teach a master class on the topic. No, my assignment was to continue the training I started in New Orleans. Again, during our walk, I asked the same question I had asked every day.

"Why was this so important now?" I asked, frustration creeping into my voice.

In light of what we knew about Mrs. Roberts and her role as the puppet master pulling the strings of the council, or what Master Thomas called a shadow witch, it seemed to me that the traditional ways no longer mattered. We were engaged in an all-out battle for power, or survival. It was probably both. Mr. Demius didn't particularly disagree. It appeared he was leaning towards my perspective more and more with each passing day. Perhaps my presence was rubbing off on him. But even if it was, he still had a valid point. One that he always included in his response.

"You might have a point there, Larissa, but we still need to follow tradition for the others on the council and for our entire community. They need to see their supreme prove she has what it takes to be the supreme. Traditions are important for our kind." Then he paused a beat, and bemoaned, "At least they used to be."

When we reached Mr. Demius' classroom, he paused and placed his hand on the doorknob. He turned to me with a mischievous glint in his eyes. "I have a surprise for you, and I need you to guess what it is before I let you see it."

I looked at him cockeyed. What kind of strange game was this?

"You cannot use the all-seeing eye, or the eye of Osiris. Use your skills to see who you will see when I finally let you walk through the door."

I understood what he was after, even without him returning my cockeyed look. He was trying to test my divination, a skill I haven't practiced in weeks. Mr. Demius leaned against the door with a determined look, making his commitment to this task obvious.

With no other choice. I settled into my task and attempted to clear my mind, which was significantly easier to do now. Easier, not easy. Thoughts and worries still clogged it from time to time. The anticipation of what was behind the door seemed to have pushed those aside for now.

I focused on a spot just in front of my toes, trying to sense anything. The anticipation of seeing two old friends grew inside me.

"There's two..." I said, still searching for the image. I saw myself walking through the door. Two shapes stood at the front of the room, and I ran to them. "There's two people in there." Their shapes came into view. One stood, and the other sat at the table at the front of his class. The shape of the one on the table was familiar. As was the quick chirps that I heard of his voice. Then it all flashed in front of me, and my hand jerked for the door.

Mr. Demius blocked my attempt, and I frowned. "Not so fast. What's behind the door?"

I jerked back and shot him a sour look. "There are two people behind that door."

"Okay," he said, "Who are they?"

"What? You don't know?" I asked sarcastically, while I made another attempt to open the door. I almost pulled it open, but Mr. Demius pushed it close with a slam. I wanted through that door badly. Behind were two witches that I had been worried about since the attack in New Orleans. I had even asked Mrs. Saxon about them, but she hadn't heard if they were okay or not. Now I knew they were fine, and if Mr. Demius didn't get out of my way, I might have to move him. There were hugs to give.

"I know perfectly well who is behind the door," Mr. Demius said, refusing to yield to my impatience. "The question is, do you?"

I reluctantly stepped back and shot him an annoyed look. "Why, of course I do, silly. It's James O'Conner and Mary Smith." Those names were the magic words. Mr. Demius swung the door wide open, and I rushed through the opening and down the steps, grabbing Mary Smith and spinning her in my arms.

"You're safe. You're safe," I repeated as she wept in my ear. It was amazing how close I felt to the woman, considering how we started.

"What? You weren't worried about me?" James said. He hopped down off the table.

I let go of Mary and hugged James. There was no crying or screaming that he was safe. I gave him something a bit more befitting him. "Nope, not worried at all. I knew this would happen. So did you. You already saw it."

Then he gave it back to me. "No, you didn't. You haven't been practicing."

"Well, I have. Just not as much as I should."

He let go and reminded me, "You need to practice it every day until you get the hang of it, and," he flashed me that car salesman smile of his, "then you practice it some more."

"That is why they are here." Mr. Demius announced as he joined us at the bottom of the steps. "Mary is here to help you with astral projection, and James is here to continue his teachings on divination. They are to be your private tutors until you know enough to teach them. Which, if I have learned anything from you, that won't be long."

I had already pieced together why they were here before Mr. Demius spelled it all out. It was the only logical reason, but seeing them prompted another thought. "Personal tutors?"

"Yes," Mary proudly nodded.

"Can I add one more to the list of students?"

"Lisa?" Mary asked, taking a guess.

Now it was my turn to nod. "Yes," I confirmed, turning to Mr. Demius. "Please. It would mean the world to her. Let her continue what she started. She is fantastic at these, too."

"It is true. She caught on quickly," James agreed. Mary clasped her hands together in front of her, and let her wide eyes do all her talking.

Mr. Demius hesitated; the momentary silence hung over the room. I was prepared to launch into another round of begging when he finally broke the silence. "All right. Who am I to deny someone the opportunity to learn in this, an institute of education?" His hand gestured around, presenting his classroom. Textbooks magically appeared on all the tables, and opened, flipping through to a page.

I could hardly contain my excitement, ready to burst through the door, but Mr. Demius caught my arm, freezing me right in my tracks.

"Where are you going?" he inquired.

"To get Lisa." I replied, looking down at the spot where he'd gripped my arm, surprised at his swiftness.

"We can work her in during another session. Right now, she needs the combat training Mr. Helms is teaching." He released my arm, and I shook it out, still feeling the pinch of his fingers against my skin. "I am glad to see you've regained your enthusiasm about training."

I shifted uncomfortably, admitting, "Well, not exactly."

I felt their collective gaze upon me, and I imagined the shock upon their faces.

"Larissa doesn't see the purpose behind this training after the revelations of Mrs. Roberts and Mrs. Wintercrest."

"Well, she has a point," James remarked.

I spun around on my heels, pointing at James. "See?"

Mr. Demius appeared unpleased with James taking my side. "No, she doesn't. Having our next supreme pass the test of the seven wonders is important for everyone on the council and all witches to see. It will instill their confidence in their new leader. Not to mention our traditions are important."

"He has a point too," James said, glancing out of the sides of his eyes.

My eyes, though devoid of emotion, conveyed my feelings perfectly as I executed a practiced eye roll. James just shrugged.

There was no avoiding it; I had to train. That didn't stop me from considering arguments to get me out of it, but each time the echoes of everyone who ever discussed this *great-plan* resounded in my mind. There had been a time when I questioned if any of them had ever really considered my feelings about the matter, but they asked, and I agreed. Why? Because it was the only path I saw for some kind of peaceful existence for myself, and those that were in my life. I saw it as the solution to all of my problems, but now new ones had piled on top of the original ones. I wasn't completely convinced this path would solve the new problems. In fact, I was quite positive it wouldn't. Mrs. Roberts wouldn't care who passed the test or not.

"I can see both sides," Mary Smith offered. She took my hands in hers. "We must deal with Mrs. Roberts, but then what? Our kind will be out there, lost and shattered. The council and what it used to mean destroyed. The people they put their faith in to lead them scarred. They will need someone. Someone they can believe in and follow. That person will need to show them they are worthy. The test is part of our traditions and is the only way the next supreme can earn that trust. Then that person will need to build on that and prove through actions that they can be the leader we need." She let go of my hand and reached up under my chin, pushing it up to make sure we were looking each other in the eye. "Larissa, I have faith that you can be that person, but you need to pass the seven tests for others to give you the chance to prove it to them."

I looked around the room at the encouraging faces and asked, "So, where do we start first?"

The consensus was to begin with divination. All agreed it was safer. Especially me. Though, safer was really a relative term.

My frustration grew and boiled over a few times during the exercises. It was another game of red car blue car, but with a simple pack of playing cards. Yes, every street magician in the world can guess what card you are holding, thanks to the markings on the card or other tricks, but I was tasked with an entirely different challenge. I wasn't allowed to touch the cards, ever. Only James could, but that wasn't the challenge. I had to guess the card before James drew it from the deck. We started with my guess coming a few minutes before he pulled the card, and then progressed to stretching it to an hour, which I did without an issue. Maybe Master Thomas was right. Magic was like a muscle and needed continual exercise to stay in shape. I wasn't about to tell him that, though.

We spent the breaks between my guesses to catch up and talk about the theory of what I was doing. James explained that eventually I wouldn't have to concentrate—I would just see it. Then the challenge I would face lay in knowing the difference between the present and the future. If I thought my first conversation with James was frustrating, then I needed to prepare myself for when I reached that point.

When James wasn't talking to me about divination, Mary was preparing me for my next venture into astral projection. The warnings Edward gave me were something to pay attention to didn't hold a black candle to the horror stories Mary told me. She knew witches that didn't respect the dangers and believed it was all just magic. They believed they could drift away, and just by thinking about it, they would return. They never did. I dared to ask what happened to them. Mary didn't sugarcoat it. Their physical bodies remained trapped in a trance, eventually succumbing to starvation or dehydration. Their spirits wandered for all eternity. The spirit can exist without the body, but the body can't exist without the spirit.

After finishing up the afternoon with that uplifting conversation, we left Mr. Demius' classroom and walked down the hall to Mr. Helms' classroom. It was my suggestion. James and Mary wanted to see Lisa. I wanted to introduce them to Samantha. We arrived a tad bit late. I could see the doors opening down the hall and people coming out. I waited until I saw Lisa, and then I called her name. "Lisa!"

She turned and saw who I was with, her eyes lighting up as she took off running.

I saw Samantha next and called her name. "Sam!" She didn't run, but approached cautiously, studying our guests.

"I have to say, I didn't see that coming," James remarked.

"Me either..." Mary began.

"Remember what I said about vampire pregnancies?"

"I just didn't expect you would go from terrible twos through preteen, and straight into those teenage years in just a matter of weeks."

"Oh, trust me, it seemed much faster than that." Looking back on it now, it felt like a blink of an eye.

Lisa jumped on James and hugged him. Her small five-foot two frame almost knocked him to the floor. Then it was Mary's turn, but Lisa was a little more careful with how she hugged her.

"Guess what Lisa? They are here to continue teaching us."

Lisa had almost let go of Mary, but upon hearing my news, she hugged them both again and squealed.

Samantha finally made her way to us, and as I was about to handle the introductions, I saw someone else heading our way behind her. I turned and groaned, hoping she would go away. But hearing that flirty singsong voice of our own version of an evil witch barbie-doll grated on my nerves and told me Gwen wasn't going away.

"Oh, Larissa. Aren't you going to introduce me to friends?" She pranced past me with one hand extended toward James, wanting a proper introduction. I didn't oblige. Instead, I watched Lisa's glare shoot daggers at the pink covered annoyance, as she introduced herself. I had seen this before.

James accepted her hand and introduced himself. Gwen stood there, waiting. Waiting for what? I had to assume was a kiss on top of her hand, which James was doing his best to let go of. Once it fell to her side, she turned and asked, "So, how do you two know each other?"

It was none of her business. Not much of anything Gwen ever forced herself into was, but that never stopped her. But as much as I wanted to ignore her, I knew that would only make things worse. So, I made up a story. Well, not really a story. I told her the truth with lots of omissions.

"I met James and Mary in New Orleans. Marcus introduced us." It wasn't a lie. It just wasn't the entire story. I wasn't about to mention to Gwen they were here to teach Lisa and me anything. If she knew, she would be nonstop with her attempts to weasel her way in, and that wasn't going to happen. Gwen looked at me, and I saw her brow furrow right before my eyes. She knew I was leaving something out. Just great.

Then it happened. It was something that gave me great joy, great pride, and horrified me all at the same time. Samantha walked right up behind Gwen and continued to James, wrapping her arms around him. "Oh, James. It is so great to see you again."

Gwen's eyes shot up as wide as physically possible before she spun around, and Lisa slapped a hand over her mouth to stifle a laugh.

5

"I wish I could have seen Gwen's face," Apryl cackled, her laughter echoing in the moment. Pamela was right there with her, falling backward in her chair as she envisioned the image I had painted of the earlier events.

"It was priceless." I said, reaching over and patting my daughter on the leg.

Samantha, however, only offered a brief comment on the matter. "She had it coming."

"Oh, she had that and more coming for a long time," Apryl added between fits of laughter. "Your mother used to give—"

"Enough of that," I interjected, cutting her off abruptly. I didn't want our conversation to veer down memory lane and reveal any embarrassing stories that were best kept from my daughter. I wasn't sure there was anything left that Mrs. Tenderschott hadn't already shared, but I didn't want to take any chances, especially with Nathan sitting right here next to me, holding my hand. He was at the heart of the conflict between Gwen and me, and I wasn't sure if he knew all the tales yet. "Lisa tells me Gwen got it a few times from you today."

Like a child caught doing something wrong, Samantha averted her gaze, but her sly smile couldn't go unnoticed. While I didn't object to Gwen receiving a taste of her own medicine, I didn't want my daughter crossing any lines. We all needed each other now, and we might need to grow some thicker skin, or learn to turn the other cheek, at least for the time being. I needed to have a little talk with her later.

"I'm sure Apryl wouldn't mind giving Gwen a little too, but we aren't allowed in the secret club," Mike complained, albeit half-jokingly.

"It's not a secret club, or even secret classes," I corrected him. "Mr. Helms is teaching everyone how to fight as a witch. Remember, he taught classes on defensive spells and magic before. Now he has added some attacking spells and magic. We need to not only defend the coven but also defeat anyone that tries to attack it."

"Larissa, do you honestly believe Mrs. Roberts will come after this coven?" Kevin Bolden asked with a concerned tone.

Samantha and I exchanged glances before we both replied, "Absolutely."

Our response seemed to stun many of those on the rooftop deck with us. Perhaps it was the speed with which we answered, or the fact we both provided the same answer. Whatever it was, there were a lot of long and shocked faces looking back at us.

"I killed her daughter," I began, and Samantha continued. "And exposed how she has been manipulating the council for her own purposes."

"That too."

"Then there's dissolved the council itself, robbing her of any power she had, creating a war for control of the world of witches," Samantha added again.

"Well, now, you are being a little overdramatic, but yeah, something like that," I conceded.

"I think she has a grudge to settle," Samantha summarized.

"Maybe she isn't," Kevin Bolden mused as he got up and walked over and settled in the seat next to me. "Maybe she isn't being dramatic enough. This is an old-fashioned battle for power. Something that has led to wars in civilization for centuries. There is no central power in the world of witches now. I don't doubt she will make her play for it now that her proxy has been removed, and I believe she sees Larissa and the remaining council members as obstacles."

I was relieved I wasn't the only one that saw it that way. She was going to storm this castle. Now the only questions left were when, and if we would be ready.

"So, you think a war is coming?" Brad asked, joining the conversation as he and Jeremy walked away from the railing they had stood out, staring at the woods.

Kevin surveyed everyone; his concerned expression remained. He even turned to make quick eye contact with Jeremy and Brad, who had settled in seats behind him. "Yes, I do. And we should be prepared. It might not be the witches."

Mike pounded his fist in the palm of his other hand. "We are better suited for fighting. Why are they bothering with that training Larissa described? They wouldn't be any match for us."

"Oh, really?" I challenged.

"Yes, really." Mike puffed out his chest in confidence.

I was about to ask Nathan to tell Mike about his experience with the witches, but before I could, someone else made an example of him.

"Put me down!" Mike yelled, kicking and grasping wildly as he floated in the air over the railing. "Put me down now, Larissa!"

"It's not me," I replied.

"So, Mike, you think you are a match for a fight with witches?" Samantha asked, sending him slightly higher in the air while waiting for his answer.

Clay rushed over to the railing and made a half-hearted attempt to grab Mike, but his hands didn't even come close. "You're on your own with this witch," he quipped, winking at Samantha as he walked away from the railing.

"Sam?" I called out in a motherly tone. Mike moved back over the deck and descended to a light landing. He shot Samantha an irked look, and I readied myself to intervene. Nathan's body tensed up beside me. Samantha just waved back at Mike with her fingers, and that anger he showed melted away. I wasn't sure if she had used something else on him or if Uncle Mike, as he calls himself, gave up.

"It's not just the witches we need to worry about."

Kevin's suggestion drew several curious glances his way.

"He's right," Jennifer agreed, although she didn't seem that confident. She looked back at Kevin with the same hope we all did. That hope that he had some point.

"Look at it this way. The witches declared a war against the vampires. Now the witches are ignoring them and fighting among themselves."

"Pearl Harbor," Jeremy blurted out before offering a clarification. "Well, sort of. They are distracted with their own battles. This would be the perfect time for the vampires to come after the witches. They could seize the opportunity, just like Japan did when the US was focused on Europe.

"Jeremy just earned himself some more history homework, but yes, that was my point." Kevin leaned toward Jeremy and whispered, "That's not why Japan attacked the US."

"And I hate to admit this, but," Jennifer began, her discomfort was palpable. The words she needed to say seemed to taste bitter in her mouth. "The loss of someone like Jean from our community has robbed them of a unifying voice. A horrible and evil voice, but he was a forceful personality, and there aren't many others speak up with a voice that is heard."

Now I knew why Jen looked like that when she said it. Those words felt like poison entering my ears, and I felt like I was going to vomit just thinking this, but she was right. "Our kind will be out there lost and shattered. The people they put their faith in to lead them are gone. They will need someone. Someone they can believe in and follow. That person will need to show them they are worthy. Then that person will need to build on that and prove through actions that they can be the leader we need."

"That sounded rehearsed," commented Brad.

"Not rehearsed. Just something I heard someone really smart say once," I replied, thinking back to a conversation Mary Smith and I had regarding the same thing. The only difference was at the time she was talking about the witches. Well, there was another difference. No one had grabbed my chin and looked into my eyes while telling me they had faith I could be that person.

"We, maybe not us, but the others will need that voice to lead them out of the darkness," added Kevin.

I sat there and tried to shrink in the gap between the cushions Nathan and I leaned back against, and begged quietly, "Don't say it needs to me." But, at the same time, I wondered why shouldn't it be me? I was a vampire. Which might work against being accepted by the witches. Something I didn't believe anyone had considered yet. If they had, they hadn't mentioned it to me. Could I honestly do both? I shook, to remove that thought from my being, and Nathan put his arm around my shoulder and pulled me closer. I hated to tell him this wasn't the type of chill he could chase away.

"We need to be ready, and I'm not just talking about defending ourselves. We have to defend the entire coven. Witches. Werewolves. Shifters. Everyone. Whether they are from our coven or not. If they are within these walls, they are our guest and we must be ready to protect our home." Kevin again looked around and made eye contact with every one of us, including myself and Samantha. There was no disagreement from anyone.

"What about others?" Clay asked.

"Well, Rob and his brothers wouldn't hesitate," Mike declared. "They are always looking for a fight."

Kevin nodded. "I'm not so sure about Steve and Stan. They are the true outsiders here. They are neither witch nor vampire. They don't really have any skin in the game. Remember, werewolves are the natural enemies of vampires and witches. Who comes out on top will impact them. Shifters really don't have any enemies. They get along with everyone."

"Did you really just say neither and nor?" Mike teased, and then planted a friendly punch on Kevin's arm.

"I'm old, remember? That is how we talked then."

"I can talk to Steve. If you want," Nathan offered. I looked up at Nathan. I had the urge to tell him to stay out of this. Even having him help recruit others would be too much involvement for me, but I knew better. He never would stand on the sideline or run away. He never has. That was why he was like this now. He was one of us, and considering what he just went through, he may have more emotional investment in this than anyone here. Just knowing that made him seem more regal than the others. He was my hero. My knight in shining armor; ready to run into hell's fire to protect me. Even with all the pain he suffered through, here he was again, ready to throw himself in the way to help others. I leaned into him a little closer. "Like you said, they are outsiders, and I used to be one, too. We got to know each other pretty well."

"Thanks Nathan," Kevin said graciously. "I can honestly say I haven't had the pleasure of getting to know Steve and his brother that well. They are pretty closed off."

"Laura and Larissa are the only ones that have gotten close enough to any of them to get to know them," Apryl remarked.

"Crap!" Laura jumped up from her seat, practically ripping her hand from Mike's. I jumped too, and Nathan's hand fell to the seat behind me.

"What time is it?" I asked, looking for anyone that had a watch or a cell phone. Brad rolled up his sleeve to consult his stylish gold band watch, but he wasn't fast enough. Laura and I met at his arm and helped him finish rolling up the sleeve and then attacked the watch face with our eyes.

With a sigh of relief, Laura grabbed my hand and rushed for the stairs.

"Sam, come on!" I yelled from halfway down the stairs.

6

This was something I had put off for far too long. Why? I wasn't sure. On all accounts, this should be a joyous occasion. That didn't mean I still wasn't nervous. When I finally mustered the courage to go forward with it, I explained the plan and process to Ms. Parrish to avoid any surprises. I felt honesty with her would go a long way to keeping our relationship on the right track. She appreciated it, and even, to my surprise, declined my offer to let her stay and watch. When she left, we settled in the center of the ritual room and waited for the last member of our party to arrive, who, despite my explicit instructions, was late. Laura and I had lost track of the time ourselves, but we managed to be a few minutes early, which gave me all the time I needed to set up.

"Keep them covered," I reminded our two non-witches in the room.

"That doesn't help. I can smell it through the top," Laura complained, holding her nose.

At first, Amy laughed, but then curiosity got the better of her, and she leaned down to take a whiff from her own cup. Instantly, her expression changed, and she realized it wasn't one of Mrs. Tenderschott's famous fudge sundaes.

"Family related spells always smell the worst," I informed them, much like Mrs. Tenderschott told me many months ago when I was the one drinking all these spells to remember who I was. This one reeked of a nauseating combination of fresh dog crap and vomit, making my eyes water.

"Why doesn't Sam have to drink any of this?" Laura questioned.

Samantha popped both hands up to her shoulders, snapped her fingers, and announced, "Witch."

Laura rolled her eyes, and Amy laughed. "She is a mini-you, isn't she?"

I looked at Samantha, knowing how much she hated the comparisons. I think she would be fine with it if it didn't happen several times a day, every day. "She's her own witch," I pointed out.

The chubby cherubs on the walls above us, which had once tormented me, now seemed to not notice me. That was a wise choice.

At the moment, I had a few minutes free and could start some redecorating.

"Sorry I'm late," Lisa gasped, sprinting through the door, each word a labored breath. "Gwen was running... drills."

"General Gwen," Laura cracked, provoking stifled giggles from the group.

"Well, have a seat. We have been waiting for you," I said.

Lisa found a seat and smoothed out her long black skirt around her. Then she took a deep breath and let it out slowly before she reached up and pulled her dreads out of her face. "Okay. I'm ready."

"All right," I responded with feigned enthusiasm. "You two can drink your special drink now."

Laura and Amy eyed the cup in front of them. They already knew it smelled bad. We all knew it. It was so strong; it assaulted your senses as soon as you entered the room.

"Come on, get it over with," I urged.

After a brief exchange of hesitant looks, they both uncovered their cups. Laura recoiled back. Amy scrunched up her face as she picked up the cup.

"Just remember. This is something you will get to rub in on Apryl. She has wanted to do this for a while."

Laura gave me a quirky smile, and then quickly picked it up and downed the potion in a single swallow. "It's not that bad," she said, looking at Amy, tears rolling down her cheeks.

"You sure?" Amy asked suspiciously.

Laura nodded, tight-lipped. Amy picked up her cup, and at first took a sip, and then downed it while looking right at me. I felt bad for her. I knew what this tasted like, and now she did too. She dropped the cup, and Laura fell forward to the floor gagging, while Amy coughed.

Now I needed to act quickly; otherwise, they'd have to endure another dose of that wretched potion. I reached over and grabbed Amy's hand, and just as we had discussed earlier, she grabbed Laura's. Laura then grabbed Lisa's. Lisa took Samantha's, and then my daughter took mine, closing the loop. And poof, just like that, we were all back on the porch of my family's farmhouse back in New Orleans.

"Wow, what a trip!" Laura exclaimed, her voice filled with awe. "I feel like we were just here." She walked over and sat down on the porch swing. "You're saying this isn't real?"

"Now, I never said that. It's a place crafted by magic, just like the coven. So, it's as real as the coven is," I explained. I opened the screen door, which didn't squeak, catching the fascination of both Lisa and Laura. The old hinges were young again. "Come on," I said, ushering them all inside and down the hall to the kitchen. Or that was my intention. Once inside, they all scattered, meandering around the hall and parlor. Each reaching out and touching an object they were familiar with from our brief stay a few months back. Lisa plopped down on the settee in the parlor. The cushion had a bit more spring in it than she remembered.

"Yea, I should have told you. The house, and everything in it, is how I remembered from when I was a young girl."

"So, the furniture isn't old?" Lisa deduced.

"Yep, but the kitchen will look old to you. Speaking of the kitchen. Let's get moving." I said, trying to urge them down the hallway and into the kitchen.

I stood at the kitchen door, ushering everyone through. A collective gasp resonated through the kitchen. I pushed through to the front and found my mother standing there in the same long-sleeved dark green dress I always saw her wearing during one of my visits. Dark green was her favorite color. She clutched at the dish towel in her hand, looking a little more than surprised at the gathering of strangers.

"Hi mom, I brought some friends," I announced with a wide grin, and then gave her a nice big hug, to smooth over the surprise.

When I turned around to introduce them, I caught Laura pointing at me. "What?" I looked around for what she was pointing at. Then I started swatting around, thinking there was a bug or bee flying around me, but there was nothing other than me looking silly. "What?" I demanded, as she continued doing it.

"Larissa!" she screamed. "You...You're not a vampire."

"Oh." I looked back at my mother and then back at my group of friends. "No, I'm not. At least not here. I am how my mother remembers me, or mostly. There are a few things that still come through. Like how cold I feel to her touch. Everything else is the me she remembers." I saw Samantha's mouth open, and I knew what was going to come out. "Sam, not now." That cut it off curtly.

"That's kind of how this place works. I am how my mother remembers me, and she is how I remember her."

"I keep trying to get Larissa to remember me someplace other than standing at the sink in this kitchen," commented my mother, warmly. "Larissa's friends are always welcome. Come have a seat, but I think we should head to the library. There is more room there." My mother laughed as Lisa and Laura turned and headed that way without having to be told where to go.

"Yea, they were with me when we were down here dealing with Jean."

"Where are you now?"

"We are back at the coven." I reached over and grasped my mother's arm as she headed toward the door. "Sam, can you stay here for just a minute?" There was one introduction that felt more appropriate to make in private. For some reason, I felt more nervous about this moment than I did making my last announcement to my mother. Even my normally confident daughter seemed to feel the same way, her hands twisted and tangled in an unending dance of anxious energy. Her eyes flitted back and forth between me and my mother restlessly, refusing to settle on either of us.

I took a deep breath, and relished the feeling that I only experienced here, and then let it out slowly. "Mom, this is Sam. She's your granddaughter."

My mother staggered backward and reached for the kitchen table. Her hand traced along its edge until she found a chair and then tumbled into it. Tears rolled down her cheeks, and her breathing was rapid.

"Mom?" I cried out, alarmed, and stepped forward toward her.

She waved me off and looked down in what appeared to be an attempt to compose herself. I hated to tell her; it was not a mission accomplished. She sat up and stared wide-eyed at Samantha, with more tears flowing now than before. Her mouth was a gaping wide smile. Her tears followed its lines around and down to her chin. She reached out with a quivering hand toward Samantha. I put my hand in the center of Samantha's back and gave her an encouraging push forward.

"Oh, my word. I kind of thought she was when I saw her. She is the spitting image of you," my mother said through happy tears.

"Oh, Lord." I held my breath, hoping Samantha would let that comparison fly by. She did and stepped forward cautiously and took my mother's hand. Samantha held my mother's hand as she sat down in the chair across from her. The same one I sat in often to talk to my mother.

"And before you ask, do you remember what Theodora told me?"

My mother didn't take her eyes off of Samantha. "Yes, so it hasn't been fifteen or sixteen years since you last visited?"

"Just a couple of months," I replied.

"Wow," she said, her voice quivering with emotion. Tears of joy glistened on her cheek. "Sam, it is so nice to meet you."

"It's nice to meet you too," Samantha said, actually sounding choked up.

Then it happened. I was waiting for it, and had wondered what was taking her so long. My mother yanked Samantha up by the hand, and met her halfway, wrapping her in her arms and squeezed her. My mother was a hugger. With how she returned it, my daughter may be one too.

"Let me look at you," my mother said as she released Samantha, but held on to both hands. "You are so pretty. Just like your mother."

A faint sigh escaped Samantha's lips, barely noticeable, but enough for my mother to catch it. She shot me a sidelong glance, her curiosity piqued. "But you are your own person, wonderful in every way."

"We are more alike than you might believe," Samantha responded, surprising me with her remark.

"Oh?" My mother asked, looking at me.

"Yes, and no," I hedged. "We are both witches. Sam shows unbelievable ability."

Samantha dropped my mother's hands, then gave a display that I wasn't even sure how to do. A mass of purple and blue energy flowed around and between her hands before crashing into a bright flash in front of her.

"A very capable witch," I said as Samantha stood there, almost posed like something out of a superhero movie. "And we also know she is at least part vampire. That is something that just showed up recently."

I watched in horror as the joy drained from my mother's face. To me, that statement was natural. To everyone else, there was a connotation that came with it.

"No. No. No," I rushed to reassure her. "It's not like that. She wasn't turned. It's something that was always there that kind of just came out. We don't know why. It just did."

My mother drew Samantha in close again, examining her closely. "Oh, I see." She released Samantha with one hand and gestured to the area around her eyes.

Samantha let go of my mother's other hand and took a step back, attempting to distance herself. My mother tried to hold on, but her grip slipped. Samantha turned away from her.

"Samantha's a little sensitive about her eyes," I explained.

"Why?" My mother's curiosity persisted.

"They're hideous," Samantha complained.

"No, they aren't." My mother approached Samantha, gently lifting her chin to meet her gaze. They locked eyes in an intense moment. "They are beautiful and make you who you are."

I watched my daughter's face light up, and I couldn't help but wonder why she reacted so differently to my mother's words compared to mine. I had expressed the same sentiment to her countless times, but it had usually been met with screams or teenage tantrums.

"You know, Theodora might be able to explain why it just came on suddenly."

Now it was my turn to look away. "Maybe." Maybe she would if we were still talking. Maybe she would if my boyfriend hadn't killed her boyfriend. Maybe she would if the witches, of which I was one, hadn't declared war and tried to eliminate all vampires.

"Larissa, what is it?" my mother asked in a curious tone.

"Mom, there is a lot I need to catch you up on."

My mother reached back for a kitchen chair and then fell back into it. "There always is." She motioned at the chairs across the table from her and I took my normal position. Samantha sat beside me. The whole time I told my mother about what happened to Nathan and how it affected my magic, she stared and smiled at Samantha. There were a few times I felt the urge to wave a hand in front of her face and remind her I was there, but I didn't. I understand. When the topic shifted to the council and what we learned about Mrs. Wintercrest, her attention shifted, and she even asked me to repeat it. She was in complete disbelief about what I said.

"Tell me again?"

"Our current supreme is losing her powers because of age, and another witch was propping her up, and controlling the council. Now that everyone knows, the council has been disbanded."

"But why? It doesn't make any sense," my mother said, still in disbelief.

"So, her little brat of a daughter can become supreme," Samantha added.

"Kind of. She claims to be doing it to ensure her family is the last remaining power family around and maintains control of the council." I added air quotes around power family.

My mother appeared deep in thought. "Huh," she breathed, and then sat back in her chair. "That is just so unbelievable. What was the family's name?"

"Roberts," I said, hoping my mother might recognize their name.

She tried. I could tell from her expression. I could also tell she was drawing a blank. "I don't recognize that name," she said, shaking her head.

"I was hoping you might. That war with the vampires I told you about is all her doing, and she is now coming after the coven."

"That's what I don't understand. Why would she come after witches?"

"It might have something to do with you killing her daughter," Samantha spouted.

"Larissa! You didn't?" Screamed my mother. I held out my hands to calm her down, but they had little effect. "Please tell me you didn't."

I could see disappointment bleeding from every pore of her being and landing right on me. It both burned and suffocated me. I couldn't imagine much I could say that would repair the disappointment she felt, but I had to try. She needed to understand that I didn't, nor would I ever, take someone's life if I didn't have to. "Mom–"

"Oh God! You did!" Her cry interrupted my attempt to explain. I saw tears again, and this time they weren't happy tears. Neither was her expression. My mother's face showed horror. I couldn't imagine what was going through her mind. Actually, I could. She had realized her daughter was a bloodthirsty vampire. The wailing that escaped her mouth confirmed that.

"Mom, it's not like that." The words burst out of my mouth at a frenzied pace. "We were captured and being held. It was her or me. It was completely self-defense." I pleaded, and then literally threw myself at the mercy of the court of my mother's opinion, and repeated my plea. "I had to, or she was going to kill me and Nathan."

The sobbing slowed, but didn't stop all together.

"I promise you, mom, I'm not like that. I had to."

"I know," she said, but continued to sob as her head collapsed into her own hands.

"Mom?" I stepped closer and placed my hand on the top of her head. I hoped she would look up at me. That she would say she understood, but when she finally looked up, the tears were still flowing, and the pain was clear on her face.

"Larissa, I know. I know you wouldn't do that without cause. It's just… it's just…," her words drowned in her sobs, and she sank back in her chair, using the sleeves of her dress to wipee away her tears. "I had hope for such a better life for you than this. I wanted you to have a life of joy, love, and magic. Instead, you have had death and violence, and now this war and power struggle you are in the middle of."

She stood up and reached out for me, collapsing in my arms in a fierce embrace. She squeezed me so hard it hurt, but I wasn't going to complain.

"I'm so sorry. This is not what I wanted for you," she mumbled into my shoulder.

"I know," I replied, though I couldn't grasp why I felt like I needed to accept her apology. This wasn't her fault. If I had to find a blame, I could go back to Jean, and make him the root of all evil. If he hadn't attacked us, I would have lived a normal life and probably already been dead of old age by now. I don't know what that life would have been like. Maybe I would have met someone like Nathan and had a normal life, with a normal family, or as normal as a witch could be. That wasn't something I wanted to dwell on. It wasn't anything anyone could change, and as far as I knew, there weren't any time travel spells. Even if there were, would I use them now? As much as my life felt like a nightmare, there were moments that felt like pure bliss, and I wasn't willing to let go of those.

"Mom, it's not your fault. It really isn't. It's just...fate." That was the only explanation I could come up with in the moment. "And I have a wonderful group of friends that help me," I added after I remembered we had quite a crowd waiting in the library. "They all came with me today to meet you."

"I'm such a mess," my mother said, pulling at her dress to straighten it up.

"Come on. They really want to meet you. Plus, I know you can fix it really quickly." I said with a wink.

And there it was. The quick gold shimmer and my mother was a picture of mid-1920's perfection. Perfect makeup and hair wearing her favorite green dress, which didn't have a single wrinkle, but there was still something. She may have looked great on the outside. There was a spark missing from her eyes, and I knew she was still broken on the inside.

7

I'm a lousy parent–and I should say Laura and I were lousy parents. Heck, maybe we classify as stepparents. Amy is our shared responsibility, and we both completely forgot one key and very important detail. She isn't a vampire, and she needs her sleep. That was something Ms. Parrish was sure to point out to both of us when we returned just after four in the morning. Amy never yawned or looked tired. No one did. Not even Lisa, who was the only other participant in our little magical excursion that needed sleep. We all spent hours talking with my mother, with everyone asking questions about the young, or as Laura phrased it, little Larissa.

Laura, Samantha, and I retired to the deck for the rest of the night, where I cozied up next to Nathan. It was an old movie night. It was always an old movie night when Mr. Bolden was the one picking the movie. I didn't care what it was. My pleasure came from just feeling Nathan beside me. He was a big part of this life that I wouldn't give up, no matter what hell came with it. Samantha sat across from us, and I caught her casting a few smiles in our direction. What wasn't to smile about? Her mother and father were together, and we were finally a family. A strange vampire and witch family, but we were one. In fact, we were up here with what we would consider our cousins. We were all one big family. Marie Norton and Jennifer Bolden mostly played the role of matriarch, and Kevin Bolden the patriarch when he wasn't horsing around as just one of the guys.

"Is that John Wayne?" Apryl asked, loudly.

"It sure is. It's the Duke," Kevin responded.

"I thought he only did cowboy movies," Pamela remarked. That comment drew the ire of every male on the deck, except for Brad, who sat back away from the screen, reading, as he often did.

"Just stop," Jen warned everyone on the deck. "Just stop or every movie for the next few months is going to be a John Wayne movie."

"That sounds like a great idea," Kevin agreed. "I have them all." Even if he didn't already have them all, we all knew they would appear. Just like anything else we ever wanted to watch. I needed to teach the coven to destroy things.

Laura pointed playfully across at Jen. "Remember, you're the one that gave him the idea."

At the first sign of daylight, we headed downstairs as we always did. Nathan walked me, hand in hand, to the stairs that led down to the door in my closet. He playfully pretended to follow me down. I wasn't sure if he really could. The floors were charmed for specific sexes. Something Mrs. Saxon pointed out to me when I first arrived. Clay tested the door in my closet once. To my knowledge, no one had tested it since. I had to assume they were still in place.

Nathan and I had discussed testing the one keeping guys and girls on separate sides a few times, but decided to respect his mother's wishes. Even if he didn't agree, that was what I was going to do. Lord knows I'd already broken enough of her rules since I'd arrived, and it always ended in major trouble. So, from now on, I was determined to be a good girl.

Our living arrangements were a topic of conversation when Nathan arrived back in the coven. I take that back. A conversation implies there are two sides talking. This was a one-sided edict. Until we were married, we needed to live separately. As she pointed out, it wasn't any great sacrifice, as we were always around each other. I knew otherwise. There was something we were sacrificing, but I wasn't going to point that out to her. I absolutely would not point out to her how hard it was going to be to resist that, but again, I had resigned myself to being on my best behavior for now.

I gave him a kiss and ignored all the immature smirks and comments from the others. Then I let go of his hand and stood there watching as he walked to his stairs. He waved as he headed down. I walked down while watching him, and almost ran into Samantha, who was doing the same. There was a collective giggle, and I looped my arm around her.

"Go get ready and we can walk down to class together."

Samantha agreed and headed toward her room.

"Oh, and today, take it easy on Gwen. I heard about yesterday."

Samantha let out the sigh-heard-around-the-world as she walked into her room and closed the door.

Twenty minutes later, I was showered and dressed. I still wasn't one to put on a lot of makeup, and my only real decision each day was whether I would wear my hair up or keep it down. Today was a down day, which meant it took me less time. Samantha was all into perfect makeup. Eye shadow, blush, and all. It had to be perfect before she left the room, and most of us had learned the hard way we should never suggest using glamor to do it. She wanted to do it on her own, and after I taught her what little I knew, Pamela and Apryl were her go to resources for help. Which was why it wasn't uncommon to see Samantha running from her room to either of theirs every morning while she was getting ready. This morning was no different. She made trips to each of their rooms and then made a stop at Marie's for her opinion on her outfit. Black skirt, black hose, and shoes, with a white shirt. It kind of reminded me of something.

"Hey, Apryl. Do you remember that school uniform we joked about on my first day?" I should have kept my mouth shut. Samantha stopped right there in the middle of the hall and looked down at her outfit and stormed back into her room with a slam of the door.

"I'd wear that uniform," Apryl remarked as I passed her on the way to Samantha's room.

"You look fine. It was just a joke. Apryl told me we had to wear—" I said as I opened her door and walked in. Samantha was inside, plundering through her closet, sending clothes flying all over her bed.

"All right mom," she said, exasperated. "Can you help me with my hair?"

"Absolutely. Up or down?" I positioned her in front of the mirror so she could see what I was doing. No matter how many times we did this, it still hit me deep inside. This was my daughter. A beautiful mini-me. It took effort each time to block tears from coming. So far, I had been successful, but I was sure there would be a day I let them slip.

"With what we are doing, I think up is best. That'll keep it out of the way. Maybe pulled back like yours."

"Are you sure?" I asked, still fighting the tears, but knowing how much she hated looking just like me.

"Yep."

Her wish was my dream. I pulled her red hair back into a single high ponytail, just like mine. She wore hers that way to keep it out of the way while training, and I wore mine that way because I was too lazy to do anything different. Different reasons, but the same result. "Let's go."

Our walk down was just like any other morning lately. Nathan waited out on the boy's staircase, waving at us as we walked down. Marcia and Tera came out of the door on the witch's floor just before we stepped down onto the landing. Both gave us a very quiet good morning. Neither were very talkative witches, but even this rather quick and impersonal good morning seemed odd for them. The door closed behind them. We both stepped down to follow them the rest of the way, but then the door burst open again and an icy wind blasted through, along with a blur of blonde and pink. Gwen whipped around on the steps, and the ends of the longest strands of her own ponytail strafed across our faces.

I grabbed Samantha's hand and jerked her to my side. Even though Gwen may have had it coming, this was not the place, nor the time. I let her proceed to the bottom of the steps before I released my grip on my daughter's hand, watching her ponytail bounce the whole way. Once she disappeared around the corner, I asked. "Do you want to go back up and change your hair?"

All I received in response was a groan, and we continued down the stairs.

Mr. Helms' class was more crowded than usual. We had more than just a couple of dignified guests lining the walls. James and Mary stood beside Lisa's table where she was talking their ears off, but it wasn't their presence that created the largest disturbance. Every single instructor and council member lined the walls of the classroom. Even Mrs. Wintercrest stood in a corner, seemingly wanting to be one with the shadows.

Samantha leaned over and asked, "What's going on?"

"I honestly don't know. Go have a seat." As she headed to our table, I made a beeline to Master Thomas and Marcus.

"What is all this?"

"You'll see," Marcus answered with a confident grin. I took a step to go back and join Samantha, but I felt a hand grab my wrist. I looked down, and then traced the hand back up to Marcus, who leaned in and said, "Stand here with us."

Okay, I took a place along the wall, which created its own murmur, and an odd look from Samantha. I just shrugged my shoulders at her. What else could I do? I didn't have a clue what was going on.

"Class!" Mr. Helms banged a fist on his table, cutting off the buzz, leaving the room in silence. "Master Thomas, the floor is yours."

Master Thomas stepped away from the wall and then proceeded down the steps. "Everyone, I am sure based on your reaction, you have noticed we have a lot of visitors with us today. It's not like we are a group that blends in. We are an eclectic bunch." There was a light laugh from a few of our visitors. Master Thomas stepped off the bottom step and joined Mr. Helms in the center of the floor. "The council and I have been discussing our current situation, and I believe we finally all agree on the threat Mrs. Roberts and her followers pose to this and potentially other covens, and to each of our futures. We agree...," he paused and looked at Mrs. Wintercrest. She shied away from his gaze. "We agree that the only way back to peace is to eliminate the threat and restore the council to what it used to stand for. Now the problem is, we don't really know how many witches support us, and how many support her. Myself and the other council members are reaching out to other covens and families we know to gauge their support. While we are hearing support from some, others are voicing a desire to stay out of it. I can understand and will respect their stance. That leaves us now in the position of having to train all able-bodied witches that want to support us to stand against Mrs. Roberts, and help put things right. The council members have volunteered their services to assist in your training. This is an opportunity that no witch has ever had before, so consider yourself lucky and honored, as we are honored to have you as our students. Today, as you go through your exercises, the council members, your instructors, Marcus and Larissa will watch and make suggestions." All heads turned in my direction. Jack gave a quiet cheer. Gwen did not. "If you have questions, feel free to ask any of us. We are here at your service. Mr. Helms, let's get started." Master Thomas gave the floor back to Mr. Helms. Each of the council members stepped away from the wall and appeared to ready themselves to get to work.

"All right everyone. Let's pair up..."

Mr. Helms assigned partners while I turned to Marcus Meridian to file an objection. "Why me? I am still a student here."

"Nonsense. You are more than thoroughly capable of doing this, and far exceed most of the council members. You are ready."

I held my reply after I heard Samantha's name and anxiously awaited to hear the name paired with her. I had to assume Mr. Helms knew better than to put her with Gwen, or I hoped he did. This wasn't a pull the name out of a hat type of assignment. After he called one name, he scanned the room with his eyes before calling the other. "Mr. Nash. You will train with Miss Dubois."

"Thank God."

"Oh, come on. I think it would be rather entertaining to see her and young Gwen go toe to toe. Don't you agree?"

I shot daggers at Marcus with my eyes, but that didn't stop his smug expression.

"Larissa, this is your place. It's time to step into it. Now, we have some work to do." Marcus stepped away from the wall and followed the other council members down to the floor where today's exercise, otherwise known as witch fight club, had already started. The safety was still on in this room, making it impossible for anyone to significantly hurt one another, but that didn't take the sting out of. I remembered that from my duels.

I watched for a few moments and noticed as many of the council members stepped in and offered words of instruction and encouragement. Then, "Oh what the hell," I stepped down and did the same. Most of my instruction was just telling someone not to be so predictable. Tera had a habit of doing the same spells in the same order every day. Everyone knew that. But when I passed Jack, I leaned in and said, "Sam likes to pose after a spell. Take her down." He smirked, and I walked away and listened. I heard the thud of someone hitting the ground and took a quick glance back. Mission accomplished. Yes, I did just tell someone how to take my daughter down, but she needed to learn not to do that. I seriously doubted Mrs. Roberts would wait for her to stop her pose before firing back.

At the front of the room, I watched Mrs. Wintercrest approach, probably the only witch in the room that would still listen to her, Gwen. The pink goddess beamed from ear to ear as she listened to the instructions from the old witch. Then she curtsied as Mrs. Wintercrest backed away. I had to roll my eyes at that.

8

Halfway through class, Master Thomas pulled Lisa, James, Mary, and me out for some intense training of our own. Dread welled up within me as I anticipated what was to come. The sight of the black candle, strategically placed in the center of Mr. Demius' classroom, only deepened my uneasiness. I couldn't believe Lisa's enthusiasm as she clapped her hands and rushed to take her place around the ominous candle. How could she be so cheerful about engaging in something so dark? Then it hit me; this came naturally to her. Lucky her. Meanwhile, I remained in a state of terror, haunted by Edward's warnings and my unsettling first encounter with Mary Smith. Despite her softened demeanor, her cautionary tales continued to resonate with me, making every step toward the candle fraught with trepidation.

"Come on. We don't have all day," Mary urged and pointed to the empty spot next to her. I hesitated at first, but then reluctantly took a seat. My eyes pleaded with Master Thomas. For what, I wasn't sure. Maybe I needed him to reassure me that everything was going to be okay. Ironic, wasn't it? If I had been practicing what James taught me yesterday, I would already know if this was going to be okay. Dang it! No, I wouldn't. I couldn't see my own future.

"Take my hand," Mary instructed, her hand outstretched toward me. How long had it been like that? I wasn't sure, but I didn't leave it there any longer. I took her hand, and moments after I did, I felt her give it a light squeeze. "Just relax." She must have felt the light tremble that radiated through my body.

"Now that I know you can both drift away and find your own way back, we are going to do something a little more advanced. We are going to go together. You might not think that is more advanced, but it is. A witch that can do astral projection can't take one who can't with her. It doesn't work that way. So, to do it together, we all have to do it, and you have to focus and concentrate on one another. We will be each other's anchor to keep us from going too far. Just remember that. Never, what some call, chase the rabbit." She paused; her gaze searched both of us for a level of understanding. "Now, please tell me you have read the classics. Lewis Carroll?"

"Alice?" I blurted. "The white rabbit. I got it."

Lisa gave me a big look of—what?

"Alice in Wonderland? Lewis Carroll? She chased the white rabbit into a hole and fell into wonderland and got lost," I explained.

Mary Smith laughed. "It's all right. What the saying means is stay on your path. Don't chase anything, no matter what it is. You will get lost."

"Got it," declared Lisa.

"Good. Now let's get to it."

The black flame ignited on the candle and the same thin black smoke as before wafted around the room. I wanted to reach out to grab it, but at the same time, I didn't want to let go of Mary's hand. It seemed I didn't need to. It had been over two months since the last time I did this, but it amazed me at how easily I could clear my mind and imagine myself floating away from my body. Then I saw what I imagined. My body was there, below me, still holding on to Mary's hand, but at the same time, the three of us were there, joined together.

"Good," Mary said, but she sounded as if she was talking underwater. "Very good. You both slipped free quickly, but this is only a small step, and I am not talking about how far you travel away from your body. This is the realm of consciousness. It's the world you know, or more correctly stated, it's the world you are familiar with. This is just a step. Now hold on tight. We are going to take another one. Relax your mind further and stare into the ether."

"The what?" Lisa asked.

"The fabric of the world. Not the lines you and I see, but the space in between them," I answered.

"That's great Larissa. You've been studying," Mary remarked. It wasn't the first time Mary had given me praise, but I felt this was almost like I was having one of those Lisa moments. Lisa was always diligent about studying and practicing. My knowledge didn't exactly come from that. I read it during my research about how to break out of the coven and find Nathan. There was no real academic intent there. "But think about it a little differently. Focus on it, but then imagine you are sinking into it. Slipping between the gaps, and repeat after me."

"I sever my bounds to the physical."

Lisa and I echoed in unison, "I sever my bounds to the physical."

"I allow my soul to pass to the plane where I may live forever."

Just as before, we repeated what Mary had said. "I allow my soul to pass to the plane where I may live forever." Then everything went black, and I felt a dark and empty dread consume me.

In the distance, faint points of light flickered. I peered in their direction and noticed they were moving. Make that they were swaying. "Lanterns?"

"Yes. Lanterns sourced from the eternal flame to guide souls through this place until they find their eternity. Some find it, some never do and search for an eternity. Girls, welcome to the afterlife. Stay close and if you feel something grab you, shake it off, and let me know immediately. We aren't supposed to be here, and they will know it. Most won't care. They will go on their way, searching for their place, but others that have lost hope of ever finding it will see us as an answer."

"An answer?" Lisa asked.

I wanted to ask what the question was, but I was too consumed with trying to absorb that we were here in the ether place, the afterlife, the resting place of souls. There were many other names I had heard before for this place, and none of them made it sound good. It was empty. Void of anything except darkness and wandering lights. I watched as one wandered in our direction. Mary pulled me in closer, but I still leaned out to look. I wish I hadn't. I didn't know what I expected to see. They were just people. The one that wandered close to us was a young girl, or woman, probably in her mid-twenties, wearing a red dress. As she passed, her head turned slightly as if to acknowledge me, but it instead terrified me, and I clung to Mary's arm. Her hollow eyes stared right through me, and I stared right through hers to the world on the other side. There was no life in her. She continued on her way, unaffected by my presence. I couldn't say the same.

Mary tugged me away from the eerie sight and into the abyss. I couldn't see Lisa on her other side; it was too dark. If I could have, I would have reached for her hand too. Lights passed us in the distance, and that was okay with me. I didn't want to be close enough to see any of them again. Like ever!

Something brushed my leg, and I let loose a blood-curdling scream. Mary pulled me close and clamped a hand over my mouth.

"Stay still," she whispered into my ear, and pulled me even closer to her. Lights everywhere stopped moving.

"Just stay still and very quiet."

Feeling her hand tremble made mine tremble faster.

A few lights started back on their original path, but not all. Some stayed still, and a few came in our direction.

"We have to go," Mary said. She took her hand away from my mouth, and I felt her other hand give mine a yank.

Lights raced toward us from all directions. I felt something brush my leg again, and then that something grabbed it. I kicked, but it didn't let go. I looked down, still kicking, and saw just a glimpse of a hand on my leg. Then a second emerged, and then a third, and a fourth. "Mary! Help me!" They pulled me down, and my hand slipped from her grasp momentarily. She grabbed me again and yanked me up closer to her. They were still there. I knew how to get rid of them and raised my hand to summon a deterrent.

"No!" Mary screamed. She shoved my hand down. "You can't use magic here."

They yanked me down and back again, and I felt their hands grabbing higher on my legs.

"Kick! Shove them off!" Mary ordered. She reached down to help pry a couple off of me, but others took their place just as quickly. Another set of hands pulled at them. It was Lisa. She was pulling them faster than they could grab me, but no matter how hard she or I fought to get clear, one hung on with a death grip and pulled me down. I felt I was slipping away from Mary again. A foot kicked into view and dislodged the hand from the impact. I felt the weight of what was on the other end of it disappear.

"Quick, repeat this. I accept my worldly bonds."

We started it together, but Lisa completed it first. I croaked out the last few words just after her. Then I watched the darkness dissolve in front of us. We were once again in Mr. Demius' classroom, and I collapsed on the floor, feeling a strange sensation that I hadn't felt in decades. I was exhausted.

9

It wasn't until this moment that I finally understood what Lisa meant when she said every trip to the underworld siphoned a piece of her aunt's soul. Something within me had undeniably withered away. It felt like life itself had been drained from me.

I had once thought of myself as a mere echo of the living, a ghostly semblance of my former self, a creature without a soul. I was so wrong. What I experienced with Mary and Lisa showed me what that truly felt like. Watching those souls roam through that muted container of gray and nothingness left me feeling numb to the world, and that feeling stayed with me long after I returned. The feeling of Nathan stroking my head used to be a moment of pure bliss, but now it was nothing. His touch was just something there. It lacked any of the feeling or provocative nature it used to possess. I needed to feel it. I need him to do the opposite of what those hands did to me earlier. They pulled life from me, and I needed him to put it back. That was why I pulled him away from all the others and had him lie down on one of the outdoor sofas below the stars. I lay down on top of him, hoping his closeness would refill me. My gauge was still on empty.

Lisa fared better than I did. After our return, she sat and discussed what she had experienced with Mary. A comparison of notes, as it were. I didn't. I couldn't. I just sat there after I pushed myself up off the floor and focused on staying upright. When Mary asked me a question, I responded with simple one-word answers like, "yes" or "no", or even the noncommittal grunt, which in itself was a stretch.

Samantha joined us and attempted to pull me out of this, whatever it was. To call it a funk would stake a claim for the understatement of the year. I had been in funks before. This wasn't that. It may sound cliché to say, but the experience took a part of me. Those empty eyes looking at me. The hopelessness in their expression, and the desperation in which they moved toward us and grabbed at me. It didn't take any major psychoanalysis to understand why they reacted how they did. These people, these souls, were drawn to us because we are alive. We were what they wanted to be, what they wanted to regain. That explained their actions. It also didn't take much to realize why I was feeling how I felt. I felt their hopelessness. That was true.

Moreso, I felt my own. That was our destiny. It was all our destinies. Forget the images of pearly gates, or open pastures with warm sun. That wasn't what I saw. It was dark and empty. There were no grand family reunions. Just souls searching around. That was what awaited us, all of us. Everyone I knew. Everyone up here on the deck with us. Yes, we were partly immortal, but that didn't mean we wouldn't be killed. And what about the others that weren't like us? What about my parents? Were they still wandering around in the dark?

I couldn't bear to think about those questions, but at the same time, I couldn't stop. It was all that had consumed me since we got back. The strength of Nathan's arms wrapped around me as we lay there didn't chase it away. Not even hearing the deep rumble of a laugh in his chest as our daughter murdered the lyrics of song after song during deck karaoke. The moment should have been humorous. It was for everyone else. The entire deck rattled with laughter. My reaction was to remind them that while those songs may be classics, she had never heard them before.

"She has a pretty good voice," Nathan remarked once.

She did, I had to admit that, but the best I could do was a, "huh."

When Apryl came over and attempted to jolt me out of my stupor, I just ignored her. "Dang. What did the witches do to you today?"

I almost wanted to tell her what I had seen, and what I now understood about life, or make that death. Maybe I should tell them all. Spread the grief around and destroy the bubble of innocence they lived in. I thought better of it before I opened my mouth. What was the point of telling them? I just stared up at the stars above. It was a clear, cool winter night, but even they looked dimmer. Their twinkle, not as brilliant and not as magical.

"Larissa, do you want to go down and help me read to Amy?" Laura offered, hovering over me. I gave my answer by diverting my eyes away from her. "It might cheer you up."

I ignored her again. This time even turning my head to look at the fascinating green cushion on the back of the outdoor sofa we were laying on.

"Come on. You can't stay like this forever," she tried again, and again I went further to ignore her, and turned my whole body to face the back of the sofa.

"Maybe she can," Apryl commented.

"Something has to be able to break her out of this," Laura remarked, undeterred.

Oh, I was about to break out of it all right. I was going to snap. I was right here. They didn't need to talk about me right in front of me.

There are plenty of places they could go to talk about me. I didn't care if they did it. Just not here in front of me.

"Fireworks!" Clay's voice cut through the tension from halfway across the deck. At least he had the decency to maintain some distance.

"No. I'm not sure that will work," Apryl responded over her shoulder. "Good idea though."

"No. I mean, there are fireworks," Clay yelled back.

I felt Nathan's body shift as he propped himself up on his elbows to look.

"See. Right there."

Fireworks weren't about to pull me out of this, but the fact that there were fireworks out there had my attention and I rolled over on Nathan's chest and looked.

I watched and waited. All I saw at first was the dark sky, but then high overhead there was a burst of color. Nathan's body jerked at the sight. Mine did too. I got up off of him and made it to my feet. As I walked closer to the railing, I saw it again, and then spun around.

"Everyone! Off the deck!"

Initially, no one moved, except to inch closer for a better view. Brad, displaying childlike curiosity, was the first to question, "Why? They're just fireworks, right?"

"No. It's not," Nathan said, with a bit of a tremble. He went to the railing as well, but not to watch. He frantically ushered people back.

"Who would be shooting off fireworks out here?" Jennifer Bolden asked, leaning against the railing struggling to see the source.

"No one. They aren't fireworks. We need to get inside." I ordered as I joined Nathan at the railing to help push the others back. Samantha was already halfway to the stairs. She knew exactly what the colorful bursts were, and I knew what they were crashing into high above the coven. "Inside! Everyone!" I pushed myself down the line of my friends that were still standing at the railing and yelled, "Now!"

I gave them a little magical push, causing them to slide back on the surface of the deck. Several of them stumbled backward before they came to a stop. "Move!" I held both hands up for some added encouragement, and they reluctantly started inside. Nathan waited for me, looking out at the bursts.

"What are they crashing into?" he asked, while watching a bright red one burst above our head.

"The protective runes we established extend over the coven," I explained. I stole one last glance before descending the stairs, and Nathan followed suit. Once his head vanished below deck, I sprinted down the stairs, creating a whirlwind of clothing in my wake. Through my room I rushed, finally emerging into the hall.

"What the hell is going on?" Apryl yelled as she exited her room. She wasn't the only one standing there waiting for answers. They all were.

Jennifer Bolden approached us, concerned, and asked, "Larissa, what is it?"

"It's Mrs. Roberts. Those bursts aren't fireworks. It's an attack."

"Psh." Apryl threw her hands down and put them on her hips. "You're nuts."

Pamela turned and was heading back to her room.

"No, she isn't," Samantha yelled, storming down the hall in their direction, freezing Pamela in her tracks. "That is the Fire of Ruel, the same attack they were using against the vampires. It's just hitting a magical barrier that is over us. If it wasn't there, we would all be burned like my dad was."

Now that had everyone's attention.

"Larissa, you're serious?" Marie Norton asked, concerned.

"Yes, I am," I said, but not just to her. I spoke to everyone. I needed them to hear me and to understand. "It's starting, and I need you all to stay up here, hidden. Let the coven protect you. This isn't your fight." I remembered the show of gravitas yesterday and wanted desperately to head it off. They meant well, but they wouldn't fare any better than any of the other vampires that had faced them. This had to be fought witch to witch. I didn't wait for an agreement. In truth, I wasn't asking, I was telling. I turned and ran, following Samantha to the door. We needed to raise the alarm.

"Larissa, not a chance." Hearing a protest didn't surprise me, but the source did. It was Laura, and she had rallied other supporters by the time I turned to respond, which I didn't really have to. I could have just kept on going, leaving them all there.

"No. You must listen to me," I pleaded. I knew I had already referenced what I was about to say, but I was going to make it personal this time. "You all saw Nathan when we returned. How burned he was, and how long it took him to recover. That happened to every vampire we saw stand up to her witches. If you put yourself in this fight, they will burn you inside and out so bad you will beg for a death that can't come. You will feel your skin burn slowly, never ending. Each burn will go deep and burn down through your muscles to your bone."

I hoped there were several shocked faces standing there. I didn't wait to look. Time was ticking away, and we needed to get downstairs. The last thing I said before closing the door, "Make sure the guys have that image in their head too. If they don't believe me, have them ask Nathan."

10

We raced down the stairs to alert Mrs. Saxon and the others. However, before we could reach them, she was already hurtling toward us, flanked by several council members. Samantha and I stopped in the grand hall and waited for them, bathed in the brilliant colors that shone in through the window. Under different circumstances, I might have found the display beautiful, much like the Fourth of July celebrations with my parents. But these bursts weren't a source of joy; they were harbingers of death, and a shiver ran down my spine each time one exploded above.

It was clear Mrs. Saxon and the rest of the council shared my sentiment when they joined us in the entry, and watched the show through the window. Their expressions lacked the quiet, and even brazen, confidence that was normally present on each of their faces. The council members stayed back away from the windows, but Mrs. Saxon walked right up next to us. I heard other footsteps coming from the opposite hall, and soon Master Thomas and Marcus arrived. After another few seconds, several curious witches emerged from the second floor.

"How long will it last?" I asked Mrs. Saxon, both of us illuminated by a green flash.

She hesitated a beat, and then answered, her voice wavering, "A while, I think. We need to add some more to be sure." The chorus of heart palpitations behind me said the council members were unsure as well. Either the sight or the fear it invoked paralyzed everyone. We didn't know how many witches were out there, or, as we just discovered, how long our protection would last. They were out there, and having to face them was inevitable. The big looming question was when.

I heard rustling behind me, and then a single set of footsteps on the marble floors echoed in the expansive entry. Marcus Meridian casually walked past me and then went right out the door to the pool deck. I exchanged a perplexed look with Mrs. Saxon. It seemed everyone shared our confusion. The only person who had the answer was now outside.

No one seemed eager to follow him. We all looked at and regarded the door as if there was cursed, or it was the entryway to hell itself. After what I had already experienced from these attacks, neither was far from the truth. What if the protection gave way while we were out there? Then I realized it wasn't any riskier than where I was standing now. These windows wouldn't stop much. I looked around again. No one had moved to follow Marcus. No one, not even Master Thomas. He and others were actually leaning away from the door, fighting against any inkling of walking out there. That was when I gave up and took the first of my timid steps forward to the door.

"Larissa," I heard Lisa call from the stairs, frightened.

I held my hand up. "It's okay." I lied. Each step was a slow and torturous slide of my foot across the slick marble. When I completed a step, I paused and made sure everything on the other side of the windows was okay before I took another step. I heard another set of feet doing the same slide behind me, and I glanced backward. Samantha was a few slides behind me. I reached back, and we joined hands. Our other hands extended out to our sides, as if we were walking a tight rope. It may have been because that was how tenuous we felt about our situation path.

At the door, we felt the tension of everyone behind us as we reached forward. I gave another glance back just before I pushed the door open. Mrs. Saxon and a few others had started their journey to the door. No one was sprinting toward it. The witches that lined the stairs had made their way down, but had stopped at the bottom. Samantha and I stepped outside into the cold, moist night, joining Marcus at the edge of the pool deck. He stood there, staring out into the darkness. I knew our eyesight was better than his, and I couldn't see anything, but I had learned my lesson a few times about assuming that something was as it looked. Perhaps he was using a spell or something to extend his sight. "Marcus, what do you see?"

"Not too much. It's way too dark. You can probably see better than I can." He paused long enough for me to roll my eyes. A bright purple flash above covered the world in a hue of lavender. It almost looked like something out of a fantasy movie, but it didn't last more than a few moments before a shot of red made everything look like it was burning. "I'm trying to see if I can tell where it's coming from and then guess how far they are away. You know this area better than I do. What's out there?"

Behind us, the door opened again, and the crowd crept out onto the pool deck. Mrs. Saxon and Master Thomas ventured a little further than the others, but stopped before they reached us. I had a good memory of what was out there, but I felt there might be someone in the coven with more familiarity, so I motioned for Mrs. Saxon to join us. She tried to ask me what it was about from where she stood, but I continued to motion for her to come to the edge of the pool deck. Master Thomas followed her, and to my surprise, Gwen and Jack both broke ranks with the others and joined us.

"What is it?" Mrs. Saxon asked, keeping her focus on the clear night sky and the colorful show taking place.

"The werewolves do regular patrols of the woods several times a day, right?"

"Yes, but they haven't been out there in several hours. If they had seen anything–"

"I know. They would have said something. Would Mr. Markinson have a map of the grounds, or could he create one based on what he knows?"

Marcus snapped his fingers and pointed at me. "I like where you are going!"

"I guess. Probably. He knows the campus better than anyone," Mrs. Saxon stammered. I could see the questions in her eyes.

Marcus reached back and put his arm around her shoulders, pulling her forward. Mrs. Saxon leaned back and shuffled her feet to fight the suggestion. "You see out there?" Marcus asked, but he didn't wait for an answer. "Every once in a while I see a flash. I need to know what is out in that area. That might tell us how far away they are. The more information we have, the better."

"I can go get him," Jack offered.

Mrs. Saxon was already shaking her head. "The doors won't let you." She turned and searched the crowd that was still on the other side of the pool. "Mr. Helms." She pointed right at him. "Go with Jack and fetch Rob and Mr. Markinson."

Marcus turned around and walked around the pool, looking at the side of the coven. He paused a few times and seemed to study various features before he continued on his trek. When he reached the end, he pointed up at the top of the coven. "That deck," he wondered aloud and then turned to look back out where he believed the attacks were coming from. His head nodded up and down in agreement with whatever plan he was putting together in his head.

"Yes, that deck," he repeated and then turned to the crowd that was watching him with immense curiosity. I was one of them. I didn't have a clue where he was going. "We need to establish regular watches. One or two witches that are skilled with runes need to be up on that deck at all times. They will need to watch for the approach of Mrs. Roberts and the others, while also re-enforcing our protection if it weakens. Um...," he counted along his fingers. "There are seventeen of us that know how to use runes. The council. The instructors. James, Mary, myself, and Larissa."

"Mr. Meridian," Lisa called out from the crowd. She was behind several people and pushed to get to the front. "I know how to use runes. Larissa has been teaching me on the side, and has shared some of her father's journals with me."

"Okay, then there is eighteen."

"Twenty," I corrected him. Marcus looked at me, surprised. "I have taught Jack and Sam as well. They are more than capable. Sam's are as strong as my own."

"Good. That gives us more than enough. In fact, why don't we do this? Shifts of four that last six hours."

Mrs. Wintercrest stepped forward, holding a finger up to stress she had a point. "Mr. Merdian. There is an issue."

"What is it, Barbara?"

There were gasps all around that evolved into a murmur. Mrs. Wintercrest, Barbara, flinched. It seemed the sound of her own first name was a slap to her. When she recovered, she responded almost defiantly. "That floor and deck is for the vampires. I don't think it is a good idea to mix–"

"I've met most of these vampires. I don't think it's going to be a problem. Larissa? Sam? Do either of you think they will mind?"

"Not at all," I responded, loud and proud. If anyone else had made that protest, I probably wouldn't have put the extra into it.

"Then it's settled."

The stir among the council members displayed disagreement, but no one said anything openly or aloud. I guessed some old hatchets were hard to bury.

Jack and Mr. Helms pushed through the crowd with an exhausted-looking Mr. Markinson in tow. The three stood there, mesmerized by the light show above. Rob pushed through, about knocking Lynn over with the large roll of paper he carried, and like the others, his attention was drawn upward.

"Wow. What's up with the pretty lights?"

"They are not pretty lights," I corrected sharply. "They are a shower of death. Now get over here. We need your help."

Rob looked at me reluctantly and then pointed to his chest. I nodded and motioned for him to come over. He started, but then stopped as another brilliant yellow flash above turned night into day.

"Gentlemen, I need your help," Marcus said, addressing them directly. With the encouragement of Jack and Mr. Helms, they stumbled forward in our direction.

Marcus met them halfway, and when he passed me, I asked, "Why not use the Eye of Osiris to see what is out there?"

He paused and leaned down to whisper into my ear. "That's a good question. Why don't you try that or another spell to see out there?" Then he stood up, cracked a half smile, and walked the rest of the way to meet Mr. Markinson. "Larissa, don't waste your time. The same runes that are keeping their magic from getting in will keep ours from getting out. We have a few holes for communication, but that is it. Good idea though."

I couldn't believe it; I felt a little flush in the cheeks.

"Mr. Markinson." Marcus reached forward and shook the hand of our resident alpha werewolf. "I'm Marcus Meridian. We haven't met yet, but I understand your pack is very familiar with these grounds, and you might be able to help me create a map so we might have some educated reference of where these witches are attacking from." There was another stir in the council once they realized what he was. I guess no one caught the flecks of gold in their eyes as he and Rob walked through.

"I actually have one." He reached back to Rob, who passed forward the roll of paper he carried. Mr. Markinson unrolled it. It was large, probably a two-to-three-foot square of paper. It reminded me of the roll of parchment we used to create our map to Nathan.

"We are here." Mr. Markinson pointed to a spot in the center of the map. "The cove is up at the top and to the right. To the left is just woods all the way to the coast. There is a small highway that runs through it. That's this line here, but as you can see, it's a couple of miles from us."

Marcus studied the map and then tilted the paper slightly in what looked like to me an attempt to line it up with where they were facing. He then extended his arm out straight in front of him, which was the direction where the attack was coming from. "It's all woods out that direction?"

"Mostly. There are a few clearings and granite outcroppings. Here, here, and the rest of these." Mr. Markinson pointed out each feature on the map. Then he looked out and studied the same flashes Marcus had when he first stepped out onto the pool deck. "Rob, your eyes are younger than mine. If you had to guess. Where would those be coming from?"

Rob watched three flashes before he stepped between the two men holding the map. With one last quick check of the scene in the woods, he pointed. "Either of these two. One is a large clearing. Probably a hundred yard square area of clearing in the forest. The other is a large outcropping of granite that is probably twenty yards wide. It's much smaller, but it has some elevation. I can see the trees behind both features beyond those flashes."

"I saw the same," Mr. Markinson agreed.

"How far away are they?"

Mr. Markinson and Rob consulted each other with a glance. "About four miles," Rob stated. Mr. Markinson nodded his agreement.

"All right," Marcus dropped his side of the map and turned to face the witches that were gathered on the other side of the pool. "We know where they are now. That doesn't mean that is where they are going to stay. We need to start our watch. Ben, you take first watch and make the teams. Larissa, I need you to teach anyone that doesn't know runes, how to use them. Your father was more advanced at this than anyone I have ever seen. You show his ability. We need to finish what we started yesterday and bring everyone up to speed quickly. Gather them up and go teach them, while I reach out to some old friends and see if we can get some help."

11

Master Thomas turned, his finger pointing first at several members of the council and then at Mr. Helms. They were the first patrol. I had my orders and started toward the door to go inside. As I passed through the mass of witches still consumed with the light show, I announced. "Everyone, to Mrs. Saxon's classroom." It was the closest of all the rooms.

"Need some help?" I turned and saw James O'Conner's smiling face. Even with the grim events happening around us, the sparkle in his eyes remained undiminished.

"Absolutely," I replied with gratitude. Then I yelled, "Sam, you're helping too." I couldn't see her, but I heard the huff.

He opened the door for me, and I walked in leading a parade of witches. "So, tell me Mr. Future. When are they coming?"

James shrugged. "I wish I knew. There are too many decisions between now and then. It is making the road foggy, but I don't think it will be long."

"That's what I am afraid of," I confessed, my anxiety growing with every passing moment.

I stood there with him at the door until the last student walked in. They all knew where Mrs. Saxon's classroom was, but, for some reason unknown to me, they waited for me. The student was now the teacher. That was such a venerable line in so many of the movies Mr. Bolden watched at night, but right now, I didn't like the feeling of it. "Let's go." I said, leading them to the hallway.

"I don't know about this," Gwen protested, stopping the procession of students. "Why should we learn from a vampire? They are the cause of all this."

That girl's voice grated on me just in normal conversation, not that we had too many of those. This time she had me imagining the image of Sarah Roberts's body dangling from my grasp with Gwen's face on it. I spun around on my heels. Samantha attempted to grab my arm, but I yanked it free and was in Gwen's face before she completed the first breath after her point.

"Really! Really! You are really going to start this shit right now! Those aren't vampires out there!" My arm jerked and pointed to the window. "They are witches, Gwen! Witches! The witches that attacked and killed vampires! Not the other way around!" I had to hand it to her, even with me standing nose to nose with her, screaming in her face, she never wavered. Never once did she give me that satisfying look of fear or remorse. If anything, she looked more committed to her cause, and that had everything to do with getting under my skin. I could choke her, or send her crashing through a wall, but what would that accomplish, other than giving me a satisfying feeling? Gwen was a very capable witch, and we needed everyone we could muster.

With a huff, I turned around and marched down the hall. Everyone followed, and I heard a murmur as we passed Mrs. Saxon's classroom. At the library, I yanked the doors open and marched up to the first table and waited for everyone else to enter. Once they were in there, I summoned the librarian. "Edward!"

Edward appeared in an instant, as he always did. "Yes, Miss Dubois. What can I do for... you?" The sight of everyone else appeared to startle him.

"Have my father's journals been cataloged in the archives yet?"

"Yes, ma'am."

"Anyone that doesn't want to learn how to use runes from a vampire can stay here and learn by reading my father's journals. There are several dozen of them."

"One hundred and three on the topic, to be precise," Edward offered.

"Good luck trying to make sense out of them without a rudimentary understanding, or," I looked right at Gwen for this next point, "having not ascended yet. You will lack the perspective to understand the what's and how's. The rest of you follow me."

I marched out and back down the hall to Mrs. Saxon's classroom, where I waited at the door for everyone else to enter. Even the last straggler, who entered with a bit of wounded pride. Ironically, Gwen sat in my old seat in the back of the class and not upfront. The balance had shifted, and I kind of liked it.

To complete the picture, I took the spot at the front of the classroom. Then, in an image straight out of Mr. Demius' class a few months back, I waved my hand across the air in front of me, producing ten glittering runes hanging there for everyone to see.

"These are the basics. There are more. A lot more, but these are the ones you need to know before we cover any others. We are going to cover three really quickly. The first one will give you a feeling of what it takes to use a rune. The other two you will need if they ask you to take a watch upstairs."

I took a few steps back to give everyone a good view of what I was about to do. With no description or explanation, I imagined a triangle with a line across it, the symbol for fire. While I imagined it in my head, I drew one in the air in front of the class. As it drew itself over and over again faster and faster, I did the same for all to see. Then, just like I had before, I thought of a patch of green grass below my feet. A flash of heat ran down my body, and then there it was. A carpet of lush green grass and a chorus of gasps. I repeated this again to get rid of it.

"That is fire," I explained. "Fire is the symbol of change. It can both create and destroy, and is the easiest to practice and develop the feeling of using runes. Imagine it in your head until it draws itself over and over again. Once it is doing that, you imagine what you want to do. If you did it right, you will know. The one rule," a rule I made up based on my own personal experience, "when you imagine what you want to create or destroy, it must be something inanimate. Nothing living except plants. It won't work with anything else." So, I lied, but I wanted to keep them from making the same mistake I had, twice. Right now, we just needed to teach them how to use a few of them. After all this was over, we could go into something more detailed and even have discussions about ethical usage.

"Now, let's divide into several groups. Sam will take a few, I will take a few, and James will take the rest. We are going to practice this one over and over until everyone can do it just like this," I snapped my fingers, and the grass appeared again in a flash. Lynn and Tera gasped. Even Gwen leaned over her table for a closer look.

We divided up the witches into smaller groups. They were going to be tiny groups, just because of the limited numbers. Gwen latched hold of James without even being assigned to him. He was really the only option for her. With our past, it just wouldn't work. Not that I wouldn't make it work. I doubted she would, especially after that little protest earlier. She and Samantha would be gasoline and fire. Even having them in the same room was a risk, and seeing the way Samantha was leering over at James giving Gwen his undivided attention, I knew I had two reasons to worry. Tera and Lynn were her students for this session. She was the only one left after Jack and Lisa grabbed me, which was fine by me. I had already covered more than the basics with them, and this gave me the opportunity to expand on that.

We worked well past the first light of day. By the time Master Thomas came in to send the witches up to get some sleep, the midday sun glared through the windows of the classroom. It cast little pools on the floor that Samantha and I avoided. Everyone had their basics down, and most had moved on to the protection runes, which were what we needed them to understand if they were going to take a watch. Lisa had progressed further than anyone, of course. She could wield most of the runes with little effort, and even experimented under my guidance with combining a few runes. Jack wanted to, but he wasn't ready yet, even though he spent a lot of time looking over my father's journals on the topic. He also still hadn't ascended yet, which limited his ability to wield them.

When they slogged out, Samantha, I and James followed. Master Thomas sent James up to get some sleep, telling him he had a watch this evening. He put his arm up to block my departure through the door. "Witches need sleep, vampires don't. You have training to do."

Samantha tried to slip by, but he stopped her as well. "Not so fast. You need training too. Just a different kind of training."

He led us down the hall. Dropping Samantha off at Mr. Helms' class for what appeared to be a private lesson. Before she disappeared behind the door, he dropped a bombshell on both of us. "Your watch is tonight at 10 pm. You will both be on the same watch as Gwen and Mrs. Wintercrest."

Samantha's head almost exploded as she spun around. Master Thomas had to lean back to avoid being slashed by her red hair as it slung around.

My hands balled into fists as every muscle in my body tensed up.

"Just wait! Wait!" He cautioned both of us. "I have my reasons. Hear me out before you send me to Antarctica or something." He searched both of us for agreement, and I wasn't sure he found it. He just didn't receive any violent protests yet. "Look, I need to have one or two strong witches on every watch, but I also need to have ones I can trust. I still don't know who I can trust on the council, and the idea of having any of them around who they may still regard as their supreme is troubling. With Gwen's obsession with the council, I am not sure where her head is. If someone on the council tried to sway her.... let's just say I'm pretty sure it wouldn't take much. With you two there, you can keep them in line."

"So, we are babysitting the queen bitch and the queen witch," Samantha spat.

"In a manner of speaking. Maybe think about it as supervising."

"That doesn't make it sound any better." I crossed my arms and gave him a hard stare.

"They are both capable witches and can help. You might just need to encourage them, and," Master Thomas paused and appeared to be conflicted for a moment. "If either of them gets out of line, you can blast them. Does that work?"

I saw a twinkle in my daughter's eye, that I used a motherly point of a finger to squash. God knows that girl didn't need any excuses to claim open season on Gwen. I still didn't like the idea of being stuck with them, but I understood his points. Heck, I even agreed with him. Most of the council had appeared to turn their backs on Mrs. Wintercrest after the truth came out, but was that really just for show? They all appeared to support her in this unjust war. Did they flap around freely in the breeze of power?

"Go on." I said, giving Samantha a little shove through the door to Mr. Helms, and then turned and walked quietly to where I assumed we were going, Mr. Demius' class. I pulled open his door. Seeing Mary Smith standing at the bottom of the steps with Mr. Demius told me what kind of day this was going to be.

12

"I don't like this," Samantha muttered under her breath. Her arms were crossed tightly across her chest.

"Sam, it's only for four hours. We can do anything for that long." I said, though I wasn't sure if I was trying to convince Samantha or myself. I glanced over her shoulder at Gwen, who was gushing over Mrs. Wintercrest on one of the outdoor sofas. I was surprised Gwen wasn't sitting there with her council binder, asking Mrs. Wintercrest to sign it. She was going to be pretty useless at what she was supposed to do up here. They both were. Mrs. Wintercrest looked more than happy to sit there and hold court with her fan club of one. If someone didn't know any better, they would think nothing had changed, and she was still our supreme. She even wore her usual zered robe, with gold rope edging.

"Ugh," Samantha sighed.

"Why don't you walk down that way?" My head nodded in the opposite direction, down on the other end of the deck, where Apryl and Jen had set up camp. "Make sure things are holding up."

"I can see everything just fine from here. Everything is holding strong." Samantha made a quick glance up above our heads.

"How do you know?" I asked, not for my benefit, but to gauge what she knew. I felt I was getting the typical teenager glance around at things and since nothing was falling down on our head, it was all okay.

Samantha looked up again, and then said, "The lines look strong. They are close together as they arch over us, and I don't see any of them giving much with each impact. What does, bounces back."

"You see the lines?" I asked, grabbing her hand and pulling her closer to the railing.

"Yes, mom. I see the lines. I always have."

"Okay, you see the ones wrapped over us as protection. What about out around where the shots are being fired at us? What do you see?"

Samantha looked out and waited for another volley. The wait wasn't long. Since the attack started, there had been a steady, almost rhythmic, timing to the assault. Right on time, another blast headed our way. A yellow one this time, and right behind it a blue one.

"I see the color, but buried in there, I see the sharp pointed lines, almost like a spear."

"Good. Seeing them lets you fight back against them. You can use runes or just magic to change the shape of the lines to block it, or send your own attack."

I heard another sigh, and this time it wasn't directed at the meeting of the Mrs. Wintercrest fan club. It was directed at me.

"Mom, are you going to use the entire four hours up here to train me? I spend almost all of my time being trained."

I wanted to snap back at her that she needed to learn everything as fast as she could, but I also knew how she felt. Every time I turned around, someone was pulling me into some type of training session or the other. Some were easier than others. Some, like today's, pulled a part of me off my bones and kept it. This trip wasn't as bad as the first trip, but it was still bad. Mary Smith never let me out of her grasp this time, and there was some comfort in feeling her presence there, but that was it. The void of any other presences, and the utter feeling of desperation that made up the place was enough to leave me feeling numb for several hours afterwards.

"No, I'm not. I'm just making sure you know what you need to," I conceded, realizing I needed to be more tactical in my attempts to teach her, while also giving her some space.

"Trust me. I got this," she said with a half-smile. "I think I am going to go check things at the other end, just to be sure." I watched her walk away, making a beeline to where Jen and Apryl sat. I was going to give her this brief break, but it wouldn't last long. We all had a job to do, and at the moment, I was the only one doing it.

I made a lap around the deck, circling the two social groups that were up there. Everything was holding just as it should, but that didn't mean I wouldn't reapply the runes and protection before we went back downstairs. A little extra wouldn't hurt anything. As I walked around the deck surveying the scenes, many questions about the attack came to mind. Mostly, why were they only coming at us from behind the coven? There was nothing on the sides of the coven or the front. Each shot crashed into the protection above us in about the same spot, but not the exact same spot. I even cast a little spotlight out around the front just to make sure there was nothing there. All I saw were trees. Behind the coven was nothing but trees too, but between us and the cove were a horde of witches casting a magical artillery at us. I wondered if they had a camp like the rogue witches did in New Orleans. I stopped and stared into the darkness for any flickers of a campfire. Every once in a while I thought I saw something, but then lost it in the colorful flash from the next attack. Another question was about how long they would persist? That was a question that only time could answer.

"How is your training going, Miss Dubois?"

The sound of her voice sent shivers up my back. Even after everything she had been through, Mrs. Wintercrest still sounded condescending.

"Fine," I answered, hoping she would go away. A glance over my shoulder found that wasn't going to happen. In the distance, Gwen had taken up the watch at the front. Right where nothing was happening. That was fine with me. It kept her out of trouble, and away from Samantha, who was down at the opposite end.

"You know, it was never personal. I don't hate you, or what you are."

"You could have fooled me," I said, slightly perturbed, but restraining it the best I could. What was she trying to do? Make amends for all that has happened? Bury the hatchet? I wasn't interested in any peace talks between us.

"I know how it seemed, but that was then, and now you know why."

My mind added what was unsaid. Those words burned deep inside and caused my body to turn all on its own. I made sure my black eyes looked right into her crows-feet surrounded brown eyes. She looked back, as stern as ever. Seeing that burned me even more, and I completed her statement for her. "Yes, I do. It's because I am a vampire."

Then she broke, but not how I expected. There was no great explosion back at me with all the reasons I was a problem because I was part vampire. Instead, she looked at me like I had just said the most ridiculous statement that anyone had ever uttered in the history of man. She threw her arm up and turned and walked back to the closest group of chairs. She sat down, but before she did, she wagged her finger at me. "If you think that is why, then you really understand nothing." She sat down.

All the lectures and accusations made by the council played in my head. Scratch that. It wasn't the council. It was her and her protégé, Miss Roberts. This woman was trying to re-write history to make herself look or feel better, and I would not allow that. "Yes, it is what I think," I said, marching toward her. "You said it. More than a few times. My being a vampire and a witch was a threat."

"No." Her finger wagged again. "You heard what you wanted to hear, child." She chuckled. Hearing that hint of joy in her voice annoyed me to no end. "What I said, exactly, was you were an immensely powerful but undisciplined witch, and with your immortal life and physical abilities as a vampire, you were a threat. I still stand by that on many levels, but notice I used the word were. You barely understood how to use your abilities as a witch, and you were, and maybe still are, emotionally driven. I feared you could have been swayed by Jean St. Claire to give him what he wanted, or worst yet, become what he wanted, but you didn't. Now look at you. You are the best of us all. I am not beyond admitting I was wrong and shortsighted about your potential, but I don't feel I was wrong about the threat you were at that time. Miss Roberts and her mother feared you for all those reasons and one more. You were a Dubois." She patted the seat next to her. "Come. Sit."

Why I stepped forward, I wasn't sure, but I corrected that action, and stepped back. "You sent me to Mordin. Classified me as an agent of evil, or something like that!" I caught myself becoming very animated.

She lifted a single hand up in front of me to stem the emotional tsunami that was approaching, and calmly said, "That wasn't me," she shook her head gently. "At that point, I knew your potential, and so did someone else. Think about it. Who did you see?"

"The decree has your name on it," I blasted back in anger. She was really doing this. She was really trying to rewrite the history that I had just survived through.

She greeted my challenge with a less serious huff. "And Eleanor Roosevelt never signed her husband's name during his declining years, didn't she?" Then right before my eyes, I watched her wilt for the second time, and as her confidence disappeared, so did the anger I felt. "Larissa, do you know what it is like to see your end coming? To feel things slipping away. I'm not talking about feeling my mind go. I'm talking about feeling my power go, feeling what defined who I was go. There used to be nothing I couldn't do. Then, in what seemed like overnight, there was nothing I could do. I was done, with no heir to pass things down to. No protégé to teach. And worst yet, I was no longer a witch. Come. Sit down, please."

She patted the seat next to her again. Without thinking about it, my legs moved toward the seat. Once I realized it was happening, I could have stopped it, but I didn't. I let them take me to the seat, and then sat cautiously. Gwen watched from the other side of the deck and grimaced when I sat. I drew no joy from her expression.

"I can honestly tell you; it is a frightening feeling. Dying may not be as frightening. There is a peace that comes with that. There is no peace with the feelings of helplessness and uselessness. I tried for a while to keep anyone from finding out, but it didn't take me long to realize they could see it just by looking at me. There were whispers in the council about who could replace me, but no one stepped forward. I once hoped Benjamin would, but he never showed interest. Then Mrs. Roberts stepped forward and approached me about teaching her daughter. Did you know I originally said no? Why would you? At that time, you weren't part of our community anymore. I did. I told her no. I didn't think I had it in me to teach anyone, and I didn't feel she was the right one to tie my legacy to. Does that sound egotistical?"

"A little," I said.

"You can be honest," Mrs. Wintercrest said with a smile. "It's just us talking. I am nothing anymore, just another witch. Well, I'm not even that anymore. And yes, it was very egotistical. If I were to train someone to succeed me, they would be tied to my name forever. Their greatness would lift my name up. Their failures would stain it. She wasn't ready, and she wasn't the right one. Her mother was pushing for her own reasons. She wanted to be supreme badly, but she lacked the ability to pass all seven wonders. She even hired the best tutors for herself, but to no avail. She always fell two short. Her daughter had shown signs of being able to do all seven, but lacked the formal training to really put up a challenge. She approached me again, and this time offered a price I couldn't look away from, an extension. It knew it wasn't my power I was feeling, but that didn't matter. I felt it flow through me, and I felt whole again."

It made me almost feel sick on my stomach to be able to relate to this woman, but I could understand better than anyone here.

"I knew when I agreed what I was getting into, and what kind of woman she was. Even if she could do all seven, she would have never been allowed." She held a hand up to her chest as if to hold back some of the soul she was about to spill before me. "Now, I am no saint. I am egotistical. That we already agree on," she held up a finger to cement that point, "and I would be lying if I said I wasn't power hungry. We all have been, for centuries. The wonderful and romantic image of the council has long since been dead. I have done a great many things I have been ashamed of, but never like her. Mrs. Roberts stopped at nothing to clear the path for her daughter, and I mean nothing. We became weaker as a people because of it, and even she realized it. Which was why she seized the opportunity you gave her to go after the vampires."

"I gave her?" I asked, curious about how I had done anything to help that woman.

"Jean was out of the picture for the first time in centuries. That set everything into motion." She looked at me. Her eyes asked a question her mouth didn't ask. Then she searched my face for that answer and sat back as if the lack of one surprised her. "You don't know, do you?

What you did. A witch confronting Jean, with the permission of several of the elders, set off a tidal wave of turmoil among the vampires. Without Jean, there were no vampires remaining that we would consider threats to us. To her, that made them an easy target."

And there it was again. Another name, make that names, lots of them, to add to my list of people whose lives I had totally ruined. I felt myself bite my lip.

"Don't do that to yourself, Larissa. You didn't know, and you did what you had to do. Jean wouldn't have stopped until he had you. You and I both know that. I knew it would cause turmoil. That was why I ordered him held until we could decide what to do with him. If we had let you kill him, or killed him ourselves, that tidal wave would have been a tsunami, and we would have risked being attacked ourselves." She adjusted herself in the chair, and settled back, staring out at the black night. Colors filled the sky directly above us, but the area she stared at was black. I sat there and wondered how she had read me so easily.

"We make decisions, and as much as we try to see what the impact of those decisions will be, we can't see where all the ripples will land. We just have to deal with it when they occur. That is just life, and something every leader needs to learn to accept. The possible outcomes of every decision are endless, and no matter what you try, you can't see all of them. You just have to accept it."

I sat there in shock. Did she just give me advice? This woman. The queen of my torment. I didn't understand what was happening. We sat there in silence for a while as I tried to make sense of it, which I couldn't. I could accept it for what it seemed, which I felt was highly unlikely. I just couldn't ignore our past. No matter how she tried to reframe it. I could also dismiss it. The chance I was being played like a fiddle was high, but that wasn't an absolute either. That left us with a silence, an awkward one, and I hated those. The discomfort of it grew as time passed, and just like it always had before, the urge to say something pushed forward. I fought back as hard and as long as I could. I knew I wasn't going to acknowledge her advice. I hadn't accepted it for what it was yet, and I wasn't going to give her the pleasure of thinking I had. This was something I felt I still needed to keep more than an arm's distance. I wasn't sure if keeping her a few miles away was far enough at this point, but here I was, stuck on the deck for another three hours with her.

"You're wrong, you know," I said, finally breaking the silence. "There is no peace in death."

She laughed. "Someone has been practicing descensum. That was my least favorite of all the test, for exactly that reason. Knowing about those lost souls makes you worried that you, or someone you know, may become one, doesn't it?"

"That and just the feeling of it."

"It's the one they say that takes something out of you, and it's true. I only did it for the test. After that, I have never used it. It's considered one of the wonders because it shows a mastery of astral projection. You just have to force yourself to get through it. If the test means enough to you, you will. If being supreme means enough to you, you will do it. I just hope it's for the right reason."

I hated to tell her; it wasn't really my reason. It was everyone else's. Which had me thinking. I didn't tell her that. My trust was still on the floor where she was concerned, but I asked a question I became curious about. "Why did you want to be supreme?"

"Oh," she sighed, and again focused out off into the black. "I was probably an idealistic young woman set on changing the world. I remember how I felt about the supreme back then. Just seeing her was magical. That is easy to be caught up in. Many still are to this day. I think it is the aura of the position, and not that person, but that doesn't change how people feel. Several members of my family had been supreme before, and that kept us active in that circle. That meant I had the opportunity that most others didn't. I could talk to her and learn from her. Just being around her was intoxicating, and feeling her hand guide me was even more so. God, I remember wanting to be this more than anything else in the world."

"But why? Was there something specific you wanted to change or do?" I finally turned to look at her. The whole time we talked, or make that she talked, and I listened. I had looked out into the night or up at the flashes. I didn't want to seem interested, and I hated that at that moment I truly felt I was.

"I would love to say there was. In reality, there wasn't. This will sound silly to you." A slight smile breached her normally grim expression. "It was like becoming the queen, and what little girl doesn't want to be the queen?" Her eyes lit up unlike I had seen before. They lost their normal leer, and I could only imagine she was thinking back to that time. "That is probably why, and it was the wrong reason. I like to think I did some good while I was here, but I am afraid I let things happen that shouldn't have." Her voice took on a cold edge. The glimmer left her eyes, and her hands fidgeted in her lap. "I should have stepped down. Instead, I let her tempt me and I accepted it. Now, that is how I will be remembered." There was a quick curt shake of her head. "It takes a special person to be the supreme, and they need to do it for the right reasons. I know Sarah wasn't doing it for the right reasons, and neither was her mother. I would ask you why you want to be supreme, but something tells me you don't want to be it. Do you?"

I couldn't answer. I was too busy trying to figure out if it was written all over my face. There was no way she could have known that. I didn't even know it. It wasn't something I had thought about. If I really wanted to do this, hadn't come up. It was always a means to an end, which brought everything back in balance. That was what I wanted. Becoming supreme was just how to get to achieve that goal.

"You don't. I can tell," she said, looking deeply into me. "But you know. That might be the best of all. So, how is your training going? Anything other than descensum giving you any troubles?"

I shook my head.

"I was serious when I said I hated that one the most. Remember, each of the tests is designed to show you have complete mastery of that ability. This one shows you are a master of astral projection. You don't have to stay there long; you just have to go while another witch observes. I don't believe I stayed there for over ten seconds during my test, and after that day, I never returned. Do yourself a favor. Don't do that one first and don't do it last. If you do it first, that feeling that sticks with you will mess up anything else you try that day. If you do it at the end, it will mute all the happy things that follow you completing all seven tests. That is what I did and regretted it. Remember, I wanted to be a queen, and when I finally became one, that feeling overshadowed my coronation. Pick a day, and do it last that day, so you have the rest of the day and all night to recover. When you are there, don't venture too close to anyone, and don't fret over what you see. They may look lost now, but they will find their family, and to them it's only a blink of an eye. "

"Is that true?" I asked.

"Do you want me to tell you if it isn't?" she responded smartly.

I didn't.

13

Master Thomas called our four-hour shift a watch. He should have called them a sentence. A short one, but it was still a sentence, with periods of outright torture. Mrs. Wintercrest, who had become a fountain of advice, chased me around the deck for most of the night. Which was more than a little odd. Just weeks ago, this woman was trying to kill or imprison me. Now she was trying to convince me it wasn't her. I had to admit there was a part of me that found what she explained plausible. It was a small part and one that was easy to ignore, but it was still there.

Time after time, she snuck up behind me and attempted to offer some unsolicited advice. Gwen was never far away. It wouldn't have surprised me to see her following us around with a notepad during our next shift. Before that happened, I planned to plead my case again to Master Thomas about the need for a change to the schedule. I came up with many other combinations, including Mr. Demius or Mrs. Saxon up there with Mrs. Wintercrest.

When Marcus emerged up on the deck for his shift, he asked for a report. I gave him an earful about my night, which included nothing about what was happening out there in the woods. He just laughed, and I gave him a frigid look that stopped that flat. Then he asked for a proper report. I told him Samantha, and I had reapplied the runes just for extra protection about an hour ago, but other than that, nothing much happened. The attack was constant and steady. Almost like the clicking second hand on a clock. It still continued overhead while I gave him the report. When the rest of his group arrived, which was mostly council members, and Jack, I told him, "You have the deck." Then I turned to walk down the stairs.

I had made it two steps when he grabbed me by the arm and pulled me back. "Cut her a little slack. Maybe she is doing what she can to right her wrongs before she has to answer for them to her maker." He released my hand and gave me an intense but persuasive stare.

I wasn't buying what he or she was selling. "She has a long list to work through."

"That might be so," he remarked, but then waved me on. "Think about it," he called behind me as I descended the stairs. There was a fat chance of that happening.

"Think about what?" Gwen asked.

"Nothing."

I led Gwen and Mrs. Wintercrest out through my room and down the hall and out. To say that was an uncomfortable few seconds wouldn't be incorrect. Scowling vampires lined the hall and didn't let the opportunity to leer at the person they considered the essence of evil walk past. And that was just for Gwen. I let them enjoy their moment, but with Mrs. Wintercrest, I made sure I was close by. The leers were still there, but they lacked the same intensity. By now, everyone knew the truth. This was a powerless witch. What had happened had happened. There was nothing she, or any of them, could do to change that, and there was nothing she could have done to stop it. She wasn't calling the shots. Even if she spoke up and told the council what was going on, I didn't believe that would have stopped either of the Roberts' from following through with their plan. That didn't mean she wasn't in the face of it.

"Good God. I'm glad that is over," Samantha exclaimed as soon as the door closed behind them.

I spun around and looked at her curiously. "What exactly are you complaining about? You spent the night chatting with Apryl when you weren't up doing a little bit of your patrol. I was the one that couldn't get away from Mrs. Wintercrest. That woman was practically affixed to my ass all night."

"Don't forget Gwen trying to hear everything you two talked about," Apryl added.

"You stay out of it." I snapped in her direction, and I watched her sink back further against the wall.

"Yea, what was that about?" Samantha asked.

"Never mind what that was about. I am going to talk to Master Thomas later about making some adjustments before our next shift. That will fix that."

"Larissa?"

"What!" I spun around and immediately checked my attitude when I saw who I just snapped at. "Yes, ma'am."

Mrs. Saxon motioned for me to come out and join her, and then let the door close.

"Stay here." My order was not just for Samantha. It was for everyone in the hallway. I didn't know why she wanted to see me and didn't need an entourage accompanying me.

"Ma'am?" I asked, opening the door. Stepping out on the landing, I heard a murmur from below and looked over the railing. "Who are they?"

Lines of witches marched up the stairs, carrying bags of clothing and other belongings over their shoulders up to the witch's floors on both sides. Women and girls on our side. Men and boys on the other.

"Marcus reached out to the rogue witches and Master Thomas contacted other covens." She motioned her hand over the masses assembled below, filing up the stairs. "We are not alone."

"It takes an army to fight an army," I mumbled, my head bowed down, and I leaned hard against the railing.

"Yes, it does," Mrs. Saxon confirmed, but I didn't need her to. I already knew it was true, and that really bothered me. I didn't care what everyone else thought. This wasn't their war. Not that I could take on Mrs. Roberts by myself. Well, I could if it was just us, and not all those fighting alongside her. I almost had her before. The chances I would get another opportunity like that seemed slim, but if I did, I wouldn't let her slip through my fingers again. I made that mistake and then corrected it with her daughter. I had one more correction to go. A good old-fashioned burning at the stake sounded good for her. I tried before and missed. Samantha almost had her.

I stood there with Mrs. Saxon for several minutes and watched the group file in. It wasn't a silent procession by any means. There was a fair amount of hooting and hollering. There were also happy reunions with lots of handshaking and hugs before each group separated and headed up the stairs to what I guess I could call quarters now that the coven seemed like a barracks. Even just that simple realization hit deep in the pit of my stomach. That hole I felt when Nathan was gone had reemerged and I couldn't stand here and let this image feed it anymore. I spied Nathan and Mike standing on their landing on the other side. I had to wonder how long he had been standing there watching me, and if he was ever going to say anything. I nodded toward the stairs, and he got the hint and started making his way down without a single notice of the witches coming up. When I headed down, the same wasn't true. Everyone on both sides stopped right where they were and watched as I descended the stairs. The hoots and hollering and warm welcomes of old friends they hadn't seen in some time fell silent. My normally silent footsteps echoed in the dead, quiet entry hall. Once at the bottom, I held my hand out for Nathan, and he took it without a word. I yanked him hard and sped out of the entry hall, leaving the stifling silence behind.

I had my choice of rooms to duck into. Why I chose the ritual room, I wasn't exactly sure. It wasn't the first room we came to by far. I had to pass most of the classrooms, the library, and the cafeteria that I had only been to a few times with Samantha or Nathan. At this hour, any of them would have been empty. Who was I kidding? The library was always empty now that I wasn't in there twice a day for my therapy sessions.

As soon as we pushed through the curtains, I dropped Nathan's hand and stormed around the room like a caged animal. My hands pulled at my hair in a desperate attempt to grasp some sense out of all this. Nathan did his best to follow me, but all that earned him was a few collisions as I changed directions erratically.

"Larissa. Talk to me. What's wrong? What was that all about?"

I paced frantically back and forth across the room. Nathan gave up trying to follow me and stood in the center of the room.

"Talk to me."

Talking was the last thing I wanted to do. I wanted to run. I wanted to escape and get as far away from all this as I could. That was the urge I felt throughout my entire essence. Even my skin crawled and wanted to peel itself from my body and make its own escape if the rest of me didn't go willingly.

"Larissa. What is it?" Nathan grabbed at my arm as I stormed past, and had it for a second, but that was all. I snatched it from his grasp and then put that arm to use.

"That!" I screamed, pointing back toward the spectacle in the entry. "All that out there!"

"The witches?" He questioned.

His question earned him a look that screamed—DUH!

"What's wrong with it? We need all the help we can get."

I finally came to a stop and stood just outside the remnants of the runes left after the last use of the room. "I didn't ask for this." I said and then looked up through the skylight. Brilliant flashes of yellow, green, and red reflected in the glass. The cherubs, another source of my torment, took in the show before looking back down at me where I guess the show was more entertaining. I shook my fist at them, but they appeared unaffected. "I didn't ask for their help."

"News flash," Nathan declared, walking toward me, his arms flying out. "This isn't about you anymore. This isn't just Jean coming after you, or really anyone else coming after you. It's bigger than you. It's bigger than any single person. Now this is about the future. That is what is at stake."

"You're wrong!" All my emotions that had built up inside flash-boiled at that moment. "You're all wrong! This is about me! It's always been! Jean was after me! Mr. Norton paid for that with his life! My real parents did too! Now this is about me because I am the only one standing in her way."

"Really? That is what you think?"

"It's what I know." I turned my back to him and stared up at those stupid cherubs. They were enjoying the show. It was probably my pain they enjoyed the most.

"You don't think there are other witches that could put up a challenge for that precious crown of supreme? What about my mother, Lisa, hell... probably even Gwen," he said with an edge of irritation that I hadn't heard often, but when I had, it was always in response to my stubbornness. "And don't forget all the vampires and rogue witches. How exactly are they tied to you? And before you say it's because you are both, really think about it. Why go after them and not just kill you when she has had the opportunity?"

"Because she thinks they are all threats to her," I mumbled, not wanting to admit he was right.

"What was that?" Nathan asked, standing right behind me. I felt his hands on my shoulders.

"Because she thinks they are all threats to her," I repeated, this time louder.

"Exactly. Whether or not you are here, she would still do whatever it took to secure that seat for her daughter and eliminate anyone that would get in the way. Just like she already told you she had. Remember?"

"Don't forget I killed her daughter." The smile that had accompanied that statement in the past failed to appear now. Instead, a shiver chased down my spine as I realized what that meant.

Nathan rubbed my shoulders. "Yes. Yes, you did. I was there, remember? You did it in self-defense."

I wanted to laugh, but couldn't bring myself to do it. Just opening my mouth to reply was a task all on its own. "I doubt she sees it that way." I shook his hands off my shoulders.

"Oh, I'm sure. A lot of this is revenge for that, but," he grabbed my shoulders firmly and spun me around. At that moment, I saw him. The old Nathan. Not the one that had emerged in New Orleans. Not the one that I had to rescue. This was my rock. The steady force that worked so hard to keep my balance, even if he didn't realize he was doing it, even when I didn't know who I was. "You have to remind yourself that this war started long before this. The war with the Rogues has been going on for years, if not decades. Remember what

Master Thomas told you. And the war with the vampires started... has really existed all the way back to the beginning of time. Witches and vampires never got along. They never trusted one another. It has just been a cold war of such. Now it's a little hotter because Jean is out of the way. When you truly look at it, nothing has changed. Her daughter was just one of many casualties of this war."

Nathan let go of my shoulders and lifted my chin with the most delicate of touches, his eyes locking with mine. "Now, there are a lot of people willing to fight for their lives, but I think they need a leader, and everyone that matters believes that is you, me included. They need you. Remember the speech you used to give me when I complained about all your training, about how you told me it was necessary so we could have the future we both want? I see it now, and I plan on having that future with you."

He pulled me closer, and then kissed me. No matter how many times our lips touched, sparks always flew like it was the first time. Normally, this was always an effective way for him to win any argument. This wasn't one of those times. I couldn't help but agree with him, kiss, or no kiss. That didn't mean I had to go along with it.

He pulled me in and embraced me. Instead of nuzzling against his muscular chest, I kept my head to the side and glanced up at the colorful attacks going on overhead. They seemed brighter than before. That could have been my glow leftover from the kiss. The cherubs looked down with puckered lips.

Nathan let go and noticed where my gaze was, and looked up as well at the light show above. "Can we go somewhere that we aren't reminded about that for just a few moments?" he asked, but then stammered, "That is, if you don't have any training to do right now."

I didn't believe I did, although no one had provided me a schedule for the day, not that they really ever did. It was still very early morning. The sun wasn't even up yet, and Master Thomas was serving his four hour watch up on the deck. The others were probably still asleep, either recovering from their last watch, or preparing for their next. I shook my head and then wondered where we could go. A devious thought entered my mind, and I felt a similar smile creep across my face. "I know where."

I grabbed his hand and led him toward the door. Then I stopped in my tracks and looked up. Another evil smile replaced the one that was already present on my face. "Go on. I need to take care of something first." I urged Nathan to keep walking.

"What?" he asked, concerned.

I held up both hands and pulled down quickly. Behind me, three stone cherubs crashed down to the floor, shattering into piles of dust.

Even though I knew the coven would put them back as soon as I left the room, I still felt a little satisfaction from it. I stood there posed and smiled. "It had to happen." Then the entire coven rumbled and heaved under our feet.

"What else did you break?" Nathan asked.

"That wasn't me." I reached my arms out to steady myself as the entire room rattled again. Cracks developed up the walls, sending a shower of dust our way. I looked up just as the walls crumbled. I knew I didn't pull the cherubs down that hard. Nathan grabbed my hand and yanked me out of the way, just in time. Now I knew how it felt.

14

We stumbled out into the hallway as the ritual room collapsed behind us in a shower of dust and chunks of stone. I fell to the ground, putting up an arm to shield my head from the falling debris, but then felt something larger and heavier laying over the top of me. My personal protector groaned slightly when the larger objects crashed into his back.

"You all right?" he asked once it stopped. The debris slid off his back and tumbled to the floor when he stood up.

"I'm fine." I dusted the fine dust that coated my black t-shirt and jeans. "Are you? I can protect myself, you know?" He and I needed to have a talk later about what seems to be his compulsive need to throw himself between me and harm. I was more than capable of taking care of myself.

"I'm good," he announced and seemed to puff out his chest, which drew a quick eye roll from me.

"You missed a brick," I said, reaching up to brush a brick fragment from the collar of his shirt. Then I twirled my right hand and a quick gust swirled around us, cleaning off the dust.

The walls and floor of the hall rumbled. I had already seen this movie once. I wasn't going to stand around for the sequel. We took off for the stairs. Inside, I knew what had happened. Somehow our protection had broken and those beautiful and colorful lights that had been harmless for the last day were now raining a revenge filled hell storm on top of us.

"Where are we going?" Nathan yelled.

"The stairs. We need to get Samantha and Amy. Then we are getting out of this place before it collapses on us." I had a feeling outside would not be much better, but at least we wouldn't be underneath all this rumble. We would have more options for our next move.

"Can you repair that shield you guys put up?"

"Probably," I replied, unsure. I didn't doubt I could put one up. I put up the first one, and then again during my shift. Chances were someone didn't properly support it during their watch. But there was something about the place crumbling around us that made that option seem fruitless. "It seems like it is too late for that!"

At the end of the hall, a figure in the dust and flashes waved us through. The sound of her voice reached our ears. "Come on! Hurry! We need to get out of here!" Mrs. Saxon screamed. Behind her, figures ran toward the front door. A door I had only used twice. Once when I arrived, and once to sneak out. Then, from out of nowhere, there was a flash, and she was lying against the wall.

"No!" Nathan screamed, and he let go of my hand and sped past me in a blur.

There was another flash. It hit Nathan, but he stood his ground and snarled in its direction before continuing on to his mother. I reached the hall and felt a dreadful déjà vu come over me. This was the second time I had seen the large bank of windows and doors that lead out to the pool, the woods, and the cove destroyed. Before it was a giant boulder tossed through it by supporters of a power thirsty vampire. Now there was an army of witches marching through, and unlike before, their leader was present. She proudly marched at the center of their line in a red robe that stuck out like a jewel in the sea of gray robe adorned witches.

I ignored them and scanned up and down the stairs for any sign of Samantha. She, Lisa, and Gwen were being led down by Master Thomas. Samantha yanked them to a stop and pointed at the shapeshifter's door. Master Thomas went in while they waited. I made a quick survey of the scene again and fought off the chills it sent through me. This was the end, and there was no way to avoid it. Plan B materialized quickly in my head. Once I saw Amy, I would send them, and as many as I could, away to some place safe. That plan included Nathan and his mother, who I ran toward.

"Not so fast," Mrs. Roberts commanded, and I felt something wrap around me, squeeze, and then throw me back against the opposite wall. "I haven't forgotten about you."

"Neither have I!" Nathan lunged at her, but she caught him in midair before I could grab him myself, and tossed him on top of me. He was a lot heavier than he looked.

"The lovebirds should be together at the end," Mrs. Roberts taunted with a gleeful cackle.

He rolled off of me, stunned. We both were. She had a little something extra in her shove that stung and stayed with us after we landed.

"Get up! Get up!" I demanded.

"I'm trying," he said, grimacing as he made it up to one knee.

I had meant the order more for me than Nathan, but he responded better than my body had, which had only forced itself up into a seated position. Nathan looked back at me, locking his eyes with mine. I felt everything sink. He knew exactly at that moment we all weren't getting out of here alive. He said nothing. His glance up the stairs at our daughter, and then over at his mother, said it all. He and I were in agreement.

In the blink of an eye, I leaned up and grabbed the back of his neck and pulled his lips to mine. Every kiss was like the first time. The tingling excitement flowed throughout my body, from my lips to the tips of my fingers. Which only strengthened the glow that had formed in my free hand. I released him and pulled back a hair's width from his lips. "Save all we can," I whispered.

He nodded and smiled. My white knight was about to climb upon his trusty steed and ride off into battle against overwhelming odds, and I was going right along with him. Or was it the other way around? It didn't matter. We never had the chance.

Before I reached my feet, I heard an enormous explosion and saw dozens of gray-robed witches flying through the air.

Nathan spun around and congratulated me. "Very nice!"

"That wasn't me!"

We both looked around for the source of the attack. I looked up the stairs, half expecting to see Samantha, or any other witches, coming out of their floor firing down at them from behind. They all looked just as confused as I was. In fact, Samantha was looking down at me as if she expected I was behind this.

Then it happened again while I was looking up at my daughter. Her head looked off to the side, and I followed it. Standing there was Mr. Helms, giving his best to the column of witches, and he was not alone. Several members of the council of mages had stayed behind to help.

As soon as the witches landed, they returned the attacks. They filled the space with balls of energy and fire coming from one direction, and colliding with something similar coming from the other side. A few made it through doing its damage. From above, a few of the rogue witches that hadn't escaped yet joined in. This sent a few of Mrs. Roberts' supporters running out of the gaping entry. She didn't seem to care. She ignored the chaos around her and strode forward calmly.

Samantha moved closer to the railing and prepared to join in just as Master Thomas emerged with Amy and Cynthia. She aborted her attack, and gathered Amy in her arms, and rushed down the stairs as fast as she could, weaving through the attacking rogue witches, dodging the few shots that came close. Cynthia followed, holding on to Samantha's shirt the whole way. Master Thomas returned a few of his own as he followed.

Mr. Helms and Mr. Demius joined from the boys' stairs, covering the escape of the werewolves and shifters. Steve and Stan stayed in their human form. I saw Steve make a quick look over at the other stairs. When he spotted Cynthia, he and Stan both ran down the stairs, grabbing her before they went out the door.

Rob and Martin never even attempted to escape out the front door with everyone else. They phased right there and stalked toward Mrs. Roberts. She raised her hand, but I was too fast for her and robbed her of whatever she had planned. With a quick whip from my hands, I sent both of them sliding through the front door with a whine. This was not their fight.

My actions drew Mrs. Roberts' attention. Had she really forgotten about me? I was still right where she had thrown me earlier, and there was no way she believed that had killed me. Nathan lunged for her, before being pushed aside lightly against the wall. My doing, not hers. This wasn't his fight, either. It was mine. I stood up and readied both hands and ran toward her. Mr. Demius hit her with some kind of purple bolt, and she didn't even flinch before sending it right back at him. It hit him on the upper thigh and sent him to the ground. Then, as she marched toward me, she did the same to Master Thomas and two of the council members. They each flopped to the floor like a rag doll.

I screamed.

The corner of one side of her mouth rose slightly in enjoyment as she watched them lie lifeless on the floor. That satisfaction only lasted for a moment. I hit her on the shoulder with something of my own. She went down to one knee, and it was my turn to watch. I saw Master Thomas stir on the ground, and then whipped my head around and gave her my full attention. First, it was a punch to the face, then a kick to the side of the head. A small river of blood streamed from her upper lip. Now it was my turn to smile in enjoyment, and this wasn't just a half smile either. I was grinning.

Nathan attempted to get involved again, but I pushed him over to where Amy and Samantha were standing.

"This is mine. Stay out of it," I commanded, making sure I had made eye contact with both him and Samantha. Then I hit Mrs. Roberts with my best shot. The blue ball of flame. But I lost control like I had that first day in Mr. Helms' class and it turned into a column shooting right at her. This time was no accident; it was on purpose. None of the flames touched her. Instead, they stopped short and formed a large orb of rolling flames. As soon as I stopped, it came back at me, leaving me against the wall again.

Mrs. Roberts stood up and wiped the blood from her lip. Behind her, the gray-robed witches closed their ranks. There were fewer of them than there were before, but these weren't running away like some others had. They stayed still and never noticed the vampires raining down on top of them from the top floor. Mike landed on three witches, crushing their bodies beneath him. Apryl and Laura landed right on the shoulders of two witches, and quickly relieved them of the burden of their heads. Clay and Kevin did the same. Witches were being ripped up off the floor and thrown around. The result of months of frustration that had built up from not being able to do anything to help other vampires in this war. There were screams and the pop of bone everywhere. It appeared to all to be happening too quick for any of the witches to respond with magic.

Mrs. Roberts stepped forward and raised up both arms, and the railing on the stairs on either side of the entry broke free from its spindles and slithered its way to me. They coiled around and squeezed. The lion's heads that made the end of each railing hissed and snapped at my head.

I dodged and jerked to keep from being bitten. Samantha ran over and grabbed one of the two heads, and attempted to twist it off. I heard the wood crack, but it never broke completely.

"Let' go! Quick!" Mrs. Tenderschott yelled, entering from what used to be a hallway. She reached inside her jacket and whipped out something I had never seen anyone use before. A gnarled piece of wood, maybe a foot long. "Vinea!" A gold flash exploded from the end of the stick and hit the constricting railings. Slowly, they both transformed into a leafy green vine that dried up and withered.

Mrs. Roberts leered at her, and then threw her head back and raised her hands to the sky. Dark clouds swirled above, and everything shook. She was uttering an incantation of some sort, but I couldn't hear anything she said over the roar of the rumble that beat a drum roll on my eardrums. She recited the words with speed and ferocity as she leveled her gaze at Mrs. Tenderschott. The women we all thought of as our grandmother looked back at me. Her features shook, and the color drained from her once rosy cheeks. She now resembled a vampire more than herself. A gust of wind whirled in and circled around the open entry, and past Mrs. Tenderschott. Then she just disappeared.

"Larissa, get everyone out of here now!" Master Thomas screamed his order as he ran towards us, but he disappeared as the gust passed him. It circled around, passing Mr. Demius, Mr. Helms, and then Mrs.

Saxon. Nathan lurched forward, but I grabbed him, and held him firm where he stood. Like a wave of destruction that started on the opposite side of the room, one by one everyone vanished, and the walls crumbled on top of where they stood. I watched as the ripple of air approached us, and threw up my best set of protection runes, and it washed over those I could cover as if we weren't there, but those it touched disappeared.

The swirling vortex above disappeared, and Mrs. Roberts collapsed to the floor briefly before her supporters swarmed her. Two gray cloaked figures rushed from the opening that used to be the hallway to the residences. They carried another individual, and the sight of him set the hair on the base on of my neck on end. He shielded himself from the sunlight that shone through the coven's destroyed roof. I would not let him get away, and I sprinted as fast as I could across the debris. Nothing else was there except him and me. My hands flexed in preparation of gripping his head and yanking it free. Something I should have done before instead of toying with him. I used a small pile of rubble as a launching pad and jumped, aiming myself to land on top of him, but before I landed, Jean and everyone else disappeared. All of them, in the flash of a portal, but before it closed, she left a warning. "I'll be back for you." I landed, and the remaining walls of the coven collapsed around us. Each staircase was now nothing more than mounds of rubble.

Several stones moved where the entrance to the hall was. Then another couple of stones moved, causing a waterfall of dust to fall from that area.

"Mike. Clay. Come help me," Kevin Bolden commanded. "We have survivors." The three of them climbed up and over debris and approached what used to be the entry to the hallway leading to the instructor's residences. Stones were still shifting in the pile, and I noticed an odd glow emanating through the cracks.

"Get down!" I yelled, but I was too late. Stones exploded up and kept flying right out of sight. Marcus Meridian stood up, dusting off his black jacket before walking up and over piles of debris, running both hands through his dark locks. He looked around in panic.

"Bring them back!" I demanded.

Marcus kept walking aimlessly, running his hands through his hair and then over his face.

"Marcus, bring them back!"

Marcus turned his back to us and walked up another pile of rock and splintered wood, and looked out. I watched the man's body take in two deep breaths that he let out slowly. "I can't."

"Then show me how, and I will." I said and went to join him on top of the pile.

He spun around and stormed down, stopping inches from my face. His nostrils flared. "I can't. You can't. No one can. They are dead. Dead. All of them. There is no bringing them back."

There were loud gasps behind me, and the sound of several approaching footsteps. Nathan was the first to arrive. He reached forward and pushed Marcus on the shoulder, turning him. "What do you mean?"

Marcus pulled free from Nathan's grasp and marched back to the top of the debris pile. "They are dead. All of them. I know what she did. It's an old, dark magic spell that is part of the forbidden lore. Just like some of our magic can create life, it can also destroy just as easy."

"That's not funny!" Nathan stormed up toward Marcus, his fist flexing. Tears threatened to breach the corners of his eyes. He hit a barrier that Marcus had erected that only I and he could see.

"Mr. Saxon. Please try to control yourself, but I am sorry. There is no way to bring your mother back. She's dead."

"All of them?" Gwen asked from way behind us.

"Yes. I'm sorry."

Marcus sat down on the top of the debris and ducked his head. Nathan went down to his knees, and the tears flowed, as did the painful wails. I was still standing there trying to absorb what was just said. They were all dead. I reached forward and placed my hand on Nathan's shoulder. What a simple and stupid and meaningless action. It in itself did nothing for him. I knew it. There was nothing that would, but that didn't stop his body from following human nature and reaching up and taking my hand.

"I knew this would happen. I knew it." I turned and wondered, of all the people we lost, how the hell Mrs. Wintercrest was still here, and alive. She stepped down from what remained of the girl's stairs and weaved her way around the piles of debris, wagging her finger at me the whole way. "You were going to bring doom to us all. I knew it-"

We never found out if she had anything else to say. I opened a portal and shoved her through. No one asked where she was sent. I don't think anyone cared. I knew. She was now enjoying my cage at Mordin. That would keep her out of trouble.

No one objected to my handling of Mrs. Wintercrest. Not even Gwen.

15

"I can't believe they are all gone," Lisa whispered. It was a phrase that most everyone who remained had uttered more than once since it happened. It was just sheer luck that all the vampires were on the side of the room I was on and found refuge under my runes, and were spared. Of the witches, only Marcus, Lisa, Jack, and Gwen remained.

Marcus sat perched up on his pile. The vampires chased the shadows to avoid the discomfort of dawn. Gwen, Jack, and Lisa sat silently against a small section of wall that still stood. Samantha sat against the same wall, but down a bit with Amy embraced firmly to her chest. I sat silently next to Nathan. There was an overwhelming urge to tell him how sorry I was, but so far, I hadn't. I just sat there, my arm around him as he mourned. Tears flowed down his cheeks, but the woeful wails had stopped just before daybreak. We all shared two common traits: a blank stare and silence.

The silence wasn't helping me. I needed someone to yell and scream. Something to be fired up and pissed off about. I felt I should be. I should be the one out chasing her down for revenge, but there was nothing. Just the hollow shell of my body remained, with two eyes that stared through holes in my skull, attempting to find some sense in all this. A completely fruitless task.

I sat there, holding on to Nathan. Hoping against hope I could take away his pain. I wanted to tell him I understood how he felt. Actually, I understood two-fold. This had happened to me twice. First, I watched my mother die, and then Thomas Norton. Both were murdered right in front of my eyes. I felt that pain, and I knew it well. The hurt, the despair, the grief, all wrapping around hate and anger that snuck through at times. So far with Nathan, I hadn't seen that surface yet, but it would. It was only a matter of time, and there was nothing I could do for him to help. I just hoped he didn't blame me for this. I was doing enough of that for everyone. This was my fault. All of it.

We all sat there in silence for a while longer. The vampires had to adjust twice to avoid the rising early morning sun. Nathan and I just scooted a few inches to stay in the shade. Each time, I had to nudge him. It seemed he had become numb and didn't notice the slight tingle. I couldn't blame him. I was numb, too. I moved more in response to the presence of the light, not how it felt. Light didn't seem to have a place in the world anymore, and the darkness felt more comfortable.

A new shadow appeared over us, and I looked up at its source. Marcus had left his seat on top of the pile of debris and now stood over me. He motioned for me to follow him as he moved back to the base of his pile. I didn't. I just sat there and watched. At his second attempt, I gave a quick look at Nathan, his head still propped up on his knees. I pulled my hand from his, and he didn't stir. Then I walked over to where Marcus stood.

"We can't stay here." He whispered. "What she did drains her, but only temporarily. Once she has recovered. She will be back. You and I both know that."

She told us as much right before she left. "Okay, where do we go?"

Marcus shrugged. "Some place safe, but first I need to ask you something first. Are you still committed to seeing this through?"

It wasn't the question I was expecting, but it was one I could willingly answer. What doubts that had roamed in and out of my head about this very topic since they proposed it were gone now. It was official. We had lost too much for me to say no now. That didn't mean my answer came out confident. "Yes, I am."

He grabbed me by the shoulders and looked me dead in the eyes. "Larissa, it is only going to get harder. I need to know. Are you really committed to doing this?"

Before I answered this time, I swallowed to clear the weakness from my voice. It only partially worked as I answered, "Yes." To enhance it, or to give the illusion of the confidence I didn't have, I nodded.

He let go of my shoulders and looked up over me and surveyed the others seated among the remains of the coven. There was a quick shake of his head, and then he walked down the pile of debris. "Follow me! All of you!"

Everyone staggered to their feet, and I went to help Nathan, but he stood up before I reached him. He looked at everything, dazed. His body was here, but I didn't have a clue where his mind was. It was probably down in a pit of emotional despair, like we all were, except his pit was deeper, much deeper.

Marcus waited for everyone to stand and for the witches to join him out in the open. The rest of us kept to the shadows. He made another survey of all of us before he turned and walked toward what used to be a hallway in the coven. He walked right at the large pile of debris that used to be multiple stories of the coven that sat atop that hall. Then, like a disaster movie playing in reverse, the debris floated up, and piece by piece, the coven put itself back together. It restored the hall perfectly before we followed him into it.

Everything looked as if nothing had happened. I looked back behind us, and the grand entry hall stood just as majestic as before. The shine across the marble floor was so deep you would swear you could dive into it and swim.

We followed Marcus down the hallway. Each of us inspected every detail for any signs of what had just happened. Everything looked like it always had. Even the doors to the library, which was where Marcus led us. I sure hoped this wasn't his idea of some place safe for us to go. Even if I considered my earlier point about how no one used the library, this wasn't exactly what I would have picked.

As soon as we entered through the door, Edward greeted us. "Master Meridian." He followed it with a slight head bow.

Marcus returned the pleasantry, "Edward."

Then he turned and found me in the crowd that was behind him. His laser sharp focus cut through everyone and then made a beeline for me. He bumped Samantha in the shoulder to get to me. Once he was in my face again, he asked, "You're sure?"

"Yes." I answered again. He turned and returned to the front of the line.

"What are we doing in the library?" Mike asked when Marcus passed by, but he didn't get an answer.

Marcus walked back through the crowd back to the front. Once he was there, standing in front of Edward, he made the request. "Edward, the vault, please."

Edward received the request curiously. Then he looked at the rest of us, even more curious. "Sir?"

"You heard me. If we are going to fight her, we need to level the playing field. The vault."

"Sir, might I remind you–"

"No need, Edward. I am well aware of the restrictions. Admittance to the vault is forbidden unless granted by the council's written decree. There is no more council. There is no more supreme. As a member of the Meridian family, I am asking you to take us to the vault. I wouldn't ask if I didn't feel it was completely necessary."

Edward considered the request for a few seconds, and Marcus stood there patiently and waiting respectfully.

"Of course, sir. Follow me." Edward turned around and floated through the library. We followed him blindly.

Who knew the library was this big? I hadn't made it past the first row of tables during any of my prior visits. We were now probably twenty rows of tables and shelves deep, and even then, the back wall was still nowhere in sight. We continued to trudge through the library. Nathan walked beside me, his hands shoved in his pockets, and his eyes focused on the spot just a few inches in front of his feet. Samantha came up and joined us at one point. She was carrying Amy, who appeared both tired and upset. The evidence of tears was still present on both of their faces, as it was on all of ours. Even Gwen, who had remained uncharacteristically quiet. Stranger yet, she was walking next to Apryl. Neither one seemed to acknowledge the other. All any of us did was walk.

I wedged my hand between Nathan's arm and his side, looping my arm around his. He ignored the little tugs I gave to free his hand, so I gave up on holding it to comfort him and settled for just holding his arm. The urge to ask him how he was doing pressed on my lips, but I resisted. It was a stupid question. I knew that. Anyone could just look at him to see how he was feeling. He was just a husk of humanity, following others. There was no conscious movement from him. If I tugged him away from the group, he would easily follow, and probably not even look up while doing it. Inside, he was a storm of feelings. It was a storm I knew well, and there was no guarantee you could ride this storm out. Even if you did, it changed you. Either the feeling of loss changed you, or the anger changed you. Both might. If only I could see behind Nathan's black eyes to see if his world was burning or if it was frozen. I could probably help him, but those black orbs hid his current state like a secret locked away, whose key had been thrown away long ago. I knew he needed time. So did the others. Mike and Brad both gave Nathan the standard guy slap on the shoulder. Which was really how guys expressed any emotion. You did something great? Here is a slap on the shoulder. Not feeling good? Well, get better and here is a slap on the shoulder. Your entire world fell apart? Here, this little tap will make you feel better.

For us that were more feminine, it was a hug. We each tried to squeeze the pain out of him, or that was how it looked. Each pulling him in close and offering our bodies as a surrogate to pass the pain along to. Gwen seemed to offer a little too much, but I let it pass. Nathan wasn't paying attention to who it was. He was just standing there, letting them do it. Well, that was true except when it came to Jennifer Bolden. He latched hold of her. She was his mother's closest friend, and both were consoling one another.

Marcus stopped abruptly in the middle of the library between two rows of tables. The rest of us jerked to a stop behind him. "Edward, can you do the honors?"

"Certainly." Edward circled around the front and hovered just ahead of Marcus. A shower of gold glitter appeared above him. It rained down on the floor, and as it did, a large red wooden door appeared.

"Thank you." Marcus turned around, looking straight at me. "Larissa, why don't you open it for us?"

I must have looked back at him with a look that questioned if he was talking to me. "Come on up and give the handle a turn. This door will only open to council members, their family members, and those granted special access by the council—"

"Then, I am pretty sure–"

Marcus cut off my interruption and completed what he was saying. "And the family members of those granted access. Go ahead."

I felt the gaze of everyone, including Edward, burning me with great anticipation. I pulled my arm from around Nathan's. He gave no protest, and just stood there while I walked tentatively toward the door and examined the big iron handle and lock. When I reached it, I stood before the door, still looking at the handle and lock. Marcus joined me up at the door and stood to the side. I asked, "Now what? Is there a spell to unlock it?"

"No, Larissa. Just turn the handle." Instructed Marcus, motioning toward the handle.

I reached forward and gripped the handle. It was cold and metal. I wasn't sure what I was expecting to feel. It felt exactly how it looked. I gave it a turn. It turned easily, with no stop, as if it were unlocked. Instead, it clicked, and the door lunged outward.

"Go on, pull it open."

I did exactly what he said and pulled as I stepped back. The door opened, and inside candles flickered to life, chasing away the darkness that was there. The light revealed endless shelves of books and tables of objects. Many of them were golden, glittering in the dancing light.

"Everyone, inside. Please." Marcus ushered all of us through. Even Edward entered. Once we were all inside, Marcus closed the door behind us, and it disappeared. Everyone fanned out, looking at the shelves and tables. I found myself drawn to the objects on the tables. Maybe it was shiny object syndrome. There were jewel adorned bowls and chalices lined up one next to another, filling several tables. Next on display were staffs. Some were as glorious as the bowls and chalices, but others were just simple wooden staffs. Then there was another table of smaller objects. There were golden and brass balls, small carved and forged figures, and wands.

"Welcome to the vault. The home of all the magic that is banned and forbidden from being taught. These shelves contain every spell the council has deemed too dangerous to be practiced. Some go as far back as three millennia." He walked along one shelf as he spoke. It was obvious he was searching for something. His voice was firm, but his pacing was distracted. "Edward?"

"Right here, sir," Edward popped around next to Marcus.

"The Journal of the Council of Corinthia, please."

"Right away." Edward sped off into the expanse of the vault.

Lisa had joined me at the table that I was most fascinated with. Her hand hovered over a pair of brass balls as she asked, "What is all this stuff?"

"Don't touch that!" Marcus scolded. He rushed over to the table and pressed her hand down close to her side. "Don't touch anything. Got it?"

Lisa looked up at Marcus with a bit of a tremble in her lips and nodded.

"That goes for all of you. These objects are not playthings. They are magically charmed items that in the right hands are wonders, but in the wrong hands are dangerous. That is why they are locked away in here and forbidden from being used."

I took a step back away from the table to avoid any accidents, as did everyone else in the room. Those that weren't looking at the objects originally were now casting cautious gazes their way. There was an eerie silence as we all stood there, studying the objects from afar.

"The Journal of the Council of Corinthia," Edward announced, breaking the silence and startling most of us. He floated there with a large brown leather-bound book floating beside him.

Marcus grabbed it and placed it on a table. "Thank you, Edward." He opened the book and quickly fanned through the pages with his hands, no magic. Then he stopped and let the book open wide to a single page and pointed at the page. "Just as I thought," he muttered before looking up at me, and asking, "This is the last time I am going to ask this. Are you sure?"

I nodded again, and said, "Absolutely."

16

He motioned for me to join him at the table, and I did so without hesitation. The others watched. I felt a duty and obligation to them, and everyone else, to finish this. In fact, this may be the point I felt strongest about what I had to do. It energized me, and I would be untruthful if I didn't recognize the desire I felt for revenge as a strong source of that energy.

"This is how she did what she did." He pointed down the page while looking back over his shoulder at Edward. "The Chronicles of Ruel, please."

"Yes, sir."

Then he looked at everyone else, witches and vampires alike, and motioned for them to join us at the table. "Everyone, gather around the table. This involves all of you. This text is from the eleventh century. In those days, the council was based in Italy. They documented the minutes and topics of every meeting in journals, just like this one. That included spells that were deemed too dangerous to be practiced, such as the one Mrs. Roberts used. I knew I recognized it."

"If it is banned, how do you know about it?" asked Pamela.

Without looking up from the book, Marcus answered, "Because, my dear, I am a student of history. Our history. I still have access to these, even in my exiled state. That access was granted to my family by the great Supremes of old. Once granted, no one can remove it, and I have spent many hours in here reading, especially the journals of council meetings."

Edward reappeared with a large red leather-bound book in tow. "The Chronicles of Ruel, sir."

"Thank you Edward." Marcus took the book and placed it next to the other book. He flipped through its pages purposefully. "If they are going to use banned magic, then we need to fight fire with fire."

I attempted to read each page as it flipped by. I saw what looked like multiple dated tables of contents. Those were probably the true minutes of the meetings, with references to the pages that documented the topics. Some pages appeared to just be reports or discussions of points. I briefly saw one talking about recognizing someone named Engus Romano for their contributions. Other pages were definitely pages of spells. Each were formatted the same way. They centered the name of the spell on the top page. Below was a paragraph or two covering its origins, use, and effects. Then there was a section called Critical Arguments. In the brief glimpses I managed of those sections, I could tell these were the arguments for why they were to be added to the forbidden list. The next page were the instructions for how to perform the spell or potion.

Marcus stopped flipping and let the pages fall open. "Mr. Saxon. I believe you are very familiar with this one." He pushed the book to the center of the table and turned to face Nathan.

The page he stopped on was titled "The Fires of Ruel".

"That I am," responded Nathan. It was one of the few times we had heard his voice since he went after Marcus.

"If you look at these entries. It tells you what the spell does, how to perform, why it was forbidden, and how to counteract it. The problem is there are too many spells in the vault for you to learn the defense of each of them. If we tried, we would be here for centuries." Marcus stopped and looked up from the books. "Well, only a few of us would still be here. What I can do is show you a few that will serve you best no matter what she and her followers use against you. That is the best I can do. I can also help arm you with a few forbidden secrets of our own that I doubt she would know."

Marcus backed away from the table and began walking along the bookshelves. "I'll get that book myself, Edward."

I moved in and took his spot at the table, and looked down at the page. Jack and Lisa did the same, crowding me. Gwen kept her distance and appeared mesmerized by the tables of objects. She looked over at each object curiously, and didn't keep the same cautious distance as the others were. To be on the safe side, I reminded her of Marcus' warning from moments ago. "Gwen, remember, don't touch anything."

She shot a look of disgust back in my direction. The frequency and the volume that I had received of that look from Gwen had minimized any of its impacts. In fact, I had found them humorous under normal circumstances, though these circumstances were not normal, and I did not find it amusing. Samantha didn't either. Her mouth was opening to say something, but put a stop to it.

"Gwen. Please."

"All right. All right."

"Samantha, can you come over here for a moment? I want you to see this." It was crowded enough behind the book, but I needed to put some distance between Samantha and Gwen. This was not the time for an internal fight. If we were going to get through all this, we needed to rely on each other.

Jack turned sideways and gave Samantha room to join us. I was thankful Gwen hadn't taken an interest in what we were looking at. I looked down again and took in the page. Its title Eradere. I only needed to read the first few lines of the description to know what that word translated to. That didn't stop me from reading all of it, including the section on why it was forbidden magic. Jack and Samantha either jumped ahead or reached that section first. I heard each of them gasp next to me. I had the same reaction, but I held it in. It seems this was an acceptable spell for many years, but that all ended when a witch used it against an entire village after they branded her sister a witch and thusly burned her at the stake.

Samantha was the first to reach to turn the page, but she paused to look at the rest of us and waited for us to finish reading. Once we had all reached the end, we gave her a quick nod, and she turned it, exposing the ritual, as it was called. I didn't have to read it to know how this spell was performed, but seeing the symbols and text there in black and white sent a chill down my spine. This was one I already knew how to perform and what it could do. Let's just say my mind hadn't made the leap to all it could do. I swallowed hard to read more of the page, hoping to find out I was wrong, but the farther I read, the more right I became.

"Sam, you're reading this, right?" I asked.

"Mmhmm."

"Don't ever do it!"

"I won't."

Jack adjusted his stance to look closer. "I'm not sure I get it."

"Oh, I do," Lisa said as she leaned back away from the table. The size of her eyes told me she had made the same leap I had, but I had to wonder if she had really realized everything.

"Lisa, did you read the last paragraph?" I asked.

There wasn't an answer, but the heads of all three witches dove toward the page. "Will that work?" mumbled Jack.

I didn't want to tell him it would, and we had all just seen it. The text discussed something that Mr. Demius and my mother had each explained to me before. The Fire Rune can both create and destroy. Just like in the exercises Mr. Demius used to teach it. First, we create a floor of grass beneath our feet, then we destroy it with the same rune. Each had hinted at the danger of using this rune. I had never considered just tapping into its destructive capability against something I hadn't created with it, especially people. I also never considered what I saw today and had just read in the last paragraph.

Witches can tap into the primary source of magic to amplify the effects of a spell. I knew from several of the council members that Mrs. Roberts, and her now deceased daughter, were Elementalist. When she reached up and the clouds swirled around her, she was tapping into that source. That probably also explained the gust of wind that appeared to carry it. If I were to attempt the same thing, I would have to tap into my telekinetic ability and push the spell outward.

"Marcus, does this apply to all spells?" I yelled, not knowing where he was in the vault.

"Ah, a very astute witch," his voice responded from some distance away. Maybe he was just a few rows, but the echoes made it seem further than that. "That is what I was hoping you would read. That same clause is at the bottom of most every spell in any of these journals." His voice grew nearer, as were his footsteps, which were now no longer just an echo. "Seeing it with that spell, I hoped would help you all make the connection faster."

"What?" Gwen turned around, breaking her trance over the objects on the table. She rushed over to the book to see what we had left her out of. Everyone else dispersed, giving her plenty of room.

Marcus rounded the corner of the bookshelf four rows away from us, carrying three large black leather-bound books under his left arm. "Larissa, do you remember what the council's greatest tool is?"

I thought for a second, and a long list sprang to my mind, and then exited my lips. "Fear, intimidation, ruthlessness, threats– "

Marcus shook his hand, and I stopped. "Those are all suitable answers," he said from just a table away. "And all part of the right answer." With a twist of his body, he threw the three books on the table. They slid a few inches before coming to a stop. "Each is part of control. Control was their greatest tool. Control through all the things you mentioned. You don't have to look that hard at history to find where fear has been used to control a population. It's practically a common occurrence. But the type of control I am talking about is what I know Master Thomas had talked to you about before. Do you remember?"

Master Thomas and I had had many conversations since I met the man. They covered many subjects. Not all of them were related to magic, but there were many about the council, and one of those stood out well. "Controlling what we are allowed to be taught."

"Exactly," he said with a snap that was very Master Thomas-esque. "If none of you had read that part, would any of you have ever thought about trying that? Don't get me wrong. Through the years, some witches have figured it out on their own. Once the council caught wind of it, they isolated or imprisoned them on some kind of trumped up charge. Their best method of control is limiting what they taught you and stunted your potential. Thus, ensuring they maintain a power edge. Just like the runes. Runes themselves were forbidden about two centuries ago because a member of the council at that time couldn't master them. So they made sure no one else could. Luckily," he snapped a point in my direction. "Some families continued to pass down the knowledge."

Marcus paused and arranged the three black leather-bound books in a particular order on the table. "Now, what I am going to teach each of you is how to tap into your natural strength, your source," he said with a fist pump, "to amplify any spell, but not just any spell. Those Mrs. Roberts won't be prepared for." He placed a hand on each of the two outside books and leaned over them. "The spells I am going to teach you are within these books. These are not journals of banned magic."

He paused and looked over at our princess in pink that was busy studying the other text. She appeared oblivious to his presence, and the activities occurring at the end of the same table she read the text at.

"Gwendolyn, I need you to hear this."

I don't know why, but every time I heard her full name, I felt the need to gag.

"In fact, I want you all to hear this. This next part is fascinating. Nathan, Mr. and Mrs. Bolden, Mrs. Norton, Mike, Laura, Pam, Apryl, Jeremy, Brad, Amy. Gather around. I am going to tell you a story that many of you believe you have heard before. Historians have debated for centuries whether these stories were true, or just folklore. If you ask me, there is a sizeable chunk of truth in every myth. That is what makes them fascinating. Fifteen hundred years ago, the world was quite a different place. Clans fought one another for control of entire nations. Leadership changed about as often as the weather did. Those that lasted longer than the blink of an eye became a name that history remembered. The way you lasted was by having the strongest army of that day. These armies comprised men on horseback with swords, long bow archers, and field troops sent into harm to kill their opponents using weapons that sometimes were nothing more than farming tools. The most prosperous of the clans may have something like a trebuchet. The most fortunate had access to something else. See, back in those days, wizards and witches were powerful allies for a clan to have. Those that had them used them to enchant their crops for a plentiful bounty, to predict the future, and as weapons in war. That was the primary use in those days. Magic itself took on a dark flavor in the dark ages. These here," he lifted his hands up, and then slapped down on the covers of the outside books, "are the Merlin diaries. Yes, King Arthur existed. Yes, Merlin existed. No, he did not age backward. That is a story that has been fabricated through other tales about his ability to predict the future. How else to explain someone's ability to predict the future than by saying he already lived it? These are the only written records of Merlin's spells. They are written by his own hand, and one of my favorite texts in this whole place. Inside here are spells I am going to teach you. That, combined with showing you how to tap into your magical center to amplify your strength, should give us an edge, magically. There is another angle that I need to talk to a few of you about."

17

After a brief introduction and explanation of the spells we needed to learn, Marcus lead us away, deeper into the vault, away from the others. There, he and Jack pushed a few tables aside to clear a space for us to practice. They both grunted and groaned as they struggled to move the old solid oak tables. I gave them a little help, but only Samantha noticed.

Behind us, Kevin Bolden was holding class. Who knew, not that I found it all that surprising, that he was a huge Arthurian era nut? To him, it seemed being able to read about the period and events that happened in Merlin's own handwriting was like Christmas morning. Jen called his reaction almost orgasmic. That was more than I wanted to know. Before we left him to his reading, Marcus flipped a few pages in and pointed out a sentence, and then made everyone promise to take that information to their grave. I thought Kevin was going to jump out of his skin when he read it. I have to admit, in all my reading, and all the documentaries I came across flicking channels, that is one place no one had ever looked for signs of Camelot.

Marcus picked five spells from the Merlin diaries. These were among his favorites, or so he reminded us of several times. Learning a new spell was difficult, but not all that challenging. Each of us had learned several dozen spells. I probably had learned a few more than that, being the one that was older than any of the others. To help, Marcus performed a few of them first in what he felt was a scaled down demonstration. It wasn't really his choice. Edward insisted on it, due to how valuable the books and objects in here were. It was a good thing too. Most of the spells involved some kind of fire, lightning, or strong wind. That wasn't all that surprising. Most of the offensive magic that existed did.

The fourth and fifth spells were the ones that were surprising. Marcus hadn't performed these, and I assumed they were more of the same. Why wouldn't they be? That was all we had learned in Mr. Helms' class. I was so wrong. Jack went first and followed Marcus' direction exactly. It was just three words: three rather corny sounding worlds. "Defendo. Repello. Attacko." There was a flash that radiated out away from Jack and along the floor. Several spots on the ground glowed after the flash passed by, then full sized armor wearing and sword wielding hollow faced soldiers grew from those spots. There was nothing to them other than armor and weapon. They snapped at attention in front of Jack. Their weapons were ready to follow his command.

"Now, if you amplify this, you can create a lot more than a dozen of them," remarked Marcus. He walked past Jack and then weaved between his private army. "A lot more. Like several hundreds."

Now I could see the usefulness of this spell in battle. You could summon an army anytime you wanted to. Almost like a guarantee that you would never be outnumbered. That was going to be useful in our battle with Mrs. Roberts. She definitely had the numbers advantage over us.

"I'm going to show you how to pull from your amplifier in a few moments, but first I want everyone else to try that spell while I set up for the fifth spell." He walked back toward the others, leaving me wondering if he had forgotten the spell and needed to refer to the diary again.

I stepped forward and gave it a shot. It worked just like it had for Jack. Gwen was next, and just like the rest of us, she created six soldiers. She stood there and admired her personal army that she had created. Samantha leaned over to me and whispered, "Thank god it doesn't create more Gwens." I had to fight to hold back my laughter. Samantha was next and practically giggled her way through the spell, but still pulled it off with a little extra umph. She had produced an army of nine, not six, like the rest of us.

"Mr. Meridian, I must protest. I don't feel comfortable at all about this."

"Relax Edward. I won't let anything happen." Marcus strolled past Edward, ignoring his concern.

"Sir, it's just too dangerous."

Edward was about to add another challenge when Marcus tossed the two brass balls along the floor. "Ignite!" The two balls shook for a second before they erupted in a whoosh of flames. When the flames disappeared, there appeared, standing there in the vault, two full size, honest to God dragons. One had a red tint on its scales, and the other had a blue tint. Both had large wings that they stretched out to either side before folding them back against their bodies.

The sight of the two beasts sent me scrambling behind the closest bookshelf. I dragged Samantha along with me. It wasn't until we were both behind the shelf when I looked up and saw the red beast looking over the top of it down at us that I realized how frivolous my attempt to find protection was.

"Whoa!" I heard Mike exclaim. Then there was the shuffling of many feet on the floor, along with the screech of chairs and tables moving out of the way.

"Return!" Marcus commanded, and both dragons disappeared.

I took a timid look around my bookshelf turned shield. There, sitting on the floor, were two brass balls. They looked rather simple and shiny. Not a scratching or spot of tarnish on them.

"These were Merlin's favorite," Marcus explained, walking over picking up both balls. "Most know the stories of King Arthur and Merlin, but most don't remember Merlin was the magical advisor to Arthur's father, Uther Pendragon. Without Merlin, it is very possible that Uther would have been overrun and ousted, or killed, and there absolutely wouldn't be Arthur. He would often call upon Merlin for help in battle, so Merlin created and imprisoned these two dragons that he would unleash from what seemed like nowhere against opposing forces. I believe you would agree it was a rather effective counterattack, especially if you consider they breathe fire. It was rather symbolic, a pair of dragons for Pendragon, or loosely translated, the head dragon."

I crept around the bookshelf, holding on to Samantha. I thought I had seen everything, but I guess I hadn't. There was a question dancing on my tongue that had to be asked. "Are dragons real?"

"They used to be. Back in the old world, but not anymore. These are just magic." He walked toward me, and I retreated a few steps. I had to admit I was leery about those two brass balls and what they contained inside.

"Edward, is he joking? Were there dragons?" Lisa asked.

"They were magnificent creatures. The last of which died off over 800 years ago. They had a bit of a temper."

I stood there in shock, along with everyone else. We each shared a similar look with one another. What else was there in the world that I didn't know about? That was a question I found myself a little afraid to ask. It wasn't the question I was leery of; it was the answer. I wasn't sure I was ready to know.

Marcus walked through everyone until he reached me. With his left hand, he reached out and grabbed my right hand, pulling it out away from my side. Then he placed what he carried in his right hand in my open palm. The brass balls felt cold on my palm, but other than that were very ordinary. "Larissa, I want you to have these. When the time is right, you will wield them."

I was about to protest when Gwen piped up and asked, "Why her?" She crossed both arms and plastered a look on her face we had all seen many times before. It hadn't been there all day, but it seemed our reprieve was over, and the old Gwen was back.

"Well, Gwendolyn," Marcus started, staring right into my eyes. "Larissa is who I trust."

His words cut her deeply, and it showed. She shrank back through the group and hid behind Mike. He made several attempts to foil her plan, but she stuck to him like glue, which brought a look of annoyance to both his and Laura's face. I was too distracted and shocked to take any enjoyment in Gwen's suffering.

"I don't—"

"I know," Marcus said, closing my hand around the balls. "It has to be you, but we still have a lot of training to do." He let go of my hand and backed away to the center of the room, where he clasped his hands and looked around. "I hope each of you are comfortable with the spells I gave you. Now we need to build on that. I need you to tap into your primary source of magic and amplify. Allow me to show you."

This part was easier said than done. What Marcus showed us looked easy and effortless, but there was a problem. He couldn't tell us how he did it. I guess to him, it was like a fish trying to describe swimming or a human describing how to breathe. It just happened. Though he admitted it took him hours of practice before it worked for the first time. He started working with Lisa and me first. His logic there was, our big "aha" moment would most likely be something physical that all could see. I guess I understood. Chances were, if I did this, I would push or throw something across the room. Lisa, with her dark magic, I wasn't sure what she would do, but most of her spells had a bit of a dark flair to them, spinning clouds and lightning flashes.

It didn't take long before I felt a strange and unpleasant déjà vu. Only this time, nothing was clogging me up and preventing me from performing the magic. I was really back at square one with this skill, but I wasn't alone. Lisa stood next to me, just about as frustrated as I was. She let hers show through several loud exhales. I let mine show by sending Marcus into a bookshelf when he told us to—just magic. Whatever that meant.

Marcus described it as a feeling of something welling up from inside. I felt something welling up inside, but it wasn't magic. It was frustration; a feeling I knew all too well. He made it sound like it just happened, and for him it probably did, and it probably would for us as well after years and years of use. He had to have learned somehow.

"Marcus, this isn't working." My hands slammed down against my side. "How did you do this the first time?"

"I don't know," he replied with a shrug. "It's been a while. I think I was seven... no, make that nine, and I did it just like you guys are, doing a core element of my magic, and then adding the spell to it."

"Wait. Wait. Wait.", I said, shaking my head while my hand cut across the air. "What do you mean, doing a core element of our magic?"

Marcus looked at each of us curiously. "Like I told you before. Use something from your core magic and add to it. For you Larissa, it would be a telekentic push, and then add the spell to it."

"You didn't say that," I informed him.

"Yea," Lisa complained. "All you said was, let it build up inside and release it with the spell."

"Well yes. Use your core magic, and when you feel it well up, release it."

I let something well up alright, and I used it to give Marcus another shove. I didn't send him to the bookshelf behind him this time. It was just a few feet, but I wanted to make sure he knew how I felt.

"Maybe I missed that," he conceded. "Give it a try." Marcus pointed at Lisa, and she was more than happy to comply. I stood there and watched her, as did everyone else. At first there was nothing, then I noticed the hint of dark clouds formed above her. It didn't take more than a second for those hints of clouds to turn into dark spirits circling above her. I took a few steps back after already having a few encounters with them during her ascension ceremony. A smile crept across Lisa's face, and then it happened. A bolt of purple lightning hit the floor, cracking it open. The crack spread, forming a chasm. Steam rose from deep down, followed by several hands.

Gwen shrieked.

"Very good, Lisa," Marcus praised. "Go ahead and put it away."

In a snap, the chasm closed, and the crack in the floor disappeared. Along with it, the spirits dissipated into thin air.

"Actually, that was kind of easy," Lisa crowed, walking back toward the others. I gave her my usual mature response and stuck my tongue out at her.

"Larissa, now it's your turn, but instead of the spell I gave you, I want you to try the troupe de force."

"The what?" I asked, looking back at him like he had two heads. I knew English and had been lectured more than once about the need for me to brush up on my Latin, but I was quite sure that was neither. It sounded French to me.

"The spell I showed you to create an army. Push out," Marcus pushed out with both arms, "and then cast the spell."

"All right," I said, unsure. It had looked easy for Lisa, and what I had learned was many things were easy for her. She can take all that practice she talks about and shove it. I honestly believed she had a knack for magic that made learning new skills, like divination, a little easier.

"Everyone, back up and give her some room." Marcus flapped his arms like he was trying to take flight. The movement ushered everyone back quite a way. I locked eyes with Nathan for a split second. He still wasn't here with us, but he wasn't completely gone, either. He looked on with a half-interested expression peeking out from the dread and mourn he wore. "This is going to be something."

I did just as Marcus had instructed and performed a little push. Nothing big, just a little shove, and relied on an old technique I used when I was younger and imagined a wave moving out from me. This time, I didn't just see it in my imagination. I saw it playing with the fabric of the world. I strengthened it a little and let the edges of it creep out toward where Marcus and the others stood. A few stumbled backward, and I pulled it back. Then I thought, here goes nothing. "Defendo. Repello. Attacko."

Bang. There were no glowing spots on the floor. There were no soldiers that grew into a full-size. There was an entire army of knights in armor and swords snapping to attention in unison. The clang of their suits echoed in the vault as a single sound. A row of horseback soldiers appeared behind them. I turned to look at them, and each of them turned in the same direction.

"The stronger–" Marcus started, walking toward me, but the quick snap of a sword almost did more than cut off his statement. Marcus was a little faster and had moved twenty feet or more back in the blink of an eye before the blade reached its intended target.

"Return!" I snapped. The soldiers followed my command and disappeared just as fast as they appeared.

"As I was saying. The stronger the magic behind the spell, the greater the numbers, and the greater their aggression."

"That makes you the perfect candidate to wield it," Mike remarked. Apryl nodded her agreement, but it appeared Marcus had a different plan in mind. He shook his head as he passed both of them.

"The dragons are hers. She can use it if she likes, but I think that is one for Mr. Nash. I just wanted to give him an example of what is possible. A target to shoot for, per se. Mr. Nash, let's see what you can do."

Jack stood there for a moment while we all watched.

"Any time you're ready, Mr. Nash, but the world doesn't have all day."

Jack stood there for a moment before he looked down at his hands. "I don't know how—"

Marcus moved forward and leaned back against the table that was directly in front of Jack. "Jack. Just focus on your core magic. This is the part that comes naturally to you, so this should be the easiest part."

Again, Jack looked down at his hands.

Marcus jumped off the table and leaned forward toward Jack. "Mr. Nash. What is your primary magic?"

"I'm not sure," he answered, still looking down at his hands. There was an unsure tremble in his voice. "I'm an empath. That's what I do best, but Mrs. Tenderschott..." Jack's voice went from a tremble to a full-on quiver at the mere mention of her name. He wasn't alone. There were a few sniffs around, and the room took on a heavier feeling. Jack sucked in a huge gulp of air and did his best to right himself. "Mrs. Tenderschott said my secondary was elemental, natural like plants and stuff."

"All right, then let's try this. Have you ever created a creeping vine? Every witch has done that from time to time to annoy someone across the room."

Jack nodded as he finally looked up at Marcus. When he did, he jerked back. I don't believe Jack knew Marcus was only about six inches away from him the whole time they were talking.

"Then let's try it, shall we?" Marcus leaned back against the table, giving Jack some room. He crossed his arms.

From back amongst the gallery of vampires, Pamela urged. "Come on Jack. You can do this." I glanced back fast enough to see the look Apryl gave her.

Jack shook his hands out and straightened his posture. With his eyes closed, I saw a vine form on the ground around his feet, but that was as far as it went. Not exactly all that impressive. Jack commanded, "Defendo. Repello. Attacko."

Four spots on the floor in front of him gave off a blue glow before soldiers appeared in each spot, and that was it. Just four of them, and they disappeared rather quickly. Marcus let his head collapse, shaking it back and forth.

"That wasn't strong enough. I barely felt the magic flowing from you. You need to try harder. Go again."

"Come on Jack." This time, Clay had joined Jack's cheering section. It wasn't long before Brad, Jen, and Kevin were all piping in. Maybe that was what he needed, a boost of confidence. He cracked a smile before he set off on his second attempt.

Maybe he needed more than that. To me, the vine looked even shorter this time, and when he uttered the spell this time, only two appeared, and one of the two was missing a weapon.

"Jack, come on. You have to give it more," Marcus groaned. He rubbed both hands down his face and then addressed Jack. "You have to focus and give it everything you have. Think about what is at stake. Think about what they just did to people you care about."

Now I felt like I was sitting outside looking in at my life. I had heard similar speeches many times, and I knew most of the time they did more harm than good. Adding that type of stress on top of someone doesn't encourage the magic to flow freely. Maybe if Marcus made Jack mad, it would. That seemed to work for me.

"Master Merdian. Could it be because Jack hasn't ascended?" Lisa suggested.

"You haven't ascended yet?"

"Not yet," replied Jack.

"What about you?" Marcus asked again, turning to direct the question back at Gwen, who was still back with the others. She shook her head. "Well then," he exclaimed. "That explains everything. You are barely tapping into what you can do." Marcus turned and walked away from us. I was about to move to console Jack. It looked like he was going to have to sit this one out. I could tell that the realization had already started to eat at him. Marcus stopped and snapped around, looking at Samantha. "What about you?"

Samantha looked over at me, and Marcus followed her gaze.

"Unsure."

"Of course," Marcus conceded with a huff, and stopped right where he was. "Go ahead and give it a try. Just like your mother."

Samantha stood up straight, and then in a blink of an eye I watched as a blue wave emanated from her. She showed good control, stopping it before it touched anyone. Then she whispered, "Defendo. Repello. Attacko." In a flash, there were three dozen soldiers standing there at complete attention. Just as easily as she had summoned them, she dismissed them. "Return."

"Okay, good. So only two of you need this. Gwendolyn and Jack follow me."

18

"Now, to pick the perfect one for you," Marcus said, surveying the objects on the table.

"Perfect what?" Jack asked.

"Wands. Since you have yet to ascend, you need a magic enhancer," Marcus responded. His hand hovered over each object on the table as if he was feeling its power. "The secret is you have to find one that matches the temperament and ability of the person. The council banned wands during the last century. Which means a witch would have to wait for their ascension to unlock their real potential. The problem with that was it was usually around the age in which most witches stopped training. That was why they created wands. To let a witch tap into it, in a controlled manner, while they were being trained. That made sure you were truly ready."

"Ready for what?" Gwen asked.

"To be a real witch," Marcus answered with a look over his shoulder at us. "Most of the witches nowadays aren't real witches. They are just shells of what we used to be. But you already know that, don't you, Larissa?"

I swallowed hard as the gaze of every set of eyes in the vault landed on me. There was a brief temptation to summon my army and take off running, but I dismissed that. "I do." I had to admit that in front of everyone, and I watched as their faces morphed into the looks that I was afraid I would see. "It's not that," I blurted, hoping to cut them off at the road they were about to cross in believing I felt I was better than all of them. "I'm not one either. Master Thomas and Mr. Demius explained it to me a while ago. The council has restricted magic and what we could be taught, and because of that, we were losing ourselves."

"Well, you are closer than anyone else I know," Marcus commented, sending a cringe up my spine while I waited for the looks to return. "Your mother taught you runes which aren't taught formally. But that is something we are going to correct. It is a new age of witches, my friends," Marcus announced, spinning around with his arms held out wide. "Everything is going to be better."

Marcus returned his hand to the table and again hovered it over the wands. It dropped low, almost touching two or three of them before moving on, but then it stopped, reached down, and picked one up. The one his hand chose had a straight shaft, but a gnarled up handle. He held it up, tip pointing to the sky, and studied it. Then he turned it length wise and surveyed it while running a finger down its entire length. The last check was looking at it straight down the tip. Once satisfied, he gave it a furious swipe through the air, and pointed it up in the air. "Illuminate."

A flash shot out of the tip of it and became the second sun. It was so bright I even felt my hand burn as I used it to shield my eyes. Most did the same, but a few looked away. Edward turned away, unable to shield himself.

"This should do nicely, but we need to be careful. Mr. Nash, follow me for a second." Marcus started toward the area he had cleared for our impromptu training. Lisa and Gwen followed, but Marcus turned and stopped them. "Stay back, for just a second."

When they reached the cleared space, Marcus grabbed Jack's hand without even asking. He yanked it straight out and turned his hand, palm up. Then he placed the wand gently in Jack's hand and curled his fingers around it. Marcus yanked his hand back and took two quick steps backward. Jack's heart rate jumped, as did that of every human in the room, including Marcus Meridian.

"Mr. Nash, do as I just did, but be sure to focus carefully."

Jack turned the wand around to examine it just as Marcus had moments earlier.

"No! No!" Marcus stormed forward and yanked the wand from his hand. Then yanked Jack's hand back out straight and placed it in its palm and closed his fingers around it. "You'll probably blast a hole through your skull if you try that again. Hold it pointing that direction, and say 'Illuminate'." Marcus stepped back again, but this time not as fast as before. He still gave Jack space.

"Illuminate!" Jack's voice cracked under the pressure, and his heart skipped a few beats once he uttered the word, but just like when Marcus performed the same trick, a bright flash shot out, illuminating the vault. This time, I turned away from the light.

"Good. You didn't blow your hand off." Marcus walked back to the table, turning his attention to the objects. His hand hovered over them again. "The process of assigning a wand to a witch is supposed to be a several month long process, and the wand actually selects the witch. We don't have that kind of time, so we will do... the... best... we... can." His hand stopped and picked up an aged, sundried, dainty wand, and began his inspection. "Gwendolyn, your turn."

Gwen gasped and made an unsteady step forward.

"Come along." Urged Marcus. He had already reached the open area and stood there waiting for her.

"If we're lucky, it will blow her hand off," Apryl whispered. Her comment earned her a slap upside the back of the head from Jen, and a few off looks from the others. Samantha hid a giggle behind her hand, as did Amy, who stood next to her. I channeled my inner mother and gave them both an admonishing look. It must have worked, because both let their eyes droop as Samantha mouthed an apology.

Gwen finally reached Marcus, and she held her hand out in front of her, waiting for him to place the wand in it. He did and closed her fingers around it. It trembled wildly, and Marcus gripped her hand again and held it steady. He spoke to her, but I couldn't hear what they said. All I could see was Gwen's huge fear-filled eyes watching his face. He let go and backed away.

"Illuminate!" Gwen called out. Her body flinched as the flash blasted from the end of the wand and up in the air high above the vault. I turned again, as did most of the vampires. Seeing it didn't blow her hand off, I guessed that was a match.

Marcus called Jack down to where he and Gwen stood. My guess was it was their turn, now that he had found the wands that match them.

"Why do I have to use a wand?" Jack complained as he passed me on the way to his lesson.

"Trade you. I still have a jar left of that sludge I had to drink."

Jack looked at me, and then held up his wand in front of his face and kissed it. "I love you wand."

With the magic excitement done for the moment. Kevin returned to the Merlin diaries. Clay and Brad appeared to share his enthusiasm as they followed. Jeremy followed them too, but didn't appear as eager as the others to rejoin the history lesson. Mike sat down in a chair behind Laura and rubbed her shoulders. She sat at a table and wept along with Jen, Apryl, Pam, and Marie, who all appeared to share the same emotion. Jen and Marie spoke while the others wiped tears from their cheeks. Occasionally, Jen and Marie paused long enough to wipe away their own. I didn't know how it happened. Maybe it was the absence of anything else, but the sadness of what had happened crept back in. That had to be it. Since we left the grand entry, Marcus had given us something to focus on.

I looked at Samantha and Amy, and the grins and giggles that were there moments ago were gone. Both were looking to their right at a single solitary figure that stood alone next to the table of objects. I went over and hugged him, hoping to feel something more than just a person standing there, allowing me to hold him. Nathan's head dipped and landed against my neck, and his arms wrapped around me, and he opened up. It started slowly and quietly, but then it grew. What inner strength he had used to hold himself together had finally failed him. The floodgates were open.

"I'm going to make her pay for what she did," I whispered into his ear.

"Not if I do it first," he responded in a cutting tone. I left it alone, knowing it would have to be me. She was too much for him to take her on alone, but this wasn't the time for me to remind him of that. It wasn't the time for me to push back on his nature to jump in the way of danger, something he had done many times. He needed this anger. It would give him strength.

Another set of arms wrapped around us, and I turned my head to see Samantha. Then I felt someone wrap their arms around our waist. That had to be Amy. Nathan let go of me with one of his arms, and then wrapped it around both of them and pulled them in closer. He would need us, too. We would give him strength.

"I'm so sorry, dad," Samantha said.

Nathan reached up and rubbed the back of her head before kissing her on the forehead. Then he buried his head against my neck. There was no doubt he was still hurting, and I knew that hurt would last for a long time. I was familiar with that feeling, but not completely, and that stopped me from trying to console him further. My parents were killed, but what had happened to me robbed me of the chance of mourning them. I mourned Thomas Norton, but I quickly realized he wasn't really my father. Not that learning that fact diminished the hurt. It still hurt. So much was happening at that time, I didn't really have time to let it soak in. The worst hurt I had ever felt was when Nathan refused to return home with me. The difference there was, he wasn't gone, and there was a chance I was going to see him again. That didn't exist for Nathan. That didn't exist for any of us.

"Larissa, a word." Marcus requested, returning from where Jack and Gwen continued their training.

I loosened my grip on Nathan, but he didn't. He tightened his, but only for a second. Slowly his grip let me go, and Amy snuck in where I was, and Nathan welcomed her with open arms.

"How's he doing?" Marcus asked as I met him halfway.

"About as you would expect." It was a generic answer, but what else was I supposed to say?

"It's devastating to lose one's parents. A rogue witch killed mine when I was about his age."

"I didn't know that."

"Not that you should," Marcus replied rather matter-of-factly. "We were in exile. News of our family was rarely reported or discussed in the community, but I still remember that day just as clearly as the day it happened. Nathan will never forget what happened. What is important is to not let it define him. You need to help him with that."

"Me? How?" The question I asked was a legitimate one. I didn't have a clue how to do that, and I wasn't even sure what he meant about it defining Nathan. Was he seeing a future where Nathan would go around hunting witches just because of what happened to his mother? That wasn't who Nathan was. I knew that.

"Yes you. Remind him that there is a life ahead of him. Make him be present for you and Samantha. Don't worry. I will help too. This is partially my fault. I should have never stood for so long on the sideline and allowed things to deteriorate in our world this bad."

I was about to correct Marcus and tell him it wasn't his fault, that it was mine, but he changed the subject to a very different subject.

"But that's not what I wanted to talk to you about. We have a problem. This," he pointed at our gathered group, "is no match for what we are walking into. We are going to need more help."

I looked around and realized he was right. If we could corner just Mrs. Roberts, we would have more than a chance, but the likelihood of that happening was next to nothing. She had arrived with a rather large army, and that was probably what we were going to find, but we had our own. "What about the spells?"

He shook his head. "Magical soldiers are more of a distraction that will discourage and chase off some of her numbers. In a true battle against witches, they won't amount to much. We need real people. We need numbers."

I looked around again. Numbers were not something we had. "What about the rogue witches?"

He dismissed that idea a little too quickly for my liking. "No. They are too scattered. Especially after what happened here. You might get a few, but that is it."

"Can't you talk to them?"

"Sure. I can put it on the agenda of the next Roque witch conference." Sarcasm dripped from every word. Marcus turned and looked deep into my eyes and explained, "Larissa. These witches have all been betrayed by the council and others more than once. They are more than happy to find a hole somewhere in the world to disappear into and live out the rest of their life, just like they were before. The time it would take to convince them to unite would be immense, and we don't have that."

"That's not true, and you know that," I firmly rebutted. "The camp. That wasn't exactly a hole. They were all together. Following you!" I poked Marcus right in the chest, causing him to stumble back from the force of my finger.

Marcus straightened his white shirt out, and returned the favor, sort of. Instead of poking me in the chest, he pointed his finger right at me, stopping just a few millimeters away. "Wrong. They were following you. What you did gave them the hope that times were changing. But we are talking about people who have been terrorized for centuries. What Mrs. Robert did here shattered that hope."

My head dropped from his gaze. Let's go ahead and add hopelessness to all the other horrible emotions I was feeling at the moment. Why not? I think it was the only one left.

"Hey," Marcus whispered. "She shattered that hope for them, but not me. I believe you can still do this, and once they see it. They will come back, and they will follow you. Just like I will."

"I don't want anyone to follow me–" I explained as I looked back up into his eyes.

"Yes, I know. Benjamin told me that many times. You just want a peaceful life. Larissa, you know this better than anyone that this is the only path to that."

I looked away, while I nodded an agreement. He was right. Just when I first started to understand that, the path seemed easier. I was just to challenge for supreme. Now we were locked in a war that had cost us more than what my happiness was worth. I shuddered at that very thought, which appeared selfish on the surface. How could I compare my happiness to the deaths of those we loved so dearly? I couldn't. I forced myself to remember it wasn't just about my happiness, though. It was a question of freedom and peace for everyone, and that included both witches and vampires. A historical quote came to my mind about how the tree of liberty needed to be refreshed with the blood of patriots and tyrants. Thank you, Mr. Norton, and his obsession with American history. I had a feeling he and Kevin Bolden would have gotten along just fine. The way I looked at it, too many patriots had paid their toll. Now it was the tyrant's turn, and I had a feeling I knew where to find one.

"I'll reach out to see who I can muster," Marcus conceded. He sounded a little defeated when he added, "It will just be a drop of the bucket compared to what we need."

I looked at Jack and Gwen, still practicing with their wands, Lisa and Samantha now practicing on their own, Nathan sitting with Amy on his lap with arms latched around his neck trying to hug the grief from him, the two tables of vampires consoling one another, another reading furiously through an old text of someone we all thought was just a legend before now while my hand rolled the two brass balls around and around subconsciously. Seeing all that ignited a spark inside.

"I have an idea."

19

"Larissa, I'm not sure this is such a good idea."

I looked over at Jen and asked, "Do we have any other options?"

"No."

"Well, then." I reached up and grabbed the brass knocker with my right hand and gave it a hefty swing to knock on the large double doors of the main entry of the white sugar plantation home. It was late, probably a little after four in the morning, but I knew the residents here didn't keep normal business hours. Through the ornamental glass in the doors, I spied several sources of lights still on, both down the hall and in the study that also served as an office, and that was just on the main floor. Both the second and third floor had a splattering of rooms with lights on. The first movement came from the stairs. First it was just a shadow, then the figure of an older gentleman in a t-shirt and jeans crossed in front of the lights and descended the stairs. I recognized him from my last visit here and felt bad I had woken poor Clarence. I doubt he had regular sleep hours, seeing who he worked for.

Clarence was halfway down the stairs when another figure appeared in the hall on the bottom floor. It was unmistakable who that was. She glided down the hall and said something to Clarence that sent him back up the stairs. I backed away from the door, not wanting to be caught peering through the glass. I didn't want it to appear that I was an intruder, considering we were here to ask for help. The door cracked open, and we were face to face with a very surprised Theodora Raudeau.

"Oh," she gasped, and then reached forward and yanked us all inside before closing the door briskly behind us. It produced a breeze that carried the cool night air past us and into the warm confines of her home. "What are you doing here?" She rushed back to her door and looked out through the glass, bracing herself on her hands as she looked. "What if someone saw you?"

"We need your help," I responded, answering her first question and ignoring her second. No one saw us. How could they? It wasn't like we had walked all the way up her sidewalk. We exited a portal. I opened it right at her door to avoid just that.

"And why should I help you?" Theodora said as she backed away from the door. There was an edge to her voice. It was sharp, not its normal smooth and seductive crooning. She turned and walked through us. "Why would I help witches?" She started her question looking at me, but before she finished it, she had shifted her focus to Marcus. I had done my best to disguise him, but she somehow saw right through it.

"Theodora what the witches have done is wrong, but we can stop them."

"Then why haven't you?" she asked, again looking right at Marcus. "I know you. You look familiar."

"I don't believe we've met," Marcus responded, confused. I let my illusion fall from him. There was no reason to hide him now.

"Not in this life, but one in the past. Perhaps your father, or grandfather." She brought both of her hands together in contemplation, just below her chin. The wheels turned inside, working through the memories of a lifetime that had spanned centuries. When the right one came to the front, I saw the lights come on behind her black eyes. "You're a Meridian, aren't you?"

"Yes ma'am. Marcus Merdian at your service." Marcus semi-bowed, and then stood up, extending his hand to Theodora. She took it while presenting her own.

"I met what I believe would have been your great grandfather while he was on the council. Long before your family's falling out with the council. Those were very different times."

"They were indeed," Marcus agreed. Then, as she turned away from him, he stepped forward and offered. "We can return things to how they were then. We can bring our worlds back to the golden era." He was trying harder than any used car salesman I had ever seen on television, but it didn't appear Theodora was buying.

"Smoke and whispers. It's all smoke and whispers." Theodora turned and walked down the hall. Her heels clicked lightly on the deep wood floors. "Come. Let's not stand there in the entry. We can talk more about your smoke and whispers."

Marcus, Apryl, Samantha, and I followed her. I didn't want to overwhelm Theodora by bringing everyone. There was also the concern about how she would react to my presence. If things went sideways, I didn't want a lot of people here. It would be more than awkward. It could be dangerous. Marcus was needed for the conversation we were about to have. Apryl and Samantha were just tagalongs. Samantha didn't want to miss a chance to meet Theodora after how I had described her. So far, Theodora hadn't disappointed. She was just as I remembered, except maybe colder.

"Sit," she instructed as we entered the library section of her home office. Samantha and I sat on one side. Apryl and Marcus on the other. Theodora took the same chair there in the middle as she had the last time I was here. She sat and crossed her legs, tugging at her black sequined dress to allow it to hang freely down to the floor. Then she placed both hands on her knee. "So, you need my help? I have to admit, I'm a little reluctant to even entertain the notion, but I will listen." There was a frigidness to her face.

I gave Marcus a look to offer the floor to him, but he returned one relinquishing that responsibility. This was my idea. Though he didn't object when I first proposed it. He was rather interested in the idea, and even upbeat about the possibility. The way I saw it, this was the only option we had. How viable was it? Well, that was something I was about to find out.

"I guess I should ask, how much do you know about all that is going on?" Theodora had always seemed rather well connected in each of our past conversations. I needed to know how much she knew, to know how many gaps I needed to fill in.

"I know enough to know the world is coming unhinged."

I leaned forward and asked again, echoing her bitter tone. "How much do you know?"

Her body jerked in response to either my question or my tone. "Well, I know about hundreds of unjust and atrocious murders of our people by witches. What else is there?" She raised a finger up, with a perfectly painted nail, and pointed it right at me, and then at Marcus. "If you are here to provide some justification, you better leave now, while I am still controlling myself."

"Not at all," Marcus finally answered. "There is no excuse, and no rationale that explains any of this, and we are trying to stop it."

"Then work with your precious council," Theodora spat. She shifted in her seat, switching her legs.

"She doesn't know," Marcus said, repeating what I was thinking as he looked across the room at me.

"I don't know what?" Theodora asked. Her tone had thawed slightly, as had her posture. She leaned forward. Almost interested.

"There is no council. Mrs. Wintercrest is no longer the supreme. She is in a cell in Mordin where I put her. Her abilities as a witch left her years ago, and another witch has been propping her up. In return, her daughter was to become the next supreme." I paused to see if Theodora had any questions. There was a great bit more to the story, but I felt it was a lot to throw at someone all at once. After a few seconds of silence, and no follow-up questions, I continued. "She, Mrs. Roberts, started the war with the vampires and rogue witches to eliminate the threat and paving the way for her daughter's rise to power. The only problem, I killed her."

"It sounds like you did the world a favor," Theodora interjected, but I held up my hand to stop any additional commentary. This next part would hit her like a ton of bricks.

"In revenge, she led her followers in an attack against our coven, killing all the instructors, most of the witches there, and the entire council. Including Benjamin."

The load of bricks fell on her and sent a hand up, covering her mouth. I knew hearing that name would make it more personal to her. Not that what was going on didn't already feel personal. There was no doubt she knew vampires that had been murdered, as she correctly called it.

"Theodora. She will not stop until she has control of everything. The witches, the vampires, and whoever else. She rescued Jean from our coven. I don't know why, but I know I don't want to find out."

"She killed Master Thomas? Ben?" Theodora whispered with a hint of a tremble in her voice.

"Yes. She killed Master Thomas, our head mistress, Mrs. Saxon. Mrs. Tenderschott, Mr. Demius, Mr. Helms, many more, and many of our fellow students."

"She used forbidden magic to do it, just like she is against the vampires with the Fires of Ruel. She has to be stopped." Marcus added.

"Then stop her," Theodora insisted. "You are both capable witches. Put an end to her."

"It's not that simple," Marcus replied.

"Sure, it is," Theodora argued. "You handled Jean. Just set a trap for her, just like you did him."

"No, it's not," Marcus forcefully rebutted. "She has an army of witches out there attacking both your and my kind right now. She has to be stopped, but with her supporters surrounding and following who they believe is the next witch to be the supreme, we can't."

"All it takes to rule the world of witches is to show them a new trick, I guess," Theodora remarked. I saw Marcus lean forward to react. His heart rate spiked. I felt it loud and clear across the room. That comment had cut him somewhere deep where his honor sat. I had ignored it. There was something else brewing in my mind.

"Maybe it is," I wondered aloud.

"Maybe what is?" Marcus asked in a huff. He was about to lay into Theodora after her little comment, and I caught a little of that energy in his response to what I had said.

"Maybe it is that simple." I leaned forward and stared at a spot on the floor. The idea behind my statement percolated in my head. There was a rational thought behind my little outburst, and it was gaining momentum. "Maybe we don't have to fight everyone." I started, still focused on the same spot. This focus, God I hated that word, helped the thoughts flow. "Maybe we just have to fight her, Mrs. Roberts."

I lifted my head and looked to make sure everyone was paying attention. They were, intensely. "If someone were to defeat Mrs. Roberts in front of everyone. What would that do?" I looked at Marcus to make sure he knew the question was directed at him.

That didn't stop Apryl from chiming in. "I think you have watched too many movies with Mr. Bolden."

Marcus held up his hand to stop any more comments from the peanut gallery as his eyes appeared to find my favorite spot on the floor. His thoughts were gathering too, and I felt encouraged that my idea wasn't immediately slapped down. I hadn't laid out my plan completely, but he seemed to understand where my mind was heading.

"It might," he muttered before looking up at me, and then at Theodora. "It's hard to say how they would all react, but in a traditional setting, that would weaken her and elevate you. You would both be seen on equal footing and open the door for a true challenge."

"You're talking about the Test of the Seven Wonders, aren't you?" Samantha asked.

Marcus nodded. "No, not exactly. I believe these witches are following who they believe is their supreme because of how powerful Mrs. Roberts is. If someone were to show themselves to be more capable, or even just confront her and show her weak, then maybe. Whatever we do, I believe Larissa is right. It needs to be a spectacle in front of everyone."

"You're missing something big here," Samantha spouted. Her hand slapped down on her lap. "All those witches won't let you just walk right up to that bitch, and there are hundreds of them."

"First, language." I admonished her, lightly looking at her, but I agreed with her choice of words. "Second," I started and looked at Theodora, "she's right. We are seriously outnumbered here, and that is why we are here. As long as Mrs. Roberts is there, our worlds, witches and vampires alike, will not know peace. I need your help. I need the help of all the vampires to stand against her and end this."

"You practiced that, didn't you?" Theodora asked.

"No," I responded sternly.

Theodora stood up and motioned for me to come with her. She stepped away from her chair and walked toward the bank of doors that led out to her garden walkway. Marcus and Samantha stood up to follow. When Theodora noticed them, she stopped and commanded, "Stay. I need to speak with Miss Dubois, alone."

Both stood and watched as we made our way to the door. Theodora reached forward and opened it. She walked through, leaving it open for me to follow. I looked back and saw concern in Samantha's eyes. I mouthed a reassuring, "It's okay. I'll be right back."

I followed her out into the cool night air that was bathed in the aroma of jasmine. It was such a pleasant smell that took me back to my youth and relaxed me. Theodora paused her stroll long enough for me to catch up. Once I was by her side, she continued. "So, let me get this straight. You want me to approach the elders on your behalf and request that they ask their people to become cannon fodder?" Her head turned in my direction as she continued walking.

I looked straight ahead as we walked past a wall of vines. "No. I am asking you to approach the elders to ask their people to take the fight to Mrs. Roberts. There is a difference. They can stand around and wait to be hunted down, or they can fight and put a stop to this."

"Good point." Her head nodded before turning back to look straight ahead. "But that is assuming you can truly end this. As we have already seen, the witches have the upper hand in every encounter."

I stopped and reached over and grabbed Theodora by the hand. She stopped and looked shocked before yanking her hand from my grasp. "I can. I can end this. I just need help to have a chance."

Theodora pursed her ruby red lips and shook her head slightly as one hand reached up and caressed my cheek. "My, you are a confident one. If only I were that confident, but I'm not. Larissa, you are just one witch."

I shook off her caressing hand, not at all happy with her condescending tone and look. The old Larissa wanted to fire back, but I knew that wouldn't help. If anything, it would show her I was immature, further fueling how she just treated me. I wanted a few beats before I responded. Mostly to reword what I wanted to say to remove any of the vinegar I wanted to add to it. "You are right. I am one witch, but I am not just any witch. I am both a witch and a vampire. I have to consider what is best for both of my people, and what is happening now, is not it."

"Your people? That's funny." Theodora responded, almost sounding annoyed. She stepped to continue her stroll, but I wasn't done yet, and grabbed her, yanking her to a stop. Again, she shook her hand free, this time a little more vigorously than before. "Larissa, when you were here, you were more focused on being a witch, and even turned your back on your vampire brethren. They may be grooming you to be the supreme of the witches, but let me remind you, we don't have a leader, and we don't need one. Even if we had one, why would it be you? You rarely care about this side of you. This is about revenge, pure and simple. Just another blood war, and we don't want to be any part of it."

"That's where you're wrong," I roared. "All of it. You are wrong about all of it. There is a leader. Your own boyfriend said it. Vampires follow who appears strongest, and so far, they have been following the wrong examples. That is also how Jean St. Claire rose to power in New Orleans."

"How dare you bring him up!" Theodora stormed off, but that didn't stop me. I kept yelling my argument behind her.

"A leader doesn't always have to have a title or wear a fancy robe. A leader can identify themselves through their actions. They show there are more important considerations than just what is best for the individual. It's about what is best for all, even if that means sacrificing what is best for them. As things are now. I could take my family and go away someplace no one will ever find us and hide. Don't think for one moment I haven't considered that many times. I have, and it's alluring. But I feel the weight of everyone we've lost and those continuing to suffer, and I owe it to them to end this. I owe it to my parents to restore witches to what they used to be. I owe it to Master Thomas to restore the council to what it used to be. I owe it to all my friends that are vampires to end this war and let them live in peace. You may think I turned my back on being a vampire, and only focused on being a witch. I agree, it may look that way, but that is only because that is the path to fixing everything for both worlds. Neither world will live in peace on their current paths."

Theodora stopped and bowed her head. "Do you think you can repeat that speech if I arrange a meeting?"

20

"So now what?" Samantha asked, pacing behind me and making me nervous.

I reached back and grabbed her. "Have a seat, please?" My request sounded more like a request than it really was. If Samantha didn't take the empty seat next to me, I was going to yank her down into it. Luckily, she took it and sat down next to me at the table with the rest of us. It was the same table Theodora, and I sat at the last time the Elders were in a conference about one of my requests. We were in luck. With everything going on, they and what remained of their followers came here for protection. The Elders stayed in one of Theodora's guest houses. Other vampires around New Orleans, ones Theodora called experts at blending in, took in what amounted to refugees that arrived with them.

"I still can't believe she is your daughter." Theodora remarked. She had become enamored with Samantha since I made the official introduction. "I mean, I see the resemblance. It is remarkable how much she looks like you, but it was only what? A few months."

"Well, what was it you reminded me of over and over about?"

"Oh, I know, but this is extraordinary."

"By my count, I am older than twenty-one, so..." Samantha eyed Apryl's Bloody Mary, made with fresh blood, of course.

Apryl caught her gaze and slid the glass a little closer to herself and away from Samantha. "Don't you dare try any magic." Samantha smiled and held out her hand before motioning for the glass to come to her. Apryl snatched the glass before it moved more than an inch and returned the smile.

"Not a chance," I responded. You're still only a few months old. Then I took a nice long drink of my own, while looking right at her. Her jaw dropped. I stopped and put my drink down. "What? I'm old, remember? Almost ninety is what I believe you remind me of when it is convenient for you." I pointed to her glass of blood. "Enjoy your drink."

Marcus looked on humorously while nursing his brandy. "Theodora, do you believe they are going to help?"

"It's hard to say." She put her glass down and leaned back in her chair. The normal air of confidence that surrounded Theodora diminished. She looked around at each of us. "Normally I would say yes. There are many of us that enjoy a good fight, and wouldn't hesitate to volunteer. But, as you can imagine, most of them have already rushed to the front lines. Some are gone. Others have gone into hiding. I believe they would be more than a little reluctant to step forward and volunteer again. Those that would be naturally hesitant to enter a conflict are even more so now. You need to remember; our world differs from the world of witches. Larissa knows this. We have just discussed this. There is no single leader in our world. There is no one that can give an order that others will follow blindly. Even if the Elders agree this is necessary, then they have to convince others to join, which is a hard ask now. They can't just give the order, and everyone will follow. Our world doesn't work that way."

By now, we all knew that the society of vampires didn't work that way. She had reminded us of that fact enough. Just like she had my accelerated pregnancy when I carried Samantha. Before she was preparing me for what was to come. Now I felt she was preparing us for disappointment. Maybe in her mind she already knew what the Elders would decide, and perhaps she was right. It sure seemed like she was if everything she said was true. But I wasn't about to give up. I had another angle. One I had mentioned earlier that I felt resonated with her enough to even entertain my presenting my proposal to the Elders. "No, it doesn't. Vampires are followers. They followed Jean St. Claire. There has to be someone of a better character out there they would follow."

"There was," Theodora started. A single tear raced down her cheek as the words got caught in her throat. "But he is dead now."

I knew who she meant, and it was my turn to be the bigger person. It was time to ignore what that person did and reach out to console a friend. "Theodora, I am so sorry about Montego. I wish things had ended differently."

She looked away, tossing her hair out of her face, and snapped. "So do I, but this is how things ended. The one person brazen enough to run into battle, like you are asking, is now dead." Her words stung, and her tone slashed. I wanted to respond. I wanted her to know how sorry I was. Her pain was so much deeper than what I felt when Nathan and I were separated. I knew he was still alive, and everyone told us we would be together again one day. She didn't have that hope. Her separation from her beloved was eternal. There was no apology I could make that would be deep enough to fill the holes that his loss left in her. All I could do was sit there quietly and take any venting she needed to do. For me to protest anymore, in her mind, would cheapen his memory. Not to mention it wouldn't help our current situation. We needed her help.

"I'm sorry," Theodora said. Her head dipped again and then landed in her hands on the table. I heard a few quick sobs. When she picked her head up, her hands rushed to wipe away any evidence that it had occurred. How her makeup stayed perfect was surprising, but that wasn't what shocked me most. "Larissa, I am sorry. It wasn't your fault. It's not even Nathan's fault. If the roles were reversed, Montego would have killed Nathan where he stood. What he did was so senseless. Will you accept my apology for both betraying you and my outburst?"

I was too stunned to reply. My boyfriend killed her boyfriend, and now she was apologizing to me about that, and it was a heartfelt apology. This wasn't just something shallow that someone did when they felt they needed to. No, she thought this one from words to tone out and it was sincere. She meant every word, but even though she did, and she was right, I still felt funny accepting it. I couldn't not accept it. That would make me look even worse, and who knew how badly that would hurt Theodora? I found some middle ground that I felt was safe to navigate. A way to give us both what we needed. This wasn't about saving face for either of us. This was about healing a wound festering between us, that had already shown up a few times, and threatened to infect our relationship, which wasn't something I wanted to do. I still meant what I promised her on my last visit. I was going to visit often and learn from her. "Only if you accept mine."

The attention of everyone at the table shifted to Theodora as if they knew the importance of this moment. I doubted they did. Each probably thought it just had a bearing on what we were here for, but this was about something that would reach well beyond today.

Theodora stood up, pushing her chair back. Its metal legs scraped on the concrete patio. She slowly strolled around the table, passing Apryl, and then Samantha. When she reached me, I looked up and felt my hands tremble. She loomed over me, with intentions that were not clear in my head. They covered the entire gambit of possibilities.

"Stand up," Theodora commanded.

I did, feeling I had little choice. If things were going to go south here, being on my feet gave me the best chance. Samantha looked on with a fearful gaze.

Theodora reached forward and embraced me. This wasn't just one of those embraces for show, or polite hugs you might receive from a relative you rarely see. There were emotions radiating from her body. She squeezed and her hand rubbed the back of my shoulder. I returned the embrace. I guess that was proof to Theodora that I had accepted hers. "Of course, I accept yours. We are sisters in this world. We need each other."

I glanced at Apryl expecting some faux disgusted look at the show of sensitivity, but my hard edged and always sarcastic friend looked to be wiping a tear from her cheek.

Theodora let go of me, but her hands draped down my arms, and grabbed hold of my own. She smiled. "Even if the Elders say no, I am with you."

"You say the vampires don't have a leader, but they will follow one if one shows up," Marcus started. "Why can't you be that leader?" he asked. His eyes directed the question at Theodora. Theodora released a nervous laugh as she let go of my hands. She placed one hand on her hip as she stared down at Marcus. I saw a lecture coming, but before she could get started, Marcus's eyes cut in my direction. "Or Larissa?"

Heads turned in my direction. I felt the weight of their attention press against me as I launched my protest. "Ah, no. I am supposed to be the leader of the witches. Remember? You were part of the scheme."

The attention his question had earned me returned to him, but he seemed unaffected. Marcus took a sip of his brandy, but held up a finger to ask me to wait for his reply before I added any more to my protest. I complied and stood there, crossing my arms across my chest. He took his time enjoying the coffee. The longer he took, the shorter my fuse became, but he timed it exactly right. Just before my fuse was at its end, he finally replied. "You are both. Why can't you be both? Unite the worlds."

Again, the attention of everyone sitting at the table followed his volley back to me, but this time there appeared to be wheels turning behind all the looks. Especially inside Theodora. Her bottom lip twitched, and I thought I noticed her tell. The twitch continued, and I knew it. She was chewing on the inside of her lip while quietly contemplating Marcus's proposal.

What wasn't to consider? His statement sounded like the secret to world peace. While I was at it, I might as well become the leader of the mortals too. From what I have seen on the nightly news, they need someone to straighten out the mess they have made of the world. It was a wonderful vision and dream, but completely impractical. It would never work. I still had doubts the witches would follow me, even after we defeated Mrs. Roberts and I had completed the Seven Wonders. The vampires had more reason not to follow me. My being part witch was probably at the top of the list.

"No," I replied, sounding rather annoyed by the suggestion. "I have been training to be the supreme, and I still need a lot of work there. Let me focus on one."

"But," Theodora started.

"No buts." I stopped before the next sentence reached my lips. Something inside me had slammed the brakes on that phrase. Theodora had already accused me of focusing too much on being a witch, and I tried to explain why. She seemed to accept it and understand, I think. She hadn't questioned me about it since, but admitting that I wanted and needed to focus on my witch side would probably bring that back to the forefront of her thoughts and concerns. I needed to walk the middle ground, and yes, I saw a place where I could exist that was equally both, but that didn't mean others would see me that way. I had to be diplomatic in my response. "It wouldn't work. My being both is always going to be a problem for either side to accept. Witches will always accuse me of being too much vampire, and vice versa. I have to pick one side." I left it at that, not stating out loud which side, though I was sure it was readily known. It had been the topic of more conversations than I cared to remember.

"Maybe, but..."

"Remember, I said no buts."

My interruption did nothing to derail Theodora's thought. She grabbed the empty seat to my left and pulled it close and sat. As she did, I sat back in my chair, while remembering one of Kevin Bolden's sessions of body language and keeping my arms folded tightly across my chest.

"You may be right, if you try to be the actual leader, but what about a close confidant or advisor to both?"

Marcus leaned forward enthusiastically and bumped into the table. "Yes. A mediator between both worlds. Seeing that you have the perspective of both. Having the supreme as a close advisor to the leader of the vampires would be—"

I started shaking my head as soon as Marcus began his explanation.

"No. No. No." Theodora did everything but stomp and bang her fist on the table with her objection. "Just like a witch to miss the obvious. Even if you forget all that has happened in the last month, no one will accept the rule of the Supreme Witch."

"I'm not saying she will lead. She can advise who ever steps up."

"And then I will be just like Mrs. Roberts," I injected, throwing my objection into the discussion. Theodora pointed at me, to echo her agreement.

"Then I guess you need to be the leader of the vampires," Apryl said, before quickly taking a drink of her Bloody Mary and attempting to hide her smile behind her glass.

"That is a possibility." Theodora practically cooed at the suggestion.

"Yes mom. Why not?" Samantha asked, leaning back in her chair toward Apryl. They were teaming up on this side of the argument. Why she had taken that side, I wasn't sure. She was like me, both, and I knew for a fact she loved being a witch. It was the vampire side she wasn't thrilled about. This was not the time for her to stir the pot and have a little fun. I mustered up a stern, motherly look from deep inside and watched as she slumped in her chair. She got the message.

"Absolutely not!" Marcus exclaimed. "Larissa is being groomed to be the supreme, and that is that."

"Groomed!" Now it was my turn to exclaim. That word burned deep. It had so many negative connotations. Come to think of it, I couldn't think of any uses of the word that were good. "Nobody is grooming me for anything."

"Larissa, you know what I mean. The training," Marcus explained. "The choice of whether or not to be the supreme is yours. It has always been. My point is, this is something that is far bigger than you. It is far bigger than anyone at this table. You are the one that can help— "

"I know. I'm the one that can help fix everything, blah, blah, blah." I had heard it so much; I had started to resent it. Maybe I didn't want to fix everything. This world had brought me some happiness, but a freight train load of misery.

I was about to launch into a tirade about that very topic when the tall and slender John Milton appeared in the courtyard. Everyone at the table knew what that meant. The Elders had reached a decision. We were all more than eager to find out what it was and hurried up from the table. Inside, the nerves were playing with my system again. I took one last sip of my Bloody Mary, hoping it would pull me back together. Then that sip turned into a guzzle of the remaining contents of my glass.

21

The four men were seated in the library when we came inside. Each stood up out of a show of courtesy that was centuries out of place. There was something that wasn't right about this picture, and it wasn't the chivalry. These four were dressed in suits and waist coats before. Tobias had sleeves with ruffles on them. Now, they were plainly dressed in simple button-up shirts and slacks. Except in Keith Taylor's case, he appeared to had opted for jeans. There was something else that made me believe these were not willfully made choices. They looked beaten. Inside and out. Their features were gaunt, and their posture and expressions lacked the stately presence they had before. Now, they were just men that were here.

Harold Leeward motioned toward one of two chairs that were in the center of the room. One of which was the one Theodora always sat in. I walked over to it and had a seat in the other one. Theodora followed me and sat in her chair next to me. The four elders sat, leaving the others standing back by the door leading in from the courtyard.

"It is good to see you again, Miss Dubois," began Harold. "We have discussed your request for assistance. I completely understand your plan and what you want to do, and why you need our help. I want to assure you that a great bit of thought has gone into this, as I am sure you put a great deal of thought into your plan, but at this time it is a no for me."

Marcus gasped behind us, and someone else moaned. I believed it was Samantha, but I couldn't be sure. I was too busy picking myself up off the floor. The way I saw it, this was our last hope. My head dipped. So, this was how two great civilizations ended. The witches kill all the vampires, and then the witches implode from inside. Would history record that I was at the epic center of all of it? Would history even record our existence at all? I was sure the vault and libraries would still exist, but no one would be able to access them. They would stay in that magic bubble Mrs. Saxon had described to me once, for eternity.

"But that is only for me. I am in the minority. Where I believe we would be best served by going into hiding to preserve our kind, my brothers feel that would only delay the inevitable."

Jonathan Smith shifted in his seat and leaned forward. "It would, and for who knows how long," he crooned with an unmistakable Cajun sound. That man was from right here. Probably someone Jean ran out of New Orleans centuries ago. "We can't run and hide forever."

"That was never your style," Tobias remarked.

"Nor yours," Johnathan responded without looking back at Tobias.

"You will need to forgive those two," chuckled Keith Taylor. "Neither of them has ever shied away from a fight. They were on opposite sides of the Civil War."

"Which we won," Tobias proclaimed proudly.

"And," Keith Taylor interjected loudly, in what appeared to be an attempt to slam the door on any further rebuttal from Johnathan. "It will be nice for both of you to fight on the same side for the same cause this time." He paused and regarded his two representatives from the North and the South to see if any shots were going to be fired for the first time in over a hundred and fifty years. The silence between them seemed to signify we were still at peace. "Miss Dubois. We will help you the best we can. I don't know what kind of numbers we can rally for the cause, but I believe when faced with the decision to return to the lives we knew or run and hide, many of our people will choose the former. Even if we tried, we can't hide forever. They will eventually find us. Then there is the matter of Jean St. Claire. He should have been dealt with promptly."

My mouth opened to explain, but Mr. Taylor would not wait.

"I know. You have your ways, which include a trial and then that prison. A quick yank should have been all he was afforded. He is a magnet of terror. He attracts the weak minded, and then twists and turns them. I am sad to say, there are many that would be drawn to such an individual and his promises of grandeur. We can't let him continue. We will help on both fronts. I just want two promises from you. First, one that you aren't leading us into a slaughter. And second, and most important of all, if push comes to shove and you have to choose between saving a friend or killing Mrs. Roberts and Jean, you won't choose the friend and let them escape, making all this for naught."

"Oh no. Absolutely not," I answered as confidently as I could, without really thinking the question through. I knew the answer I gave was the one he wanted to hear, and that was all that mattered right now. That didn't stop the question he asked from rattling around in my head. Each bounce off the inside of my skull and back the other way tore at my soul. The pain I felt confirmed a suspicion that had developed some time ago. I actually had one. There was no right answer to the question, other than to tell them what they wanted to hear. In reality, I just couldn't see it in absolutes. It would have to be based on the situation, but more importantly, the person. I absolutely couldn't let Nathan or Samantha go. That was a fact. There was a short list of others that fell behind them. The others may, I guess, depend on the situation. Even thinking that way made me queasy. It was that or the Blood Mary I had gulped before coming back inside.

"Good, that is what I needed to hear," replied Keith. He looked across at Tobias, who nodded his agreement. "Now, do you know where they both are?"

I looked back at Marcus. I had a hunch, but I wasn't completely sure, and the last time I tried a spell to locate someone, I read the wrong one.

"I wouldn't worry about that." Marcus answered. "If you can gather your side, I can lure them out to a place of my choosing."

"Excellent." Jonathan clasped his hands in front of him and turned to Harold, who sat next to him. "Won't you join us?"

Harold stared straight ahead.

"Harold. We need you," Tobias urged. "If we show a united front, that will convince more to help. This is our chance. If we don't act now, and wait, it may be too late later."

Harold stayed focused straight ahead as he answered his fellow elders. "I'm afraid I just can't find my way through that argument to that conclusion. I understand your points," he said, finally regarding each of them as he spoke. He then stood up and walked to the center of the room and tugged the wrinkles from his shirt. "When we have the option to remove ourselves from the violence and seek safety, why should we run headlong into that violence? In the name of peace, but that is only if you are successful. What if you aren't? Then what have each of our brothers died for?"

I watched as the two of them bowed their heads, and I felt my hopes sink with them. They were considering his argument. And why wouldn't they? It was well delivered. The best orator in the world couldn't have done it better. Well thought out, the points made sense, points that contained a ton of logic. What I was proposing made no sense and was based on a ton of hope.

22

"Why don't you come lay down?"

Well, at least Nathan looked back at me. It wasn't a great look, but it was a look. It was the first break in his zombie-like state in a day. "I don't need to sleep. You know that."

"Oh my. You can speak."

There was that look again, and I felt bad about my comment. He wasn't giving me the silent treatment to be mean to me. He was giving the silent treatment to the world because he was angry at it. His anger wasn't just limited to a part of the world, either. It was the entire world, and I understood. No matter where he looked, he saw something that reminded him of her. I was in the same boat. Everywhere I looked reminded me of Mrs. Saxon and everyone else we lost, too. That was why when we were faced with a decision of where to come, I chose here, my old home in New Orleans. It was somewhere everyone was familiar and comfortable with. Unfortunately, there were people included in that "everyone" that we didn't want to know where we were. That gave Marcus an opportunity to show us a new trick. Needless to say, we now know how the coven was created. We were now staying in one of our own. From the outside, everyone saw my old family home, abandoned and run down. Inside the magic bubble, it was just as we left it.

Even sitting out here on the porch, with Nathan standing up at the railing, no one would see us from the outside. That didn't mean I wasn't still a little on edge. For the first few hours, every rustle out in the trees caused me to leap up and stand ready. Each time it was just the wind, but that didn't stop me from standing there and watching the tree line for a few more minutes just to be safe.

"I'm sorry," I apologized to Nathan for my curt reply. "I know you don't need to sleep. I just thought you might want to relax some. You can head up to the bedroom or lie down in the parlor."

"I'm fine."

"Nathan, you're not, and it's fine. None of us are fine." I got up out of the rocking chair and approached him from behind. I stood there, almost afraid to wrap my arms around him. Not because I was afraid of him. I was afraid of his rejection. Slowly, I put one hand on his side, just above his waist. It was a test to see his reaction. When he didn't move, I slid my arm the rest of the way around him, and then looped my other around him, clasping my hands in a death grip. Once I had him, I wasn't going to let go. I gently kissed his neck. "You're not fine, and it's fine." I kissed his neck again. "Your world has been destroyed. It's okay to–"

"Nothing's okay, and you don't need to remind me of what has happened to my world. I am well aware of it. It's not like you would understand."

"Actually, I think I do," I reminded him, sweetly.

"Not a chance." He tried to shake my arms off of me. "How could you even come close to understanding?"

I didn't want to do this, but I felt it might help him to know I could truly understand. Maybe, just maybe, it would allow him to open up to me. I let go with my left hand and flashed it in front of his eyes. When my hand dropped, it was daylight, and my father's '24 ford was parked next to the house. Out in the driveway lay two motionless bodies. One smaller than the other. "We can go talk to my mother, if you want. She is pretty wise. I always feel better after I talk to her."

His head dipped, and I let the world return to the present day. That was long enough of that. I did it for his benefit, but just those few moments pulled me down even deeper. The fact that it was even possible surprised me. "Maybe you do," he whispered breathlessly.

"I was serious about talking to my mother. She has a way of making people feel better." I re-clasped my hands around him and squeezed.

"Maybe. We will see." His hand found mine, and our fingers laced together naturally, and I nuzzled my cheek against the back of his shoulder. I would be lying if I said I didn't miss the warmth I once felt when he held me, but at least I knew I wasn't making him cold.

We stood like that for a long while and watched the night sky. I swear I saw a shooting star and quietly made a wish. But as time hadn't backed up two days, I knew the wish hadn't come true. A few moments later, the first peach hue of the coming dawn found its way across the horizon and signaled the start of another day.

"How long did they say they needed?"

"Tobias said to give them a day, maybe two. Theodora will let us know once they are ready."

I felt Nathan's body twitch first, then he turned and leaned across the banister. His hand that held mine, now pried itself away, and then pulled himself free from my grasp. Right before I lost contact with him, I felt his body tense up. "So, I take it that isn't Theodora?"

"Where?" I asked, rushing to his side, and leaning across the banister myself for a better look.

Nathan threw his arm up to hold me back. I was glad to see his protective streak wasn't gone, but it was completely unnecessary. I saw what he saw emerging through the tree line, and I shoved his arm away to go greet them. Nathan grabbed my hand as my foot hit the top step. I snapped my head around to look at him and yanked my hand free. "It's fine. There is no danger."

His face was twisting and twitching, and I could tell inside he was about to crack. I stepped back up onto the porch and took his hand in mine.

"Nathan, look at me."

His eyes rose to meet mine.

"We are safe here. Nothing can get to us. And we are especially safe from those four smelly mutts. Now I need to step out there so they know we are here, and I can pass them through. You can come, or you can stay here and watch me. Either way, I am going to be fine."

Nathan looked out at the four approaching figures. His grip loosened, and I went and greeted our guests.

As I stepped through the barrier, I looked back at my house and saw what everyone else would see. A place that hadn't been touched in over eighty years. All the repairs I had performed the last time we were here erased to restore the illusion of vacancy. I didn't venture far from the edge of the magic bubble. Maybe I was a little leery of anyone watching and seeing me standing there as four of the biggest wolves you had ever seen bounded their way toward the lavender field toward me. They stopped, but I didn't give them much of a chance to say hello before I threw all four of them through a portal that landed them on the porch inside the bubble. I hurried through after them and closed it.

"Still sore at me about that day in the woods?" Mr. Markinson remarked as he returned to his human form.

Martin, Rob, and Dan were a pile of fur struggling to get their feet. As each phased back, they turned and gave me their vote of dissatisfaction at how I had greeted them. I didn't care. These were dangerous times and caution was the word of the day. When each realized Nathan was standing behind them, their mood changed and softened. The three of them mugged Nathan.

"We heard," Mr. Markinson leaned over and whispered. "That is why we figured you would be here. We ran all day and all night to get here, just in case."

"We had no other place to go, and Marcus felt he could protect this place."

"I don't know what your plan is, but all the Lycans will fight." He hugged me, which felt like hugging an oven. "This has to end," he said as he let go of me.

"Lycans?"

"You really need to study your Greek mythology, Miss Dubois," he smirked. "Werewolves." Then he turned and joined the others and hugged Nathan.

23

The amount of food four werewolves could put away in a single sitting still surprised me. I know they had to be hungry. They ran hundreds of miles. I still wasn't sure how they made it all this way in just two days. Martin bragged they had made it to Tennessee the first day, but had to slow up because of the mountains. I topped him by saying I would just open a portal through the mountain.

They were napping and snoring loudly in a full-on food coma on the floor in the parlor when Jack ran down the hallway and back to the library. He had volunteered to take a watch for a while. All the sitting around was making him feel antsy, and he felt some fresh air would do him some good. I readily agreed. It gave me a few minutes to go back to my father's hidden office. The journals weren't there anymore. The council had claimed them and added them to the communal library. What I was in search of was his presence. To sit here at his desk and roll the pen he used to write those journals around in my fingers felt like it brought him closer. I thought about visiting my mother, but I knew if I told her all that was happening, and what was about to happen, it would worry her. That was if I told her the truth, but I wasn't sure I could hold things together enough to lie to her.

"Theodora is here!" Jack murdered the silence of my father's office, sending me jerking back in the chair. The color had drained from Jack's face. If mine had any, I was sure it would have done the same. We all knew what her presence meant.

I stood up and walked out of the office. Nathan sat on the sofa in the library with Amy sleeping on his lap. Samantha sat next to him doing something I hadn't really seen her do freely. She was reading one of my old books. Not that there was much else to do. The TVs I added during our last visit were still there and working. The werewolves, or what I will now call lycanthropes because it sounds fancier, turned the one in the parlor to a sports network before falling asleep. I told Samantha she could change it, or turn the one on back here in the library, but she didn't want to wake anyone.

As I exited the room, I caught Nathan passing Amy off to Samantha. He did everything but support her head, and she did a wobbly turkey neck dangle before Samantha caught her head and gave her father a roll of the eyes. If we survived all this, it would be the first of many, I hoped.

I held back in the hallway and waited for Nathan. He walked instead of shuffled, but still hung his head as he did. I grabbed his arm, gently, to stop him, and he looked up. Marcus had explained eventually the hurt would turn to anger, again. That hadn't happened yet.

"You can stay back here with Sam and Amy." His gaze narrowed, and I added, "if you want."

"I need to be part of this."

I didn't fight him on that and took his hand and walked down the hallway and out to the porch. It was midday, and the sun blazed overhead in the clear sky. Theodora stood there under a black umbrella. I spun open a portal in front of her, and she stepped through, landing on the steps of the porch. She mounted them with haste and closed her umbrella once she was under the protection of the porch's awning.

"Is there somewhere we can talk?" she asked with a grim look on her face. Seeing it, and her request, without any of her normal polite pleasantries, had me worried.

"My father's office," I volunteered.

Theodora didn't hesitate. Her steps were quick and purposeful inside. Something was definitely wrong.

"Nathan, can you show her to the office?" I asked. "I need to get Marcus."

Nathan took the lead and showed her the way down the hallway and back to the office. Theodora paused slightly and her head turned to regard the mass of sleeping humanity in the parlor as she passed. The sound of her heels on the wood floor attracted the attention of the vampires that were hanging out in the kitchen. Heads poked out through the door and watched as she passed by. Mike watched her particularly closely and earned a slap from Laura.

"Kevin, can you join us?" I requested, from the bottom of the stairs.

"Sure," he agreed, stepping through the group gathered at the door and followed Nathan into the library.

I rushed up the stairs, and went to my parents' old room, the one I had offered Marcus so he could get some rest. Lisa and Gwen were in my old room. Our current situation seemed to have caused what would normally have been reluctant roommates to push their differences aside. Things were bigger than what was really a childish spat. Though Gwen brought a lot of it on herself.

I knocked first and then opened the door. The room was dark, but I could see fine. My knock had woken Marcus, and he sat there looking disoriented. Why not? He had maybe two or three hours of sleep and now woke up in a strange place.

"Theodora's here. She wants to talk."

"Okay." He rubbed his face with both hands before flicking on a candle. I closed the door, not wanting to see what he slept in. It didn't take long for the door to open and he emerged, in perfectly pressed black pants and some kind of red jacket with gold accents. It looked regal. "Where is she?"

"My father's office."

"All right," he yawned, and started down the stairs.

I followed him, having to control my pace to not run him over. His steps were sleepy steps all the way to the bottom, where he paused again for another yawn before he turned to head down the hall. I paused myself, but for a different reason. There was someone else that I felt needed to be part of this conversation, especially after what he had pledged to me earlier this morning. I crept into the parlor and stepped over Rob's sprawled out body and leaned down and tapped Mr. Markinson on the shoulder. At first, he attempted to swat my hand away, but after the second attempt he roused awake, and looked up at me, startled.

"I need you to be part of this conversation."

"Oh, okay," he stammered, contorting his body to get up bumping no one else. His presence was an odd contrast to that of Marcus Meridian. There were no perfectly pressed pants and coat. Mr. Markinson wore wrinkled clothes that were a little too baggy for him. They were some of my father's old clothes. They were the best I could do. I offered to conjure up some, but he refused that offer and said what I had would work just fine for him. The others didn't hesitate to take up my offer. Martin even rejected a few outfits at first, as not his style. My fourth attempt was what he called "perfect".

Mr. Markinson followed me back to my father's office, giving its opening through a false door hidden in the bookcase an interesting look. Once inside, I closed the door, not knowing what Theodora wanted to discuss. If this was bad news, I didn't really want anyone else to hear it until we, the larger we of myself and Marcus, heard and understood it.

Theodora stood in the center of the room. Her black umbrella lay across my father's desk. She pulled her black lace gloves off her hands and slipped the black hood she wore from her head. Her expression was blank, but stern, as I watched her and waited for her to start.

443

When I watched her black eyes scan the room, I realized a few introductions were needed.

"Theodora, you remember Marcus from last night, I assume, and this is Mr. Markinson — "

"A werewolf? I can tell from the smell." She pursed her lips. Mr. Markinson looked down at the floor and let out an awkward smile.

"He is their instructor at our coven, and has pledged their assistance." I paused and searched for the word I needed to use," in this matter." I winced at that choice, but nothing else came to mind besides the obvious ones of war and battle, but depending on what Theodora was about to tell us, neither may be the truth.

"Assistance?" Theodora asked with a curious gaze in his direction.

"Yes ma'am. I can speak for all the lycanthropes. We will fight. We have to. If this doesn't end now, what is to stop the witches from targeting us? Not to mention, they killed the people that took us in when we had nowhere else to turn. Our closest friends. They were our family, too."

Theodora threw her head back and laughed, which created a host of nervous gazes around the room. She brought herself under control, but grinned as she wondered aloud, "Werewolves and vampires fighting together. What has the world come to?"

Her grin appeared to be contagious as both Marcus and Mr. Markinson shared it. Nathan didn't. He stood there grimly, and because of him, I did my best to hide my amusement. This was no time to smile or act happy.

"So, the vampires will fight?" Marcus asked.

"Of course. We told you we would." She acted almost offended by his question, but even I had that question in mind. With how she arrived, I was worried there was a change of heart. "Even Harold has agreed. I'm here to go over the plan. Our side will be ready tonight."

"I thought he was dead against it," I asked, surprised.

"He was, but Tobias can be rather convincing."

"Tonight?" Marcus asked.

"Yes, that is, if you want us that soon. They are on their way here now. Most have moved here for protection."

Marcus reached up and rubbed the back of his neck. Then walked around the room in thought. He stopped as he reached Mr. Markinson. "Can you have them ready by then?"

Mr. Markinson nodded.

"Good. Then tonight it is?" He questioned, looking right at me.

"Tonight," I agreed.

Marcus walked to the center of the room and leaned forward, propping himself against my father's desk. "Everyone will meet here just after dusk. The witches will open portals to transport everyone to a place close to where we Mrs. Roberts and the others will be gathered. Then we make our move." He stood up and circled the room again. "How many vampires are we talking about here? A couple of dozen?"

"A few more than that. Try over sixty. The number's still growing," Theodora replied. Her head twisted around, trying to keep up with Marcus.

"And you?" Marcus asked with quick regard to Mr. Markinson.

"Not quite that many, but enough."

My mind did the quick math. This was way better than I had expected. If it was just us, we wouldn't stand a chance. Did we have enough now to stand better than a chance? I didn't know. I saw how many Mrs. Roberts had with her when she attacked the coven, and she could have more.

"Master Meridian," Theodora said, addressing Marcus rather formally, even for her. "I'm not sure what your plan is, but if you can get just a few of us close enough, we can take care of your witch."

Marcus continued his march, but now he waved his hand in the air to dismiss that suggestion with urgency, as if it were an offending odor. "No. We have already talked about that. This needs to be a spectacle. All of her followers need to see what happens, and it needs to be one of us." He stopped and stood up straight, clasping his hands behind his back. "This isn't just about taking her down. It is also about changing minds. If it's a vampire, or a werewolf for that matter, it could do more harm than good."

"It would darken the lines of division, and strengthen their cause," Mr. Markinson muttered.

"She would be a martyr," Nathan whispered.

Marcus continued his walk, patting Nathan on the shoulder as he passed him. "That's the last thing we need. We need everyone to see this and experience it." He pounded his right fist into his open left hand. The sound echoed in the room, and I jumped, causing several surprised looks. This was as tense a moment as I had ever experienced in my life. This was no time to fall apart. I locked my shoulders back as straight as I could get and channeled my inner marble statue as Marcus continued his circle.

"Do we know if they are all camped together?" Theodora asked.

"Probably not," Marcus replied, looking past Mr. Markinson and right at me. His gaze stayed locked as he continued to walk. There was an urging in his eyes, but for what? Then it became clear when he asked, "Isn't that right, Larissa?"

I thought back to the last question and his response. If he was hoping I could add more, he was unfortunately mistaken. It wasn't like I knew where they were. Even if they were where Mrs. Roberts took me that one time, I wasn't going to be much help. The last time I was there, I came in through another magic portal right into her chambers. I didn't see what was around, and outside that little cabin we entered, that was the portal. I didn't see any camp there either. Not that I could look around much. I was just along for that ride. He should know that. I had already told him about what had happened many times. Each time, he asked for more and more details so he could figure out where she was on his own. What else was there and why would he think I would know? I wasn't the only one wondering. The entire room was, and all eyes were on me as I stood there, thankfully like a marble statue, while inside my mind did cartwheels through the memories for any detail I was missing.

The absence of one made me wonder if the answer wasn't in that memory. It wasn't something as tangible as a picture or a place. Was it something more basic? What could it be? The question again. It was about where all the witches would be. Marcus didn't believe they were camped together. What would be that reason and where would they be? An answer came to me, but I had to ask myself if it was too simple. That didn't stop me from saying it out loud first before I had that answer. "They are all back at their covens to control the message and keep control of the masses."

"Exactly. They will stay with their own covens to maintain control and identify any threats so they can be quickly dealt with before they become a real problem. That is my bet. If they camped together, people could freely ask questions among their own covens, and who knows? Some covens might rise against them, and that isn't what they want. They want all witches aligned behind them. So, they go off, do the wishes of the new, and acting, supreme and then return home as if nothing really happened and try to keep everything as normal as possible. That is my bet. I could be wrong, but I doubt I am."

"It makes sense," Kevin Bolden agreed. "Look at every dictator throughout history. Controlling the masses through the control of information. If people don't see or hear of the atrocities, they never happened."

I guess all those hours he spent watching old war movies and documentaries up on the deck finally paid off, and he knew it too. A prideful smirk had made it to his face.

"Mr. Markinson, will you be able to gather everyone by tonight?"

"That won't be a problem."

Marcus stopped his circle, which I was grateful for. Watching him had made me dizzy. He looked across the room at Mr. Markinson and raised his eyebrow as he leaned slightly in his direction. "You're sure?"

"Watch!" Mr. Markinson said, with a defiant glimmer in his amber eyes. He took off, opening the hidden door himself, and ran down the hallway. We followed him all the way out to the porch. He stood there just at the edge of the magic bubble and looked back in our direction. With a point toward the woods, I knew what he wanted, and I opened a portal so he could exit. His clothes shredded right before our eyes as he phased into the biggest gray wolf I had ever seen. Make that the biggest one I had now seen twice. He sprinted out into the woods.

We stood there and did exactly as Mr. Markinson requested; we watched. He ran across the fields and then disappeared into the darkness of the woods. Then we heard the loudest howl I had ever heard. It seemed terrifyingly out of place. Maybe one too many horror films had conditioned me to only expect that sound when the moon was up high in the sky. At the moment, there was no moon. The sun was still shining in all its brilliance. Silence fell over the scene again, but only for a moment. What Mr. Markinson had just done was place a call. We were now hearing the responses.

"Well, that answers that," remarked Marcus.

"What's all the noise about?" Rob asked from behind us. I turned and watched as he attempted to rub the exhaustion out of his eyes. Once his hands were clear of his eyes, he looked back at us, probably mirroring the look we were giving him. "What?"

24

Theodora left not long after Mr. Markinson ran off into the woods. She had affairs to attend to. Jack asked how she could think about business at a time like now. I didn't have the heart to tell him she wasn't talking about that kind of business. It was a somber topic that each of us handled differently. Mr. Markinson gathered Rob, Martin, and Dan together after he returned and talked with them. I wasn't in there with them, but I didn't need Jack's empathic ability to feel the heaviness in the room as I walked by.

It appeared everyone dealt with it differently. Marcus sat silently outside, as if in meditation under the warm sun. He looked so peaceful. I was jealous. Lisa had mentioned the ultimate price of what we were about to do once to me, and almost appeared joyful going on about how her mother talked to this person on the other side, and her grandmother talked to this other person. It seems her culture viewed death differently. It's not an end, but a beginning. I guess I could see that too. My mother still existed, just in a different way and different place than the living. If something happened to me, Samantha could come visit me, and she could bring others to visit me. That was assuming they were still around, and I wanted to make sure that happened.

I searched the house for the quietest of its occupants. They were all in the back library watching a movie. A comedy of all things. They didn't share the same somber concerns the others did. I hated to break it to them. No matter how invincible they felt, they were still in danger. Many vampires like themselves had been hurt and even killed by Mrs. Roberts and her followers. I was considering that type of outcome for myself. Seeing them sitting there, smiling, and laughing quietly, only to avoid waking or disturbing others, boiled a bit. It even had me questioning why I had sought them out. The person I had elected for what was the most important responsibility in the world was the one laughing and having the best of times. He sat there in jeans and a white wife-beater. His hand over his mouth, struggling to contain his laughter. The grin on his face escaped past the edges of his hand. A grin that all but disappeared when I stepped into the room and requested, "Mike, can I talk to you for a minute?"

Mike walked out to a chorus of "ooos" from everyone else in the room. Amy sat next to Laura and pointed, giggling as Mike made the trek across the room and out into the hall, where I waited. As he approached, I moved down the hall and out to the porch, only stopping at the door to motion for Mike to follow. I wanted privacy, and with everyone's enhanced hearing, just out in the hall wouldn't do. We needed more space.

I stood there waiting for him by the railing with my back to the door. The century old squeak of the screen door announced Mike's arrival, but I didn't turn. I waited for him to walk up and join me at the railing, but leave it to Mike to not take the hint or see the signs. He stood there, cluelessly, behind me. After a few seconds, which was me giving him the benefit of the doubt, I waved him forward next to me. Once he arrived, I realized I wasn't prepared for this conversation. I didn't even know how to start. Even if I did, the large frog that had hopped in and made a home in my throat threatened to choke off any attempt to make a sound. I coughed to clear it and to give myself a few more seconds to plot an approach.

"Larissa, did you just invite me to come stand here and look out at the fields and woods?" Mike asked with a suspicious glance.

"No," I croaked, and coughed again to clear it. "I need to ask a favor."

Mike turned and faced me, leaning against the railing. "Sure, what can I do for you?" He flashed his million-dollar smile, and I felt the impulse to roll my eyes. I wondered if I had made the right selection. After one look at how he stood there. All muscular, brazen, and confident, I knew he was the only choice.

"This is hard to ask, but it is very important."

"Sure, what is it?" he asked, his grin dimmed ever so slightly. The gloominess of the topic had already started casting its shadow.

"If something were to happen to me, I need you to promise that you will grab Nathan and Samantha and get them as far away from everything as you can." I tried to hold it together as I made my request, but my restraint was short-lived. A tremble developed inside, and quickly escaped from where I tried to lock it away. I tightly clasped my hands together to hide it. All that did was redirect it up my arms and into the rest of my body. Mike watched me, wide-eyed and gaping mouth as the procession made its way through my body.

He reached over and grabbed my shoulders with both hands. "Larissa, nothing is going to happen," Mike said, trying his best to be reassuring while his eyes traced the shaking up and down my body. "I'm serious. This is going to go just like you planned."

"Mike," I said, or attempted to say. His name barely made it out of my mouth, and only the "M" and "K" were sounds. The rest were just breathless spaces.

"Stop it. It's going to be fine."

My head shook back and forth, and this time, I was in complete control of it. Or make that even partial control. The movement back and forth was me, but the rapid shaking wasn't. "Mike, just promise me. It's important. If you can, grab others like Lisa and Jack. Even Gwen. Please!" I meant to make that sound like a forceful command, but it came out as a pathetic sobbing plea.

"Stop!" Mike succeeded at what I had just failed at. His strong arms yanked me forward, and he wrapped them the rest of the way around me. "We aren't going to have this talk."

"Yes, we are," I said, recovering a little of my native defiance. "I need you to promise. I need you to do this for me. Will you?"

He loosened up his grip and allowed me to back away. Our eyes met, and I saw what I had hoped to see the first time I asked him this favor; understanding. "Yes, you know I will. You're really worried about this, aren't you?"

"Yes," I said, the pain of the thought that ran through my soul each time I considered the possibility caused my eyes to dart from his gaze. A single tear sprinted down my cheek. Mike was quick to catch it with a finger.

"I got you. You don't need to worry about that. Okay?"

I turned to meet his understanding eyes again and nodded as I reached up to brush away the two tears that threatened to make their own trip.

"You came to the right vampire, too. I'm the strongest. Ain't no one going to stop me." He smiled. I couldn't help but smile and giggle through a sniff.

"That is one of the reasons I picked you."

"Just one?" he asked, feigning disappointment. "What were the others?"

"You are more aggressive than the others. I know if you set your mind to something, no one is stepping in your way."

"That's just my awesomeness," he joked as he pulled me in for another hug. This time, I returned the favor and wrapped my arms around him. He gave me a big bear hug squeeze. I hated to tell him; he couldn't crush me. I couldn't crush him either, for that matter. "Don't worry. I got you, and I have your back, too."

"Them before me," I said, my voice muffled by his shoulder.

I felt a shudder through his body just before he answered, "Of course. Them before you."

25

After Mike and I walked back inside, he headed back to join the others in the library. He must have missed something hilarious in the movie. Clay's laughter thundered down the hallway. Mike looked back at me a few times as he walked back. The weight of our conversation had drowned the levity of the mood he had enjoyed before we talked, and I had to admit I felt a little guilty of taking that from him.

Once he disappeared through the door. I stepped up on the first step and then took another. My legs weighed a ton, and each step up was an arduous task of torture. At the top, I stood and leaned against the newel post, and rested. Not so much for my body, but for my spirit. That was what was weighing me down. The physical was ready to go, but my spirit was torn to pieces with worry, and I had hoped I would have felt better after talking to Mike and getting his promise, but I didn't. I felt worse. Things felt more real now.

I took a step away from the newel post, but my hand hung on to it with a death grip. With a yank, I pulled it free and threw it forward to the closest doorknob. I turned it, and it opened. I slipped in quickly and yanked it close behind me, startling the one occupant that I already knew was inside. I had just watched her walk up the stairs ahead of me as Mike made his way back to the library.

"Larissa, you scared me!" Lisa gasped, spinning around at the sound of the slamming door.

"I'm sorry. I need to talk to you." I said. My body plastered against the backside of the door. I must have looked frightful. Lisa came to me right away and grabbed my hand.

"Larissa, you look like you have seen a ghost."

I wanted to remind her I was naturally pale, but I knew what she meant. That was exactly like I felt. Actually, maybe it was Lisa that was seeing a ghost, and that ghost was me. I felt like nothing more than a shell of myself roaming around. She led me over to the bed, where I sat.

"Is that what it is? Did you see a ghost? Maybe your parents?" Lisa asked as she sat down next to me. "It's really common and not at all what the movies and other popular culture makes you believe."

I placed my other hand on top of the one holding mine and gulped in a huge breath of air that I didn't really need. Maybe it was an action that my body felt would relax me. It didn't work if that was the intention. All it did was weird me out even more, and forced me to exhale it. "Lisa, I need to ask you a favor."

"Sure, anything," she agreed, concerned. "You know there is nothing I wouldn't do for you."

"Good." I turned and faced her, steadying my nerves. Seeing who I considered my best friend, a sister, though I never really told her that often, smiling back at me helped. "If something happens, I want you to get Nathan, Samantha, and anyone else you can out of danger."

Her smile melted, and I prepared for her to try to comfort me that nothing was going to happen, just like Mike had a few minutes ago. My counter arguments were going to be the same, with a lot of insistence.

"I had already planned on doing that if I felt things were going wrong," Lisa said, leaning forward. "Jack and I talked about it last night. If things turn badly, we are going to get everyone out. It would be better to live to fight another day, then it all end right there."

Huh. I sat there, shocked.

"We already talked it all out. There is a spell that I have been dying to try that would sweep a portal across all of us and send us back here. I showed Jack how to do it outside earlier. It seemed to work. It took us and Gwen back up here. That wand really helps Jack focus his magic. Just don't call it a wand in front of him. He doesn't like that word. He prefers to call it a magic sword or staff."

I felt my shoulders slump. Was it relief, or was it worry? I wasn't sure.

"Relax," Lisa said. She pulled her hand from mine and then reached over and pulled me in for a hug. "This is about all of us, and we have each other's backs." She let me go, and I almost fell back on my old bed. Oh, how great it would be if I could do just that and wake up back in my teens and this all just be a terrible dream. Actually, that's not right. That's not right at all.

"You know, I think back to everything that has happened. The death of my parents, my being turned into a vampire. Then the death of Mr. Norton. Jean and all his creepiness. What happened with Mrs. Saxon, Mrs. Tenderschott, and the other instructors and witches? All of that. This might sound horrible to say," which it did, and I felt horrible and selfish at the thought I had just completed, even before I said it out loud, "I wouldn't change anything. Because of all this I met you, Apryl, Laura, and Pam, who are the sisters I never had. I met Nathan, who has changed my life in the most wondrous of ways. Then there are Sam and Amy. I wouldn't give all that back to undo all the bad."

Lisa reached over and put her hand on my forehead. I backed up, but she grabbed the back of my head to hold it still. She shook her head as she removed her hand. "Nope, you're not running a fever. Since when have you become Mrs. Sunshine and Rainbows?"

"Not quite," I replied, forcing myself to hold back the tears that threatened to race down my cheek. "It just is what it is, and I–" The emotions inside choked off my voice.

"Larissa. I understand. We all do. It's how we all feel about one another. Don't worry about any of this. We are all looking out for each other." She looked at me sternly, which was a first for Lisa. This was a side I hadn't seen from her before, ever. Silly and mischievous, I had seen. Stern and serious? That was a big nope. A pointy finger emerged from her hand and planted itself right in my chest. "You need to get all these thoughts out of your mind. Tonight, you need to be as focused as ever. I do too. I am even going to tap into one of my mother's old rituals to pull in a little extra darkness. We need to be at the top of our games. Got it?"

"Yes," I nodded out of fear of what she would say or do if I said no. Her eyes were glowing yellow, and I had a feeling she had already tapped into that extra darkness. Inscriptions and symbols faded in and out on her skin. When I could see them, they appeared to crawl up and down her arms and neck.

"Good," Lisa said, and her eyes and arms returned to normal. Lisa gave her body a little shake. "God, I like how that feels," she exclaimed. Then I think she noticed the shock on my face, and she smiled back sheepishly. "Sorry, I had to try it a little before I went for it fully. There is more to the ritual."

I stood up, off the bed, and shuffled a few steps away. "Then I better let you get to it," I said, hoping she would buy that excuse for my leaving.

Lisa looked back at the last moments of sun coming in through the window. "Yes, it looks that way." She turned back. "Larissa. Let's not worry about what is going to happen. Let's just go give them hell. If things go badly, then we get out of there and give them hell another day. We won't stop until we have stopped them."

"Okay," I said, unsure what else to say, and shuffled closer to the door. With my hand on the knob, I turned back, and remembering all she had said, what she and Jack had already planned, and everything she meant to me, I said, "Thanks, Lisa. Thanks for everything."

Maybe it was just a single lapse in who I was that let it slip out, but it was a sentiment I meant. These were people I was closer to than anyone I ever remembered from my old life. Even Clay, Mike, Jeremy and Brad were like the brothers I never had, and Rob, Martin, and Dan were those cousins that came in for the holidays that you always got into trouble with. We were more family than anything I ever remembered. That was a thought that felt weird to think about here in my old family home where I was raised, but maybe it wasn't. This was my family's home, and I was here with my family. I stood there at the banister at the top of the stairs after I left the room Lisa, Jack, and Gwen were using. Below me was a room with my sleeping cousins. Two of my siblings, if I included Gwen in that category, were down in the kitchen. Maybe I could consider her my evil stepsister.

I walked down the stairs just as Jack and Gwen rounded the corner. Jack started up the stairs while Gwen paused at the bottom, eyeing me leerily. I stopped and waited for Jack to reach the stair I stood on and then grabbed him and hugged him. His arms hung limp to either side.

"What's that for?" he asked as I released him.

"Just because." I said, and I started down the stairs again, leaving him standing there dazed and confused.

Gwen looked up, now looking surprised by what she had just seen. She stayed locked on me as I descended the stairs all the way to the bottom, where I now stood just a foot or so away from her. Then I reached over and hugged her. She froze and was as stiff as a board in my arms.

26

It didn't matter what room I sat in. The retreating line of sunlight on the floor counted down to the inevitable. It was a silent countdown outside, but in my head the tick of the count rattled me. I was thankful I hadn't "fixed" the old grandfather clock in the hallway. I didn't need it chiming the hours before doomsday. As a distraction, I tried to sit with Laura, Samantha, and Jen to watch movies, but I honestly couldn't tell you what we were watching. They were just images that passed before my eyes, with dialogue and music that never reached my ears. The others appeared to immerse themselves into them. Laughter was constant. At least for a bit. As the afternoon wore on, I noticed even that had tapered off, and one by one they all started looking at the clock up on the bookcase, or out toward the hall where the light of the waning day shone through.

The kitchen was a terrible option, and it had nothing to do with Gwen and Jack constantly coming in and out. The big window over the sink gave me the perfect view of the sun setting behind the trees to the west. There was no hiding from that, and that view amped up my anxiousness to an all-time high, but I knew I wasn't the only one. It appeared Gwen ate when she was nervous. If I had known that, I would have given her a few more things to be anxious about over the past year to see if she could gain a little weight. What was looming over all of us was really getting to her. So much so, she even sat down at the table across from me and slid over a plate of cookies she had cooked. I didn't hesitate to take one, and my stomach didn't object to the sweetness of peanut butter. We sat there, just looking each other in the eye as we ate. She glanced a few times out the window, and each time I noticed her next swallow was a little slower. I stopped at one, not wanting to push my system, but Gwen had another while I finished the rest of my first one. We spoke no words, but we didn't need to. We both knew what was on each other's mind. Jack came in and just paced. I wanted to ask him to stop, because it was annoying me, but I didn't. That was his way of dealing with the stress of the moment, and I needed to let him do just that. In fact, walking seemed like a good idea. The longer I sat, the more antsy I felt, and the more thousands of thoughts clouded my mind. Lisa warned me about not being focused. Would a little walk help? There was only one way to find out, and I wasn't going alone.

I got up and walked back to the library without saying bye or anything else to Gwen. Behind me, I heard another crunch and had to assume she had started on a third cookie. My presence in the library's doorway drew a flurry of attention. Everyone seemed to believe I was there for them. Each probably guessed I was going to talk to each of them individually after I pulled Mike aside earlier. My eyes glanced around at my friends, and I felt a little weepy. Clay leaned forward to stand, when my eyes paused on him, but I waved my hand and then pointed to Nathan and Samantha. A tension that I hadn't seen in everyone else melted slightly and they settled back down where they sat.

Nathan got up from the old leather chair in the corner and then reached down to help Samantha get up off the floor where she was all stretched out watching the movie. They walked without reluctance over to me in the doorway, but stopped short of walking out into the hallway on their own.

"Let's take a walk."

Nathan looked down the hallway and out the door. He was probably making a note of how dark it was. His head dipped for a second, but when he looked back up, there was a half-smile on his face. "That sounds nice."

Out the three of us went. Any warmth the sun had imparted on the day was gone. The cool night air was setting in, and a layer of dew covered the grass. As a kid, I loved this time of night. I swore that was when the lilac smelled stronger than any other time of the day. I closed my eyes and took a big sniff. The fields of lavender and lilac were gone and had been for decades, but that didn't mean there weren't a few plants remaining out there in the unkept land. What I smelled in that sniff proved there were quite a few still there.

"You can still smell them, can't you?" Nathan asked.

"Yes," I answered with my eyes still closed. I could picture them too. The smell wasn't as strong, but that didn't stop my mind from bringing back memories of what they used to look like.

"It's like I never left." I felt my hand reach down toward the ground, hoping to find a bunch of lilac. As a child, when my father wasn't watching, I would pull up as big a handful as I could and just hold it up to my nose to smell. If he caught me, which he did a few times, I would hear a few scolding words telling me to not do that, but at no time did he raise his voice or make me put them down. He instead watched and smiled while I smelled them, anyway. Why not?

It would be a waste to just throw them back on the ground without enjoying them.

My hand felt the wet grass and weeds, but I dug deeper for what I knew was there. I kept searching around. The weeds felt rough and stringy against my fingers. The touch of what I was looking for was well known to my senses, even after all these years. I felt it brush the tip of my fingers. My hand attacked down and grabbed its target before slowing pulling it up out of the weeds. When it finally cleared all the overgrowth, a handful of purple flowers emerged. Fighting the instinct to cram the bunch under my nose, I held them out to my daughter. "Take a sniff."

Samantha leaned forward and sniffed. Then she leaned even closer and sniffed again. "Oh, my God. They smell so sweet."

"I know. This is what I went to bed smelling every night, and what I woke up to. I slept up there in that room," I said, pointing up to my window on the second floor. "If it wasn't raining out, I would have the window wide open. If it was raining, I had it cracked open so I could still smell them."

"Can we keep some in our rooms back at the coven?" Samantha's voice trailed off as she realized what she had asked. I watched the elation from her first smell of fresh lilac disappear.

"Sure. That would be great." I quickly said, hoping to stop her descent into that realization. That wasn't what this was about. "This was my life growing up. Every day, my father and his farm hands worked in the fields. They harvested lilac and sent it to New Orleans, where it was shipped out to be used in perfumes and soaps, or up the river to cotton mills where they used it to dye the fabrics they created. When we weren't out here, we were entertaining friends of my parents, attending church and school, really anything any normal family would do. Witchcraft was just part of who we were, but it wasn't us." I handed a few of the flowers to my daughter and dropped the rest. I took her free hand in one of mine and then took Nathan's in the other and started walking through the field. "Most of the families my parents associated with were witches, but you wouldn't know that from the outside. Everyone had a seemingly normal life. We gathered for dinner parties, afternoon visits, birthdays, weddings, and holidays, and none of the holidays were particularly related to anything to do with being a witch. We were normal. Yes, I attended magic classes, and my mother and father handed down their own knowledge to me, just like I have and will continue to do with you, but that was it... well, except for the occasional use of magic during our gatherings. Maybe if someone wanted a hors d'oeuvre off a tray that was across the room, they would help themselves, but that was it. I know now that my father and mother both did a lot more with their magic as part of the coven to help the area, but they kept that from me. Sam, the reason I am telling you all this, yes, you are a vampire and a witch, but neither of those define you. You can be anything you want to be. It is your choice." I shook her hand. "You can be whatever you want to be."

"Mom, I know that," she said, releasing my hand and draping her free arm around my shoulders.

"I just wanted you to know that. I wanted you to know what my childhood was like and how my parents raised me. I'm afraid the world I brought you into has been full of poor examples of how witches and vampires should live. I didn't want you to think that was how you needed to live."

She pulled me closer. "Oh mom. I've had plenty of good examples too. Mrs. Saxon." My eyes darted to Nathan as Samantha spoke her name. He stayed strong, but appeared to nod. "Mrs. Tenderschott, all the vampires, even Mike, and you. Trust me, I know. You don't need to worry about that. I'm not going to become a Mrs. Roberts or a Jean St. Claire." Samantha let go of my shoulder and I saw her hand go up and rub her chin. "You know... I might become a Theodora. She has some style."

"Okay, that's a good point." I agreed, while Samantha struggled to maintain her deadpan expression. A hint of a snicker broke through. I knew she was being funny, but I felt the need to add a vote to that choice. "Theodora has been around for centuries and has managed to live among all three worlds without issue. I wouldn't dismiss her as an example too quickly."

"She does have great style," Nathan remarked. I yanked hard down on his arm to remind him who was still holding his hand. He looked at me with that boyish grin he sometimes had. I felt something stir inside, and looked ahead of us at the old barn, and back at the house.

"Sam, why don't you go on and head back to the house and fix you something to eat? I want to show your father something before it gets too dark." I hoped my daughter wouldn't smell through this or call bullshit on the too-dark condition in my request. Nothing was ever too dark for us. "You haven't eaten all day," I added for some extra re-enforcement.

"I don't feel much like eating," she said.

"I know," I said as I turned and caressed her cheek with the palm of my left hand. "But you need your strength for tonight, and a little rest wouldn't hurt you. This staying up all the time is new to you." Really new. It had only been a month since she realized she never really felt tired and stayed up for a few days at a time. The same with eating. She still craved certain food. More than I had. I had only rediscovered my sweet tooth. She had several favorites.

Samantha leaped over and wrapped her arms around my neck. "I love you, mom."

"I love you too," I replied, melting on the inside. "Now go on."

Samantha let go, but her hands ran down my arms and gripped my fingers as she stepped away. Our fingers lingered tip to tip for a few moments until we could no longer touch. After a few more steps, she turned and headed back toward the house. I turned and yanked Nathan forward with me to my father's old barn. It no longer sported the nice bright red paint job I had magically applied to it during our last visit. Now the only coating on the old worn boards was filth. I had always considered that place dirty and avoided going into it unless I had to. Now that wasn't even the word. I pushed a hand in front of me, sending a little telekinetic push through the building to clear out any creatures that had now taken up residence in it. The push might have been a little too hard. The building creaked on its foundation, but luckily, it didn't fall down. It scattered a few birds out of the upper loft. Just to be sure, I sent a little breeze through it, tapping in to one of the many elemental tricks I had perfected to the point of being nothing more than the flick of a wrist while thinking of wind. Two more birds scattered, and I hoped that was it.

Just as we entered through the door, I felt Nathan pause while I tried to imagine what the inside used to look like, followed by the fire rune. The symbol drew itself over and over before I sent it out away from me. A wave of fire shot across the ground and up the stairs to the loft. What was once old was new again. I walked Nathan up the stairs to the loft and its mattress of fresh hay. With a clear view out of the large second-floor opening of the sun barely hanging above the horizon, I shoved him down on the hay and fell down on top of him. My hands pinned his down above his head to keep him from resisting. How his body reacted to me showed no resistance. If this was going to be the last moment I saw the sun, I was going to make sure it was enjoyable.

27

"Come with me."

When Nathan and I arrived back, it was pitch black outside. Theodora was walking across the fields toward the house, and Mr. Markinson had headed out to gather the other werewolves. Inside, there was an eerie and heavy silence. There were no shows on any of the televisions. No one was in the kitchen. They were all lingering inside the hallway at the bottom of the stairs or in the parlor. To say you could cut the tension in the air with a knife would be an understatement. If you tried, the silence would have screamed back.

I grabbed Samantha by the hand and yanked her up the stairs to my parents' room. We passed Master Marcus on his way down. He was dressed to the nines in black slacks and a long red jacket. I guess whatever made him feel comfortable is what he needed to wear. I had something else in mind, and comfort wasn't exactly at the top of the list. We stormed through the door of my parents' bedroom, and I dropped Samantha's hand as I ran to her closet. I pulled everything she had hung up out and threw it on the bed, then I stood there and admired what was hanging behind them.

"Sam, come here."

Samantha joined me in front of the closet. We stood there side by side, in the mirror my mother had in the back of her closet. Something of mirror images ourselves. In the reflection, I saw Samantha's eyes examine the garments hung to either side of our reflection, and then her jaw dropped.

"Pick one."

Samantha reached in, her hand lightly touching each garment that was hanging in the back of the closet. Back behind all the normal clothes my mother wore were her robes and gowns that were worn for her more ceremonial purposes. Her hand settled on a dark green robe that was bejeweled up and down the sleeves.

"Go on. Put it on." I urged. "If we are going to do this, we are going to do this as Dubois."

She pulled it out and admired it for a second before taking it off the hanger.

I had my eyes fixed on one garment from the moment I opened the closet. I knew it was in there, and if Samantha had tried to reach for it, I would have politely redirected her. It was something I had seen my mother wear only once. She said it was for special moments, such as my coming out party as a witch. Well, if there was ever a time for me to wear it, it was now. I pulled out the long black dress and matching robe and carefully put it on. It was old, and I worried the fabric and the threading that held it together might have weakened over time, but it hadn't, and it didn't feel old. It felt brand new as it slid against my skin.

The reflection of myself in that dress transported me to another time. A time when I sat on the bed as a young girl and watched my mother put on this very dress. Many people had told me I resembled her, but it wasn't until now that I really saw so much of her looking back at me. Then I looked at Samantha, who had just finished tying the green robe on. She reached up and pulled her hair back, much like my mother did back in the day, and there she was again. My mother was absolutely a part of us.

I walked over and shared the mirror with my daughter. We each gave each other a silent look. Samantha's hand reached for mine. I gripped it and gave it a few reassuring squeezes. While looking at our reflection in the mirror, I said, "It's going to be okay. You are a very capable witch, and more powerful than any others you will face. Just stay calm and focused, and everything will work out." Samantha nodded, but in truth, I wasn't sure if it was her reflection I was talking to.

We left the room together and walked down the stairs. I expected to draw a lot of attention, but little did I know we were going to be out done, and it wasn't Theodora who stood at the bottom of the stairs at the center of everyone's attention. She didn't even notice us as we descended. She was too busy checking out Lisa, who stood there with her dreads all pulled back under her head wrap, and a ton of charms hung around her neck over her long red dress. When we reached the bottom as she was explaining the significance of each charm to Theodora, Jack, and Mike. Mike seemed to be obsessed with one charm that was in the shape of a very curvy woman. His hand reached out more than once to grab and caress it.

Lisa looked up from her charms and spotted us leaping at both of us, hugging us around the neck. "You guys look so great," Lisa squealed before releasing the headlock she had us in and backing up. "They are going to be in so much trouble tonight. So much heritage helping to power us."

I grabbed Lisa and hugged her again. I didn't share her enthusiasm, and anything I could say would only dampen it. So instead, I just hugged my friend, and hoped she could feel the warmth I felt about her through my cold touch.

"All right," Marcus clapped from where he stood by the front door. If he wanted our attention, he had it. Every head in the place had turned in his direction. "Let's walk outside where the others are so we can talk about the plan."

Marcus turned and pushed open the front door. He didn't exit himself. Instead, he stood and waited as each of us exited out before he followed behind me. I turned, out of habit to make sure the door was closed, but Marcus had already taken care of it, and even waved his hand over the lock, which I heard click. He gave me a wry smile once he realized why I was watching him. He walked with me down the steps of the porch and out into the front drive, where what I could only describe was a horde of vampires on one side of the driveway and several packs of werewolves already in wolf form on the other side.

Marcus walked up and shook the hand of Mr. Markinson and pulled him close, and said, "This is perfect. Thank you so much." Then he walked across to Theodora and did the same before walking to the center of the driveway. He stood straight and clasped his hands in front of him. There was a quick turn to each side to regard the two groups, with a slight nod to each.

"There are no words I can say that will express the level of gratitude I have for the sacrifice you are willing to make. We are living in dark times. If we do not act, they will only become darker. Inside, remember you are the light that will chase away that darkness. Hold on to that light. Feel its warmth and let that feeling power you through. We are on the side of the right. We are on the side of peace for all of us." Marcus paused and bowed his head and lowered his voice. "Many sacrifices have already been made, and they will not be in vain." He looked up, his eyes stern and steady. "We will not be denied."

Marcus released his hands, allowing his arms to hang loosely at his side. His body lost a bit of the edge it had just had. "Larissa and I will go ahead first. We must draw all the witches together, or this won't work. Once we have them assembled and we know for sure where," he stopped and chuckled, "We will attack."

Marcus spun open a portal and held out his arm. "Larissa, shall we go set the trap?"

My legs trembled as I attempted to free them from the ground I stood on. First one step, and then another. Both steps were laborious, but I knew what was ahead of me was inevitable. That didn't make the walk that much easier, it just kept me from battling with myself over stopping and running the other way. That was no longer an option.

Samantha stepped forward and grabbed my hand, and then took a few steps with me.

"No, Sam. Just your mom and me for now. She will be fine. Trust me."

I looked at my daughter's concerned face and mouthed, "It will be okay." She hung on to my hand as long as she could until we finally lost grip of one another. We both held out our hands, still reaching for each other as I continued trudging to the portal. Once at it, Marcus motioned for me to enter first, and even waited until I was fully through before he moved. For a split second, I felt I had been tricked, and the portal was going to close behind me, but Marcus took two steps and then stepped through. Then the portal closed behind us.

We found ourselves standing on a stone bridge that led up to a stone castle with the largest wooden door I had ever seen in front of us. I walked over and leaned over the stone wall to my left and looked down into the abyss below. It was darkness, fog, and more darkness. If I fell, I might fall forever, but that might be a more preferred option than what stood before me. This place looked familiar, and another glance at the stone walls told me where I was.

"How did you know how to find this place?" I spun around and asked Marcus. This was a place I had been only once, and it wasn't of my own free will either. I was pulled, hovering above the ground, through a door of a shed in the woods. Then I was in what I guess was Mrs. Robert's throne room. Now I stood here at what appeared her front door, somewhere high up in the mountains with snow-covered peaks off in the distance.

"Let's just say, I know Mrs. Roberts, and leave it at that."

I shot a look at him as he knocked on the door. Its echo thundered both inside and out.

"Can you make yourself look like someone else really quick?" Marcus asked, just as the lock in the door clunked loudly, sending another echo through the peaks.

"Who?" I whispered back in a panic, but all Marcus offered me was a calm shrug. I had to come up with an idea quickly. Lisa or Samantha were the first ideas that popped into my mind, but then I remembered Mrs. Roberts saw them. The next idea wasn't one I was happy about, but it was all I had as the door creaked open. With a quick wave of my hand, glitter fell down on me, revealing blonde locks and a pink dress that made me sick to even think about.

The door opened and exposed a world of darkness. I waited to see if Marcus would walk in, but he didn't. He stood there and waited, so I did the same. The sound of footsteps echoed out of the darkness, and I peered through to see if I could see who was approaching. There was someone. I could see their shape. He was tall with broad shoulders, which was why I assumed it was a male. What was also obvious? They were not exactly in any sort of hurry. He was casually strolling to the door.

"This is going to be uncomfortable," Marcus muttered under his breath. He shifted back and forth where he stood.

The figure finally stepped into the wedge of light that shone in through the opened door. I was right. It was a male, and he was tall, and a tad bit older. Strands of gray hair weaved through his short, dark hair. He extended a hand to Marcus. "You're the last person I expected to find at the door." He said. His voice had a deep rich tenor to it

Marcus took his hand, and I watched as the muscles in the man's exposed forearm below his rolled up white sleeve twitched as they shook each other's hands.

"Gregory. You never know where you might run in to someone." The two men continued to shake each other's hands long beyond the point where it had become uncomfortable. Their knuckles were white with strain. When they finally released each other, Marcus flexed his hand a few times. I wasn't sure if it was to stretch or to force blood back into his fingers. Marcus looked up at the man, who had a few inches on him, and stated. "I need to speak to her."

"I imagined you did. Why else would you be here?" He turned sideways, removing himself from the opening of the door. Marcus entered, and I fell in line behind him, but a large hand reached down and put up a stop sign right in front of my face. "Not you. Just him."

"She's with me," Marcus turned around and said.

Gregory looked down at me with a curious gaze. He leaned down closer and studied my face. I sure hoped I hadn't missed any details in my split-second transformation. If I had only given myself blonde hair and a pink dress, this might be a problem.

"And you are?" he asked, leaning down to my eye level.

"Gwen..." I stammered, realizing I didn't know Gwen's last name. With how cold we were with each other; I didn't really have that much of an interest in knowing anything personal about her. I had to make up something. "Gwen Gale," I finally spouted, realizing it sounded even stupider out loud than it did in my head.

"She's a witch, and she's with me." Marcus held out his arm, waiting on me, and I slid to the side and around the imposing Gregory, watching him the entire time. He never tried to stop me, but he never stopped watching me as I slipped by him and through the door. I shuffled quickly to join Marcus in the darkness, which only became darker once the door slammed behind us. The darkness was short-lived. Lanterns high above us flashed to life, casting a bright flickering light across the large stone hall. The shadows in every corner danced with every movement of the flame.

Gregory walked around us and took the lead. "Follow me, your majesty?" he mocked. Marcus didn't react. He did as requested and followed Gregory down the hall, and I followed him.

We passed four doors that all looked alike and then stopped at the fifth door. "Wait here." Gregory opened the door and stepped inside. I expected Marcus to let out an exhale or something, but he just stood there, admiring the stonework on the wall. There wasn't much else to admire. There were no pictures, windows, or anything. Just stone and doors, with more stone followed by more doors.

After a few seconds more, the door opened again, but Gregory didn't come out. He stood just inside and invited us in. I walked in, and fought to keep my eyes from surveying the room of my torture. The floor to the right was the same floor Nathan and I laid on. In the center was that hideous throne, with fresh burn marks on it. I half expected her to have had those already cleaned off. My eyes darted against my control to the wall where I had tossed Sarah Julia Roberts' lifeless body. The corner of my mouth curled up at that memory.

The door slammed behind us, and I turned to look. We were now alone, and my nerves raced while my mind thought of every type of ambush imaginable. There was only one other door, but that meant nothing. She could come from anywhere. The gold flash I saw through the archway that led out to a balcony behind the throne was exactly what I meant. It appeared and disappeared, then she appeared through the door, rushing toward Marcus with open arms. Her bright red dress flowing behind her in an imaginary wind.

"Marcus, my dear. I was so worried you were killed in New Orleans." She hugged him, and I felt something roll up from deep in my stomach. When she offered her cheeks to him to kiss and he obliged, I had to fight even harder to keep it down.

"Sharon, it's good to see you. Luckily, I have survived so far."

"It is very fortunate," she said. Her arms draped down Marcus as she backed away and made her way over to her dreadful throne. "And now that you are here, you have nothing to worry about. I will keep you under my umbrella of protection. No one, and I do mean no one," she settled down on the throne, "will dare to touch you."

"I appreciate that, Sharon. I honestly do." Marcus approached the throne, but I stayed back. I just couldn't make myself come closer to that woman. No matter how congenial she appeared at this moment, all I saw was the monster that stormed into the coven and wiped everyone out. "But that is not why I am here."

She sat back and looked down her nose at Marcus. "I imagined not. Then what brings you here?"

"An offer," Marcus said, stepping to within just a few feet of her. "To end all this."

Sharon Roberts turned in her seat away from Marcus. He had lost her attention, but that didn't stop him. He continued. "If you return Jean St. Claire to the vampires."

She waved a dismissive hand with a harsh exhale. Then she pointed in my direction.

"Child, who are you?"

"Gwen Gale," I said, this time making sure not to stammer. She looked me up and down once, and then crossed her legs, one over the other. Her foot bounced as she looked away from Marcus. Her hands played with one another. It appeared the mere mention of the topic had caused Marcus to lose her attention, but that didn't stop him, and what he offered pulled her right back and stunned me.

"They will give you Larissa Dubois."

I wasn't sure who was more stunned by that offer. Her or me. She showed it, and about fell off of her throne. I, on the other hand, had to stand there emotionless, all the while I was trying to figure out if Marcus had just betrayed me or not. I wasn't sure if he knew he needed to choose his next words carefully.

"Larissa Dubois? That's a nice try," Sharon said, trying to compose herself. "But it's not something they can deliver on."

"Well, actually," Marcus held his hand out palm up, and light projected from it. In the middle of the light was me. I was sitting there on my knees with my hands tied behind me. "They already have."

Seeing the image caused my fingers to twitch uncontrollably. It brought back more than a few memories that I didn't want to relive. I had to tell myself, it's just an image, but there was a part of me wondering if it was a vision of the future, and that just added to the anxiousness that built inside, and now threatened to explode out.

Sharon Roberts leaned forward. Her eyes were as wide as a child's on Christmas morning. She surrounded the image with her hands and spun it all around, studying it from all angles.

"There are advantages of her boyfriend being a vampire," Marcus added.

"Well, isn't that heartbreaking," Mrs. Roberts crowed. She sat up and looked right at Marcus. There was an intensity in her gaze I hadn't seen before from her. Not even when she stood there and lectured me about her master plan. She studied the stone-steady expression on Marcus' face and the corners of her mouth curled up. She pointed a single finger at him and asked, "You're serious. This isn't some kind of trick?"

Marcus closed his hand, and with it, the disturbing image disappeared. He put both hands behind his back and stepped one step closer to Mrs. Roberts. "No trick. This war you have going won't serve the best interest of anyone in the end. It needs to stop, and it needs to stop now. This is the way. If you broker this trade, in a great show of leadership in front of everyone, you would be the default supreme. Everything else would be forgotten. Any threat to your rule would be gone."

Sharon Roberts leaned back and looked up at the stone ceiling. "You do have a point," she admitted. "You do have a really good point, but would every threat really be eliminated?"

"The most immediate ones," Marcus quickly offered.

"Really? What about you? One could consider you a threat. With your family name and all."

Marcus laughed loudly, which seemed to bother Sharon Roberts. Her face scrunched up, and she leaned back as far as she could against the back of the throne. His outburst seemed to offend her, and for a moment, I forgot he had just offered my life up to her.

"Sharon, I can assure you," Marcus said through the remnants of his laughter. "If I were. I wouldn't be here making this offer." Marcus adjusted his stance and leered up at Sharon Roberts. "And I would have just come in here and yanked from that throne to take my family's rightful place." Then he smiled up at her, almost maniacally. The weight of his threat made the silence suffocating, and Marcus knew it. He let it last for several seconds before he let the pressure out. "But rest assured. That is not my intention. I always hated that hideous throne. It's all yours. I just want all this to end, and I know what you need to make it happen." He rocked back on his heels, and shifted his hands to in front of him, where he clasped them again. "So, do we have a deal?"

"Okay. All right," Sharon Roberts agreed, but did so sounding reluctantly.

"Great. Not that I want to tell you how to do your business, but I believe you should make a spectacle of it. Gather everyone together for the swap, and make some kind of grand announcement about ending the hostilities. I'm sure you can think of a magnificent speech to revel in your moment."

"Yes, that's not a bad idea." Her finger tapped her chin as she considered his proposal. I was sure images of me being dragged up on some grand stage were playing in her head. Even images of my death.

But I think I finally understood what he was doing. I was the bait. I wasn't happy about it, and even if he believed that was my way to get close to her, if he thought I was going to let someone drag me up on to the stage tied up as part of some show, he has another think coming.

"Oh, one thing that I neglected to mention," started Marcus, drawing Mrs. Roberts to the edge of her seat. "It has to be tonight."

"Tonight?" she asked, surprised.

"That is one of their terms. It's tonight, or it's all off. Their rules, not mine."

She sprang up out of the throne and walked around behind it toward the door that led out to the balcony. She never went through the door, just merely stopped in the door. I guess she needed some fresh air to aid her decision.

"This is a once in a lifetime opportunity," Marcus pressed, with all the tact of a used car salesman.

"All right," she agreed with her back to us. "But I pick where."

"Agreed."

Sharon Roberts spun around, still standing at the door. The night wind ruffling the long skirt of her dress. "The original coven. In two hours."

"Deal."

"You do remember where that is? So many of the newer generations don't know about the birthplace of magic."

"I do," stated Marcus. I was glad he knew where it was. I didn't. I hadn't even heard of the place. "Now, if you would excuse us. I need to deliver the message and make arrangements."

"Of course. It was great to see you again, Marcus." Then she looked past him and at me, regarding me for only the second time. "And you too Miss Gale. I hope to see you again. Maybe you would like to serve on my court at some time."

Marcus turned and walked out through the door Gregory had led us through. I followed right on his heels. I half expected to find him waiting for us outside in the hall, but he wasn't. We walked swiftly down the hall. Lanterns dimming behind us, restoring the place back to the darkness that was there when we arrived. The main door was still open, but as we exited out of it. It closed.

"Court," Marcus scoffed, breaking the silence. "More of a cult of ass kissers." He spun open a portal, and we walked through it and back to the driveway in front of my old farmhouse.

I gave Marcus a quick shove, sending him to the ground, and then returned myself to my normal appearance before I screamed, "Why didn't you tell me I was the bait? And there is no way in hell I am going to be paraded around as some kind of prisoner."

28

I stood over Marcus, leering down at him. Our appearance and my actions had caused a bit of a stir among those gathered around us. The murmur was almost deafening, and they had closed ranks around us to find out what was going on. Right up front was Samantha. Her hands were already flexing.

"My mother is not bait," she roared, and her hands rose up, ready to give her a response to anything Marcus had to say. I stepped in front of her and held up an arm to hold her back. It was possible I had overreacted just a tad, and Samantha and others were feeding off of my reaction. I did my best to calm down, or to at least look calm outwardly, no matter if I was calm inside or not.

Marcus didn't appear too afraid, but he did not try to get up. He just laid there, propped up on his elbows.

"Sure, she is. She has to be, and she knows it." He looked at me and then leaned to one side, offering me the other hand to help him up. I didn't take it. I wasn't exactly satisfied by his answer, and instead stepped closer, and crossed my arms so there was no confusion. I would not take his hand. At least not yet. He got the message and wiggled his way up to a seated position. "Larissa, you are the only reason she is going to assemble everyone together, which is what we need."

"Okay, but I will not be paraded up there like some kind of prisoner." There was more than my pride talking here. Things could go haywire in a heartbeat with this plan, and I would be trapped up there, tied up, just like she would want me.

"No one said you would."

I cocked my head to one side and reminded Marcus, "Really? What about that image? The one you showed her of me on my knees with my hands tied behind me."

"An illusion only. Just to make her believe it." Marcus struggled up to his feet all on his own and took a few steps backward to put some space between him and those that had gathered closely around us. If he had taken another step backwards, he would have bumped into the front porch. He brushed himself off. "I needed to sell her an image that she would not only believe, but one that would inspire her.

Something that would tap into her ego. The more I tapped into that, the more her own aspirations will blind her. She is exactly where we want her."

Marcus scanned the faces of the gathered group. "The trap is set. Now we will spring it on her." He looked at me, confused. "You didn't honestly believe I was going to hand you over to her, did you?"

I felt hesitant to answer. The thought seemed so stupid now, and to say I felt a little embarrassed, well, I did. "Yes, in a way."

Marcus walked toward me. "Larissa, nothing would be further from the truth," he explained while covering the distance between us.

"I know that. I knew you would never hand me over completely, but I was worried you were going to deliver me to her as part of the plan. That can't happen."

"It won't. I won't let it," he assured me with a look and a pat on the shoulder. "This is all part of the plan. Once everyone is all assembled and waiting for you to arrive, that is when we spring it." Marcus walked past me and toward the center of the driveway again. The same place he stood in the last time he addressed everyone. "Everyone gather around." He held his arms out to pull everyone in. "Two hours. In two hours, Mrs. Roberts will gather all her supporters at the original coven for a prisoner exchange of sorts. She will hand over Jean St. Claire to us, and we will hand her Larissa Dubois." Another murmur showed signs of developing, but Marcus raised his hand up in the air and put an end to it. "Which there is no way we are going to do. Sharon Roberts' guard will be down, and everyone we need to see what is going to happen will be in one place. That is when we will strike."

Marcus pulled both hands tight into a prayer, and then exploded them outward. A flash raced across the ground, behind it the ground rolled and changed. Vampires and werewolves scattered, jumping to avoid the changing ground. Grass became stone. Sky became forest. The moon shifted slightly in the sky. The farmhouse and field disappeared. The flat landscape became rolling hills with dips and rises. Old stone columns burst through the ground and rose a dozen or more feet in the sky. They created an arch around a single stone platform that unfolded itself on the ground.

"This is the original coven. It's in the woods to the north of Old Salem," Marcus announced. "We are not really there, but I wanted you to see what it looked like." Marcus walked toward the platform. "I have no doubt this is where she will be waiting." He stepped up onto the stone platform. "This will be her grand stage for her spectacle, just as it was for the supreme to give speeches and instructions to the masses many centuries ago." His hand reached out and attempted to trace the horizon line of the landscape. "If you can't tell, this is down in a depression which makes this a natural amphitheater. That is not an accident, and we will use it to our advantage. They will all be gathered here."

Hundreds and hundreds of red shadows appeared on the slope of the hill that led down to the stage. Some stood. Some moved. I jumped out of the way of one and right into the middle of another. Gwen shrieked when one walked through her. A few people, me included, giggled at that.

Myself, Lisa, Jack, Gwen, Samantha, and Larissa will open portals to bring everyone just on the other side of the rise. There we will crest the hill. A line of yellow figures and shapes appeared at the top of the hill. The shapes took form and became people and large wolves. "We will have the high ground, and they will be surrounded. Now, I want to make something perfectly clear. I will give them one chance to surrender. But just one chance. Any that want to leave can. If Sharon gives up, then she gives up and will face a trial as mandated by our laws. If she doesn't, she will not have another opportunity." He searched through our gathered numbers around him and pointed at Jack, Gwen, and Samantha. "You three will be on opposite sides and will unleash your little surprises left by the great Merlin. Send those troops over the hill from each side at the same time. Have them rush the crowd. They will fight back, and after the initial confusion, they will realize these troops are not real. That is when we unleash hell and give them something real. Our goal is not to kill, but to subdue, but if you need to, you know what to do. Larissa and I will make our way to the stage. I hope in all the confusion, no one will see us coming, but just to be sure, Larissa, let the balls fly." He paused and looked around the mass of people. His head nodded up and down as the image of the first coven dissipated around us. "Is everyone clear?"

There was a chorus of vocal agreements. Marcus reached down to the ground and grabbed a handful of dirt and tossed it up into the air. It never hit the ground. Instead, it became the sand inside of a golden hourglass. "When that runs out, we will go."

The crowd dispersed and everyone intermingled together. Marcus motioned for me to come with him, and I did. Samantha, Nathan, and Jack attempted to follow, and I expected him to stop them like he had before, but he didn't.

"Wait up," Lisa called, running to join our group. I noticed Gwen followed behind her; probably not wanting to be left out.

"I have a little surprise," Marcus said as he turned around and revealed a growing portal. The image on the other side produced a squeal from Lisa. James O'Conner and Mary Smith stepped through. "I thought we could use a little extra help."

Lisa ran and hugged James before Samantha could reach him. I was going to have to watch those two. Nathan raised an eyebrow at the sight. I made a beeline for Mary Smith. "Oh my god, Mary, I am so glad you're alive."

"That makes two of us," she said, returning my hug. "I heard what happened at the coven. Marcus told us. I'm so sorry. We are going to end this tonight. No one else is going to die." A little of the old Mary made her way into that declaration, and I was actually glad to hear it.

We walked back toward the house where everyone else was mulling around. Nathan grabbed my hand as we walked. "You know it's not too late."

"Too late for what?" I asked.

"To take off and find a life way away from all this."

I stopped, but Nathan kept walking. Our arms stretched between us, until it was too much, and I pulled him back like a spring. He turned around and looked at me. Even though his eyes were blank and black, I still saw pain. It was all over his face, and in his body language. The confidence was gone. His head tilted down, almost dangling from his slumped shoulders.

"And now you want to do that? Not all the times I mentioned it before?"

He looked around me awkwardly. "Yep." His head guided his eyes all around the area above and beside my face, but never at my face. I gave his hand a hard yank, trying to pull him back from wherever he was. His gaze finally found me. It looked away briefly and then returned. "We've lost so much. I don't want to lose any more." His voice trembled as he spoke, and then his eyes glanced away. "Not to mention we need to get our daughter from your friend over there."

I followed his eyes, and saw Samantha talking, alone, with James. That was something I would have to nip in the bud rather shortly, but there was something else more important at the moment. I reached up, grabbed his chin, and yanked his face back to mine. I couldn't believe what I was about to say. It sounded so responsible to be coming from me, but it was the right thing to do. "It's because of all we have lost that we need to do this. We owe it to their memory to stop this right now."

Nathan reached over and yanked me up against him, hard. Not that I was complaining. His arms squeezed me into one of the biggest bear hugs I had ever felt. "I know you're right; I just don't want you to be right. I want you and Samantha by my side the whole time. Got it?"

I didn't answer, and looked over at the base of one of the magnolia trees that lined the driveway.

Once he saw who was sitting there, he knew what I was thinking, and let me go. "She can't come with us."

"I know. I thought about sending her off with Samantha, but as much as I don't want it to be true, we need her. She is probably my equal, just never tell her that." I left Nathan standing there, watching as I walked toward the tree and the two individuals that sat under it. I knew what I had to do and readied myself for a protest.

When I arrived, I kneeled down beside Amy and Marie, who sat at the base of the tree. "Look. I want you to go with Marie someplace, and I will come get you when we come back."

Amy said nothing, but I saw Marie prepare her protest. It was a good thing I had my counter ready and beat her to the punch. "Nope. Don't start. You have done enough. You saved me and paid a horrible price for it. I am going to open you a portal back to our old home. I want you and Amy to go there and wait for us to return." I looked down at Amy. "I think I still have some stuffed animals in my room you'll enjoy, and loads of books."

Marie tried to speak again, but I cut her off with a light, "No." Then I opened the portal that took them right into our kitchen. Marie stood up and hugged me. I felt a wet tear running down her cheek when it pressed against me. "We will be fine," I whispered. Then Amy hugged me. Marie held out her hand, but before Amy took it, she ran off and crashed into Laura with a big hug.

Laura bent down and returned it. Over Amy's shoulder, she looked at me and mouthed, "Thank you."

Amy ran back and took Marie's hand, and I watched the two of them walk into the home I had lived in for over seventy years.

I stood there feeling weepy, watching the space they had just walked through. Marcus announced it was time, and I heard the crowd gather behind me. There were lines of vampires and werewolves behind the witches. I took my place beside Samantha, and Nathan behind me, right where I could keep an eye on both of them. Marcus watched and waited until the last of the werewolves had phased. A few howled. I looked through the crowd and found Mike. We made eye contact, and he nodded. Then I looked along the front lines and found Lisa two columns over. Gwen was between us, and Jack was on the other side of Lisa. Lisa and I locked eyes, and I cut my eyes in the direction of Samantha. Lisa understood the message and nodded, and the writing appeared again on her skin and her eyes turned golden. I can't really say we were ready, but that didn't matter. The time had arrived.

29

Marcus explained he would leave and gave us the instructions to wait three minutes before we came through. Just to make sure we knew when to arrive. He set the hourglass again, but this time with only a thin layer of sand in it. Probably three minutes' worth. We were all ready to watch him walk through and then wait for the time to run out, but Lisa realized something, that I guess with everything else in my head had slipped my mind.

"Marcus, we don't know how to get there."

He turned around with chagrin. He should have realized it, too. Details. Details. Details. That would have been great. He would have walked through. We would have been here with no way to follow him, and he would be there wondering where we were. That would have been a bit more than awkward.

"James, have you ever been to the first coven?"

James shook his head.

"Mary, I'm guessing you haven't either."

"I've been to Salem once, but that is as close as I can take you."

Marcus pursed his lips in thought. "Astral location is probably only an option for two. Make that three of you. Sorry Mary."

"I've read about it, but have never done it," I said, wanting to make sure he understood I was in no way an expert. That was one option I wanted to see ruled out.

"It's quite easy. You locate my astral presence and use it as a way finder," he explained. I cocked my head to the side and crossed my arms. "Yea, that's no good. Well, that really just leaves one option. Come along, we will make it quick."

Marcus spun his arm, and a portal opened. He stepped through and waved urgently for us to follow. I stepped through and felt the cold chill of the Salem night air. We were on the other side of the hill, right where he wanted us to be. Behind us was a dense forest that stood majestically in the darkness. Ahead of us, a glow from torches illuminated the top of the hill, and voices, a lot of them, drowned out the natural sound of the night. They were there waiting, just like Marcus had explained.

"Okay, now you have been here. You should be able to find your way. Get." He motioned for us to leave as urgently as he motioned for us to come through just moments before. The portal started to close, but just before it disappeared, he leaned through, "Remember, three minutes." It closed, and the hourglass flipped.

Lisa, Samantha, Jack, Gwen, and I took our positions in front of our groups. James and Mary stood between us. All eyes watched as each grain of sand fell from the top down to the bottom of the hourglass. Each grain seemed to defy gravity as it fell slowly to the bottom. We waited, anxiously. I peeled my gaze from the sands of time and looked over at Samantha. She was focused and leaning forward, ready to run. Her hands flexed open and closed, ready for whatever came to her. She was a warrior, and so much like her mother, and I guess her grandfather. Ready to jump into anything without a second thought. I looked back up at the glass as the last grains fell. Then, the world flashed with gold glitter as five portals opened, and we rushed through into the chilly Salem night air.

We were through, and we closed each of the portals. Gwen, Jack, and Samantha were conjuring their forces. In the distance, I heard Marcus's voice. He was addressing the assembled witches. I tilted my head to the side, trying to point an ear in the direction of his voice. He didn't seem to be up at the front. He was closer than that. I walked forward a few steps up the incline of the hill. I was right. He was just over the top of the hill.

"... Now on this auspicious night, allow me to hold my end of the bargain and bring the vampire elders and their prisoner, Larissa Dubois." He said with the enthusiasm of a circus ringleader. The crowd erupted in a cheer that was a little too grand for my liking, considering what they were cheering about. Marcus crested the hill and walked down a few steps to make sure he disappeared from their view.

He looked around and smiled at the image of large garrisons of knights with a few on horseback to either side, and one directly in the center behind the hill. With a bow, he said, "Unleash hell."

Samantha pointed forward with her right hand. Jack and Gwen did the same with their wands, and the troops rushed the hill. I started up the hill. Nathan was close behind, and Mr. Markinson and Martin had made it up to my side. Having two of the largest wolves I had ever seen beside me gave me a sense of security. Having another two dozen or so of their friends behind us didn't hurt either. They were growling lowly. Rob had moved up next to Samantha, and so had Mike. Clay and Rob had taken similar positions next to Gwen and Lisa. Brad had Jack's back.

We all stopped midway up the hill and watched as the knights crested the top of the hill. Then they stormed down the other side. Screams filled the air, as did flashes of color. Howls erupted from behind us as the thunder of paws racing up the hill rattled the ground.

Apryl ran up and grabbed me by the arm. "Let's go! Let's get you to the front and end this!"

She dragged me a few steps before it clicked, and I followed her up and over. The image was one of complete chaos. Hundreds of red-robed witches running and fighting. Many of them hadn't figured out the knights weren't real yet. They were still firing offensive spells through them, which sometimes hit other witches. The werewolves were trampling anyone in their way. They showed great restraint, not biting and tearing them apart with their massive teeth. I felt that would only last until the first witch fought back. The same with the vampires. Mike and Clay were tossing witches over the hill like feathers. The others had cornered groups of witches and were surrounding them.

Apryl got in the action and tossed two out of our way. I shouldered a few more. Mrs. Roberts and I locked eyes when I was halfway down the hill. She turned and scampered toward the edge of the platform, but I sent a huge shot of fire in her direction, creating a wall of flames. That sent her retreating to the other side. I met her there with a bolt of lightning, and she bounced back to the other. She wasn't getting away, and she knew it. She prepared to fight back, but then it all stopped.

"Everyone! This is over!" Marcus announced from high above the scene. "There is no need for anyone to die today. Surrender and leave peacefully and all will be forgiven." He floated down to the platform, next to a surprised Sharon Roberts. Feeling the attention shift back to her, she righted herself and straightened out her ceremonial red robe, and then reached up and threw her curly blonde locks over her shoulders. "Sharon, surrender and the bloodshed ends now."

I pushed my way through the rest of the way to the platform. Gwen, Jack, and Samantha stood up on top of the hill. Each pulling their troops to a stop. This was the chance Marcus said he would give them. The only chance. What happened next was their choice.

"Hello Larissa." The voice sent chills down my back from behind. I knew that voice. I dreaded that voice. His gnarled-up hands grabbed me and threw me off the platform, and I landed face first on the hard cold ground.

I rolled over fast enough to see Jean St. Claire leaping off the stone stage at me. He leered at me with an expression nightmares were made of. My nightmares, that I had when I didn't even sleep. My hands raised, and I sent him screaming off to the left in a flash of fire and smoke that traced his path into the old Greek revival column he crashed into. The column cracked, and the rubble rained down on top of him. I caught another flash out of the corner of my eye and saw Marcus moving just in time. Mrs. Roberts had given her answer, as did most of the witches.

They had finally realized the knights weren't real and were ignoring them. I looked back at the rubble of the destroyed limestone column. It was shifting, but Jean hadn't forced his way free. Just to be sure, I pushed a gust of wind in his direction to send a teetering piece of limestone back on top of the pile. I heard a muffled grunt after it crashed down.

With Jean secured for at least a moment, I turned to the gathered group of witches. They were now ignoring the knights, and walking right through them, with no fear of their attack. The vampires and werewolves were stepping in to re-enforce things. I heard the first cries of death come from a witch. A bright flash followed, and then a mournful howl from a wolf. I looked and saw one fall, with a familiar burning. Mary Smith rushed toward it, as it cried and writhed on the ground in pain. These were just the first of what would be many, and I felt that deep. My head knew it going in, but my heart wasn't ready to experience it all again.

I searched frantically for Nathan and Samantha. At first, I didn't see them, but I searched away from the melee and found Samantha still up on the hill. She was firing shots from up high. I watched as she expertly cast a spell, not at a group of witches, but between a group of witches. The ground fell out between them, sending them scattering. She was being a disruptor, while avoiding causing anyone any injury. Lisa and Gwen were doing the same. Nathan was still missing. I searched again, praying he wasn't in the middle of all that. Knowing how he had that tendency to run toward danger, it was a logical concern. Panic fueled my first steps to a full-on sprint toward the mass of witches, vampires, and werewolves. While I ran, I kept searching for him, and for Mike, hoping Mike remembered his promise.

"Duck!" I didn't wait to see who said it before I dropped to the ground. My body slid because of its forward momentum. Behind me, I heard the thump of two bodies tackling one another. I slung my body around, and quickly raised a hand, calling on the fabric of the world to push one of the two individuals that were locked in combat. It caught both of them, sending my target further than my hero. I jumped up to my feet and offered Nathan my hand. "You have to stop jumping between danger and me."

"What? And let Jean get you again." We both cast a look in the direction I sent him. Knowing Nathan was in the line of fire, I didn't want to give it my full force, so he landed just a few feet away. He stood there looking at us, in some kind of odd standoff while the world around us erupted in screams, flashes of fire and light, and the rumble of the ground. That didn't matter, though. At the moment there were only three of us, and in my mind, I felt this was the final standoff, and I no longer needed to be concerned with Nathan. He was a vampire, and virtually still a newborn.

We walked toward him, and he walked toward us. A pair of hands slapped us both on the back. "Don't leave me out of the fun." Clay stared over our shoulders at Jean like a rabid animal. He was fangs out and rage building as he pushed through us on his way to Jean. He had a score to settle with Jean, but I hated to break it to him, my score was bigger.

"Whoa, wait a minute," I said. Now it was my turn to grab his shoulder from behind. Clay tried to shake it off, but my grip was firm. He turned, eyes bugging, ready to feast. "We do this together. We all have something to take out."

Clay looked at me, and then at Nathan and growled a low, "Absolutely."

The three of us walked toward Jean like some kind of badass vampire gang. Jean walked toward us but had seemed to have lost a little of his animalistic edge he had earlier when he came after me. Now he was more confused than anything. He held his arms out and asked, "What? Can Larissa Dubois not fight her own fight?"

"This isn't just her fight!" Clay shouted back.

Jean looked taken aback by this response, and he stopped and stood there studying Clay.

"Remember me?" Clay asked, his arms outstretched. His fingers clawed at the air, ready to sink into tissue.

"Ah no," Jean started, and then he stuck his finger up on the air and looked at Clay pridefully. "I do. I sent you to deliver her to me." Then he turned to look at Nathan, and practically giggled like a schoolgirl. "Wow, and you must be that poor idiot that threw yourself between me and Larissa the last time." He studied Nathan up and down. "You're some of my best work, it would seem."

"And you will be mine!" Nathan growled.

That amused Jean, who again giggled while clapping his hands together at this chest. "Very poetic, my dear boy. Very poetic."

While he was distracted, I cast "grandeur" and pointed at the ground beneath Jean. I hadn't tried this particular spell in years. Make that decades. The last time I tried something similar, it was a potion in Mrs. Tenderschott's class. A flash shot from my hand to the ground, and the grass and wildflowers beneath Jean's feet grew uncontrollably, wrapping themselves around his legs. When they tightened, he looked down, surprised, then he looked up.

"Not fair," he pouted. That pout lasted a few kicks into his attempt to break free. When nothing budged, and instead tightened even more around his calves before growing up to his thighs, that pout changed to an expression I enjoyed.

I held my hand up and let sparks fly from the ends of my fingers. "I'm a witch. We aren't to be trusted, remember?" None of us waited for his answer before we sprinted for him.

He screamed, but I doubted anyone there would help him. I even heard him call out to Tobias, who stopped what he was doing for just a brief second to look in Jean's direction, but then he appeared to nod his okay to the three of us and went back to subduing witches. Jean called out other names, but I didn't recognize any of them. To me, they were just random attempts for help, but each time I looked around just to be sure. Not a soul moved, and only a few looked in his direction.

Seeing the lack of regard for this once great vampire should have been sad, but I didn't feel that way at all. I didn't care. What I found shocking were the smiles of approval we received from those few that looked in his direction.

Any belief Jean had that he would survive this melted away before our eyes. That defiant and ego-fueled grin he always wore dropped as he looked into each of our eyes. I believe he was able to read our intentions. Not that there was any big mystery about what those intentions were. If he had asked, I imagined we would have rather enjoyed telling him what we were about to do, blow by blow.

I shared a look with Nathan and Clay. This was our time, and nothing could stop us. Or so I thought. As soon as we stepped forward another step, it happened. I saw the ground heave first before the flash. When the flash arrived, a loud crack accompanied it. I flew up and over Jean, and from this vantage point, I could see two things. The weeds and grass that had restrained him were now receding, and Mrs. Roberts had rescued him yet again.

I hit the ground hard and rolled over to see Nathan and Clay land close by. Jean didn't take the opportunity to attack us. Instead, he retreated to the side of his protector, who was still battling Marcus and had the help of a few other witches. Behind him, we were losing. Some of the vampires were in retreat. The werewolves weren't stopping, but their numbers were limited and most of them were limping. Something had to happen to turn the tide, but what?

My mind searched for a spell that might help or serve as a distraction. I had nothing in my head, but I remembered I had something in my pocket. I reached inside, I felt the two large round objects. My hand fished them out and threw them into the air as far as I could. I waited for them to fall down until they were just above everyone's head, and I yelled, "Ignite!"

Two large dragons flashed to life. Their wings flapped, sending a blast of air down and along the ground, pushing people from their feet. This was definitely a distraction. Everyone stopped and looked as both of the mythical beasts took flight and circled above. When they circled for the second time, both blew a long stream of fire down at the ground. No one waited to find out if this was real or not. The witches dispersed, but they didn't get far. What remained of the vampires circled around them and held them there. With a flick of my wrist, I sent both beasts to perch on two of the large marble columns. Then sat there, atop those columns, watching over everyone.

Mrs. Roberts didn't wait to see what our next trick was. She opened a portal behind her and rushed through it with Jean and a few of her core supporters that were lucky enough to be up on stage with her. Marcus leapt to the stage and spun his own inside hers, preventing it from closing.

"Come on Larissa! We need to move!"

30

I jumped through the portal and back into what I would now consider the infamous throne room. This time, Mrs. Roberts wasn't perched on that hideous chair or giving any grand speeches. She was running for what appeared her life as she, Jean, and a handful of her supporters exited out through the door we came in during Marcus' negotiation session. Marcus and I gave chase, but the echo of several sets of footsteps in the stone walled room told me we weren't the only ones. I looked around to see Lisa, Samantha, Clay, Brad, and several other vampires flooding through the portal that was now stuck open.

"Stop them!" someone cried from behind.

I wanted to remind them that was the goal, but it seemed senseless to have to do it. Instead, I attempted to loop a telekinetic rope around Mrs. Roberts or Jean to pull them down to the ground, but each time I tried, I missed. They were moving fast. I needed to go stronger and faster. I could easily do it faster, and it didn't take more than a second before I was leading the pack, and just outside of arm's length of several of Mrs. Roberts' supporters. I tried again, but this time tapping into something stronger. There was no rope this time. I sent a little pulse down the fabric of the universe while thinking of an Athame. It didn't take more than a split second for the symbol to construct itself and draw itself over and over again. A little pulse of fire blasted away from me through the fabric of time. One by one, the supporters in front of me fell to the ground like dominoes.

Mrs. Roberts opened another portal in the wall in front of her and pushed what appeared to be a rather reluctant Jean St. Claire through it before she jumped in herself. I slowed enough for Marcus to catch me, but he never slowed, and he did exactly what I thought he would. He spun his own inside hers, holding it open before jumping through too. I followed, landing in an expansive rose garden that spanned across rolling hills.

Lisa landed just behind me. Adrenaline was the only explanation for her keeping up with me. Mrs. Roberts' supporters, on the other hand, were falling by the wayside, unable to keep up with the pace of the chase. I gave a few of them an evil eye as I ran past, almost wanting to make them pay for their support of that evil woman, but that would be to what end? Nothing, that's what. I didn't want to be just like her. I wanted to appear just and benevolent, not abusive, and vindictive. I could only hope the vampires behind me showed the same restraint. Was that something I could leave to chance? I didn't know, considering everything that was going on. I couldn't chance it. "Leave them!" I turned and yelled back, never missing a step.

I didn't turn to check to see if my request had been complied with. There was no screaming, so I had to assume it had. My target now was Mrs. Roberts, who was in the clear and slowing with every step. I sent a fireball in her direction. She still had enough to turn and defend herself with the same. Now I know I could reach her; this was her endgame. I reached out and pulled the fabrics of the world, and she slowed further. I threw a Besom out to protect myself and anyone around us. I wasn't sure it would be enough, but I had to do something, considering what I was about to try. With a combination of air and earth elemental runes fired in her direction, I knocked her to her knees. It was either the blast of wind or the upheaval of the ground that did it. Either one also knocked Jean over. Now we had them where I wanted them.

"Dang it!" I screamed as Mrs. Roberts opened the portal through the ground below them. Or I assumed it was her. I never saw her arm spin. All I saw was her hand pressed against the ground, and the portal exploded open from there. She and Jean fell through the hole. Marcus did his magic yet again and opened one of his own before it closed, then jumped in. I did the same and realized I should have looked before I leaped. There was nothing except darkness below us as we fell, and I screamed again. I wasn't the only one. Lisa and Samantha both screamed as they fell.

I kept searching below us for the ground, but there was nothing.

"Time to learn a new trick," Marcus exclaimed. "Aim wind downward."

"What?" Gwen screamed.

"Aim wind downward."

Lisa went first, and we all zoomed past her. Then Samantha did it, while also aiming it below Apryl and Clay. I tried next and finally understood what Marcus was asking us to do. My fall slowed to something that was more akin to a float, and it wasn't just me. The more I aimed, the more people I could carry down with me. Clay, Apryl, Brad, and several other vampires were caught up in my column of air, and just in time, too. Below us, treetops came into view. With a few shifts of my hand, I sent puffs of wind to the right and then to the left, to weave us between the tree canopy and down to the forest floor.

When we landed, it was just us. Mrs. Roberts and Jean were nowhere to be found. She knew where she was going and probably descended a little more gracefully and expediently. How much of a head start they had? No one knew. But there were several vampires that stepped forward and pointed to our right like bloodhounds tracking a fugitive. Samantha pointed too, and I searched my sensations to confirm they were all correct. That was the direction.

Several vampires streaked forward ahead of everyone else, and I mumbled, "Oh, crap," before taking off myself. I believe I knew what they might do if they reached her first, and I couldn't let that happen. Not that I would have minded. Both she and Jean deserved it, but it would not accomplish what we had set out to do. I had to get there first.

The haunted forest in *The Wizard of Oz* had nothing on this place. I ran through tall, towering trees and shadows dancing in the moonlight. All that was missing were the moving trees throwing apples at me. It looked and felt eerie, and that was before the wind howled through the treetops, producing a chorus of groans and pops. I had planned to add a few screams and groans to that. I just needed to catch up with them first, and for the briefest of seconds, I saw them shoving an overgrown fern out of the way. I had them.

Giving it my all, my strides transformed into leaps. I tried again to use magic to draw them closer. This time, producing a slight wave in the ground beneath their feet. Call it a mini earthquake, that was more of a rolling wave than an actual destructive quake. It worked, and again Mrs. Roberts, her last remaining supporter, a gentleman in a brown suit, and Jean St. Claire were on their backsides. They were in my grasp, but to make sure, I allowed my mind to imagine a huge lasso around them and attempted to pull them right to me with a single yank. I yanked. In my mind, the loop tightened. In real life, they slipped through another portal Mrs. Roberts had opened in the ground beneath her. This was getting old. I cast a look behind me and saw the others following. Marcus was several vampires deep in the posse. I pointed down and jumped through the open portal. Order, Larissa! Order, Larissa! Marcus always opened one of his own inside the portal to hold it open. I jumped through first, before trying to open my own, hoping that would hold it open. Not that I knew it would work for sure. I hadn't done it before. I hadn't even tried it before. No matter. I forgot to open a portal inside hers before I jumped through. It closed behind me.

We landed back in the throne room, falling through the door to the right of the throne. I slid across the wood floor to the other side. Mrs. Roberts, her last supporter–Mr. Brownsuit and Jean stood there watching as I slipped right past them and into the wall on the other side.

They stood over the top of me and leaned down. I wasn't sure who was leering more. Jean or Mrs. Roberts. Mr. Brownsuit tried, but I believe he was just doing it because the others were. Jean's hands rubbed one another briefly before pushing the sleeves of his white shirt up to his elbows, and his large black eyes narrowed. All I could do as I laid there, looking up at them, was wave. "Hi." Then I let out a huge gust of wind from the palm of my hand, sending them all back against the far wall.

Before they hit the wall, I hit my feet, using a bit of wind myself to push me up right. I wanted to be ready in case Mrs. Roberts tried something before her re-introduction to the wall Samantha put her through once before. She didn't, but Jean rebounded off the wall and leaped across the room at me.

"You're mi–" he started to scream, but I stopped him, grabbing his head as he passed. I jumped, arched my back, and then recoiled with all my might, slinging him by his head back into the wall. It was a move Mike showed me, and I rather liked how it caught your target off guard. He hit with a loud crack and slid down the floor, shaking his head. There was no doubt he was going to feel that impact for quite some time. Even the sound it made hurt.

I landed back on my feet like a superhero with one fist on the floor. A flash of blue passed by my head on the way down. When I hit the ground, I had to twist to one side to avoid a flash of red.

I looked up and saw Mrs. Roberts' hands waving around in the air. Nothing had appeared yet, so I knew she wasn't done, and I had at least a blink of an eye to react. I pushed against the stone floor below me to charge at her. My mind was already reciting the third surprise Marcus had provided me with. It was time to see how much she enjoyed being frozen and floating just above the ground. Turnabout was fair play. The stones below me disintegrated to dust as my foot and hand pushed down against it. Then I sank into the floor up to my waist in an odd grey dust that still had lines on it and looked like a cobblestone floor.

"Crap!" I didn't just think about it. I screamed at it.

Two laughs erupted from the other side of the room. I tossed a few fireballs to shut that up and then tried to break free. The more I struggled, the more I sank. I pushed down with my left hand, hoping to lift myself up and free. My head dropped as my left hand became stuck. Now I was up a creek, and one of my paddles was stuck. My right hand shot down instinctively, but I stopped it before it reached the floor. Getting both hands stuck would be my end, and the source of that end was now enjoying my predicament.

They were no longer laughing. They were smiling and looking rather proud of themselves. Almost like conquering heroes who were about to win the final battle of some great war. The victory parade through downtown would be next. There may not be a parade for this, but I had no doubt Mrs. Roberts would celebrate. Maybe it would even be my execution, if that didn't happen here in the next few seconds, if my last idea didn't work.

Using the one free arm I had, I spun it around in a circle and the golden glitter rained. I knew where I was. I had been here a few times, and I knew where I came from, which meant... yep, here comes the calvary. I pointed at my achievement and almost yelled, "Tada!" which would have been pretty stupid. No one came through. Not a soul. And looking through the portal, I didn't see anyone either. Great! I had missed them.

Where I had opened it was where I had fallen through the one Mrs. Roberts had opened. They either weren't there yet, or had already passed the spot and were still running, thinking they were still behind us.

Well, my end was here, but I would not go down without a fight, or make that a huge fight. Even with one hand, I planned to do some damage, and started with everything I could. Fireballs. Runes, and every spell I could think of. Inside her own throne room, it was blazing hot, cold and windy, raining, and electrified with lightning strikes. I pulled a few of the stones out of the wall behind them and projected them right at Jean, sending him to the ground hissing. Mrs. Roberts was too busy fending off anything I could throw at her. I even threw in some nuisance type of spells like glamour, changing her into a dog just to mess with her. With only one hand, I was rather limited on what I could do other than delay the inevitable. That didn't mean I would not do just that.

Out of the corner of my eye, I spotted a figure running toward the portal. I couldn't make out who it was, but that didn't matter. It was help, and help was what I needed. I amped up my efforts as I waited to see who was coming to my rescue, while I hoped it would be Marcus or Lisa. It was neither. I knew it as soon as the leg stepped through.

"What the..." exclaimed Gwen as she looked down at my current situation.

I pointed to the other side of the room. Gwen's head jerked in that direction, and then her whole body jerked flat against the closest wall. Her skin always had a healthy glow, but now it was pasty white, and her eyes were so dilated all you could see was the black of her irises.

She looked rather vampire-ish to me, and if this were any other moment, I would have called her on it, but this was not the time or the place.

"Gwen? Gwen Gale?" Mrs. Roberts asked, stepping forward. A shudder went down my spine at both the name and the reaction. I sent a gust to push her back, but she leaned hard into and held her place. "You don't need to be afraid."

Mrs. Roberts held her hand out, and I watched in horror as Gwen's body leaned forward.

"You don't need to be afraid at all," she repeated. Gwen's eyes jumped back and forth between Mrs. Roberts and Jean as she stepped toward them.

"Gwen, stop!" I yelled.

"Don't listen to her," Jean cracked, but Mrs. Roberts cut him off with a single hand before he could say anything else. She brushed her blonde hair back behind her ears, and she straightened her robe.

"Gwen, you don't need to listen to her. She is an exiled witch. Come on over here and let me help you."

Gwen kept walking.

"Gwen! Stop!" I reached out toward her and threw a few protective runes at her; unsure what Mrs. Roberts or Jean might do to her. Then I attempted to pull her back, but each time I looped that imaginary rope around her, it disappeared before I could pull. I was sure Mrs. Roberts had something to do with that.

"Gwen. Come over here. Join me. I could even help groom you to be the next supreme. I saw you with Marcus, so I know you must be a very capable witch."

Her voice was smooth and melodic even to my ears, but it seemed the words were the music Gwen really needed to hear. Her hand reached up to her chest as she squeaked out, "Me?"

"Yes, Gwen. I could make sure that happens. Come on." Mrs. Roberts reached out again and put on her warmest smile.

"Oh, holy hell!" I exclaimed, and made another attempt to pull Gwen back, but again, my attempts were thwarted. A quick glance from Mrs. Roberts confirmed my suspicion of who was responsible for that.

"Just come on Gwen. Come over here and help us get rid of Larissa, and you could be my right hand."

"Gwen, stop!" Marcus stepped through the portal as did Lisa, and several vampires, including Theodora and Tobias. Jean pointed at them before stepping behind Mrs. Roberts and back into one of the few shadows in this torch lit room.

"I should have known not to trust you, Marcus," Mrs. Roberts hissed through gritted teeth. She pointed right at him and then snatched her hand back with a violence that made the air bleed. "No matter. Like you said. This has to end, and end it shall."

I reached my one free hand up, hoping Marcus would yank me free. It dangled there in the air as he provided what, in my opinion was a completely unnecessary rebuttal. "You're correct about one thing. It ends tonight."

Less talking and more action was the order for the day, and I shook my hand in the air one more time to grab his attention. If that didn't work, I had more drastic plans. A hand finally grabbed mine and lifted me partially out of the ground. I looked up and found Lisa pulling with all her might. I knew I wasn't that heavy. Nathan's hand then grabbed on top of hers and yanked me up and free. My feet landed down on the same spot, but it was now solid again.

"Marcus, this is your last chance. Join us. We can rule together."

'Nope," he replied frankly, with a shake of his head. Again inside, I was wondering if we were going to stand here and talk all night, but when I saw the corner of Marcus' mouth curl up, I had my answer. "Now Lisa!"

Lisa swiped her arm swiftly from side to side, and a line of gold glitter went from one side of the room to the other. The throne room melted away. What came into focus was the stone platform at the bottom of the hill in the first coven. Out there on the hill were what remained of her supporting witches. Seeing them all watching us told me why we were here. The audience. Everyone needed to see it.

"This is your last chance," Marcus offered, but he didn't sound sincere. Maybe it was because he, me, and everyone else that was here knew she would say no. The large blue fireball that sent Marcus and three vampires leaping off the stage captured her answer. I gave my rebuttal that was less wordy than the one Marcus gave before. Mrs. Roberts didn't get out of the way, and I enjoyed seeing her sprawled all out on the ground.

"Gwen, defend me!" she ordered. Her voice was scratchy and weak.

For a second, I considered taking out Gwen too, but something inside stopped me. I needed to see her make the first move. If she did, then I had a reason. She never did and just stood there looking down at Mrs. Roberts, now frozen on the ground. Which was really my doing. Encased in that fireball was another spell that Marcus taught me just for this moment. He called it mummification. I was sure it had a better, more grandiose name in some book back in the library or in the archive. But having been a victim of it twice, I can attest it is a rather accurate name. Now Mrs. Roberts was a victim of it. Her restrained form rose off the ground.

"Gwen! Jean! Defend me!"

Gwen may have stayed still, but Jean did not. As I stood there, controlling Mrs. Roberts' flight. Jean rushed at me from the other side of the stage.

"Someone! Help!" I screamed. Both dragons looked down from their perches on the columns behind the stone platform and just watched. So much for their help. Of course, if they did, we probably all would be a little toasty. "Help!" I screamed, with Jean just a few feet away. I was faced with the choice of releasing Mrs. Roberts or bracing myself for the impact of Jean's hit. Neither was one I was looking forward to. Out of the corner of my eye, I saw a blur of figures rushing past me. They knocked me down, breaking my concentration. Mrs. Roberts hit the ground just a split second before Jean was tackled and restrained.

I made it up to my knees and saw a pile of vampires struggling. Hands yanked at Jean's head while his hands struggled to keep his head attached. Leading the tug of war was, surprisingly, Tobias. Four others were helping him, while Nathan and Mike held him on the ground. My triumph to my knees was short-lived. Samantha knocked me to the ground just in time to avoid being hit by some glittery blast. We were both flat on the ground, when another one flew over our head, and then I heard a scream that was music to my ears. It was reminiscent of when I killed her daughter.

I hopped up to see what the cause of the scream was this time. Whatever it was, it was good news, but then was stunned beyond words. Samantha, I think, expressed it best for both of us when she yelled, "Way to go, Gwen!"

Mrs. Roberts, the self-proclaimed supreme that was behind all of this, was struggling for her breath against a sparkling thread that extended from Gwen's wand and wrapped right around her throat. Gwen pulled back with all her weight, tightening the thread's grip on Mrs. Roberts' life.

I wanted to celebrate along with Samantha, but there was a nagging voice in my head. I couldn't believe I was about to say what I was, but I had to. "Gwen! Stop! She has to live!"

"She has to pay," Gwen growled. "She took the lives of the only people who ever made me feel like family. She has to go."

"Gwen–" Marcus started, but Lisa walked forward and placed her hand on his arm, cutting him off. She continued to walk slowly across the platform, studying the mass of vampires that struggled in the center as she passed by.

"Gwen. I know exactly how you feel. She took my family too. Mrs. Saxon, Mrs. Tenderschott, and all of them were my family, too. They took me in when no one else would. Everyone feared my dark side, but instead they taught me to embrace it. To be who I am. Her death won't bring them back." Lisa passed by Mrs. Roberts, letting a finger run across her forehead and up and over her head. As she did, a little red line developed where her finger had touched, and blood dripped. "As satisfying as it would be, it will solve nothing, and take us further from who we are." Lisa reached out and touched Gwen's hand, holding the wand. "We are witches, and the council has rules. Let's not lose who we are. She has taken enough from us already."

Gwen lowered her wand, and as she did, Marcus spun around and threw his hands in the direction of Mrs. Roberts. A white fog raced across the stage and surrounded her form. Then Mrs. Roberts floated up above the ground.

I looked at the assembled witches and saw a surprising show of agreement. Lots of nodding and discussions. The vampires had left the fight and were assembling at the front, watching the struggle for Jean's life. It started as a murmur, then one by one voices broke free. Each voice cried for Jean's life to be taken, and that appeared to energize those struggling with him. Tobias now leaned back with all his weight, attempting to pull Jean's head from his neck. There was a deathly scream from Jean as the torque of the pull began to work. Then a surprising request reached out from the horde. "You can't kill him!"

Another voice made a similar request, and then a third. Then it started. All out melee among the vampires. Those that wanted Jean dead rushed to the stage. Those that didn't, grabbed and fought those that did. I looked at the pile as they wrestled for Jean's life and then looked up at Lisa. Our eyes locked, and I knew we were having a shared thought. I just couldn't believe what the thought was.

A few vampires made it to the stage and joined Tobias' effort to remove Jean's head from his body. If I was going to do this, I had to act fast. I stepped forward and pushed through those gathered for a closer view of Jean's death, and then I did it. The one thing that I think surprised everyone up there, including myself.

"Stop!" I screamed. I reached in and pulled Tobias off of Jean and then pushed his assistants back. "Just stop! We are better than this. We may not have the same laws as the witches do, but that doesn't mean we are animals. Jean has wronged more people than we can count. Trust me, I know, but we can imprison him in Mordin for eternity."

The fighting below us stopped, and every single vampire looked up at me there, perched above Jean. Those that had been struggling with Jean backed away, shocked, and almost looked fearful. I shared the same shock. There was no part of me that saw Jean's fate ending this way. I don't think Jean did either. He attempted to stand up, and I slammed him down on the ground with my foot, keeping it planted firmly on his back. I could have hit him with some magic, but I was standing here in front of vampires. I needed them to see me as a vampire, and not a witch.

"Nathan! Clay! Find something to tie him up with until we can transport him." Nathan and Clay turned to run off, but Jack quickly waved his wand around in several circles, producing a long rope that he gathered and handed to them. They took up position over Jean, and I stepped aside, but not too far, just in case he tried something. Both set to hog tying him, and Jean grunted a few times as Clay tightened the knots, pulling his feet up closer to his back.

31

"Are you ready?" Lisa asked, standing behind me and looking at me through the reflection in my mirror.

"I think so." I looked back at her in the mirror I stood in front of. She and Samantha were rapidly adjusting my mother's white robe on me. I wanted to wear the green one again, but Samantha objected to my wearing the same thing twice, and even went to New Orleans herself to pick this out of the closet. She added a few gold touches to it on her own before she showed it to me. It was a little flashier than I would have agreed to, but it was fine.

"One wonder left," I said, looking right at Lisa's reflection.

"Yep," she agreed, looking at me with a snicker. "Then it's all over, and the world is how it should be."

I let my black eyes roll. Lisa popped me upside the back of my head. Samantha giggled. That was all she had done for the last few days, was smile and giggle. Either it was because of everything that was going on here, or James O'Conner's presence, who I had seen her sharing a few moments around the pool.

After the events of the first coven, we originally returned to New Orleans, but after a bit, several of us felt drawn back here. Imagine our surprise when we arrived and found the coven standing as if nothing had happened. Well, let me take that back. The building was here. The classrooms, our rooms, and even the library were just as we all remembered. Edward was even here waiting for us. But that was it. Inside, it was empty. We were there, but no one else was. The instructors that made this building something were gone, and they weren't coming back.

Staying here felt uncomfortable, and I offered everyone a home in New Orleans, but that seemed to be problematic. Our world was different now. In so many ways. The first night, we all sat outside around the pool with a large fire roaring in the fire pit. Too many memories haunted us on the inside, and as much as we were thinking about them, we weren't speaking about them. We weren't speaking at all. It was Jennifer Bolden who first broke the silence.

"We have all lost friends here, but they are not forgotten. We can either leave this place, or stay here and honor their memory by stepping in and continuing their work. Kevin and I will continue to welcome vampires in and help them acclimate to the world."

Mr. Markinson announced, "I will do the same for werewolves and any shapeshifters. It's a similar world. That is how it should be." His voice trailed off.

"Great," said Jen. Then she looked over to where Lisa, Gwen, Jack, Samantha, Nathan, and I were sitting. I knew what she was waiting for. It couldn't be Gwen and Jack. They were students. Lisa was also a student, but she was a little more advanced. That left me, which was laughable on so many levels. My head dropped, weighed down by the disappointment in myself. I should be the one that stepped up, but that was no longer in the plans.

"I'll step in and continue what they started here," Marcus offered from the log he sat on. "It's my responsibility."

Shame washed over me, and I lifted my head.

"Larissa, no. You have other responsibilities now," Marcus said, and no one seemed to disagree.

I kept my head where it was and accepted his words. He was right. There was a higher calling. Even higher than this.

"I'm sure I can recruit a few others to help."

"Give me a few years and I would be happy to," Jack offered.

"That's a deal," Marcus accepted with a smile. "You too Gwen." He looked over everyone else, including Gwen, who sat next to Lisa and Samantha in the back. It was beyond the oddest group of three witches I had ever seen. Just a week ago, I don't think this would have been possible, but we aren't the same people we were back them. This world wasn't the same place it was then, either.

It's been 3 days since then. Two days ago, the who's who of witches arrived at the coven as Marcus' invited guests. I was one of many that told him it was too soon, but he insisted we couldn't wait, and we were ready. I had to wonder if anyone was truly ready for the test of the seven wonders.

Nerves filled my stomach on day one. At least the easy ones were scheduled first: telekinesis, pyrokinesis, and transmutation. Day two was Concilium, vitalum vitalis, and divination. Those weren't hard, for some they were more difficult than the others. During the ceremonial parts of the test, Marcus explained the order as steps. Most witches can perform the first three. Many can perform some, if not all, of the second three. But only a select few, usually just one in a generation, can perform all six, and the seventh one. You didn't have to be a master of divination to see what was coming.

Each of the days started the same. We all dressed in our own ceremonial robes. A change Marcus made from the tradition considering what all had transpired at the hands of witches wearing the red ceremonial robes. Then we paraded down to the ritual room. Only witches were permitted inside, but that didn't stop everyone else from gathering and cheering us on with words of support. Once inside, it was just like any of the ascension ceremonies I attended. The subject being tested would sit in the center, while all the other witches stood around them. Traditionally, there wouldn't be a circle of runes around the center for protection like there was during an ascension. Nothing we did during the test was that dangerous to those watching. But recent events had convinced us a set of runes might be needed. So, I set to painting them on the ground to create a ring that no other magic could cross, just to keep anyone from helping or interfering with the test. It's not that we didn't trust some of those attending, but it was only a week ago they were trying to kill us.

Today was no different, if you ignored the dread that hung over what today was. Once Samantha, Lisa, and I were properly dressed, and Samantha's hair was perfect, she is still refusing to use magic, so it takes forever; we made our way out to the hall and down the stairs, stopping at the second floor to gather Gwen. Big surprise, her robe was pink again. Jack waited at the bottom of the stairs for us, and just like the first two days, he led the way down the hallway to the room.

I think everyone else knew what today was, too. The normal cheers we walked in to were gone. Everyone, and I mean everyone, was silent, and that was quite a feat for some of them. Marcus waited for us at the door, and bowed as I passed by, "Your majesty." I made a note to talk to him about that later. We had already discussed this, and he wasn't to address me in that way. No one was really.

We walked in through the door, and Lisa stopped just short of the black robes that surrounded the room. Samantha almost ran into me from behind as I jerked to a stop. I was about to reach forward and check on Lisa when she spun around, grabbed my hand, and yanked me to the side. Panic filled her eyes, and I understood it. What awaited was not a pleasant experience, by any definition of the word.

"Lisa, are you okay?" I whispered.

Her hand trembled as it gripped my own. "It's not too late. You don't have to do this."

"Lisa, it's the only way," I said, reassuring her. "It's all for the best. It really is."

Lisa seemed unsure, so I grabbed her other hand and massaged the top of it with my thumb. "You got this." Her eyes trembled in their sockets. "Just go in and out, and it will be done in a minute."

That didn't seem to help.

"Not even a minute. It will be seconds. That's all."

"It's not that," she said with a quiver in her voice and a tear forming in her eye. "I'm not ready to be supreme. I'm too young. I'm too inexperienced. My magic is too–"

"Dark," I said, answering for her. Now I understood, and I had waited for this to come up after we had made the decision two days ago. I was not to be supreme. That would be Lisa. She was more than capable of passing the test of the seven wonders. Hell, she was probably more ready for it than I was. The grand plan had changed, and in my opinion things changed for the best. This was how it had to be. The vampires needed a leader to look up to. Now there wasn't exactly a seat in the community that allowed you to rule them all. The elders were impressed with how I not only approached them for help but also took control while also sparing Jean's life. Everyone saw what I was willing to put on the line to restore peace. I couldn't believe my ears when Theodora proposed what she did. I could take a seat at the head of the elder council, to rule and advise on everything that is vampire related. She went a little too far, suggesting I could use the throne Jean had in his mansion in New Orleans. That thing now was nothing more than splinters. I had taken care of that. That was another move that resonated well with the vampires.

To say the idea intrigued me was an understatement. It fascinated me, and the more and more I thought about it, the more fascinating it became. I approached Marcus about it, who I expected to be dead set against it, but he wasn't. He wasn't in the least. He nodded, and then quickly said, "Then Lisa will be supreme."

Lisa about fell out of her chair at hearing that. It took a few hours to convince her. Her concerns had nothing to do with passing the test of seven wonders. We all knew she could. She had a better handle on the elements of the test than I had at that point. Her objections were to everything that the title came with. I explained why I felt this was a good idea, and that was when Marcus suggested a merger, or a peace accord, between our two worlds. "Lisa will be the supreme, and Larissa will be an honorary member of the council, allowing some representative of vampire causes. An airing of grievances as you would. She, if Theodora and the others are okay with it, can even return to be a guest instructor here from time to time."

The offer in my mind was too good to be true, and that had nothing to do with my avoiding the test of the seven wonders. A few days ago, this would have been impossible. My being part witch would have prevented it. Theodora had said as much, but things had changed. My actions changed them, and the people of my other half needed me, and I could be the bridge between both worlds to make sure this would never happen again.

My, our, final decision shocked Nathan and Samantha. Both brought up how many times I talked about being supreme as the solution to everything. It was, but so was this in a much bigger way.

"Lisa, this is how it needs to be. You are going to be a wonderful supreme, and I will follow you everywhere." I pulled her in for a hug, which her trembling body accepted.

"Just remember, you are sitting at my right hand to help, correct?"

"Absolutely. I wouldn't be anywhere else," I said, still holding her.

"Then let me get this over with, and then it's your turn," Lisa said, letting go and backing up and taking her place in the center of the room. She pointed at me, and gave me a devious smile, "And no running away from this." I felt my knees buckle as my mind thought ahead to what was planned for this afternoon.

Lisa sat in the center of the room and prepared herself. Mary Smith stepped next to her and placed a hand on her head. She would be the observer to certify that Lisa performed. Where Mary had taken us to the underworld several times, the roles were now reversed, and Lisa would need to take her. From the outside, we couldn't tell what was really happening. All we saw was a quick flash of black smoke around Lisa, and I thought I saw the spiritual presence inside of it. Then Mary's head dipped, and her body stayed standing but hung limp. That lasted for only a few seconds, and then Lisa collapsed forward onto the floor, and Mary opened her eyes, and looked at Master Meridian, nodding.

Gwen and I stepped into the center and helped Lisa to her feet. She felt like a rag-doll in our arms, and following what Mary Smith had instructed us on earlier, we carried her out of the room and down the hall through our gathered friends, who watched on in silence. We approached the stairs, when Miss Wynona, one of the new council members, who seemed to take a liking to Lisa's style, and had mimicked how she dressed, even though the mid-thirty-year-old blonde wasn't part of the dark magic world, stepped in front of us. Gwen attempted to maneuver us around her, but Wynona was rather insistent on stepping in front of us each time we attempted to sidestep her.

"My supreme, I just need a moment," Wynona requested.

"Your supreme needs rest," Gwen said, taking control of the situation.

"This matter requires her immediate attention though," Wynona insisted, attempting to hand Lisa a leather-bound pad.

"It can wait," Gwen said again, this time forcefully, as she stepped forward toward the stairs.

It did not deter Wynona. She stepped right in front of Gwen again and then stepped up on the first step of the stairs to block our ascent. By now I was becoming perturbed with her presence and was about to send her on a little trip, but Lisa's calm demeanor took over and in her weakened state she asked, "What is it?"

"My supreme," Wynona curtsied, "I apologize for the interruption. I know you have been through a great test today, but we have been holding this until a supreme was in place. By our laws, I need your approval on the council's recommendation to commit Mrs. Roberts and Mr. St. Claire to Mordin for the rest of their lives."

Upon hearing the request, it appeared Gwen understood the urgency about the same time as I did. I reached out and took the leather-bound binder and opened it for Lisa. Inside was a decree that looked similar to the one that labeled Master Thomas and me as hostile entities and committed us to Mordin. The only thing missing was the signature and the wax seal of the supreme. Both of which Wynona was ready to assist with. After she handed the pad to me, a feather pen and a stamp with melted wax appeared in her hands.

Lisa read over the decree, and her hand reached for the feather, but stopped. "Is it too late to change a portion of this?" Lisa asked.

"No ma'am. You are the supreme. You may change whatever you like," Wynona replied. "Just state the change, and it will be so."

"I remember something Larissa told me about Mordin," Lisa said, looking at me out of the side of her eye. "Mrs. Roberts and Mr. St. Claire are committed to Mordin for the remainder of their existence. During that period, their treatment is to be humane. Food, shelter, and care are to be provided as appropriate for their kind. Mrs. Roberts will receive human food. Mr. St. Claire will receive animal blood. Mrs. Wintercrest is to be released from Mordin, to live out her retirement in her families home in New Orleans. Her needs will be cared for, but she is to have no contact with any coven."

Just as Wynona had explained, the sentences in the decree faded and then reappeared, documenting exactly what Lisa had requested. Then she reached for the feather and signed her name and then affixed her stamp.

Wynona reached over and took the binder from my hand. "Thank you, my supreme." Then she rushed off down the hall.

"I will start my rule, being compassionate," Lisa said, as we mounted the stairs.

"You will start your rule with a nap," Gwen countered. Lisa was in no shape to argue as we carried her up to her room.

"Just give me an hour or so," Lisa requested as we laid her down.

"Take all the time you need," I said, rubbing her forehead as she settled down. "We can even push this off for a few days. You need to rest."

"Oh, no!" Lisa snapped back, pushing up off her pillow, but then her body and its drained state melted back into the bed. "This is long overdue." Her head turned toward Gwen. "You get her ready, and don't let her back out." Then she looked back at me. Her eyes almost begging. "You need this. I need this. That is why I said we decided to do this after this part of the test. It will help us recover. Hell, something like this will help everyone recover after all we have been through." Her head rolled back and looked straight up at the ceiling. "That's an order from your supreme," Lisa said, closing her eyes and fading off.

Gwen grabbed me by the arm and pulled me out of the room. "Come on. We have things to prepare."

"I think we should wait," I stated once we were out in the hall, hoping to appeal to Gwen's sense of logic. "Everyone has been through so much, and Lisa needs to rest."

Gwen was having none of it. "You heard her," she said insistently. "Now, you need to get dressed, and I need to tend to the final details downstairs." Gwen twisted me around and pushed me toward the door leading to the stairs.

"I'm wearing this," I said, surrendering to what felt like was my inevitable future.

"I was afraid you were going to say that," Gwen said with a tsk. "How many breaches of tradition have we had today?"

I could have counted a few of them up, but I didn't bother, and just sheepishly apologized, "Sorry."

Gwen shook her head. "Upstairs for you. We will come get you when it's time." She pointed up the stairs rather insistently.

I didn't fight her. Some alone time with my thoughts sounded like a good idea. I needed to prepare myself for what was to come. I hated being the center of attention, and while Lisa was the center for the last few days, now it was my turn again, and that made my stomach queasy. Oh, to just fade into the shadows.

"If you want, do something with that hair," Gwen called up to me as I stepped up on our landing. I held my hand behind me as I walked through the door. A single finger gave her my response. "Love you too, sister."

There was a time, hearing that come from her voice would have been fighting words. Now, it wasn't exactly something that caused a surge of warmth all over, but it was progress. We needed each other after all that had happened. Plus, I couldn't ignore that she kind of saved my life. Now I just needed to drag Samantha to the same spot. That I had a feeling wasn't a simple task.

I went into my room and sat on the bed, just looking around my room. It had only been a few months since I first stepped into this place, and so much had changed. Scratch that, everything had changed. Nothing was how I thought it was. I had such a simple view of the world, and my motivations were so self-serving. That stack of books, there on the floor next to my bed, and the one on my desk, where I read the wrong spell from, were all here so I could fill a need I had. Now, I had so much more to consider. Was I ready for that? Could I even do that? Those were all the questions that I still had about my new position in the world. I had to be ready. That was the only answer that kept coming to each of those questions. I had to be ready, and any answer other than that would have repercussions well beyond the little circle I considered the known world.

With a quick wave of my hand, I sent all seven books back to a table in the library. Edward could take care of putting them back where they went. There were two books left, but I couldn't force myself to part with them, not that I wanted to. I no longer needed them. Actually, once I remembered who I was, I didn't need them at all, but that didn't mean they weren't important to me. A dear woman gave them to me, and they had her name on them. I found a place of honor on the desk for Mrs. Saxon's Elemental Based Spells, Volumes 1 and 2, but then it hit me. Was this the last time I saw this room?

Where I was going to live now wasn't a question I had given any consideration to yet. I hadn't even thought of it. Would I live here? Would I go back to the family farm? Was I even allowed to stay here? Though I didn't know why I wouldn't be. I was sure Lisa, or someone, would bend those rules. My lips quivered as I felt myself turn a little weepy. I turned away from my room and stared out the window, but that didn't help. Outside that window were the woods, and way out there under the sun was the cove.

I must have lost myself in the memories of the strolls through the woods, and out to the cove, because I didn't hear anyone knock on the door, and I didn't hear them come in after they gave up waiting on me to answer. All I saw were Samantha and Amy standing there dressed in their best. Samantha had optioned for a robe of her own creation, in blue, instead of one of my mother's old robes, but I could see inspiration from those garments in the ornamental beading and gold edges. Amy, I had a feeling wore what her sister had picked out for the occasion, though the pink chiffon looked more like something Gwen would have picked out. Her blonde hair was in tight curls. I couldn't help but to rush over and touch them lightly as Amy spun around modeling her dress.

"Laura did her hair," Samantha said, with a quick tussle of a few of Amy's curls, drawing a look up at her.

"You look perfect," I said, leaning down to give her a hug.

There was a knock on the door that I actually heard. I stood up and walked over and opened it. On the other side, stood Lisa all decked out in her red ceremonial robe with gold lining, something reserved for the supreme, and Gwen in a robe that could barely be called off-white. I almost asked her about those tradition violations she mentioned to me earlier. She was clearly skirting one.

"Are you ready?" Lisa asked.

"Are you?" I returned.

She laughed. "I'm fine. A few moments to talk to my mother and aunt was all I needed. This is all about you."

Gwen looked down the hallway and then back at me. She shifted nervously back and forth where she stood. "Ready or not. We need to get moving. Need I remind you that our guests were trying to kill each other only a few days ago?" That brought a smirk to everyone's face.

The door at the end of the hall exploded open, and Apryl came sprinting down the hall, wearing a dress for only the second time that I had ever seen. The first being the Christmas party. This was a blue number, matching the color of Samantha's robe. I detected a little bit of coordination here. If I saw Pam and Jen wearing blue, I would know for sure. "Come on. What are we waiting for? I'm not sure how long the peace will last downstairs."

"See!" Gwen screamed, pointing at Apryl.

"All right. All right," I conceded. I wasn't sure why I was feeling so nervous about this. I should be eager. "Let's go."

Gwen smiled and reached for Amy's hand. Amy took it. "You lady, we need to get you into position downstairs." They headed off down the hall.

"If being a witch doesn't work out, I think she has potential in another career," Apryl remarked as Gwen walked off the floor gleefully.

"She does enjoy this stuff," Lisa agreed. "She takes it seriously." Lisa looked at Samantha and Apryl. "You two need to get to your spots, or you will face her wrath."

"Come on Sam. Let's get down there to make sure the guys don't screw this up." Apryl put an arm around Samantha, and they headed off the floor, leaving Lisa and me behind.

"Well," Lisa said with a sigh.

"Well," I responded.

Lisa looked at me and said, "I'm not sure why I am nervous at all about this. This is nothing for me, but it is forever for you."

I rolled my eyes, letting them land looking up at the ceiling.

"In all seriousness. When you arrived, none of us really knew what to make of you. Of course, we thought you were just another new vampire student, but then as we unraveled who you really were we found out you were so much more, and I am not talking about you being a witch, or the daughter of a prominent family, or any of that. You are a loving, caring, loyal person who would do anything for those you care about, and we all became the same way about you. We call ourselves sisters because we are all witches, but with you, it is so much more. Larissa, you are the sister I never had, but always wanted. I love you, and I will always be by your side."

I felt a tear running down my cheek but didn't reach up to wipe it. I let it run and lead the way for the others.

"Oh, you are going to mess up your makeup," Lisa said, fighting back her own tears. She waved a hand over both of us, repairing our makeup just in time for more tears to streak through it.

"Lisa, I love you like a sister too. There is nothing I wouldn't do for you," I choked out.

"I know," Lisa said, grabbing my hand. "And there is nothing I wouldn't do for you. Let me show you." She gave my hand a tug, leading me down the hall.

"What did you do?" I asked.

"You'll see."

"Should I close my eyes?" I asked as we reached the door.

"Nope," Lisa said, opening the door of the vampire floor and leading me out to the landing. She paused and reached over toward my neck, grabbing the simple golden chain that I always wore, and tugged the charm that hung from it free from the robe I wore. "Let's go."

Below in the grand entry were two columns of chairs with an aisle down the center. April and Brad were walking down the aisle, arm in arm. A quick glance up to the front confirmed my thought. Jen, Laura, Apryl, and Pam had coordinated with one another. Each wore the same blue dress. At the back, by the front door, stood Gwen behind pedestals covered with flowers. She was busy coordinating everything and holding Samantha and James O'Conner back until it was time for them to begin their procession down the aisle.

"Now I know how Gwen felt, losing a man to a Dubois," Lisa remarked sarcastically.

"Oh, stop it. I need to remind him she is only a few months old." I felt Lisa jerk my hand at that comment.

503

"You ready?" Lisa asked. Gwen stood at the bottom of the stairs, looking straight up at us.

"Yes," I said confidently, and with that we took our first step down the stairs, and the wedding march on violin started. I only then noticed the cherubs from the ritual room floating out in the air above everyone playing violins. They sounded nice, and I decided to let them enjoy the day. As we started down the stairs, all eyes looked up at me. Witches were on one side, which included the new council members, friends, and rogue witches that I also considered friends. Vampires were on the other side. At the bottom of the stairs, Gwen instructed Lisa to continue her trek around the flowers and down the aisle. As she emerged from behind the flowers and stepped on the aisle, every witch bowed their head out of respect for their supreme.

With Lisa gone, Gwen took up the responsibility of holding my hand. I guess they were afraid I would run. Not that I had done that before, much. "You ready?" she asked, as we walked slowly around the flowers and toward the aisle.

I really wished people would stop asking me that, but I understood. She positioned me right in the center of the aisle, and everyone turned and looked right at me. In unison, the vampires all bowed. Theodora sat midway up the aisle, dabbing tears from her eyes.

"Wait here for just a second," Gwen instructed me.

I sure hoped it wasn't going to be longer than a second. All this attention was making me nervous. Ahead of me, at the end of the aisle, stood Marcus Meridian, flanked on one side by Lisa, Samantha, Apryl, Jen, and Pam. On the other side were Jack, Mike, Clay, Brad, and one other person, my future, Nathan. He stood there in a tux, looking every bit the cover of a romance novel, and I felt my insides melt. Mike was rubbing Nathan's shoulders, and I giggled, realizing he was feeling nervous, too. A hand gripped mine, and I was prepared for Kevin to ask me if I was ready, but then I saw him peering back at me from the first row of seats, and he wasn't alone. I had to blink twice. There with him were several gray presences that I knew Lisa was responsible for. Seated next to him were Mr. Demius, Master Thomas, Mrs. Tenderschott, and right next to him was Mrs. Saxon, who held a handkerchief up to her cheek, dabbing away tears.

My own tears flowed down my cheeks, and I looked at Lisa. This was her surprise. I mouthed, thank you, but she just pointed back at me, and it took me a few seconds to understand why. If Kevin was seated up front, who was here to walk me down the aisle? Seeing the head of my mother turn and look at me from the first row on the witch's side answered that question, and I felt my knees give. The hand squeezed mine re-affirmingly, and I turned my head.

"Daddy," I cried.
"Hi, Larissa."

THE END.... For Now!

The story continues with a new class and some old favorites in winter of 2024 with "The Crystal of Ankhryn"

After centuries of strife, the world of witches has entered a period of tenuous peace. Not all are happy with the peace, and factions both old and new reemerge, threatening to push it over the edge. But for now, gone is the oppressive rule of the council, and gone are their controls over what magic can be taught, but maybe some magic should stay buried.

A fresh group of orphans have arrived at the coven, and while the last group of students settle into their new rules as instructors and leaders on the Council of Mages, they face the same struggles their predecessors did. They must teach this new generation how to be witches, while helping them heal from the loss of their families. But as each of them knows personally, grief is the strongest of all emotions.

One such student, Megan, is so grief stricken that she turns to a formerly forbidden source of magic to bring her parents back to life. This source was lost centuries ago, but anything lost can be found if you look hard enough. Her search draws attention, reminding many of the long forgotten object's existence, creating thoughts of possibilities, and schemes to resurrect witches of the past, to rule the future.

Welcome back to Coven Cove and strap in for a new quest with a new generation.

Pre-Order NOW!
[Amazon US Store](#)
[Amazon UK Store](#)

But up next....

Enjoy this sneak peek of a new series due out in the first part of 2024.

She was born to kill them, then she fell in love...

Maria Foster's move to Savannah, a small coastal town in Georgia, could have been the most boring move she ever made. But not much of her life was boring. She has lost count of how many times she and her grandfather have moved. He reminds her often that it comes with their responsibility. That responsibility, being a vampire hunter. They either move on after the job is done, or fleeing when they have been found, like now. She has never stayed in one place, or been the same person, for long. She has had so many names she has almost forgotten who she is. But once she meets the mysterious and alluring bad boy Adrian Starling, and his brother Elijah, Maria's life takes a thrilling and terrifying turn. She has never met a real vampire, until now. She finds herself balanced on the edge of a knife -- between desire and obligation.

Blood Moon captures the struggle between defying our instincts and satisfying our desires. This is a love story with fangs.

"Blood Moon"
- An optical illusion created by the scattering of light through the Earth's atmosphere.
- A sign of the start of the end of days.
- A sign portending death.
- The opening of a path to explore the darker side of yourself...

1

September 30th
Dear Diary,

    Okay, so this whole diary thing is kinda weird, but like, whatever, right? People in movies always start with "Dear Diary," so I guess that's what I'm supposed to do. I honestly don't know. This is my first-ever diary entry, and it's not even really a diary. Thanks, Grandfather. I turned sixteen today, and he handed me this old-school, leather-bound journal thing. Brown and boring. Super sweet of him, right? Not. It's my official journal to record my encounter and kills now that I have "arrived." Like, what even is that? He's been training me forever, but I've never seen an actual vampire. Not that I'm complaining, but I mean, do I really want to be a vampire hunter? No one bothered to ask me. My grandfather and his "associates" just decided it for me. Apparently, it's in my blood or whatever.

    So, I'm supposed to hunt vampires, but I've never even met one or seen one up close. Makes total sense, right? So, no kills to brag about in the journal, and zero encounters. He's trained me like some kind of ninja, but he keeps me away from the real action. Fine by me, honestly. I'm not dying to meet vampires. I'm not even sure how I feel about this whole vampire hunter gig. It's just what I am, apparently. Predestined. Birthright and all that jazz.

    I asked Grandpa why he's kept me away from vampires and not taken me on his hunts, and he just said I wasn't ready. No explanation. It used to bug me, feeling like an insult. Now? Don't care. I just wanna be me, survive high school, and hang out with my friends. Speaking of which, birthday wish? A car or my driving permit, instead of this journal. That was a big no and no. Most of my friends get theirs on their birthdays, but not me. Why? Grandfather's rule number one, no attachments, no real names, no records. We're ghosts, blending in and *disappearing. I'm Maria Foster, but here I'm Elizabeth Winters. Not the coolest alias, but whatever. Lana Perez was the coolest. I wish I could be her again.*

That rule makes school trying. I'm to just do the work, learn, and don't get attached. No activities, no real connections. Easier said than done. Blending in means not being a total loner, but not too social either. Perfect balance. I've got it down, mostly. Sometimes I slip up and let someone get too close. I Can't help it. I'm human. Sometimes hearts speak louder than brains. I'm worried tonight's one of those times. My brain was screaming no, but something else, I'm not so sure it is my heart, was screaming yes. It has screamed yes before, but not as loudly as tonight. My grandfather will kill me if he catches me sneaking out, but that wasn't my biggest concern. That was the concern that I had slipped up again, and Lucas, the nerdy gamer I met at school and spent hours at his house playing video games with, had become an attachment.

"Want these?" Lucas asked, holding my panties on his finger.
"Keep them."
"A souvenir?"
"A reason to come back."
I looked back at the clock on Lucas' nightstand. It read 2:12. I didn't plan on staying this late. I didn't plan on a lot of what happened this evening, but it did. Just like I didn't plan on stumbling over his shoes on the floor as I searched his room for the rest of my clothes without making a huge ruckus and waking his parents. My hand located what felt like my shirt and I pulled it on. My skirt was right next to it on the floor, and so were my flats, which I slipped on.
"Maria, you could stay the rest of the night and leave before my parents wake up." Lucas suggested, sitting up in bed with a smile so white I easily see it in the pitch-black room. His hand reached out for mine. I didn't yank mine away, but I didn't grab his either. I just let the distance between mine and his remain. It was a familiar distance. One that defined what Lucas and I were. One that defined most all of my relationships, if you could call what Lucas and I had one of those.
"My grandfather would kill me." He probably will anyway. I knew what Lucas was going to suggest next, that my grandfather was fast asleep, and I would be home before he knew it, but that was a lie. He was still up in the living room waiting for me, just like he did every night. Part parental, part other.
"He wouldn't know. He Is probably asleep."
An easy prediction to make from an outsider's view of my life. Perception is often not even close to reality. "Trust me. He already knows." A check of my cell phone confirmed that. Several texts asking if I was okay. Then about a half dozen ones just with '911' in it. That is

our code for an emergency. An absolute overreaction to a missed curfew. Especially when I did it as often as I did.

I held up my phone and shook it for Lucas to see while giving him that awkward and quirky smile that says he has already caught me.

He mirrored my smile and got out of bed. I diverted my eyes. Why the sudden shyness, I didn't know. It's not like I hadn't seen him like that for the last few hours. When he attempted to hug me, I hurried to his bedroom window, putting that distance between us. With both hands on the window, I quietly slid it open.

"Maria, you can use the front door."

I ignored Lucas and stepped out into the slanted room just below his window. "See you at school tomorrow." He leaned out the window, and I quickly kissed him. Why? My brain didn't give me a response when I asked, and I rolled my eyes at myself while walking to the trellis. The climb down from the second floor was easy. Easy for me, and not because I had done it a few times. It was child's play. I only looked back once up at the window I came from. Lucas was there watching me, so I gave him a quick wave. Distance girl. Distance.

Halfway down the block, I felt an urge to look back again, but I resisted. When it returned, I cringed. I knew my own rules, and any such feelings completely breaks them. Lucas wasn't someone I would consider a boyfriend. He was just someone I considered. Someone I consider when I want to hang out. Someone to consider when I want to go out. Someone to consider when I want to do what we did tonight. Someone just to consider when I want anything. He was not alone. There are others. I only considered some for certain things, like Rob Carter, despite being the quarterback of the football team and the desire of every girl in school. I only consider for a few things, and not the one he wanted. I don't fall for that whole more muscles than brains jock type. They have their purpose. Their uses, but that was it. I wanted depth, and he is anything but deep.

Most, including me, considered Lucas a little nerdy. He reads, and not just what they assign in school. He reads a lot, which fascinated me. There were never any awkward silences between us. There was depth there, and I like depth, which was hard to find in this shallow, superficial world.

What was I doing? It's like I was making an argument about why Lucas could be that one. That one I dropped my shields for. I can't, can I?

Absolutely not. I shook my head to clear the thoughts from my head. Blaming the afterglow of what had just happened for it. But then again, thoughts crept in and not about the sex. That little smile I see when he looks at me across our chemistry class. The way he waited for me at my locker every morning. The way...

A cool breeze chases me around the corner and to my home. Feeling it on my mid-section shocks me out of my internal discussion and forces me to check the buttons on my shirt. Thankfully that happened, or I would have walked in with my shirt only half buttoned. I probably forgot to do it in my rush to leave. Walking in like that would have earned me a little more of a tongue lashing than I was already in store for from my grandfather. Or was I?

The front windows I expected to see glowing from the light inside were dark. I could clearly see that from several houses away. In fact, all the windows on this side of the house were dark. This wasn't a good sign. It's an ambush. He was probably sitting there in the dark, just waiting for me to open the door. Probably with his cane in hand, waiting to slam it down on the floor to scare the crap out of me. To be sure, I walked by and checked the other side for any signs of life. I found nothing. Every window down that side was dark. Even the little half bathroom window, which should have a little glow to it from the nightlight he kept plugged in, so we didn't bump into anything. I've told him several times I didn't need that anymore. It's more of a thing you would have for a child, which I was not anymore. That was a bigger sign than anything. He never turns it off. I was being set up. That was for sure. Well, two can play that game.

Instead of going in through the front, I walked down the driveway and headed for the backdoor. It's unlocked, which I didn't find too surprising. Even with all the precautions my grandfather takes, it wasn't unheard of for him to forget to lock it from time to time. I go behind him nightly to double check. That always brought a smile to his face. He attempted to take credit for it, citing his blasted training.

Everything was dark inside, just like I expected. It was dark and quiet. The television wasn't on. No radio. Not even a fan, which my grandfather always slept with. I crept down the hall while I debated going to the living room, where I knew he was waiting on me, or heading straight to my room. There are both good and bad to each decision. There was no way I was going to avoid the lecture, but I could delay it. That might raise the intensity, though. Might as well just take my medicine and get it over with.

I put my purse down on the counter in the kitchen and headed down the hall to the living room. Out of nowhere, a hand wrapped around my face and over my mouth, clamping it shut and then yanking me backward into my room. I tried to turn around to see who or what, but I felt a long wooden rod press across my back and pin me against the wall face first.

"Don't scream," whispered my grandfather. "Understand?"

I nodded, and he removed his hand. The pressure across my back let up enough so I could turn. I found myself looking right into the whites of my grandfather's eyes. "I'm sorry I am late." I expected a lecture, not the accosting I just suffered. This was extreme, even for him.

"Not that. Grab your bag and follow me. Now." The cane dropped to his side, freeing me from the wall.

"Bag?" I asked, as I started for the kitchen where I left my purse.

"Bag," he whispered back intensely. "They found us." Then he points at my closet. When I saw my grandfather holding his bag, the bag, in his left hand, panic filled in on top of the confusion. If he had that bag in his hand, it meant one and only one thing. I grabbed mine from the closet, being careful not to jostle any hangers or the door. With it firmly in hand, the panic ratcheted up about the looming threat that must be there; I realized this was the end of who I was.

"Let's go," he whispered and then hurried down the hall for the backdoor. Now I knew why the backdoor was unlocked. He prepared a quick egress path. When my own footsteps joined his down the hall, I heard something fall to the floor in the living room. My pace quickened, but my grandfather continued to move slowly until we reached the backdoor, then we ran for the car. I slammed the door shut as the first dark creature emerged from the house and gave chase.

The car cranked without issue, which was not the norm, and my grandfather put it in reverse, backing out just as the pale face of our pursuer came into view. He leaped at the hood and landed with a thud. I finally broke with what I promised my grandfather earlier and screamed. I screamed my lungs out, and when I thought I couldn't scream any more, I find more air just as another pale figure rushed out the front door, hitting the car with his shoulder, sending it skidding across the road.

When it stopped against the curb, my grandfather slammed it into drive, and sped off with a chirp of the tires. I turned to watch; they gave chase for a bit and then stopped. That didn't mean I turned back around and stopped watching them. I watched as they stood there. Only after we made several turns and I didn't see them following, then I turned back around, but that didn't stop me from looking in the rear-view mirror, watching that life disappear behind us from time to time. Once it disappeared into just the darkness of night, I settled in for the ride.

We drove long into the night. My grandfather constantly fiddled with the radio, trying to tune in the weak signals of the stations in the towns we passed. He wasn't after anything particular, setting on everything from talk radio, sports, country music, and about a half an hour of some evangelistic church preacher reminding us we were all sinners every minute or two. Praise the Lord! According to what he said, he was the one that could save our wretched souls. Too bad we drove beyond the range of his station before he could bring us to salvation. Eventually we reached the official middle of nowhere, which was too far for any signal to reach, so he turned off the radio, leaving us with the rumble of the engine, and the sound of the tires on the road.

"How the hell did that happen?" I yelled, finally breaking the silence of the last few hours. I wasn't asking anyone in particular. My focus was out on the moon, which was illuminating the flat featureless landscape that lined the freeway we were traveling.

"I don't know. I took precautions, just like I always do, but somehow, they found us."

"I know." I reached over and patted him on the shoulder. My frustration wasn't aimed at him. It's just the situation we find ourselves in. My grandfather took precautions to keep this from happening. He always did, and so far, this had only happened once before. Not to say we hadn't left our home in a rush under the cover of darkness before. I lost count of how many times we had so far. All but once before was because he finished his job. This was only the second time like this. The twitching in my grandfather's jaw meant the machine inside him was running at full power. Details were being reviewed for anything he missed, and revisions were being made to my training to adapt, one of his favorite words.

"Why were you out walking in the open so late?" The question was calm leaving his lips, but the expression was stern, and intense. The next statement echoed how he looks. "You darn well know the night is when they are active. How stupid..." My grandfather bit off that last comment, and even took a glance out of his own window, away from me, instead of focusing on the road ahead.

I didn't know how to answer. He was one hundred percent right, and even worse, I didn't even consider that fact. At that moment, I was just being a teenager. Of course, I am anything but. My childhood was anything but normal. A parade of schools, homes, and friends. I think we were at one place more than a year, maybe two. Even then, it wasn't much more than a year. I spent days listening to my grandfather tell me the history of our family and undergoing physical drills to improve my reflexes and coordination instead of playing with dolls or learning to ride a bike. I could do a backflip when I was six. If I didn't flip back away from where I was standing, the rope my grandfather swung at me would smack me in the head.

Life as a teenager wasn't much different. The training now included offensive moves. It was something my grandfather added after he felt I was able to defend myself and survive. A status he forced me to prove against what he called one of his brothers of the order. The man was someone I had never seen before. We never had many visitors. Just one or two passing through from time to time. He never really introduced them to me, keeping them hidden in a backroom. Ironically, their comings and goings were always at night, like ours.

"Are you listening to me?" He sounded agitated as I came back to the present, accepting this was just another move, like the so many times before.

"Yes. Sorry, grandfather. I don't know what I was thinking. It was just my birthday, and I..." I stopped myself. Something about admitting the truth to him of what I was thinking about and what I was doing seemed worse.

"That rule is for your own protection, and one you must follow." He let out a sigh and then brushed a hand across his brow. He was tired. I could tell. My hand reached for my phone to check the time, but my empty pocket reminded me I left it on the counter. But, then again, he would have had me throw it out the window shortly after we left town, anyway. No attachments. Nothing that could be traced. Thems the rules, as he always says.

"Why don't you pull over and let me drive? You must be tired."

"I'm fine," he said, but his eyes were barely open. "Where were you tonight? I tried calling you as soon as they showed up. I really should have left."

"At a friend's."

"That late?"

"Yes, we were watching a movie." It was just a little lie to save me a larger lecture. "I'm sorry. It won't happen again."

He sighed again, rubbed his eyes, and then let that hand crash down on the armrest next to him. There was something about his demeanor. Something I hadn't seen before as he sat there shaking his head a little from side to side. "Look," he started. The sting was gone from his voice, and it wasn't from exhaustion. "I know it's hard. You want the life you see others having. We just can't. Remember, we don't choose our life. Life chooses us. Our only choice left is if we will live it..."

"And we can't say no," I said, completing his speech for him. It was a mantra I have heard him say for as long as I could remember. I even pointed out once that there was really no choice at all. He didn't really disagree with my point. "I know. It won't happen again. Now, why don't you pull over and let me drive?"

"Okay," he agreed.

At the next offramp, he turned on the blinker and pulled off and into the closest gas station he could find. I offered to gas us up while he grabbed some snacks and drinks. He didn't answer verbally, just walked toward the store. He returned with a grocery bag of sodas and sandwiches and put them in the back seat next to the two bags we grabbed on our way out. I saw the same scene that he did. He stood there and took it in for a few seconds. Everything we own, the total of our lives, there in two bags in the backseat. But, it's like he said. We don't choose our life. Life chooses us. He didn't want to be a vampire hunter, and neither did I, but that is who we are.

"I keep going over it. It was just a recon, but somehow they followed me. I didn't know until they came in through the door."

He appeared shaken. My grandfather was not a young man, but he had nerves of steel and reflexes like a ninja.

"They just followed you. That's all. Nothing you did wrong."

"Not possible." He shook it off.

"Just stop thinking about it and try to get some rest."

He didn't fight my suggestion, opening the passenger side and collapsing down into the seat. He leaned back in the seat and slammed the door shut. I filled the car with as much gas as I could physically get in it, then took my spot in the driver's seat of his blue and rust colored 1970 Impala. The shocks squeaked as I shifted around and adjusted the wheel. I leaned over and hugged him. His arms attempted to hug me back, but the exhaustion I knew he felt had set in.

"Where to?"

"Get back on the interstate and keep driving west until you find some place to stop for the night." He settled back in the passenger seat and leaned against the door.

"And then what?" I asked, but I had a feeling I already knew. This wasn't my first rodeo with this. It didn't matter if my grandfather had completed his assignment or not. Our departures were always in the middle of the night. No goodbyes or anything. We just disappeared from where we were, hoping anyone we had crossed paths with would forget who we were quickly.

"You know the protocol. We go somewhere safe...," he replied, already half asleep.

"Yep, and we wait," I whispered under my breath, turning the key, and pulling the shifter on the column to "D". The car lurched forward under my less than graceful touch. Maybe if he had gotten me my learner's permit and given me a few lessons, I would be smoother. At least I didn't have to shift. I pulled out and worked my way back on to the interstate and did as he said, drove west, watching the signs for a hotel of some type, well not any type. If my grandfather were awake, he would pick some off the wall, hope you aren't killed by the caretaker, rat infested location to pull into and rent a room for the night, or a couple of days. How long we would need to stay there we never knew. I was looking for a brand name. Something that will have clean sheets and towels, and maybe a working television.

I passed a few exits that had signs for the brand name chains. Something inside wanted to put more distance between us and what we had just left. Not that I felt there was a chance they would find us.

It had never happened before, and I wasn't sure if that was even the reason for feeling that way at all. The further away we were, the easier I found it to put that life behind me. To consider it as a distant memory. Why this time felt harder? I wasn't sure.

After another hour, I pulled in, and following my grandfather's training and example, I pulled the car around the back, and walked around the entire hotel looking for... to be honest, I don't know what I was looking for. We haven't gotten that far into my training yet. I mean, I had seen vampires before, kind of. Just flashes here and there when they chased us. After a second lap around the two-story square structure with a pool in the center, I found myself standing at the office door and so far no creatures lurking in the shadows had attacked me. It must be safe, so I went in and reserved us a room for the night. Our standard room. Nothing in the interior. It had to be exterior facing, with the car parked right outside the door. What I wouldn't give for pool side? Not that I would go for a swim. Well then again, maybe I would just to relax. Just watching the water and the reflected ripples it created would be a relaxing view. Instead, we had that luxurious view of the rear of a green 1970 Impala, which I was now backing into the parking space in front of our room.

A little nudging was all it took to move my grandfather from the passenger seat to the bed in the room. He sat down on the edge of the bed and dropped his bag on the floor, still half asleep, and attempted to stand.

"I need to clear the room," he mumbled.

"You need rest," I said, while doing my best to help my grandfather slide up further on the bed to the pillow. "I can take care of the room."

There was no protest at my suggestion, just a point at his bag on the floor. I knew the objects I needed were in there. I had watched him do this more times than I could count since the death of my parents when I was six. The first time I thought he was nuts, but now I understood both the symbolism and importance of every step. Some of which I thought were overkill. I could only imagine what the housekeepers thought about us once they saw a room we had cleared.

I opened his bag and dug through it past the few changes of clothes he had packed in his emergency bag. At the bottom was the simple wooden box I needed. I pulled it out and placed it on the floor, carefully opening the top and laying out the contents in the order in which I would need them.

First were the cloves of garlic dangling on the end of ropes and a handful of old rusty iron nails. Every door and window leading to the outside needed a clove dangling over it. He didn't pack a hammer. He never had. I watched many times as he stood on a chair holding a clove on a rope in one hand and a nail in the other hand. With a single violent stab, he affixed it to the frame, every time. It took me a few times to make it stick in the frame, but I finally got it. The windows took less of an effort. Then it was time for the vial of holy water he kept packed. There wasn't much left, so I needed to use it sparingly. I dabbed a bit on my finger and ran it along the edge of the windows. I was afraid there wasn't enough to surround the door, so I just ran a little on the door handle. The cloves should cover it. My next-to-last task, placing crucifixes on the floor in front of the door, and on each window ledge. He had six packed for that purpose, but I only needed three. That left me with the last task, which I felt was the one that made us the scourge for hotel housekeepers across the country. What I needed was not in my grandfather's little wooden box. The box wasn't big enough to hold it. It was the bag that was under the clothes in my grandfather's emergency bag. A simple bag of salt. With it, I drew a line in front of the door, and a circle around the bed. With that done, I repacked the box and the bag of salt.

"The call," my grandfather moaned.

Oh, yes. The call. I reached back into the bag and pulled out a simple white card with a phone number printed on it. I stood up and walked over to the other bed in the room, and sat, studying the simple card the entire time. This was another step I had never performed before, but I had seen him do it many times and knew exactly what to do. My hand picked up the receiver of the room phone, and then I dialed the number. It rang twice before the other end picked up the call. I counted to three, slowly, and then hung up and leaned back against the pillow. Sleep was something I probably needed, but it probably would be nothing more than a distant desire. My mind was racing faster than the cars on the interstate outside.

Pre-Order NOW!

[Amazon US Store](#)

[Amazon UK Store](#)

Stay in Touch

Dear Reader,

Thank you for taking a chance to read this book. I hope you enjoyed it. If you did, I'd be more than grateful if you could leave a review on Amazon (even if it is just a rating and a sentence or two). Every review makes a difference to an author and helps other readers discover the book. Also recommend this to your family and friends that enjoy similar books, and if you are active on TikTok post a review there using the tag #CovenCoveSeries.

To stay up to date on everything in the Coven Cove world and other new releases, click here to join my mailing list and I will send you a **free bonus chapter** from "The Secret of the Blood Charm".

As always, thank you for reading,
David

A big thank you to my beta reading team. Without all your feedback, books like this one would not be possible. Thank you for all your hard work.

Coven Cove © 2023 by David Clark. All Rights Reserved.
All rights reserved. No part of this book may be reproduced in any form or by any electronic or mechanical means including information storage and retrieval systems, without permission in writing from the author. The only exception is by a reviewer, who may quote short excerpts in a review.

This book is a work of fiction. Names, characters, places, and incidents either are products of the author's imagination or are used fictitiously. Any resemblance to actual persons, living or dead, events, or locales is entirely coincidental.

David Clark
Visit my website at www.authordavidclark.com

Printed in the United States of America

First Printing: November 2023
Frightening Future Publishing

Printed in Great Britain
by Amazon